The Complete Diaries of Young Arthur Conan Doyle

Edited by

PROF. RICHARD KREVOLIN

&

DR. JOHN RAFFENSPERGER

First edition published in 2017

Hardback ISBN 9781787051669

Published in the UK by MX Publishing
335 Princess Park Manor, Royal Drive,
London, N11 3GX
www.mxpublishing.co.uk

Covers painted by Ewa Czarniecka,
graphic design Kyra Dunn, compilation Brian Belanger.

To our esteemed editor, Nancy Cohen, our wonderful agent, Paula Munier, Renee Braeunig, Melanie Jappy, Kathy Copas, Colleen Sell, Dr. Wally Duff, Dr. Glenn Shepard, John Haslett, Penny Macleod, Steve Callender, Katja Bressette, Katia Haddidian, Coach Bob Orgovan, and the Sanibel writing group four.

Contents

Adventures in The Wild West, 1878 1

Adventures in Russia, 1881 197

Adventures in America, 1883 433

Dr Joseph Bell, The Model For Sherlock Holmes and The Medical Life of Sir Arthur Conan Doyle 629

EDITOR'S NOTE

I have always been a collector of Sherlockiana and a medical history scholar. As a result, when I heard that a trunk of Sir Arthur Conan Doyle's personal effects—which had been willed to J.M. Barrie and held by his estate for almost eighty years—was finally coming up for auction at Sotheby's, I eagerly placed a bid. Luck was on my side, and I was fortunate to win the old footlocker from the estate of Sir Arthur Conan Doyle's dear friend and classmate at the University of Edinburgh who created Peter Pan.

I hauled the heavy treasure home and opened it in the living room of my little apartment. But, all that was inside was a smelly bunch of old, heavy wool blankets and rusted medical instruments. I felt like a fool for spending so much money on a bunch of trash.

As I was about to close up the chest on yet another disappointing purchase related to my obsession with Sherlock Holmes, I took time for a closer look, just to be sure. It was then that I noticed a little compartment on the inside of the lid of the footlocker. I slipped my hand in and, to my astonishment, pulled out three leather-bound, hand-written journals.

Stunned, I sat down in my kitchen and cracked open the first one. A folded piece of paper and a lock of red hair fell out. I smoothed out the yellowing paper and was shocked when I read:

It is July 7, 1930. I am gravely ill and do not think I will live through the night. And so, it has become incumbent upon me to deal with these treasured journals from my medical-school days that reveal the most personal details of the formative moments of my young life.

Due to their private nature, I thought it would be unseemly if they outlived me. An hour ago I walked them over to the fireplace in my library determined to burn them. But, when the

heat of the flames licked their spines, I rescued them, like a mother hen grabbing her ducklings just before a waterfall.

Instead, despite some reluctance, I will place these journals in my old footlocker and ensure they are well-hidden. A message in a bottle that, perhaps, will someday be discovered by one who has learned the powers of careful observation . . . Or will be left, unnoticed, to disintegrate over the years.

~ Sir Arthur Conan Doyle

And so, almost one hundred years later, with the publication of this volume, Sir Arthur Conan Doyle's dying choice to recover his journals so that they might one day see light is now being justified in these pages. You, dear reader, hold the first of the "lost" diaries of Sir Arthur Conan Doyle, written in 1878 while he was a nineteen-year-old student at the University of Edinburgh Medical School.

This volume details the story of Doyle's first year of service as the clerk for Dr. Joseph Bell, as well as shedding light on the origin of many of Robert Louis Stevenson and J. M. Barrie's most famous characters.

I now entrust this diary to you, my dear reader. I hope you gain as much pleasure perusing its pages as I did when I first discovered it buried deep within the wooden confines of that ancient treasure chest…

~ Dr. John Raffensperger, Sanibel Island, Florida, 7:56 a.m. February 29, 2016.

Adventures in
The Wild West, 1878

25 September, 1878

"Mr. Doyle, for heaven's sake, open your eyes and mind! Observe, deduce, and connect. Employ your faculties of reason, however limited they may be. The tiniest of details might be the key to reaching a proper diagnosis and saving a life. Otherwise, abandon a career in medicine, try your hand at writing and see how well that goes."

I squeezed my hands into fists and tried to blot out the professor's taunts from my mind. Dr. Bell is utterly maddening. He was riding me hard just because earlier in the day I had misdiagnosed a hernia in a squalling baby. There are many times I would gladly plunge a scalpel into his heart—that is if he had one.

I didn't think it was humorous, but, as Bell's pretentious, willowy voice subsided, my classmate's giggles grew into howls of laughter and the stomping of feet. Damn them all for having fun at my expense!

Let me explain. It was late afternoon and uncomfortably hot in the amphitheatre of the Royal Edinburgh Infirmary—too hot for my wool suit. Ah, if I only owned another lighter one I would be wearing it, but alas, as a poor medical student it was all I had . . .

I was fulfilling my responsibilities as Dr. Joseph Bell's outpatient clerk, tasked with examining his patients to arrive at a tentative diagnosis before he discussed the case in front of a class of medical students. I had been chosen to replace his former student clerk, my mate John Watson, when he decided to leave university and enter the military.

The great amphitheatre was packed with students and still had the stench of carbolic and chloroform from the morning's operations. I was in the anteroom with the last of the day's nearly fifty patients. He was a huge brute of a man around forty with a long, red beard that barely hid a hard, pocked face. His shoulders and muscular biceps bulged through a thick woolen shirt, and his black, homespun pants were stuck into mud-stained, cowhide, knee-high boots. He slurred his words and walked with a shuffling gait.

"Your name, please," I asked.

"MacLure."

"What's the matter?"

"It's me fingers," he said.

"Well, what about your fingers?"

"See for yourself."

Before my very eyes, he held up his right hand. The fourth and fifth fingers turned from a deathly white to blue and then to a dull red color. I had never before seen, nor read about, anything like that dramatic color change.

"Mr. Doyle, my next patient, if you please," Dr. Bell called.

I led Mr. MacLure into the amphitheatre, fully expecting Dr. Bell to ridicule my findings.

Dr. Bell cleared his throat. "Mr. Doyle, you have examined the patient, aye?" he asked.

"Aye."

"We eagerly await your diagnosis."

"From the patient's shuffling gait and slurred speech, he appears to be under the influence of strong drink."

"You observe nothing else?"

"Um, well, well . . . It's his fingers. They change color."

"Is that all?"

"That is quite serious, is it not, sir?"

"You noted nothing else?"

"Nothing, sir."

"What about the tobacco stains on his beard and the ulcer on the top of his right ear?" Bell asked.

I looked at my feet while a classmate chortled. "I don't know, but can't see that they have any connection to his illness."

And this was the moment he made that oh so humiliating statement, "Mr. Doyle, for heaven's sake, open your eyes and mind! Observe, deduce, and connect. Employ your faculties of reason, however limited they may be. The tiniest of details might be the key to reaching a proper diagnosis and saving a life. Otherwise, abandon a career in medicine, try your hand at writing and see how well that goes."

Dammit all! How can I be so dense? Dr. Bell and I can gaze at the same patient and yet, somehow, he always seems to notice minute details that I miss and draw conclusions that I can never reach.

"I don't see how a tobacco stain can—" I countered. Before I could finish Dr. Bell cleared his throat. "Laddie, sometimes I wonder if you have the cerebral facility for a future in the medical arts."

His words stung. I blushed, but did not defend myself. My job as clerk is to make an initial appraisal of the patients. Once again, I had failed miserably . . .

"Please tell us, sir. How do the ulcer and tobacco stains relate to his medical condition?" I asked.

"The ulcer is undoubtedly the result of an old case of frostbite, and tobacco aggravates this disease." Bell rose from his chair. "Doyle, please return to your seat and let me question this man further."

I hung my head and stumbled to my place in the front row of students.

Dr. Bell circled the man, peering intently, first at his hands, then his face, and, finally, his gaze fell on a slender leather holster hanging from the patient's belt, flat against his buttock. He returned to his chair and stretched out his legs.

"Mr. MacLure, are you employed as a gravedigger at Greyfriars?"

The man's face contorted and his eyes shifted about the room as if seeking an escape. "No, Doctor. Never been near Greyfriars."

Bell's voice turned sharp. "Unfortunately, the mud on your boots tells a different story—one that is a bit more truthful."

MacLure's face went pale, and, in a moment, the tips of his fingers turned from blushing red to dead white. I thought back to last year when several young people had gone missing. They all were presumed to be dead and all had last been seen walking by Greyfriars Kirkyard. For many months all of Edinburgh was filled with fear of walking at night through that part of town.

"Well, then, Mr. MacLure, if you are not a gravedigger, what is your profession?"

"I got no job right now."

"Eh, but you once were an iceman on the high lochs?"

"Aye." MacLure's eyebrows went up in surprise. "How did you know?"

Bell rose from his chair and took the patient's right hand. "You noted how his fingers underwent a rapid color change. They turned from red to white and are now changing back to blue. This is a sign of Raynaud's disease, named for our French colleague who first observed this phenomenon in 1862. It occurs mainly in women, but also in men who work in the cold or have repetitive injuries to their hands. Damage to the small blood vessels reduces blood flow to the fingers and toes. On warming, an increased flow of blood causes the color changes. Emotional distress, as from telling a lie, also causes the fingers to change color."

I was dumbfounded, when Dr. Bell, quick as a cat, reached around the patient and removed a slender steel spike from the holster at his belt. "This ice pick is used to divide blocks of ice, aye?"

MacLure did not respond.

Bell held the sharp pointed steel pick in front of MacLure's face. "You were acquainted with Professor Corcoran, were you not?"

"Damn you to hell!" The huge man lunged at Bell, who neatly stepped away.

I wanted to help Dr. Bell, but I froze and stood there like a daft galoot.

Fortunately, a couple of the other medical students dove onto the brute, but it was like taking down an oak tree. MacLure did not budge until two more students plunged down the steps and jumped onto him. The four of them wrestled the giant to the floor of the amphitheatre.

"Call the police!" students cried. MacLure struggled violently until Dr. Bell went behind the brute, grabbed his head, and dramatically held the ice pick at the back on his neck, the point pressing into the flesh. "See here, gentlemen. By inclining the head forward, I can easily press the pick through the foramen magnum at the base of the skull, directly into the medulla oblongata and on into the center of the brain. The victim will die instantly, with no more than a barely detectable pin prick on his neck. An autopsy will demonstrate what appears to be a spontaneous cerebral hemorrhage."

During the tense seconds while Bell held the ice pick tight against MacLure's neck, I remembered the horrible moment in Professor Corcoran's anatomy lab last year when I recognized Allison Davies, a fellow student, on his dissecting table.

At first all we saw was her cold, marble-white body, as lovely as the Venus de Milo. Professor Corcoran opened her skull and revealed clots on the surface of her brain. The professor sliced open the brain and found hemorrhaging within the cerebral cortex.

In fact, all of Corcoran's cadavers seemed to have brain hemorrhages. Suspicion fell on Corcoran, but, until this moment, there had been no proof of foul play.

"Doctor Bell, wait. How is this man related to the cadavers in Professor Corcoran's anatomy laboratory?" I had to ask.

"My dear Doyle. Observe, deduce, and connect. I would wager that our Mr. MacLure was formerly in the employ of Corcoran and is 'The Greyfriars Killer!' "

There was a great hubbub of excited conversation. MacLure grunted and tried to escape, but Bell pushed the ice pick a bit deeper into his neck until he drew blood. Could it be true? I had little doubt that Bell, with his powers of observation, had proved that the bodies in Professor Corcoran's laboratory were the victims of the vicious MacLure. No wonder the professor always had perfect bodies for dissection.

Suddenly, with one final burst of energy, MacLure screamed and threw the boys off. He got his hands around Dr. Bell's neck just as a half-dozen police officers burst in and grabbed him. MacLure gave up. The officers dragged the Greyfriars Killer off to prison.

Dr. Bell straightened, cleared his throat, and the smallest hint of a smile etched itself on the side of his mouth. "That is all for today, lads. Thank you very much."

As I packed my books, I could not help but admire Dr. Bell's observational and deductive skills. I was in awe of this brilliant, extraordinary man and knew I needed to document all aspects of my time with him as a clerk.

Just as I was about to file out of the great amphitheatre, a messenger arrived with a letter for the good professor. I followed the messenger as he made his way to Dr. Bell and handed him the stained envelope, which was marked 'URGENT'.

"This is most unsettling. The envelope was postmarked in Chicago on July 11, yet it only just arrived today." He slit open the envelope and scanned the letter.

"Read this, Mr. Doyle," said he.

Dear Dr. Joseph Bell,

As the President of the Board of Trustees of Rush Medical College, I wish to cordially invite you to perform a series of lectures and demonstrations on the antiseptic surgical techniques practised in Edinburgh. These lectures will inaugurate the mid-term which begins on October 12. An honorarium of one thousand pounds sterling will be paid to you upon completion of these lectures and we shall also cover food, travel, and lodging for you and an assistant. I am enclosing steamship and rail tickets for your journey from Glasgow to Chicago.

I also wish to retain your professional services on a personal matter. As you know, I own one of the largest railroad companies in America. I care deeply about my employees, and several young gentlemen who work for me have suddenly collapsed, ceesed breathing, only to then have died within minutes of some enigmatic illness which has defied diagnosis by our best physicians. I pray that you can be of some assistance to me in solving this perplexing mystery.

Yours, very sincerely,

Angus Duncan, Chairman of the Board of Trustees

"Mr. Doyle, what is strange about this letter, aside from the rather lengthy delay in its delivery?"

I re-read the letter. "Um … Eh … Nothing I can see, sir. It appears to be an ordinary invitation."

"Not exactly, lad … Please, note the thickening of the upstroke on the letters 'L' and 'H' in the second paragraph when the author applied firmer pressure to the pen. Also in the second paragraph, the word ‘ceased’ is misspelt. The author’s hand trembled when he signed his name. And why did he use the word ‘solving’ rather than diagnosing? I deduce that he suspects foul play in the death of his friends and fears for his life.”

I examined the letter again. Dr. Bell’s keen ability to analyze handwriting had enabled him to detect slight elements which I had missed.

“Angus Duncan was my classmate at the Academy. He was a bit of a scoundrel and the black sheep of his family, but, upon emigrating to America, he made a fortune during the Civil War and is now a respectable railroad baron.”

Dr. Bell then studied the steamship tickets. “These tickets are for the *Devonia* that sails from Glasgow on the morning tide tomorrow,” he said in his high-pitched voice.

He consulted his gold pocket watch. “And we have missed the last train to Glasgow. Doyle, be quick—there is not a moment to lose. Harry will drive us.”

“But, sir. It is more than sixty miles, and, surely, I can’t go with—”

“Of course you will accompany me. You are my clerk. If we act post-haste, we can make it in time.”

He swept up his leather instrument case and was out of the door onto Lauriston Street. In an instant he spotted Harry, his footman, waiting in a barouche carriage. “Home, Harry, with great alacrity . . . Mr. Doyle, get in. Quick, quick.”

It was ludicrous. I had my studies, and we would never make it in time. I glanced at Dr. Bell, ready to object.

He instantly knew my thoughts. “My dear Doyle, quit being an *auld strangy wifie*. The game’s afoot and we are about to embark on the greatest adventure of your young life.”

“But, my studies—”

“On this trip, I assure you, you will receive an education far beyond what you could get at university.”

“Aye, but I can’t well afford to just—”

“Aye, ye can. I’ll pay you a stipend for your time. I shall give your mother your entire year’s clerkship salary in advance. You will finally be free from worry about money.”

"How do you know so much about my . . . I have never told you—"

"Observation. And where is your sense of adventure, laddie? At your age you should be ripe for a journey."

He had me there. I had always yearned to go on a grand adventure and try my hand at being like my heroes in the adventure books. How could I refuse such an opportunity?

Our carriage dashed past the castle in a drizzling rain, then on to Princes Street where old ladies were still selling pies to students under the gas lights. Harry whipped up the matched bays and we were off to Dr. Bell's grand residence at 20 Melville Place.

As I sat next to him in silence in the coach, I wondered why this esteemed man of science cared about me. Was he merely looking for a buffoon to mock in America or did he truly see some unrealized potential in me?

Several times I tried to muster up the courage to talk to him. Soon we pulled up to his home and he lurched to the door with his unsteady gait, the result of nerve damage from diphtheria that he had contracted from a young patient.

He was no sooner through his front door when he shouted for his valet. "Willum, pack the Gladstone bag and my steamer trunk. We shall be gone for a month." He thrust a handful of bills into Harry's hand. "Take young Mr. Doyle to his lodgings and give this money to his mother. Be quick!"

I felt like the Prince of Wales as I sat with Dr. Bell's footman in the open carriage while it raced through the yellowish fog of *Auld Reekie*.

"Whoa! Whoa!" Harry yelled ten minutes later, as he stopped the horses in front our squalid rented rooms on Heriot Row.

I flung open the front door. Maw was home, but my Da was probably at the pub getting stinking drunk. "Maw, I am going to America with Dr. Bell," I said. Harry came up, touched his cap, and gave Maw the envelope filled with my clerk's salary for the whole year. Maw and I hugged for a moment. "Don't tell Da about the money."

"I'll save it for your return."

"No, buy a new dress for all the girls, get Innes new shoes, and save the rest for food this winter."

"That's kind of you, Arthur, but what about your studies?"

"Dr. Bell said that I'll learn more in one month in America than I would in two at years in school."

"But, how will you pay—"

"Dr. Bell promised me a stipend on this trip. I shall be back by winter term. I must hurry and pack."

I had only the clothes on my back, but Maw found an extra undershirt and her home-knitted heavy wool stockings, and gave me her bright red wool scarf. I put my meager belongings into a cloth bag along with Macaulay's *History of England*, Cooper's *The Last of The Mohicans*, and a collection of short stories by Edgar Allen Poe. I also packed a blank notebook so I could record my experiences with Dr. Bell. Perhaps, one day, I will have material for stories. Maw also scrounged up my favourite things to eat—a few apples, a pear, a box of sardines, and a packet of butterscotch candies.

I left, but ran back in to give my Maw a big hug. She cried, but I pecked her cheek with a kiss. "I love you, Maw. Thanks," I said.

Harry whipped up the matched bay horses and we were back at Dr. Bell's home in minutes. The doctor was in the library, before an open gun cabinet, loading a stubby British Bull Dog revolver and a handful of .44 calibre cartridges. It was a deadly weapon at short range. "Is that really necessary?" I asked.

"I daresay we may encounter ruffians in Chicago," he said, while carefully hiding the gun in a compartment of his instrument case.

We lay our bags and a wicker basket on the floor of the carriage and covered ourselves with a rug. Harry gave a command and we went at a trot through the streets of Edinburgh. When we reached the macadam roadway, Harry urged the horses to a gallop.

Dr. Bell wore a top hat and a black overcoat about the city, but, now, he was clad in a heavy Inverness cape coat and a deerstalker wool cap with earflaps, raiment usually worn by countrymen. I remembered Dr. Bell made many a cold trip to care for his patients. We were beyond the city, and galloping furiously through open country, when he extinguished his beautifully carved Meerschaum pipe, slouched down, and went fast to sleep. He was obviously accustomed to late night calls to the country.

My thick tweed coat repelled the drizzling rain like a duck's downy feathers, but cold water seeped in around my collar and, soon, I shivered from the wet and cold. I pulled Maw's old scarf tighter, and, after a while, drowsed off.

I was awakened by Dr. Bell's voice. "An extra guinea if you change the horses within five minutes." We had stopped at a livery stable to exchange our exhausted horses for a new team. With straw sticking out of his hair, and rubbing sleep from his eyes, the stable boy brought out new horses. Within five minutes, we were on our way.

Dr. Bell opened the wicker basket and removed a silver flask and a quantity of foodstuffs wrapped in a napkin.

"Mr. Doyle, a sip of this may warm your weary bones."

I waved it off. After seeing what liquor had done to my father over the years I had made a vow never to take a drop of spirits.

"Ah, laddie, a wee dram is good for the body and soul," said he.

He was right. A sip of the malt whisky warmed my stomach. Suddenly, I was ravenous. My last meal had been oatmeal and milk at breakfast, almost a day ago.

"My maw packed a snack," said I.

"Save it for later. My cook packed these viands for our journey."

I started on a chicken leg and then devoured a sandwich. By the time I had finished smoked salmon and rum cake we were nearing the outskirts of Glasgow. It was still many a mile to the steamship docks on the Clyde.

The Tollbooth tower clock struck five as we trotted through Glasgow Cross. Dr. Bell roused from his slumber. "Harry, faster! The ship leaves on the tide."

We were not going to make it. Harry bellowed and cursed at the horses. I prayed that the ship might leave a few minutes late.

At last, we reached the docks as the eastern sky grew lighter. I was barely able to make out the black funnel of our ship amongst the masts and derricks.

"*Devonia*, hold for special passengers. HOLD GODDAMNIT!!!" Harry commanded, with a thunderous shout.

He whipped up the tired horses for the final dash, and we arrived just as the dockhands were releasing the hawsers that held the gangplank.

Dr. Bell gave five guineas to Harry. "You've done wonders to-night. I am deeply grateful. Get yourself a pint, some food and rest," said he.

He would not trust the instrument case to the ship's men, but insisted that I carry the precious load. It was heavy, and I was anxious to get aboard the ship. At the top of the gangplank, I was stopped dead by the sight of a pale and lovely face looking out at the dock.

Sad, tearful green eyes. Flaming red hair hanging in ringlets about her pale, delicate features. A lovely, ethereal angel.

The most beautiful creature I had ever seen was standing before me.

And then, she waved.

My heart raced.

Of all the men on the ship, she chose to wave at me!

I smiled, and, as I was about to wave back, I sadly realized that she was waving at a lad of no more than twelve years who happened to be standing on the dock right behind me.

"Miss Yates, stop that mewling. Jimmy needs you this instant," a sharp, gruff voice suddenly intoned.

She turned and disappeared. What was I thinking? My medical studies came first. I had no time for women.

My euphoria vanished into the mist as I heard a familiar voice. "Doyle, there is no time to dawdle. Hurry along and take my instrument case to our cabin."

I grabbed the bags and grimaced. Was I his lackey? I wanted to throttle Dr. Bell.

26 September, 1878

By the time Dr. Bell and I settled in our cramped quarters my wet clothing left puddles of water on our stateroom floor. I sneezed and had a fit of shivering as I carefully stowed the instrument case beneath Dr. Bell's bunk and then collapsed onto my own.

I was cold, wet, and tired, yet, for the first time in a year, I was free from the Edinburgh Infirmary and the pressures of university. I was grateful for the change. For a few days, I would be a man of leisure.

The purser, a muscular black man, brought the Gladstone bag, trunk, and my cloth bag.

With a flourish, he unpacked the trunk and arranged Dr. Bell's clothing in our closet. He then removed my shirt and the extra stockings from my bag and stacked my books on a small shelf. He did all of this with a genuine smile on his face. When he was finished, he turned to me with a quizzical look. "Is this all, sir?" he asked.

"Aye, that's it. What is your name?" I inquired.

"My name is Bub, once a slave, but a freeman now. Sirs, the first gong will announce breakfast after the ship is underway." Dr. Bell gave him a shilling while I struggled out of my wet coat.

"Good heavens, Mr. Doyle, have you no dry clothing?"

"Only a shirt and a pair of stockings, sir."

"We are first-class passengers. You can't go about looking like a pauper, laddie."

But, I am a pauper, and a dirt poor one at that, but no laddie. I am a man of almost twenty-years! Why did Bell always ride me so hard? "Try these," he said, just as I was about to make a tart response. He took a dark green wool jacket and grey trousers from the closet.

We were of about the same height, both over six feet tall, but, from playing rugger and boxing, I had more muscle. The coat was tight across the shoulders, but, left unbuttoned, the fit was not too bad and the trousers were perfect.

I felt like a true gentleman, rather than a poor student, and was instantly ashamed of myself. The professor had a streak of humanity after all. Warmth returned. "Thank you, sir," I managed to say, after a fit of sneezing.

The ship's engine rumbled, and a great blast from its horn announced the *Devonia*'s progress down the Clyde. A gong sounded with a sharp *clang*. "That is for breakfast," I said.

"I am not the least hungry." Dr. Bell laid out writing material, his books and papers on the small desk under our porthole and set to work on revising his manual of surgery.

The first-class saloon in the middle section of the ship was as fine as any gentleman's club. There were tables for six. Wood paneling and portraits of great ships lined the walls. Off-duty ship officers were at one table, but it was early and there were only a few other diners.

I had no sooner selected a table where I could be alone with my whirling thoughts about Dr. Bell and that red-haired girl when a white-coated waiter poured a cup of strong tea from a silver pot and left a tray of toast and marmalade.

This was followed by rashers of bacon, fried and boiled eggs, potatoes, a mutton chop, and kippered herrings. I felt obliged to eat everything, and, out of a sense of duty and moral obligation, I also forced down an apple tart, a pear tart, and another cup of tea.

The ship was vibrating as we steamed with the tide down the River Clyde. The wind that blew across the deck was invigorating, but, after the long night and hearty meal, I could not fight off drooping eyelids and a feeling of lassitude.

I journeyed back to our cabin. Dr. Bell was inside, reading and chewing on a gangly ginger root. I climbed into the upper bunk.

27 September, 1878

I slept until well past noon yesterday, and awoke to a peculiarly unpleasant sensation in the pit of my stomach. Dr. Bell was still at the small desk, his legs stretched out, while he read from a textbook of surgery and wrote a few lines on a sheet of foolscap. The entire room was rolling, and even the papers and ink pot on the desk slid from one side to the other with the ship's motion.

"Tsk, tsk, young Doyle. You slept away the best part of the day. We are well out in the Firth of Clyde and shall soon round the Mull of Kintyre to the North Channel."

I hardly heard his words when I was overcome with the two terrible sensations of whirling about and nausea. I tried swallowing back the copious amounts of spit and acid, but they kept coming back up. I made it to the side of the ship just in time.

My prodigious breakfast splashed into the sea. For the rest of the day and night I gagged and heaved into a bucket provided by the gentle purser, Bub.

"Ah, my boy, you should know ginger root is a capital remedy for *mal de mer*, but it is only effective as a preventative, not as a cure," said Dr. Bell.

By this afternoon, we were well out in the Atlantic Ocean and the ship was steadier. I held down a spot of tea and set out on unsteady feet for a walk. Passengers were lounging on deck chairs covered by heavy blankets, but there was no sign of the red-haired girl.

I then ventured onto the more crowded second-class deck and down a series of ladders to steerage, where hundreds of poor emigrants slept in their clothing on hard tiers of shelves. The noise and stink of vomit and unwashed bodies was unbearable. *This is where I really belong*, I thought, and, for a moment, I was ready to abandon my first-class cabin.

There was no sign of that wonderful and mysterious red-haired girl.

Back on the open deck, I filled my lungs with a bit of fresh air and felt better. I even thought about food once again. Halfway down the port side, just aft of the funnel, I came across a lanky, pale fellow with long brown hair and a wispy mustache wearing a stained velvet coat. He was resting on a nest of coiled rope and canvas, scribbling in a notebook, with his face to the warm sun. It took me a moment to recognize him—he was an old mate whom had been several years ahead of me at Edinburgh University.

"Stevenson, old fellow, what are you doing here?"

"Arthur, I could say the same to you, you old sod." Robert Louis Stevenson swept away a lock of dark hair that hung over his eyes.

"You first, and then I'll tell my tale."

"I'm off to California to meet the woman I love. What about you?"

"I'm with Dr. Joseph Bell, a faculty member at Edinburgh. I am his outpatient clerk, although, sometimes, I feel more like his valet than a medical assistant. The doctor is to give lectures in America."

"Ah, yes. I remember Bell is a great surgeon, second only to Lister himself. And Lister, you know, helped my dear friend, William Ernest Henley, the poet. London doctors had amputated one of his legs for tuberculosis of the bone and wanted to take his other leg as well. Lister kept poor Henley in bed and saved his one leg with surgery and carbolic dressings. Your field is dreadfully gory, Arthur."

Stevenson's face turned unusually pale, and he was wracked with a deep cough. He got up from his nest and barely made it to the railing to spit out a gob of yellow mucous. The poor man was little more than skin and bone and appeared to be deathly ill. "I prefer the gilded fantasy of fiction," said he.

"I remember seeing you with Henley on the surgical wards. Weren't you studying law then?" I asked.

"Engineering first, and then the law, aye. All the while, though, I felt as if I was lost upon the seven seas. A man without a calling . . . But, you, my dear friend, don't seem to have that problem. Your true love is the medical arts, aye?"

"Well, medical school has been a long, weary grind of botany, chemistry, anatomy, physiology, and subjects that seem to have little bearing upon the art of curing."

"Ah yes, the dull, mind-numbing grind of studies . . . Why do you think I am here and not back there?"

"In all honesty, I yearn for adventure and dream of sitting at my desk and penning famous tales like Poe, but that will never happen. I come from a humble background and shall practise medicine so that I will always have two pence to pay the taxman."

"Quite the pragmatic choice, but . . . I prefer your dream life . . . To be able to support oneself only through the might of the pen. That would be a dream come true."

I gestured to the men swarming up the mast, setting the sails to catch the following breeze. "Well then, mate, why don't you write of this adventure? Spice it up a bit with some buried treasure and pirates and I'll wager you might garner the interest of a London publishing house," said I.

"I could not. I haven't the skills nor imagination."

"Then, like Shakespeare himself, base your characters on real figures, such as Henley."

He coughed. "What do you mean?"

"Henley, with his wooden leg, could serve as the model for a murderous pirate. Can't you just hear the thump of his stump on a tavern floor or the deck of a sailing ship?"

"I would not want to offend poor Henley, especially after he's been through so much."

"You need not worry if you alter his character a bit. Make up a fitting moniker. Let us see . . . With only one leg, you might call him something like 'Short John' and give him a murderous craving for silver coin."

"Hmmm . . . That is a thought worth considering. I often carry pencil and paper with the hope of someday capturing a good yarn." Poor Stevenson had another fit of coughing.

"And you might also consider consulting with Dr. Bell about your lungs."

"You sawbones are all alike. The doctors in France recommended a year at bed rest and the Germans prescribed hot baths. It is all tomfoolery. For me, the prescription's simple—travel, a warm woman, and a hot climate. I do not intend to waste away in bed, but will live as I like and shall die with my boots on."

“I see. And speaking of women, Robert, have you spied a lovely lass with wild red hair on the ship?”

“Ah yes, Arthur. I see that working with Dr. Bell has also helped your powers of observation.”

“Do you know her, by chance?”

“I do.”

“So tell, my friend . . . Tell all.”

“I would, but I do apologize. I have a pressing engagement . . .” He started to get up. I grabbed him by the forearm and implored him with a stare and my firm grip. “I give in . . . Her name is Rebecca. Rebecca Yates. She is a nurse to the spoiled brat son of a Presbyterian minister.”

“By the name of?”

“James Balfour. The insufferable man is a distant cousin of my mother and recently dismissed from a church in Aberdeen. “

“I see . . . Hmmm . . .”

“Oh, Arthur, do join me to-morrow night for the evening’s entertainment in the companionway between steerage three and four.”

“I can’t make it. I must be sure to study my medical texts and keep my diary up to date.”

“Dear, misguided Arthur, put your beloved books aside and live. It should be quite a frolic. I promise such a bevy of busty lassies. You’ll soon forget red-haired Rebecca.”

“We shall see.” I smiled and bid Robert farewell.

28 September, 1878

After the evening meal I scribbled down the day's events, read for a few hours, but needed a break, so I met Stevenson in his second-class cabin just forward of the companionway. His room was little more than an open space in the deckhouse, lit by a wildly swinging lantern. Through a side door there were glimpses of the night sea. Couples were already whirling about, dancing to the music of a fiddle.

Down below on the first landing, near coils of rope and a huge capstan, a half-dozen Irish girls danced a lively jig. Stevenson was right. Several of them caught my attention, but their green eyes never rested on me. They were more interested in the sailors. After a few pints of beer I was eager for a dance or a kiss, but those thoughts were unworthy of Rebecca. And, besides, the lassies had picked out their sailors.

The evening wore on, and the company grew to at least thirty or forty people, including a few from the first-class cabins. The fiddler played a bastard doggerel from the music halls accompanied by onlookers keeping time by beating tin pans with spoons.

As the evening came to a close, a particularly comely Irish girl, with painted lips and a saucy smile, climbed on the capstan and danced to a rousing jig. She kicked up her legs and, at the end, turned her back on the audience, flung up her skirt, and aimed her backside at the audience. There was wild applause and shouts of "More! More!" but, at that very moment, the bosun arrived. "All turn in!" he bellowed.

I bid Stevenson a bleary "Good night," and staggered back to my cabin.

29 September, 1878

After only a few hours of sleep, during the deep dark of night, I was awakened by beating on our door. Dr. Bell, in his nightclothes, opened the door to reveal the ship's Captain and two armed sailors.

"Dr. Bell, sir, sorry to trouble you at this ungodly hour. Would you be so kinds as to see a gravely ill passenger?" the Captain asked.

Dr. Bell threw his heavy Inverness cape coat over his night clothing, while I quickly donned my tweed coat. The wind had come up again, and, as we made our way to the passenger's cabin, we were assaulted by sea spray. Clouds closed in on the ship's masts making the night even gloomier.

The victim was the same Irish girl who had danced so madly on the capstan only a few hours ago. The swinging lanterns provided only a fitful light, but one of the sailors produced a bullseye lamp to illuminate her body. The poor girl's swollen, black tongue protruded between her lips, and her eyes bulged as if in mortal fear. There was no pulse or heartbeat, but the body was still warm.

"She is well beyond my care," Dr. Bell said.

"I thought as much. Can you determine the cause of death?" asked the Captain.

The skin on her neck was red, badly abraded, and her throat was almost cut through just beneath her jaw.

"Death was certainly due to strangulation. Note the twist marks. I should think she was attacked from behind. The murderer used a twisted chain or heavy cord about an eighth of an inch in diameter," Dr. Bell said.

There was another strange finding. Her bodice was open, and written with the girls own lip paint across her breasts was the word "Tzabel." Neither of us, for all our study of Latin, Greek, and French, knew the word. It was a mystery.

"Captain, I suggest that you maintain absolute secrecy about the mode of death and this word," Dr. Bell said.

His head was sunk in thought while I made ready for bed. “It is unlikely that an ignorant sailor committed this crime. I believe the murder was the work of an educated man,” said he.

4 October, 1878

Nothing eventful has occurred over the past few days, thus, I have not written any new entries here. Today, fresh rumors are flying about the ship. Many passengers are certain that a crewman committed the fiendish murder. Women will not walk about the decks alone, and even the men have taken to carrying personal weapons.

This morning, I paid a courtesy visit to the sick bay in the hope of furthering my education in regards to the practise of medicine at sea. The ship's doctor was a trembling American with a purple nose and broken veins in his cheeks. One glance at his untidy desk and nearly empty medicine cabinet told the story of a man long gone to drink. As I looked at him and his quarters, I tried not to think of my own Da.

The ship's doctor gave heroic doses of mercury to the crew for their chronic venereal disease and prescribed opium in alcohol for the passengers so that they might sleep through the voyage.

Desperate for better care, several passengers requested a consultation with Dr. Bell. These culminated in Bub bringing a request for Dr. Bell to see a sick child. My heart quickened when I saw that the note was signed by none other than a Mrs. James Balfour.

I followed the good doctor, carrying his black medicine bag, hoping to meet or at least see Miss Rebecca Yates. When Miss Yates, herself, opened the door, I was overcome, turned red in the face, and lost the power of speech.

Dr. Bell bowed and introduced himself to the Reverend Balfour and to his wife. I stood, blushing, holding the black bag. "My capable assistant, Mr. Arthur Conan Doyle," said he.

The minister was a mild-mannered, meek man of about forty who stood aside while his wife wiped tears from her eyes and showed us to the bedside of their five-year-old son. Her deeply lined face was creased with worry and she wrung her hands. "Oh Doctor, thank you for coming. Poor Jimmy hasn't had a moment's rest. I fear it is typhoid."

I would never have noticed, but Dr. Bell's eyes were immediately drawn to the heavy twisted gold watch chain that crossed the minister's chest from one vest pocket to another.

"Has anyone in the family been ill? Reverend Balfour, do you feel well?" Dr. Bell asked.

"I was a trifle indisposed last night, but am quite well this morning."

"Just to be sure, I should check your pulse. May I use your watch?"

"Certainly."

The Reverend Balfour snapped open his heavy gold watch and passed the instrument with its peculiar chain to Dr. Bell, who ostentatiously held the man's wrist while counting his pulse. I was puzzled when Dr. Bell ran a fingernail over the length of the gold chain. Had he, with his famous powers of observation, noted a detail that I had missed?

"Your pulse is quite normal. May I ask a question?"

"Of course," the minister said.

"Are you acquainted with the word Tzabel? T-z-a-b-e-l?"

"That is old Hebrew for Jezebel, an evil woman, the wife of Ahab, in First and Second Kings." There was no trace of nervousness or anxiety in his voice. Reverend Balfour could have been preaching a sermon.

Suddenly, a look of comprehension passed over Dr. Bell's face. Had he deduced who the killer was?

Jimmy made a most piteous cry, demanding attention. Dr. Bell did not speak, but sat by the boy, chin on his hand, and turned his penetrating gaze to the lad. Without a word, he placed his hand on the boy's abdomen. Jimmy clenched his eyes and writhed in pain.

I was certain the poor child was suffering from the last stages of peritonitis when Jimmy half opened one eye to peer about the room. Then, when he thought no one was looking, a brief smile came over his face as if he were having a grand old time being the center of attention.

Dr. Bell probed his abdomen for an enlarged liver or spleen, then counted the pulse. “Young man, please open your mouth and stick out your tongue.”

“What did he eat last evening?”

“He cleaned his plate of beef, potatoes, gravy, bread, milk, and a bit of pie. We all had the same meal, but it couldn’t have been the food,” his mother said.

“When did he have the raspberry jam and chocolate?” Bell asked.

“We never allow him to have sweets.”

Dr. Bell wiped his finger across the edge of the lad’s mouth and displayed a sticky red smear with tell-tale raspberry seeds. Next, he held up the lad’s right hand. “If you will, Mrs. Balfour, please sample this brown substance on his right index finger. It is chocolate, a Dutch chocolate if I am not mistaken.”

I had peered over his shoulder and had seen none of these clues. Again, I felt like an oaf, unfit to practise medicine.

“Your son’s greedy, that’s all. He’s a glutton. Give him a dose of castor oil and no food for the rest of the day,” said Dr. Bell, with an uncharacteristically harsh tone. He was usually so gentle with children.

The mild-mannered Reverend Balfour was suddenly transformed. His once-placid face became contorted into a dark rictus of hatred. His lips pulled back, exposing yellowing teeth, and his eyes sunk into slits buried within horrid wrinkles. In an instant he had become a beast—an aged, horrid beast with outstretched, claw-like fingers.

Balfour took up a sewing case and swung it with all his might at Dr. Bell’s head. “Damned bloody bastard! No one calls my son a glutton.”

Dr. Bell ducked, and the sewing case smashed against the wall of the cabin, where it splintered—sending needles and thread flying about the room. The Reverend Balfour swayed as if he would fall, but, then, lurched across the small room towards Rebecca. “It was you, witch! You gave him the chocolate!” His scream ended with a hideous choking and gurgling in his throat.

I blocked him before he reached the poor girl, who had collapsed into a heap against the wall. Then, we watched in horror as the minister's right arm jerked with uncontrollable spasms and his right leg collapsed.

He fell to the floor with his legs jerking convulsively. Powerful neck muscles, contracting like iron bars, pulled his head backwards until I thought his neck would dislocate. He lapsed into unconsciousness.

As his mouth clenched tightly and his breathing became labored, Dr. Bell urged, "Doyle, open his mouth. Don't let his tongue fall back."

What was I supposed to do? I hesitated and trembled when Rebecca handed me a spoon. I stood there, doing nothing, until she grabbed the spoon, jammed it through the clenched teeth, and pried open the man's mouth. I pulled myself together and grasped his slobbery tongue. His breathing became less labored.

"A light. I need a light, please." Dr. Bell said.

Rebecca lit a candle, which the doctor held before the sick man's eyes. The pupil of his right eye contracted normally in response to the light, but there was no reaction in the left eye. "The fact that his left pupil doesn't contract in the light doesn't bode well. Has he had these spells in the past or complained of headaches?"

Mrs. Balfour sobbed uncontrollably and could not answer. "He has suffered unbearable headaches for the past year and has had similar, though milder, spells," said Rebecca. "Dr. Balfour was dismissed from his church when he had an attack during a service and smashed the altar," she barely whispered.

The epileptic fit had passed, but the Reverend Balfour was in a deep coma. His tongue no longer fell back in his throat, but he struggled to breathe, with harsh, labored gasps. Dr. Bell again knelt by the man and carefully probed the left side of his head. "Mr. Doyle, feel this."

There was the slightest elevation and irregularity of the scalp above and behind his left eye forward of the ear. "What is it, sir?" I asked.

"Elementary," said Dr. Bell. "This is a case of Jacksonian epilepsy, caused by a tumor pressing on his brain. I fear he is hemorrhaging from the tumor. We must elevate the bone to relieve the pressure on the brain and, if possible, remove the tumor."

Dr. Bell rose to his height. "We must operate immediately. Have the sick bay scrubbed with carbolic until it is sparkling clean. We will need freshly laundered, boiled linen." Under the circumstances, I could not understand how he was so calm and determined.

"But, sir, trephining the skull is dangerous, even in a hospital."

"Believe, me this is for the best," said he.

Rebecca commandeered two housekeepers to scrub the sick bay walls and floor with strong soap. I washed the operating table and a desk for the instruments with dilute carbolic acid.

Dr. Bell ordered the Captain to slow the ship and put her on a stable course.

"Damn, we will be late to New York!" The angry red-faced Captain spluttered.

"It is the law of the sea. You must obey a doctor when there is a medical emergency," Dr. Bell said.

Bub and another purser carried the unconscious man to the newly scrubbed sick bay and, as gently as any nurse, placed him on the table with the left side of his head uppermost. A moment later, Dr. Bell walked in and his face fell. The small room was only illuminated by a tiny porthole. "This'll never do. There's too little light for a delicate operation."

Stevenson, sensing a possible story, had slipped into the sick bay. "Dr. Bell, if you will, I have an idea."

"And who, exactly, are you, lad?"

"Robert Louis Stevenson, at your service. I have a bit of experience with lighting and would like to try something if you'll allow me . . . Doyle, hand me those oil lanterns and that looking glass."

Dr. Bell grew interested. "Hmm . . . Aye, but Stevenson, can you create a bright light?"

"We shall see," Stevenson said as he placed four lanterns on a shelf above the operating table. With a calculating eye, he placed the mirror in front of the lanterns, which he angled down to concentrate light at the patient's head.

"Stevenson, where did you learn that ingenious trick?" I asked.

"I'm from a family of lighthouse engineers and I even gave a paper on mirrors and light to the Royal Society." He turned up the flames, bathing the patient's head in light as if he was outdoors on a sunny day. Amazing!

Bell ran his hands through the bright light. "Quite ingenious."

I set out the scalpels, chisels, trephine, forceps, needles, and stitches, all freshly soaked in carbolic, on a clean white sheet. We then rolled up our sleeves and scrubbed our hands with a mild carbolic solution. Our patient remained in a deep coma, but he breathed better and his pulse was strong.

"Lassie, can you thread needles?" Dr. Bell asked.

"I have threaded needles since I was five years old," Miss Rebecca Yates replied.

"Good. Thread the needles with silk and keep the instruments in good order," he replied.

Bub, clearly a man of many talents, had shaved and washed the minister's head. It shone in the bright light.

Bell turned to Bub. "Hold his head, like so, with the left side uppermost. It must remain steady. Mr. Doyle, you must be my assistant. If he awakens during the operation, you may have to give him a few drops of chloroform."

I began to panic and could not for the life of me remember the location of the temporal lobe. But, fortunately, Dr. Bell knew exactly what he was doing.

He studied the head as if it were a laboratory specimen. After a moment, he took up a scalpel, and, gently, with its tip, marked the line of incision on the scalp. It was curved above and just forward of an imaginary line drawn between the eye and the ear. "Doyle, here is the line of incision. Press with all your might down on the scalp, please."

This was a job usually reserved for senior surgical house officers. I had never assisted at an operation and felt bile rising in my throat. My right hand commenced to tremble when blood trickled from the scratch.

"Doyle, there is no time to dilly dally. Buck up, lad. Press on the scalp."

Well, I thought, I will use my muscle. After years of playing rugby I was strong. I pressed as hard as possible. There was hardly any bleeding. From the semi-circular scalp incision, he stitched an artery and laid back the scalp to expose an irregular area of bone.

The trephine was little more than a carpenter's brace connected to a round bit designed to bore through bone. When he had made three openings down to the membranes surrounding the brain, he connected the holes with a hammer and chisel.

His only words were, "Bub, if you please, hold the head as still as possible."

Though just a beginning student, I could identify the hard grey tumor that bulged up from the membranes covering the brain. Bell cut around the tumor until the gyri and sulci of the temporal lobe of the brain came into view.

I was completely carried away by seeing a functioning human brain inside a living man's skull. Dr. Bell jolted me out of my reverie. "Please Doyle, help. I can't see to do my work unless you mop away the blood."

With fifteen minutes of concentrated work using forceps and knife, he removed the plum-sized tumor and dropped it into a metal tray.

Dr. Bell used firm pressure and a few stitches to stop blood that trickled from open veins on the surface of the brain. Every time he held out his hand for more stitches, Miss Yates had the needle threaded and ready.

He replaced the bone, sutured the scalp, and applied the carbolic dressings. It was over. I had concentrated so hard on the operation, I forgot my distress, and although my legs trembled, I had passed a milestone in my medical career.

Miss Yates took her leave to care for Mrs. Balfour and Jimmy, and Dr. Bell sent word to the Captain that all was well. Soon, we were steaming at top speed on our original course.

Dr. Bell insisted that our patient remain on the sick bay table until he awoke from his coma. He watched over the unconscious man with brooding eyes. It was near midnight when Stevenson strolled in with a flask of French brandy. He listened to my worried query.

"Dr. Bell, will you notify the Captain about your suspicions of Reverend Balfour? He is surely the murderer."

He gave me a queer look. "The murderer is gone and departed. Reverend Balfour is an innocent man," said Dr. Bell, just as he left for our cabin.

"What does he mean?" I asked Stevenson.

"Dr. Bell must believe it is as if the Reverend Balfour is two people in one or that he has two personalities. The real Balfour is an innocent man. When Dr. Bell removed the tumor, he took away the religious maniac who killed the girl," Stevenson replied. "I would argue that he should not be held liable for the actions of his second, evil self."

Stevenson took a generous pull from the flask. "You know, it might be worth a story," he said, rather idly.

The Reverend Balfour moved an arm, and his eyes fluttered. I checked the pupils of his eyes. They were equal, and he breathed easier.

"You know better than me. If a small tumor can cause a mild-mannered man to become a murdering maniac, could a potion, some sort of witch's brew, do the same?" Stevenson asked.

I thought of my experience at the Hospital for Incurables. "Aye, the brain can react to disease, drugs, or injury in mysterious ways. If you someday return to Edinburgh, look up Dr. Jekyll in the chemistry department. He would certainly be able to provide more information."

Stevenson furiously scribbled in his notebook and offered the bottle. I had to keep my wits about me and refused. "Tell me more about Miss Yates."

He laughed. "You poor, poor sod. You're smitten. Her parents died last year from typhoid fever, leaving her and a young brother in deplorable circumstances. She is distantly related to the Balfours, so the minister took them in. The girl was supposed to be a nurse to the lad, but the wife makes her work like a scullery maid. When he became ill and left the church in Aberdeen, he found a position as a missionary to a tribe of Indians in the far west. He sent the lad to a foundling home and kept the girl to look after his son. I pity the poor heathens who must listen to his dogmatic rants."

I mulled over this tragic story until our patient stirred. He again moved his right arm, and both his eyes flickered for a moment. He uttered a long sigh and grasped my hand. There were more signs of slight, but encouraging, improvement as a new day dawned.

As I sat with him, I was having visions of sweeping Rebecca off her feet and taking her back to Scotland when, suddenly, she entered the sick bay holding a tray with a pot of tea and plate of eggs and bacon. She glanced at Stevenson, but rewarded me with a lovely sunny smile. "Arthur, I have been thinking of you. Poor man, are you famished and exhausted?" she asked.

Her hair was swept back and tied in a severe bun. She wore a drab grey gown, but, to my eyes, she was a vision of loveliness. Without another word, she poured tea and handed me the plate. "Enjoy the food. I must go back to Jimmy now."

She was gone before I could thank her, but, for the next few minutes, her words "I've been thinking of you" danced in my mind.

Then, a sad thought struck home. We were destined to never be together. We were both penniless. I had another year of school and more years before I could support a wife, much less her young brother.

A moment later, Bub entered and told me that Dr. Bell had paid him to look after the Reverend Balfour and I was free to go.

5 October, 1878

After an exhausted sleep I awoke to Stevenson's knock. We strolled a bit and took our usual place in the sun behind the ship's funnel. We had been chatting for a good hour or two when we heard a low moan that could have been wind sighing through the rigging or even a sea bird. Yet there was an immediacy to it that caught our ears.

When the moan became a scream, we leaped to our feet and followed the sound to behind a small deckhouse that served as a sail locker. It was there that we saw a huge sailor attempting to force Rebecca into the locker.

He had one hand to her throat and the other was ripping the front of her gown. We both leapt forward to rescue her. Stevenson reached the man first, but was batted away as if he were a common housefly.

I moved into the fray, but the big sailor loosened his grip on Rebecca and slammed his fist into my mid-section. The blow forced me to my knees, but afforded me a moment to watch the man.

His face was red with lust and rum. His nose was twisted from some long-lost battle. There was a gold hoop ring in one ear and a sheath knife at his belt. A green tattooed sea serpent twisted up one bare arm.

I regained my feet and jumped up as he aimed another blow. I had flailed away with boxing gloves at other students at the university, but this was not a gentlemen's match.

I narrowly avoided his punch, but, as he cocked back his arm for a killing blow, I remembered something I had learned from dissecting an arm in anatomy class: The ulnar nerve behind the elbow is extremely sensitive. With all my might, I aimed my clenched fist at his elbow, where I landed a terrific blow one inch above the medial epicondyle. He must have felt a horrible lightening-like pain because he roared and threw Rebecca in a heap on the deck.

Even though his right arm now hung uselessly at his side, he charged with his head down and reached for my neck with his good left hand.

I stepped to my right and barely avoided being pushed into the ocean. He had his knife half out of its sheath now, and if it had not been for his drunkenness, I would have surely been run through and killed on the spot. Instead, his knife sliced through the air a few inches from my ear.

I swung at his face, but he ducked, and my blow hit his shoulder. I heard the *snap* as his collarbone broke. Before either one of us could get in another blow, the third officer and three sailors subdued the brute.

I felt more than a twinge of jealousy when Stevenson got to Rebecca and whispered consoling phrases into her ear. He even covered her bare bosom with his seedy velvet coat. Stevenson was a ladies man, and I feared that he might try to take advantage of her distress.

I dashed over and wrapped my tweed coat around her shoulders. Instantly she stepped away from Stevenson and threw her arms around my neck, sobbing convulsively.

I held her close. She moved her head onto my shoulder. We clung together until her sobbing stopped. Holding her was such bliss, such pure sweetness.

"Oh Arthur, you were magnificent. I wish we could spend more time together, but I must get back and help the Balfours."

As we walked to the Balfour's cabin I asked about her life. She still clung tightly to my arm. "When my parents died, I vowed to earn money so I might study medicine in Edinburgh." She said this wistfully as if it were merely a dream.

"Oh, Rebecca, that is possible. The university allows women to study. Some professors don't believe women have the constitution to dissect a cadaver, but Dr. Bell is offering special anatomy classes to a few women. He believes women can be good doctors."

I did my best to comfort her, but she was still trembling when we arrived at the Balfour's cabin. Without another word, she again wiped her eyes, sighed deeply, and then entered the small second-class quarters. Immediately, I heard Mrs. Balfour accuse poor Rebecca of inviting the sailor's advances. "You have dishonoured God and will never know the Lord Jesus!" I turned away with a heavy heart.

6 October, 1878

I attempted to pay Rebecca another visit today, but to no avail. Dr. Bell had sent the minister back to his room, so she nursed him day and night and suffered from the demanding brat, Jimmy, and his angry mother. I spent my time reading medical texts and writing last night's diary entry.

Today, after ten long days at sea, we ended our voyage. We docked at the Battery on the southernmost end of Manhattan Island. Stevenson was the first off the ship, hurrying to take a train across the continent. As he disappeared into the crowd I wondered if I would ever see him again.

As we were packing Bub brought a note from Rebecca. "Please, come to me, immediately, at the place where you usually meet Mr. Stevenson," it read.

She was leaning over the rail, staring at the water and the distant buildings. Worried that she might be about to leap overboard, I ran and took her hand.

"I thought I might never see you again," I said.

"I wanted to thank you for saving me from that brute before we parted forever."

"Forever? Is that Indian reservation so far that we shall never see one another again?"

"Arthur, please." She bent closer and touched my lips with her index finger. As I tried to kiss it, she pulled it away. "You must never tell a soul what I am about to tell you."

"I promise."

"The minister is not going to the Indians. That is just a story to fool people. Just before he became ill he met an American who was traveling in Scotland. This man invited him to preach down South."

"Why would he invite a Scot to preach in America?"

At first, she did not say anything. For a long moment, we watched gulls making great swooping dives in the ship's wake to find tidbits of garbage in the salty water.

"I don't know all the details, but I have a sense that it has to do with a pro-slavery secret society. You see, the Reverend Balfour always preached that the Bible says Negro people are God's disobedient children, the cursed children of Ham, and therefore destined to be slaves to white men."

"But, that is ridiculous. I have read the Bible and I don't see how anyone could reach that conclusion."

"I don't know, but it all scares me. And he mentioned something about us meeting him in a big city on a big river in the middle of America."

"Wherever you end up, Miss Yates, please write and tell me."

"I shall, Mr. Doyle. Where will you be?"

"You can always address the letter to me care of the Rush Medical College."

For a moment I held her close and felt her heart fluttering like a small bird. She pulled away, and, without another word, ran off to the Balfour's stateroom.

Suddenly, I felt empty, forlorn, as if my life had come to a crashing halt. A minute earlier, the world had felt so warm and welcoming and full of promise. Now, it was a lonely, cruel place.

"Doyle, my lad, come. We have work to do." Dr. Bell called and insisted that I join him in visiting our patient. I was red-faced and clumsy in front of Rebecca, but managed to assist with the dressings. "Doyle, take care. Mind the antisepsis," said Dr. Bell. Reverend Balfour had no fever and Dr. Bell found no sign of inflammation in the wound. Our patient could speak, and, although weak, he had full use of his extremities. We learned that the family was to stay with the Reverend Henry Ward Beecher in Brooklyn prior to their trip to the Southland.

Dr. Bell insisted that once the Reverend Balfour settled down in America he seek the services of a former Edinburgh physician to mind the antiseptic dressings. Balfour promised and we exited his stateroom.

I took one last longing look at Rebecca. There were tears in her eyes.

Back in our tiny cabin, Bub was folding and packing Dr. Bell's clothing. "Mr. Doyle, I want to ask a question," said he.

"Why of course, Bub."

"Sir, I can read and write and I've studied lots of medical books. I wanna be a doctor for my people. Can I go with you and Dr. Bell to Chicago as your personal valet? I can sure take care of your things, run errands, and keep your boots shined. And maybe you and the doctor put in a good word for me. Maybe you can help me get into Rush Medical School in Chicago."

I had never known a man of color. The occasional black man in Edinburgh seemed out of place and often menacing, but Bub was different. I liked him, and it would be good to have someone who knew the customs of America with us. I took the matter up with Dr. Bell.

Dr. Bell liked the idea, and we quickly struck a bargain. Bub became our valet and all-purpose assistant for his board, room, and ten dollars a week. I promised to teach him Latin medical terms and some anatomy.

"We can't keep calling you 'Bub.' What name was given to you at birth?" Dr. Bell queried.

"I once had the name of my master, but I ain't used it since I escaped and went up North. I'm scared of using that name because that man is liable to snatch me back."

"But, that's illegal since Mr. Lincoln signed the emancipation proclamation."

"Don't matter. My old master's a ghost and the law don't apply to spirits. He claimed all his slaves are his property forever, no matter what paper Mr. Lincoln signed."

"No one is going to take you back to slavery . . . Out with it . . . You must have a name."

"Rufus 'Bubba' Freeman is what I like being called now."

"I understand. But, before you got that name, what were you called?"

"Well . . ." He looked around nervously. "They used to call me Rufus Bedford Forrest."

"As in General Nathan Bedford Forrest?"

"Yes, sir."

I made a thrust with an imaginary sword. "The dispatches to the London papers carried stories about his exploits. He killed many a Union soldier with pistol and sword."

"The papers reported his death about two years ago, so you need not worry about him," said Dr. Bell.

We all shook hands. Down on the dock Rufus hailed a hansom cab, packed our things, and off we went to a bank to exchange our pounds and shillings for dollars. Then, to my great surprise, Dr. Bell ordered the cab to the nearest haberdasher to outfit me with a suit of clothes and new shoes.

I preened before the mirror in my new grey suit with a fine white shirt and a cravat. Just as my head was filling with thoughts of my splendor, I heard my mother's voice echoing in the back of my mind, and my spirits fell. "Arthur, you must never live above your station. Remember who you are."

Was Dr. Bell decking me in fine garments to show me off to his rich American friends as a sort of well-dressed, trained monkey?

7 October, 1878

I felt much better this morning after having eaten a big porterhouse steak, oysters, turtle soup, and ale in the hotel dining room last night.

Early this morning, Rufus proved his worth by guiding us through this strange, crowded, bustling city to the station just in time to catch the train that would take us across half a continent.

Our compartment had couches that the porter folded down at night and made up with fresh linen for sleeping. Rufus stowed our bags, but, as usual, I was in charge of the instrument case.

Dr. Bell settled in our compartment and returned to writing *A Manual of Surgery* and smoking his meerschaum pipe. Meanwhile, I explored the observation car, read my books, and searched the passing landscape in vain for some sign of Cooper's Mohicans or at least a Mohawk squaw.

I am sad to report that I did not seen a single red man between New York City and Chicago. I had to be satisfied with the villages, cities, large fields of corn and wheat, and great herds of cattle that we whirled past. It was all so different from our wee country in the north of Britain. The dining car was as elaborate and the food was even better than on the *Devonia*, but I had little appetite.

Rebeccca's lovely tear-stained face haunted me wherever I turned. She was always in my dreams, on the pages of my books, and, once, the sight of a young red-haired girl made my heart leap. But, she was not Rebecca.

Rufus was a quick student. By the time we arrived in Chicago he understood the basic physiology and anatomy of the heart and lungs. I asked him about life as a slave, but he preferred to talk about his future in medicine. "I'm gonna set me up an office in Chicago and help all the poor folks who can't afford to go to a fancy white doctor. White. Colored. Chinamen. Indians. Don't matter. I'll give 'em all the best doctoring in the whole state of Illinois."

I scribbled these last notes just as Lake Michigan came into view. The rail line went through the dingiest part of Chicago, but

Angus Duncan met us with his gilded grand carriage driven by a smartly uniformed footman. Mr. Duncan had indeed made a great fortune in America. His elegant fawn-colored trousers, dark brown waistcoat, and the heavy gold chain across his vest would made me look like a country bumpkin if it was not for my fine new clothes.

However, Dr. Bell bowed to no man, but greeted his fellow Scot and introduced me as his assistant. Perhaps it was the fine clothes or my Edinburgh education. Either way, I had gained confidence and walked a bit taller.

Rufus sat with the Negro coachman in the driver's seat and we were off through the streets of Chicago. I was dazzled by the new buildings that had been erected in the seven years since the Great Fire. We soon turned onto Prairie Avenue, an elegant tree-lined street with one great mansion after another that had most fortuitously escaped the flames which had devastated so much of this city.

Duncan, like Dr. Bell, was a widower. Once we arrived at his three-story home, built of pink limestone and brick, a maid ushered us into a paneled living room. A lively fire crackled and blazed in a marble fireplace while we had tea and scones and little jam-filled delicacies that reminded me of home.

After tea the two men exchanged stories about their school days, and Mr. Duncan talked about how he had built a great railroad empire in the West and South. They were still talking and having a dram when I went off to my room and fell into a massive four-poster bed.

8 October, 1878

This morning, we went straight to the Chicago County Hospital. The morning clinic in the huge amphitheatre was attended by a few Rush professors and a handful of noisy students. It was only then that I realized American doctors greatly oppose Lister's new antiseptic method. Just as the clinic was about to begin, an angry student shouted, "No women! Get out!" The center of the commotion was a small elegantly dressed woman who beat her assailants back with an umbrella.

Dr. Bell raised his hand. "Behave like gentlemen or this clinic will be terminated. In Edinburgh, I welcome members of the fairer sex interested in the medical arts, and I shall do the same here . . . As should you."

The male students sullenly took their places. Bell offered his hand and escorted the woman to a place in the front row. She was a dark, sensual Mediterranean lass with twinkling grey eyes and black hair. The wrinkles about her eyes and lips did not detract from her beauty. The boys may not have liked women in their classes, but they ogled her attractive figure in tight-fitting skirt and shirtwaist.

"Thank you, Professor. We, in America, admire your courage in teaching female medical students and your interest in the nursing profession. I am Emilie Droussard" she said.

When patients arrived and the clinic started, the students settled into learning and were not so very different from my classmates in Edinburgh.

I took notes as the Rush students presented their cases. There was the usual run of patients with hemorrhoids, broken bones, and consumption, but nothing tested Dr. Bell's acumen until a student wheeled an impish little man of perhaps forty years into the small amphitheatre. He complained of a lump and pain on the right side of his abdomen. The Rush professors had diagnosed a tumor of the kidney.

The patient sat on the edge of his stretcher, dangled his legs, and grinned like a monkey. Dr. Bell looked at him, "Good morning, Mr. Ericsson. I see that you suffered an injury in the recent war."

The man proudly pointed at a scar just to left of center in his chest. “Yes, indeed, it was a Confederate ball. Special delivery on the first day at Shiloh.”

“Your rib must have blocked the bullet from your heart.”

The patient had a broad smile when he twisted around to show another scar on his back. “Oh no, sir. The ball went all the way through and festered. The surgeon drained a pint of pus and found the bullet.” Mr. Ericsson then proudly removed a conical lead bullet from his trousers pocket. “Here it is.”

Dr. Bell had the gleam in his eye that I had come to recognize when he was about to spring one of his great surprises.

“Would you be so kind as to stand up and drop your trousers?”

“Excuse me, Doctor. There is a lady present.”

“Please. Indulge me, sir.”

Ericsson blushed crimson, but dropped his pants.

“Gentlemen, normally the left testicle descends first and hangs lower. Please note that our patient’s right testicle hangs lower than the left. This is a sign of situs inversus, a condition in which all organs are reversed. He survived the gunshot wound only because his heart is on his right side rather than the left. His spleen, normally on the left side of his abdomen, is the mass noted on his right.” Dr. Bell sat back in his seat, folded his hands and cast an appreciative glance at the woman.

The Rush professor of surgery, Moses Gunn, who had made the diagnosis of a kidney tumor, scowled and rose to examine the patient. He first put his ear to the patient’s chest and then minutely felt his abdomen. “Gentlemen, our distinguished guest, Doctor Bell, is correct. I bow to his diagnostic skill.”

The students stamped their feet and clapped their hands. Amidst the uproar, a young man entered the amphitheatre and urgently spoke with Dr. Gunn, who then turned to Bell.

“One of our interns, Dr. Murphy, has a patient in the emergency room. Would you care to come along?”

“By all means,” Dr. Bell replied.

The patient was a perfect specimen of manhood, certainly no more than twenty-five years old, muscular, and well-formed. Unfortunately, he was quite dead.

"It happened only a few minutes ago. A policeman was investigating a horse theft at a livery stable and he observed the victim walking as normal as could be with a group of men. Then, suddenly, he said, 'Oh,' walked a pace or two more, stumbled, and fell to the ground," Dr. Murphy explained.

During Doctor Murphy's recital of the history, Dr. Bell minutely examined the body. "Were there signs of life when the policeman found him?"

"He was gasping for air and his eyes were wide open. It was as if he was pleading for help. That's why I rushed him to the hospital," the policeman, evidently an experienced detective, replied.

"Is this case similar to other recent deaths in town?"

"Why yes, many of their attributes are the same," Dr. Gunn replied.

"I thought so. The specifics seem to echo the collapsing men mentioned in Angus Duncan's letter which summoned us here. Dr. Gunn, can you arrange for an immediate post-mortem examination?"

The hospital morgue was an ill-lit room in the basement, equipped with a rough wooden table, a tray of rusty instruments, and a bucket of water to sluice away blood.

The body was extraordinarily flaccid and I could not help but notice the victim's open, staring eyes. It was as if he had watched his own death from some faraway place and had begged for mercy.

Dr. Gunn, with practised ease, slit open the body from neck to belly and examined each organ in turn. There was nothing abnormal.

Dr. Bell sniffed at the contents of the stomach which held nothing more than partially digested bits of beef and bread. He then held his chin in one hand and closed his eyes for a long moment. Then to the policeman, he said, "Describe again, in as much detail as possible, your observations."

"It was as I said. The gentleman was walking as normal as any man with a group of friends. When he fell, his friends were immediately upon him, holding his hand and slapping his face. They would have removed his body if I had not found signs of life and insisted on taking him to the hospital."

"And did you observe anything unusual?"

"Not really, but it was a little strange that his friends did not go to the hospital. They abruptly left the scene."

"Did you notice anything else?"

"No, everything seemed perfectly normal . . . Although, there was a lady in black who seemed to be part of the group, but the moment the man fell to the ground, she rushed away."

Dr. Bell offered his hand. "Sir, you have uncommonly good powers of observation."

"Thank you, sir. It is part of our job," said the policeman.

"One more thing, officer. Before you leave would you be so kind as to please turn the body over?" The policeman rolled the corpse onto its stomach.

"Aha, there it is." Dr. Bell pointed to a speck of blood and a puncture wound on the man's left buttock. "This man may have been injected with curare, a deadly South American poison that causes near-instantaneous paralysis and death."

"Are you saying this was murder?" Dr. Gunn asked.

"Indeed, murder most foul."

"But, we must prove it," Doctor Gunn replied.

"Doyle, my instruments, if you please . . ."

I opened the leather case, and, from the rows of gleaming surgical tools, Dr. Bell selected a straight scalpel, forceps, and two hooked retractors. He then, with great care, opened the puncture wound and dissected through the layers until he paused and murmured, "Doyle, hold the tissues apart with retractors."

I separated the skin and fat as he deepened the incision to a layer of muscle at the very end of the wound.

"There," said Dr. Bell. "A few drops of the poison that were not absorbed after death occurred." He selected a glass syringe and drew up the whitish fluid.

"To prove the cause of death, I shall require a small animal. A rabbit or a cat would do nicely."

Within half an hour, two students returned with a sack that contained a writhing, spitting, clawing, grey rat. It was the size of a small cat and rather fearsome-looking. It took two students to hold the rat, a picture of violent activity with ears laid back, until Dr. Bell drove the needle home injecting the deadly white fluid.

Instantly the rodent went limp and collapsed, but, curiously, he struggled to breathe for nearly ten minutes. During this time, his eyes were wide open, and I swear he seemed to be pleading with us to spare his life.

"There, gentlemen—all of the exact symptoms of curare poisoning. The man and the rat died from a lethal dose of this deadly poison used for generations by natives in South America."

That evening, Angus Duncan and Dr. Bell shared a bottle of port. "Angus, your suspicion of foul play in the cases of the collapsing men is well-founded," said Dr. Bell.

"What? How did you know?"

"Your handwriting gave you away. You must insist on a police investigation."

"The Chicago Police are more concerned with taking bribes than investigating crime, but I shall notify the Commissioner. Your help will be most appreciated."

10 November, 1878

Over the course of this last month, I have been busy. So busy that I have failed to record my thoughts in this journal. But, I shall fill in all the blanks of the past few weeks now in these next few pages.

I assisted Dr. Bell as he repaired crooked legs, operated upon joints infected with tuberculosis, and repaired cleft lips. Rufus quickly learned how to clean instruments and swab down the skin of patients with carbolic solution. I have assisted at surgery, and Dr. John Murphy, the delightful, red-haired Irish intern, gave the anaesthetic for all our surgical cases.

At first, only Dr. Gunn and a few students were present, but, as news of Dr. Bell's incredible results with the antiseptic method became known, more and more students and physicians began attending his clinics.

Every single day, Emilie Droussard sat in the front row, avidly taking notes and occasionally asking questions. Dr. Bell seemed to take great delight in her attention. Additionally, by the end of the week even lay people were drawn to witness Dr. Bell's feats of surgical skill.

During the afternoons, Rufus and I had the run of Rush Medical College, which was just across the street from the hospital. Most of the students were rough, uneducated country laddies, but still good fellows.

Beyond the hospital and medical college, it seemed like every other establishment in the city was a saloon, gambling den or brothel. I had no money for gambling and was not interested in the offerings of the painted ladies, since I know too well the horrors of venereal disease. Even when tempted by a particularly attractive wench, the vision of Rebecca's lovely face always appeared to keep me from committing an unspeakable sin.

To-night, after working all day, I invited Rufus to Peachey's Saloon, a good Irish pub that sells an honest mug of ale. A group of Rush Medical College students had congregated there to drink. In the center of a gang of students, an overgrown Wisconsin farm lad by the name of Carl Lindborg was telling stories, to roars of laughter. Over six feet tall, with massive arms and legs, he had a huge head of curly blonde hair, rosy cheeks, and a baby face. As he spoke, he held a lit El Perfecto in the side of his mouth and punctuated the best moments in his story with a wave of the cigar.

I tried to push my way inside the circle around Lindborg. "Excuse me. Pardon me," said I, but nobody budged. Did bringing Rufus make me an outcast?

Lindborg heard my Scottish accent. "I hear that a Scotsman knows how to drink," he barked.

"I was born in Scotland, but have some Irish and English blood, so I wouldn't exactly call myself a Scot. The name's Arthur Conan Doyle."

"Well, Artie . . ."

"The name is Arthur."

He pointed the El Perfecto Cigar. "Whatever you call yourself, my friend, might you be interested in challenging this wee American lad of Swedish descent to a chugging contest?"

"It would be my pleasure to teach you a lesson on how to drink, sir, but I believe it would be more fitting to propose an arm wrestling match instead."

"Even better. I have milked cows my whole life and never lost an arm wrestling match." As the other students laughed and snickered, suddenly the circle around him parted and I was ushered into the center.

Carl and I struggled and grunted and strained for a good minute or two before he bested me. Within five minutes we were smoking cigars together, and I could not help but like this giant of a lad who must not have been more than eighteen.

As Lindborg and I chatted, he continued to imbibe while I smoked deeply on one of his cigars. Next thing I knew, we were discussing the scarcity of bodies for anatomical dissection in Chicago. Our discussion inspired Carl. "Artie, I have me an idea."

"It is Arthur."

"Either way, follow me." He led me and a group of medical students to a uniformed copper sitting on a stool at the far end of the bar. The police officer was eating a late dinner of boiled eggs and a pig's foot.

Lindborg pushed a pint across the bar to the officer. "Paddy, my friend, would you care for a drink?"

"I would not turn down a pint," said the copper.

After Paddy had several mugs of good beer, as well as a dram or two, Lindborg patted his back. "Paddy, my dear old friend, may we borrow your wagon for a bit?"

The policeman nodded and we were off. Carl and his lads stopped at their lodgings to gather spades, shovels, a large canvas bag, a chisel, and a hammer. It appeared as if this was a common student activity. A half-dozen of us, including Rufus, piled into the four-wheeled wagon drawn by one poor horse.

We traveled through the darkened streets, mostly north and east by my calculations, until we were beyond the city limits. As we drew nearer to Lake Michigan a cold rain, driven by a northeast wind, sprung up. We plodded along until a large, decrepit sign announced 'GRACELAND CEMETERY'.

For a moment, I wondered if we were any better than MacLure, the Greyfriars Killer, but then I reasoned that what we were doing could save a good deal of lives. I proceeded along with Lindborg.

Inside this dreary place there appeared to be several acres of gravestones surrounded by a broken down fence. The wind sighing in rows of trees and the patches of fog lent a ghostly aura of gloom. I shivered with cold and had real misgivings about the whole enterprise. "Carl, we shouldn't be doing this."

"Look here, Artie. You can stand there and look down on me from your high and mighty Scottish pulpit, or you can roll up your sleeves and help. Either way, we are going to do this."

"CALL ME ARTHUR! And what if . . ."

"I can't afford to think about what ifs . . . The other medical schools have the money to buy bodies, but, if we want to learn anatomy, it is up to us to provide the specimens. And so, what choice do we have?" said Carl.

Rufus stepped forward, "I'll stand here as your lookout. Mr. Doyle, why don't you stay with me?"

I paused, considered his proposal and sighed. "Alright, then, Rufus and I shall be your lookouts."

Carl and his boys continued until they came to a fresh grave in the pauper's section. With the help of a shaded lantern, the boys set to work shoveling the loose wet dirt until their spades struck the wooden coffin.

I shivered in my bones at the hollow awful sound. It was one thing to dissect a body—an innate thing—beneath a bright light and quite another thing to bring up a fresh corpse from what was supposed to be its final resting place.

The combination of the sighing wind, the flickering lights, the brush of tree limbs, and the shadows playing amongst the statues and gravestones was more than enough to take away my thin veneer of rational scientific thought. Perhaps there really were spirits and ghosts that haunted places such as this.

Lindborg, with practised ease, chiseled off the top of the coffin. The boys removed the body, placed it in the canvas bag, and carried it to the police wagon. The boys passed a bottle to me. I quickly got over my qualms and looked forward to testing my knowledge of anatomy against the Americans.

Within the hour, we returned the wagon to Paddy and the body was safely on the dissecting table in the anatomical laboratory. The corpse was that of a well-dressed, well-formed young man. He was clearly not a pauper. While we removed his clothing, the body was face down on the table. "My God, there is a puncture wound in his left buttock," I gasped.

We then turned the body face up and stepped back in horror. His neck had been slashed from ear to ear, leaving a gaping bloody wound.

It was then I noticed the open, desperate eyes that, though dull and dead, seemed to plead for mercy—just like the rat. There was also the unmistakable odor of carbolic acid about the man's neck.

Carl and the rest of our tipsy companions quickly sobered at the sight of that ghastly slashed throat and the eyes, dulled by death, but still wide open, pleading for an answer as to why he was murdered.

The other students faded away from the dissecting room leaving just me, Carl, and poor Rufus alone with that awful corpse.

Before he came to Rush, Carl had been apprenticed to a busy surgeon and had seen his share of wounds and death, so he was not shocked.

He even had the presence of mind to lower the shades and darken the windows. "The murderer would not be happy to know that we have discovered his victim," said he.

At first I did not understand, and then it struck me. When Dr. Bell had made his clever discovery of homicide, he had unwittingly thrust us all into danger. Yes, like it or not, we had stumbled upon a series of dreadful murders and, as a result, we would surely be thrust into a truly perilous game. Truly, "the game was afoot," as Doctor Bell often said.

"Rufus, please fetch Dr. Bell immediately," I said.

11 November, 1878

In the wee hours of the morning, Dr. Bell arrived, accompanied by Angus Duncan. Dr. Bell quietly inspected me and Carl and shook his head disapprovingly. "Doyle. Please remember, we are guests in this country. You must promise to refrain from engaging in unlawful activities," said he.

"Doctor Bell, sorry, sir, but—"

"Robbing graves is a criminal offence."

"Sir", I stammered, "It . . . It was only a prank and the students—they are doing it for the sake of their studies. They need anatomical material."

"Even in the name of medical research, it is still illegal."

"How did you know this cadaver was stolen?"

"Elementary, lad, elementary. 'Tis the power of observation, as I have attempted to instruct you." There was a ghost of a smile on his lips. "Graceland Cemetery is well known for its fine stand of Hazelnut trees and there is a Hazelnut leaf stuck to the underside of your muddy left shoe."

His astounding observational skills once again amazed me. If only I could learn to observe, deduce, and make a correct diagnosis.

Dr. Bell then circled the corpse, observing it with great intensity and sniffing its odors.

Mimicking the technique I had seen Dr. Bell use in the past, I put my chin on my knuckles and studied the cadaver. The body was undressed, but the well-tailored suit of clothes we had removed suggested that he had been a gentleman. Even in death, the facial features were symmetrical, and the body was well-built. Aside from the puncture wound and slashed throat, there were no other outward signs of injury and nothing to indicate that the victim had attempted to defend himself.

"Roll the body over, and a probe, please," Dr. Bell requested.

I handed him an iron probe. The probe entered the puncture wound at a slightly upward angle. The wound appeared to be two inches deep. By measurement, the corpse from the crown of the head to the heels was about five feet ten inches.

"The needle that delivered the poison was thrust from somewhat below the wound in an upward direction, suggesting that the assailant was shorter than the victim," Bell surmised.

After he had minutely inspected the body Dr. Bell turned to the slashed throat. The wound was cleanly incised as if the assailant had used an extraordinarily sharp instrument.

With steel hook retractors, Carl and I separated the edges of the wound. Dr. Bell gasped. "This is no ordinary slashing. The killer was a gifted surgeon who dissected each layer with supreme precision and avoided the great arteries and veins."

We eagerly peered into the wound. "Great God in Heaven! There's no thyroid gland!" Dr. Bell exclaimed.

Indeed, the thyroid gland, a reddish, paired organ shaped like half of a peach, was missing. It normally covered the trachea and the jugular veins, but in this case it was gone. The wind pipe and great veins were uncovered in the depths of the incision, and the vessels that had supplied blood to the gland were now neatly divided.

Mr. Duncan, who had silently held back away from the corpse, finally found his voice. "Who could have committed such a dreadful crime?"

"This was clearly the work of a devilish surgeon. Angus, we must notify the police at once."

"The police have done nothing to investigate the previous cases and I fear they will do nothing about this. Instead, let me send for my good friend, Allan Pinkerton," said Duncan.

Every Scot knew of Pinkerton, a native of Glasgow who founded a famous detective agency. He was a source of national pride because he had once saved Abraham Lincoln from assassination.

Pinkerton arrived in a carriage drawn by four fast horses just after dawn. He was stocky, with a high forehead and a bushy, black beard. He was accompanied by two detectives. After greeting us brusquely he examined the body in minute detail and then took a series of photographs. “Gentlemen,” said he, “You are no longer needed. I shall take this case from here.”

Dr. Bell and I looked at each other. Duncan jovially clapped Dr. Bell on the shoulder, “That’s enough for one evening. Gentlemen, it has been a long night. Let us all repair to the Tremont Hotel for breakfast.”

We went off in two carriages. Rufus came along, but refused to enter the dining room. “I’ll get me a bite in the kitchen,” said he.

The sumptuous dining room, decorated in gold gilt, overlooked Lake Michigan. Carl Lindborg and I were out of place in our shabby clothing and dirty hands, but we took our place at the table and set to work on ham steak, fried eggs, and sweet rolls slathered in butter and jam.

When the party settled down to coffee and morning cigars, Allan Pinkerton tapped his glass for attention. “Gentlemen, to solve this case I need to know as much information as possible, so, at the request of Mr. Duncan, I have decided to hear from our medical colleague, Dr. Joseph Bell.”

Dr. Bell, in his usual manner, laced his fingers together over his chest and spoke in his quiet, squeaky voice laced with a wee bit of a Scottish brogue. “We have two victims with similar puncture wounds. In the first, we proved the presence of a poison that caused paralysis and death within a few minutes. The poison was undoubtedly South American curare. The second victim was rendered helpless by the same poison, and, either while still alive, or immediately after his death, the assailant removed his thyroid gland.”

“Hmm. Well . . . What, exactly, is the function of this gland?” Allan Pinkerton asked.

“We know very little. However, Swiss surgeons have observed a decline in all body functions, especially intelligence, after the removal of enlarged thyroid glands. The condition resembles cretinism that occurs in children born without a thyroid gland.”

“What would be the purpose of removing the gland from an apparently healthy young man?” Angus Duncan asked.

“I have no answer for that. The Swiss have implanted various glands from animals into patients with declining sexual and mental function, but, thus far, their experiments have failed.”

When a memory of a lecture by our chemistry professor flashed into my mind, I could not help but add my bit to the conversation. “Sir, at university back in Edinburgh, Professor Brown proposed a series of experiments using fresh extract of the thyroid gland to increase intelligence. Is it possible that this murder is part of such an experiment?”

Dr. Bell glanced my way with fresh interest. “Doyle, my lad, you may have hit upon a motive, but I believe it is still far too early for us to know for sure. What we do know is this. The perpetrator is undoubtedly a well-trained surgeon with a detailed knowledge of chemistry. His use of carbolic acid indicates that he wanted to keep the gland free from infection for some as-yet-unknown use.”

I was across the table from Pinkerton and Bell, who were sitting together. The detective’s expression went from concentration and interest to a rather condescending smile and annoyance. “Professor Bell, you and your assistant may thrive in the world of academia, but detective work is a bloody and dangerous game that provides little room for a bookish gent such as yourself. I thank you and now hope that you will stick to your ivory tower and let me and my agency do what we are famous for.”

A crimson blotch rose on Doctor Bell’s cheeks, and he stabbed the air with his long, delicate index finger. “First of all, let me point out that one person could not have poisoned the victims and carried off their bodies alone. There must have been a gang. And sir, don’t you at least want to know how the poison was delivered?”

“Ah yes, you have a theory about that, as well, I presume.”

“I do, indeed.”

“Well, let’s have it.”

“A hollowed out walking stick, or, perhaps, an umbrella with a plunger connected to a retractable needle at the tip of the stick, could easily deliver the poison. A type of *sword cane*, if you will. The victim would be unaware of his assailant’s approach until he felt the prick of the needle, and then it would be too late.” As he spoke, Dr. Bell jabbed Mr. Pinkerton in the back with his index finger.

Pinkerton jumped to his feet, "Touch me again, sir, and I shall break that finger of yours!"

"Sir," Dr. Bell smiled gently. "I was merely demonstrating the murderer's technique."

I had, during the conversation, been idly looking about the room and spotted a woman wearing a flowery hat. Her face was hidden by the hat and a newspaper. When Dr. Bell spoke she crumpled the paper, and I had a glimpse of her black curly hair and worried eyes. She looked like the woman who had attended Dr. Bell's clinics, but, before I could make out her features, she turned away and hurriedly left the dining room.

A tall, distinguished man with a droopy mustache and greying hair met her at the door. They paused long enough for me to see that he was wearing a grey suit with a decoration in his lapel. She carried an umbrella even though the day promised fair weather.

Refreshed by the meal and several cups of strong coffee, we left for the medical school with Angus Duncan. "Angus, I fear that Mr. Pinkerton cares little for our observations," Dr. Bell mused.

"He does things his own way. He and his agents have solved many crimes involving train robberies and counterfeiting; however, he is still smarting from his failure to capture the notorious James Gang."

The day's clinic began with the usual bustle of house officers (what the Americans termed "interns") and students, arriving to take their places in the theatre. There was more than the usual interest today because the patient was a young woman with a tumor on the side of her face. Several local surgeons had declared her beyond help.

Carl, Rufus, and I scrubbed with greater care than usual to remove the grave dirt from our hands, and Dr. Bell insisted that we wear a clean butcher's apron over our clothing. Unruly students were noisily shelling and munching on peanuts in the back row until Dr. Bell shot them a stony glance. He never tolerated nonsense from students—whether in Edinburgh or America. When he removed his frock coat and rolled up the sleeves of his white shirt, several older surgeons guffawed.

"Are you not afraid of soiling your white shirt?" one of the surgeons asked.

"Better to soil one's shirt than the wound," Dr. Bell answered.

The operation was long and intricate, since Bell had to dissect the tumor without damaging the nerves that controlled facial expression. After he was done, and when the girl had awakened from the ether, Dr. Bell sighed with visible relief. He then answered questions concerning the antiseptic method.

It was not the first time that he lingered after a clinic to talk with Emilie Droussard. He seemed quite charmed by the twinkle-eyed lady. I overheard her say that she was anxious to introduce a Nightingale type of nursing service to a hospital. I did not catch the name of the city.

We were both dead-tired, but Carl was eager to dissect the cadaver. Several students had already opened the abdomen under the watchful eyes of Dr. Gunn, but the intestine had gone putrid and, despite wreaths of tobacco smoke, the smell was overpowering.

Several students were especially keen to dissect the intricate plexus of nerves in the neck that led to the arm. Rufus seemed oblivious to the smell and eagerly followed our work, asking questions all the while. Carl and I took turns poking and cutting into the body.

Sadly, muscles and nerves are never as clear as depicted in a book. We first stripped away the skin and then separated muscles and dissected beneath the clavicle.

I set out to display the origin of the median nerve with a great deal of confidence, but the scalpel and forceps soon became slippery with fat and, for a while, I was hopelessly lost. Together, Carl and I finally found the junction of the medial and lateral cords of the brachial plexus that formed the median nerve. It was then easy to trace the median nerve in its course next to the humerus bone.

The dissection had taken so long that most of the students had drifted away. It was early evening before we decided to have a beer and a bite to eat at Peachey's Saloon. Just as Rufus went off to visit his new friends at the Tremont Hotel, the dean of the medical school thrust a letter in my hand. The name, Rebecca Yates, was on the envelope, and my heart soared.

I wanted to tear open the envelope, but decided to wait until I could savour her words in the quiet of my room. Carl loitered to clean and put away his dissecting instruments while I left the building with my mind on Rebecca.

There was the sound of hurrying footsteps, and I was dimly aware of something moving in the periphery of my vision. But, when I halted, scanned the street, and listened, I did not see anything in the gathering darkness. I should have waited for Carl, but memories of Rebecca's kiss had overtaken my senses.

I paused in the midst of my fantasy. The street was suddenly silent, deadly silent. Why had I walked out alone?

In a moment of terror, I remembered Dr. Bell's theory of the walking stick filled with poison and started to run.

Hands grabbed me. Sharp pain shot through my arms and back. It was not the sting of a needle. Ruffians wrenched my arms behind my back and forced me to the ground. I struggled until rough hands held a cloth soaked in chloroform over my face.

I fought against the sweet fumes. And from a great distance heard I a soft, melodic American-accented voice, "Take care. He will make a fine specimen."

12 November, 1878

Early this morning, I woke up and thanked God that I was still alive. I was in Carl Lindborg's bed. He was sleeping on the floor next to me. When he saw me trying to get out of bed he jumped up. "Artie, please –" said he.

"It is Arthur."

"Either way, don't get up too quickly. Just sit back and tell me what you remember."

Through a chloroform haze, I told him that I recalled bits and pieces of my attempted abduction—rough hands dragging me, my heels bumping on the cobblestones, flashes of light, someone screaming, fists flying, shouts, curses.

Carl half-carried half-led me through the streets of Chicago to Angus Duncan's house and into his parlor. I was still groggy and had only partially regained my senses. Dr. Bell and several other gentlemen from Rush Medical College were having breakfast together when we arrived.

"Good heavens. What happened?" Angus asked.

I told them what I could of the moments before being overcome by the chloroform. Carl stepped in and told them how he had finished his work, and, fortunately, emerged from the dissecting room just in time to see two thugs drag me across the road to a four-horse carriage.

He screamed and tackled one of my assailants, but the other knocked him to his knees with a terrific blow to the back of the head from a stout, gilded cane. Carl went down screaming, "Help! Murder! Police!"

There were no police, but a group of medical students leaving Peachey's Saloon ran to our rescue and swarmed around the thugs. After an exchange of kicks and blows they dragged me from the carriage and pulled Carl back onto his feet. Then, the coachman whipped up the horses, the thugs jumped on, and the carriage rushed away from the scene.

Angus Duncan put down his china tea cup. "These days in Chicago, I have heard of more than one instance of thieves using chloroform on their victims," said he.

"However, these do not sound like common thieves, sir, for when was the last time you have heard of ruffians having a four-horse carriage?" Dr. Gunn interjected.

In his usual way, Dr. Bell asked a penetrating question. "Mr. Lindborg, please try to remember—and do be specific—did you see anything different or unusual about the carriage?"

Carl rubbed his forehead and thought for a moment. "It was very dark, but it seemed to be an uncommonly fine gold-leafed carriage with spirited horses."

"Did you hear anything?"

"The thugs cursed, and at least one student cried out when he was struck down. Amid it all, I do seem to remember a woman's voice from within the carriage."

A dim memory stirred. "Yes, I heard her say the words, *'Take care. He will make a fine specimen,'* " said I.

"Just before the coach drove away I also heard someone saying a general would be damn angry. It could have been a woman's voice. I'm not sure. If those goons hadn't attacked me from behind, I swear I could have taken them all." Carl added.

"Doctor Bell, Is this episode related to those two recent deaths and your theory of murder by poisoning?" Dr. Gunn asked.

Dr. Bell mused, "Well, one need not rush to any conclusions. All one can do is try to separate the probable from the possible and the impossible."

"In that case, what do you find to be probable?"

"Ahem . . . I do think it is fair for one to conclude the following. The term 'specimen' is an unusual one to be used in the context of a common robbery, but not unusual for use in a scientific experiment. For example, Doyle is similar in stature and age to the two recent victims. Angus, tell us, what were the physical characteristics of the first two victims?"

Angus pondered a moment. "By Jove, they were both well-built men, of about the same stature and age as young Doyle."

"Were autopsies performed?" Dr. Bell asked.

"Relatives took charge of the bodies even as they lay on the street. There wasn't a funeral, as far as I can remember, because the men lived in a different city."

"Would it be difficult to exhume the bodies? I believe these murders are the work of a well-trained surgeon," Dr. Bell said.

"I cannot believe that anyone in the medical profession would murder in cold blood for the purpose of removing an organ," Dr. Gunn replied.

"The case of Dr. Corcoran in Edinburgh, who paid for the bodies of recently murdered victims for anatomical dissection, was not so terribly different. He defended his actions by claiming that, since the victims were already dead, he could use them for teaching anatomy, thereby benefitting humanity," Dr. Bell said.

Dr. Isham, a professor of medicine at Rush, spoke for the first time. "That reminds me of Dr. Eli McGillicutty who grafted skin onto burn victims after the fire of '71."

"What ever happened to McGillicutty?" Dr. Bell asked.

"There was a great scandal when he experimented with grafting animal skin onto humans. All of his patients died. Some called it murder. He claimed it was to advance science, but county commissioners removed him from the hospital staff. McGillicutty has since disappeared," Dr. Isham replied.

The meeting broke up and the doctors went their separate ways. Doctor Bell was to present another clinic. "Doyle, my boy, you have had a difficult, perilous night," said Dr. Bell. "Take today off and rest until you feel up to snuff. Oh, and here is five dollars. You have more than earned it."

I was grateful for the chance to rest, but, even after several cups of hot tea and generous helpings of eggs and ham, I still felt awful and went to my room. I was too restless to sleep and tried to read my medical textbooks for an hour or two, but I could not get Dr. Eli McGillicutty out of my mind. He sounded exactly like the sort of physician who might experiment on human beings. The idea of human experimentation was deeply disturbing, especially when I considered that I just narrowly escaped being the subject of just such an experiment.

But, then, we would not have anaesthetics, ether, and chloroform if doctors had not experimented on medical students and taken the drugs themselves.

I am venturing deeper and deeper into the heart of this mystery and this great, enigmatic American nation. I am filled with questions. Much of what I have always thought of as absolute in my life is beginning to shift and alter. What is right and what is wrong no longer seem as clear to me as they once did.

As I set down these events of the past few days, I realize we are embroiled in a complex mystery. Even Dr. Bell does not seem to have any answers. With those confused thoughts, I am finally ready to drift off to sleep.

13 November, 1878

Bright sun was streaming through the windows when I awoke. It was early in the morning and I must have slept a good ten hours . . .

And I must have been dreaming about skin grafting for burns because the idea of it popped into my mind as soon as I was awake. Out of what I justified as professional curiosity, I was determined to learn more about Dr. McGillicutty.

"Where can one find old newspaper stories?" I asked the cook during a grand breakfast in the kitchen.

"Ask at the Tribune downtown," she answered.

It was a cold day, but clear and brisk and good for a walk. So, I strolled north on Prairie Avenue with the railroad tracks and chuffing trains close by. Horse-drawn trams, hacks, and wagons of all description filled the bustling streets. Workmen were busily erecting new homes and buildings as high as six stories. A fellow on the street said they were planning one that would go up to eight stories and have a steam elevator. But, since Chicago is so flat there, were no interesting vistas, and my view of the lake was perpetually blocked by tall buildings.

My thoughts turned to my beloved Edinburgh. From almost any street in *Auld Reekie*, one may view a heathery shoulder of the Pentland Hills or glimpse a ship tacking down the Firth of Forth to the North Sea. Aye, perhaps I was homesick. It was just that the new buildings in Chicago did not have the character of our Parliament or St. Giles, and there was nothing so fine in all of Chicago as the statue of Charles the Second astride his charger.

Finally, I reached the Tribune building just off State Street. The lobby was grand, with brass railings and gas lights. I found a clerk wearing a green visor behind a desk. The worthless scamp ignored me for a good while. "Where I might find old copies of papers?" I asked.

"In the archives," said he.

"And where might the archives be?"

The smirking rascal ignored my question until I leaned over the desk and flexed a muscle. "Through that door, down to the basement. If you can't locate what you're looking for, ask for a drunken gent by the name of Fogarty," he finally answered.

I went down smooth, worn, stone stairs to the dingy basement. The sign on the door said 'Archives.' I proceeded through a dark corridor to a dim, musty room filled with stacks and stacks of newspapers and folders filled with clippings. I made my way through the jumble and came to a desk lit with a green oil lamp. Behind the desk was a gnome of a man with a small head of thick brown hair. He shuffled papers with hands as delicate as a child's.

I cleared my throat. "Are you Mr. Fogarty?"

"And, what in hell do you want?" was his reply.

"Um, eh, well . . . Information on a doctor by the name of McGillicutty."

"And who in the name of hell are you?"

"Doyle. I am a visiting medical student from University of Edinburgh."

The gnome cackled with laughter. "I might have known . . . Doyle, eh? Irish, are you?"

"My father is of Irish descent."

"And, I suppose you are a good Catholic."

"I was raised Catholic."

He cackled again, "And, now, you're a damn backslider. I suppose you take a drop now and then."

I did not respond.

The little man pulled a bottle from his desk drawer, took a generous swig and pushed the bottle across his littered desk. "Have a pull and then we shall see about Dr. McGillicutty."

"Thanks, but, no thanks." I wanted to keep clear head.

"More for me, then. Yes, I have information on every damn politician, business man, and half the crooks in town. You can't tell one from another and, yes, there is a file on McGillicutty. I know that bastard well."

When Fogarty rose from his chair, he was less than five feet tall, but he quickly skipped through the stacks of newspapers and returned with a folder. His small stature reminded me of my mate Jimmie Barrie from university. Then, I remembered Dr. Bell's statement that the assailant in the poisoning cases was of small stature. "Have you had any medical training, sir?"

"Hell, no. Studied literature at Oberlin . . . Lot of good it did me."

"I see . . . Um, eh . . . This must be a dismal place to work."

"Ach, you get used to it."

He cleared a space beneath the oil lamp and spread out a series of clippings and advertisements. The first story, dated November 1871, described Dr. McGillicutty's remarkable results in the treatment of burn victims. A brief biography listed him as an 1860 graduate of the Eclectic Scientific Medical School in Nashville, Tennessee where he had won the prize for anatomical dissections. Next, he was a surgeon to the Confederate Army. In 1863, he had resigned from the Army to study in Paris and Vienna.

A photograph showed Dr. McGillicutty wearing a formal suit of clothes and a black silk hat. He had a thick black mustache. Gold-rimmed spectacles were perched on a thin, almost aristocratic nose. He appeared to be highly respectable and the sort of practitioner that one could trust with his life. He also appeared to be of short stature . . .

There was another article about his dismissal from the County Hospital. An advertisement, dated 1874, included a close-up photograph of his face and head without the hat. He was balding and his spectacles were perched lower on his nose. He still appeared to be a solid practitioner, but something was a bit askew about his eyes.

Dr. McGillicutty, in the advertisement, offered the highest quality drugs: cocaine, opium, quinine, digitalis, and extracts of all known plant remedies. The next advertisement was more interesting.

REJUVENATION THERAPY
DR. MCGILLICUTTY'S GLANDULAR EXTRACT
REVIVES SPIRITS, RESTORES YOUTH
&
INCREASES PASSION IN BOTH SEXES

When I saw the word 'glandular' my heart skipped a beat. I hurriedly recorded the information in my notebook, drew a rough sketch of the doctor, and pushed the folder back to Fogarty. "Where is this Dr. McGillicutty now?"

"Ah ha, aren't you the nosey bugger? Any more intelligence will cost you a drink, sonny boy."

Fortunately, Dr. Bell had given me the five dollars, so I could afford a few drinks. His destination, Hinky Dink McKenna's Saloon, was several blocks away in a shabbier part of town. On the way there we passed several mansions where young men and well-dressed young ladies were coming and going. Piano music and feminine laughter filtered out through open doors even though it was the middle of the day.

"Are there always parties here?" I asked.

"Aye, this is Mother Brigit's." He paused for a moment and pointed to an especially gaudy mansion. "The finest sporting house in the world. You can hire a young virgin or an experienced older vixen to teach you the ways of the world. Take your pick."

Hinky Dink's Saloon was a big raucous tavern with a long mahogany bar, scratched wooden tables, sawdust on the floor, and dozens of men lifting a glass. We had no more than arrived at a spot on the bar next to the lunch counter when the barkeeper slid a double shot of whisky to Fogarty, who downed the liquor with one gulp. I had a beer, and we helped ourselves to free pickles and tasty roast beef sandwiches.

He showed no sign of intoxication, but, when he commenced talking about Dr. McGillicutty, he nearly shouted. "McGillicutty, the bastard, promised that if I took ten bottles of his medicine I would grow a half-foot taller and be able to please a woman all night long. The damn stuff didn't work, but he claimed he was brewing a new formula just for me."

Several men put down their drinks and cocked an ear in our direction. "Where is Dr. McGillicutty now?" I asked.

A crafty smile came over his face. "Well, ain't that a bit of a secret?"

"Please, I must know."

He looked at me for a moment and then relented. "I happen to know he has his own private hospital."

"Where?"

"It's in one of me files, somewhere in the archives. Come back to-morrow with a bit of cash and I'll have the address for you."

I reached for money to pay for our drinks and felt Rebecca's letter. How could I have forgotten?

I tossed some coins on the bar, ran into the street, and, with great care, slit open the envelope with my pen knife. I scanned the single page with her delicate writing and then read it through a half-dozen times.

Dear Mr. Doyle,

I must thank you again for your kind assistance and pray that this finds you in good health. The Reverend Balfour is regaining his strength and has had no more spells. We are staying with the Reverend Beecher, a very famous minister who was a good friend of President Lincoln. His sister wrote the story ***Uncle Tom's Cabin.***

The Reverend Beecher is a strange man for being a minister, since he was involved in a scandal and was accused of seducing young women in his parish. Of course, these malicious allegations are false. He is a kind man who treats me with great sympathy, almost fondness, but he has changed his opinion about slavery and now believes, like the Reverend Balfour, that the black people should not have been freed. Sadly, his health is failing and I am not sure how much longer he will be of this world.

Now, I have exciting news. Since the Reverend Balfour is feeling better, next week we shall travel to Memphis. Perhaps we shall meet again there after all.

Sincerely Yours,
Rebecca Yates

In the letter, there was not a word expressing any feelings for me. My world turned upside down. I folded the letter, tucked it my notebook, and turned back to the saloon. I wanted to get dead drunk, but the vivid image of my own father lying drunk on the floor crossed my mind. Shame and anger welled up in me. I refused to ever become like him.

Maybe I should just go to a sporting house and find out what it's really like to enjoy the pleasures of the flesh. But, Dr. Bell would not approve. Why should he? He is so different than me. Everything has been so easy for him. He comes from long line of medical aristocrats. His father was a third generation physician, while my father, a struggling artist, has never had a tuppence to his name.

However, it is also true that Dr. Bell has not lived without suffering. He lost his wife and his only son, yet he has never veered from his life's course. When I thought about that, I knew I must do the same. I lifted my shoulders and decided that I will NOT be deterred from a career in medicine by one small setback. I am done with feeling sorry for myself and with romantic yearnings. Miss Rebecca Yates can dally with her elderly minister all she wishes. I am through with her.

14 November, 1878

Immediately after Dr. Bell's morning clinic we went to the children's ward to select patients for surgery to-morrow. The young physician, John Murphy, pushing a dressing cart, led us on rounds, giving a brief history of each of the sick little patients.

Even though the hospital is relatively new, the ward was damp and chilly. Columns blocked light from dirty windows. Dr. Bell clucked at lazy slatterns who swept dirt into corners or under beds, but he tousled the hair and joked with small lads and complimented the girls.

Boys and girls were not separated on the ward, and most beds had at least two small occupants. Apparently there was little interest in children or their diseases because, aside from Dr. Murphy, Carl Lindborg and Rufus, there was only one physician present on the floor.

More than once, Dr. Bell raised his eyebrows. "All this poor child needs is fresh air, sunshine, and good clean milk," he said. Yet these items seemed to be in short supply. At least half of the children suffered from tuberculosis of the bone or lymph glands, and the rest had broken bones from being kicked by a horse or run over by an omnibus.

For surgery the next day, the professor selected a child with tuberculosis of the spine and a large abscess, and another whose chest was filled with fluid, collapsing the lung. I knew he would save both lives.

My feelings about Bell keep shifting. In Edinburgh, he seemed to take pleasure in ridiculing me and I had wanted to curse at him. Now I see that his hard veneer is merely a necessary coat of armour to protect a sensitive disposition. Do all physicians have to harden their hides to survive? I wonder if I can develop the necessary toughness to carry on as a doctor . . .

I said nothing for fear of antagonizing my new friends, but I could not help thinking that a rich country like America must learn to take better care of these poor sick children. Scotland is an old, poor country, but there has never been a speck of dirt on the floors of the Royal Infirmary.

Near the middle of the ward, we came upon a girl of perhaps three years of age who was breathing with terrible difficulty. Her little chest caved in each time she attempted to draw in air, and her lips and fingernails were dusky blue.

"This little one is suffering with the croup," said Dr. Murphy, just as the child gave up her struggle and stopped breathing.

Dr. Bell fixed his eyes on the dying child. "Her vocal cords are completely obstructed. Mr. Doyle, my straight bistoury, please."

I desperately looked at Rufus. I thought he had brought the instruments. He had assumed that I had them. I could barely get the words out. "I'm sorry sir; the instrument case must be in the clinic."

Bell's voice was filled with venom. "You left the instruments?!"

"Aye sir. I'm terribly sorry."

"Then at least find me some carbolic acid, PLEASE!"

I sprinted through the ward until I found a vial of carbolic and then ran back to Dr. Bell with it. Without another word, he removed a small silver pocket knife from his vest pocket and cleaned it with the carbolic.

Then, with no hesitation, he held the child's chin back with one hand and, with the other, sliced an incision down the middle of her neck. Black sticky blood oozed from the wound. With another stroke, he cut into the child's windpipe and twisted the blade to separate the tracheal cartilages.

Dr. Murphy stepped forward and mopped a glob of mucous away with a bit of gauze. The child's chest heaved. She took in a lungful of air through the opening and coughed out plugs of mucous. Her breathing settled down, and, like a miracle, color came back to her cheeks. Murphy ran to obtain a proper tracheotomy tube.

Dr. Bell rarely became angry, but, in this instance, he was steaming. He cuffed my shoulder with an open hand. "Mr. Doyle, at the very least I expect my clerks to be dependable. This child might have died because of your negligence!"

I left to fetch the instrument case. By the time I returned, he had settled down and was discussing the treatment of esotropia (the condition of being cross-eyed) with Dr. Murphy and the physician who had tagged along. I had some interest in eye diseases and listened intently, then thought of the spectacles perched on the nose of Dr. Eli McGillicutty and the slightly off-center appearance of his eyes.

After we had finished the rounds I screwed up my courage to speak. “Sir, I may have information on the murder cases.”

“Doyle, I would prefer that you concentrate on assisting me only in the care of medical patients. Please, do not let your concern about crime interfere with your medical duties. Mr. Duncan is having second thoughts about our involvement in this crime. I shall be having lunch with him shortly.”

Damn him! Bloody Dr. Bell could drop the case, but I was not going to go away so easily. I was determined to find the wretches who had attempted to kidnap me and learn more about skin grafting.

I saw the doctor off in a cab to his lunch. With great trepidation, I turned the damned instrument case over to Rufus with strict instructions for him to immediately go to Mr. Duncan’s home.

The horse drawing the omnibus was spavined and limped on its hind leg. The driver used his whip, but it was not until mid-afternoon that I arrived at the Chicago Tribune building. I immediately went to the basement archives only to find Fogarty asleep in his chair behind his desk. I cleared my throat. “Mr. Fogarty . . . It is I, Doyle. We have an appointment,” I announced.

He opened his eyes and gave me a bleary look. “Doyle? I don’t know any Doyle. Who the hell are you?”

“Sir, you promised to give me information on the whereabouts of Dr. Eli McGillicutty if I returned today with some cash.”

“Are you a damned spy—a damned bloody Pinkerton?”

“No sir. I am Dr. Joseph Bell’s medical clerk.”

“Oh, you are with Ding Dong Bell.” His witticism sent him into cackles of laughter and he seemed to wake up. “That mad Scottish quack.”

“Please, you were to tell me about Dr. Eli McGillicutty’s whereabouts?”

"You should ask the Colonel down South in the red house. I don't remember—"

"Mr. Fogarty, does this help you remember?" I held out a two-dollar gold piece. His eyes cleared, and he opened a drawer filled with empty bottles. "Damn, I can't think without some whisky. If you want me to find McGillicutty's damn bloody file, go around the corner and fetch me a bottle. "

I purchased a pint of Old Crown and hurried back. I could not have been gone more than half an hour, but, when I returned, the archives section was pitch dark. I struck a wooden lucifer friction match against the brick wall and made my way, step by careful step, through the corridor.

When the friction match spluttered out, I bumped into Fogarty's desk. I lit another match, and, in the flickering yellow light, I saw Fogarty sleeping with his head down on his desk. The oil lamp had been knocked over.

I lifted the lamp out of a pool of what looked like oil and then realized there was dark blood all over the desk. I dropped the whisky bottle and touched Fogarty's neck. He was not asleep, but, quite . . . Dead.

Something protruded from his mouth. "Holy God!" I uttered, and stepped back from the desk just as the lucifer match burned my fingers and flickered out.

I stumbled my way back up the corridor and into the front office of the paper. "Murder! There's been a murder!" I hollered at the top of my lungs.

The next minutes passed in terrible confusion. One of the clerks went into the archives with a lantern, returned immediately, and vomited on the floor. In the chaos that followed, there were screams for police. "Notify Mr. Medill!" someone yelled.

Within minutes, two constables arrived on the scene. After being equipped with lanterns they went into the basement. I followed and beheld an awful spectacle. Fogarty's chin rested on the edge of the desk and a long knife protruded from his mouth.

Lamp oil and blood soaked the papers on the desk. One constable reached for the knife. "I don't think we should touch anything," I warned.

The constables, more accustomed to dealing with vagrants and drunks than murder, readily agreed, and we returned to the first floor. The clerk, who yesterday had directed me to the archives, pointed in my direction. "There, that man. He is the murderer!"

The constables drew their revolvers and pinioned me against a large marble column, pulling my arms back and applying handcuffs. I was the victim of rough frontier justice—tried, sentenced, and executed by the mob before I had a chance to prove my innocence.

Fortunately for my health and longevity, a distinguished bearded gentleman, dressed entirely in black and wearing a silk top hat, had entered the room and quickly restored order. Much to my surprise, he was accompanied by Angus Duncan and Dr. Bell.

The gentleman was named Mr. Joseph Medill. He was the owner and publisher of the Tribune and had been the Mayor of Chicago after the Great Fire. He had been having a long lunch with Duncan and Bell at the Union League Club when he was summoned.

The constables described the scene in the basement, but their English was rather poor and the powers of observation were even poorer. "Fetch Allan Pinkerton," Medill ordered, after listening a moment.

Then, Mr. Duncan asked that I be released. Dr. Bell drew me aside. "Doyle, what in God's good name is the meaning of this?" he whispered.

I quickly explained my interest in Dr. McGillicutty and locating the newspaper file. "The murdered man is in the basement." I said.

Mr. Medill, sweeping his cane from side to side, quickly cleared the room. "I should've fired the damned Irish drunkard long ago! And the damn democrats had a hand in this, I will wager."

Medill was still ranting when Allan Pinkerton arrived. "Who found the body?" he demanded. I stepped forward.

"Lead the way," he commanded.

During the hour or so since I had found the body, blood had congealed on the desk, but nothing else had changed. Mr. Pinkerton was about to remove the murder weapon. “May I examine the body?” Dr. Bell asked.

Pinkerton stepped in front of Bell. “The man is clearly dead. A doctor’s opinion would be of no use now.”

“I disagree.” Dr. Bell stepped around Pinkerton, wrapped a handkerchief about the hilt of the knife, and gently moved it back and forth; the head moved with the blade since it was solidly imbedded. “The murder weapon entered slightly from the left of his mouth, went through the back of the throat, and is imbedded in the vertebra. From the volume of blood, I would wager that the tip of the blade severed the right vertebral artery. He may have temporarily recovered from the initial shock of the blow, only to die when he strangled on his own blood.”

I held the grisly head while Allan Pinkerton used all his strength to remove the knife, which he identified as a bayonet, with the letters C.S.A. stamped on the blade.

“Have not seen one of these since the war,” said Pinkerton.

“What does it stand for?” I asked.

“Confederate States of America.”

Mr. Pinkerton seemed to have completed his investigation and, after wrapping the bayonet wrapped in cloth, he left the scene.

Dr. Bell motioned me to stay. “Look at this,” said he.

Fogarty had scrawled something in his own blood on the desk top. The words were nearly illegible, but they seemed to say c*innte faoi ghlas*.

I wanted to solve the mystery right then and there, but Dr. Bell urged me to return post haste to the hospital and take over the care of the little girl with the croup.

Her breathing was still labored and her big brown eyes reminded me of my little sister, Ida. As she coughed and struggled for air, I knew something had to be done for her. I devised a method to aspirate her trachea using a syringe and a tube and, after a while, she took some broth and bits of bread. Her breathing sounded much better, and I felt good about being able to help her.

When Dr. Murphy arrived to take over her care just before midnight, she was peacefully asleep. As I walked home, I realized that I was able to perform the aspiration without freezing up. Was it because the little girl reminded me of my little sister, Ida, or that Dr. Bell was not watching, or that I did not think about any of it, I just acted?

I shall never know. But, for the first time in a long time, I thought that maybe, just maybe, I might become a tolerable physician.

When I returned to our lodgings, to my surprise Dr. Bell was still awake and going over his notes. I expected another severe chastisement. Instead, he invited me into his room and motioned to a chair next to his blazing fire.

He poured out a dram of sherry for himself. "I know this might sound redundant, but, now, please indulge me and tell me everything that happened between you and this man Fogarty."

I started from the beginning and told him everything, from the time the thugs accosted me outside of the anatomy lab to my conversations with Fogarty. I showed him the sketches I had made of Dr. McGillicutty. Doctor Bell grunted his approval and leaned back in his chair with his right fist under his chin. He tapped the sketch of McGillicutty. "Pinkerton suspects this man has connections to the foreign socialists who are intent on destroying Mr. Duncan's railroads by murdering his employees. He may be our man."

"But, only the first two victims were employed by Mr. Duncan," said I.

"That's true, but we don't know anything about the most recent victims. Now, tell me in more detail anything that you have not mentioned about the events of today."

"Well, Fogarty seemed to hate the Pinkertons and he said something strange along the lines of, 'Ask the Colonel down South in the red house . . . ' I could make nothing of it. But, I do believe the words he wrote in his own blood are Gaelic."

I passed the page of my notebook with the words *cinnte faoi ghlas.*

"Aye, indeed. One would tend to think that he would write in his native tongue during his last moments. I shall have a chat with Mrs. O'Flynn as to their meaning."

At the mention of the cook's name I wondered what delicacies might be in the kitchen. I had missed dinner again. She had promised roast duck with orange sauce, but, due to the awful events that I had been involved in on this day, I ended up going to bed hungry.

And now, I cannot sleep . . .

So here I am, writing this entry to try to get my mind off my growling stomach. I came on this little adventure to see America, but I never dreamed that my life would almost be snuffed out by thugs or that I would be involved in solving a series of murders!

What have I gotten myself into? When Bell asked me to accompany him I should have flatly refused. Aye, my family is poor, but back in Scotland I was safe and happy and my stomach was always full. AND no one was trying to kill me. Maybe I am not cut out for a life of adventure, after all.

15 November, 1878

I awoke this morning, hungry as a bear, with no thoughts at all about my grim musings of the past night.

The morning operating clinic went quickly, and, after the usual discussion, Dr. Bell announced that he was about to perform a post-mortem examination on an interesting case. Word had gotten about that Fogarty was to be the subject.

There was a rumble of displeasure and almost-lewd remarks when Emilie Droussard insisted on remaining to witness the post mortem examination, but Bell silenced them with a hiss and a wave of his hand.

The diener rolled the corpse, covered with a sheet, into the amphitheatre while Bell arranged his instruments. The audience was silent when Bell drew back the covering and revealed Fogarty's body, which was the size of a small, hairless lad with undeveloped genitalia. Fogarty's lips were drawn back in a rictus of terror and his eyes were wide open.

"Gentlemen, you will agree that we have a most unusual case. This man, nearly forty years of age, has a body which has not developed beyond childhood. Our task is to determine the cause of this condition."

Bell made an incision from the neck to the pubis and quickly dissected the organs, which he placed on a pan beside the body. The heart, lungs, and stomach were perfectly normal, but the liver was in the advanced stages of alcoholic cirrhosis.

He then carefully placed the testicles, adrenal gland, and the thyroid on the pan and pointed to each with the tip of his knife. "Observe, these glands, the ones that we believe regulate the body—are atrophic."

Bell turned his attention to the gruesome head with the open mouth and congealed blood on the lips and gums. "Now, we will see a most rare abnormality of the pituitary gland."

He rolled the head from side to side. "What have we here?" He pulled the hair aside and demonstrated a smear of blood around a small hole in the back of the head. "It is a puncture wound."

He then drew his long, razor-sharp knife across the back of the head, from ear to ear and rolled the scalp back over the forehead, so that, when replaced, the face would appear to be untouched. Whatever instrument had made the puncture wound had penetrated deeply into the skull. "Doyle, look here." With the tip of his knife, he removed a small fragment of metal imbedded in the skull. "Take this and keep quiet," he whispered in my ear.

I palmed the bit of metal, turned my back to the crowd, and slipped it inside my billfold.

Bell then sawed through the circumference of the skull and removed the skull cap, revealing the glistening brain with its convolutions, sulci, and veins. The physicians and students in the audience leaned forward with rapt attention. Perhaps some of them had never seen a human brain before.

Emilie Droussard's delicate features were deathly pale. I was surprised because she had witnessed operations and organ removal with equanimity, and I did not expect her to appear affected.

Bell then removed the brain, and, with infinite care, dissected the pituitary gland and held it up for all to see. "As anticipated, the pituitary gland, the supreme regulator of the body, has failed to develop. This undoubtedly caused Mr. Fogarty's small stature."

"Gentlemen, come, I want all of you to see the small size of the sella turcica, where the pituitary gland normally resides. Older textbooks refer to this saddle-like depression in the sphenoid bone as a 'Turkish chair.' "

When the crowd moved in closer to Fogarty's body, Emilie Droussard quietly left. Out of curiosity, I followed her out to the street.

She was adjusting her shawl, not far away, when a stooped, sallow-faced fellow came up to me. "You are one of the doctors caring for my little girl in the children's ward. I can't thank you enough."

"You should thank Dr. Bell. He was the one who saved her life."

The man poked his head close to mine. "I was in Hinky Dink's Saloon when I overheard your conversation with Fogarty. Since you helped my little Gracie, I kin tell ya this. If you want Dr. McGillicutty, there he goes." He pointed at a man walking in the opposite direction down the street.

"Damn," I thought. McGillicutty had been in the audience all along. McGillicutty was stooped, had a bad limp, and his hat was pulled well down over his eyes. No wonder I had not recognized him in the audience. He was climbing into a hack less than a block away.

I started to go after him. "No need to run after him. He lives at the Marshall Hotel at State and Van Buren." My sallow-faced friend spoke from the corner of his mouth and scuttled away before I could thank him.

Dr. Bell was still lecturing, and it would not hurt to delay my meeting with Dr. McGillicutty, so I returned and watched while Dr. Murphy neatly sewed up the incisions in poor Fogarty and Dr. Bell lectured on glands. He is as knowledgeable on the subject as anyone in the world, but very little is really known about them.

The amphitheatre was very warm and the session bogged down in a discussion of philosophy and even Darwin's theory. I found myself drifting off to sleep.

16 November, 1878

My day was filled with more lectures and dissections, so I was not free until late in the day. In Chicago, as in Edinburgh, dusk comes early, especially on those overcast days with a foreboding of snow. The Harrison Street Omnibus took me to State Street which was only a short walk to Van Buren.

The streets were filled with disreputable men, poorly dressed women, and raggedy lads. Many carried unlit torches, and there was an air of excitement in the crowd. I hurried on, ignoring the moving swarm of people, and kept a hand on my wallet. The Marshall Hotel was a hastily slapped-together structure next to a gambling parlor and across the street from an empty lot filled with rubbish.

I shivered against the wind, and a knot of cold fear clutched the center of my chest. I started to freeze and then stopped myself. What was I doing? Did I have the nerve to do this? Was it foolhardy to pursue a criminal alone? Was I merely trying to prove my worth to myself and Dr. Bell?

I hesitated, but pressed forward into the shabby, dark lobby where a clerk directed me to the corner room overlooking State Street. "Who is there?" The gruff question came in answer to my knock on the door.

"My name is Doyle, assistant to Dr. Joseph Bell."

I was not sure how he would respond. "The door is open. Enter." The voice had a strange tone, but was not unpleasant.

As soon as I walked in I backed away—repulsed by the overpowering odor of decay—and covered my face with a handkerchief. By the light of a single candle stuck in an old wine bottle I made out a bed, table, and a chair. Then, as my eyes adjusted, I saw movement under a pile of blankets on the bed. The dim figure gradually sat up and swung his legs off the side of the bed.

"Mr. Doyle, you have been looking for me?"

The voice had a peculiar resonance, and, as the figure gradually came into the candle's light, I saw a face disfigured by deep crevices, flat red patches, and a sunken nose. It was nothing like the photograph of Dr. McGillicutty. Was this an imposter to throw me off the scent? Maybe he had syphilis.

"Um, are you . . . Are you Doctor McGillicutty?" I stammered.

"None other."

"But, you don't look like your pictures."

"Mr. Doyle, you have followed me from the hospital, aye? I was there and saw you. I had to witness the post-mortem examination of poor Fogarty. He was one of my patients, you know?"

I took a step forward, but he held up his hand and motioned for me to come no closer. The hand was misshapen and the tips of the fingers ulcerated.

"Have they taught you about leprosy at Edinburgh?"

I recoiled in panic. "There might have been a lecture, but I don't remember."

His laugh was hollow and mournful. "Study my face and hands."

"But, I thought leprosy was only in the tropics."

"You are seeing the revenge of a monkey. I caught the disease from an experimental animal."

"What sort of experiments?"

"I worked on glandular extracts, looking for a cure for poor unfortunates like Fogarty."

"Then, you are the one. You murder men for their thyroid glands."

"No, no, no… Please, look at these hands. I have not operated for a long while." He waved his misshapen hands for me to inspect, although from a distance. I realized he was right. There was no way he could have performed delicate surgery with such deformed digits.

"But, you know about glandular extracts and—"

"Yes. My experiments with monkeys demonstrated that extracts of fresh tissue reversed the effects of total thyroidectomy. Sadly, I had to work on live, awake animals because, otherwise, anaesthetics reduced the potency of the glandular extracts I needed."

"And you used curare to prevent the animals from moving while you were experimenting on them?"

"Exactly. Until, one day, I administered too low a dose of curare to a poor creature, and the monkey awoke in mid-operation and bit me. The damn animal infected me with leprosy."

"Sir, I believe that someone knows of your work and is killing humans to obtain the thyroid."

"You are correct. I suspect it is one of my former associates. Doyle, if you can stand the sight of my poor broken body, I would be willing to share all I know with you."

"Yes, Doctor, should we talk here or . . ."

"I haven't had a morsel of food all day. Let's go out and get something to eat. You know, your mentor, Dr. Bell may be the only surgeon in the world who can truly understand my work."

My heart went out to the wretched man. I wondered what it was like to have a horrible, incurable disease and feel death hovering over you. I shivered again and felt a premonition of ominous things to come.

The poor man pulled on gloves and turned the brim of his hat down over his face. Together, we exited his tiny room. As we made our way down the street to his favourite restaurant I made out a band of armed men lurking in the area just past the hotel. As if in a bad dream, I watched as they raised their weapons and took aim. *Dear God. Is this the end?* I dove into the shadows just as shots rang out. I was unscathed. Dr. McGillicutty was not so lucky. A fusillade of bullets struck him down.

Instinctively, I crawled to his aid, barely avoiding injury myself when a slug tore through the sleeve of my heavy coat. McGillicutty had bloody holes in his chest. The sound of gunfire was suddenly drowned out by shouts and the clip-clop of horses on the pavement.

Was it a diversion to mask the murder? The night was lit by hundreds of blazing torches carried by demonstrators shouting for justice and higher wages. I huddled with McGillicutty on the sidewalk as a phalanx of mounted men dressed in white hoods and robes marched by, followed by men and lads shouting and carrying banners denouncing capitalism. All of them were oblivious to poor Dr. McGillicutty.

I held two fingers against Dr. McGillicutty's neck. There was no pulse. He was beyond help. Knowing it was too late for him, I escaped the raucous hubbub through an alley while I still could.

I could still hear the shouts and gunfire behind me as I crept between buildings until I was away from the demonstration. When I was finally in the clear, I broke into a dead run to Mr. Duncan's mansion.

In order to avoid disturbing anyone, I decided to go around the back and through the servant's entrance into the kitchen.

By this time it was so late, and I was able to sneak through the entire house and make my way to my room without being spotted.

Once I arrived in my quarters I was so exhausted that I was asleep before I could take off all my clothes.

17 November, 1878

I slept almost till noon and then spent most of the afternoon walking the streets of Chicago, thinking through last night's events. When night fell, I returned to Mr. Duncan's house where many fine carriages lined the front entrance to the mansion. As I walked by the great living room I stopped and listened to agitated conversation. ". . . What business do Southerners have up here?"

"I attribute it to all those bastard foreign anarchists."

"Yes, and don't forget the damn socialists."

I paused long enough to recognize the voice of Allan Pinkerton. "Gentlemen, my men will put down this riot and shoot the instigators."

"That's all well and good, but what is the Klan doing in Chicago?" another voice asked.

Pinkerton's voice rose. "Gentlemen, please, let me finish. There appears to be a group of Southerners who are attempting to ally themselves with local union organizers to disrupt our nation."

There was a stunned silence. "How, in the name of God could that happen?" asked a gentleman with a fevered voice.

Pinkerton went on. "Gentlemen, yesterday one hundred Gatling guns and a thousand new Winchester repeating rifles were stolen from the armory. I fear that they will be used to arm troops in the South or to foment uprisings among disgruntled workingmen right here in this fair city. Either way, it is not good."

I had heard enough and crept up the stairs. I was surprised to find the door to Dr. Bell's room wide open. "Doyle, please join me for a bit of supper."

I set to work on smoked turkey, a bit of pork roast, preserved strawberries, tea, and bread smeared with butter. Dr. Bell sipped Mr. Duncan's fine malt whisky and gazed into the blazing fire. "The Americans seem to have themselves a bit of a crisis," said he. "But, enough about them, what have you been up to, my lad?"

I had to make a clean breast of it and confessed that I had left the hospital to pursue the investigation. Dr. Bell humphed and harrumphed as I told him of my encounter with Dr. McGillicutty. The whole while he sat with his fingers laced over his chest, looking deeply into the flames. When I came to the part about the doctor's leprosy, he shook his head. "Sad, so sad."

When I finished my dismal story, he became alert and had that glint in his eye that I knew so well. "Damn it, Doyle, do you realize that your meddling may have caused that poor man's death?"

"I don't think . . . How could—"

"Who knew you were meeting with him and that you were involved with the investigation?"

"I am so sorry." I hung my head and wished that I had never come to America. "I didn't . . . Well, I never meant to cause him harm."

"Just answer my question."

"The father of the little girl with croup knew I wanted to meet Dr. McGillicutty. He seemed to be an honest workingman."

"Who else?"

"Well, there were many other people in the tavern that day."

"So, there were others who could have overheard your conversation with Fogarty?"

"Yes, and oh, there was that woman."

"That woman?"

"The one you are fond of who attends the clinic."

"I am not *fond* of her. She is a student of the medical arts. Nothing more and nothing less."

"She left the post-mortem early and may have overheard my conversation with the girl's father."

"Hmm . . . Now, Doyle, I regret to say this, but do you realize that your meddling may have also bungled our entire investigation?"

I felt awful. "I am so sorry, sir. Is there anything I can say or do—"

"On the other hand, you may have turned up an important clue. Fogarty was murdered to prevent him from revealing Dr. McGillicutty's location and some unknown person or persons killed the doctor to prevent him from discussing his work and his comrades with you."

I was overcome by guilt and remorse at my folly and was scarcely listening. He squeezed my arm to bring me out of my guilty funk.

"Doyle, please lad, listen to me. What were McGillicutty's exact words? Are you certain he said comrades instead of colleagues or classmates?"

"I think he said comrade. What difference does it make, sir?"

"My lad, have you learned nothing on this trip? You must not only learn to observe diligently, but to listen carefully and analyze the meaning of each word. Obviously the word colleague refers to a close associate, such as a physician's partner. The word comrade, on the other hand, is often applied to one's friends in a military outfit."

"Heavens above. That reminds me." I hastily consulted my notes. "Dr. McGillicutty was a surgeon in the Confederate Army."

"Exactly, lad, and a Confederate bayonet killed Fogarty . . . Yet I cannot connect his statement about going south and a red house with anything concrete related to these murders."

"What about those three words scrawled in blood by Fogarty? Did you discover their meaning?"

"Mrs. O'Flynn confirmed that *cinnte faoi ghlas is* Gaelic and means 'sure lock.' "

"Sure lock . . . That could be the name of a type of lock box or a safe." I said.

"Aye, most likely. Do you think Fogarty may have been directing you to a specific safe that contained some item of great value?" Dr. Bell asked.

There was a gentle knock on the door.

"Who is there?" Dr. Bell asked.

"Rufus."

"Come in, please."

Rufus stumbled into the room and stood before us, speechless. He trembled and twisted his cap in his hands.

"Rufus snap out of it, man. What the devil is wrong?" Dr. Bell asked.

"They's coming after all us freedmen. To make us slaves again. I gots to go back to the *Devonia*. Get clear out of this country."

"Mr. Freeman, please calm down. Have a drink to settle your nerves."

Dr. Bell filled a crystal glass with several fingers of malt whisky. Rufus gulped it all down in one swallow.

"President Lincoln freed the slaves and the Thirteenth Amendment assured their freedom. You have nothing to worry about," said Dr. Bell.

"They killed poor Mr. Lincoln and those ghosts marchin' in the street gonna tear up that 'mancipation proclamation. My lady friend's a housekeeper at the hotel and she told me that she was brushin' a man's suit when she seen them ghost clothes."

"Ghost clothes?"

"Yes sir. White hoods, long white robes. He had a set in the closet just like they was wearing on the street."

"Who is this man?"

"Captain Andrew Spencer. He was in the rebel army and rode with General Forrest. He got his right hand blowed off at the battle of Corinth and turned plumb mean."

"Did he stay in the rebel army?"

"Yes, sir. The doctors fixed a hook on his right arm so he could grab things. He kilt prisoners at Fort Pillow after they surrendered. Those poor bluecoats knelt down and begged for mercy, but he kilt them in cold blood. They called him Captain Hook."

"Can you describe his hook?"

"It was made out of iron, curved like this and sharp at the end." Rufus bent his finger in the shape of a half circle.

"Doyle, let me see that fragment from Fogarty's skull."

I handed him the sharp metallic sliver. Dr. Bell drew the lamp closer, placed the fragment on a slip of paper. He minutely studied the bit of metal with a magnifying glass. I fidgeted and wondered why a small bit of metal was so interesting or important. "Doyle, tell me what am I doing and why."

"Um . . . Ah, well, you are trying to determine if that metal is iron or steel or—"

"No, Doyle. Sometimes you appear rather clever. But, then, there are other times when you seem a bit dense."

"Sorry, sir."

"Shush. Please sit in that chair and imagine what you would do if I attempted to drive a knife into your mouth."

"I would clench my teeth and resist, moving my head from side to side."

"Exactly. And, unless it was tightly held as the knife was thrust in, your head would move back. As a result, there would not be enough force to penetrate the vertebra."

Dr. Bell then clasped the back of my head with his left hand and drove an imaginary knife into my mouth.

"See. Most likely, the assailant drove the point of an instrument into the back of poor Fogarty's skull and held it, while, with his left hand, he drove the bayonet from left to right into the vertebra."

"Captain Hook, or should I say Captain Spencer, is most definitely our man," I said.

"Not so fast, my laddie. Have I not taught you to be wary of jumping to false conclusions?"

I hung my head in shame. "Aye, sir."

"Mr. Freeman, what do you know about the people in these white robes?"

"They's the ghosts of soldiers who got killed in the war. They ride at night and burn crosses and hang poor Negroes that ain't done nothin' wrong. They's used to be found only down South, but now they's haunting the night right here in Chicago."

"Mr. Freeman, my friend, let me assure you there is no such thing as ghosts. These people garbed all in white are flesh and blood, just like you or me. Now, please, if you will, give me a moment to think."

Dr. Bell stretched his legs to the fire and for several minutes was lost in thought.

After what was probably no more than five minutes Bell sprang up out of his chair and paced the floor. “Mr. Freeman, do you know the Captain’s room number at the hotel?”

“I can find out.”

“Doyle, to-morrow, go into town and purchase a half-pound of gunpowder and two ounces of sulphur. Mr. Freeman, secure a porter’s uniform for yourself. And to-night, both of you, please get a good night’s sleep. There’s a good deal of work to be done.”

Rufus and I nodded in agreement. “Yes, sir.”

“Excellent… Gentlemen, the game is afoot.”

18 November, 1878

America is a strange county. It is a nation so full of energy and in such a rush to be a world leader, yet still so backward. For example, Americans have the quaint idea that sulphur is a sovereign remedy for many ills including pains, fevers, and upset stomachs. I found sulphur in a chemist shop among other patent remedies. "Take a pinch of the sulphur in a tablespoon full of molasses. You will be set right in no time," the chemist advised.

He, then, kindly directed me to a store that sold gunpowder and a variety of firearms. I could not ignore the irony of visiting a gun shop in order to cure one's ills . . .

I purchased the gunpowder. While paying the bill, I looked longingly at the Winchester rifles, Colt six-shooters, and a wide variety of pistols, daggers, holsters, and all the equipment necessary to subdue wild animals, Indians, and all the other deadly dangers lurking in the wilds of the American continent.

After my recent narrow escapes I was determined to purchase a weapon to defend myself. The .45 calibre Colt revolver really took my fancy, but I settled on an easily concealed two-shot .32 calibre Remington Derringer.

"If you are concerned about personal protection, may I also recommend this item?" the clerk asked. It was a thin, very sharp stiletto about five inches long that would fit into a sheathed strapped to one's leg or forearm. It would be instantly available in case of an attack. I thought back to my assailant on the *Devonia* and could not resist. I walked out of the store with the stiletto in a sheath, firmly strapped just above my right ankle under my wool stocking. With a gun and a knife, I felt like the hero, Hawkeye, in my favourite American adventure book, *The Last of the Mohicans*. For the first time since arriving in Chicago, I felt safe.

The rest of the day, I worked in the laboratory with Carl Lindborg. We dissected the intricate tendons and nerves in the hand of our cadaver. Carl was such a good fellow that, after swearing him to secrecy, I told him of my adventures with Fogarty and Dr. McGillicutty.

"Artie, these are violent times here in America. Everything might be quaint and safe in good old Edinburgh, but here we're in the grips of a terrible financial recession. Why do you think I left our farm in Wisconsin? Ever since I arrived here in Chicago, there have been strikes and killings over wages and worker's rights. It's worse down South, where people are boiling over with resentment against the carpetbaggers and President Hayes who they think stole the last election." Carl spoke with the fervor of the downtrodden. "Still, for the sake of Dr. McGillicutty, shouldn't I investigate fur—"

"As your friend, I beg you to be careful . . . With that said, there is nothing I like more than a grand adventure. If you want to be foolhardy and get to the root of these murders, I am the man to go with you and keep you safe."

Later, Dr. Bell brooded over Carl's words but made no comment. Finally, he looked at me. "The authorities are unable to solve these murders. The Pinkerton detectives scoff at our methods. A less stubborn man would quit right now, but I owe it to my old friend, Angus, to continue our investigations. I trust we shall get to the bottom of this mystery over the course of this very evening."

"But, how?"

"Well, dear laddie, all we have to do is follow my plan."

A few hours later, Carl and I were wearing our very best suits and smoking fine cigars as we strolled into the lobby of the Tremont Hotel. We looked like two fine young dandies out for drinks, dinner, and a night on the town. We were not alone. Stylish ladies and gentlemen were scattered here and there, chatting on stuffed leather chairs. Others were drifting in and out of the dining room. We finally settled into a pair of chairs next to a low table in a corner not far from the grand open staircase.

I placed a folded newspaper beneath the table. Hidden inside was a rolled-up sheet of paper holding a small quantity of gunpowder. I had twisted each end of the paper to contain the powder as well as to work as a sort of fuse. When Rufus, dressed in a porter's uniform, raised his hand, I applied my cigar to the twisted end. When it began to 'sizzle,' Carl and I casually strolled towards the entrance.

Just as Dr. Bell predicted, exactly ten seconds later there was a loud *whoosh*, flying sparks, flames, and a dense cloud of yellow, sulphurous smoke. People ran to and fro, coughing, gagging, screaming, covering their faces with handkerchiefs, and making for the exits.

Almost immediately, a bell clanged and more guests swarmed down the main staircase. Rufus dashed through the smoke and stamped out the flames, but the sulphur continued to smolder.

The smoke cleared, but the pandemonium continued. I noticed a petite lady hurrying down the staircase. Even though her face was covered, there was no mistaking the elegant Emilie Droussard on the arm of a ramrod-straight gentleman wearing a grey suit and gloves.

Porters and clerks scurried about, attempting to restore order. Carl and I waited for a full ten minutes, as instructed, but Dr. Bell did not appear. After a few more minutes of waiting for him Carl and I went from perplexed to deeply worried.

Next thing we knew, as a few guests were venturing back up the grand staircase, Rufus and a girl in a maid's uniform ran up to us. Rufus could barely get out the words, "They killed him!"

"Who?" I asked.

"Dr. Bell!"

Great heavens! We ran upstairs and found him lying, absolutely still, in a pool of blood in the corridor outside the open door to room 203.

There was a long gash on the side of his face. With each faint heartbeat more blood pumped out onto the oriental rug in the hallway. Dr. Bell was still alive, but barely. I should have reacted, but, for all my training, I trembled. Dr. Bell, who usually told me what to do, was unconscious and bleeding. Carl staunched the bleeding with a folded handkerchief pressed against his scalp. I looked into Carl's calm face and saw that he was a natural physician, while I—I was the son of a drunk and a dreamer.

"Look at me! Snap out of it, Artie, for God's sake, we must get him out of here."

I snapped out of my trance. "My name is Arthur, can't you learn?"

"Never mind. We need to get him to Mr. Duncan's house right now or he could die. Our safest route is down the servant's stairs and through the kitchen out to the alley. Follow me."

I held pressure on the wound while he and Rufus carried the doctor. As we walked through the kitchen we kept our heads down and tried to ignore the firemen and police who were restoring order. And then, I felt a hand on my shoulder.

I froze and looked up into the eyes of a burly, red-faced Chicago policeman. "Where you two going so fast? Is that man alive?"

Carl spoke up. "We are medical students assisting an injured guest, sir. This man is badly injured. We are taking him to the County Hospital."

The policeman seemed satisfied with Carl's response. We kept moving. During the journey to Mr. Duncan's house, Dr. Bell moaned in pain and appeared to gain consciousness.

Carl and Rufus put the doctor to bed. The deep laceration did not reach down to the skull and appeared to be due to a glancing blow. The profuse bleeding subsided to a slow trickle after I dressed the gash with carbolic gauze and applied a large pressure bandage.

I was beside myself. Would Dr. Bell live through the night? Had I failed him? Would he be in this horrible condition if not for me? If I had dressed the wound poorly and it got infected, I could never live with myself.

I wanted to stay by Dr. Bell all night, but there was nothing left to do. Rufus and Carl forced me to go back to my room to get some sleep. I wrote out the day's events and even prayed for Dr. Bell . . .

19 November, 1878

When I awoke in the morning, I went straight to Dr. Bell's room and knocked on his door. There was no answer. My heart sank: was he dead?

Then, I heard his voice from the kitchen. There he was, healthy enough to sip at Mrs. O'Flynn's homemade chicken soup. It looked scrumptious, and I joined him for a bowl.

The bandage was clean and his skin was no longer deathly white. At noon, after he had insisted upon eating a bowl of Scottish oatmeal, he was sufficiently recovered to relate a rather disconnected, garbled version of his adventure.

"When the fire alarm sounded, I dashed up the servant's staircase to the second floor undetected. Rufus's lady friend provided a key for me to enter Captain Spencer's room. Just as Rufus said, there was a grey officer's uniform with the insignia of a major general in the closet. My memory is still clouded, but I think there was a white hooded robe and several articles of women's clothing."

Dr. Bell's head drooped on the pillow for a long minute, and he covered his eyes with both hands. "If only I could remember more specifics," said he.

"Were there any documents?" I asked.

"Aye . . . Good. Press me, my dear Doyle . . . Help me clarify my thoughts."

"Professor, what did the documents say?"

"I remember . . . A list of names . . . Jefferson Davis . . . Wade Hampton . . . It seems to me that the name Beecher was on the list . . . There were other names, but I just can't remember."

"Did you see Spencer's iron hook appendage?"

"No, but the door to the adjacent room was ajar. I remember now. There was a table with retorts, mortar and pestle, various sized bottles and test tubes, and syringes with needles."

"Chemical apparatus and equipment for medical experiments?"

"Aye, exactly. But, at that very moment, I was struck from behind and was barely able to stagger into the corridor before collapsing and losing consciousness."

"Did you see your assailants?"

"I sensed that there were two large men."

For a moment, Dr. Bell's eyes took on their familiar keen twinkle. "Now, my dear Doyle, everything I've taught you about observing the world comes into play. Tell me. It is vitally important. Did you see anyone come down the stairs?" he asked.

"Well, sir, let's see . . ." I paused. "Carl and I were so nervous about setting off the charge of gunpowder that I didn't notice. "There were dozens of people milling about, making for the exits."

"Think hard."

"Ah, yes. There was a man dressed in a grey suit, walking rather stiffly. I am certain Emilie Droussard was at his side. I may have also seen them together the morning we had breakfast at the hotel."

"Was there anything unusual about his right hand?"

"He wore gloves."

"Was the woman holding his right or left arm?"

"I think she was on his right side, holding his right arm."

"Did that strike you as unusual?"

"No."

"Now, Doyle, a man usually offers his left arm to a lady, so his dominant right hand is free."

I saw the trend of his thought. "Then, if his right hand was useless, he would offer his right arm to the lady."

"Exactly. Captain Spencer or, as he is called, 'Captain Hook', was wearing an imitation hand, covered with a glove. But, why would he be with Emilie? Hmm . . ."

20 November, 1878

Dr. Bell has spent a good deal of time in his bedroom staring off into space, or in the library huddled with Angus Duncan.

Meanwhile, I have been attempting to keep up with my medical studies by attending lectures and assisting in the anatomy laboratory. This morning, Dr. Bell requested that I attend a meeting with Allan Pinkerton and Mr. Duncan.

Dr. Bell sat up in bed with his hands folded and explained the purpose of the meeting. "Doyle, Mr. Pinkerton has ascertained that our suspects have absconded from the hotel, leaving no clues as to their destination. Further investigation has revealed the identities of the most recent victims. They were newly recruited Pinkerton detectives assigned to Mr. Duncan's Chicago, St. Louis and New Orleans's railway. However, none of them have ever reported for work."

I helped Bell walk down to the great drawing room where Allan Pinkerton and Mr. Duncan were having tea.

"These poor devils were murdered to prevent their work in protecting the railways." Pinkerton spoke with a great air of superiority.

"But . . ." I tried to introduce my thoughts. He rose and cut me off with a wave of his hand.

"Listen to me, lad. I know about these things, and their deaths have nothing to do with your ridiculous theory of organ removal."

"But, we have absolute evidence in one case that the thyroid gland was removed, and the equipment Dr. Bell found could very well have been used to prepare a glandular extract from the thyroid." My Irish was up. The man was a pompous ass.

Mr. Pinkerton ignored my outburst and spread a map of the United States on the desk. He tapped the route of the railway from Chicago to New Orleans. "Whoever controls this railroad can move troops to Chicago and control the western half of the country. It is then only one day to transport a Southern army, augmented by communists and Molly Maguire's, to seize Pittsburgh and other major industrial cities. The Federal Army is spread thin attempting to control Indians. So, if the rebels choose to attack, there is actually very little we could do to stop the South from taking over the country and restoring slavery."

"Does that explain the presence of Captain Spencer in Chicago?" I asked.

"Young man, that is none of your business."

"Allan, you are mistaken. Mr. Doyle has risked his life to unravel this mystery. It is very much his business." Angus Duncan's reply was somewhat testy. I was happy for his support.

"But, he is a foreigner and only a student," Pinkerton retorted.

"I trust him and you must, too, sir." There was a pregnant pause as both men stared at each other and then looked at Bell . . .

Finally, Pinkerton nodded. "Oh, very well. After the Civil War the federal authorities charged Captain Spencer with murder for killing soldiers after they surrendered. He escaped to Mexico and joined Maximillian's army, then went to Venezuela where he made his fortune in gold mines. Sadly, the Hayes administration has pardoned all war criminals. He has returned, is dangerous, and is determined to restore the Confederacy."

"Who is Emilie Droussard?" I asked.

"All we really know is that after her husband was killed at Vicksburg she became a Confederate spy," Pinkerton answered.

There was a pause in the conversation until Dr. Bell commented. "Aye, Doyle, our enemies are quite brilliant. If we are to stop these butchers and survive this investigation, I daresay we must be even more clever . . ."

22 November, 1878

Dr. Bell disappeared yesterday. When I saw him this morning, there were subtle changes in his appearance. His cheeks were drawn, and lines had appeared in his face. Even his hair was darker and unruly. I looked more closely. "Doctor Bell, are you still not well?"

"Why do you ask, lad?"

"Well, as you have taught me, I'm trying to make subtle observations. For example, it seems to me that in just two days your hair has changed from pure white to a dull grey-brown."

"Bravo, my dear Doyle. Bravo. It appears as if all my efforts in training you have not been in vain, after all." He flung down a copy of *The Chicago Tribune*. "Read this aloud, laddie."

Bell watched me read with a twinkle in his eye. "Edinburgh surgeon, Dr. Joseph Bell, has been visiting our city and is reported to be seriously ill and near death. If his health improves, he will return to Scotland."

"This makes no sense. Why would they write this?"

"Doyle, are you familiar with *Didelphis Virginiana*?"

"Excuse me?"

"You might be more familiar with this creature by its common name—the Virginia opossum. When this creature senses danger, he curls into a ball and feigns death."

I thought for a moment and then smiled. "And you intend to play that same game to lure our opponents out into the open."

"Astute, my lad. Quite astute. Maybe my lessons are finally paying off."

Another of Bell's peculiarities is the daily reading of newspapers from all different states in America. As he reads one paper after another, he discards them into a stack. I have read in the discarded papers about such things as Nez Perce Indians fleeing through Montana to Canada, Texans fighting over the Mexican border, and Irish miners being hung in Pennsylvania.

So, then, I was not at all surprised when he handed over a copy of *The Memphis Daily Appeal.* "They have struck again, Doyle. Look."

He pointed to an article on the third page which mentioned a young man collapsing on the street and his body immediately being removed. And then he pointed to a story on the back page which announced a series of sermons by the Reverend Henry Ward Beecher and the Scots minister, the Reverend James Balfour, on the subjects of slavery and social Darwinism.

"What do you propose we do about it?" I asked.

"I must go there, but in disguise. I owe it to my old friend, Angus, to see this through. He has paid a hefty fee to get us here and has entrusted us with solving this enigma . . . But, my dear Doyle, you are under no obligation to continue with what will be a dangerous mission. Feel free to return home to your mother."

"Sir, I may be many things, but a craven lad who runs home to his mother, I am not. And, by and by, I have always wanted to visit Memphis in Tennessee, as well."

"An epidemic of yellow fever has been raging through that fair city since August. Thousands have already died."

"That does not change my mind."

He chuckled. "I expected you would say that . . . And you must know, if you go, Doyle, your life will be in danger and you will have to pose as a Pinkerton man."

"A Pinkerton?"

"You will be disguised and will need a sturdy companion. You will be well paid, and there might be a reward if this case has a satisfactory outcome."

"I know the perfect bloke."

"Your mate, Mr. Lindborg, I presume?"

"Why, of course."

"It is agreed then. Allan Pinkerton will prepare two sets of papers for you and Mr. Lindborg. The first will establish you as medical volunteers to assist with the yellow fever epidemic, and the second set will identify you as special security agents for the Illinois Central Railroad."

Carl was eager for the adventure, and, together, we went to the Pinkerton Detective Agency. It was located in an imposing three-story building with a huge sign along the second story which read 'THE EYE THAT NEVER SLEEPS'.

When we entered the building, a clerk conducted us to the office of the general superintendent where we signed the payroll and obtained our two sets of papers. The pay was six dollars a day, and our task was to 'keep an eye on things.' Under no circumstances were we to partake of hard liquor or behave in any way that would dishonour the agency.

On our return, Dr. Bell gave us further instructions. "When you arrive in Memphis, stay at the Peabody Hotel and volunteer to aid the sick. At night, spend time in the saloons, pretend to be intoxicated, and brag about being security officers for the railroad."

"For six dollars a day I can do that," said Carl.

"Wait, sir, is that all?" I asked.

Dr. Bell sighed, "Above all, always stay close. Never let each other out of your sight and follow one another when you are on the streets. The poison curare primarily affects skeletal muscles. If you ever feel a pinprick, it may be a poisonous needle. You must concentrate on nothing else, but breathing with your diaphragm. That is less affected by the poison."

"I'm sorry, sir, but what does being a Pinkerton have to do with curare and practicing breathing?"

"Well, dear laddie, you and Carl will be bait for the killers. I would do it myself if I was younger, but alas . . ."

"You mean, we may be in danger from the killers who use curare?"

"Aye, this is a deadly game. Lad, you may back out if you wish."

"No, I am armed and with Carl. We will have no fear of those ruffians."

I spoke with great bravado, but with an undercurrent of fear. And then, despite my determination to put Rebecca out of mind, I wondered about whether she was with the Reverend Balfour in Memphis and if I might see her again.

23 November, 1878

I did not sleep well last night and dreamed about poison and ghastly medical experiments. I greatly admired Dr. Bell's deductive talents, but did his cognitive faculties overshadow common sense and his ability to empathize with the plight of others?

The idea of posing as Pinkertons smacked of lunacy and sheer madness. Several times in the wee hours of the morning, I vowed I would march right over to his room and tell him to get another poor sod to serve as his live bait.

In the end, it was clear we were committed. Both Carl and I needed the money. I am already in too deep and must not let down Doctor Bell or Carl.

Rufus came early to help pack. "Mr. Arthur, those folks down south don't take to strangers from the North. Don't you trust nobody and be careful."

"I shall."

"I want to go with you."

"No, Rufus. You stay with Dr. Bell."

Rufus bobbed his woolly head. "Guess you is right. I'll stick with the doctor, but they's one white man in Memphis you can trust."

"Who?"

"Mr. Josiah Burk on Second Street."

He then took a common pin out of his wallet and a pinch of black soot wrapped in a scrap of paper. "Hold out your wrist." He dipped the pin in the soot and pricked the inside of my wrist, leaving an almost microscopic black dot. "Show him this mark. He helped slaves escape to the North."

I finished writing these bits of conversation and my sad ruminations. I then gave this diary to Doctor Bell with a folded note that said, "Sir, if we don't return, please give this to my mother."

An hour later, Carl and I climbed aboard the crowded smoking car of the *St. Louis Flyer*. It was ten o'clock in the morning as we rattled through Central Illinois. I was tired and morose at leaving Dr. Bell and the dangers that may lie ahead. Carl was jubilant.

"Carl, how can you be so calm?"

Carl puffed on his El Perfecto cigar and smiled. "In just ten days on this job, I am gonna earn sixty dollars. My pa don't see that much money for a year of hard work. It will save our family's farm and pay for Rush Medical School next year."

"That's all well and good, but you won't be able to collect your sixty dollars if you're DEAD!"

"Doyle, you Scottish worry-wart! We'll be fine . . ."

I began to settle down and watch the never-ending prairie, fields of corn, and sluggish rivers. Carl never stopped talking, puffing his El Perfecto cigar, and pointing out landmarks. He had a natural understanding of the land and botany. He knew the names of the rivers Kankakee and Illinois, and recognized the small towns. Later in the journey, the land was bleak and flat compared to the braes of Scotland. I felt a pang of homesickness and had images of a girl with red hair in the heather.

24 November, 1878

(I am writing this from memory since I did not have my journal for several days)

It took all day to get to East St. Louis where the train cars were loaded on a ferry boat that crossed the Mississippi River. We pulled into the Relay Depot in St. Louis just after four o'clock in the morning, pretty well covered with grit and soot and hungry as bear cubs. In the depot we had fried egg sandwiches and about the worst cup of coffee I ever tasted.

Our old train needed work, so we got on a new one bound for Memphis. Although, the word *new* probably should not be used since the locomotive had an old pokey engine . . . The train had a coal car, a luggage car, and three passenger cars. One was a smoker, but it was filled. We had to get on the second-class carriage where there were only a few empty seats. I remembered Doctor Bell's last admonition, "Boys, don't get separated," but there was nothing to do. I sat next to a grizzled, bearded old farmer, and Carl found a spot a few seats forward.

The talkative farmer took a chaw of tobacco. "We ain't got nothing to worry about on this train, no sir. There's Pinkertons on board, you know, but they's probably dressed like ordinary folks," said he.

I gulped. If he only knew. "Really? Um, eh . . . Why would you think there are Pinkertons on board today?"

"To protect all that cotton money. Why else?"

"Cotton money?" I asked.

"Why, every year, bankers up North send a safe full of money to Memphis to buy cotton. And when they do, they always hire extra guards."

I was beginning to feel uncomfortable. No one said anything about guarding a safe full of money . . . And, speaking of safes, could this farmer sitting next to me be making a reference to Fogarty's *sure lock* safe?

I must have looked nervous because the farmer offered a bottle of whisky. I overcame my scruples and glugged a healthy swallow. It was rotten homemade stuff, not like smooth malt Scotch whisky.

I tried to relax by looking out the window. We were south of St. Louis. The train wound through hills and over streams and rivers on rickety bridges. I was keeping my eyes peeled for Indians when we entered a dense forest that was what I always imagined America would look like. There were occasional patches of corn and shacks, but, unfortunately, no red men.

When the train stopped at a village, I decided to get out and stretch my legs. I looked around. The whole town seemed to be nothing more than a general store, a blacksmith shop, and a few run-down log cabins.

The grizzled old farmer had followed. "Ain't nothing but poor folks here. The damn Yankees took everything we had. 'Bout time we drove the dang carpetbaggers back up North where they belong," he said, and spit a stream of tobacco juice.

"Were folks hereabouts sympathetic with the Confederates?" I asked.

"You're damn right we were. I reckon things get any worse, we're gonna raise us another rebel force."

The train whistle blew. We boarded and took our seats. Carl was sound asleep a few rows away.

The train lurched and swayed on the curves at thirty or forty miles an hour until we came to a hill and down a long curve to a valley. The train was not going more than ten miles an hour between a cliff and a small river. All of a sudden, the air brakes screeched and the train crashed to a stop.

Our carriage shuddered and stayed upright, but the engine and the coal car slipped off the rails and went into a ditch. Folks in our carriage were jostled and shook. I slammed into the seat in front and the farmer fell into the aisle, but no one was badly hurt.

I looked out the window and saw men on horseback riding down from the hill, whooping and hollering and swearing something awful. They fired at the train. One shot shattered a window in our car. Suddenly, an ear-piercing *BOOM*! came from the baggage car up ahead. Pieces of train flew in the air then rained down to earth. The bandits continued shooting guns and whooping.

"Are those wild Indians?" I asked.

"Nah, more likely to be them James boys. They blew the safe. Good for them."

Women screamed and children cried. Everyone tried to hide their valuables. I checked my little pistol and felt for the stiletto. Should I make a brave stand and take out one of the bandits? Pretty soon, two men carrying large revolvers, their faces covered with masks, came into the carriage. One fellow was tall, skinny, and sandy-haired, and the other was big-bellied and wore a black, broad-brimmed hat.

The tall, skinny fellow pulled down his scarf to reveal whiskers and a snub nose. "You folks just stay still, put your hands up, and no one'll get hurt."

He held his revolver to the conductor's head and pulled back the hammer.

"Show me them Pinkertons."

"Yes, sir, Mr. James." The conductor pointed first at Carl and then at me. I tried to pull the .32 Derringer from my coat pocket, but the old farmer grabbed my arm. "Put that damn pea shooter away before you get us all killed."

"But—"

"Shush your mouth. That there fellow is Jesse James."

James and his partner came down the aisle, smiling and joking as if they were having the best time in the world. The dark-haired, fat gent carried an open feed sack. He stopped before a rather plain-looking woman and smiled as if she was a real looker. "Please, ma'am, put your money and jewelry in the bag."

Jesse James was polite as he could be to the passengers, but he turned mean and surly when he stopped at my seat. "So, this is one of those damn Pinkerton fellas? I oughta blow off your damn head!"

I hunkered down and tried to look innocent. Carl, blazing with his hot temper, rose to his full height and stared at Jesse James. "The name's Carl Lindborg and I'll lick you and your whole gang."

Jesse smiled. "You can start by licking my ass," he answered.

James and his gang howled with peals of laughter. Jesse walked over to Carl and poked his revolver into Carl's ribs. "This here Colt can blow a hole right through your gut. Say one more word and you are dead meat."

I threw aside caution. "Mr. James, please don't shoot! He likes to talk tough, but we aren't Pinkertons. We're both medical students going to Memphis to help with the yellow fever victims."

James jammed his big Colt revolver into my ribs. "Your accent sounds like that blowhard Pinkerton."

"Aye, I'm Irish, but grew up in Scotland and proud of it."

"Pinkerton can't get men no more, so he gets boys to do his dirty work, eh?"

"Lemme kill 'em, boss." The fat gunslinger begged.

"Nah, they might come in handy later." He trained the revolver first on me, then on Carl. He pulled back the hammer and squeezed the trigger. I figured Carl was a goner, but the revolver made a harmless click. Carl went pale as a sheet. Jesse grinned. "Scared, aintchya? If you boys are good, I might let you live a while longer. Some fool might be willing to pay ransom for your sorry tails. Take off them duds and your shoes, so you won't get any ideas about escaping."

"No, we ain't gonna—" Carl protested.

Jesse whacked his mouth with the butt of the heavy revolver, leaving a trickle of blood running down Carl's chin. Carl's eyes went blank, but he did not pass out. We sat down on the floor of the car and pulled off our shoes, then our pants and coats. The fat man kicked me in the ribs. "Shirt, too."

The gang collected more loot from other passengers, then herded us off the train like we were a couple of sheep. I silently thanked Maw for making me wear heavy wool underwear and that she had knitted my stockings out of good Scottish wool. Fortunately, my stiletto, our only weapon, was still strapped to my ankle under the stocking.

The gang finished stuffing jewelry, greenbacks, and gold pieces into their saddle bags. The big-bellied fellow aimed his pistol at Carl's chest. "C'mon Jessse, lemme kill 'em both right now before we go," he said.

Jesse James looked us over. “Nah. Let’s keep ‘em as carrots to attract those Pinkerton donkeys. We’ll let their stink fill the air. That damn Allan Pinkerton’ll come sniffing around. When he does, we’ll set a trap and nail that Scottish bastard.”

They tied my hands with flat leather thongs and lifted me onto the rump of a horse behind the saddle. When they bound my feet under the horse I was helpless.

They did the same to Carl and we set off on a hard ride. We mucked about through dense woods. Then, one of the gang members yelled to another to go up a stream bed so as not to leave tracks. I tried to forget I was a captive and, instead, imagined I was a character in a great American adventure novel by James Fenimore Cooper. I was not used to praying, but I sure prayed that these desperate men would take pity and turn us loose.

Every so often we stopped so one of the boys could look back for a posse. We were up in the hills where it was colder and snowing. I shivered, and my hands were numb from the tight thongs. It was not until after we came to a ramshackle log cabin that one of the gang finally cut my feet loose. I fell to the hard ground. It hurt, but nothing was broken. We could not walk, so they dragged us into the cabin and shoved us into the corner on the dirt floor. Jesse tied us together with a lariat and hitched one end to a post. We were not going anywhere soon . . .

The musty cabin, lit by one oil lamp, was foul from grease, old sweat, and sour piss. We were tired and thankful to still be alive. I struggled to stay alert and remembered Dr. Bell’s admonition to be observant. I hung my head so as not to attract attention, but let my eyes rove around the room, searching for a means of escape. It was a plain log cabin with a low ceiling and two small windows. A table cluttered with whisky bottles and cards was in the middle of the room surrounded by homemade split wood chairs. An iron cookstove and a kitchen counter were near to the door. Straw sleeping pallets were scattered about on the floor, but there was no other furniture. I noticed the gang had hung their coats on pegs by the door, but they kept their guns close by. I did not see any hole where we could slip through and escape. It looked hopeless.

Because we would not be going anywhere soon, Carl and I ultimately gave in to our fatigue, rested our heads upon each other's shoulders, and drowsed off in an exhausted sleep.

25 November, 1878

Come morning, I woke up to the smell of cooking grease and the sound of Carl's snoring. A bedraggled old woman fried corn meal mush, eggs, and pork belly on the stove.

I noticed that the left sleeve of her dark brown dress was pinned up just below the elbow. The poor woman had no forearm.

Carl awoke and blinked the sleep from his eyes. "Look . . ." he said.

In the opposite corner of the cabin, a man tossed and turned on a straw pallet with his foot poking out from under a pile of quilts. The red, swollen foot was partly plastered with a brown mush. The fellow mumbled about escaping from jail and hiding in the woods, but he did not make sense. He was plumb delirious.

I figured they would give us a scrap of food, but Jesse and his gang ignored us. The gang ate their breakfast on the rickety wood table. There was not a morsel left after they were done eating and scraped their plates on the ground outside the door. We heard the sounds of saddles slapped on the backs of their horses, and then hoofbeats, when they rode away.

Carl and I were alone in the cabin with the wounded man and the old lady. As the day progressed, the old lady bustled about while the wounded man moaned and hollered. I had not had anything to drink for almost a whole day, but had to pee so bad, I almost bust. "It's just a dirt floor, let it go," said Carl. I did and felt a lot better. The smell was no worse than the rest of the room.

Just at dusk the gang returned and flung a small deer on the ground. The old lady, with one hand and the stump of her other arm, skinned and gutted the animal while the men smoked and passed a whisky bottle. Later, our mouths watered while the men ate venison stew. We were powerfully hungry, but they did not even give us scraps.

As everybody ate, the room grew warmer and I sensed an opportunity. I pointed at the injured fellow. "What happened to him?" I asked.

"Got shot in the foot after robbin' a bank last week," said Jesse.

"What's that brown stuff his foot is wrapped in?" Carl asked.

"A plaster of chewin' tobacco," said the dark-haired fellow with the big belly, who they called Cole Younger.

"He looks pretty bad. Why don't you let us have a look? I wasn't lying. We really are training to be doctors," I said.

"Just listen to the lies. Ma, do they look like the Pinkertons that killed Archie? I should shoot them right now," said Jesse.

I leaned close to Carl. "What's he talking about?" I asked.

"The Pinkertons thought they had Jesse and his gang trapped and blew up his house, but Jesse got away. They killed his little brother, Archie, and his mother lost her arm. Most folks down here sympathize with him and hate the Pinkertons."

Mrs. James lifted the oil lamp close to our faces with her good hand and looked closely into our eyes. "Naw . . . These are just two scared boys. Don't look like no Pinkertons to me."

Our medical training might save us if we convinced these desperados that we could save the life of the injured man. Trouble was we did not have antiseptics or ether or even clean bandages. But, if given the chance, we could make a show of treating the wound and hope they didn't know the difference.

"We got to string them up anyway, on account of they know too much," Cole Younger said.

The injured man was delirious. He let out a piercing cry of pain.

"Hell, Cole, what's the rush? Maybe they can help Ace. Untie their hands and give them a chance to show what they can do," the old lady said.

Her word was law. Jesse untied our hands and held the lamp while we looked at the foot. The bullet had left a big hole that oozed pus just below the ankle. The whole foot was swollen, red, and hot, with red streaks running up the leg. A chaw of tobacco was sticking out of the hole and tobacco juice was smeared over the wound.

My heart sank right down to my socks. It looked hopeless until Carl spoke up in his best country accent. "Thank you, Ma'am. Now, please boil up a kettle of water and give us a bottle of that there whisky. We'll have your boy right as rain in no time flat!"

We cleaned the wound with soap and water and poured whisky into the jagged hole. It still looked bad. The edges of the skin were green and the sole of the foot bulged out. I thought even Dr. Bell could not help this man.

"There's pus in there," I said.

"Ma'am, we just need us a sharp knife to drain that there pus." Carl said. I thought of the stiletto still strapped to my leg under my long johns, but did not dare mention it.

The old lady hunted through the shelves and came up with a straight razor. "Here, take this. It's sharp, but don't get no ideas. If you even think of using it for anything other than helping Ace, Jesse will blow your head off."

"Yes, ma'am." Carl said.

Carl plunked the razor in the boiling water and then fished it out with a couple of forks. When the razor cooled, Carl felt the swelling and squinted a long time at the evil mess of torn, infected flesh. Ace had passed out from the fever and hardly moved when Carl made a cut that went across the sole of his foot.

I was pretty nervous until he sliced deeper down to bone and about a pint of green stinking pus welled up out of the wound. We poured in more whisky and tied the foot up in a bandanna that had been boiled.

Jesse's mother nodded. "You boys know doctoring alright. Mebbe we should put you to work and keep you around for a while."

"Hell no. Don't make no difference. They seen our faces. We gotta string 'em up in the morning." Jesse said.

"Why wait? Let's have a necktie party right now." Cole Younger, the meanest man of the bunch, waved his pistol.

"No, damn it. Just tie them up," Jesse said. Cole, the drunkest of the gang, tied our hands, but he fumbled the knots. I could have slipped my hands out of the binding, but waited until the gang finished playing cards and drinking whisky. They finally settled down on the dirt floor for the night at what I judged was about one o'clock in the morning.

26 November, 1878

They were snoring up a storm when Carl gave me a nudge. "Doyle, this might be our only chance."

I worked my hands loose and got out the stiletto, then cut the knots on Carl's thongs. He untied my feet and we crawled towards the door. We each took a heavy coat from the pegs and escaped out the door. It had not stopped snowing and it was cold. There was white everywhere, which enabled us to see, but also meant that the gang could easy follow our tracks.

"Let's steal a horse," I said.

"They would catch us in no time. We've got to stay in the deep woods. Listen close. These nights are cold, and the snow half-melts during the day, but freezes over with a crust at night. It will be hard for them to follow us on foot or horseback, but I got an even better idea," Carl whispered. He stopped by an old whisky barrel behind the shed.

"What are you doing?" I whispered.

"Going to make a way for us to slip away on top of the crust and move at a faster clip."

Carl ripped away the rusty metal bands that encircled the barrel and removed four curved staves. We listened to see if the noise had roused the gang, but there was no sign they heard us. Carl sneaked back into the cabin. In a moment, he returned with a skillet covered with old bacon grease and a coat pocket filled with bread and hunks of venison. "There was still food left on the stove," he said. He smeared bacon grease on the bottom of the staves. "Keep those leather thongs. And now take your skis and let's get going," he said.

"Skis? What are skis?"

"Those staves."

"Huh?"

"I'll explain later. Just grab 'em and follow me."

We tramped off through the snow, but it was bloody cold and hard going. We were leaving tracks, but I was more thankful than ever for Maw's heavy wool stockings and the woolly long johns. The stolen coat helped a lot. At the top of a hill, we stopped at a narrow path that led into the woods.

"Use the thongs to tie your feet to the staves and we will zoom down this hill."

"Carl, I have never been on skis," I said.

"Ain't no time for lessons. Do as I do. Aim your feet downhill and push off," he said.

I felt clumsy on the skis and was scared, though I had no choice but to follow Carl down the hill at an alarming speed. We had no more started than I heard shouts and the *BAM! BAM!* of Colt .45 revolvers and the sharp *CRACK!* of a Winchester rifle. They were probably firing at the noise we made. Even though I am writing this a week later, I can still feel the wind as a bullet whistled next to my ear. Fortunately, the gang was still at least half-drunk, and the muzzle blasts must have ruined their night sight.

We slid into a dense stand of brush and trees and were out of their sight, but the gang still kept shooting.

I fell down in a snow drift and struggled to get back up. "Crouch low, keep the staves parallel, and bend your knees." Carl said. We started down the hill and I fell to the side, but I righted myself and held my arms out to try to not fall.

I started to get the hang of it and imitated Carl, crouched low, and whizzed down the hill. Despite our being earthbound, it felt as if we were flying. I gained speed, but the gang must have heard us again as they started another barrage of gun fire. I heard one bullet whiz through the brush. I ducked, though the bullet was a long ways away.

Carl reached the bottom of the hill first. He stopped himself, discarded his staves, and grabbed me as I zoomed by him. "Get rid of your skis and follow me," Carl said. We took off into the dense woods.

Over the course of my short life, I have spent very little time in the country and no time in the deep woods, so I was not feeling especially confident. After a few minutes we did not hear any more shooting.

The sound of howling replaced the sound of bullets. My thoughts turned to wolves and bears and how they might be more dangerous than the gang. But, Carl was comfortable in the deep woods. He forged ahead through the snow, so I stumbled along in his path.

"Carl, do you know where we are going?"

"Don't worry your Scottish head. This is nothing. Once my little brother and I were hunting and got lost in a snowstorm, but we stayed warm by moving and survived. By the time we got back to the farm my parents thought we were dead. Keep moving. We will find a stream and follow it until it leads to a river. There are always towns on rivers."

It was dark and terrifying in the forest. And cold. My feet felt like they were solid chunks of ice. The only thing that seemed to keep us from freezing was to continue walking and talking. Carl kept up a steady conversation—much ado about nothing—which went something like this:

"Arthur, in a fight, who do you think would win; Natty Bumppo—you know, Hawkeye from *The Last of the Mohicans*—or Ivanhoe from Sir Walter Scott's book?"

"Nobody, Carl. They are both fictional characters."

"I know. But, still, if they were in the woods and had to battle to the death, who do you think would win?"

"I refuse to have this inane conversation, Carl. They are not real people."

"All right, then. If Genghis Kahn and Alexander the Great met each other here in the woods and had to fight to the death, who do you think—"

"They lived in completely different eras. It would be physically impossible for them to ever meet."

"I know. But, still, what if . . ."

He kept me awake and going, but I was exhausted. I, grew careless, and tripped over a root. Carl bent down and offered me a ham-sized hand. "Carl, let's rest here for a few minutes," I pleaded.

I pulled the canvas coat tighter. We huddled close together for warmth and rested a few minutes, but the cold was still brutal. Carl's teeth chattered. "We have to go before we freeze to death," he said.

We struggled on together through the black night. Carl talked and talked so we would stay awake and keep our spirits up. Though we eased our hunger by sharing small bites of the food we had stolen from the James Gang, we had no relief from the cold until the early morning sun warmed our cheeks and the snow started to melt.

We stopped going long enough to sit down with our backs to a chestnut tree and chew some chunks of hard bread and venison. Carl got sort of dreamy and talked about his hopes of marrying a pretty nurse and being a country doctor in Wisconsin. That got me to thinking of Rebecca, and my heart warmed.

We got up, stiff and cold, and kept going until we came to a bubbly creek flowing over smooth sand. Our wool socks were already wet and crusted with ice and snow, so we waded into the creek, figuring it would lead to something bigger. The water felt almost warm; at least it was not freezing. We pushed aside brush and stumbled over stones as we walked. My feet felt almost warm for a spell, but soon were, again, like chunks of ice. By that time, my head was sore and my leg muscles burned. I was in a foul mood and wanted to go back to Scotland. This was a lot more adventure on the American frontier than I had bargained for. Perhaps I did not want to be like an American frontier hero in a James Fenimore Cooper novel after all.

"As long as we continue downstream we will come to a town." Carl was reassuring and I felt better. We rested a while under a big cottonwood tree, soaked up the warm sun, drank cold stream water, and finished off the bread and meat. I would rather have had bacon and eggs.

"Let's get going. If we can figure which way is east, we will come to the Mississippi river after a while, if we don't reach a town first," Carl said.

It was mid-afternoon when the creek went under a bridge on a dirt road. I collapsed with my back against the base of the bridge. "Carl, I'm sorry, but my feet are frozen and I can't go one step further."

He slumped down next to me. After we had been sitting for a wee bit we heard the sound of a wagon creaking down the road. I thought of the James Gang and felt a stab of fear in my gut, but it was only a lad of not more than sixteen years old driving a hay wagon drawn by a sway-backed mule.

"You fellers look plumb worn out," the boy said.

"Worn out, cold, and hungry. We were robbed in a train holdup." Carl said.

"Where you headed?" The lad asked.

"Memphis."

"That's an awfully long walk."

"We were hoping to get to the river. Can you give us a ride?" Carl asked.

"Naw, the load is already too heavy and I got to get this hay to Cape Girardeau."

I looked the boy square in the eye and pulled the stiletto from under my stocking.

He threw up his hands. "Now fellers, don't cut me."

"I don't mean you no harm. I'll trade this knife for a ride and something to eat," I said.

He admired the sharp killing blade, took the knife, and turned it over in his hand. "Well, ok, fellas. Climb on if you want and I'll take ya. And have some bacon. You can lay back there in the hay and cover up with this here blanket."

Cold bacon never tasted better, and the hay and blanket warmed our bones. The cart clacked and bucked its way over the dirt trail while we huddled together to stay warm. I watched the green woods of Missouri pass by until it got dark. The boy pulled off the road and we spent the night, warm as bugs, under the hay.

27 November, 1878

We arrived in Cape Girardeau at around nine o'clock in the morning. The lad, whose name was Travis, gave us bread and molasses for breakfast. It was still cold, so he let us keep the blanket.

We got off the wagon at the livery stable and limped through town towards the river. A pot-bellied fellow with a shiny badge swaggered towards us. He hooked his thumbs in his belt. "We don't want no good-for-nothing tramps in our town. Beat it or go to jail," he said.

"We aren't tramps. My family owns a 400-acre farm in Wisconsin," Carl replied.

"You damn well look like tramps. Get the hell out of town."

We skedaddled on out of town to the steamboat landing on the great muddy Mississippi River.

I sat on a bench overlooking the river, and, after a few minutes, fell asleep. Carl went off talking to the roustabouts until he met a bloke from Wisconsin who got us a job shoveling coal on a decrepit little cargo steamboat. The Captain was glad to have new hands and gave us some old clothes to wear. We were still in our stocking feet, but did not look any worse than the other coal stokers.

We took turns all day shoveling coal into the furnace to keep the steam boiler going. The boat chugged along, stopping every so often to take on bags of grain bound for Memphis. Whenever we could, we snuck out to the deck to get a glimpse of our surroundings and watch the river roll by.

I wanted to write about the journey, but did not have paper or pencil. Instead, I froze the river, the flocks of ducks, and the muddy banks in my memory for a future story. Whenever the fire got low, the first mate cussed and threatened to throw us overboard. I threw big chunks of wood and coal on the fire and ran back on deck so as not to miss anything.

When our shift was over the first mate let us eat leftovers, mostly fried catfish and cornbread. We drank river water after the mud settled and bedded down on grain sacks where we slept like dead men.

28 November, 1878

We did shifts in the morning and afternoon until, in the distance, I made out buildings and tall church steeples up on a bluff. Memphis looked like a fine city, but down by the river there were tumbled-down stores and shacks on muddy streets.

The deckhands lowered the gangplank down onto a cobblestone landing where steamboats were lined up for near a half-mile. The mate gave us burlap bags to wrap around our feet. "I'll pay you two bits apiece if you help us unload," he said.

Carl and I readily agreed. We fell in with the black deckhands and passed the hundred-pound sacks of corn to the next man in the line up to the warehouse. I was strong from playing rugger and rounders, but it was bloody hard work.

Big Bart, a six-foot-four black man, was the leader of the workers. "You the first white boys I seen who know how to work," he said.

We all jollied and joked and had a pretty good time. After we collected our two dimes and a nickel I sat next to Bart who offered me an apple.

"You sound British?" he asked, as we ate together.

"I'm of Irish blood, but I'm studying medicine in Scotland."

"So what brings you to these parts?"

"We were robbed by the James Gang. Lost everything and we need help. A friend said we should see Mr. Josiah Burk in Memphis. Ever hear of him?"

"No." Bart turned cold and distant. "I don't know no Mr. Burk."

"Well, do you at least know where Second Street is?"

"Don't know that neither."

Bart got up to leave, but I grabbed his shoulder. I showed him the black spot on my wrist. He paused and squinted. "Who made that mark on you?"

"My friend, Rufus Bubba Freeman."

"He must have been a slave at one time."

"Yes. That's right. He used to be known as Rufus Bedford Forrest."

His face crinkled with a big smile. “Hmmm… In that case, you keep on this here road until you are up on the bluff and come to Second Street. Turn right and go down a ways. Mr. Burk lives in the white house.”

It was near dark when we found the white cottage surrounded by old trees.

“We better go around to the back door, especially considering we’re still wearing these dirty old rags from the steamer,” Carl said.

I hung back and let Carl do the talking when a little old lady opened the door just a little. “You men looking for food?” she asked.

“No, Ma’am, I’m a Wisconsin farm boy and now, we’re medical students coming to help with the epidemic. We were robbed and come to see Mr. Josiah Burk,” Carl said.

The lady opened the door another few inches and squinted at us through little half-rim spectacles. She could not have stood more than five feet tall. She wore a bonnet and a long calico dress buttoned up to her neck.

“Land-sakes, you boys look a fright.”

I guess we did look pretty bad. My shirt and trousers were soot-covered and torn. The fact that we did not have shoes made us look worse than the usual tramp. Carl was in just as bad a shape and neither one of us had washed or combed our hair in a week. “Come in, come in and I’ll call my husband,” she said in a kindly soft voice.

She took us into her warm, cheery kitchen lit by two oil lamps and heated with a big iron cookstove. We both drooled at the sight of a big piece of ham, a loaf of bread, and a bowl of apples on the table.

“Josiah, two boys are here to see you.”

Mr. Burk was a stout man with hair gone to grey and dressed in a black frock coat, shiny black trousers, and a white shirt. He looked solemn enough to be a minister, but, after he said thee and thou a few times, we learned that he and his wife were Quakers. I held out my wrist towards the lamp so that they could see the tiny black spot.

"Remarkable. I have never seen that mark on a white man."

"A black man said we could trust you," I said.

He stroked his beard. "Mrs. Burk and I helped many a slave to freedom before the war."

The Burks took us in and gave us supper. Mrs. Burk drew a hot bath. After Carl scrubbed down with rough, homemade soap I jumped in while the water was still hot. It felt so good to be clean and warm. Our bedroom was a lean-to out back with only one sofa. Carl took the floor. "Sleeping on a nice warm hardwood floor is nothing," he said. "Back on the farm, we had so little room in the house, I'd often sleep on the dirt floor of our chicken coop."

In minutes, Carl snored. I could not sleep, so I wandered to the kitchen. Mrs. Burk was reading a religious tract. I slumped down on a wooden kitchen chair across from her.

She had white hair and watery, sad grey eyes that reminded me of my dear, poor mother.

Mrs. Burk poured boiling water from a copper kettle onto dry tea leaves in a plain white cup. "Drink this," she said.

It was a dark, strangely soothing brew. In a moment, I emptied the cup and felt drowsy. She took the cup, swirled the remaining leaves, and looked intently at the bottom and sides of the cup.

Her old grey eyes took on a new luminosity. I sensed a change in the room and the intensity of her gaze. "You are troubled by a dark, inky past. For a young man, you've experienced great sadness and much death. It's your Irish blood and the Romani blot." Her voice was a mere whisper, but every word went into my very soul.

I shivered at the memories of the harsh beatings and my rigid education at the hands of the Jesuits when I was a boy. I had forsaken religion for science, a move that caused my Maw great sorrow.

Mrs. Burk looked back down into my teacup. "I see an older woman—dying. Your grandmother, perhaps. You're just a young boy, crying at her bedside."

The shock of my grandmother's death came back with the full force I had felt while still a young boy. Her passing started our family on the path to poverty and ruin, and it was the reason I was sent away to live with relatives and the Jesuits.

"Now I see another woman, a wisp of a girl, but beautiful. She tugs at your heart, but she is not of your faith and would bring great sadness to your mother. You must not marry her."

I came alert with a start. My mind whirled. Did this old woman have the gift of second sight? Could she see the past and divine the future? My scientific background and Jesuit teaching told me no. But, then, was she speaking of my dear Rebecca? I was overcome with shame and guilt that took my breath away. I had abandoned the faith of my parents, and I had eagerly run away on this trip, leaving them in their poverty. I should have stayed in Edinburgh to help out.

I felt awful. How could I be such a bad son? I stumbled away and sank into bed.

29 November, 1878

I awoke on the sofa to the smell of bacon and sausages that reminded me of home. It took a minute to realize I was in the middle of perilous America. Mrs. Burk had generously mended our clothes, so we looked halfway decent for the first time in days. The Burks also had a storeroom with old clothes and shoes for runaway slaves that they now shared with poor travelers like us. I found a pair of boots that almost fit. A little lamp black made them look respectable.

"So, you boys want to use your medical learning to help with the yellow fever?" Mr. Burk inquired while we were at breakfast.

"Yes, sir," we answered.

"The epidemic is almost over, but there still are sick folks at St. Mary's who need help."

"Was there a lot of fighting around here during the war?" I asked.

"Oh yes. The Union took Memphis early in the war, then the Rebels raided the fort several times," Mr. Burk said.

"Ever hear of a Confederate officer named Captain Hook?"

"He was bad. A very bad man. Funny you mention him. I just overheard some folks saying that he is rallying his old troops to make mischief again."

I felt the urge to record this information and my experiences, but had neither pencil nor paper. "Sir, I can do chores or give you a nickel for a notebook or a pad of paper and a pencil."

Mr. Burk rummaged through an old rolltop desk and produced a pad of cheap foolscap and a pencil stub. "It's worth a nickel," he said.

I thanked him, took the paper, and offered to do chores, but he sent us on our way with handshakes and smiles.

We could see the church from a long ways away. The imposing St. Mary's was a big stone structure with a high steeple that had been made into a hospital. The yellow fever epidemic might have been nearly over, but there were still at least fifty poor, sick souls lying on cots in front of the altar. A nun in starchy white met us at the door. She looked us over with a critical eye.

"Do you boys have medical experience?" she asked.

"Yes, Ma'am. We are medical students and want to help."

She pointed to a heap of wrapped bodies. "First thing, carry out the ones that died last night."

The corpses were already wrapped in sheets, so we could not tell what they looked like, but they were light as a feather. When we finished stacking the bodies on the cart like so much cordwood, another sister gave us buckets of water and towels to clean new patients.

All day, we cleaned black vomit, changed beds, and held patient's heads while they took broth. It was more like nursing than medical work, but it felt good to help these unfortunate souls. No matter how awful my problems seemed to be, these folks had it much worse.

The new patients were out of their heads with fever, their teeth chattered from chills, and they bled from their mouths, eyes, and noses. The skin of the some patients had turned yellow, and even I could see that many were doomed to die from kidney or liver failure.

It was late afternoon when Carl and I took a break and rested on a cot. A nice-looking lady holding a pot of coffee walked over to us and sat down next to us. "You boys must be plum tuckered out. Have some coffee," she said.

"Thank you, ma'am," said Carl.

She poured each of us a cup. "This is the first time I have seen you boys."

"We're medical students from Chicago," I said.

"They say the epidemic is about over. Good thing, since my gals are getting tired of seeing these poor folks die every day. The sisters pray for their souls, but there ain't much else we can do," she said.

"It's awfully hard, but important, work," I added.

"Where are you boys staying?"

"We don't have lodgings yet," I said.

"If you behave and leave my girls alone, I can give you a meal and make room for you at my place. Go to Angie's Hotel on First Street right on your way to the docks. Go in by the back door and say Angie sent you."

"That's very kind," I said.

"There was a nurse with a funny accent like yours who was here yesterday."

"Did she happen to have flaming red curly hair and sparkling green eyes?" I asked.

"Why, yes, she did."

"Was her name Rebecca?"

"I think so."

My heart skipped a beat. "Do you happen to know where she might be staying?"

"She didn't say."

I had vowed to give up on Rebecca, especially after Mrs. Burk's strange message that had gone straight to my heart. Yet I could not get her out of my mind as I blindly followed Carl through darkened streets. It was raining and the wind was whistling off the river when we finally came to First Street.

The area was mostly lit by red lanterns in front of dismal shacks and saloons. Angie's Hotel was a higher-class place, though not by much. The kitchen was clean, but the cook, an old black lady with an enormous apron across her fat belly, was not very friendly.

"Why ain't you usin' the front door, like every other man?" she asked

"Angie sent us here."

"I 'spose you wants eats?"

"Aye, a bit of food would be much appreciated," said I.

"I kin give you beef stew and fixin's for fifteen cents."

We shelled out thirty cents in dimes and nickels and tucked into beef stew, homemade biscuits, and gravy served out of tin plates at the kitchen table. The cook sat with us. "These are the best vittles I've had in a long time," Carl said.

She smiled for the first time. "You kin call me Ma, like all the girls. You boys is more polite than most men who come here. Would you like a helpin' of apple pie?" she asked.

"Yes ma'am," I said.

She served up two slabs of pie filled with sliced apples, cinnamon, and sugar. "Oh, I've never, even at home, had such good pie," said Carl.

"Yes, it is quite lovely," I added.

"Nobody ever called my pie lovely 'afore," she said.

"How's business?" Carl asked.

She sighed. "Ain't been much of anything you can call business since the epidemic, 'cept last night when a crowd of old Confederates come nosin' around. I din't like them fellers at all."

We were scraping the bottoms of our plates and licking our spoons when a little, blonde, skinny girl flounced into the kitchen wearing a wide-open, tiny housecoat without a stitch of underclothes except for black stockings and loose slippers. She was no more than sixteen years old if she was a day. The girl acted like we were not even there. "Ma, kin you let me have a pitcher of warm water for washin'?" she asked.

The cook filled her pitcher from a bucket on the stove. Then, the little, blonde girl acted like she had just noticed us. "Oh my. Well, hello there, gentlemen. Are you boys lookin' for fun?"

Carl and I smiled shyly. "Sorry, ma'am, but you see we're Pinkerton agents on official railway business," said I.

"I don't care if you're the crown prince of Wales. You oughta be in the front room with the girls."

Carl cleared his throat, but could not speak. She gave Carl a lascivious smile, twitched her hips, and sat down on his lap. "Hello there curly. You big, beautiful, sweet boy. Do you mind if I sit down for a minute?" She kicked a leg back and forth and played with a lock of Carl's hair.

"Um, eh . . . Ah . . ." Carl stammered.

"Curly, I ain't got nothin' to do to-night and I'm sure lonely. Why don't you follow me to my room? I can sure show you a good time . . ."

Carl's face turned beet-red and his jaw started to work, but all that came out of his mouth was hemming and hawing. "Hmm . . . Emm . . . Ummm . . . Ah, sorry, ma'am. You seem nice and all, but we best be on our way." Carl jerked up to his feet and the little girl practically fell to the floor.

"Now, Curly, you ain't very sociable."

"You can stay as long as you want and socialize, but I got things to do." Carl said to me.

Carl burst out the front door. I was sort of reluctant to leave, but followed him into a pouring rain. Carl's face was still flushed with a rosy hue and I could not help but laugh at him.

"What's so funny?"

"I've seen you stand up to Jesse James, but one little girl made you squirm like a wee lad with ants in his knickers," I teased.

"Well, um, eh, that there place is one of those houses of ill repute. We might have gotten a disease if we stayed there too much longer," said Carl.

"Carl, you can't catch venereal diseases from food and furniture."

"Still, it was, um . . . Well . . . I've never done . . . You know . . . and I'm gonna save myself for my wedding night, and I don't wanna talk about this no more!"

Misty halos formed around the gaslights and the eery light made for a dreadfully unnerving feeling. I looked back over my shoulder at every little noise and jumped at the clatter of hooves and jingling spurs. A troop of fifteen or twenty men on horseback cantered down the street, two abreast. Every man wore a long red shirt, carried a rifle, and had a set, dark expression.

"Keep your head down and walk straight ahead," Carl said.

"Who are those men?"

"Red Shirts. One of the White Militias that go night-riding to scare the blacks."

I grabbed Carl and pulled him into an alley. "Carl, people are talking about Confederates. I thought the war was over years ago."

"The war over slavery didn't really end. The Southerners won't give the black people equal rights. They don't let them vote and, in the end, they want to restore slavery. They say the Republicans stole the last election and Northerners are sick of the whole thing and don't really care what happens."

"So, in a way, the war is still going on."

"You might say that . . . Now, we have to secure our lodgings and get out of this rain."

"Dr. Bell said we should go to the Peabody Hotel."

"We've only got ten cents apiece."

"Never mind. It won't hurt to try."

The Peabody was about the swankiest place in Memphis, but we walked right up to the desk like we always stayed in the finest hotels all our lives. "Hello, dear sir. Might there be any messages for Mr. Arthur Conan Doyle?" I asked.

"Why yes, sir." The clerk, without batting an eye, took an envelope and a key with a tag numbered 215 from a cubby hole. The envelope was stuffed with greenbacks, enough for a week's pay for both of us, and a scrap of paper with two words: 'Keep quiet.'

The door to room 215 was unlocked and did not make a sound when I pushed it open. To our great astonishment, a tall, thin man smoking a Meerschaum pipe, sat with a binaural stethoscope pressed against the wall. It was Dr. Bell. And there was good old Rufus, squatting on his haunches, shining shoes. He had stayed with Dr. Bell just as he promised.

Bell put his finger to his lips, motioning for us to be quiet, and offered the stethoscope to me. I adjusted the ear pieces and pressed the bell against the wall to hear snatches of conversation and the tinkling of glasses. *"Why not just shoot him . . . It must appear to be a natural death . . . It is perfected . . . That bastard in Chicago knows . . . The depot in . . ."*

I could not make out all the words, but Dr. Bell had a page full of notes. Carl gasped when he saw the names: Wade Hampton, Jubal Early, Martin Cary. We moved away from the wall and spoke in whispers.

"Those are names of Lee's Confederate generals who never surrendered," Carl said.

"They are plotting assassinations as we speak," Dr. Bell said.

There were more notes, something about a Reverend, that I could not make out. "It sounds as if they are planning more assassinations with the curare poison," I said.

Then an awful thought crossed my mind. If ‘that bastard in Chicago’ was Dr. Bell, his life was in great danger.

Or maybe, they were referring to me . . .

I am in my own space now and the others are asleep. Dr. Bell thoughtfully brought my precious diary, so I am setting down everything I remember since leaving Chicago. This is a strange land, so different from Scotland. American doctors still do not believe in the germ theory and reject Lister’s antiseptic surgery. After thinking about our narrow escape the James Gang is not so different from the highland robbers so prominent in our Scottish lore.

Aye, we are in danger, but even forbidden thoughts of Rebecca, and the possibility of seeing her again, are a tonic.

2 December, 1878

Early this morning, Carl and I went to the cathedral and I asked about the red-haired Scottish beauty. "Try President's Island. There are more patients quarantined there," a nursing sister finally told me.

Carl and I spent some of our salary on new clothes, cigars, and beer and sandwiches in a saloon, where we listened to the gossip. Recalling our original plan, we let it be known that we were Pinkertons working for the railroad. Everyone shied away as soon as they heard our accents, and one fellow called us *damn carpetbaggers*. After we left the saloon Carl went back to the cathedral, but I hurried down to the landing to catch a ferry to President's Island.

Once on the island I walked into what seemed to be an old warehouse, which is now a makeshift hospital filled with the worst cases. I looked down a long corridor filled with beds and she was there! Her red hair stood out like a bright star in a dark evening sky.

"Miss Yates?"

She looked up from wiping vomit off a small lad and tossed a limp lock of hair from her eyes. Her voice was dull and tired. "Oh, Arthur, is it really you?"

"Yes, it is me. I found you."

"Oh, Arthur." She fell into my arms and sobbed. "They're all dead. Jimmy is the only one alive."

I held her and tried to soothe her anxiety. It took several moments for me to understand. The Reverend and Mrs. Balfour had died of yellow fever. Jimmy, their son, was here and near death. The poor boy was feverish, delirious. I could barely feel his pulse.

"Rebecca, please, come with me. You are so tired and in danger of contracting this terrible disease."

"No, I must stay with Jimmy to the end."

I begged her to come with me. Dr. Bell would surely look after her and Jimmy, but she insisted on staying with the sick child.

I was torn between staying with Rebecca and going back to Carl and Dr. Bell. I, too, had a duty.

"Do you have a place to stay?" I asked.

"Yes, with the Reverend Beecher who is also not well. I am needed here."

"I shall bring Dr. Bell to see Jimmy," I said.

I hugged her and left to catch the ferry back to Memphis. Was it fate? Had this terrible disease led to our reunion?

It was dusk when the boat touched the dock in Memphis. As we moored a steam launch backed out into the river. In the fading light, I could make out a tattered sign on the launch which read—SHERLOCK-MEMPHIS LINE.

The word 'Sherlock' startled me.

I paused for a moment and thought of the bloody words, *cinnte faoi ghlas.* Sure lock. And now, here it was again, that strange word. Sherlock.

I jumped onto the dock. As the launch steamed downriver, nosing against waves with its stack belching smoke, I sprinted down the dock to see the sign better and ensure that my mind was not playing tricks on me.

The launch was already too far away to read the sign again. I turned to a grey-bearded black man who was fishing with a long cane pole at the edge of the dock. "Excuse me, sir, may I ask—did you see that boat, the one that said Sherlock?"

The old man merely looked down at the worn wooden planks of the dock. "I don't want no trouble, sir," said he.

Then, he pulled in his line, picked up a can of worms, and hurried away.

I chased after him. "Please, sir, is that boat going to Sherlock?"

"Leave me 'lone. I don't know nothing about no Sherlock." He said these words and disappeared down an alley.

I returned to the docks, questioned two stevedores, and received a similar response. Everyone seemed frightened of the very name, Sherlock. It was most peculiar and mysterious.

Could it be the same name that Fogarty had written with his bloody, dying hand? I would have asked more questions. Instead, I dashed to the cathedral to find Carl. He was still there, spooning broth into the mouth of an old man. After he had finished we hurried back to the hotel as I told him about Sherlock.

When we arrived back at the Peabody Hotel, it was quite late and Dr. Bell and Rufus had already retired.

3 December, 1878

At six o'clock this morning, Bell was up reading his newspapers and drinking coffee. We knocked on his door to let him know about what had transpired. Rufus was putting a final polish on his boots.

"Sir, I found Rebecca Yates. The Balfours are dead from the fever and Jimmy is very ill. Rebecca is looking after the boy on President's Island."

Before I could tell him about Sherlock, he held up his hand. "Oh, so sad, so sad. The Balfour clan is one of the most important in Scotland. We must save Jimmy's life."

"But, sir, your identity will become known if—"

"Never mind, Doyle, my lad. A life is at stake. Bring my instrument case. Doyle, Carl, we will need both of you. We leave at once."

Dr. Bell hailed a cab. "Hurry, man, to the ferry landing." The ferry was not running. Dr. Bell dropped his disguise and became the commanding presence I knew so well.

"Hello!" he shouted at men on a fishing boat. "A ten dollar gold piece for a ride to President's Island."

"Who is in charge?" Bell shouted as we entered the makeshift hospital.

There was no answer. Dr. Bell went from one poor wretch lying in putrid vomit to another. Before our very eyes, an old woman threshed about with fever, chills, and delirium.

"Damn, this is intolerable. We would never stand for this neglect of the sick in Edinburgh."

Then, like a beacon of light, we came to Rebecca, still at Jimmy's bedside. Her lovely face was streaked with tears and she was worn from overwork. Carl, my big unfettered friend, appeared to be struck dumb when he saw her.

Without a word, Dr. Bell threw off his coat and knelt by Jimmy. The lad was delirious with fever and crying weakly for his mother. His lips were parched and cracked, and his eyes were sunk into his head. It was a dreadful sight. One did not have to be a trained surgeon to see that the lad was near to death.

"When did he last drink?" Dr. Bell asked.

"He hasn't had a drop of liquid since yesterday morning. I have tried, but he will not swallow," Rebecca responded.

"We must get him out of here. This is no place for a Scots lad of the great Balfour clan to die. Doyle, wrap the lad in my coat."

I bundled Jimmy and carried him in my arms. Dr. Bell led our little party out of the quarantine hospital and down a muddy path to our boat.

Dr. Bell steadied the boat while I gently put Jimmy on a seat next to Rebecca. "Doyle, where can we find a quiet place with clean linens, drink, and food?" he asked.

I thought for a second. "There is the cathedral, but it's just as crowded as the quarantine hospital. Everyone in the city is frightened of the disease."

"There must be someplace we can go."

"Let me think . . . Well, aye . . . Carl and I met a woman, Angie, a kindly soul, runs a sort of a hotel which is not far away."

"It would not be proper," Carl said.

"Never mind, Angie's is the only place," said I.

As we burst into the front room of Angie's Hotel the half-clothed girls screamed, but, when they saw the sick lad, the girls shed tears and helped us up to Angie's room on the second floor. All the while, Dr. Bell gave no evidence that he was shocked by the licentiousness around him.

Angie's room was opulent, with a brightly lit gold chandelier, a frilly four-poster bed, paintings of cherubs on the wall, and a large plaster saint in a lighted niche. Dr. Bell rolled up his sleeves and went to work. "Doyle, soak sheets in cold water and bring a pitcher of lemonade with sugar and salt."

The young girls of the house scurried about fetching sheets and pitchers of ice water. Rebecca soaked the linens in icy water. Carl and I wrapped Jimmy in the sheets. "Hurry! Where is the lemonade? And bring chicken bouillon," said Dr. Bell.

A particularly fetching lass, wearing only a shift, ran into the kitchen and helped Ma, the old black cook, make enough lemonade for half the city. Then Ma took up a kitchen cleaver, went into the backyard, and killed a chicken to make the broth.

We forced lemonade, fortified with malt whisky, between Jimmy's lips. Most of the drink spilled down his chin, but, eventually, he took the liquid. His teeth chattered with the cold, and his skin took on a bluish tinge, though his temperature receded.

"Ah, we must not go too far. Now, we shall apply warmth," said Dr. Bell.

The girls filled brass bed warmers with hot ashes from the fireplace. We removed the icy sheets, and, with the warmers and blankets, we warmed the boy until Dr. Bell was satisfied.

We continued the vigil through the day and into the night. Rebecca slept, slumped in a chair, while we took turns at the bedside spooning lemonade and broth into the boy.

4 December, 1878

Carl was on duty during the dark, wee hours of the morning when human vitality is at its lowest. Jimmy gave one last small sigh and stopped breathing.

Carl put his hand on the boy's chest. "No! The poor fella . . . He stopped breathing!" he shouted.

Dr. Bell, who was sleeping in a rocking chair, came awake, leaped to Jimmy's side, placed his mouth over the lad's, and forced his own breath into the child's lungs.

After a few moments—moments that seemed like an eternity—Jimmy took a breath, then another. We continued the vigil, which seemed more and more like a death watch. But, in the morning, when sun came streaming through the window, he was no worse.

I had my hand on his feeble pulse. Carl and Dr. Bell closed their eyes and had forty winks. Ma tip-toed into the room with a pitcher of strong root tea. "This is an Indian remedy. Us slaves used it for the fever."

Rebecca and I took turns forcing spoonfuls of the murky brown liquid down Jimmy's throat. By mid-morning, his eyes fluttered and his pulse was stronger. He swallowed more tea and lemonade then drifted into a quiet sleep. By mid-afternoon, Jimmy was able to take an entire cupful of broth and his cheeks gained a hint of a pink glow.

They said it was a miracle that a child so young had survived a bout of yellow fever. The young ladies of the house were in and out of the sick room, sometimes bringing little treats. But, mostly, they fluttered about Carl, playing with his curly hair and making him blush.

Dr. Bell quietly shared a dram of malt whisky with Angie, but I had eyes only for Rebecca. I thought it was the Indian tea, but Dr. Bell scoffed and said it was the salt and whisky in the lemonade that cured little Jimmy. However, I noticed that he put a sample vial of the murky brown liquid in his medical bag. I would wager that he was going to bring it back to Edinburgh for analysis.

When we left, Angie and her girls made a fuss over the lad. The little blonde girl curled his hair and planted a big kiss on Carl who seemed to have lost his fear of 'painted ladies'.

Mr. Payne, the Reverend Beecher's host, sent a regal carriage for Rebecca and Jimmy. I wrapped Jimmy in blankets and carried him into the carriage. Rebecca insisted that I accompany them to the Payne's grand mansion.

Half an hour later, we drove through the stately gates and into a grove of old Rowan Oak trees. It seemed as if we rode for another mile until we finally reached the three-story brick mansion. The proud façade featured porticos, tall windows, and a wide veranda. A servant opened the door and welcomed Rebecca.

I carried Jimmy to a third floor room once occupied by the Balfour family. The lad cried for his parents and was weak as a newborn kitten, but his body was mending well.

"The Reverend Beecher will be stopping by in a moment. I'd like you to meet him," said Rebecca.

I had heard and read a good deal about this Reverend Beecher. His sister was the author of *Uncle Tom's Cabin,* and his adultery trial in 1874 was the most famous of the century. In his prime, the Reverend was a tall, handsome fellow with a high forehead and flowing black locks that hung down below his ears.

It was told that, during his long sermons, Beecher howled high-flown moral platitudes, used slang and humor, banged his fists, and stamped his feet. Even though he was more than fifty years old, he was rumored to still have dashing looks and the romantic air about him of a much younger man. Like many of the women who heard his sermons, I wondered if Rebecca had amorous thoughts about the old lecher.

When the Reverend Henry Ward Beecher greeted us, I was struck by his pallor and how different he looked from what I had imagined. His skin was dry and he lacked vitality. He was sickly, moved with difficulty, and his breathing was labored. He held out a quavering hand when Rebecca introduced me as Dr. Bell's assistant.

"Ah, Mr. Doyle, I am pleased to meet you. Mrs. Balfour regaled us with her praises of you and Dr. Bell. I wonder—is it a coincidence, or God's divine will, that you and the great doctor are here in this very city? My fondest wish is to have a medical consultation with him."

"Sir, I am sorry, but—"

"I am not as young as I used to be and I must gather my strength. I have to complete my great work."

"Dr. Bell is not seeing patients right now."

"Yet, he just saved the life of young Master Balfour."

"He would prefer if you kept that to yourself. Please don't mention his presence in this city."

"Even better. We shall have a clandestine consultation and it will be our little secret. You see, I need his opinion on my treatment. My physician has great faith in glandular extracts, but I want Bell's opinion."

"Who, may I ask, is your physician?"

"Dr. Edward Droussard."

I was taken aback. "Sir, do you mean Emilie Droussard?"

"Not Emilie. Edward. He has a most brilliant scientific mind and he is most up to date in his practice."

"Still, I believe that Dr. Bell can't—"

Beecher grabbed my shoulder. "Droussard is providing me with the very latest treatments to restore my vigor and endow me with eternal youth, but I want to seek counsel from Dr. Bell."

"But—"

He shook me. "I TRUST YOU WILL ARRANGE THIS, YES?"

For an apparently ill man, his grip was quite strong. "Um, aye sir. I will relay your desire for a consultation to Dr. Bell. If he does agree, I hope you understand that he must remain incognito," said I.

"Excellent . . . Ah, to fly about as if I was a young boy again," the Reverend Beecher said, with a smile.

I offered my farewell to Miss Yates, but she was preoccupied with Jimmy and did not even wish me well.

I was devastated by the cruel, cold distance that she had imposed between us, but I pretended to not be hurt, held my head high, and made my way back to the carriage, never once looking back.

5 December, 1878

After breakfast Carl and I spent the day wandering around Memphis, trying to discover more about Sherlock. We came up empty-handed. It was not until dinner at the Peabody Hotel with Dr. Bell and Rufus that we learned more of the sinister plot of our foes.

"Doyle, did you observe anything of import in town today?" Dr. Bell asked.

"No, sir. Unfortunately, it was a day of constant cul-de-sacs or, as Carl would say, 'dead ends.' "

"Well, one would have been better off spending one's time investigating those places where the walls have ears."

"I don't follow, sir."

"My dear Doyle, sometimes the apparently most common personage might provide the one missing clue necessary to unravel a mystery. For instance, all day long, Angie, that most estimable of hotel keepers, happens to be privy to some most damning conversations."

"My Lord." Carl could not control himself and jumped up. "What'd she say?"

"Well, Carl, if you'd just calm yourself, I shall tell you. You see, on more than one occasion, she has overheard former Confederate officers talk of overthrowing the government of the United States. They only lack a charismatic leader to convince the Northern states to repeal the Thirteenth Amendment that freed the slaves. They hope that this leader, whoever he is, will become the next President of the United States."

"But, sir, that is not possible. There are too many good, God-fearing people in this country to allow such a thing to occur."

"Sorry Arthur, but that's not true." Carl shook his head. "Most Northerners are still sick of war and not interested in the plight of former slaves. Many of our leaders are conciliatory towards the Southern whites."

"But, how could—"

Dr. Bell cleared his throat. "Doyle, consider the politics of our day. The most prominent minister in the land, The Reverend Henry Ward Beecher, is preaching Darwin's theory of survival of the fittest. He has renounced his former abolitionist views and thinks the blacks would be better off as slaves under benevolent owners at least until the twentieth century."

"Speaking of the Reverend Beecher, I met him when I went I returned Miss Yates and Jimmy to their lodgings."

"Doyle, you must tell me these things."

"I did not tell you because I know how you want to remain incognito here in Memphis and, well, he was begging for a consultation with you about his glandular treatments."

"Ah yes . . . It is all starting to make sense." The good doctor took a puff from his Meerschaum pipe and exhaled a cloud of smoke. "I appreciate you trying to protect me, Doyle, but, indeed, I shall be more than happy to advise the Reverend. In fact, it might be the only way we may learn more about this curious case."

"Maybe you can do better than us. We spent the whole day trying to learn more about a ferry boat with a sign, 'SHERLOCK-MEMPHIS'."

"Hmmm… Tell me what you observed."

"Well, when we saw it, I thought that maybe this might be the same 'sure lock' that Fogarty wrote about in his blood."

Dr. Bell sprung from his chair. "Bravo, Doyle. You have found another piece of the puzzle. Aye, of course. The poor man, in his death throes, wrote the word Sherlock in Gaelic. It must be the name of a town or village. Rufus, get busy. Ask your new friends here in town about this name."

"Yes, sir, I'll ask my lady friend. She'll know."

"But, Mr. Freeman, isn't she in Chicago?"

"Oh, I gots a lady friend here, too."

Everybody at the table laughed. I winked at him. "Mr. Freeman, you sly devil, you," I said.

Rufus looked coy and laughed with embarrassment. . .

6 December, 1878

In the morning, Carl and I arranged for Dr. Bell to see the Reverend Beecher. Rufus spent a few hours in town trying to get more information about the place known as Sherlock.

During lunch, Rufus gave his report. "I had to pay a dollar 'afore anyone talked. Some folks say the place is cursed. Others say it be a house with haunts. Even white folks won't go there."

"Bosh, that just sounds like a bunch of old wives tales," I said.

"No, suh. It's the truth. Sherlock was once a rich cotton plantation on a piece of low land dat jutted into the river, but da river come up and wash most of it away. A few years later, during high water, da river cut a channel dat made the tip of the land into an island, and then, well . . ."

Suddenly, he shifted his feet, his body tensed, and he shook nervously. "I can'ts tell you no more. No, suh . . ." Dear Rufus, who was our intellectual equal and had learned anatomy and physiology, had become scared, superstitious, and was talking like he was still a slave.

"Please Mr. Freeman, there is no need to get alarmed. If you will be so kind, tell us more . . . What is on the island now?" Dr. Bell asked.

"Dat island is done gone and growed up with weeds and bramble thickets and dey's rattlesnakes and wild beasts that walk on two feet and screech somethin' fierce. Everybody says ain't no people left there, but dey's an old, scarlet-colored plantation house on a hill with a buncha other little old cabins next to it. Da black folks say ghosts of dead Confederate soldiers live dere and when dey's a full moon, da walls of dat place run red with blood, and lights flicker, and Lucifer's smoke pours outta all the winders of dat ole place."

"Hmmm . . . I would like to visit this island. Where exactly did you say it is?" Dr. Bell asked.

"'Bout fifteen miles downriver."

"We must reconnoiter there this afternoon."

"No suh." Rufus twisted his cap and rolled his eyes. "No, suh, Docta Bell, dat ain't a good idea."

"I understand. I appreciate your concern, but it is imperative that I pay this island a visit. Please tell me how to find it. Can we take that ferry boat?"

"It don't go there no more."

"But, Doyle said that it had a sign which read—"

"Dat sign on da steam boat musta been from de old days."

With a flurry of orders, Dr. Bell arranged for a suitable vessel to take us all to inspect Sherlock. Rufus agreed to come only if he did not have to get out of the boat. Dr. Bell said that we must stop at Payne's mansion on the way to the dock so that he might have a consultation with the Reverend Beecher.

Rufus hailed a cab and we all set off to the mansion. "Are you really certain that visiting the Reverend Beecher is a good idea, sir?" I asked Dr. Bell.

He patted my arm and smiled. "Why, Miss Yates should be there, Doyle. Don't you want to see her?"

"I, um . . . Well, aye, but, still . . ."

"Doyle, a truly dangerous plot is afoot." Dr. Bell paused, lit his pipe, and exhaled a fragrant cloud of smoke. "We must see Beecher. He may be the only one who can lead us to the heart of this mystery and to the sinister mind that lurks behind all of these deaths."

"That makes sense, sir, but, how, then, is all this connected to Sherlock, an uninhabited island?"

"If what I have deduced is correct, Doyle, you will soon see for yourself."

Half an hour later, we arrived at the Payne mansion. Rufus refused to go inside. "Dem folks owned 'bout a thousand slaves 'afore the war and dey still treats black folks bad," he said. Carl decided to stay with him, so it was just Dr. Bell and I who knocked on the door. A few moments later, the Reverend Beecher ushered us inside.

He appeared weak, but he talked eagerly of his upcoming operation as he walked Dr. Bell to the library. "Doctor Bell, have you ever read Ovid's Metamorphoses?"

"Aye, of course. Why do you ask?"

"Well, do you remember Ovid's retelling of the myth of the child-god Iacchus?"

"Aye, the puer aeternus—the eternal boy who never grows old."

"This myth has always meant a great deal to me because as a young boy in Litchfield, Connecticut, I had a dear, dear friend, Peter, who died at the tender age of eight. He was such a sweet, gentle soul. He was musical and loved to play the pan pipes. When a child dies so young, in the minds of those who loved him he never grows old. It is as if sweet Peter lives on in a never, never land where he is a puer aeternus—an eternal youth."

"Reverend Beecher, I'm sorry to say this, but, as a man of science, I find it hard to believe that this operation will give you eternal youth."

"It is my heart's desire. And, mind you, it is not a selfish one. I only dream of it for the sake of salvaging this great country from ruin."

The Reverend Beecher talked about his great work of recanting his original abolitionist views. "I shall convince the North to remedy its mistakes and save the country," he said.

We listened to Beecher talk on an on for what seemed like an hour until Doctor Bell interrupted. "Sir, we must be on our way. May we now return to the topic of your operation?"

"Yes, of course. I am sorry, but politics have become my new religion, so to speak. My doctors have assured me that my ill health is due to a lack of glandular secretions. The injections I've been receiving are not helpful, so the next necessary step is a surgical implantation of tissue directly into my body."

"What is the origin of the glandular extracts?" Dr. Bell asked.

"I presume they are of animal origin."

"I agree that the Swiss have had some limited success with glandular implants, but only in very specific conditions of proven deficit."

"According to Dr. Droussard, the surgical incision is the only danger. He is willing to do the operation, but you are one of the world's best surgeons and use the new antiseptic technique. I trust there will be little risk and it would be my pleasure to have Mr. Doyle give the anaesthetic."

Dr. Bell's interest quickened at the name Droussard. "I insist on having my entire team, and I must inspect the local hospital facilities."

"It must be done in absolute secrecy. My doctors conduct experiments in a perfectly modern laboratory with suitable facilities for surgery," said the Reverend.

That was the end of the consultation. We left the stately mansion without a single glimpse of Rebecca.

It was a pleasant Tennessee day. The air was cool and crisp as we walked to the docks. Our vessel was eighteen feet long with four oars, a mast, sail, and tiller.

We set off downriver in high spirits. Carl and I each took a pair of oars. Rufus was at the stern with the tiller. Dr. Bell lounged on the bow seat and scanned the shores with a powerful telescope. A contrary southerly breeze precluded use of the sail, but with the strong current we made rapid progress.

After leaving Memphis the shoreline became low with innumerable small creeks and inlets. Dr. Bell pointed out hawks, shorebirds, turtles sunning on logs, otters, and even a black bear on the shore. It was a little after three o'clock in the afternoon when we rounded a bend and saw before us a small heavily wooded island and, much to our surprise, a two-story house—painted a bright scarlet-red.

We shipped our oars and drifted another quarter of a mile while Dr. Bell minutely surveyed the island. He passed the handsome brass instrument to me, and, after adjusting the lens, I examined the island, commencing with the scarlet house and the surrounding scarlet cabins.

The main building appeared to be an old-style Southern plantation house, and the cabins were probably slave quarters. There was no sign of human occupancy, but, over the door, outlined in black, was a flag. And it was not an old worn flag. It was new and bright red, with a blue cross and three white stars in each arm of the cross.

The rest of the island was densely covered with vegetation, right down to the water. I passed the telescope to Carl. "It's a Confederate battle flag," he said.

"Lemme see," said Rufus. He took a long look through the telescope. "Dat ain't just any Confederate battle flag."

When he passed the instrument back to me his hands shook. "Dat dere is the flag of old General Forrest. I told you this was a bad place."

We had drifted to within two hundred yards of the north end of the island when I heard a loud series of booms. Dr. Bell fell to his knees. "Gentlemen, get down!" he cried.

Rufus, Carl, and I all followed Dr. Bell's lead and dropped down to the deck. We heard a high-pitched noise as a volley of bullets whistled over our heads and splashed into the water on either side of the boat. I could see little puffs of gun smoke coming up from the edge of the island, but our assailant was well-hidden.

Dr. Bell coolly scanned the shore. "Whoever is shooting at us isn't visible, but he's no ghost. Gentlemen, please pull hard. We need to get out of range."

Carl went to his seat and pulled an oar to turn the boat. In my desperate attempt to duck from the bullets, I skimmed the water with my oars and fell backwards.

Carl managed to turn us towards the middle of the river and I thought we were safe. That is, until a few moments later when we were caught in an eddy current. The violent whirlpool spun our craft like a merry-go-round, further and further into the middle of the mighty river.

Suddenly, Dr. Bell grabbed my oar from me and his expert rowing brought us to the edge of the eddy. "I didn't know you knew how to row, sir," I said.

"Doyle, my lad, to you I might appear to be an old fogey, but, in my youth, I happened to have been the single scull champion of Edinb—"

Before he could finish his sentence, a final furious current took us back towards the island where we were greeted by another volley of rifle fire. A bullet smashed into a plank just at the water line of our boat. Instantly water poured in and we sank lower.

Dr. Bell and I kept rowing as Rufus and Carl tried to plug the bullet hole. Water poured in. Rufus desperately bailed with his hat while Carl cupped his hands and threw water overboard. Despite their best efforts, the boat settled deeper and deeper into the water.

We could not land on the island and the other shore was too far for us to reach before the boat sank. It looked hopeless. "Sir, any ideas on how we should proceed?" I asked.

"Stay with the boat, laddies, and have faith that this too shall pass!" Dr. Bell shouted.

We were down to the gunwales, frantically bailing with our cupped hands and hats when a low mournful wail rang in our ears. A steamboat was coming our way, a lovely grand vessel traveling upriver at a great speed. Her stern wheel chunked away; black smoke and sparks flew from her twin stacks into the rapidly darkening night.

She did not slow as we waved and shouted. No one on board saw us. To make matters worse, it appeared as if she was going to blindly ram our sinking vessel. Rufus and Carl pulled furiously on their oars. We narrowly escaped being rammed, but the boat had filled with water.

"I cain't swim!" Rufus shouted.

"Hang on to the boat!" Bell replied.

Suddenly, from behind the steamer, a small boat rowed by two powerful deckhands came our way. With extra-ordinary timing they arrived just as our boat was about to sink beneath the waves of old muddy. Our poor cockle shell was just barely afloat when our rescuers pulled us onto their little skiff and brought us to the steamer.

Within minutes, we were safely aboard the steamboat, *Natchez*, which was bound from Vicksburg to Memphis. The crew escorted us, dripping wet, through the grand ballroom, with a band and dancing couples, to the officer's quarters.

In all of America, I never saw anything as grand as that Mississippi River steamboat. The gilded decorations, gorgeous furniture, oil paintings, splendid food, abundant drinks, and hand-carved gambling tables took my breath away. She was a glorious embodiment of this young nation. Bold. Brash. Full of steam and power and energy.

Maybe it was our narrow escape from danger that filled us with a certain euphoria, or maybe it was the hot New Orleans coffee fortified with some sort of sweet, syrupy fluid that they served us as we were wrapped in warm blankets. Either way, it was as if we were snatched out of hell and carried into a heavenly abode. I will never forget those several glorious hours we spent on the *Natchez.*

By the time we docked in Memphis we were dry and warm. Dr. Bell seemed most bothered by the fact that the tobacco for his meerschaum pipe was a soggy mess. People often wonder why doctors are so addicted to this vile weed, but they need only endure the stench of an anatomy laboratory to understand.

"Doctor Bell, I would be happy to fetch pipe tobacco and pick up an El Perfecto cigar for myself," Carl said, with his usual good nature.

"Carl, I appreciate the offer, but it's getting late. You and Arthur should get some rest."

"I don't mind and would enjoy stopping by Angie's for a hot bowl of stew," said Carl.

"Do you want stew or that little blonde?" I teased.

Carl laughed. "The stew."

"Only if Arthur goes with you."

"This has been a most eventful day. I am exhausted and feel I must record everything in my diary before going to sleep," I insisted.

"I don't mind going alone. I'll only be an hour. I'll run to the tobacconist and then Angie's and be at the hotel in no time."

"No Carl, please, it may not be safe," Dr. Bell said.

Carl smiled, turned, and began running off into town.

"Doyle go after him!" Dr. Bell admonished me. "Rufus, please go with him. It is dangerous, too dangerous for any of you to be out alone. I will go to the hotel and wait there."

We did as he said, but, by the time we got started, Carl had gotten a good lead on us. In a near panic, we searched the streets and alleyways. He was nowhere to be found. We went to the tobacco shop. It was closed. A loud party was in progress at

Angie's. I slipped around to the back door. "I ain't seen hide nor hair of Mister Carl," Ma said.

After searching for over an hour, not knowing where else we could look, we gave up and went back to the hotel. When we returned Carl had still not appeared, but Dr. Bell was waiting in the lobby with a letter in hand.

My Dearest Dr. Bell,

My carriage will meet you at the hotel nine a.m., to-morrow. The operation we discussed will take place at noon, when there is the best light. I look forward to seeing you then and thank you for your assistance in advance.

Your Most Humble and Obedient Servant,
The Reverend Henry Ward Beecher

7 December, 1878

In the wee hours of the morning, I had a bad dream and awoke, certain that Carl would be snoring in the next bed. But, when I looked around the room, there was no sign of him. My nagging fears for his safety turned into a sinking sensation. Was he in the clutches of those evil people? Paralyzed and near death from curare? I ran to Dr. Bell's room and banged on the door. There was no answer.

I found Dr. Bell in the lobby pacing back and forth, empty pipe in hand.

"I should never have let him go after that damn bloody tobacco," he said. "I notified the police and sent a wire to Angus Duncan requesting assistance from the Pinkertons."

We again prowled the streets and alleys and visited Angie's. There was no sign of my friend, the best of America: an optimist and a trustworthy Wisconsin farm lad. Carl always had a smile on his face and never let anything oppress him. He had led me out of a freezing forest and saved my life more than once. I wondered where he could be and whether he was safe.

By nine o'clock in the morning, we were a dispirited group, waiting in the lobby for the Reverend Beecher. I was for putting the whole thing off until we found Carl, but Dr. Bell grimly observed that in all likelihood the minister would lead us to the fiends who had abducted Carl. The carriage arrived, but I was too distraught to pay attention to the two armed horsemen who followed the Reverend Beecher.

To my surprise, Rebecca was sitting next to the minister. *What a cozy arrangement*, I thought. We settled ourselves on the opposite seat, leaving room for Rufus who carried the instrument case. The Reverend's face twisted into a smirk. "Is his presence necessary, Doctor Bell?" he asked.

"Aye, absolutely. Mr. Freeman is an integral member of my surgical team. Your operation cannot proceed without him," Dr. Bell replied.

Rebecca's eyes were downcast. She did not meet my gaze. "Jimmy is almost back to his normal self," she murmured.

I leaned across the narrow space that separated us. "That's good. How are you?"

"Happy because now I shall have time to nurse the Reverend Beecher after his operation."

"I see." I turned from her and gazed out the window.

"Arthur, where is your friend, Carl? I thought for sure that he would be here to assist in the operation," she asked.

"He's gone missing," I said.

"Oh, I am so sorry. I had hoped to see him again. I hope he will be all right."

To my great consternation, Rebecca spent her time arranging pillows or tucking the minister's feet under blankets. Every so often I glanced at her, hoping that she might be looking at me. But, it was as if I never existed.

We galloped in a southerly direction, past fields left fallow for the winter, then through dense woodland and swamps, for at least an hour. We stopped by a trail that led through a desolate, forbidding swamp.

It was then that I noticed the two silent men who had followed us on horseback. They and our driver held Winchester rifles. One man led the way on the trail beneath dark, low-hanging clouds. The rain started with a drizzle, but quickly became a downpour before we reached the waiting steam launch. We huddled in the shelter of the small deckhouse as we chugged downstream past ancient trees hung with a greyish moss. I moved as close as possible to Rebecca, who was hunched in a corner.

She said nothing, but, to my surprise, she took my hand as if she were searching for comfort or reassurance. My heart did a flip-flop, but, in a moment, she removed her hand and silently moved closer to the Reverend Beecher.

Our vessel touched ground, and, while balancing on a narrow gangplank that ended in a muddy path, a great flash of lightning revealed the scarlet house and surrounding cabins on top of the small hill. We were on the back side of the island. Evidently the river continued around the southern edge to join the Mississippi.

Our silent guards cradled polished new Winchester rifles in the crook of their arms. "Why are you armed?" Dr. Bell asked.

"Damned dangerous in these parts. Alligators and rattlesnakes and the like," one replied, as he spit a stream of tobacco juice.

We were walking up a muddy path when I spotted a crumpled, soggy El Perfecto cigar, Carl's favourite smoke, beside the path. I had the wild hope that we would find him alive. As we trudged up the path through driving rain towards the scarlet house I heard chattering, howling, and crying. It was as if the house had a nursery filled with babies who were making an eerie, almost inhuman sound. The rogue at the head of our column bought his rifle to his shoulder and scanned the trees on either side of the path.

Rufus, for all his superstitions, seemed the least concerned about our surroundings. He proudly carried the instrument case at the head of our dreary column. Dr. Bell kept a grim silence and stolidly treaded onward. I caught up with him to gain strength from his resolve. There was no chance to tell him about the cigar because the Reverend Beecher insisted on stopping to catch his breath. "Don't waste our time. Get along," one of the armed men said.

"I understand the need for secrecy since I am destined to be the next President of the United States, but I demand an explanation for the guns," said the Reverend Beecher with an angry scowl.

There was no answer because the Reverend Beecher took a feeble step, slipped on a stone, and went down. Rebecca helped him to his feet and on we went.

We finally reached the scarlet plantation house and the howling and chattering reached an otherworldly pitch and then died out . . .

It had once been a grand mansion, but now the columns were askew and most of the floor boards on the veranda were rotting.

One of our keepers shifted his Winchester and, with a large key, unlocked the front door beneath the painted battle flag. We stepped into a long corridor containing odd pieces of once-elegant furniture. It ran the length of the front of the house, and by the light of oil lamps I identified four doors leading off the corridor. The chattering and crying, which had ceased when we entered the corridor, started back again, this time with greater intensity and a note of madness and anger.

To my amazement, the door to our left opened into a clean whitewashed room. Rain beat against a skylight that admitted light the color of cast iron. Oil lamps helped relieve the gloom.

There was a plain wooden operating table in the center of the room beneath the skylight. Shelves filled with medical supplies lined the walls. Next to the operating table was a small table with a wash basin, soap, and towels. The room was heated by an old-fashioned open fireplace.

My eyes swept across what was to be our operating room. In addition to the entrance, there was another closed door. Did it lead to another room or to the outside? A tall, stooped woman clad in the white floor-length dress of a proper operating room sister was in charge. A bonnet pulled low obscured her hair and features. Upon our arrival, she ceased stacking linen on a shelf and half turned with a folded towel over her right hand.

"The table is freshly scrubbed and prepared for the Reverend Beecher. You may place the instruments there." She pointed to another table covered with a white sheet. "I trust everything is satisfactory."

Dr. Bell swept the room with his eyes. "Aye, the room seems well-organized, but where is the Reverend Beecher's physician?"

"Dr. Droussard will be here after he secures the glandular material."

"I understand the desire for secrecy, but why have we been threatened with firearms?"

"Our men are armed to discourage trespassers and to protect you from wild animals. We are quite removed from civilization."

Dr. Bell nodded to Rufus who placed the instrument case on the edge of the table. The minister, holding Rebecca's arm, tottered into the operating room. He removed his coat and shirt and, almost eagerly, stretched out on the table.

"Prepare both arms, please. The doctor may implant two glands," said the nurse.

Rufus soaked the instruments in carbolic and Rebecca, at Dr. Bell's instructions, swabbed both of the Reverend Beecher's arms with the antiseptic.

Dr. Bell was quiet and pensive. His interest in the operation appeared to be as much curiosity as scientific interest.

The preparations for surgery proceeded normally until Dr. Bell instructed Mr. Freeman to give the chloroform and Miss Yates to handle the instruments. I would normally have given the anaesthetic, but assumed he was giving Mr. Freeman the experience because this operation was a mere incision through the skin and fat.

The wild chattering and raucous noise had died down. I became aware of a low moaning, almost gurgling, sound from the back room. Fearing the worst, I could not help but creep towards the closed door. While everyone concentrated on the Reverend Beecher, I quietly inched opened the door.

Suddenly, large, rough, powerful hands grabbed me by the shoulders and covered my mouth, stifling my outcry. The door was closed and I was overpowered and forced to the ground. It happened so quickly, I was afraid that my companions, busy with their preparations, were unaware of my predicament and would not notice my disappearance.

As I struggled against my assailants to get to my feet, I felt a slight stabbing sensation in my right buttock. A moment later I lost voluntary motion, first in my legs, then my arms. I was still perfectly aware of my surroundings, with unimpaired vision and hearing. However, when they roughly placed me on a table, I realized I was no longer able to hold up my head.

With my death likely imminent from suffocation, I remembered Dr. Bell's advice to breathe with the diaphragm, the muscle that separates the abdomen from the chest cavity. I concentrated every fiber of my being on the phrenic nerve that innervates the diaphragm.

But, I could not budge my diaphragm. My chest felt heavy and dead. I was going to be asphyxiated. I wanted to scream. I wanted to breathe.

I did not want to die.

I focused all my mental energy on my phrenic nerve until there was a flicker of movement. I felt a minute flow of air enter my lungs. I flexed my diaphragm again and again in an attempt to maintain a tenuous hold on life.

I heard a low gurgling together with a constant trickling sound that, at first, I thought was water. To my horror, it was the drip, drip, drip of blood.

They had left me with my head turned to one side, and as my vision cleared, I looked upon a dreadfully horrific scene.

Carl, my best mate in America, was naked from the waist up and strapped to a table. A gowned, hooded figure held back his head while another, similarly attired, dissected with knife and forceps deep into a bloody hole in his neck.

The paralyzing drug that they had given us both still had me in its hold, but Carl started to squirm as they probed his neck in an attempt to remove his thyroid gland.

Suddenly, Carl jerked and attempted to struggle free. He moaned and his eyes rolled towards me with a startled look of recognition.

I wanted to reach out to help him, to do something, but I was incapable of movement.

The surgeon, or rather I should call him the detestable butcher posing as a surgeon, continued with painstaking slowness to dissect through the nerves, blood vessels and muscles of Carl's neck.

There was a steady drip of blood, and occasionally a crimson spray when the sharp knife cut through an artery.

I willed my paralyzed muscles to stir, but could not force even the merest twitch of movement. I felt a constant sensation of suffocation, as if I was being held under water by a giant hand and could not rise to the surface. I felt lucky to occasionally get a tiny gasp of air into my lungs.

I momentarily went unconscious from lack of oxygen, but something—call it a deep-seated atavistic need to survive—forced the diaphragmatic muscle to quiver now and move the merest whiffs of air into my body.

The high-pitched chattering increased. Something banged and knocked at a side door. The surgeon continued slowly dissecting Carl's neck.

I drifted in and out of consciousness while the operation on Carl proceeded step by agonizing step. I had no sensation of the passage of time, but concentrated on each shallow breath. Carl's moans and gurgling respirations became weaker until, with one final gasp, his beseeching eyes turned to me. *Kill me. Now. Please*, they seemed to plead.

His life's blood drained out onto the floor and I knew he was knocking on death's door. My foggy, oxygen-starved brain understood. They were not implanting glands into the Reverend Beecher from animals, but from human beings. They had kidnapped Carl to implant his thyroid into the Reverend to re-invigorate him. It was a hideous, detestable plan.

But, yes, now I understood. The nurse had said they would implant two glands. I was to be the next subject.

Rough hands straightened my body into a supine position and tilted my head backwards to expose the flesh of my neck to the surgeon's knife.

The memory of the scene that followed is both a confused blur and a vivid nightmare.

The chattering increased to a frenzied howl, and the door on the opposite side of the room swung open. A horde of screeching and howling monkeys flew out through the door and descended on the hooded figures ripping, clawing, and biting.

The surgeon and the medical assistant attempted to defend themselves with surgical knives, but the frenzied animals tore away their hoods and robes and overcame them.

Suddenly, a small woman's body with long, flowing locks of raven hair passed before my eyes, and I realized that the surgeon was none other than Emilie Droussard. She covered her face with her hands to protect herself, but the animals were not deterred. They ripped her skin and bit deep into her neck, chest, and head. Blood spewed everywhere.

She screamed as they bore her down to the floor. Her blood mingled with Carl's. She struggled against the mad primate onslaught for another moment and then, mercifully for her, she passed out.

One large, fierce monkey fastened on to the back of her assistant who I now realized was the tobacco-spitting man with the Winchester rifle who had walked us to the scarlet house.

The man beat the animal with his bare hands and struck it with the butt of his rifle, but to no avail. As he staggered from their onslaught, his arms flailing furiously, two monkeys shredded his face with their razor-sharp incisor teeth.

As if possessed by demons, the ferocious monkeys tore his eyes from their sockets. He emitted an unholy scream and sunk, lifeless, to the floor.

Throughout this ghastly uproar, I fully expected the monkeys to attack me and Carl. We were helpless and the next victims.

A monkey even jumped onto my chest, but, instead of ripping me to pieces, to my amazement, it merely sniffed and jumped down.

Suddenly, the once-ferocious monkeys became docile as family pets and scampered about, ignoring the bodies and lapping up human blood.

Two of the animals leaped up on to the surgical table, sniffed Carl, and made sad, mewing sounds. Carl stirred. He was still alive! My heart leaped with joy.

However, his chest hardly moved, and I was certain that, without medical attention, he would surely die.

It all made sense when I dimly remembered surgical scars on the monkeys. These simple primates had been subject to dreadful experiments, yet, somehow, they had survived. Now, they had taken revenge on their tormenters.

Suddenly, the room went grey, then black. Dr. Bell later said my eyes were wide open, but I was unconscious when he and Rebecca burst into the room.

They heard the ruckus and, fortunately, arrived just in time. Rebecca thought I was dead and, with quick thinking, grabbed the bellows from the fireplace. “Dr. Bell, he isn’t breathing!” she shouted.

Dr. Bell immediately pumped air into my lungs. They said I initially showed no signs of life.

At the first twinge of returning muscle activity, I weakly brushed the wooden nozzle away from my mouth, coughed, spluttered, and took a deep breath. "Save Carl," I said.

Poor Carl was near the end of his life, but if there was one man in the world who could save him it was Dr. Joseph Bell.

"Aye, he has a faint pulse!" Dr. Bell shouted. "Miss Yates, please, my instruments . . ."

Rebecca snatched up clamps, needles, and thread. In the merest twinkling of an eye, Dr. Bell sutured bleeding arteries and veins. The bleeding stopped. Dr. Bell had trained in the old days before anaesthetics, when surgeons operated with great speed. His fingers flew, and it was only minutes until he had stitched the terrible wound.

In the midst of the frantic efforts to stitch the wound, Carl had stopped breathing. Dr. Bell responded to this new emergency and pumped air into his lungs with the fireplace bellows. Carl did not respond. Dr. Bell, a staunch churchman, looked to heaven, and I am certain his lips moved in prayer, entreating God for a miracle.

Dr. Bell kept pumping the bellows. Suddenly, Carl took a weak breath, coughed, sputtered, and came back to life. To our great joy, he was alive.

If the monkeys had come a minute later, Carl would've been dead, and if Dr. Bell and Rebecca hadn't arrived shortly after the monkey attack, I would've been dead, too. Yet, it was as if some sort of divine force had wanted us to survive and so, we were both saved.

(I do not remember a great deal about my rescue. Therefore, I must admit that the details as written were related to me by Rebecca and Dr. Bell after these events took place. They also told of the events as they transpired in the adjoining room of the scarlet house in the few minutes before my rescue. Ergo, the following text is his tale as they related it to me after it occurred.)

Doctor Bell, with his usual way, dictated the following between puffs on his pipe: *I was focused on the operation, dubious, yet I must admit, also excited about, the possibilities of a great scientific breakthrough. Lister's antiseptic technique made it possible to remove or repair diseased organs. If this operation succeeded, organ implantation could become a reality.*

Rufus had administered sufficient chloroform and the nursing sister indicated the organ was nearly ready in the adjacent room. I had made a mere scratch of an incision on the Reverend Beecher's right arm. "Doyle, please finish the incision down to muscle. You need the practise," I said.

When you did not respond, I looked around and realized that you, laddie, had disappeared. I put down the scalpel and demanded to know your whereabouts.

The nursing sister insisted that I continue with the operation. I expressed concern and adamantly refused until she revealed your whereabouts.

As I looked at the nursing sister, I observed something. You see, my dear Doyle, once again, it was observation that saved the day...

For the nursing sister was no woman.

I tore off her white bonnet and flung aside the towel covering the right hand only to reveal an awful hook. As you may now have guessed, the nursing sister was really Captain Spencer or, as he is better known, Captain Hook.

The villain jumped away from me. He seized Rebecca just beneath her jaw with his terribly sharp hook and, with his good hand, pulled a long-barreled revolver from beneath his white dress. His face was contorted with rage and he had the strength of a mad man.

I immediately poised the scalpel over Beecher's chest.

"Damn you! I shall plunge this knife into his heart. Release the girl."

He was far gone into madness, but Rufus flung himself at the Captain. The man fired his pistol, but the gun caught on his long dress. His aim was poor. The bullet grazed Rufus on the side of his chest. The ragged wound was bloody and painful, but not lethal.

Just before he collapsed, Rufus seized the weapon. Thankfully, the open instrument case was close at hand. I reached into my secret niche and withdrew the Bull Dog revolver.

My first shot splintered the doorway. I aimed again, but Hook used Rebecca as a shield and I lowered the gun.

(Here, Miss Yates took up the narrative. She spoke in a low, almost inaudible voice, while twisting a handkerchief. She was clearly under great emotional strain as she spoke, but I felt it important to convey her story in order to complete this narrative.)

It all happened so fast. He dragged me backwards and said he would kill me if Doctor Bell didn't continue the operation. I felt helpless and terrified as the cold metal of his hook dug into my throat.

With his last ounce of strength, heroic Rufus pushed him off balance and took his gun. When Doctor Bell fired, I wrenched free. He then fled down the corridor, tearing off the dress as he ran. In his flight, he knocked over an oil lamp. Oil spilled and burst into flames. The fire spread through the old furniture and dry wood. He reached the front door and disappeared. "Down with tyrants!" he screamed.

(Dr. Bell took up the narrative again here.)

When I reached Rebecca, the corridor was already filled with black smoke and flames were licking at the walls. Captain Hook had disappeared, but a door at the end of the hall opened and a man holding a rifle and a whip stepped out.

When I fired, he ran and disappeared around the corner, apparently following Captain Hook into the approaching night.

To my amazement and utter horror, a pack of shrieking monkeys emerged from the door and ran through the flames and smoke. They ignored us and scampered out of the house.

After I had seen to Rebecca and staunched the bleeding from Rufus's chest I then proceeded to help you and Carl.

(I shall now continue the narrative from my own perspective.)

As Carl and I began to recover, Dr. Bell and Rebecca dragged Rufus into our 'operating room'. They then pulled the Reverend Beecher from the approaching flames. He was still recovering from the anaesthetic. They slammed the door behind them, but the smoke poured in through the cracks around the doorstop.

Flames were rapidly consuming the house, smoke was filling our room, and we could not see a way out. A quick inspection of the 'operating room' revealed the windows were barred on the outside and there was no other door.

We considered making a *run* through the flames to an exit, but the floorboards started collapsing, and we seemed destined to die of asphyxiation in this ghastly room in this gruesome scarlet house.

A few feet away from me, suddenly I heard Emilie Droussard. "Dr. Bell . . . Please . . ." She slowly raised her bloody arm and pointed to a shelf.

Dr. Bell knelt by her side and listened to her nearly inaudible, wispy voice "It was a mad dream . . . My casebook . . . Take it. You will see . . ."

Her arm fell back and her eyes closed. She made a deep shuddering sigh. Her eyes fluttered open, "If only . . . The implant . . ." Her voice drifted off, and then her eyes brightened for an instant. "To hays . . . Below the tomb!"

She said nothing more, but took another raspy breath. Her eyes went dim with the blank emptiness of death. Dr. Bell then reached for her casebook, a leather-bound notebook sitting on an overhead shelf. Dr. Bell slipped it into his coat pocket.

Rufus groaned in pain and Dr. Bell tried to assist him.

Meanwhile, the smoke continued to fill the room, and Rebecca was the first to succumb to the fumes. She slumped and fell to the floor. She struck the hard wooden floorboards with a loud *FWUNK*. I was dizzy and still badly shaken, but knelt by her side, fanning her face and massaging her hands. I coughed and wondered how much longer we could survive the smoke and flames.

Things looked grim. The smoke was growing thick. We were lost.

"Doyle, how is Rebecca?" Doyle shouted through the haze of smoke.

"Her pulse is steady and her breath is shallow."

Rebecca opened her eyes. "What happened?"

"You fainted."

"Doyle, did you hear the hollow sound as she hit the floor? It sounded hollow. Please inspect the floorboards!" Dr. Bell yelled.

The smoke made it hard to see, but I ran my hands along the floorboards by Rebecca. I noticed nothing unusual. The floorboards were old and worn.

Just as I was about to give up, my hand struck upon something cold and metallic. Brass. There was a round, tarnished brass door-pull set deeply into a plank in the floorboards.

"I found a trapdoor handle . . . You were right, Dr. Bell. How did you know?"

"Elementary. Did you not interpret the hollow sound as Rebecca fell?"

It was a trapdoor that led to a flight of stairs, then into a cavernous basement dug out of the earth and lined by crude bricks. Like priest-holes in old English homes, many pre-Civil War homes in America had trapdoors that led to tunnels. We were saved, thanks to Dr. Bell's great powers of observation.

Dr. Bell and I supported Rufus while we made our way down wet, moss covered wooden stairs into the dank subterranean room. The Reverend Beecher, now fully recovered from the chloroform, followed us. And Carl, my magnificently strong mate from Wisconsin, struggled to get to his feet. Unfortunately, he was still very weak and, as he tried to stand, he collapsed back to the floor.

Rebecca, poor, sweet Rebecca, felt better and helped Carl to his feet and down the stairs of the tunnel.

Once everybody was safely below the ground, I slammed the trapdoor against the dense smoke and breathed a sigh of relief. Dr. Bell gently lowered Rufus to the earthen floor and I struck a lucifer.

By the flickering yellow light we made out dozens of wooden crates labeled 'U.S. ARMORY, WINCHESTER CALIBRE .45-70 RIFLES.' Were these the guns stolen from an arsenal in Illinois? I had no time to ponder the question. It was pitch dark when my match went out.

I used up all but one match while exploring to find an exit. There was nothing. I pulled slivers of wood from a crate and, with my last match, created a makeshift torch.

I held the burning slivers high and explored more until I felt a slight draft of fresh air from a side tunnel leading down and away from the crude basement.

"Follow me." I went ahead with the dim torch and our motley parade trudged in the dark towards the draft of fresh air. Rebecca supported Carl and Dr. Bell helped Rufus. The Reverend Beecher complained at every step while we crept along the muddy tunnel. I may have stepped on a rat, but stifled a scream for fear of upsetting Rebecca. She cried out and batted at a spider web in her hair. The spider was a black, wicked-looking creature. I never liked creepy insects, but I brushed it away and stepped on it.

We had been in the tunnel no more than a few minutes when a terrific explosion shook the earth. Bricks flew from the walls and all around us the tunnel began to collapse.

"My God, there must have been enough powder and ammunition there for a small army," said Dr. Bell. "Hurry, before we are buried alive."

We moved as quickly as we could under the circumstances. Fortunately, we soon saw a speck of light, which grew larger as we moved closer to it. In a moment, we emerged into some brush only a few yards from the big river. The tunnel entrance was well-hidden by trees and foliage. Muddy footprints in a worn trail leading to a crude landing indicated recent use.

I searched, but the steam launch that had brought us here was gone, most likely taken by Captain Hook and his rifle-toting crony.

Flames and dense smoke still shot skyward from the old scarlet plantation house and were spreading fast to the cabins. We watched as the house collapsed into a veritable crematorium for Emilie Droussard and her accomplices. Meanwhile, the storm moved on, leaving a yellow haze that marked the sun setting across the great river.

About an hour later, a side-wheeler packet boat pushing a flat-bottomed barge had paused in mid-river, evidently to watch the spectacular pyrotechnics. We shouted and waved. Finally, Dr. Bell fired three quick shots from his Bull Dog revolver.

The Reverend Beecher finally proved of some value when he shouted in his best stentorian voice. “HELP! HELP! We have injured men here!”

She was the *Lucy B*, an elderly tug pushing a barge upriver. Her great wheel churned mud, but she edged close enough to our landing for husky black deckhands to help us aboard.

On board, we huddled among bales of cotton, trying to make Carl and Rufus comfortable. Carl had lost a lot of blood and had used all of his remaining energy to get through the tunnel. He was pale and weak as he rested on the cotton bales.

Rufus coughed and spit blood as if the bullet had grazed his lung. More blood oozed from his chest wound. Fortunately, the bullet had entered his lower chest and exited from his side. Dr. Bell swabbed his wounds with carbolic and applied a tight bandage torn from his shirt.

Rebecca, now fully revived from inhaling smoke, took over his care with great tenderness. The five of us huddled together and sat away from the Reverend Beecher. The old fellow was angry that we had not implanted the thyroid gland. He was still convinced the operation would have made him into a new man. Even now, he could not believe that his doctor was a fraud.

We reached the Memphis landing a few hours later and, with difficulty, roused a drayman and his wagon.

With my energy somewhat restored by the fresh air, I went ahead and informed the Burk’s of our plight. They were more than willing to take in my injured companions and tend to their needs. Upon arrival at the Burk’s house, Rebecca, Dr. Bell, and I carried Rufus and then Carl into the home of the friendly Quakers.

Rebecca shook her red curls. “I shall have nothing more to do with the Reverend Beecher. Please, Mrs. Burk, I have a little money and will pay if you can let my ward, Jimmy, stay with you for a few days while I care for these two injured men.” Her eyes flashed with an emotion that I had never witnessed in the girl.

“Of course, dear, you may stay as long as you wish.”

So, Miss Yates stayed with Rufus and Carl.

Soon thereafter Dr. Bell and I retired to the hotel where I am once again at my desk with pencil and paper recording the events of this incredible day. I am at this moment reading out loud to Dr. Bell, who is kindly correcting some of my observations. To the best of my memory it is all true. I am glad to be alive and looking forward to spending the remainder of my time in America wooing Rebecca. How can I ever thank Doctor Bell for saving my life? Someday, I shall immortalize this man with my writing.

8 December, 1878

In the morning, after a sound sleep, Dr. Bell and I picked up Jimmy from the Payne's mansion and delivered him to the Burk's house.

On the way, I asked Dr. Bell about the Reverend. Beecher. "You need not worry about that old scoundrel. The sly old dog slithered back to Brooklyn on the first train. The old fraud tried to swear me to secrecy before he left and said he would pray for us."

We brought young Jimmy and all of his and Rebecca's luggage to the Burk's home. Rufus and Carl were on makeshift pallets in our old lean-to bedroom. Their wounds were clean, but both patients were in considerable pain. When we arrived with Jimmy, Miss Yates was administering laudanum to Carl. My friend gazed at her with what were clearly love-smitten eyes and, when she put down the bottle of medicine, she caressed his hand and returned his loving gaze. Was it possible? Had they fallen in love overnight?

Rebecca rose, hugged little Jimmy and then gave me a mere glance. "Mrs. Burk will allow me to stay as long as it takes to restore Carl and Rufus to health," said she. She smiled warmly as she spoke. In that moment, a spark flashed between Rebecca and Carl and I knew that they had taken a fancy to each other.

Despite all my efforts to woo her, she had instead fallen for my friend from Wisconsin, and he was just as smitten.

I must admit, as I watched them stare deeply into each other's eyes, I did feel the sharp stab of green-eyed jealousy. Our star-crossed love was not to be. At first I was angry, but then I felt happy for my mate, Carl. It was a struggle, but I became resigned to focusing on the other dreams in my life: finishing my studies, learning medicine, and, someday, writing about my adventures in America. Even with a broken heart, I would wish them well. She was the pretty nurse that Carl had longed for. Perhaps the prophecy of Mrs. Burk's tea leaves was correct and marrying her would have upset my Maw. My scientific mind would not accept the occult, but perhaps there are unknown mysteries.

Aye, it is disappointing and hard to accept. Surely, there has to be someone else out there for me. Somebody who wants me as much as I want them. I am still only nineteen and have the rest of my life to learn the ways of women.

Back in the kitchen, over cups of Mrs. Burk's coffee, Dr. Bell lit up his pipe. "I wish I could say all's well that ends well, but, alas, we still aren't free to return to Scotland."

"Why?" I asked.

"Our friend, Captain Hook is still at large."

"Aye, but he is no threat."

"Doyle, my lad, do you remember Emilie Droussard's dying words?"

"Something about 'to hays below the tomb.' "

"Something bad is afoot, but I am baffled."

Rufus overheard our conversation and weakly lifted his head from the pallet. "Sir, dey's only one tomb important to those damn Confederates. The good folks up North buried Mister Lincoln in a fine tomb in Springfield, Illinois."

Dr. Bell nodded. "They might steal the body, but that would not further their cause. Hmmm . . . Let me ponder this. Doyle, let us take a walk. The fresh air might help."

It was a sunny, fine day with just a bit of a breeze. We strolled back to the Peabody for lunch, and as is his habit, Dr. Bell stopped in the lobby to check the newspapers.

"My God. Doyle, read this." I took the paper and scanned a long article on the front page about the travels of President Rutherford B. Hayes from Washington, through the Midwest to Kansas, and back through Springfield, Illinois. The President was to end his tour with a final address at Lincoln's tomb at four o'clock in the afternoon on the ninth day of December.

I gasped. "That was her message. Not to hays, but to Rutherford B. HAYES."

"Aye and BELOW the tomb. President Hayes will be delivering a speech on the balustrade BELOW the obelisk marking Lincoln's tomb, and he very well might share Lincoln's fate if we do not intercede by four o'clock in the afternoon to-morrow," said Dr. Bell.

TO-MORROW! The President was going to be in Springfield in one day. We had to get there if we were to stop something awful from happening.

"Get a cab! We must warn Angus at once!" Dr. Bell shouted.

I hailed the first cab. Dr. Bell offered the driver a gold eagle to reach the central depot and the telegraph office within five minutes. The driver whipped his horse to a furious gallop. By his gold watch, the time was four minutes later when we reached the depot.

Dr. Bell presented his scribbled message to the operator, an obese gentleman with a flowing white beard dotted with brown dribbles of tobacco juice.

"Please send this urgent message to Mr. Angus Duncan in Chicago," Dr. Bell said. The message read: *Alert the Pinkertons. Potential tragedy to occur to-morrow at Lincoln's tomb at four o'clock in the afternoon. Must be stopped.*

The operator chewed his gob of tobacco while reading the message, paused for a moment, then aimed a stream of brown spit at Dr. Bell's feet. "You damn Yankees have done enough damage."

"I am a subject of her British majesty. A Scot, to be specific. Not a Yankee."

"If you ain't Southern, you're a damn Yankee in my book. I would be damned to hell before I send this message for you, even if I could. Big ice storm up North, all lines are down, bridges washed out, ain't even no trains runnin'."

"Please route the message to another line. I shall pay you in gold," said Dr. Bell.

"Hell, no."

"I shall call the police."

"Go ahead. They locked up the last carpetbaggers who came into town. Sure they would be happy to lock you up, too."

The operator was correct. No trains were running north. Dr. Bell consulted the station map. "It is over three hundred miles to Springfield. If we ride day and night we can make it in time."

I disagreed. "Doctor Bell, horses won't be able to get us there in time. Do you have any other ideas?"

“You are probably right. Well then, if we can ride these horses to Cairo, Illinois, we might be able to catch a train there.”

We obtained two good horses and saddles and immediately set out at a gallop on the only road heading north. The first fifteen miles sped by, but our horses were tiring and my backside was already sore as a boil.

We were on the outskirts of a small town when we spied a crowd of men, lads, and women around some sort of show in an open field. As we drew closer we saw a hot air balloon being inflated.

“Whoa!” Dr. Bell shouted. “This demands investigation.”

A portly man in a set of white overalls paced in front of the balloon on jerky steps while wringing his hands. “Ladies and Gents. Just one dollar a person for a full twenty-five minute ride in the world’s largest hot air balloon . . . Boys, be the first to tell your friends you kissed your girl while five-hundred feet in the air.”

A few young fellows scuffed their feet and looked interested, but no one opened their wallets. We drew closer to see a wicker basket connected to the balloon that was tethered to the ground with ropes. Above the basket, flames from a metal tank heated the air that inflated the balloon.

Dr. Bell inspected the contraption. “Sir, can your balloon go as far as Springfield, Illinois?”

“Well, well, well . . . Lookee here, lookee here . . . Hear that there accent, folks? Yes, they come all the way from England to ride Oscar’s world famous balloon.”

“We are from Scotland, not England,” said I.

“Either way, you came to the right place, gents. Yes sir, it is your lucky day.” He held a finger to the wind. “If this south wind holds, she could probably take you all the way back home to Wales.”

“Scotland.”

“And the fee, sir?” Dr. Bell asked.

“Since you gentlemen came all this way, I’ll give you a special discount. Remember, this is the world’s largest balloon and a once-in-a-lifetime opportunity. Take a ride! Take a death-defying ride and make history!” he said, as much to the crowd as to us.

"The fee, sir?" Dr. Bell asked once again.

"Because the British have been such great friends to these here colonies and you are so beloved, I shall give a special fee reserved customarily for family members. And gents, this fee will be a special offer, a never-to-be-repeated price, so if you don't grab it the instant I quote it—"

"PLEASE, just tell us the fee!"

"A mere one hundred dollars."

"That's highway robbery!" I yelled.

"I tell you, gents, and this is the God's honest truth, one hundred dollars for a chance to ride in the world's largest balloon is a steal. An unheard of, never-to-be-repeated deal. At that price, gents, you are robbing me."

Dr. Bell shook his head in disgust. "We shall give you the horses and saddles now, and twenty dollars upon arrival, if you can get us there by three o'clock to-morrow."

"DEAL. You gents drive a hard bargain. And please do not tell another soul about this special rate that I only give to friends from across the pond in merry old England." He extended his hand and shook Dr. Bell's. "The name's Oscar. Oscar Blithe. My balloon is named *Blithe Spirit*. Now, climb in the basket and off we go."

We introduced ourselves and climbed in. "Make haste, sir. We have no time to lose, and need to go as soon as possible," Dr. Bell urged.

"As you wish. We'll be off in a moment. Just need to turn up the heat."

The balloon itself was constructed of panels of red, white, and blue silk. The gas tank, suspended just within reach above the basket, was equipped with a valve to control the flow of gas, and a flint and steel igniter that made a spark when the operator pulled a string.

After we crowded into the basket Mr. Blithe opened a valve. Blue flames shot upward sending hot air into the balloon. The great silken bag inflated and tugged at its mooring line. "Let her go!" Oscar shouted.

We hauled in the ropes and we were up and away.

When we were high over the tree tops, Oscar shut off the gas and we sailed through the sky in absolute silence. It was so perfectly peaceful, unlike anything I had known. I felt tension and worry draining away. Happily, I had brought my diary and a pencil with me so I could record the experience.

I was calm and tranquil for the first time in many days. The sighing wind and clear skies were a balm to my soul. It was utter serenity—that is until Oscar broke into my thoughts.

"You folks are in for a real treat. It's a clear sunny day and you can see forever. We're following the river to Cairo. Then, if the wind holds, we will strike a compass course to Springfield." Oscar stated this with so much enthusiasm that I was convinced we would reach Springfield in plenty of time.

At one point, Oscar gave up on his travelogue and began fussing with the gas burner. My gaze rested upon the great river, which twisted and turned for miles and miles like an endless serpent. There were sandbars, shores lined with greeny-grey trees, and a few villages hugging the river banks. Steamboats glided along, belching clouds of dense black smoke.

I scarcely had words to describe the magnificence of this land, which made me wonder if I could ever really be a good enough writer to share my adventures with the world.

This was the first time I truly had the opportunity to study Dr. Bell in repose. He had removed his great cape and the wool hat with earflaps that so effectively repels the icy, whistling winds and drenching rains of our Scottish climate. His eyes were closed against the sun and he folded his hands over chest. I could not help but sketch his aquiline profile and jutting jaw to fasten that moment in my memory.

The wind was starting to die, which meant our speed diminished. Dr. Bell came instantly awake, reached for his great curved pipe, tamped in tobacco, lit up and watched the smoke drift skyward.

"Mr. Blithe, we are slowing. If you please, canna you make mair speed?" he asked, with a pronounced, rarely used Scottish burr.

"I'll give her some more gas. We'll get a better wind if we go higher up," Mr. Blithe said.

He opened the valve and pulled the igniter string again. Immediately, a blue flame roared out of the tank and the balloon lifted higher and then even higher.

We flew along as fast as a railway train, but Oscar said we were going no more than twenty-five miles an hour. Either way, I figured that we were going more than fast enough to get us to Springfield in time.

Riding in the balloon was a welcome, tranquil experience and a great relief after being shot at in Chicago, nearly hanged by the James Gang, almost drowned, poisoned by curare, scared half to death by vengeance-seeking monkeys, and losing Rebecca to my mate.

However, the placidity was occasionally broken by our balloonist. As we passed over a sizable village, farm, or town, Oscar waved and yelled 'hallo!' to folks gathered below. The people looked upward as if hearing a voice from heaven and then waved and hollered back. From our vantage point, they were as small as dolls. Oscar was a lively fellow and had evidently entertained guests before.

"Would you fellows care for a little snack or drink of homemade hooch?"

Oscar hoisted a jug and glugged down a half a cup of raw hooch.

"English balloonists serve champagne," said Dr. Bell.

I wolfed down a half-loaf of hard black bread and a moldy hunk of cheese cheddar. I even took a sip of Oscar's homebrew. Dr. Bell tipped up the jug for me and then helped himself to a long drink.

Dr. Bell touched his lips with a handkerchief. "Not up to a good Scottish malt, but, not bad, not bad. Mr. Blithe, we must not get behind our schedule. Please, make haste."

"Have no worries, my friends. I will have you in Springfield within the hour," Oscar responded.

Except for the wind and the occasional roar of the gas flame, it was once again tranquil. I rushed to write down my final thoughts because, surely, our adventure was soon to be over. Sadly, too, all was over with Rebecca. I searched for a word that could help me move on and the one that came to mind was *exorcise*. Yes, I would erase her from my thoughts and remember this grand landscape.

While I was writing we passed over a lake. With no warning a whirlwind struck the balloon. Suddenly, our basket was swinging madly, like a pendulum. I was forced to put aside my pencil and cling to a rope for dear life. The basket tipped, made a great splintering noise, and spun like a top. I was certain we would fall to our death. Dr. Bell, for all his fearlessness in the face of danger, was deathly pale.

Oscar remained his jovial self. “Ain’t nothin’, boys. Just warm air rising from that lake down under. Old *Blithe Spirit* has seen worse than this. Have some more whisky.”

I held tight and felt the bread, cheese, and homebrew burn the back of my throat. I swallowed and tried not to throw up. We must have been a thousand feet high. The setting sun was almost covered by streaky white clouds. There were more ominous clouds ahead, and the wind was changing fast.

“Mr. Blithe, damn all, we are veering too far to the east. You must keep us on course to Springfield!” My spirits rose. Dr. Bell’s voice once again had that familiar commanding tone.

Oscar shielded his eyes. “Yep, that there hill should be on our left. We are a might off course.”

“How can that be? You are supposed to steer this contraption and keep us on course!”

“Well, sir, that is the thing with hot air balloons. They ain’t like a horse and buggy. You can’t just keep ‘em right on course, especially if God don’t blow wind the right direction.”

“You said you would get us to Springfield.”

“Well, sir, God’s the pilot and we just go along for the ride. Ain’t nothin’ me or you or nobody else can do about it.”

“And you chose not to mention this until now.”

“Yes, sir. I reckoned that you being a big college professor, you already knew that, but maybe I mighta been wrong.”

“Sir, our British balloonists regularly stay on course aross the English Channel,” said Dr. Bell.

"This ain't no damn channel," Oscar replied.

Dark clouds crowded the horizon, dusk fell, and, suddenly, our blissful day turned ominous and cold. Dr. Bell pulled his cape coat tighter, and I wished I had mother's wool scarf.

Oscar took a long drink. "She will go down when the air in the balloon gets colder. Don't you worry none. Things are gonna be just fine. Who knows? We might even land within a few hundred miles of Springfield."

I grabbed my head in disgust. Dr. Bell harrumphed loudly.

We did drop down a ways, but, then, in the dark, it was hard knowing if we were high enough to clear the trees. We swooped over a small town and, judging from the lights, we were barely over the rooftops.

"Dang, we ain't high enough, need more hot air. I'll light her up," Oscar said.

He pulled the string. The flint and steel made a spark, but no flame.

"Damn, we must be outta gas. Probably shoulda checked that out before we lifted off."

Dr. Bell covered his face and groaned. "Aye, that would have been a good idea."

Oscar snapped the flint and pounded on the gas tank, but there was no flame. We dropped lower and lower, and, suddenly, I saw two glittery rivers just ahead. Oscar saw them, also, and hopped on one foot, then the other.

"Boys, I got good news for you. That there first river's the Mississippi and the second's the Ohio, which means that if we can clear the first and land before we hit the second, we are as good as gold."

"If?"

"Yes, sir. You see, right there between the two is the town of Cairo, Illinois. Cairo's perfect. From there, you'll easily catch a train to Springfield. So, all I gotta do is figure out how to land this thing now and make sure we don't sink in either of them there big rivers."

"You don't know how to land?" asked Dr. Bell.

"I was just joking. Of course I do. I mean . . . I just ain't never landed in the dark, ain't got that much experience. Always figured landing at night was too dangerous."

"Great God in Heaven, preserve us," Dr. Bell groaned.

A long pregnant silence hung like an ominous cloud over us. We barely breathed as we silently floated over the Mississippi. The murky water rolled on with little waves and whitecaps. Even if we landed in the water, our basket might float, but we would surely freeze.

A sudden puff of wind, pushed us to the far bank of that massive brown river and we floated over a glade of trees. "Now! Now! Now! Cut loose those sandbags if you don't want to drown in the Ohio!" Oscar shouted.

Dr. Bell opened his penknife and, with a quick slash, cut the ropes. Two sandbags fell away and we rose a few feet before settling down again. For a frightful moment, the basket touched water. Oscar cut loose two more bags. We rose twenty feet or so and glided across the Ohio River.

The wind picked up speed. We whirled through the gathering darkness with tree branches dragging at the basket. An updraft gave us another bounce for a moment, and we sailed on into the night.

I was down on the floor of the basket when Dr. Bell fell across my legs.

"Mr. Blithe, get this thing under control!" he shouted.

There was another jolt and we dragged and bumped against tree branches. Oscar sprawled across Dr. Bell and groaned. "Ain't nothing left to do. I done tried everything, but I ain't got the experience. My cousin, Lester, crashed and died in this very same basket just a month ago. Nobody in the family wanted it, so I inherited the balloon, basket, and a month's supply of gas."

I looked heavenward, but, instead of sky, saw only the crazy balloon fluttering like a half-empty sac. I hardly remember the next few seconds. Dr. Bell struggled, was almost on his feet, then fell in a heap. Oscar covered his face. "Hang on! She's gonna hit!" he shouted.

Our basket with the collapsed balloon crashed down, down through the branches of a giant tree. The gas tank struck Oscar, then we splintered wood and crashed through a roof.

The basket split in half. Oscar went flying and landed on his back, cuddling his jug like a baby. Dr. Bell was nowhere to be seen, and I was down on all fours amidst a furious flutter of wings and angry squawking. I wiped feathers out of my eyes and, when my head cleared, heard angry barking, snarling and a boy's voice in an excited shout. "PAW! PAW! THEY'S THIEVES IN THE HEN HOUSE. GIT THE GUN!"

A light went on in a farm house not thirty feet away and the back door opened. I saw an older woman who wore a long white nightgown and carried a lantern. A skinny old fellow stood in the doorway, raised a long gun, and *BOOM*!

Oscar had struggled to his feet and raised the jug, which shattered in a charge of birdshot. More pellets rattled on the chicken coop and made tree leaves go a-flutter. The shot further enraged a great snarling mastiff with bared teeth who tugged at a rusty chain.

The old fellow, his nightshirt fluttering at his knees, rammed home another charge. We were caught in the light.

I was still down, batting away a huge rooster, when Dr. Bell arose to his full six feet, two inches. His cap was askew. The two bills were over his ears and an earflap covered one eye. With his outstretched arms, his billowing cape looked for all the world like wings.

"Mon, Yir dinnae need the gun! And control yon beastie. We arna thieves, but poor fulk fallen from the heavens." I could scarcely understand Dr. Bell's Scottish burr, or why he was speaking that way, but the old lady went to her knees with hands clasped prayer.

"Oh, blessed Lord, you sent an angel from heaven!"

Dr. Bell walked towards the old lady with the measured steps of a highland lord. "Gude lady, dinnae fash yerself. We shall gladly pay for the damages to your chicken coop."

Dr. Bell held in his hand a glittering ten-dollar gold piece.

"Hallelujah, we are saved!" the woman cried. "Is that real gold?"

"From the United States mint," said Bell.

"Ma, boil up some coffee. Show these folks hospitality."

We crowded into a kitchen with a wood stove and a plank floor. The old lady set a kettle over a crackling fire and crushed coffee beans with a hammer.

I chocked down the foul, bitter brew and, once again, was glad to be alive.

Dr. Bell toyed with his cup. "Mr. Blithe, you promised to deliver us to Springfield."

"I reckon you can get a train in Cairo and be there in no time at all. I dun' pretty good considerin' the circumstances and all, and, on account of you fellers are Scotchmen, I'll reduce the charge to ten dollars. But, don't tell a soul you didn't pay the full price."

"Damn, you scoundrel, we aren't even in Cairo."

The old farmer hitched up his nightshirt and scratched a skinny leg. "If you got another one of them ten dollar pieces, I kin drive you into Cairo in time to catch the train."

"Can I go along?" Oscar asked.

"It's a deal." Dr. Bell handed over the gold coin to the aged farmer.

We piled the shredded balloon, the basket, and ourselves in wagon drawn by two balky mules and set off through brush and across fields in the direction of Cairo. I drowsed off, but jerked awake when a hoot owl screeched. Oscar claimed he saw a wolf, but, then, he had a good imagination.

It got easier when we came upon wagon tracks that, after a bit, led to a road. Finally we reached the outskirts of Cairo.

The mules ambled on the dirt road past big houses that belonged to steamboat captains and a building that Oscar said was the Customs House—which also served as a post office and courthouse.

There was not a single light or a soul on the streets. Not even a night watchman could be seen. We reached a fallen-down frame building with a porch and rocking chairs that Oscar said was a public house.

"I'm stoppin' right here. You lads go on another block to the train depot. The agent keeps the place warm," the farmer said.

We said our goodbyes and went to the cheerless depot. There was no sign of an agent, but the ancient wood-burning stove had a few glowing embers. Dr. Bell and I flopped on the floor and dozed off.

9 December, 1878

It was just light, maybe six o'clock in the morning when the Cairo stationmaster kicked my ribs with a hobnail boot. "Damn tramps. Get out of my station," he said.

"We aren't tramps," I said.

"Oh pshaw, you can't fool me. You talk like some foreigner."

Dr. Bell jumped to his feet. "Sir, we are in this country as guests of Angus Duncan who owns the railroad." He pulled out his wallet and waved a fistful of American dollars at the uncouth man. "We demand immediate transport to Springfield, and damn the expense."

"Well, this is a different story. The next train ain't due for another hour. You boys might as well go across the street and have breakfast."

Dr. Bell had toast with jam and I polished off a half-dozen fried eggs, ham, and biscuits with gravy. Bell paid a dollar and we rushed back to the station.

The agent was nowhere to be found, but Dr. Bell wrote out a telegram to warn the Pinkertons and added a note for the agent, "Urgent. Send as soon as possible," and left a gold ten dollar coin.

We paced, back and forth while Dr. Bell puffed clouds of smoke. At half nine a slow-moving goods train, with a tired wood-fired steam engine pulling two cars, chugged into the station and wheezed to a stop. The name *GLADYS* was painted in red across the boiler.

Dr. Bell hailed the engineer. "Ho, we need immediate transportation to Springfield. It is a matter of life and death. Your president is in danger."

"Ach, now. As surely as my name is Billy O'Toole I'd help you gentlemen, but ya can't fool me with a damn cock and bull story."

Billy O'Toole climbed down off the engine and ran a hand through sparse hair. I recognized a fellow Irishman by his merry eyes and red nose with broken veins. Billy clearly enjoyed a drink.

Dr. Bell took in the situation with a single glance and jingled gold coins.

"Mr. O'Toole, you will be generously rewarded and I shall put in a good word for you with Mr. Angus Duncan who owns the railroad."

"Ah, you are two pretty boys. This is a freight, don't carry no passengers. How do I know you ain't Pinkertons trying to catch me out with a bribe? My old pal, Tommy Jenkins, on the St. Louis line, lost his job when he let his drinking pals ride a freighter. I ain't gonna make the same mistake."

"Mr. O'Toole, consider our money as honest payment for passage, not a bribe. You have my word," said Dr. Bell.

"I wish I could help, but, no, sir. You can't fool me."

"Just one second. The broken blood vessels in your nose might at first appear to be windburn, but I would wager that they are telangiectasia rosacea resulting from your over-reliance on alcohol; further confirmed by the fact that even though your back pocket is empty the dye of the material is worn away in the faint outline of a flask. You drink on the job, and the pork grease under your fingernails and the scent of ham on your sleeves indicate that you are stealing cargo," said Dr. Bell.

"Well, you don't say." Billy hung his head, then came up with a sheepish smile. "Why shucks, if you boys don't mind ridin' old *Gladys* with the freight, come on board and we are on our way. You got two choices, ride with the smoked pork or sit on the grain sacks."

Dr. Bell sniffed. "Those are our only choices?"

"Yep. Now I'll fire her up and go like lightning, but we gotta cross the Big Muddy River."

"Never heard of that river," said I.

"Ain't on no map, but this time of the year she runs pretty fast, and there is so much mud the fish can't see the bait. Trouble is, the only bridge is mighty shaky. Some days, I gotta wait till the water goes down."

"We shall take that risk, sir. Sally forth," Dr. Bell replied.

The bags of grain were a might uncomfortable, but we snuggled under a canvas tarpaulin. It was not so bad. The old train did not go like lightning but, instead, puttered along at a snail's pace. It was bloody hard to be patient and then the train shuddered, clanked, sputtered, and jerked to a stop.

Billy clambered down from the cab and wiped his nose. We joined the little Irishman on the banks of a raging muddy stream. "This here is the Big Muddy River and there is the bridge."

He was right. The iron tracks were laid on a slender wooden trestles that trembled with each wave. A tree branch, rolling with the fast current, struck a wood piling. The bridge shook and creaked.

Dr. Bell opened his fine gold watch. "We must hurry on. The President's address starts in four hours. If that telegraph operator sent our message, the Pinkertons might save the President, but they will not know to look for Captain Hook. The entire country may be in dire straits."

"Aye, we are in a dire rush, but will the bridge hold?" I asked.

"*Gladys* is a heavy load, old bitch, but there's a 50/50 chance we kin make it." Billy twinkled with a crafty smile. "Now boys, let me see the color of your money."

Dr. Bell peeled off ten dollar bills. "Who was *Gladys*?" I asked.

"Yep, *Gladys*. That's what I call the old lady. Been driving her for ten years and she ain't never let me down. Named her after my schoolteacher, Miss Gladys Connors. She was one helluva woman. She used to lay my head between her thick thighs and cane my rump when I was bad."

Dr. Bell gave Billy a fist full of greenbacks. "Let us waste no more time."

"Boys. Old *Gladys* needs a head of steam. You . . ." he pointed at me. "Get up and heave wood into the boiler. We all three climbed into the engine cab.

"Yes, of course . . ." He cleared his throat. "So, as I was saying . . . *Gladys* can be mighty temperamental, and I shut her down because to get over this bridge we're going to need a full head of steam, especially considering the state of that there bridge."

Dr. Bell and I looked at the bridge. Across its entire span it seemed to be constructed of spindly timbers. And the current in the Big Muddy River swept against the wooden pilings at its base with a force that shook the entire creaky structure. It looked awfully dangerous, and I sincerely doubted that *Gladys* could traverse it safely.

Billy took a long pull at a bottle and offered me a drink. I could not say no to a fellow Irishman, so I had a long swallow, opened the furnace door, and threw chunks of wood on the fire.

"I presume you will cross the bridge slowly and with great care," said Dr. Bell.

"Hell, no, that ain't the way." The fire roared and the steam gauge topped the last red mark. Billy put her in reverse. We chugged about one hundred yards away from the bridge and came to a halt. Billy took another pull at the bottle. "Let her rip!" he yelled.

Black smoke poured out of the stack. The fire roared. Billy let off the brake and sounded the whistle. "Hold on, boys!" he whooped.

The wheels turned faster and faster until we flew. I could have sworn we left the track. *Gladys* pounded down the slope, gaining more speed until we hit the bridge. Billy kept his head out the window with one hand on the throttle. His hat flew off, but he ignored that and gave another pull on the throttle. Dr. Bell, as excited as a wee boy, yanked on the whistle. The mournful cry sounded across the little valley, but did not drown out the frightful *CRACK!* of breaking timbers.

I closed my eyes, said a good Catholic prayer, and crossed myself.

Dr. Bell did a little jig. "Aye, boys, that was grand. The grandest thing, I ever saw!"

We were across and safe. I looked back in time to see crumbling timbers and iron rails splashing in to the Big Muddy River. The bridge collapsed.

"Damn all, how am I to get home?" Billy complained. He turned obstinate, slowed at every village, tootled the whistle at every dog, child, and woman and refused to press on with more speed.

It was almost a quarter to four o'clock when we pulled into the Springfield depot. Bell anxiously consulted his watch. We had nearly fifteen minutes to save the President.

The station was deserted except for the agent, and there were no hacks, cabs or carriages.

"You will have to hoof it, but the tomb is only two miles away. The whole county's already there to hear the President," the agent said.

We set off at a brisk jog, but, after a half-mile, Dr. Bell became short of breath and slowed to a bare walk. "My dear Doyle, it is up to you. Take my revolver and run. Go, laddie, go!"

I tucked the Bull Dog pistol into my pocket and set off like a madman. I found a pace, ran well and fast, but my boots sunk into wet ground and I slipped on patches of melting snow. In a few minutes I passed latecomers and then, suddenly, saw the tall pointed obelisk of Lincoln's tomb where I heard snatches of a stentorian voice.

Damn it all to bloody hell! Hayes had started early. Was I too late?

From a distance, I saw four flights of balustraded stairs—two flanking the entrance and two at the rear. Both led to a level terrace where the President stood in front of an ornate parapet. Patriotic red, white, and blue banners and streamers fluttered from flag poles. Dignitaries surrounded the President. I was uplifted by the display and paused to listen. Hayes, in full throat, waved his arms. "We are gathered today to honour the saviour of our union—" he roared.

Stern-faced Pinkertons with rifles at the ready were on guard. They stood in front of the tomb and on the balustrade looking out over the crowd. They were intent on protecting the President and seemed competent. Things appeared to be in order with nothing amiss.

I breathed a sigh of relief. The Pinkertons were on the job, and, besides, the country folks and city people were purely innocent.

I looked around the cemetery and saw people stretched as far as the eye could see. There had to be a few thousand spectators spread out on the grassy lawn in front of the tomb, on the steps, the terrace, the balustrade. A few young bucks had climbed the bronze statues for a better view. Far in the back, folks listened from open carriages.

President Hayes must be popular because people clapped and hurrahed. Enthusiasm was in the air. Venders wandered among the crowd hawking peanuts and beer. Children played tag in the mud. There were picnic hampers, and young couples held hands. Even though the day was overcast, it was more like a jolly holiday than a national event. Her Majesty, Queen Victoria, would not allow such nonsense.

I pushed through the crowds on the lookout for Captain Hook, especially beneath the terrace because Emilie Droussard had said "below the tomb."

Nothing looked suspicious. All was festive. Did Bell's telegram get through? Perhaps the Pinkertons had already found Hook and his accomplices.

I began to relax and idly listen to President Hayes, when someone brushed my shoulder. "Well, lad, have you observed anything of note?" It was Dr. Bell.

"No, sir."

"Perhaps I was mistaken and there is nothing to fear," he said.

The clouds parted for a moment, and I had to squint to see over the crowd towards the west. "Sir, look over yonder. What a gallant band of horsemen. They must be farmers, late arrivals." The band came on at a brisk trot. I counted twenty or more men riding two abreast.

Dr. Bell shielded his eyes. "How curious; they are accompanied by two large wagons and seem to be riding with purpose. Doyle, do you recognize those types of wagons?"

"If I am not mistaken, they are the great Conestoga wagons used to carry settlers west to California. The first appears to have a load of baled hay," I said.

The wagons were a hundred yards away when the wheels sunk into a patch of deep mud. The drivers whipped up the struggling animals with cries of "Gee up!"

Four massive draft horses were hitched to each wagon, but the wagon wheels appeared to be stuck. The horses struggled forward and pulled the wagons to drier ground. One wagon came to the last row of spectators. The other dashed onto a small knoll in the back of the cemetery.

Bell was suddenly alert. His eyes twinkled as if he were in the amphitheatre solving a ticklish clinical problem. "Doyle, my lad, observe those horses. They are under great strain. They sweat and are well-lathered. Their nostrils flare and, man, look at those deep ruts left in the mud. There is more than hay in those wagons. What do you deduce from these observations?"

"They carry a heavy load, especially the wagon moving towards the knoll. But, sir, they are only farmers," said I.

"Doyle, those men are no ordinary farmers. They are expert horsemen."

"Yes, yes, of course. They wear slouch hats and peculiar long coats. Perhaps they are cowboys," I said.

"Doyle, use your head. Those coats are dusters, perfect to conceal weapons. They ride like cavalry men." Bell sniffed the air like a bloodhound and slapped his head. "Damn it! I smell gun oil. Those men are heavily armed. I was wrong. Droussard's last message was not *below the tomb*, but *BLOW THE TOMB*!"

"Bloody hell!" I exclaimed.

"Follow me!" he shouted, and set off at a run towards the nearest wagon.

President Hayes made a rousing statement. Amidst the cheers one wagon halted on a shallow decline almost in the midst of the spectators. The other continued to slowly move forward and came to a halt.

We were within a few feet of the first wagon when the driver threw down the reins and pulled off his long coat. The uniform was old and patched, but unmistakably Confederate cavalry. The man was a veteran of many a campaign. He was a hard, grizzled-looking man who wore sergeant's stripes.

At his side, in a brown scabbard, was a long, deadly sabre. He paused and puffed hard until the cigar jammed between his teeth glowed brightly. With frantic haste, he tore away the canvas covering and hurled bales of hay from the wagon to reveal wooden crates marked 'US ARMORY'.

With a long knife, he tore open one crate in the middle of the pile to reveal bundles of red sticks. The wagon was filled with dynamite, enough to blow up the monument and kill the president and thousands of innocent people. The confederate jammed a long fuse between sticks of dynamite, jumped from the wagon, and unrolled the fuse as he went.

Nobody, not one of that crowd, noticed. Folks whistled, shouted, and roared with applause at the President's speech. The noise was deafening.

"Somebody, stop that man! Stop him!" I waved my arms and tried to attract attention.

It was no use. I jerked my head at the sound of pounding hoofbeats. There, not twenty feet away, a fellow on a chestnut horse coolly took aim and fired his Winchester at me. I ducked, stumbled, and fell face down. The bullet made a small geyser in the soft mud by my face. I was up and running again, with bullets whistling in the air. Dr. Bell saw my plight. He was closer to the wagon and there was no way I could get there in time. With a burst of speed, he dodged the whistling bullets and reached the wagon just as the sergeant put his cigar to the fuse.

The fuse sizzled and sparked. The enraged sergeant drew his sabre and swung the steel blade in a deadly arc. Bell ducked and, with one motion, pulled out his meerschaum pipe and smashed the heavy bowl on the man's temple. The sergeant went down. In an instant Dr. Bell snatched the sabre and sliced the burning fuse with all the élan of a clansmen in Bonny Prince Charlie's army. Bell then jerked the remaining fuse away from the dynamite.

He had done it. Dr. Bell had saved the day.

The now-shortened fuse spluttered out into thin air and the dynamite sat silently in its box with an unlit squat fuse.

I ran towards the wagon to congratulate him, but, before we could celebrate, one of the other horsemen riding a big chestnut stallion at full tilt, dashed towards us. His whip stung my shoulder as he passed. "Damn you both! Get out of the way!" he shouted. My attacker rode like an old veteran, a cavalryman. I realized, with a horrible certainty, that these men were hard core survivors of Nathan Bedford Forrest's troops. These were the villains we had been searching for across America.

As I leaped away from the next strike of his whip, I noticed that the other wagon driver had moved again and parked his four-wheeled cart behind some trees on top of the knoll overlooking the crowd and the tomb. That driver then jumped into the back of his wagon, tossing the hay off the wagon and onto the ground.

As he did, he began to expose a most distressing sight. Under the bales of hay was a large canvas which, when ripped away, revealed the big, ugly snout of an artillery piece aimed directly at the tomb.

I had studied military weaponry at university and knew that a cannon of that size could send twelve-inch shells hundreds of yards in the air. If a shell of that calibre struck the tomb, the entire structure would surely collapse, killing hundreds of people.

"Doyle, the revolver! Use the revolver!" Dr. Bell yelled, as President Hayes paused between phrases.

I heard him, but so did everybody else nearby, and bedlam ensued.

The riders on now-frenzied, bucking horses dashed in a great circle while throwing off their long coats. Each one had a pistol in their belt and a repeating Winchester rifle in hand. Every man wore either a faded Confederate uniform or a red shirt. "Sic Semper Tyrannis! Long Live the South!" they shouted.

The crowd took notice and, though many people screamed and began running in different directions, some simply laughed and clapped as if this were another Wild West show.

The riders created a diversion with their shooting and shouting. Dr. Bell, with his long legs pumping, was on a mad, limping run towards the second wagon.

By now, I had the revolver out of my pocket and, with great leaping strides, ran towards the deadly cannon. The officer, in the gaudy uniform of a major general, lit a match and leaned over the touch hole of the beastly cannon.

I was yards away when Bell shouted. "Doyle, for God's sake, shoot!"

I had no experience with fire arms, but, with trembling hands, I pulled back the hammer and pressed the trigger. I missed, fired, and missed again. At the sound of my revolver, the Southern officer paused long enough for Dr. Bell to reach the lead horse in the team. He grasped the halter and pulled. The horse balked, but, with frantic effort, the good doctor hung on for dear life. He turned the horses head. The team reacted to the lead horse. They pulled as if one animal and jerked the wagon into a sudden motion. The general lost his balance and dropped the match. He fumbled in his pocket for another. The wagon made a quarter turn. He struck a flame and ignited a few grains of powder in the touch hole.

I watched, horrified. The cannon roared and shot flames. The great *BOOM!* rocked me back. The shell flew, but not at Lincoln's tomb. Miraculously, the shell crashed and exploded harmlessly in the cemetery to the north. Headstones, earth, and trees erupted in a great geyser, but no one was hurt. Dr. Bell had succeeded in turning the wagon away from its target. The President was safe.

My first thought was for Dr. Bell. Had he been in the path of the shell?

When I saw him, he was flat on his face, but unhurt. I breathed a sigh of relief when he opened his eyes.

The Pinkertons came at a run and roughly shackled the old major general. The Confederates fired wildly and charged through the crowd. When two of their riders fell, killed by the Pinkerton's intense fire, they hesitated, then galloped away. More than one farmer in the crowd blazed away with squirrel rifles and shotguns.

The undaunted President resumed his long speech. "Please, fellow citizens. The danger has passed. Let us forgive our Southern brothers—"

The people—all those farmers, city folk, veterans, and children, now stunned into silence—edged in closer with renewed interest in the President's words. Meanwhile, the Pinkertons and volunteers helped the injured into makeshift ambulances.

Among the gaping, church-quiet audience I had lost track of Dr. Bell. Along with the others, I made my way closer to the tomb and rather idly noticed a poor elderly man with a white cane. He wore a black hat pulled low over his face and a brown coat, with long, ill-fitting sleeves that hung well below his wrists. I assumed he was a sad, blinded veteran of The Great War, perhaps injured at Shiloh or Gettysburg.

He stumbled, and my heart went out to him. He tapped his cane and limped a short distance towards the memorial. People stepped aside and made way for his deliberate progress. He stopped, pulled his dirty beard, and seemed to be listening to the President. He went on, slowly, but always towards the President, as if he wanted to be closer. Perhaps he was deaf as well as blind. Still, I took a closer look.

Something was not quite right, but I could not put my finger on it. The cane was brand new. The handle was unusual, too intricate for a poor man's cane. I instantly thought of Dr. Bell's *sword cane*. No, the idea was preposterous. I could not let my imagination run wild.

President Hayes went on. "This is a great era, a time for forgiveness. Let us seek peace with our Southern brothers . . ."

The tap, tap on the marble staircase continued. The blind man was almost on the terrace behind the President when he stopped and cocked his head as if listening. I assumed the poor man was a disoriented or confused veteran. A Pinkerton guard watched him briefly, then looked away across the crowded field.

The fellow moved on, deliberately now. For the first time, he raised the tip of the cane as a blind man will do if searching for an obstacle. It seemed to be a perfectly normal gesture. At that instant, the clouds parted, and bright sunshine flooded the terrace. It was as if God had shed a beam on the President to bless his salvation from the would-be assassins.

The shaft of sunlight reflected off bright metal at the tip of the cane. Why was there suddenly new metal on the cane? Instantly, the pieces of the puzzle fell into place. I envisioned with great clarity the puncture wounds of the curare victims. The so-called blind man had pressed a button in the head of the cane and flicked out what I knew was a deadly needle. I was sure he was preparing to kill the President.

Even with that clarity of thought, I could not fully believe it until the man stopped his hesitant tapping and lunged towards the President. I watched, mouth open, but could make no sound. I was paralyzed with inaction. Where was Doctor Bell? I felt worthless until, suddenly, I came to my senses and saw the blind man's right sleeve had ridden up his arm a bit, revealing a hook instead of a hand. It was him. Captain Spencer, better known as Captain Hook.

My heart was pounding. Panic filled my mind. But, I had to act immediately. At that point, it was not about me, or my drunken father, or anything else in the world, except saving lives. I heard Dr. Bell's voice in my head and all he had taught me about using my mind to uncover the truth and then act on it. I had overcome enough obstacles over these few days and had survived each one. I knew I could do this. I knew I had to do this.

"Damn you! Captain Spencer, HALT!" I screamed, as loudly as I could. I drew the pistol, aimed, and pulled the trigger. There was only a sharp click.

The President, alerted by my frantic cry, stopped in mid-sentence, and, with unsuspected agility, dodged to one side. The deadly can missed the President.

Hook turned his eyes, murderous with hatred, on me. His face twisted. "You again? Damn you, boy!" He lunged at me with the cane held point-first. "Justice! Down with the tyrannical North!" he shouted.

Before he could attempt to attack the President again, I made a flying tackle, hit his knees, and felt his hook swipe across the top of my head. I rolled and smashed a fist into his groin. The hook slashed across my cheek. I made a terrific kick that snapped his femur. We rolled together down the steps.

The man was incredibly strong and was able to keep going despite any pain in his groin and leg. I rolled onto my back and there, above me, he was poised to plunge the tip of his cane into my neck. I heaved him away and rolled down one step. Like a tiger, he was upon me again, but, this time, I grabbed his arm, and, with all my might, forced the poisoned cane away from my body. He held onto the cane and attempted to rise, but I kicked his broken leg. He crumpled, and the deadly tip entered his stomach. The curare worked its way through his body. He had impaled himself with his own deadly weapon.

In his last paroxysm, his mouth opened, and his tongue moved, but he could not utter a word. He went limp, took his last breath, and died, practically in my arms. His death came surprisingly quick. I supposed it was because he had loaded the cane with an extra strong dose of the poison to kill the President. His eyes had the same pleading look I had seen in Carl and the poor rat.

I expected immediate accolades, but, much to my amazement, the opposite was true. "That's him! He tried to shoot the President!" cried the gathering crowd. A half-dozen Pinkertons pinned me down, applied steel shackles to my hands and feet, and dragged me away to a barred police wagon.

The cries hushed. President Hayes made a last comment about forgiving the South before his guards hurried him away to a place of safety. The Pinkertons roughly tossed me into the police wagon, on my way to a prison cell.

When we arrived at the police station about twenty minutes later, the guards dragged me inside while a crowd gathered outside. "Lynch the damn bastard! Kill the assassin!"

While the crowd screamed for my blood, the guards threw me face down onto the floor of a filthy, solitary cell. I was still shackled and beset by an angry mob. Where was justice? What a damnable country. I risked my life to save the President and my reward was to have the entire populace of Springfield wanting to hang me.

Where was Dr. Bell? Was he, too, under suspicion? It wasn't until later that I learned he had gone off to send an urgent telegram to Angus Duncan. He searched for me, not realizing I was in a dirty cell.

I remember that long, dreadful night. My hand still trembles as I write these words. On that cold stone floor, amidst pools of filth and chittering rats, I vowed to give up travel and adventure and settle in dear old Scotland to practise medicine and, who knows, maybe even write.

10 December, 1878

It was almost noon before the authorities identified Captain Spencer, a.k.a. Captain Hook, and later still before Dr. Bell, with the aid of Angus Duncan, came to my rescue. I was never so glad to see his dear homely face.

Dr. Bell put out a hand, ignoring my mud and filth-covered fingers. "Come now, laddie, you must be famished. Join us for a wee dram and meal."

"Aye, sir. Aye."

The lynch mob had dispersed, the railroads were cleared, and Mr. Duncan's personal gilded railroad carriage waited to take us back to Chicago.

As we sat in the luxury of Duncan's private carriage a fierce northeast wind blew gusts of snow against the windows. The carriage creaked with the cold, but a crackling blaze in an iron stove warmed my bones. Our belongings were still in the Peabody Hotel, but Mr. Duncan shared warm clothing and provided a fine meerschaum pipe for my use. Its fragrant smoky aroma filled the air and, in between puffs, we imbibed hot toddies, ate fresh oysters, boiled shrimp, and a strange soup, gumbo, fresh from New Orleans.

After I could eat no more Mr. Duncan and Dr. Bell relaxed with drinks and read the latest newspapers. I selected a Herman Melville novel, *Moby Dick,* from Mr. Duncan's library and settled down in a soft armchair to read about the adventures of Ahab.

A few moments later, Mr. Duncan laid down his pipe and newspaper. "I am sorry to say, gentlemen, but the newspapers make no mention of your adventure. There is nothing to corroborate your story. I am especially doubtful of your ludicrous tale riding in a balloon."

"The agent in Cairo and the President's guards will surely confirm our story," I instantly replied.

"Ah my dear Doyle, you do not understand. The station agent and the train driver will deny us to their deathbed for fear they will be accused of taking bribes. The Pinkertons are so humiliated by their inability to protect the President that they have hushed up the entire episode. The American public will never know how a couple of foreign sawbones saved their President," said Doctor Bell.

"How do they explain the explosives, the cannon, the armed men, or Captain Hook?"

"The Pinkertons claimed it was all good fun by a band of rowdies to celebrate the President's visit. The Americans fire guns and cannons just for fun. The crowd trampled Captain Spencer's body. The President was led to believe he was a harmless, poor old veteran."

"How can they obscure the truth?" I asked. "Uch, it makes no difference. Someday, I shall put it all in a book for the world to read so they will know what REALLY happened."

Duncan made a face, as if he had swallowed a sour pickle. "Mr. Doyle, you are a fine young man. Calm yourself. Would England admit that a couple of Americans, including one who is practically a boy, thwarted a plot to kill the Queen?"

That bit of repartee left me at a loss. Dr. Bell winked, put down his glass, and picked up a leather-bound book. "Angus, if you desire confirmation of our story, listen as I read from Emilie Droussard's casebook. She gave it to me as she lay dying."

Dr. Bell flipped through its pages. "The first part is mostly a diary starting at the beginning of the war. She learned the fundamentals of medicine from her father, a prominent New Orleans physician, but gave up hopes of becoming a doctor when she married a dashing officer. General Butler executed her father on a charge of treason and a Union sniper killed her husband at Vicksburg."

"Clearly, she had good cause to hate the North," murmured Duncan.

"She became a spy for Nathan Bedford Forrest and, with her elegant good looks, she had access to Union officers in the border states. She passed secrets through Dr. McGillicutty, a Rebel surgeon who introduced her to Captain Andrew Spencer, one of Forrest's men. She, in fact, assisted McGillicutty when Spencer lost his hand. This re-kindled her interest in medicine, but, after the war, every medical school in America refused her admission."

"Women have no place in medicine," said Angus.

I disagreed, but did not argue the point.

Dr. Bell ignored him and continued. “She gained admission to a medical school in Switzerland and, there, she again met Dr. McGillicutty who developed an intense interest in the implantation of monkey glands to rejuvenate ill, old men. McGillicutty was far ahead of his time. His work with grafting skin to the victims of the Chicago Fire was outstanding, but unappreciated. His determination to carry on led him to the remote scarlet house in Sherlock, which was the only place he could do his experiments in peace.”

“All that makes sense. But, so far, you have told us nothing of a conspiracy to restore the Confederacy,” said Angus.

“I was getting to that. Captain Spencer, or, as he was so aptly called, Captain Hook, never surrendered. The government charged him with murder because of his involvement at Fort Pillow and would have had him hanged. Instead, he ran to Mexico, joined Maximilian’s army, and later fled to South America.”

“Yes, many Confederates fled rather than live under the Union,” Angus added.

“Spencer was driven by a lust for revenge. He made a fortune in gold mines and, incidentally, collected a large amount of the curare poison from the natives. He returned to this country, but, like so many other veterans, was in failing health. That is how he came to be re-united with Emilie Droussard and Dr. McGillicutty.”

“Then, I was correct. McGillicutty was involved,” said I.

“Yes, McGillicutty’s experiments failed because of his difficulties in anaesthetizing the animals. The monkeys became wild and dangerous. He could not find a dose that would allow the animals to live and yet keep them paralyzed for the surgery. Emilie conceived of administering the drug with a syringe attached to a long pole placed through the cages. That, of course, led to the poison cane that killed, silently, from a safe distance.”

“Wait. When did they start to work on human subjects?” I asked.

“Well, at first they gave liquid extracts of the glands to Captain Spencer. Here is a quote from her casebook. *‘20 minims aqueous extract of a monkey’s thyroid gland injected into the Captain.’* A second notation one week later read, *‘Captain is agitated, pulse 120, no improvement in physical condition.'* This failure led to further experiments with human glands."

Mr. Duncan took a long drink of this toddy. "Again, I regret saying this, but this whole plot sounds rather hard to swallow." He spluttered on his drink and had a long coughing spell.

"I know. It is representative of the horror of medical science sans ethics. For example, here is a description of their first 'specimen'. '*Male schoolteacher, carpetbagger, aged twenty-two years. Paralyzed with curare, thyroid gland removed while specimen still alive. Extract injected into Captain Spencer. Improved.'* "

"Was McGillicutty involved at this point?" I asked.

"No, Doyle. He objected to using humans and abandoned the project, but, Hook, with his renewed energy, commenced recruiting men for his rebel army. His efforts led him to Chicago. There, according to Droussard, is where they hit upon the plan to use railroad guards as their specimens. The men were all young and strong. In addition, their loss would weaken the railroad's security and allow for their ultimate attack on the United States government."

"Diabolical. I feel awful about my poor men. I must set up a fund to help their families," Angus murmured. "Well, gentlemen, I do apologize. Sorry for ever doubting your story."

"Good . . . Then, we shall be in need of this no longer." Dr. Bell snapped the casebook closed, walked to the fireplace and, with a puff of his pipe, dropped the book in the flames.

The pages caught fire. Maybe it was all for the best to spare the country from another dreadful story of rebellion. For now, it was best to allow healing. Perhaps I should even destroy my own journal. I lacked heart, but promised myself that this journal would never see the light of day while I lived. Our exploits, and the American adventure, would forever remain a secret.

"Arthur Doyle. Mr. Arthur Conan Doyle?" We had just disembarked from our coach as the porter shouted my name.

I lifted my arm, "Aye, that's me."

The porter handed me a telegram from Carl.

Rufus is better. I must lean on Rebecca to walk any distance, but we sometimes go to the river and think of you. Jimmy is fine. We shall return to Rush, but you will be gone. Please write to us when you are home.

The telegram mentioned nothing of marriage, but deep in my heart I know Carl and Rebecca are meant for each other. I was pondering this thought when we reached Mr. Duncan's mansion. "Laddie, you did me proud. But, I am curious . . ." Dr. Bell paused to sip from a glass of golden single malt whisky. "How did you know the assassin was Captain Hook?" he asked.

"It is rather elementary," said I. "My dear Doctor Bell, it was a great surgeon who taught me to observe and deduce in order to make the proper diagnosis."

With that, I lay down my pen and close this diary.

~ Arthur Conan Doyle, student.

Editor's Elementary Endnotes

Sir Arthur Conan Doyle once said, "It is a capital mistake to theorize before one has data." And so, my dear reader, before you close this extraordinary manuscript discovered by my colleague, Dr. John Raffensperger, there are some historical facts that I believe you should know about the actual life of the real Arthur Conan Doyle, et. al.

Fact. Arthur Conan Doyle embarked on his medical studies at the University of Edinburgh in 1876 when he was nineteen and Edinburgh was the world's center for medical education and surgery. The university was renowned for its curriculum, which included studies of the humanities as well as science. Joseph Lister had transformed surgical practise with his discovery of antisepsis that banished infection from wounds and was the world-famous professor of surgery.

Fact. The impoverished Arthur Conan Doyle barely had the admitting tuition and was forced to periodically support himself as a ship's surgeon or an assistant to country doctors. He also earned money by writing short stories. In 1878, one of his professors, Dr. Joseph Bell, appointed Doyle to be his outpatient clerk.

Fact. Dr. Bell had contracted diphtheria from a patient while he was a house surgeon. The disease affected his vocal cords and his gait but did not prevent him from becoming one of the foremost surgeons in Scotland. In addition to teaching students and running his large personal practice, Dr. Bell wrote textbooks, edited medical journals, and was the secretary-treasurer of the Royal College of Surgeons. Bell was especially gentle with children and, when his term at the Royal Infirmary expired, he became the first surgeon to have a ward at the Royal Edinburgh Children's Hospital where he continued to operate and teach.

Fact. Bell could deduce a patient's occupation, nationality and place of origin from such details as the calluses on their hands, mud on their boots and their accent. With his uncanny powers of observation he made rapid and accurate medical diagnoses. In the position of clerk to Dr. Bell, Arthur Conan Doyle briefly examined new patients to make a preliminary diagnosis. He then presented the patient to Dr. Bell in the great amphitheatre of the Edinburgh Infirmary in front of medical students and house officers.

Fact. When Doyle became his clerk, Dr. Bell was 36 years old, sparse, lean and tall with an aquiline nose and black hair. He had long sensitive fingers; his gray eyes twinkled with shrewdness. This is almost the exact same description that Dr. Watson made of Sherlock Holmes during their first meeting at 221B Baker Street in *A Study In Scarlet*. Indeed, Conan Doyle ultimately confirmed that Dr. Joseph Bell was his model for the great detective.

Fact. The esteemed authors Robert Louis Stevenson and James Barrie were real-life contemporaries and colleagues of Doyle at Edinburgh University.

And so, just as we began this endnote, let us also end with words of our esteemed hero, the real Sir Arthur Conan Doyle. "*How often have I said to you that when you have eliminated the impossible, whatever remains, however improbable, must be the truth?*"

~ Prof. Richard Krevolin, Los Angeles, CA. 11:41 a.m., February 29, 2016.

Adventures in Russia, 1881

7 June 1881

Despite my adventures in America with Dr. Joseph Bell, and even though I am a senior and will soon graduate, he continues to humiliate me in front of the entire class for my trivial errors in diagnosis. Professor Bell is a brilliant diagnostician and the most popular teacher in the medical school, but I sometimes feel like lashing out at him with curses and expletives.

Take today's Friday afternoon clinic: Dr. Bell walked in at exactly two o'clock sharp. Sun streamed through the sooty windows of the great surgical amphitheatre of the Royal Edinburgh Infirmary. Medical students filled tiers of hard-backed seats overlooking the 'cockpit,' which doubled as operating theater, as well as Bell's clinic.

I had recently finished my term as Dr. Bell's clerk, and now, another poor, trembling third year student, Josiah Weeks, was in my place, organizing patients to see the professor. I pitied poor Weeks and did not envy his position, although I could sorely use the extra funds from the measly salary that accompanies the post.

There was a sprinkling of visiting doctors from all of Europe, as well as America, to observe Dr. Bell's brilliant operating skills and his diagnostic acumen. Dmitry Gorchakov of the St. Petersburg faculty of Medicine and Surgery, a great bear of a man with a bushy, black beard, had taken notes during clinics and operating sessions for the past week. He was especially interested in Dr. Bell's operation for joint excision in cases of tuberculosis and injuries. The Russian spoke broken English with a thick, guttural accent, but I suspected he understood our language better than he let on.

Meanwhile, I was idly thinking about Miss Jean McGill, a pretty new nurse who was sitting a few rows back, when Dr. Bell turned his keen gaze upon me. "Mr. Doyle, if you please, what causes Mrs. Connor's cough?"

Mrs. Connor, the patient in a plain, black skirt, black coat, black hat, and black, ankle-high shoes, was spare and stooped with a sad, sharp, lined face and nearly-white hair. She had walked haltingly, resting on the arm of Weeks, the third year clerk, to a chair in front of us students. Connor could have been anyone's grandmother. Weeks, a nervous boy of perhaps nineteen years, had stammered out the information that Mrs. Connor's cough had resisted all treatment for the past half-decade.

For the life of me, I couldn't think of a plausible diagnosis. Aye, I had seen several coal miners with such a cough, but never a woman. The patient hung her head and seemed to gaze at the floor, when she took a rag from her handbag, covered her mouth, and coughed out a gob of bloody phlegm.

I mumbled, "Well, sir, um, eh, she could have tuberculosis or chronic bronchitis?"

"Indeed, Mr. Doyle." He paused for a painful moment. "I'd recommend visiting the bursar's office this afternoon," he advised.

"Why, sir?"

"Well, laddie, the bursar can issue a refund of your tuition, since it appears as if you have yet to learn how to truly examine a patient after four years of medical school."

The other students burst out in raucous laughter. I flared with anger, my cheeks grew red, and I was barely able to hold my tongue.

Dr. Bell's fierce, probing eyes twinkled with pleasure. After our trip to America a few years ago, I felt a close kinship with him. Being that my father was a worthless drunkard, when I was admitted to Edinburgh, I had hoped that Bell would fill his shoes as the sober authority figure and a mentor. Alas, upon our return, he seemed to coldly withdraw and resume a formal teacher/student relationship.

Nay, he was not truly malicious; but neither was he kind and forgiving. I looked up at him and Bell leaned back in his chair. "Doyle, how many years have you been under my tutelage?"

"Several, sir."

"And what is the single most important precept I have taught you?"

"Never assume anything. Look at every situation with fresh eyes, observe fully, and then deduce properly."

"Aye. 'Tis good to know that at least your ears work . . . Now, let us begin again." Dr. Bell folded his hands over his chest and stretched out his long legs as he questioned the patient. "Good afternoon, Mrs. Connor. Did you have a good trip from Lancashire?"

"Yissir, but for the childer was after giving me cheek on the train. I coulda give 'em a smackin'. "

At the sound of her lilting voice, Dr. Bell rose from his chair, went to the patient, and gently touched her cheek, then carefully examined, one by one, her fingers.

"You left Connacht during the famine?"

"Yissir, when me poor ma and pa passed on for lack of food."

"When did Mr. Connor die in the mines?"

"It was twenty years ago, near time when our only boy passed on. The mine caved in."

As cutting and cruel as he was, I still couldn't help but be filled with awe and respect as he unraveled a patient's history; keenly observing telling, minute attributes, weaving them together in his mind, and then using this web of seemingly disconnected information as the basis for an accurate diagnosis.

As he rubbed his chin, my classmates had become quiet as so many mice. Bell now had their attention; this promised to be one of his better performances and those rough-hewn boys were overcome by the woman's sad, but gentle, visage.

"Hmm. Aye... Mr. Doyle, bring that shiny new stethoscope of yours and please give a listen to Mrs. Connor's lungs."

I turned her chair away from the students, and after she loosened the front of her

blouse, I applied the stethoscope to the apex and then the base of her lungs. Her chest was filled with mysterious crackles, bubbling, and wheezing.

"Well, Mr. Doyle, tell us, what did you hear?"

"She has rales and wheezing, sir."

"Do you still think the diagnosis is tuberculosis?"

"It is possible, but I don't know anymore, sir," I answered.

Dr. Bell dictated two prescriptions to his clerk. "Mrs. Connor, each morning, burn a quarter cup of the leaves of Jimson weed and inhale the smoke. In the evening, put a teaspoon of dried sage and fifteen drops of oil of eucalyptus in a cup of boiling water and drink the tea. You will feel much better." The good doctor gave Mrs. Connor his arm and personally helped her to the anteroom.

There was a stir amongst the students until Dr. Bell returned, drew a hand across his pure white hair, and spoke. "Gentlemen, this is one of the more simple cases we have seen today and yet, not a one of you made the necessary observations. I regret to say that it is a result of your innate presumptions and prejudices. Never let them get in the way of a proper diagnosis. Observe, deduce, and diagnose with a clear mind and open eyes."

What was he getting at? I was confused and stupefied.

"Dr. Bell?"

"Did you, Mr. Doyle, or anyone, note the slip of paper pinned on her coat? It was yellow, the color of tickets for the Lancashire line. She has the dialect of West Ireland, and many of the poor Irish were forced to work in the coal mines of Scotland after the great famine. Coal dust is still embedded in her skin. When evaluating the lungs, carefully examine the finger nails. Mrs. Connor's nails are slightly blue, pitted, and down-curved, a sure sign of chronic oxygen deprivation caused by long-standing lung disease. The diagnosis is silicosis, better known as 'miner's lung.' The word, silicosis, as you surely know, is derived from the Latin, *silex*, or flint. When miner's inhale dust in the mines, the silica becomes imbedded in the alveoli of the lung. Any questions?"

We students remained perfectly mute. Not a one of us stirred, overcome by Dr. Bell's great powers of observation and his quick wit. One student finally raised his hand.

"Aye," Dr. Bell said, pointing to the student.

"Sir, that makes sense for a man who toiled in the mines, but how does that apply to a woman?"

"Don't assume anything just because she's a woman… Ah, one of the great tragedies of Scotland. I would venture to say that when her husband died, she was forced to labor in the mines to support herself. Next patient, please."

He was a ten-year-old boy whose flushed, feverish face was contorted by pain. The clerk rolled him into the amphitheatre on a cart. "Jamie McLeod here has a pain in his stomach," he said. At the poor boy's side was his mother — a poorly dressed, tearful, young woman twisting a handkerchief with both hands.

Dr. Bell did not question and harass us students in his usual way. Instead, he went to the cart and immediately put his finger on the boy's pulse. There came over his face a look of intense concern. He closed his eyes and pursed his lips. "Now, mother, how long has your boy been ill?"

"He's been down with pain in his belly these five days, sir."

"Can he keep down his food?"

"No sir. He throws out every mouthful and hasn't had even a drop of water this past day."

"Have his bowels moved?"

"No sir."

The professor loosened the boy's trousers and gently ran his hand over the abdomen. The child winced and cried out when he touched the right lower quadrant.

Dr. Bell absently stroked his chin. "In the past, we would have diagnosed your son with a severe case of inflammation of the bowels, but these days, there are physicians in America who would posit that your son is suffering from a disease of the vermiform appendix. However, we would have to do exploratory surgery to know for certain."

"Do whatever you need to, sir. Just ease his pain."

"Mr. Doyle, fetch my instrument case, please," Dr. Bell instructed.

The appendix? There was nothing in our textbooks about the appendix. Aye, my anatomy professor had mentioned it in passing, calling it a useless organ with no known function. We all murmured and twisted in our seats, not sure what to make of Bell's diagnosis. Meanwhile, the Russian sitting behind me leaned forward, straining to understand every word.

When all was ready, the junior clerk dripped chloroform on a mask over the boy's face. When he was asleep, Dr. Bell swabbed the abdomen with carbolic, attached a trocar to the syringe and, after a moment's hesitation, plunged the sharp steel probe into the boy's abdomen. We all held our breath. He pulled back the plunger, and the syringe filled with yellow, creamy pus.

"By Jove, the Americans are on to something," Dr. Bell said and then looked at Weeks. "Take this young man and his mother straight to the Royal Hospital. Find Dr. John Hetherington and tell him that I said that this lad needs to have his appendix surgically removed immediately."

As Weeks led the boy — still groggy from the chloroform anaesthetic — and his mother out of the theater, there was a great clatter of horse's hooves and a jangling of bells on Lauriston Street. An agitated police officer burst into the amphitheatre. "There's been an accident at the quarry!"

In the next instant, two burly orderlies carried a groaning, bleeding, bearded man on a crimson-stained stretcher into the amphitheatre. Something about him was familiar, but I could not place him nor was he in any condition to identify himself. Who was he and why did I feel like I knew him?

His legs below the knee were a jumble of bloody boots, mangled skin, and muscle, with white, jagged bone protruding from his torn trousers. Bright red blood bubbled up from lacerated arteries. His right hand was a scarlet mess.

In a flash, Dr. Bell with his two assistants cut away the man's clothing and applied tourniquets above his knees. The furiously spurting blood slowed to a trickle; a great sigh of relief went up from the students.

Dr. Bell removed his coat and rolled up his sleeves. "Mr. Doyle, please administer the anaesthetic," he said. I adjusted a cloth mask over the poor man's nose and mouth and poured a few drops of chloroform. His moaning soon ceased and his clenched jaw relaxed.

For a moment, I thought he was dead, but there was a faint pulse at his neck. The gentleman wore a fine tweed jacket, but at the time, I was too busy with the anaesthetic to wonder at his clothing.

Dr. Bell and his assistants scrubbed their hands, then swabbed the patient's legs with a solution of carbolic, while the clerk arranged the instruments on a clean towel. There was a sense of great urgency as he cut through the skin and layers of muscle, sawed bone, ligated arteries, and stitched up the skin. He amputated both legs just above the knees within twenty minutes of the time the patient had entered the room.

I stopped the chloroform, but the poor man remained unconscious. We worked furiously to save his life. Dr. Bell ordered coffee enemas, and we attempted to force brandy down his throat, but to no avail. He sank lower and lower.

Suddenly, he stirred, opened his eyes, and murmured with a slight Irish accent. “It was no accident. No accident.” Damn! I couldn’t determine his identity. His voice was familiar, but a beard and scars covered his face.

Bell hovered over him as his bloody hand rose and he uttered a few words. He seemed to be saying, “Proof… Dr. Hutton correct… No God… End of the old regime.”

With that effort, his entire body seemed to shrink into itself. His chest rose in a great sigh as he gave a shout with his last breath. “Tsar must die!”

The students and observers had left, but the Russian surgeon had stood by Dr. Bell’s elbow. Now, he stepped back as if struck. “No, no, no…” he murmured. “We will save the tsar. We have blood. Blood for transfusion.” All of a sudden, the Russian grabbed his notebook and stomped out of the amphitheatre.

Proof? Blood? The tsar?

What did it all mean? I was lost, and needless to say, no matter who our patient was, Dr. Bell and I were both upset at not being able to save him. We were the only ones left. “Doyle, please clean the corpse,” Dr. Bell said.

As I did, I opened his clenched hands and found a scrap of paper. A clue. Was this his proof?

Dr. Bell, who had been slumped in his chair in utter defeat, took the paper, spread it flat on the sink, and gently mopped away some clotted blood, which had dropped on it. On one side was a sketch of a small animal, somewhat like a lizard, and on the other was an address: 41 Maitland Park Road.

The professor then minutely examined the corpse, muttering all the time. “Well-tanned, a once-handsome man, and a fine tweed jacket; this is no ordinary quarryman.” He then delicately sponged away the blood from the dead hand. Two fingers had been blown away, and in the middle of his hand was a dark, thick scar from an old wound — one that penetrated through the palm of the hand. There was an identical scar in the center of the palm of his left hand.

"Sir, what was that about the tsar?" I asked.

"Doyle, when was the last time you read a newspaper?"

"It's been a while, sir, with studying for my examinations and all …"

"If you were aware of current events, you'd know that anarchists assassinated Tsar Alexander II three months ago, on March the first."

"Aye, I may have heard about that."

"This is a case for Scotland Yard," he said. "Now, Doyle, go home, get some rest, and meet me in the morgue tomorrow morning."

While walking home, the words "No God" and "Tsar must die" kept reverberating in my mind.

Who was that injured man?

Why did he seem so familiar?

8 June 1881

I was busy with a cadaver, tracing the optic nerve from the eye through its foramen to the brain, when the two men interrupted my work. They were from London and had the bearing of military men.

Indeed, the short bull of a man, with greying red hair that poked in clumps from under his derby, introduced himself as such. "Sergeant James O'Grady of her Queen's Own Rifles at your service, sir." He had bright blue eyes and a freckled face that was toughened from years in the sun. His broad girth and strong musculature was such that I would have liked to have him on my rugby team.

The second man was nearly six feet tall and elegantly dressed in fawn-colored trousers, a black frock coat, and a grey jacket. I immediately recognized the ribbon of the Victoria Cross on his lapel and, almost as a reflex, stood at full attention. He did not offer to shake hands. His lips barely moved as he introduced himself, displaying the finest example of the British stiff upper lip I had ever witnessed. "Colonel Sir Cameron Beachy-Edwards." I judged him to be at least sixty years of age. He was pale and slender, almost to the point of emaciation, as if he had suffered some terrible disease, such as typhus or dysentery.

The colonel didn't waste time or words. "Conduct us to the morgue."

I nodded. "Follow me," I said. We immediately set off down the corridor to a flight of wooden stairs, then through a door, smudgy with many hands that had handled body parts, into the cold, damp basement morgue. It was no surprise to see Dr. Bell already folding back the sheet that covered our deceased patient. I studied the bearded and scarred face once again. Who was it?

Sergeant O'Grady took up station by the door while the colonel stood with his hands clasped, staring at the dead face. Then, he minutely examined the dense scars on the man's face and the palms of the dead man's hands.

"Oh, dear God, it's Foley."

Foley?! I staggered back, away from that dreadfully maimed body. Was that why he seemed so familiar? Could he be Declan Foley? Foley is not an uncommon name, but my mam was a Foley and said Declan was a relative, perhaps a distant cousin. When he was stationed in Edinburgh, he often came to our house for Mam's cooking. One Christmas he brought a huge ham with sauces and a dessert. I was very young at the time and clung to him like he was my real father. I would run all the way to the castle to watch when he drilled the troops for the noon gun ceremony. I called him 'uncle' and loved it when he tossed me into the air and always caught me on the way down. He took me on long walks and to the museum, where told me the names of all the stuffed animals and where they were from. He was an amateur scientist as well as a soldier. When I last saw Uncle Declan, he wore his red officer's coat and a sword. He was off to the war in Afghanistan. I had often dreamed of him, gallantly slashing the heathen with his sword for the Queen and country. When pa was away on a drunken spree, I would frequently yearn for Uncle Declan's strong protective arms. The last we had heard, the poor man had died during a battle. This couldn't be . . .

The colonel wiped his eyes, seemed to be overcome by emotion, but gathered himself. "He was a lieutenant in command of a troop of Gurkha border guards while gathering intelligence in Baluchistan when he was captured by the Russians. Recently, we learned that the fiends turned him over to Moslem women who pinned him to the ground with stakes driven through his hands then propped his jaws open with a stick. Those sadistic women took turns squatting over his face and urinating into his mouth. Most men drown during this bizarre ritual, but Lt. Foley and another intelligence officer survived. Foley did not return to his regiment. Little is known about the other man, but we think he killed an officer of the Okhrana, took his identity, and disappeared into Russia," Colonel Beachy-Edwards said.

"What a horrible story! What happened to poor Foley?" I asked.

"He wandered around Eastern Europe. Recently, we learned that he came home and entered Cambridge under a pseudonym to study geology. Needless to say, Declan was a changed man as a result of the torture," the colonel said.

I studied the dead man's features. "Oh, my God! It is Uncle Declan!" I exclaimed.

"You knew this man?"

"My mother's relative, Declan Foley, was reported missing in action a few years ago. We assumed he was dead."

"As we did, too."

"But surely, he would've contacted us once he returned from . . ."

"Actually, Declan avoided family and old friends once he returned, changed his name, and dedicated himself to his study of geology. As I said, he was a changed man."

"I still can't believe . . ."

Dr. Bell cleared his throat. "Come here, laddie, and take another look."

"Aye." I studied the bearded, well-tanned face of the corpse. It was much more wrinkled and leathery than I remembered. There were new scars, but I saw the resemblance to my mam.

Aye, it was definitely him. He had the high cheek bones and the grey eyes of a Foley. He even had the same heart-shaped face as my mam. We had failed to save him. My eyes wandered to the stumps of his legs. Tears came to my eyes.

Dr. Bell saw I was deeply affected. "Tis him, aye?" he asked.

"Aye." I answered. "Dr. Bell, what did we do wrong? Why couldn't we save him?"

"We tried, laddie. We did everything in our power. There is no reason to feel shame."

I felt as if my uncle had been delivered to me for a reason. I swore I would — I must — find his assassin to redeem myself for our failure to save his life. The best surgeon in Scotland had been unable to save him. My years of study seemed futile. I would try to honor him. "Dr. Bell, we must discover his killer," I said.

"Aye." Dr. Bell said, "We will try… I am sorry, laddie. Were you and Declan close?"

"My father . . . Well, you know about my father. When I was a young lad, Declan was like a father to me, and I called him 'uncle.' Mam and I always looked forward to his visits. Oh, how my mam's face lit up when he appeared in the doorway. She loved him so."

"Then, we shall do everything in our power to solve his murder."

"Aye, thank you, sir." I brushed away my tears.

Dr. Bell, touched by my emotion, gently held my shoulder. "There, there, laddie. There, there."

"Thank you, sir. Sorry about that."

"Don't mention it. But remember, you are a physician; buck up and keep a professional demeanor." Dr. Bell replaced the sheet covering the corpse. "Let us adjourn to more comfortable surroundings. My cook makes an excellent breakfast tea."

It was in this moment when I most appreciated Dr. Bell and felt guilty that I complained about his abuse.

At Dr. Bell's house, O'Grady and I wolfed down boiled eggs, buttered toast with jam, and a rasher of bacon, while Dr. Bell and the colonel sipped tea. The colonel lit a cigar. "Who is Dr. Hutton?" he asked.

Dr. Bell took down from his bookshelf a heavy volume, *Theory of the Earth* by Dr. James Hutton. "Dr. Hutton was trained as a physician, but spent his entire life studying geology to prove that the earth was made over millions of years, not in the biblical six days."

"Balderdash. Sounds like one of those Darwinians. That goes against all authority."

O'Grady lifted his hand. "Sir, if I may be so bold. Lieutenant Foley was born a Roman Catholic, but, ever in search of the truth, he became an atheist and often talked about inciting the peasants to overthrow the Russian tsar if he could prove to them that the tsar's power was not derived from God."

"Perhaps Foley found something at the quarry that proved Dr. Hutton's theory," Dr. Bell said. He blew a cloud of pipe smoke and leaped from his chair. "Let us go there. Doyle, call James to bring up the landau," said Bell. He also took a telescope in a long case and one of his fine English shotguns. “We may see grouse on the moor,” he muttered, while stuffing cartridges into a pocket. It was not the season for bird shooting.

The day was overcast with a fine mist but not enough rain to put up the folding top of the chaise. We spun along in fine style to the abandoned quarry, three miles outside of Edinburgh. “James, stop here,” Dr. Bell commanded. We were perhaps two hundred yards from the granite face of the open quarry.

He intently scrutinized the exposed rock with the telescope. After a few moments, he passed the instrument to the colonel. “See the horizontal lines of the granite overlying the vertical lines of limestone. According to Dr. Hutton, the granite was formed over millions of years by upheaval of the earth on top of the limestone.”

“Doesn’t prove a damn thing,” the colonel said, handing the telescope to me.

I trained the instrument, first on the granite, then on the underlying limestone. After a bit of focusing, I saw the tracing of a lizard-like animal, exactly like that of the sketch in Foley’s clenched fist. “There, a fossil. I’d like to take a closer look,” I said, and began moving towards the face of the cliff. The others followed, stumbling over rocks and uneven ground.

I was nearly fifty yards away when the entire cliff face dissolved in a terrific explosion. The force of the blast sent us to the ground beneath a rain of pebbles and clouds of dust.

I was still dazed when I heard Dr. Bell. “After him!” he shouted.

A figure ran for all he was worth high atop the cliff. O’Grady went off like a scared hare and disappeared among the trees on the hill. The colonel followed but after a few steps, slowed and sank to the ground.

I followed the professor around the hill towards the road. It seemed longer, but in a matter of minutes, we met O’Grady and glimpsed a dark figure on a dappled, light grey horse pounding away towards the city. Dr. Bell fired two shots after the man, but the distance was too great for his light loads of bird shot.

I trained the telescope on the retreating figure. “There is something wrong with the animal’s right rear leg!” I shouted.

We criss-crossed the rough ground until Dr. Bell found hoof prints. "Aha! Here is a perfect print. Doyle, you are correct. The shoe in this print has a loose nail. We will find our man and I will wager that he is in the theology department."

Colonel Beachy-Edwards limped back to the chaise while the three of us explored the blasted rock face of the old quarry. Except for a faint imprint of a fish's tail, there was no sign of the fossil that my poor uncle had sketched.

After we presented our findings to the local police, the colonel and O'Grady took the next train to London. "You fellows have things well in hand," the colonel said as he waved goodbye.

Dr. Bell's close friend, Detective Willie McGregor found the dappled, grey horse with a sore right rear hoof at the second farrier he visited. He sent a message to say it was, as Bell had predicted, owned by Ian Stewart, an anti-Darwinian professor of theology.

Upon receiving the detective's message, we hurried to meet him at the professor's door. There was no response to our knock, but after butting the door open with my shoulder, we found Stewart attempting to escape by the back window of his flat.

He was wild-eyed and, at first, denied all knowledge of the explosion or of Foley.

"Hold his hands, please, Mr. Doyle." Dr. Bell said. I grabbed Stewart's hands. Under the careful gaze of detective McGregor, Bell scraped beneath the nail of Stewart's index finger with the blade of his penknife. He soon collected grains of powder on a slip of paper. "There," he said. "Gun powder of the type used for blasting."

The man wilted and admitted that Foley had come to him asking for the whereabouts of Dr. Hutton's cliff, with evidence that the world was millions of years old.

"He was clearly mad — mad as a hatter. He planned to take proof that God didn't make the world in six days to that atheist Karl Marx. In doing so, he aimed to give Marx the proof he needed to destroy the divine right of kings and emperors to rule. He wanted nothing less than to shake up all of Europe, dethrone the royals, and start a revolution."

My God! I thought to myself. This was not the Uncle Declan I knew. He had changed into a truly dangerous man; it was no wonder he was murdered.

Detective McGregor questioned Stewart further until the man admitted to the deliberate murder of Lt. Foley to "…save the world from these godless communist lunatics."

21 June 1881

It has been close to two weeks since the incident with Declan and the arrest of Stewart. Things have been uneventful. I have not mentioned a word to mam because she thought he died a few years ago, and bringing up these sordid affairs would only hurt her further.

Yet, with that said, the events surrounding my uncle were troublesome; I wanted to discover more about his past. Today, after morning ward rounds, Dr. Bell took me aside. "Doyle, I have been invited to St. Petersburg, Russia and will need an assistant."

I almost died several times on my trip to America in 1878 with Dr. Bell, so needless to say, I was a bit hesitant. When I did not eagerly reply in the affirmative, Dr. Bell showed me a letter.

"It might be in your best interest to accompany me, laddie."

"How so?" I asked.

"Well, you might be able to learn the truth about your deceased relative, Declan. Here, read this." He handed me the letter, which was written in English on heavy parchment. The handsome, embossed letterhead consisted of an open book beneath a gold, double-headed eagle.

Dear Professor Bell,

The faculty of medicine and surgery would be honored if you would consent to give a series of lectures and demonstrations of the antiseptic technique of surgery with special emphasis on your treatment of joints infected with tuberculosis. The Academy will pay all expenses for you and an assistant. There will be formal receptions and private consultations. We would especially value your assistance in training a special corps of surgeons to treat victims of attempted assassinations.

Sincerely, and gratefully yours,
Aleksey Sechenov, Professor of Physiology
St. Petersburg Academy of Medicine and Surgery

Dr. Bell must have known how troubled I was about Uncle Declan. His last words referenced the tsar, so perhaps the answer did lie in Russia. Furthermore, in another week, I would graduate with a bachelor of medicine and master of surgery; sadly, there were no prospects for work for me, so there seemed to be few other options open to me. “Does it pay well?” I asked.

“Aye, lad, you will be remunerated handsomely for your time, that I assure you.”

“Well, then, yes sir, I would welcome the opportunity.”

“In that case, come to my home at seven o’clock tomorrow evening to discuss the details.”

22 June 1881

I arrived at seven o'clock. Dr. Bell had started on a bottle of good Madeira and a round of cheese when his man, Willum, escorted me into the small study. The professor rose from his desk and took my hand in a firm grip.

"Doyle, good of you to come." He was as excited as a school boy as he pushed aside the bottle. "On August the sixth, the *Servia*, a Baltic-American liner, arrives in Liverpool to take on coal and passengers on her way from America to Copenhagen and St. Petersburg. We will have first-class accommodations. This is especially fortuitous in that it coincides nicely with your graduation."

"Aye, the timing is perfect. I will graduate in a few days and then celebrate with a journey to Russia," I said. "May I ask, sir . . . Is Russia still dangerous? It is not so long since the war in Afghanistan and there is still considerable anti-British sentiment there, aye?"

"Doyle, sometimes you can be a right numpty, laddie." He slashed the air with a stout cane and pressed a hidden button on the silver mounted knob. A wicked steel blade sprung out of the cane. He parried, slashed, then, quicker than my eye could see, he held the point of the blade against my neck. "Be an old stick in the mud, or join me for a bloody good adventure."

"Sir, I can't think with that blade at my neck."

He lowered the cane sword. "So, what do ye say?"

"I have read about the Russian government's purchase of the new Colt revolvers from America. Your sword cane will not prevail over a six-shooter."

"Ah yes." He slid a drawer out of his built-in gun case and selected a Webley .455 calibre army pistol. "This, as you may recall, fits nicely in a corner of my instrument case."

"Sir, you fired at the notorious Captain Hook with a British Bulldog, a smaller revolver. I don't believe the Webley will fit in your case."

"You may be correct. No matter. I shall adjust the case to take the Webley. Now, Doyle, this is the maiden voyage of the

Servia. It is built for the comfort of the rich and famous. According to this brochure, first-class passengers are expected to dress for dinner, and in Russia, there will be formal receptions and perhaps a ball or two."

"First class, sir?"

"Aye, Doyle, we will be traveling in grand style."

"But I no longer have a formal suit."

"Angus Duncan gave you a tidy bit of reward money for your part in saving the American President from an early demise. I presume you still have some of it."

I was deeply embarrassed to admit that most of the money had gone to provide care for my father in the asylum and to my mam for my brothers and sisters. "No. Um, well, actually, I don't have any left …" I stammered.

"Lad, you need to be more careful with your savings. Here." He handed me several pounds. "Armstrong's on Grassmarket Street will tailor a dinner suit for you."

I was preparing to leave when there was a knock at the door. Willum brought a middle-aged man into the study. "You might remember me as Sergeant O'Grady," he said."

I hardly recognized the man with black hair, dressed as a gentleman's valet, who only vaguely resembled O'Grady. "I am to be Dr. Bell's personal valet on your trip to Russia," he said.

"I have no need of a personal valet," Dr. Bell said.

"I suggest you read this before you decide whether you truly need me or not." O'Grady took a folded letter from his wallet. "You are to burn it immediately after reading the message."

I unfolded the paper. ***The carrier of this letter is a special agent of Her Majesty's Secret Service. He will accompany you on your journey to Russia***. The slashing signature was merely, 'Roberts' — none other than General Roberts, hero of the legendary march from Kandahar to Kabul that ended hostilities in the second Anglo-Afghan war.

Clearly, there was more to this humble-appearing sergeant than met the eye. "My apologies, Sergeant O'Grady. I'd be honored to have you as my valet." Dr. Bell said with a wink.

O'Grady replied with a soft grunt, cleared his throat, and spoke, not as a tough sergeant but as a refined gentleman's servant. "Hereafter, sir, refer to me as Mr. Lionel Tatum."

Dr. Bell poured a double measure of single malt whiskey for each of us and fed the letter into the fire. "Tatum, you had better move your things into the house so we can become better acquainted."

Armstrong's Men's Haberdashery on Grassmarket Street was shadowed by the palace. When I stepped through the door a bell tinkled far away in a dim back room. The floor creaked, and it took a moment to become accustomed to the gloom. My mam had stitched or knitted most all of my clothing, and I had been to a haberdashery only once before, when I traveled to America with Dr. Bell. "Kin I help you, sir?" the proprietor asked.

"I am traveling to Russia and need a formal white tie dinner suit," I said.

Mr. Armstrong, a pallid, old bloke with wire-rimmed glasses, looked me over as if he was an undertaker sizing me for a casket.

"Ah, sir, it will be a pleasure to provide you with suitable attire." He began with a measuring tape and a mouthful of pins, muttering about the amount of cloth needed to cover the breadth of my shoulders and height of nearly six feet two inches. He also measured me for a bespoke formal shirt and recommended a set of studs.

"Mr. Doyle, the climate is quite warm in Russia at this time of year. May I suggest an additional lightweight suit?"

My only jacket was of heavy tweed and hardly suitable for warm weather. I selected light grey linen for the new suit and left hoping I would have enough dosh to pay the bill.

6 August 1881

The great day of our departure has finally arrived. I have graduated and am now officially a doctor, but I have no job, no money, and few prospects for gainful employment upon my return. I have vowed to worry about such matters later and, for now, focus on solving the mystery of my uncle's untimely demise.

Beyond that, life at home has been filled with sorrow and woe. I couldn't keep my secret and had told my mam about Uncle Declan because she should know the truth. She cried for days and grieved even more about my trip to Russia. Sometimes, I have now come to believe, the truth is not the best medicine.

Aye, time and again, she begged me to stay home, but I convinced her that this experience would be an important part of my medical training and would provide me with the seed money I most sorely needed to start my practice. Finally, she reluctantly gave me her blessing.

Meanwhile, Da is still in the asylum. He is not drinking but is no better. I try to visit him every day, but it is always uncomfortable. On most of my visits, he does not recognize me and, when he does, he speaks of sprites and faeries.

And then yesterday, we started to argue. As our disagreement grew, he had a fit and the attendants asked me to leave. I could not tell if he had epilepsy or delirium tremens. It was horrible to see the man I once worshipped now demented, frail, and sickly.

Da's one saving grace is his art, and thankfully, he is drawing again. One day, I picked up one of his sketchbooks and marveled at his stunning images of faerie folk. If only he hadn't been cursed with a penchant for whiskey, he might have made these fantastic images years ago. He could have become a famous and well-paid artist like his brothers, and we wouldn't have had to live in squalor for all those years…

If only…

It is now time to stop daydreaming and to look forward.

Truth be told, I'm rather relieved to be departing Edinburgh for another adventure, but I will miss the Auld Reekie. I always do when I go away. Maybe I will even meet my future wife in the land of the tsars. Who knows?

Either way, I will now look like a proper gentleman because my new suits were completed yesterday. So, as I write this, I am decked out with a white tie, white shirt with a winged collar, silk stockings, and shiny, pointed shoes. It is all splendid beyond my wildest dreams.

Aye, I am now ready to taste life amongst the upper crust and could imagine squiring Jean the pretty lassie, to a great ball at the Edinburgh Palace. Yet, as I packed my things, I fingered my life savings, the measly sum of one shilling and six pence that remained from what Dr. Bell had given me. Oh, how it made me yearn for the day when I will be a famous surgeon with grand sums of money.

When we arrived in Liverpool, the yellow waters of the Mersey were covered with steamships and sailing vessels bound for every port in the world. Tug boats chugged back and forth while stevedores hooted, shouted, and unloaded cargo amidst a tangle of horses and wagons.

The *Servia* had only that morning arrived from Boston. And it was now moored to the Prince's Dock at the foot of Bath Street. She towered majestically above other vessels. The stars and stripes of the United States and the Baltic-American line pennant fluttered at her stern. Sailors wearing smart, white, duck trousers, and blouses lined her deck. The captain, with yards of gold braid on his sleeve, and surrounded by the ship's officers, waved goodbye to disembarking first-class passengers. With trumpets flashing in the sun, the band played a rousing version of "Rule Britannia" in deference to arriving British passengers.

Drawn by a prancing, chestnut mare, our cab pulled up amidst carriages and broughams carrying what appeared to the glittering royalty of England. Aye, this was the maiden voyage of a new steamship, pioneering a route from America to the Baltic states and Russia, and I wagered that many of its passengers would be of royal blood or important political figures or captains of industry. We waited for the passengers from America to disembark, and then, we began to make our way up the gangway.

Lionel Tatum, now completely at home as a manservant, passed Dr. Bell's trunks and my lone Gladstone bag to the stevedores. Dr. Bell insisted that I carry his precious instrument case, the lantern slides, and the projector.

I was at his side, toiling up the gangplank, feeling shabby in my hot, heavy tweed jacket when I caught the scent of orange blossoms. Next thing I knew, an absolute confection of young womanhood with the most magnificent, curly, chestnut-colored hair I had ever seen, brushed my arm as she regally extended her hand to the ship's captain. I was instantly smitten. Could this be the future Mrs. Arthur Conan Doyle? I would readily spend my life with her and envisioned sharing romantic days and evenings together in our bedroom.

I tried to appear uninterested and gave her an innocent, sidelong glance. Was it my imagination, or did she favour me with a smile and a whimsical toss of her head?

I lost her in the crowd when immaculately clad waiters bowed and offered glasses of champagne to us first-class passengers. I chugged my glass of the bubbly, and a smartly-clad steward led us up a paneled staircase to our stateroom on the upper deck, just aft of the landing and the library.

Dr. Bell handed him a gold guinea while 'Mr. Tatum' unpacked our bags before discretely withdrawing to his own less sumptuous cabin on a lower deck.

At Dr. Bell's suggestion, I chewed ginger root to guard against the *mal de mer* I had suffered during our passage to America. We were on deck while tugs pushed the *Servia* away from her dock. The band struck up "Heart of Oak" and then the "Navy Hymn." We spent the splendid afternoon watching the flats and low hills of Liverpool Harbor slip by until the ship passed Anglesey Island and headed through the Irish Sea to the St. George's Channel and Cape Cornwall.

As the sun set, we were back in our quarters. I was struggling with the studs and tie of my new outfit when Dr. Bell appeared from the dressing room, resplendent in a dress blue kilt with black and green stripes, a velvet Barathea jacket with silver buttons, and a tartan waistcoat. He had a dirk and silver, mounted, sealskin sporran with the crest of Clan Bell, a hand holding a dagger. Mr. Tatum straightened the Professor's black tie and adjusted the silk flashes on his plaid stockings then helped me with the studs and made a trifling adjustment to my tie. "Doyle, you are now a doctor and graduate of Edinburgh, the greatest medical school in the world. Hold your head high and bow to no man, whether he be an English lord, German baron or Russian count," said Dr. Bell.

All heads turned in our direction when we marched, side by side, into the splendid paneled dining room, bright with the new Edison incandescent electric lights glowing from a great chandelier. A small orchestra played dinner music while a crowd of perhaps two hundred smartly-clad passengers milled about sipping chilled wine.

The lovely lass who had brushed my arm on the gangplank was across the room, clinging to a devilishly handsome man with a long scar on his cheek. He appeared to be in his late twenties and wore red trousers with a silver-buttoned, dark blue tunic. She was stunning in a long, flounced, light green dress with a plunging neckline. Her hair was piled high on her head with soft ringlets framing her angelic face.

Before I could push through the crowd to reach her side and introduce myself, the ship's captain struck a bell and announced dinner. We found our places at a long table covered with white damask, set with bone porcelain plates and highly polished silverware. My gaze was still fastened on the captain's table, where the lovely creature was engaged in animated conversation with her dinner companion. The cad's leer was riveted on the glorious pink flesh of her upper bosom. Damn him for ogling my future wife!

Dr. Bell, seated at the head of the table, engaged in a discussion with a Russian count on the surgical aspects of the recent assassination attempt on James Garfield, the American president. I was next to a stout American who guzzled glass after glass of wine. After smacking his lips, he nudged my elbow. "What's your game, fella?" He asked.

"Oh, a bit of rugby and I've been known to box."

"Nah, sorry 'bout that. What I meant was — what'ya do for a living? In other words, how do you make enough filthy lucre to pay to travel first-class?"

It was a rude question, typical of an American. I was a bit short with him, hoping he would leave me alone. "I am a physician."

"Oh, I see, doc." He applied himself to the wine for a minute or so, then spoke with slurred speech. "My name is Adam Gritz. Electric boats are my game. By God, the world will take notice when we teach those Russkies not to kill our president."

"Excuse me?"

"Everybody knows the Russians killed Garfield."

"Sorry, but the papers here in Scotland claimed an American citizen of French descent named Charles Guiteau killed him," I said.

"Ah yes, that was the papers said. In truth, his real name was Gitorski and he was part of an intricate Russkie plot. All those damn Russians want our gold in Alaska."

I did not challenge the American and assumed his conspiracy theory was the drunken meandering of a deluded fool.

I love a sumptuous meal, especially while traveling, and I was famished. For the next two hours, I consumed oysters, consommé, salmon with mousseline sauce, creamed peas with roast sirloin, curried chicken, a gargantuan portion of squab with cress, guinea fowl baked in a delicious dressing, a black currant sorbet, buttered new potatoes, a double lamb chop, fresh asparagus, pâté de foie gras, and at last, peaches in jelly with a chocolate éclair.

The waiters served Turkish coffee in tiny china cups while sailors cleared an area in the center of the room beneath the glittering chandelier. Captain Veery struck a bell to get everyone's attention. "Ladies and gentlemen, the ship's company will now offer real seafaring entertainment. I present, for your pleasure, Billy and the Horn Pipers," said the captain.

The seven sailors wore identical, tight-fitting, white, duck trousers, singlets and black, hard-soled brogues. They launched into a merry tune with a tin whistle, a fiddle, and a squeeze box.

Suddenly, a young, sandy-haired lad with bright white teeth danced to the front of the stage. With arms tight to his chest and with legs kicking and stomping, he danced a hornpipe while singing "Blow the man down," "Maid of Amsterdam," and "Paddy lay you back."

The music became slower and solemn while Billy, in the very image of a captain, scowled, shaded his eyes, peered through an imaginary telescope, and then began to chant.

"*Captain Bligh, that silly man*
Was master in command.
He was growling day and night
An answer for his complaints."

Billy turned toward the three chanters.

"*I flogged the men, flogged the men,*" he sang, with his arms flailing.

"*He flogged his men, OH,*
Captain Bligh, he flogged his men, OH," the chanters answered.

As sweat soaked the muscular frame under his singlet, Billy gracefully bowed to the audience and the program came to an end. There were cheers and much stamping of feet. Ladies crowded about the performers, and more than one opened her purse and dropped golden guineas into the hands of the sailors.

Later, after an hour or so in the smoking room with a fine cigar and more than one brandy, I wobbled, unsteadily, out on deck and leaned against the railing for a breath of salt air. I couldn't have been there for more than a few seconds, when, much to my surprise, I sniffed orange blossoms and was immediately enveloped in a dark cloak and pushed against the deckhouse.

At first I struggled to get free, but she pressed her lips over my mouth. I felt her soft flesh and was filled with pleasure until she forced the cold muzzle of a pistol into my ribs. "If you cry out, I'll put a bullet in your spleen," she whispered.

More than thinking about any threat, I was caught up in the pleasant sensation of soft lips on my skin and even softer breasts pushing against my chest. So, I grunted and kissed her again. She responded with passion, and after a moment, she whispered breathily with her lips delicately brushing my ear. "Look carefully. Who is on the deck?"

For the first time, I became aware of two men at the railing perhaps thirty or forty feet down the deck. Their heads were together as if in earnest conversation, but in the mist and dark, they were barely visible.

"I can hardly make them out." I replied. She adjusted her hips, so we were pressed together, full length, toe to nose. The pistol was probably a fake, and the sensation was quite delicious.

"Damn you! Pay close attention," she chided.

I squinted and whispered. "It could be Gritz, an American engineer. The other may be your dinner companion."

Her lips, with her mouth slightly opened, returned to mine, and the hand with the pistol went around my neck. We snuggled like lovers for another moment, until she pushed me off balance and silently ran aft, away from the men at the railing.

I was totally mystified, slightly dizzy, and more than a bit aroused from the whole affair. I remained frozen in place, savoring the lingering scent of orange blossoms. Who was this woman? What was she after? Why wouldn't she stay with me? Why did she have a gun?

I remained by the rail for a few more minutes, eagerly hoping for her to return, but she never did. I reluctantly went to my berth just aft on the same deck, my head still swimming with her citrus scent and the lovely soft sensation of her voluptuous body pressing against me.

7 August 1881

Sun was streaming through the porthole when Dr. Bell, rather more roughly than necessary, shook me awake. I had a pounding headache and my stomach was queasy, although the ship was hardly rolling.

"Laddie, you can't sleep all day. Up, up. Time for breakfast."

I rolled out of the bunk, dressed, and made it to the nearly-empty dining room. I did not have much appetite, but after several cups of tea, I managed to put away a rasher of bacon, several fried eggs, and toast with marmalade.

A short nap was in order, but when I returned to our cabin, the stunning young lady who smelled of orange blossoms was there, sitting with crossed legs on a comfortable chair. She wore a tight-fitting purple dress with a bit of lace around her neck. As she swung her foot back and forth, I could not take my eyes away from her elegant lower leg and slender ankle. She opened a large purse and withdrew a yellow, tin box marked 'Kyriazi Freres' and selected a cigarette.

I was taken aback at her behavior, and Dr. Bell pursed his lips with disapproval. She held the cigarette to her lips between her index and middle fingers and smiled. "Well …" she said. I fumbled for a lucifer and lit her cigarette. She drew in a lungful of smoke, expelled the cloud through her perfect nostrils, and turned her luminous eyes on Dr. Bell.

"Colonel Sir Cameron Beachy-Edwards informed me that you attended Declan Foley when he was fatally injured. I am anxious to learn about his last moments and what, if anything, he found at Hutton's quarry. What were his last words?" she asked.

"What was your relationship with Lt. Foley?" Dr. Bell asked.

"Lieutenant Foley was my husband."

Jings! I could hardly believe it. Last night, I had been kissing — my 'aunt'?!!

Dr. Bell raised an eyebrow, "Aye, and you are?"

"Penelope Walshingham of the Norfolk Walshinghams. My father is the fourth Earl of Leicester. I was one of the few women to study at Cambridge." She paused to dab her eyes, sniffed, and went on. "Lieutenant Declan was the only man who showed me kindness. My parents disapproved of his lowly birth, but I am a free thinker and we wed in secret a few weeks before his death."

She gave no sign that we had met — not only met, but feverishly kissed one another — the night before. I was stunned.

How could this elegant, sophisticated lady have been married to Uncle Declan? I remembered his great beard, his face ravaged by scars and suffering. How could she have been drawn to him? Aye, she said that he showed her kindness, but none of it seemed to make sense.

I have to admit, this mystery only added to her allure. I felt as if I was being drawn into a whirlpool of emotion and, well, lust, if not love. It made no difference that this stunning creature was actually my relative through marriage. Now that Uncle Declan was dead, she would need someone to take care of her and I most certainly could be the one. Uncle Declan … I had no idea that he had remained alive the last couple of years, never mind taken on a bride.

I could hold my tongue no longer. "Excuse me, Miss Walshingham, or should I call you Mrs. Foley?" I asked.

"Since our marriage was secret, and seeing that he is no longer alive, I prefer to be referred to as Miss Walshingham."

"Aye, then answer me this, ma'am. When did Declan decide to take a bride?"

She glared and tossed her head. "Dear child, that is none of your business."

"Oh, but it is my business," I answered, angry that she had referred to me as a child. "I am Arthur Conan Doyle. My mother is Mary Foley and Declan was our relative."

"Oh my! Declan never spoke of any family. It is only recently that I discovered his real name was Declan Foley. Please, give a poor widow a moment." She began sobbing and removed a lorgnette from her bosom, placed it on her delicate nose, and looked me up and down. She gave no sign that she remembered our ardent embrace only a few hours before.

She finally stopped weeping. "How are you associated with Dr. Bell?" she asked.

Dr. Bell answered for me. "Mr. Doyle is a recent graduate of the Edinburgh University Medical School, as well as my assistant."

"I see. And my dearly departed was your relative."

"Well, aye… I called him 'uncle.' "

"So, you, like me, must also be devastated by his loss."

"Aye, and I will do everything in my power to assist you in ensuring his murderer is brought to justice."

"Good. Please, tell me about his last moments."

I told her everything and remembered his final words, "A tsar will die."

"Ah, poor Declan was horribly abused by the Russians during the war but didn't blame the people. He vowed vengeance on the tsar and his foul government."

With that, she tossed her head and ground out the cigarette in an empty teacup. I was torn between a desire to take her in my arms and a yearning to slap her for her appalling behavior. Abruptly, tears drizzled down her lovely cheeks again.

I couldn't help it. In that moment, I was overcome for sympathy for her. What I would've given in that moment to kiss away those dear droplets.

And then, I thought — *is it appropriate to have feelings for the woman who was my 'aunt'? Or at least had been my aunt until Uncle Declan was killed …?*

At that moment, there was a knock. I leaped from my chair and opened the door. The first officer saluted rather stiffly. "Dr. Bell, Captain Veery requests your assistance. A passenger has died," he said.

The stateroom of the deceased was a few doors away from our own and not far from where Penelope had so pleasantly accosted me a few hours ago. We crowded into the room. Surprisingly, Penelope followed us. The captain and the ship's doctor, a middle-aged gentleman, were staring glumly at the corpse. The dead man, stretched on his back across the bed, had silvery-grey hair, was fully dressed, and appeared to be about sixty years of age. “This is all that remains of Lord Asquith,” said the captain.

Asquith’s fine features and neatly trimmed mustache marked him as definitely upper-class. The first officer swished at a common housefly twitching its wings on the man’s upper lip and was about to close the man’s eyes.

“Please, don’t touch a thing,” Dr. Bell warned, rather sharply.

The officer shrank away from the corpse and wiped his lips with a white handkerchief.

“Sorry,” he muttered. “It’s like he is staring right at us.”

“Doyle, can you make a diagnosis?” Dr. Bell asked.

“It appears as if Lord Asquith has suffered a sudden heart attack or a lethal brain hemorrhage.”

“Yes, that is what we are supposed to believe. But look carefully. His fingernails and skin are dead white, as if he lost a great deal of blood.”

“But, there are no signs of blood loss, lacerations, or bleeding.” I said.

Dr. Bell put a hand on the body. “He has been dead for no more than six hours.”

“If it wasn’t a natural death, then what?” asked first officer.

“I can’t say as of yet.”

The Professor ran his fingers through the corpse’s hair, peered into his eyes, nose, and ears, gently pulled down the lower lip, and sniffed at the mouth. “He smoked Cuban cigars.” Bell examined the hands and fingernails and, with some difficulty, opened the left, clenched fist. He minutely examined the fingers and nails with a small magnifying glass.

“There are no signs that he fought an assailant.” He then directed us to remove clothing from the corpse and, much to my great surprise, inspected the abdomen and thumped the chest as if examining the lungs of a live patient.

“Ah, dull to percussion. There is blood or fluid in his left chest. Turn him over, very carefully, so his left side is up, please.”

He adjusted the light and, with his hand lens, minutely observed every inch of the chest. “Ah … Here it is.”

He had discovered a tiny wound, just lateral to the vertebrae, that was hardly larger than a needle prick.

"Oh, please, that little pin prick could not possibly have killed the man," the captain said.

"Death was due to a slow, but massive, hemorrhage into his thoracic cavity from a small wound in his aorta, the largest blood vessel in the body. I would wager that the weapon was a slender needle or even a hat pin. I trust that an autopsy will prove me correct. Only a highly trained assassin would know exactly where to insert his weapon in order to fatally penetrate the thoracic aorta," Dr. Bell said.

The ship's medical officer spoke. "We don't have the facilities for a proper autopsy."

"I will not disturb the passengers," Captain Veery said.

"Sir, you have a murderer on board your ship. We need every bit of information possible in order to find the man."

Dr. Bell stooped and commenced a minute examination of the floor and the furniture, then went into the adjacent bathroom. There, he sniffed the air like a bloodhound on a scent.

"Doyle, now is a grand opportunity for you to use your keen, young senses. Please identify that odor."

I inhaled a nose full of air and sensed, first, a lingering odor of brandy, cigar smoke, and something else, something rather sweet that I could not name.

"Brandy and cigar smoke," I said. "And something else, but I can't seem to put my finger on it."

"Very good. Asquith drank a quantity of brandy after dinner and then he smoked at least one Cuban cigar. There is something more …" He sniffed again, *Papaver somniferum*, better known as opium."

"Opium is in so many common medicines that it probably means nothing," said I.

"Laddie, it means that either Asquith or his assailant used opium, perhaps combined with tobacco," Dr. Bell said.

It was not my place to argue with the professor, but the faint odor reminded me of a long distant pleasant memory. I couldn't put my finger on it, but I knew that it was certainly not opium. Bell paced back and forth for several minutes, hands clenched behind his back, with his eyes darting around the room from the corpse to the floor to the walls.

"Here is what took place . . . The murderer waited for Asquith, knowing that he had consumed a quantity of alcohol. He was in this room, perhaps crouched beside the bed or in the bathroom. He waited until Lord Asquith turned his back and then inserted the weapon. Asquith would have ignored the faint pinprick and slowly bled to death over the course of several hours."

"Ahem." Captain Veery cleared his throat for attention. "How ridiculous. Mere speculation," he spluttered.

"I think not! An autopsy will prove that I am quite correct. Asquith was a British citizen and his murderer is on this ship," said Dr. Bell.

"Damn your impertinence, Dr. Bell! I will have none of this. My master-at-arms will investigate. There will be no autopsy, and the body will be handed over to the British Consulate when we dock in Copenhagen!" shouted the captain.

"Nay, sir. By then, the body may be decomposed and the murderer will escape. Doyle, fetch my instrument case and ask Mr. Tatum to join us, if you please."

Tatum and I arrived at Asquith's room the same time as the chief master-at-arms, the ship's police officer.

Dr. Bell unlatched the case, slid out a separate compartment, and removed a revolver. "Mr. Tatum, I presume you know how to use a Webley .455."

"Yes, sir, that I do." Tatum admired the well-oiled, gleaming weapon and checked to see that the cylinder was loaded with bullets.

"Mr. Tatum, use force, if necessary. The ship's officers are to line up against the far wall and witness my findings."

Tatum thrust out his chest and sucked in his belly. "Over there, lads. As the Dr. ordered. Against the wall!" he boomed, in a voice suitable for the drill field.

The master-at-arms clenched his fists and growled. "No damn lackey gives orders to my captain!"

With a calloused thumb, Mr. Tatum pulled back the pistol's hammer and aimed at the master-at-arms. The captain's face was violaceous, and an artery throbbed at his forehead. "Obey the man," he said. The ship's officers formed a ragged line with their backs to the wall.

Bell then took command of the room. "Gentlemen, what you are about to witness is not for the faint-hearted; I urge all of you to pay the utmost of attention. Mr. Doyle, my scalpel, forceps, and scissors. Oh, and please fetch a stack of towels."

I did as he asked. Then, with a few deft strokes of the knife, the professor sliced through the chest wall and cut away the anterior portion of a half-dozen ribs, opening the left chest. "A-hah! There, gentlemen — the left thoracic cavity is filled with blood and clots." "My word!" the ship's doctor gasped.

The first officer wilted into an unconscious heap on the floor.

I was feeling a bit queasy. "Mop the blood, Mr. Doyle. Make yourself useful," Dr. Bell said in a slightly mocking voice.

I clenched my teeth, held my tongue, and did as I was told. Dr. Bell assumed his accustomed role as a medical school professor. "Now, gentlemen, please, one at a time observe the thoracic aorta, the largest blood vessel in the body. It courses from top to bottom of the chest cavity. The hole was in the upper portion, where the aorta hugs the thoracic vertebra. The defect, at first, was no larger than a pinhole, but just as the flow of water enlarges a small leak in a dike, cardiac contractions forced more and more blood to enlarge the pinhole. Gentlemen, this is a case of cold-blooded murder. The perpetrator is a skilled assassin with a good knowledge of human anatomy," said Dr. Bell.

"Confound it! Our passengers will not stand for interrogations," Captain Veery said.

"Perhaps, that won't be necessary. Please allow me to see your passenger list."

"Come to my cabin within the hour," the captain replied.

Without thinking, I blurted out a statement of confession. "Sir, I was with Miss Walshingham, just outside this stateroom late last night. Two men were not far away."

“Eh, what is that you say?” the captain asked. I repeated my statement, adding that Miss Walshingham was on the deck prior to my arrival.

The captain was annoyed and simply dismissed my comment. “Humph. Coincidence, nothing but coincidence,” he said.

Mr. Tatum, with elaborate courtesy, turned to Penelope and offered her the crook of his arm. “Miss Walshingham, please join us for tea.” We returned to our stateroom. Dr. Bell rang for tea.

“Miss Walshingham, what is your role in this affair?” he rather pleasantly asked.

My dear Penelope rolled her eyes, and large tears coursed down her cheeks.

“I am not at liberty to discuss the matter.”

“Were you having a romantic liaison with Asquith?”

“Of course not. I scarcely knew him. And, ahem, sir, I am a grieving widow.”

“Then why were you outside his room at about the time of his death? Perhaps you stuck him with a hat pin in a moment of passion.”

Her eyes blazed, hot with anger. “Damn you! I am a courier for Naval Intelligence and had a message for Lord Asquith. My instructions were to deliver a letter to him on our first night at sea. The entertainment went on so long I didn’t go to his stateroom until nearly three o’clock in the morning.”

“Aye, so you say,” Dr. Bell said. “Did you enter the room?”

Penelope selected a cigarette from the tin box. I leaped up with a fresh lucifer and lit the cigarette. She exhaled a cloud of smoke before speaking. “The door was ajar. I entered, but he was reclining on the bed, sound asleep. I did not disturb him and turned to leave, only to be accosted by . . . him.” She jerked her hand towards me.

Damn, I thought, *is this an act?* Her entire performance only added to her air of mystery and my desire.

“The message, please,” Dr. Bell said. She hesitated, but Mr. Tatum prodded her with a sharp look. She removed a pale blue, unmarked envelope, sealed with a blob of red wax from her handbag.

The professor slit open the envelope with a penknife and unfolded a sheet of heavy, blue paper.

Dear Percy,

I am praying that you have a pleasant and rewarding journey to St. Petersburg.

Give my fondest regards to Alexi.

Sincerely,

A.V.

Penelope was so close to me that, as we read the letter over Dr. Bell's shoulder, I thought I distinctly felt her pressing into my side. Sadly though, she took no notice of me and, instead, stared at the letter with intense interest.

Dr. Bell frowned, lit his pipe, and puffed clouds of smoke while carefully perusing the letter.

"Note the strong downward strokes of a modern fountain pen. A small blob of ink escaped when she dotted the "i" in *rewarding*. Alexi must be the new tsar, Alexander the third.

"Who is A.V.? I asked.

"Doyle, you should be ashamed of yourself to ask such a thing," Dr. Bell said.

"Why? What does it stand for?"

"The Queen used the name Alexandria Victoria before her coronation," Penelope said. "How could you call yourself a Scot and not recognize the initials of our Queen?"

"There must be more." Bell held the paper up to the porthole. "Ah-ha, look at this." Faint marks became visible as he moved the page in the sunlight.

"I do believe there is an additional message," Dr. Bell said. He struck another lucifer and held the flame beneath the letter. Nothing appeared.

"Some forms of invisible ink require a chemical to become visible. I will wager the chemical is in Lord Asquith's cabin."

"The captain has sealed Asquith's room." Penelope said.

"There are alternative ways into a room," said Dr. Bell, as he selected a delicate chisel from his instrument case. "Aye, this will do nicely."

Penelope and I shielded the doctor as he inserted the thin metal between the door and casing. There was a faint *click*, and he was in the room, leaving us on guard. I was glad that, once again, we were alone together, and I reached out for Penelope's hand. "We must provide a distraction. Shall we re-enact last night's dalliance?" I whispered to her.

"I say – you're cheeky, but I like that. That's the Foley in you." Penelope leaned against the door, clutched me to her bosom, and planted her lovely lips on mine. She may have been play-acting, but I passionately returned her embrace and kisses.

Suddenly, there were footsteps on the deck, and through a half-opened eye, I made out a couple who hurried past while averting their gaze. In hardly any time at all, certainly not long enough to satisfy my hot-blooded, rampant lust, Dr. Bell appeared at the threshold of the door.

Penelope pushed me away and smacked my face with her opened hand. "How dare you!" she said.

"My heavens!" Dr. Bell blushed. "What has gotten into you, laddie? She's your bloody aunt!" He shook his head as if reprimanding a child.

Before I could explain, he held up a small bottle labeled 'tincture of iodine.' "It was in his shaving kit," he said.

Back in our room, Dr. Bell poured a few drops of the iodine on a bit of cloth and gently swabbed the letter.

ODQB C RSNOY ZKDBW LTRS MATO VHKKHD HR LHRBGOUHNUR VHKK AD SQNTAKD

Penelope snatched the letter. "This is my responsibility."

"Not unless you can break the cipher," Bell said as he pulled it back from her.

"Damn you! Give it to me!" she shouted.

Tatum's big hand closed on her wrist. "Leave it be, Miss. Your only job was to deliver the message."

Penelope's face hardened. "You are hurting me." Tatum released her.

"The letter is useless unless we break the code. Dr. Bell has assisted the Secret Service in other cases. I suggest we leave the letter with him and get on to the captain's cabin."

"I am going with you," Penelope said.

"The letter can wait. I, too, will attend to the Captain," said Bell.

The captain's quarters were richly furnished with teak chairs, a desk, and a table. A Persian carpet and paintings of maritime scenes completed the picture of a man at the peak of his career in command of the greatest passenger ship ever launched.

I felt decidedly out of place. The chief master-at-arms and Billy, the handsome, horn-piping sailor, put the passenger manifest at our disposal. Most were American citizens, Swedes, Norwegians, Poles, and a Finn or two returning to visit their homeland.

Bell paused, his finger on the name of a lone Japanese passenger. "The Japanese have plans to annex Russian territory and would be more likely to assassinate the tsar than a British diplomat." There were a large group of American names, including the engineer, Adam Gritz. "Doyle, use your charm to mix with the other passengers and learn more about the Americans. Some of them still hate Britain."

I jotted down a list of names. "Right, sir."

Bell paused over a name. "Is Count Carl von Wittenberg — a Prussian?"

Penelope blushed. "He is from Berlin — a naval architect and great friend of Wilhelm II."

"Wilhelm II will be the next emperor of Germany. The man hates both England and Russia," Bell said.

"He is the grandson of Queen Victoria," Penelope said.

"True, but his father, Frederick is ill, possibly with cancer. Wilhelm will ascend to the throne within a decade. He blames the English for his deformed arm and the woman he loved has married a Russian prince."

Bell paused and stared at the captain. "So much for the passengers. What about your crew?"

"My men are the finest sailors in the world, Americans and Danes, one or two Norwegians. They are above reproach."

"Doyle, if you please, socialize with the passengers. See what you can learn and later meet me for tea," Bell said.

I sunk ankle-deep into a lush Persian carpet in the lounge and gazed with wonder at oil paintings and the array of bottles in front of a mirror behind the bar. The lounge was an elegant enough place to commence my investigations.

I nursed a pint of ale while listening to jovial American doctors discussing their plans for study in Vienna and Berlin. They were above suspicion, but another group of Americans, clustered about a table and talking in low tones, aroused my interest.

I moved to an empty chair and heard only snatches of their conversation, which was mainly about the shooting of President Garfield. They had, it seemed, served under Garfield while he was an officer in the union army and were on a commission to improve the U.S. Navy. Their destination was Germany. There seemed to be no reason to suspect their involvement in Asquith's murder.

I was about to leave when a tall, stringy fellow with a long, pointy mustache, wearing high leather boots and a large brimmed cowboy hat, jostled my arm, spilling a bit of my ale. He laughed. "Pardon me, partna.' This damn ship rocks worse than a painted pinto being gelded." He held out his hand. "Howdy. Cowboy Bill, at your service."

He already had a few too many ales, but he was friendly enough. I'd met my fair share of eccentric characters in America and I'd always enjoyed their company. I figured it was worth befriending this gregarious bloke and hearing what he had to say. "Pleasure to make your acquaintance, Bill. Let me guess — you're an American."

"Yessir! Born in West Virginia and, as of late, a resident of the great lone star state of Texas. Yee ha!"

I loved his energy and couldn't resist bragging a bit about my time in America, "Have you ever heard of the notorious James Gang?"

"Hell yeah! Those damn bastards wanted me to partner up with them and be in their gang." With my mate, Carl, I'd escaped near-death by that gang when Dr. Bell and I were in America. So, although I wasn't exactly sure how much was true and how much was the ale speaking, I decided to let him keep talking. "You see, back way yonder, when I was merely a stripling poking cows, them boys wanted me to help wrangle a few thousand head of steer, but I plum refused. Where'd you say you're from?" the American asked.

"I'm from Scotland. The name's Doyle, Arthur Doyle."

"Well, Artie, good to meet ya. Most of you limeys are usually too snooty to shoot the breeze with old Cowboy Bill, but you seem to be cut of a different cloth — maybe a Scottish tartan, eh?"

"Bill, what brings you on board this vessel?"

"I shouldn't tell you this, but you seem like a good hombre and so I'll spill the beans." He lowered his voice to a whisper. "I'll be damned if I ain't bringin' a whole cage full of Texas rattlesnakes to them hifulatin' Russkies."

"What?" I whispered.

He spoke louder. "You got cotton in your ears, boy? I got me a whole mess of rattlers in my quarters. Lassoed them critters behind the head and stuffed 'em in a feed sack. If you see any mice on board, tell me, since those critters will soon be needing some vittles."

"Why do the Russians want rattlesnakes?"

"I was told they're gonna be used for medical 'speriments. I don't really care as long as they pay… Now don't mean to be rude, but rumor has it that there are some poker games and dancing painted ladies below deck, so I'll be seeing you around." And with that, he was off…

I surveyed the other passengers, who seemed totally innocent, and departed from the lounge. Once I got out on the deck, the ship was in the Channel crashing against heavy seas and a north wind. I struggled on the pitching vessel to reach our stateroom, when, just ahead, a fellow who had been leaning against the guard rail fell to the deck.

I grabbed his coat just in time to prevent him from rolling into the sea. His legs beat up and down on the deck and his jaws were so tightly clenched, he was scarcely breathing. He looked to be around sixty years old.

I had seen the same symptoms of epilepsy in my father and immediately wrapped my fingers in a handkerchief. His jaws were tightly clenched, but with difficulty, I forced his mouth open. He took in a great deep breath.

Soon after, he relaxed but was confused. He was small and fragile as a chipmunk with a high, bald forehead and a great, black beard. I helped him to his feet. “Come to the lounge. You could use a tot of brandy,” I said.

“Brandy, no. Vodka, yes.” he said.

After downing half a glass of the clear, fiery liquor, he offered his hand and spoke a decent English with a strong Russian accent. “Bah. Damn London doctors could not cure my illness. Who are you, boy?”

“Arthur Doyle.”

“*Dobry den*. I am Fyodor . . . Fyodor Dostoevsky.”

“The great author?”

“Hah, yes, I have heard of that man. He’s not so great these days . . . These days, the mediocre Dostoevsky is only great at one thing – drinking.”

“And when you aren’t drinking?”

“I gamble.”

“And when you aren’t gambling?”

“I write drivel to pay for my drinking and gambling.”

“I would give up medicine if I could write drivel as well as you.”

He lit a cigarette and coughed up a gob of phlegm. “Writing’s a fool’s folly. I would’ve been better off if I never put pen to paper. It only leads to poverty, suffering and prison,” he said.

“Maybe so. But, still, I’d like to try my hand at it one day. At university, our French professor had us read French translations of your dark and brooding stories. They are brilliant psychological tales. All about suffering…”

“Suffering is the key to our redemption. And redemption is nigh impossible. So, in the end, life is a folly, and it is only through drink that one might find momentary escape.”

“Well then, sir, may I buy you another drink?”

"No, it is my turn. You saved me from falling into the sea. Tonight, be my guest on the steerage deck for vodka, discussion, and entertainment. And then, we shall see if you are truly cut out for the life of an author."

With that, Dostoevsky left and I made my way to Bell's stateroom. After the ale and vodka, and with the ship's erratic movement, I could hardly wobble. I gratefully sunk into an armchair, accepted a cup of tea, and reported my observations of the passengers. Penelope was sitting primly as a nun with pinched lips and a cold, fixed expression on her darling face.

Dr. Bell listened to my recital of the passengers with his chin resting on his hand.

"None of them sound like a killer. Meanwhile, I've made progress. The cipher is a simple transposition of letters."

Percy, stop D. Alex must live. Willie is mischievous and will cause trouble.

"We believe the Queen chose Asquith to protect Alexander III from a secret assassin," Mr. Tatum said.

"Wait, who is Willie?" I asked.

"The very same Wilhelm of Germany we discussed earlier."

"Then, who is D?"

"David." It was a soft, almost involuntary, answer. "Poor, poor David." Penelope wiped her tears and turned away.

Dr. Bell put a comforting hand on her shoulder. "There, there, lassie…"

"Who is David?" I asked.

She cleared her throat. "Captain David Campbell was my husband's best friend. After they escaped from the Russians, they found their way to a field hospital in Kabul. My husband recovered from his injuries and, after resigning his commission, bounced around Eastern Europe before going to Cambridge for geology. They say David was a brilliant linguist and a student of the Russian people but never regained his health. In his delirium, he vowed to kill the tsar."

Penelope paused to sip tea. "Captain David Campbell escaped from the hospital and disappeared. He is thought to be somewhere in Russia," she said, in a flat, dead voice.

"If Campbell kills Tsar Alexander III, there will be a major war between England and Russia. The Queen's intelligence agents must know of his intentions and sent Asquith to prevent a murder and international conflict." Mr. Tatum paced the room and continued talking. "He has had time to reach St. Petersburg. It is up to us to stop him. In the years ahead, England needs Russia as an ally."

"We still don't know who killed Lord Asquith. Who would have the most to gain by the tsar's assassination? Doyle, do you suspect any of the Americans?"

"An American at dinner swore revenge on the Russians for killing their president but seemed to be a harmless drunk. I don't trust that Count von Wittenberg."

"Penelope, tell us more about this German fellow."

Was it accidental? On purpose? Penelope spilled her tea and then rubbed the dark stain on her dress. "I hardly know him. He is just a casual acquaintance."

Dr. Bell sat up straighter and fiddled with his pipe. "He is German and probably an enemy of Russia. Surely, Miss Walshingham, you can learn more."

"We should also consider the Russian students in steerage. I have made a new friend who invited me to a party," I said.

"Good. Do look in on them this evening."

An hour later, Penelope and I met Dostoevsky. He was still pale and walked with a stumbling, feeble gait. I held his arm as we descended stairs into the depths of the ship. The air grew dank with the smell of cooking and unwashed bodies in the crowded steerage compartment. At the lowest level, we entered a cramped, ill-lit room. A dozen plainly dressed men and women, all about my age, were smoking and drinking. As we entered, their animated conversation stopped and hostile faces turned our way.

Dostoevsky gestured toward us. "Mes amis."

I felt suspicion mingled with curiosity, despite Dostoevsky's introduction. The hostility broke when, to my great surprise, Penelope rattled off what must have been a joke, in Russian. They laughed and offered drinks. She went off with three men to a table in the corner. They greeted her with what seemed an easy familiarity. Could they have been students at Cambridge? It didn't seem likely.

"They are elitists, radical students who have studied with Marx in London and want to overthrow the tsar," Dostoevsky whispered.

Perhaps, it was my Irish half that hated authority, but I sympathized with the students. As I looked around the group, I was drawn to a buxom young woman with a long braid of blonde hair that hung down over her back. She caught my eye and smiled. "I am Vera Nayechev," she said, in good English.

I took her hand. "Dr. Arthur Conan Doyle."

"Ah, how delightful. I am a medical student."

"I am with Dr. Joseph Bell who is to give a series of lectures. Perhaps, you will attend his demonstrations in St. Petersburg. So, why were you in England?"

"We studied with Karl Marx in London. Our task is to teach the peasants and make them understand the tsar is not their 'little father,' but their oppressor."

Before I could gather my wits to answer, a bulky fellow with red hair and beard pulled her aside and gave me a fierce scowl.

Dostoevsky raised his hand for silence. "Calm yourselves, please. The new tsar is more kind and generous. Revolution will only lead to anarchy and the death of us all. We must support all Slavs and bring peace to Russia."

Vera Nayechev pulled me closer. "He is sick and old and should not speak like this. Nicholas I put him in prison and sentenced him to death, but at the last minute, he commuted the death sentence and sent him to Siberia. He should be anti-tsarist, but he has sympathy with our oppressors," she said.

The author left after his speech. Vera, rather stealthily, rubbed the inside of my wrist with her hand. Was it just an absent Russian gesture or an invitation? While I dallied with Vera, I kept an eye on Penelope. She didn't touch a drop of alcohol and remained in deep conversation with the Russians.

I had more vodka and dozed off but awakened when two white uniformed sailors placed a cauldron of beet soup and a platter of dark bread with a round of cheese on the table. Was it my imagination, or was there a whiff of that same sweetish odor that Dr. Bell thought was opium? Almost always, Bell is correct, but in this case, I thought he was definitely wrong. Yet, I could not place the odor. What was it?

The party broke up in the wee hours of the morning and I took Penelope to her room, expecting at least a long, goodnight kiss. Instead, she rather rudely pushed me away without even a friendly squeeze. Had I done something to offend her? Might she have been upset that I was sitting with Vera?

8 August 1881

In the wee hours of the morning, as I lay in bed trying to sleep, a pleasant memory returned. The sweetish odor was associated with food, but what kind of food? It reminded me of a special meal, but what was it?

I dozed off and dreamed of our traditional family Christmas dinner and my mother's lovely, glazed, baked ham, studded with cloves. When I awoke, I knew, instantly, that the faint odor in Lord Asquith's room had not been opium, but, rather, was cloves.

Over breakfast, I told Dr. Bell of my theory. He listened with rising excitement. "Very good, lad. Very good." He struck his forehead. "Yes, of course, cloves … I should have known. In the Far East, natives smoke cloves mixed with tobacco instead of opium. Someone on this ship smokes clove cigarettes. Doyle, see if you can learn more."

I was on deck, idling along, when I ran into Billy, the horn piper, scrubbing the deck. "Morning sir," he said.

"Billy, have you been with the ship for long?"

"Since she was commissioned, sir."

"Do you know of a crewmember who smokes clove cigarettes?"

"No, sir, I don't."

I slipped him an American silver dollar. "I am curious. It is a pleasant smoke. Let me know if you find a man who mixes cloves and tobacco."

Billy smiled. "I shall make inquiries."

He returned to his work. I poked into the crew's quarters and sniffed the air, but found nothing. By the end of the evening, Billy had not reported back. This struck me as strange but I was tired, so I came to my room to get some sleep.

9 August 1881

We were at breakfast when the first officer approached us. "Excuse me for interrupting your breakfast, but the doctor requests your immediate assistance in the sick bay," he whispered.

He could have been asleep on the sick bay examining table, but the body of Billy the sailor was in the first stage of rigor mortis. A stoker had found his body crumpled in a passageway forward of the crew's quarters. Fortunately, the officers and masters-at-arms had whisked the body away to the sick bay before the passengers were up and about.

Billy had been the picture of health. His body was tall and athletic — a blue-eyed, blonde Viking. Who could have struck down this man and why?

I was dumbfounded and guilty. Was I responsible for his death because I set him to discover the user of clove cigarettes? It was with great trepidation that I told Bell of my involvement.

Dr. Bell flicked open his pocket magnifying glass and commenced a minute examination; first the head and neck, then hands and arms, and on down the body to the feet. There were no marks of violence, no bruises, no hair or skin beneath the fingernails suggesting a scuffle. There was the odor of beer in his mouth, but nothing else. He searched the skin for a tell-tale pin prick — a place where an assailant could have inserted a long needle into the brain or the chest.

"A mirror and a light, please," he said.

Bell adjusted the gaslight, bent the head back, and I shined reflected light from the mirror while he examined the interior of the nasal cavity with a speculum.

"Well, well, look at this."

There, high in the back of the nose, were a few drops of blood. "Very clever. The assailant grabbed Billy from behind, bent back his head, and inserted a long needle into his nose. The assailant knows human anatomy well enough to stab through the thin base of the skull and on into the brain. Billy was instantly paralyzed and died within minutes."

Neither the ship's doctor nor Captain Veery argued against an autopsy. Dr. Bell, rather casually, assigned to me the task of slicing through the scalp and sawing off the skull cap while he took his usual morning stroll on deck. He returned, an hour later, just as I was lifting the brain from the base of the skull.

"There, a needle track. Doyle, hold the lens while I dissect." The faint needle went from the base of the brain upward through the vital respiratory center.

He put down the scalpel and wiped his hands. "Aye, indeed, our Billy did find the murderer. Unfortunately, before he could bring the villain to justice, he became one of his victims," he said, almost to himself.

I felt awful for being involved in sending him to his untimely demise, and when the autopsy was complete, I returned to our cabin and sulked for a bit.

That afternoon, the ship disembarked passengers at Copenhagen, but none of the crew left the ship. After another long dinner, I couldn't sleep and prowled the deck until quite late. We had entered the Baltic Sea and now had a strong wind on our stern. The ship rushed through the waves. There were fleeting glimpses of the Big Dipper and the North Star through ragged clouds.

It was peculiar that we were on a southern course, rather than east to St. Petersburg. I stopped to light a smoke and noticed a figure in a long, dark cloak forward of the bridge. As I watched, I became more and more convinced it was Penelope. What was she doing, alone on deck at this time of night?

I caught up with her. It was indeed Penelope. I immediately hoped for another passionate embrace or a little snuggle, but she drew back into the folds of her dark cloak.

"Are you following me?"

"No, I chanced to be on deck, and there you were. Would you care for a drink in the lounge?"

"Leave me alone."

"But, there is a murderer about. You might be in danger. I will not leave until you are safely in your room."

It seemed like a calculated move, rather than a romantic impulse. She flung her arms around my neck and offered her lips for another passionate kiss. “Help me,” she breathed. “Come along and be of some use.” As if under a spell, I followed without a word. She led the way forward to a hatch cover. “Lift it,” she said.

I followed her down a steel ladder forty or fifty feet deep into the very bowels of the ship. It was a cavernous space, as dark as a black, tropical night. She fumbled in a voluminous purse, found a lucifer, and lit a small bulldog lantern. In the flare of the light, I could see three large crates in the center of a cargo hold.

“This is supposed to be a passenger ship. Why is it carrying cargo?” I asked.

“Don’t ask questions. Stay on guard,” she hissed.

Penelope shined the lantern about the cavernous space and focused on three huge wooden crates chained to bolts. The words ‘Brooklyn Navy Yard’ were printed in large, black letters on the center crate.

I clung to the ladder for support against the rolling ship and felt, as much as heard, the relentless crashing of waves against the bow. Penelope moved about, probing here and there with a folding knife until she disappeared on the far side of the crates. I was left alone in pitch dark, clinging to the ladder and feeling more and more sea sick from the pitching and rolling of the ship. Hot acid rose in my throat.

I spit foul saliva onto the steel floor and swallowed. What was she looking for? Seconds lengthened to minutes. Except for occasional flashes of light from her lantern, the hold was chill and completely dark. I shivered when the thought of a tomb crossed my mind. Was it my heightened imagination, or was there a faint tremor in the ladder? I heard the faintest scrape of shoe leather against a steel rung and I thought it was the killer with his lethal needle coming to murder both of us.

In the darkened hold, the figure descending the ladder was invisible, but his raspy breathing and the scrape of his shoe came closer and closer. Where should I go? How could I stay alive? I was close to panic. We were in a trap and the killer had us at his mercy.

I didn’t dare call out to alert Penelope but braced myself for an attack. At the very moment the figure reached the bottom rung, Penelope emerged from behind the crates. She shined the lantern directly on me, and in an instant, a small revolver appeared in her other hand. Was it my imagination? Was she aiming the gun at me or the intruder?

The *click* of another revolver was only a foot or so from my ear. I lashed out at the shadowy figure by the ladder with a fist and struck solid bone. His gun went off with a tremendous roar, but the killer went down without a sound.

In an instant, I had him in a choke-hold, yet he was already unconscious from my blow to his head. I twisted the revolver from his inert hand just as Penelope cried out. "For God's sakes … Don't kill him!"

"Penelope, are you hurt?" I screamed.

Did anger flare in her eyes? For an instant, I had the feeling she had expected the intruder and that I had interrupted a secret meeting. Then, her demeanor seemed to change and Penelope almost cooed. "I'm fine, shaken but unhurt. You're as dashing a young man as your uncle. Bravo. I owe you a kiss."

My anger drained away. She shined her lantern on the intruder's face. He was the American engineer, Gritz, unconscious but still breathing. Penelope went through his pockets and found nothing, then searched the inside of his waistcoat. There was only a thick wallet, but she wasn't interested in the contents. "Damn. Oh, damn," she muttered. "It isn't here."

"What are you looking for?"

She flashed another hard look. "Nothing, nothing at all… Now, Arthur, sweetheart, listen to me. This has to look like an accident."

"How?"

"We must take him to the deck and you report to the ship's officers. Please, Arthur, if you care for me, say nothing about this incident. I cannot tell you more, but you must trust me. It is part of my secret work as a spy for the Crown."

She believed in me to help make things right for her. My suspicions melted away. It was impossible to refuse this beautiful woman, and besides, she was practically a relative, even though Uncle Declan was dead. However, I also knew the body would be too heavy for me to carry on my own. "Sorry, Penelope. I want to help, but his body is dead weight and there is no way I can carry him straight up that ladder," I said.

Penelope swept the revolver from the floor and leveled it at my chest.

"Fine, I can kill you and give him another good rap on the head. You will both be dead. It will look like you killed each other."

"But why would you do that?"

"Your uncle is dead, so what if another Foley joins him?"

What a ghastly creature! I half-wondered if she was joking, but realized she was serious, clearly mad, and without any scruples. Though I wanted to abandon her right then, I still enjoyed the thought of her passionate kisses and, if I wanted to live, I could not resist her gun, her steely eye, and the tension of her finger on the trigger. "Aye, then. Let us give it a try," I sighed.

"That's a good lad." She smiled. "I would not want to harm you."

"You always get your way."

"That I do."

It was a long and weary task. With great difficulty, I hoisted the man's dead weight on my back with his arms crossed in front of my chest. There was a ripping sound as Penelope tore strips from her dress, which she twisted into ropes.

She then bound his arms across my chest so I could carry him with my hands free to grasp the ladder. Up we went, rung by each painful rung, as I dragged two hundred extra pounds on my back. I was near exhaustion when I reached the closed hatch. It was dogged down and wouldn't budge.

I couldn't let go of the ladder to turn the locking handle. The man on my back moaned and feebly moved, as if he was waking up. It was a devilish situation. I could have dropped the bastard. "Goddamnit! We are trapped!" I gasped.

"Idiot! God knows how you made it through medical school. Let me by," hissed Penelope, who was still below on the ladder.

By moving aside only a few inches, Penelope was just able to climb by. She angrily bumped me as she went up the ladder and released the locking handle, opening the hatch. The engineer moaned as I moved through the hatch and collapsed on deck. He opened his eyes and began to move once again, but Penelope smashed the butt of the revolver against his head and he went back out cold for a second time.

"What? Woman, are you completely insane?"

"It was nothing."

"Nothing? You could've killed him!"

"I didn't hit him that hard. He has to be unconscious long enough for us to get away. Report him to the officers and take him to sick bay."

The third officer and the master-at-arms believed my story of finding the victim passed out on the deck during an evening stroll. The American engineer was unconscious, but breathing regularly. The ship's doctor examined him in sick bay.

"I would wager the fellow had a bit to drink and fell on deck; happens all the time," he said.

"I will be happy to stay with him," I said.

"That would be kind of you. It's getting late and I want to retire for the night."

"I'll sit with him until he comes around," said I.

"Fine. And if you'd lock up when you go, it would be much appreciated."

I nodded and the ship's doctor departed. Penelope arrived in less than an hour wearing a stunning new evening dress. She tucked the cleaned and reloaded revolver and his fat wallet into the engineer's waistcoat pocket. When the fellow woke up, there would be nothing missing. She was very clever, but what was behind her actions? Did she really spy for the Crown, or could she be some sort of double or triple agent?

When the fellow woke up, he was disoriented and amnesic. I offered to walk him back to his quarters, but he refused and shakily left the sick bay. After locking up, I went on deck for fresh air and a bit of a walk. I stretched my back and shoulders, which ached from carrying the damn engineer. I wearily sat in the shadow of a lifeboat to have a smoke.

The ship was entering a narrow channel that led to a brightly-lit naval shipyard in the city of Kiel. A tugboat guided the

Servia alongside a long embankment with a huge steam-driven crane ablaze with gas lights.

The passengers were still sleeping off another large dinner, but to my amazement, the German, Count von Wittenberg, accompanied by the Americans, appeared on deck.

"Where is Mr. Gritz?" the count asked.

"Don't know. We haven't seen him since dinner," one American said.

The count spat on the deck. "*Mein lieber gott*! Damn imbeciles! Find him."

German workers swarmed onto the deck, opened the forward hatch, and led massive cables down into the hold. In less than half an hour, the three large crates were lifted out and deposited on the embankment. The crane then rolled away, and another machine with a long conveyer belt poured coal into the hold.

The Americans appeared, assisting the wobbly engineer, now a familiar figure, out of the darkness. At the same time, Penelope, shrouded in a cloak, glided to Count von Wittenberg. There was a moment's conversation, then she disappeared as silently as she had arrived. The entire affair was most mysterious. The pouring of the coal appeared to be a cover to hide the unloading of the secret cargo.

So then, the question remained — what was the secret cargo? What was in those three huge crates, and why was Penelope involved with the German, as well as the Americans? Why was she so cozy with the Russian students? Was I really in love with her, or was this another one of my infatuations? My poor head whirled with these contradictory thoughts.

Dawn was breaking as the ship churned into the Baltic Sea. I returned to my cabin and rolled into my bunk without even undressing.

10 August 1881

My rest was short-lived. It seemed as if it was only minutes after I had gone to bed that I was awakened by Mr. Tatum, who entered our cabin with a pot of strong tea, cups, milk, and sugar on a tray. Even thought it was quite early in the morning, Dr. Bell was already at his writing desk.

I roused and splashed water from the basin over my face.

"Well, Doyle, what were you up to last night?" Dr. Bell asked.

I toweled off the water and gratefully accepted a cup of tea from Mr. Tatum. "I was with Miss Walshingham and aided an unconscious passenger who fell on deck," I said.

"Were you up and about when the ship stopped in Kiel?" Mr. Tatum asked. How did he know? I didn't want to be caught out in another lie. "Yes," I answered.

Mr. Tatum did not seem the least bit surprised. "Miss Walshingham will join us following breakfast," he said.

Penelope entered our quarters. "What is the meaning of this?" she imperiously asked.

"If you, as you say, are a courier for the Royal Navy, explain your relationship with Count von Wittenburg and your interest in the cargo that was unloaded in a German port." Mr. Tatum said.

"The count is an old family friend." Penelope tossed her head as if in contempt of Mr. Tatum. "We were merely admiring the sky when the ship stopped in Kiel."

"Surely, the count confided in you about the contents of the crates from America?" Mr. Tatum asked.

"I wouldn't know."

"Miss Walshingham, do you have anything further to say about this matter?"

My heart melted when she inclined her head with a toss of her lovely hair. "No, nothing. Nothing at all," she barely murmured, before turning on her heels and walking out of the cabin.

By that afternoon, we were in the Gulf of Finland and still had not discovered the murderer. The captain reluctantly agreed to Bell's request to search the crew's possessions.

We followed the tall, surly master-at-arms through the crew's quarters. There was the usual grumbling over the confiscation of alcohol, knives, and a small Smith & Wesson pistol. However, the officers found nothing that could have been the murder weapon.

Dr. Bell followed, rather nonchalantly swinging his cane and puffing his pipe, yet, he intently inspected each man's possessions, which were laid out on the bunks.

We came, at last, to the galley. Much to our surprise, one of the cooks looked to be Chinese.

"You assured us that your crew was made up entirely of Americans and Scandinavians, did you not?" Dr. Bell asked.

"We don't count the cooks as crew," Captain Veery gruffly responded. "See here, this man is harmless." The captain took a step towards the Chinese cook, and then, suddenly, all hell broke loose.

The Chinaman spun about, threw a pot of boiling water at the huge master-at-arms, who ducked, but the Cook came on and, with a violent, skull-crushing kick, felled the master-at-arms. "English dogs!" shouted the Chinaman, as he spun about and smashed a two-handed blow to the abdomen of the second officer.

He let out a loud "Hee-yah!" with each blow.

I went in for a tackle, lost my balance, but was close enough to see the yellowish tints in his eyes and sweat dripping off his chin. "Death to English! Hee-yah!"

His long, high-pitched scream ended when he whipped a long knife from the back of his belt. In an instant, he held the long, curved blade to the captain's throat. "Release me in St. Petersburg or the captain dies!" he shouted.

I stood, frozen, incredulous at the Chinaman's impressive martial arts skills. Dr. Bell, however, remained cool as ever. "Damn you. Unhand him," he said.

"No. I will kill him first."

With a mere twitch of his hand, Dr. Bell flicked out the blade of his cane and drove it through the Chinaman's right arm.

"Ahh!" Spittle streamed from his lips as he dropped the knife and writhed on the deck in great pain, his right hand paralyzed and useless. Bell had severed the median nerve.

The master-at-arms and the first officer subdued the howling Chinaman and tied his hands behind his back.

Meanwhile, Bell examined the cook's seaman's bag and found a carved wooden box, which contained a beautiful set of slender steel needles varying in size from one to eight inches in length. I had never seen anything like them, but it was clear that they were the murder weapons. Dr. Bell continued his search and withdrew a fifty pound note tucked beneath the lining of the box. "Captain Veery, is this not a lot of money for a cook?"

"Indeed, the man must have been a thief as well as a killer," the captain said. "I will place it in the crew's fund."

Dr. Bell slipped the brand new note into his wallet and, with a clever sleight of hand, gave the captain a different bill. In the excitement, the episode slipped my mind until much later.

An hour later, Penelope, rather breathlessly, joined Bell and me in our stateroom. Dr. Bell blew a cloud of smoke. "He was a practitioner of acupuncture, one of the most ancient of the healing arts, and for reasons yet to be known, he used his knowledge to commit murder. It is even more puzzling because, according to the first mate, the cook was educated by British missionaries in Hong Kong."

Penelope put down her cup. "Lord Asquith's last assignment was Chairman of the British Committee on Opium in Shanghai. The missionaries bitterly opposed the British practice of selling opium to the Chinese."

"Indeed, you are a knowledgeable young woman. Selling opium and enslaving a nation with a heinous addiction is inexcusable, yet murder is never a solution." Bell pressed his fingers together. "Ah, the fifty pound note. Now, there is a mystery," he mused.

Her face contorted into a featureless mask and Penelope rose abruptly. "I must pack," she said. Penelope swished out the door of our cabin while Dr. Bell watched her lovely retreat with amusement, or was it a speculative look? Did he believe the darling girl?

Later, Penelope and I went on deck to see the Russian Baltic fleet at anchor off the Kronstadt naval base on Kotlin Island. The *Servia* gave three long blasts of the ship's horn and dipped the U.S. flag as we steamed past cruisers, destroyers, and torpedo boats.

"Your friend, the German count, is taking a great interest in the Russian fleet," I said.

"He is to be the naval attaché to the German Embassy," Penelope answered.

Merchant ships from all over the world were anchored in the harbor, and a small trim yawl wound through the huge anchorage. Two tugs nudged the *Servia* alongside the long, stone-covered embankment at the passenger port on the west end of Vasilievsky Island. Once the *Servia* reached its slip, the crew let down the gangplanks with a great clatter of chain.

Armed guards from the British and American embassies came aboard and conducted a grim procession off the ship with the shrouded bodies on stretchers followed by the chained and manacled Chinese cook. He was docile as the guards dragged him across the deck, but in front of Penelope, the Chinaman jerked to a halt. Hatred spilled from his eyes as he spit a glob of mucous at her feet. Her face went dead-white but she said nothing.

The British soldiers roughly hauled at his chains. He followed, docile as a whipped dog, but on the gangplank, midway between the ship and shore, he shrieked, wrenched free, and jumped to his death in the frigid water. The passengers gasped and fled the 'bad luck' ship to waiting carriages.

When we were disembarking, I had hoped for a kiss, or at least a fond farewell, but Penelope left the ship arm in arm with the German, Count von Wittenberg. She never so much as glanced my way. Was it my imagination, or was she being coerced?

As the couple neared the line of waiting carriages, a black phaeton, drawn by a pair of fine-looking horses, drew up across the street. Penelope appeared to be confused, twisted her arm from the German's grip, and seemed to recognize the two men in dark suits and derby hats who rushed from the phaeton. Count von Wittenberg threw an arm around her shoulder and tried to push her into his carriage. Then, just as the carriage door was about to close, the two men wrenched her free. Had she intended to go with the count? Were the strangers abducting Penelope?

I flung open the instrument case and fumbled for the secret compartment. In an instant, I had the Webley revolver out and held in wobbly hands. Though I had fired a gun before, I still felt nervous. My intention was to fire a warning shot, but Mr. Tatum roughly restrained my arm and took the gun. "No, Doyle. Don't!" he said, in his Sergeant-Major voice. "Don't interfere."

I slumped, utterly defeated, and watched helplessly as the wretches tumbled Penelope into the light carriage and sped away towards the city.

I was still reeling from her apparent abduction, when, in the tumult on the dock, Dr. Aleksey Sechenov, our host at the medical school, arrived in a sumptuous blue and white carriage drawn by matching grey horses.

Two liveried footmen whisked our baggage to the boot while my new friend, Cowboy Bill, directed two stevedores to carry a stout cage containing a mass of hissing, writhing rattlesnakes to a waiting wagon. "Ah my limey friend, young Doyle. Did you have a good voyage?" asked Cowboy Bill.

"It was certainly unusual and eventful."

"Come visit me and my snakes if you have time in St. Pete."

"I will."

"And speaking of snakes, hope you kept yours in your pants the whole trip, eh pardner?" he asked, with a wink.

Before I could answer, a footman handed me into the carriage. I sat on a plush velvet seat across from Professor Sechenov who was elegantly turned out in fawn-colored tight breeches and a grey coat. "Is St. Petersburg safe these days?" I asked, still a bit shaken and unsure of the meaning of Penelope's abduction.

"Oui. There have been a few problems with student anarchist groups, but I trust that you will be as safe as in Edinburgh."

Sechenov's soft voice soothed my frazzled nerves. He explained how Peter the Great had built this city on marshland with slave labor. I was soon lost in wonder as we sped past wide canals with granite embankments, magnificent brick and stone buildings with white trim, then down a wide avenue along the Neva River. Magnificent buildings and cathedrals with blue, onion-shaped domes glowed in the soft golden afternoon light.

"How beautiful!" I pointed to a long building with two columns. "What is that?"

Professor Sechenov answered in impeccable French, which I learned was the language of the Russian nobility and intelligentsia. "The stock exchange."

Within a few minutes, we turned onto another broad street, Bolshoi Prospekt, and then into the driveway of his home, our quarters during our stay in St. Petersburg.

An obsequious footman led us through a drawing room — well-lit with gold chandeliers and filled with dark, well-upholstered furniture — and then up a curving staircase to the second floor. Dr. Bell enjoyed a bedroom with an adjoining sitting room, while I had a simple, but adequate room overlooking a garden and the buildings of the university.

After a bit of discussion, our host found a room for Mr. Tatum on our floor, rather than in the servant's quarters. A few minutes' exploration revealed a small rear stairway that led to a pantry, the servants' quarters, or the kitchen. Another possible exit was from the balcony down a convenient rain pipe to the garden. I was nicely settled when it was time to dress for dinner.

The guests assembled in the dining room consisted of St. Petersburg's leading physicians, government officials, aristocrats, and Dr. Piragoff, a high-ranking military officer and surgeon known for his work with the wounded of both sides during the Crimean war. There were toasts to the tsar and the Queen, then to Dr. Bell, the guest of honor.

When they learned that I was neither a nobleman nor a professor, but little more than a peasant, I was soon ignored and left to my own devices to enjoy the caviar, champagne, and to overhear the somber undertones of the guests.

I soon learned that the royal family, in mortal fear for their lives, was in virtual isolation at Anichkof Palace. The secret police were scouring the city for anarchists, terrorists, and members of the intelligentsia who were suspected of plotting to kill the new tsar.

I suddenly thought of Penelope. Was she in the hands of the secret police because of her relationship with Uncle Declan and Captain David Campbell? Or did British agents take her to the British ambassador with the message? Would she search for the officer who, crazed by vengeance, would kill the tsar and throw all of Europe into war?

I could not know the answer, but I was certain that our stay here in St. Petersburg would be filled with danger and intrigue. It was sometime after two in the morning, when the party broke up and I stumbled, dazed by drink, to my room. Waiting at the door, the porter passed an envelope into my hand.

Dr. Doyle,

If you will, please join me with a group of fellow students for lunch at The Beranger at noon tomorrow.

Vera Nayechev

I was intrigued and planned to join them at noon. The rest of the day was uneventful. The bed with a down filled mattress felt wonderful.

11 August 1881

The Beranger, a coffee house, was evidently a favourite meeting place for university students. Dark and musty, it was packed with young people drinking and smoking. There were no empty tables and no Vera.

Then, I made my way through thick tobacco smoke to the stairs and up to the second floor. There she was, at a table overlooking Nevsky Prospekt, St. Petersburg's main street. Vera looked as she did that night when I was with Dostoevsky on the ship, but she was calmer and more refined. She was with three men, one of whom was the sour, stocky, red-headed fellow with the beard whom I had met on the *Servia*.

"Ah, Dr. Doyle. Welcome. Please, sit… Are you enjoying your stay in our fair city?" she asked.

"Yes, I love the architecture. Reminds me of Paris," I answered.

"Ah, so have you spent a lot of time in Paris?"

"No, but I have read a great deal about Paris, and St. Petersburg reminds me of what I think it would look like."

"Peter the Great yearned for this city to rival Paris in its beauty. If only the modern tsars were as enlightened as Peter."

I had only a moment to order tea when the red-bearded one fixed me with piercing, green eyes. "You were present when Foley died, yes?" he asked.

"Yes."

"What were his last words?"

I had to think for a moment, and then remembered his words. "He said something very strange. He mentioned a Dr. Hutton and no God and the end of the old regime."

"He said this?"

"Yes, but his final words were, 'Tsar die.' "

Red relaxed for a moment. "He was one of us."

"Silence!" Another student, a slight, owlish fellow with round, dark glasses, raised his hand. "How do we know we can trust this damned Englishman?"

Vera interjected on my behalf. "He saved Dostoevsky's life."

"Bah. That old man can write, but sometimes I question his loyalties, too."

"And this boy's people, the Irish, were persecuted by the English Crown. He has a natural sympathy with our cause," Vera said, as she put her hand on top of mine.

"Aye, I have Irish blood, and aye, I am a friend of anyone who befriended my Uncle Declan." I said.

"I like this Irishman! I am Sviazhky. Welcome to Russia. Lt. Foley was your relative?"

"Aye."

"Any relative of Foley is a friend of mine." Red embraced me with a bear hug. "I had a good feeling about you since I first laid eyes upon you. Your uncle was studying our Russian people and intended to go among the peasants, disguised as a priest, to explain Darwin's theory, debunk God, and stir up the serfs against the church and the tsar."

I was more perplexed than ever. "But he was an English military officer who fought against your country in Afghanistan. I don't understand."

"He knew he was fighting the tsar and the nobility, not the people. He swore vengeance and joined our group in London."

"What exactly does your group believe?"

"For our revolution to succeed, we must break the peasants of their habit of obeisance to the church and the tsar. They actually believe that he is anointed by God and this belief must be destroyed."

I nodded and glanced at my watch.

"I apologize. Dr. Bell is giving a demonstration at two," I said. "Sorry, but it will not look good if I am late. I should go, but hopefully, I will see you there."

When I arrived at the medical school lecture hall, distinguished physicians and the school's faculty were seated in the front row. Sun poured in from a skylight and lit the space. The walls were whitewashed and the tile floor showed old blood stains. Glass-fronted cabinets held surgical instruments and rolls of gauze. As in

Edinburgh, the room was both a lecture hall and operating theater. What seats were still open rapidly filled with excited students, as motley a bunch as my Edinburgh classmates. Vera and her group sat down near the center, surrounded by roughly-clad young men from the country. Furthest in the back were rather elegant, bored, young aristocrats.

I sat with Dr. Bell in the front row, still at somewhat of a loss to explain my encounter with the young anarchists. Professor Sechenov stood behind a podium and spoke in French. In fact, all the students and faculty spoke French in class.

Sechenov removed his pince-nez and peered at the audience. "Our first patient is paralyzed by a spinal cord tumor. I have invited Dr. Joseph Bell, an esteemed Professor of Surgery at Edinburgh Medical College, to perform the operation. Dr. Bell, if you will . . ."

Dr. Bell went into the cockpit. I followed to assist or give the anaesthetic, but was immediately anxious. Operations for spinal cord tumors were rarely, if ever, successful. Was this a cunning Russian trap to make a foreign doctor look bad? I had thought Dr. Bell would teach and maybe see some patients, but I had no idea we were about to engage in major surgery.

The patient, on the wheeled stretcher, was an attractive woman of perhaps thirty years. She was on her back, covered with a sheet. Dr. Bell was clearly not prepared for surgery, and I wondered how he was going to handle this unusual situation.

"Good afternoon. May I have your name, please?" Dr. Bell asked.

"Lydia Sorokina," she answered in a low-pitched, barely audible voice.

"Miss Sorokina, how long have you been paralyzed?"

"Almost three weeks."

The professor drew back the sheet, exposing her muscular legs. He examined the soles of her feet and barely touched a callous on her great toe.

"You are a ballerina?"

“Yes, I danced with the Bolshoi,” she whispered. Her eyes filled with tears. “Today, I can no longer dance, and that is why I am here. It is my dream to dance again.”

The professor palpated the muscles in her thighs and calves and struck the patellar tendon at the knee with a reflex hammer. The lower leg responded normally with a jump. Next, he held her ankle and tapped the Achilles tendon. At each tap of the hammer, a muscle contracted and her ankle flexed. He stroked the sole of her foot; the great toe turned down, a normal Babinski reflex.

He then checked her sensation with a long needle. There was no response to a light pinprick or even when he drove the needle a half-centimeter into her skin. She did not flinch.

“Dr. Doyle, would you determine the level of sensory loss?”

I hesitated, then pulled the sheet below her waist, exposing her breasts. The young students in the gallery whistled and made lewd remarks. Professor Sechenov silenced them angrily. “Enough of that, please!”

I overcame my timidity and, commencing at her thighs, first touched her skin with a wisp of cotton, then with a sharp pin. She made no response until, at the level of her umbilicus, she winced at the prick of pin. She had no sensation below the level of her umbilicus. The level of sensory loss had no connection to the nervous innervation but was in a perfect ring around her body and, seemingly, bore no relation to her muscle paralysis. I was completely confused.

Dr. Bell watched her responses with lowered eyelids while a mere hint of a smile played over his lips. It was then that I knew he was up to one of his old tricks.

Suddenly, he upended the stretcher. “Dance again, young lady,” he said.

Had Dr. Bell lost his mind? The students and faculty sucked in their breath as the surprised young woman slid off the stretcher and landed on her feet.

For a second, there was silence. Then, she gathered the sheet about her breasts and shook her fist at the professor. “Damn you!” she shouted.

She walked out on her own two feet and left by the side door. There was much chatter amongst the audience. "Gentlemen, please, quiet down. This is a case of hysterical paralysis. Clearly, there was no need for an operation."

Many of the students clapped and cheered. Dr. Bell had done it again. Under pressure in a foreign city, he had displayed his mastery of the entire field of medicine and, indeed, the science of psychology.

The professors in the front row were silent until Sechenov stammered a few words. "How did you make that diagnosis?" he asked.

Bell cleared his throat and raised his hand to his chin. "In cases of spinal cord injury or tumor, the deep tendon reflexes of the legs, mediated by the lumbar and sacral nerves, should be absent. Her reflexes were hyperactive, suggesting an emotional state. The loss of sensation to the level of the umbilicus, as demonstrated by my associate, Dr. Doyle, bore no relationship to the normal patterns of the thoracic nerves. Gentlemen, if you enquire closely, I wager you will find a psychological reason to explain why the patient cannot dance."

Dr. Sechenov tapped the lens of his glasses against his thigh. "Yes, she was dismissed from the Bolshoi a day prior to the onset of symptoms."

Sechenov restored order with a glance and cleared his throat. "Next, Dr. Bell has been so kind to agree to demonstrate the anatomy of his operation for joint excision on a fresh cadaver."

Surgeons have often practiced and demonstrated operations on cadavers because it is easier to identify bones, nerves and tendons without the constant flow of blood to obscure the anatomy. This corpse was covered with a shroud, except for his ankles and feet. With a great sense of self-importance, I opened the instrument case on a table and arranged the scalpels, chisels, hammers, probes, and forceps, as if for a real operation. It struck me as unusual that the skin of the 'patient's' feet did not exhibit the usual lividity of death, but was absolutely dead white. I was not sure what to make of the strange pallor.

The professor removed his coat, rolled up his sleeves, and, rather dramatically, took up the razor-sharp, steel scalpel in his right hand.

"If this was an operation, instead of an anatomical dissection, we would first prepare the skin and all instruments with a solution of carbolic. However, since this man is deceased, it is not necessary."

He then applied the knife and incised the skin from the lateral malleolus of the ankle down the lateral side of the foot. There was an immediate muffled groan, and then a piercing shriek as the 'patient's' foot lifted from the table.

"Good God!" Dr. Bell stepped back and, with a single motion, applied the scalpel to the cloth and opened the shroud. He exposed the face and torso of a strongly-built, middle-aged man. His colorless lips were drawn back in a rictus of terror.

"Heavens, the man is alive!" Dr. Bell shouted. "What is the meaning of this? Is this some type of prank?"

"No, no, no. I apologize." Professor Sechenov's face went livid. He turned to his assistant. "Pavlov, this is an outrage. What is going on?"

"He was the subject for this morning's experiment; we removed all his blood. He should be dead. Dead!" Pavlov exclaimed.

With that declaration, the patient's head jerked up and down. His eyes closed. He shuddered and then became completely still. His skin was white as fresh snow, and his lips were colorless. If he was not dead when he was wheeled in, he was truly dead now.

"I am appalled." Dr. Bell lifted the right arm of the deceased. "What is this?" There was a long incision down the medial side of the arm and the brachial artery was severed. Bell sniffed at the man's mouth. "It appears as if some damned criminal performed surgery on this man without anaesthesia. What in heaven's name is going on here? This is barbaric!"

"Let me explain." Dr. Pavlov was perfectly at ease. "I am a doctor and not a criminal. I injected cocaine into the skin this morning. The operation was completely pain free. I drained blood from the artery for my work on blood coagulation. This man was found guilty of plotting against the tsar; he chose to be an experimental subject, rather than face torture and a military firing squad."

In an instant, Dr. Bell's rage gave way to his keen scientific interest. "Wait, did you anaesthetize the skin, rather than administer ether or chloroform?"

"Exactly! German chemists have isolated the active ingredient of the South American coca leaf." Pavlov held out a small container of a white powder. "Test a bit on your tongue. Your entire mouth will go perfectly numb."

Dr. Bell applied his index finger to the powder, then placed it on his tongue. "Yes, by God, my tongue is completely numb!" he exclaimed, after a moment. He bit down and drew blood from his tongue. "By Jove, Doyle, we must try this new drug. It will revolutionize surgery!"

Pavlov shook with excitement. "Simply dissolve the powder in water and inject the solution into the skin. The patient will feel nothing." Pavlov gave the container of cocaine to Dr. Bell. "Here, Doctor. Test it."

Dr. Bell placed the vial in his jacket pocket and then appeared as if all was normal. I thought, for sure, he would refuse to continue a sham operation on this newly-deceased man, but Bell didn't think twice about going ahead.

"Well, gentleman, since our subject is now truly dead, we will proceed," Dr. Bell said. And, just like that, he continued.

Dr. Bell was a church deacon and highly ethical. This was totally out of character for the professor. Had the cocaine affected his judgement?

It seemed as if his love of science blotted out his finer instincts. Had his moral principles had suddenly deserted him? He lectured as he dissected and demonstrated the anatomy of the foot and ankle with unusual brilliance.

I was horrified and repelled by Bell's display, but the others were taken in by his charisma and brilliance. The audience was truly captivated.

At the end of the demonstration, in late afternoon, Bell was mobbed by professors and doctors from all of St. Petersburg who excitedly begged him to dinners and to see their patients in consultation.

I was sickened. The more I watched these great men of science, the less I wanted to be a doctor. I had worked my whole life to become a man of medicine, but here was the heartlessness of pure science. I wanted no part of it.

12 August 1881

This morning, I couldn't shake my sick feeling about my fellow scientists. I was thinking that I should go home, give up medicine, and focus on my dream of becoming a writer. After further inner debate, though, I decided that, alas, I was too desperately poor to try anything else, especially a riskier career such as writing, so there was no alternative for me but the practice of medicine.

Thus, this morning, I dragged myself through the streets of St. Petersburg to attend lectures on chemistry and bacteriology given by two scientists with German accents. I understood most of the lectures and tried not to fall asleep.

At noon, I met Vera Nayechev for lunch. "Fyodor has spoken of your kindness to him and wishes to consult with you about his lung congestion," she said, while we ate delicious small pancakes, called blini, topped with caviar and hot soup.

I did a bit of sightseeing and, at four o'clock, reached Dostoevsky's small flat. I opened the door to the odor of decay and sickness mingled with stale beer and cabbage. A subdued group of students, writers, and a publisher was eating and drinking. Sviazhky, with the red beard, gave me an immense bear hug. He wore a grave expression on his face. "Fyodor's health is deteriorating. He is near the end," he said.

"When I saw him on the *Servia*, he appeared to have epilepsy," I said.

"It all started when he was arrested, then shackled hand and foot in the St. Peter and Paul fortress years ago. For months, he ate nothing but stale crusts of bread."

"What was his crime?"

"There was no crime. The secret police accused him of plotting against the tsar and sentenced him to death by firing squad. A priest insisted he confess his sins and kiss the cross as they led him into Semyonovsky Square. The tsar's men put a hood over his head and tied his hands, but at the last minute, Tsar Nicholas I commuted his sentence to eight years in Siberia."

"How terrible."

"Yes, and his story is not uncommon. That is why so many people want to see the end of the tsars."

After perhaps a half-hour of pleasant conversation and drinking vodka, Sviazhky flung his arms around a middle-aged man who appeared from an adjacent room. "Doyle, this is Golovinsky, the son of a man who was in Siberia with Fyodor. He is now one of Fyodor's most trusted friends."

Golovinsky gestured to me. "He is ready for you."

He took my arm and led the way into the author's small study. Dostoevsky, reclining on a chaise lounge, raised himself and languidly offered a thin, pale hand, criss-crossed by blue veins. "Ah, my young Scottish doctor. Welcome to St. Petersburg. I am glad to see you."

His face was pallid, with just a hint of freckles over his cheeks, and his beard was matted with a yellowish scum. He lay back on the lounge, covering his mouth with a soiled, blood-stained handkerchief and was convulsed with a moist, gurgling cough.

I spent a moment looking at the shelves of his books. I could not read Cyrillic but recognized many of his novels and stories. He had lived a writer's life, a life I had always dreamed about but never had the courage to pursue. This man was pure bravery, yet look at where it had gotten him — frail and sickly and dying in a hovel.

I vowed to do whatever I could with my limited skills and the meager supply of medicines in my instrument bag. Several students crowded into the room, as if expecting a miracle from the foreign doctor. There was no way that I, a recent graduate, could meet their expectations. I tried to comfort him by putting my hand on his shoulder. "So Fyodor, tell me how you are feeling."

"My cough has become insufferable and my doctors can do nothing."

"I will try to alleviate your suffering."

With my best, assumed, professional manner, I counted his pulse at the wrist. The beats were rapid and erratic, not a good sign. He had another paroxysm of coughing while I removed his shirt to percuss and auscultate his lungs. His thin chest was sunken and the ribs were prominent. There was no subcutaneous fat and only a few strands of muscle. I placed the middle finger of my left hand on his chest wall and tapped it with my right index finger. The percussion note sounded like a hammer striking an empty drum, except at the apex, where the note was flat and dull.

This was a sign of a fluid-filled cavity. One hardly needed a stethoscope to hear the gurgling rales in both lungs. I surmised that Dostoevsky was in the end stage of pulmonary tuberculosis, aggravated by years of smoking cigarettes, poor diet, and general ill health. I guessed his ailment originated in the ordeal of imprisonment and Siberian exile while he was a young man. There was little to be done except to palliate his symptoms. I poured a strong dose of laudanum into his bedside cup and wrote a prescription for menthol.

"Take as much laudanum as you wish to decrease the cough, and get this from your chemist. Place a tablespoonful in a kettle of boiling water, and inhale the steam with a towel or blanket over your head twice a day."

It was a useless nostrum, but I had learned from Dr. Bell to always prescribe something to give the patient hope — no matter what.

Dostoevsky thanked me. I lingered a while, talking with Golovinsky and Vera at the window as a half-dozen students from the flat sauntered toward the main street. Suddenly, a troop of mounted police, the Okhrana, cantered into Kuznechney Alley and, with no warning, began to beat the students with their rifle butts. "Disperse, disperse! No meetings allowed!" the policemen barked.

Two students fell with bleeding heads. Others cowed under the blows and meekly submitted to the shackles and chains. An older, stout woman — what the Russians called a babushka — showed great courage and dashed her handbag in the face of one of the officers who was beating a frail young man on the ground.

She attempted to run, but to my horror, the captain of the troop took deliberate aim with his pistol and brought the fleeing woman down with one shot. Blood spurted from her chest as she lay on the cobblestones. Then, the police dragged the shackled students away, leaving the dead woman under a dispersing cloud of gun smoke.

"This happens every day," Vera whispered. "It is the great tragedy of our lives. These horrible Okhrana round up suspects and take them away to the fortress — the ones that they have not already killed, that is."

"Is there no justice in this forsaken place?" I shouted, without thought of my hosts.

Dostoevsky finished a wracking, gurgling coughing spasm. "Watch out, my young Scottish doctor. This is not Edinburgh. If you are too loud, they will come for you, too," he said.

"Thank you, my friend," I answered.

Then, with a glance to Golovinsky, I thought I heard Dostoevsky speak. "Only one more, then I will be at peace. Now go," he whispered.

Vera took both of my hands with a firm grip. "Doyle, we should leave, but be very careful, please. I don't want you to come to harm. Keep your eyes open and your mouth shut."

I thanked her for the advice, which sounded like what Dr. Bell had said all through medical school.

It was near dusk when we left Dostoevsky's flat. Bright red sprays of light reflected from western clouds but the day had turned gloomy. Vera tucked her arm through mine and we cautiously walked out onto the street. Ah, I felt a growing warmth for this strange, but delicious young woman who was concerned for my well-being.

"Come, Dr. Doyle, we will not allow the secret police to spoil our day."

She held me so close that an observer might have thought we were lovers. Was she, like Penelope, playing me for another purpose? She was a sensuous, full-bodied woman with a scent of roses. I was attracted to her bosom thrusting against a thin blouse.

We lingered at the Bronze Horseman — the bigger than life statue of Peter the Great astride a magnificent horse — and watched the Neva peacefully flow into the Gulf. I loved the way she thrust herself against my body and enjoyed inhaling her scent.

She pulled me towards her. "I must leave, but let us meet again at the Beranger, let us say, at three o'clock," she said. The brush of my mouth on her face soon turned into a very satisfactory lip-bruising kiss.

"Yes, tomorrow at three o'clock."

Upon my return, Bell was jittery, nervous, and poised with a syringe and a needle over his bared left arm. "Ah, good! Doyle, you are just in time to witness a great surgical advance. I shall inject three cubic centimeters of cocaine and water into my skin."

He inserted the needle, depressed the plunger, and immediately relaxed.

"Now Doyle, plunge the point of your penknife into the area of injection."

"Sir, I couldn't do that. The pain would be intense."

"Nonsense. Cocaine renders the area pain free. Think what this means to the future of surgery."

With that, he stabbed the needle deep into his arm. "Look, there is no pain."

I was worried and perplexed. Since he first tried cocaine at the lecture, Dr. Bell's behavior had alternated between bouts of euphoric hyperactivity and dreamy lethargy. I was sorry about his use of cocaine and yearned for the old caustic, cutting Bell.

I excused myself and went to my room to study and mull over the day's events. My thoughts, as they seemed to inevitably do, soon turned to Penelope. Where was she now? Was she in the clutches of the secret police in some horrid prison cell? What was the role of our mysterious Mr. Tatum? He posed as our valet, but went off on mysterious errands, and once, I heard him speak of the 'embassy men.' Was he watching over us or pursuing his own affairs?

13 August 1881

In the morning, Dr. Bell ate a good breakfast and seemed to be his usual self. We accompanied Professor Sechenov to the morgue. Dr. Bell was to demonstrate a point of anatomy involved in excision of the wrist joint, an operation used in the treatment of tuberculosis.

All morgues are dismal, but this fetid, ill-lit place was more dungeon than anatomical laboratory. We passed the mutilated victims of the secret police on the way into the dissection room where the pathologist, in his rubber apron, waited by the body of an elderly man. "No one claimed the body."

"What do you know about him?" Dr. Bell queried.

"The police found him in Semyonovsky Square with his hands shackled and his mouth stuffed with dried bread," the pathologist said.

Bell paced around the table and minutely scrutinized the body. "There is no doubt about the cause of death. There are five bullet wounds to his chest and the back of his head is blown away. It appears to be an execution."

"I agree."

"Wait." He pointed at his lower arm. "What is this? There seems to be some sort of note tied to his wrist."

The pathologist pulled the note and translated in stilted English. "I am a ridiculous man." The words made no impression on the others, but I recognized the first line from a story by Dostoevsky. But what did they mean? Why would a murderer quote Dostoevsky?

"Why would anyone kill an old, harmless man?" Sechenov asked.

"Wait, this reminds me of another peculiar message." The pathologist rummaged around on a desk littered with scraps of paper, bottles of specimens, and soiled instruments. "Ah, here it is — from the body of another elderly man with identical wounds."

He read from a soiled slip of paper. "I am a sick man, a spiteful man."

Dr. Bell dissected the metacarpal bones and the flexor tendons at the wrist with more than his usual enthusiasm and skill while lecturing in rapid-fire French.

Meanwhile, I pondered the words, *I am a sick man, a spiteful man.*

Aye, they comprised the opening line from another short story by Fyodor Dostoevsky. There had to be a connection between the notes with the quotes on them and the strange deaths of these elderly men, but what was it?

By now, I had lost interest in the anatomy lecture and I wanted to think more about the notes, so I decided on a walk to the Beranger. I must admit, I was also hoping that, as I walked, I might see Vera, even though it was before three o'clock. Why did I always become infatuated with the latest good-looking woman to cross my path? Aye, the delicious Jean, the nurse, was a mere distant flicker of my imagination. Penelope? *Well*, I thought, *she is a darling girl, but she is perhaps too prickly for me*. I was in luck. Aye, Vera was already there, sipping tea alone at a table overlooking Nevsky Prospekt. I was worried that the Russian students might be jealous of my excessive attentions to her, but they shared everything; food, drink — and even their women.

We sipped our tea and ate small cakes while Vera, in an undertone, told me about the disappearance of another student.

"Dear God, is there no justice here? How can people be treated that way?" I asked.

She gripped my arm so hard the muscle ached, while a tempestuous light came into her dark, slightly-upturned eyes. There was a hint of a wild Mongolian ancestry in her high cheekbones and the tiniest of slants of her eyes. "My dearest Doyle, please come with me tonight and you will see real Russian justice."

I could not say no; we arranged to meet at midnight.

We wore dark cloaks against the light rain and huddled in the misty shadows of the old regimental headquarters overlooking Semyonovsky Square. I grew sleepy and would have been happy to leave, but Vera clutched my arm and insisted that we stay, even through the night, if necessary. To keep me from falling asleep, she gave me kisses and rubbed my back. Her attention was so lovely that I would have happily stayed with her for the whole night.

Shortly after the clock struck three, the gentle clip-clop of approaching hooves could be heard, and soon, two darkened carriages entered the square. We scarcely breathed while two men jumped from one of the carriages and erected a small platform with a sturdy pole in the center of the square.

I heard a piteous, stifled cry from the second carriage, then, two men dragged a struggling victim to the platform and bound him to the pole. His face was, for a moment, bathed in the light of a hooded lantern. A small, hunched, feeble figure then emerged from the first carriage and slowly approached the platform. "It is him."

The hunched man held a large silver cross to the victim's lips. "Damn you. Kiss the cross." The victims head inclined and his lips touched the cross. There was a long, gurgling cough and five muffled shots. I was horrified by it all. How could they call this barbarity justice?

The man's body sagged against the pole.

Then, a final shot rang out — the *coup de grace* — to end the victim's suffering. The two carriages vanished as quickly as they had arrived. A moment later, the square was silent. It didn't seem possible that six shots would not arouse the neighbors.
"Why haven't the shots stirred anyone?"

"Our people are afraid. Gunfire usually means the secret police, and no one wants to create trouble," Vera whispered.

"He may be alive. We must help that poor man."

"No. Leave him alone."

Heedless of Vera's warnings, I set off toward the victim. "It is our duty."

Vera followed me. "Dr. Doyle, stop. No."

I reached the poor man and I struck a lucifer. His eyes were filmed over by death. The lifeless lips barely touched a large crucifix hanging around his neck and resting on his chest. The dead man wore the vestments of an old priest.

There was nothing to be done; Vera dragged me away. No one appeared — not the secret police or any citizens — and we were lucky to escape without any problems. We walked along the river, thankful for the darkened, misty night. My confused thoughts would make nothing of Vera. Was she a vicious anarchist, bent on murder, or, as I had once hoped, a medical student who valued and saved lives? How could justice be cruelty and revenge? Most of all, I missed Edinburgh and my old life…

18 August 1881

I haven't had a moment to put down my thoughts in days, so I am glad to finally have time to write.

First, the day after I last saw him, Fyodor Dostoevsky died of a massive lung hemorrhage. He had said goodbye to his family and friends and seemed to have been ready to pass to the other world. A huge gathering of almost forty thousand people came to see the funeral in the Alexander Nevsky Square. Many great men spoke of how his stories had changed and inspired their lives. He had a deep understanding of the human heart and mind that few others had expressed. I suspect that he will be translated into English soon and become known as one of the world's greatest novelists.

Otherwise, we have begun a grueling routine. Dr. Bell visits hospitals and demonstrates surgery while I attend Professor Sechenov's lectures to improve my knowledge of anatomy and physiology.

Although the students in Vera Nayechev's small circle welcomed my presence and are interested in my thoughts, the better-dressed upper-class students either take no notice of me or go out of their way to elbow me aside. So, my experience with the Russian people has been mixed. Some seem to adore my accent and habits while others disdain me.

After a lecture on the circulation of blood and cardiac function yesterday morning, the same seedy fellow with a patched coat and a scraggly beard — who had been in charge of the first demonstration — approached me as we were leaving the lecture hall. He spoke in heavily-accented French. "I am Ivan Pavlov, assistant to the professor. You are Dr. Bell's assistant, yes?

"Aye."

"Would you like to visit our laboratory?"

I hesitated. Would there be live patients — experimental subjects — in his laboratory? I was repelled as well as fascinated. "Yes, of course. I would enjoy seeing your work," I said, solely out of curiosity.

"Excellent. Please follow me." We walked through a maze of university lecture halls and classrooms to a new building on the outskirts of the campus. As we talked, I became aware of his brilliant, but one-track, mind. Pavlov was not interested in medicine to benefit sick patients, but in learning how the nervous system functioned.

I was on the verge of asking about Cowboy Bill and the rattlesnakes when Pavlov spoke first. "There is another project. Our beloved tsar has ordered a study of blood coagulation."

"Ah, yes. On our very first day, one of your subjects was not quite dead when he was used in Dr. Bell's lecture."

"Yes, that was an unfortunate error. Science can sometimes be difficult. But when you get to the lab, you will see that we are doing important, groundbreaking work that will help all of mankind."

I heard whining and an occasional bark even before we entered the laboratory where a half-dozen pitiful dogs were in the center of the room. Heavy ropes immobilized each animal to a wooden frame, and rubber tubes connected their mouths to an apparatus that collected and measured their excretion of saliva. Another tube led from their stomachs to a similar apparatus. As a dog lover, my first instinct was to release the poor animals but it was not my lab.

"Once you see our experiments, you will understand how they will change the way we live." Pavlov said. "My experiments demonstrate psychic salivation and gastric stimulation in response to a secondary stimulus."

He blew a whistle; the dogs howled and whined, and within a few moments, saliva and gastric juice flowed into the measuring glasses.

"These dogs have learned that the sound of a whistle is often accompanied by food. I have named the phenomena 'conditioned reflex.' "

"Igor, turn on the generator." An elderly man — with a long, white beard and wearing a soiled smock with dark pants stuffed into knee-high boots — put down a broom and shuffled to a large box mounted on wheels.

Pavlov held a two-pronged stick that carried heavy wires from the box, which, evidently, was an electric generator.
"Igor, turn the crank."

The professor then touched the wires to a large, black and tan hound who was salivating copiously in anticipation of food. A spark jumped from the wires to the dog. The poor animal stiffened and let out a piteous, low moan. The flow of saliva and gastric juice stopped almost instantly.

Pavlov's eyes glowed with satisfaction. "A noxious counter-stimulation overcomes the animal's anticipation of food. Just think … with a combination of pleasurable and noxious stimuli, we can control the masses. If every prison in the world had such a mechanism we could end crime."

On the surface, it seemed promising, but I was deeply disturbed about the idea of conditioning people to please authority. In the wrong hands, this science had the potential to become truly dark and terrifying.

Ivanov, the student with the dark-rimmed, owlish glasses, was at a table anaesthetizing a dog with drops of chloroform. I smiled and nodded, but he ignored my gesture and continued working.

When the dog was asleep, Pavlov took a scalpel from a tray of dirty instruments and slashed open the dog's neck. There was none of the practiced grace of a surgeon, but his straightforwardness was effective, and within minutes, he opened the carotid sheath and isolated the vagus nerve.

"Igor, the wires."

With a few shuffling steps, the old man brought the generator and handed Pavlov the wires which he wrapped around the nerve.

I was mystified by the procedure, especially when Ivanov attached a rubber diaphragm to the dog's leg. A tube led to a stylus that moved on a revolving drum of smoked paper. It was a kymograph, a German invention that recorded physiologic observations.

"Start recording," Pavlov ordered.

Ivanov flicked a switch, and the spring loaded drum rotated, while the stylus moved up and down recording the animal's heart beats.

"Igor, turn the crank slowly."

The dog convulsed at the electric shock.

"Igor, you fool. I said turn the crank SLOWLY."

It was cruel. I wanted to scream, but held my tongue and vowed to rescue at least one of these poor creatures from this fate.

The elderly man hunched, and I swear there were tears in his eyes. He turned the crank several slow revolutions. The low current to the nerve slowed the heart rate. It was a brilliant demonstration of how the brain could, through the vagus nerve, control the heart.

"I am determined to unravel the mysteries of the brain and its control over the body," he said. "Igor, have you cleaned the cages?"

Igor stroked his matted beard, mumbled in Russian, picked up his broom and a bucket, and shuffled off to the next room. He had no sooner gone through the door when he emitted a terrible scream of terror and pain.

I immediately rushed to his side. The snakes were out of their cage and Igor had already collapsed into the writhing, hissing nightmare of slithering rattlers.

I seized the broom and struck at a huge rattlesnake coiled around his arm, its head only inches from his face. There were already fang marks on his hand, and the old man's eyes were insane with fear.

I batted at another huge reptile within striking distance of my own leg. I jumped back, but the fangs penetrated my thick woolen trousers. I struck out at the writhing snake again and again, but the blows only made it more viciously determined to sink its needle-like fangs into my flesh.

The old man screamed and howled in pain and fear.

Time stood still as I wildly flailed to keep them off poor Igor while defending myself. I was weakening when Ivanov appeared with the generator. He furiously turned the crank and jammed the wooden stick with bare wires into the mass of snakes. They writhed with increased rage but turned away from Igor and the electricity. They hissed and struck at the wires but retreated to the cages.

"Don't hurt them! The snakes belong to the tsar! If they die, he will have us killed!" Pavlov shouted.

He blew a long blast on his whistle and tossed a box containing live, white mice into the cage. The hissing, coiling mass of snakes, in a fury of blood and snapping jaws, devoured the mice.

I crouched beside old Igor and, with my penknife, slashed double X's across fang marks on his upper arm, then with my lips attempted to draw out the poison. Hot blood gushed into my mouth at first, but soon, the blood flow slowed to a trickle.

It was no use. He stopped breathing, and even as I held my hand over his chest, his heart made its last feeble thump.

"Damn! The old fool. I warned him one hundred times about those snakes and he never listened. Ivanov, find another caretaker without delay," Pavlov said.

The whole experience had left me shaken and deeply upset. I was troubled by Pavlov's cruel experiments and his inhumanity to poor Igor.

"Dr. Pavlov, I have medical duties to attend to. Please excuse me."

"Ivanov, show him out," said Pavlov.

Ivanov walked with me until we stopped in front of a small cage which held a shivering pup. "His mother died during an experiment," Ivanov said.

The pitiable beast was mostly brown but he had an appealing white patch around one of his sad eyes. He wriggled when I lifted him from the cage and hid him under my coat. Ivanov chuckled while we made our way to a dimly-lit worker's café tucked away on a refuse-strewn alley. The place smelled of stale beer and cooking. Ivanov ordered vodka. My nerves settled after I tossed down two glasses.

The pup was content to stay in my arms. He whimpered and shivered until Ivanov shared a bit of sausage and I fed him boiled potatoes.

"My oldest sister lives on a farm. She has room for another dog and will give him a good home," Ivanov said. He improvised a leash with his belt. "Doyle, you are a brave man, risking your life for poor old Igor."

"Anyone would have done the same."

"Pavlov gave Igor the job for food and a place to sleep. For that little bit, Igor loved Pavlov. It was more than most of the landowners give their serfs." Ivanov slammed his fist on the table. "No one cares a shit for the poor in Russia!"

"It is not much different from the way the English treat my Irish cousins," I said.

"Are you interested in justice for the poor?"

I paused, wondering where this would lead. "Of course. But, tell me, please, why is Dr. Pavlov interested in snakes and what do they have to do with the tsar?"

"The tsar is deathly afraid he will bleed to death after an attempted assassination, and there is a bleeding disease that kills infants born to every royal family in Europe. He gave a small fortune to the university to find a cure for bleeding. Pavlov took on the task because he is one of those fools who worship the tsar."

He paused and drained a glass. "Ho there, more vodka." The waiter refilled our glasses.

"Aye, I understand, but why use snakes in the research? They are extraordinarily expensive and extremely dangerous."

"For their venom. You see, he injects a small amount of venom into convicted criminals to cause uncontrolled hemorrhage. Then, he tries to cure the bleeding with blood transfusions from other criminals. It is all part of a grand experiment for the tsar."

Before he continued, a stranger slid into the seat next to Ivanov. "Dobry den," he said, before continuing to speak to him in Russian.

Ivanov responded in Russian.

I had learned enough Russian to understand 'Good afternoon' (*Dobry den*), but I was unable to understand their conversation and wondered why they didn't speak French or German like most students or members of the elite in St. Petersburg.

The newcomer was not old, but a mass of uncut, white hair stuck out from under his soft cap. His beard was flecked with grey, and there were heavy lines around his deep-set, watchful eyes. He spoke and dressed like a typical worker, but all the same, there was something not quite right about him.

"Doyle, meet my friend, Dmitri."

We shook hands. The stranger's rough, callused hand was clearly accustomed to hard work; my doubts about the man faded as I watched him speak with Ivanov. He appeared to be a good-hearted soul.

"Dmitri needs work. I will recommend him to Dr. Pavlov for Igor's job."

I felt left out when Ivanov and the new man continued to converse in Russian and used a dinner date I had with Vera as an excuse to leave. My meeting with Vera did not go well. She seemed distracted and paid little attention to me. After dinner, we walked along the Neva, but Vera barely spoke. Though it could have been a romantic date in the pleasing yellow glow of the fading evening sun, she was cold and distant. It felt, instead, like an evening with a stranger, a distracted stranger. After a chaste, unsatisfactory kiss, she suddenly turned and hurried away.

It was perplexing and disappointing; I went to my room to read about the blood's circulation through the cerebrum, when Dr. Bell banged on the door.

"Ah, Doyle, there you are. Come quickly! An emergency … Bring my medical bag. Professor Sechenov has requested an immediate consultation on one of his private cases. He is already with the patient. The situation is dire."

He seemed to be his old self, and I hoped that he had stopped the cocaine injections.

"Mr. Tatum, hail a cab, this instant!" he shouted.

Tatum was waiting with a hack and off we went at a brisk trot.

"Who is the patient?" I asked.

"Count Michael Ignatov," Bell said.

"He is the interior minister and directs the secret police, the tsar's right hand man." Mr. Tatum said.

The minister's grand house had lights in every window, and the curving driveway was lined with footmen carrying flaming torches. An elegantly dressed young woman, wringing her hands, met us at the door. “Oh, hurry, please hurry! My dear husband is desperately ill.”

An agitated footman in full livery led us through the waiting room and up a flight of gilded stairs to a room where Professor Sechenov rocked back and forth on a chair, with his hands to his face. “It is too late. He is dead,” Sechenov said, between moans.

The rather corpulent man, dressed in a fine silk dressing gown, was face down on a thick Turkish rug. His hands were stretched towards the casement of a floor-to-ceiling window that overlooked the Neva River.

While Dr. Bell knelt by the dead man, I took in the beautifully-furnished room. A table set up for chess was by the marble-faced fireplace. The ashes were warm. A decanter of port with a single glass stood on a second table. The room was filled with books, trinkets, and souvenirs from far countries. Portraits of men in military uniform looked down from the walls.

From the positions of the ivory and ebony chess pieces, it appeared that play had been in progress. If that was the case, then why was there only one chair at the table, on the white side of the board? The second chair, with a pillow on the seat, was off to one side.

“Except for a touch of gout he was perfectly healthy until this evening, but he had many enemies and feared for his life. He sent a message that he couldn’t urinate and felt strange. I arrived within an hour. He was already beyond help,” Professor Sechenov said.

Dr. Bell inspected and sniffed the body. It appeared that Ignatov had been struck by a sudden attack of angina or a cerebral fit. When satisfied with his minute inspection, he turned the body onto its back. Ignatov’s face was bright red, the eyes were open, and his lips were drawn back, almost in a smile.

“Doyle, can you identify the cause of death?”

“From the color of his face, I should think he had an attack of apoplexy brought on by the excesses of drink and rich food,” I said.

“I don’t think so. Professor Sechenov, what do you think?” Dr. Bell asked.

"I suspect foul play. It appears that he had a visitor — a chess player, perhaps an agent provocateur – most likely, the killer."

"Nay, I think he was alone at the time of death."

"Why?"

"My dear professor, the white bishop is poised to attack black's f-seven position when the white knight moves to g-five. It is the classic Philidor attack that can be blocked by any novice. The second chair was not for a player, but arranged so the count could place his gouty foot on a pillow. The count was studying moves to overcome the attack and was alone when he died." Bell said.

"No, I respectfully disagree. It is quite possible that a killer entered the room, throttled him, and left unseen. This is a matter for the police," Sechenov said.

"I don't think so; please observe his eyes."

Sechenov looked as Bell had requested. "What about them?" he asked.

"Doyle, your turn to make a diagnosis."

I went down on hands and knees and peered into two deep, black holes. "Sir, the pupils are widely dilated."

"And what does that mean?"

"The stroke affected the optic center in his brain."

"Dammit, Doyle! Don't be such a simpleton! Have you never heard of *belladonna*, from the Italian words for a beautiful woman? At one time, women used eye drops of belladonna to dilate their pupils so they would appear more seductive. Another name for belladonna is 'deadly nightshade,' a potent poison. This is a clear case of death by poison."

"Yes, that's it. I agree. And I would wager that he was poisoned by those damn terrorists. This is a police matter. By God, we must find the culprits before there is another assassination!" Sechenov shouted.

I immediately thought of the medical students. Any one of them could have prepared the poison, but, how could they have administered the drug? The police would think along the same lines and would suspect Vera and her radical friends. Though she had all but ignored me during our date, I did not want to see her imprisoned.

"That is unnecessary. Please refrain from calling the authorities. The police will find nothing," Bell said. "Professor, you said he called for help with urinary retention. That is another symptom of belladonna toxicity and suggests a slow onset, rather than an acute ingestion. In other words, this process has been going on for some time. Doyle, please remove the bandage from his right foot."

As I unrolled the bandage to reveal his swollen, gouty great toe, a sticky, greenish ointment smeared over my hands. Meanwhile, Dr. Bell hunched over the corpse, rubbing his chin while deep in thought. I wondered about his thought processes and gradually felt a slight giddiness, a pounding headache, an increase in heart rate, and my skin was hot.

"Sir, I don't feel so well."

"Doyle, your face has gone bright red. For God's sakes, lad, wipe your hands before the stuff kills you."

I became lightheaded, dizzy, and felt like flying out the window to soar over the Neva. Though he said it could kill me, it was a wonderful sensation. Dr. Bell dragged me away from the window, seized the decanter of Port wine, and with a handkerchief, vigorously wiped the ointment from my hands.

Sometime later, I awoke, stretched on a couch. An attractive house maid dabbed cold water on my face. I was giddy, with blurred eyes. The drug must have affected my moral senses because I lightly caressed her bosom; she giggled and gently kissed my forehead until two footmen carried me away to a carriage.

Later, with Mr. Tatum's assistance, I fell into my own bed. In the morning, I awoke with a headache. Was the episode real or a hallucination?

It was nearly ten o'clock when I made my way to the kitchen. After two cups of strong, sweet Turkish coffee, I felt like myself again.

Dr. Bell greeted me. "Laddie, you had a close call."

"What happened?"

"The ointment contained belladonna, a hellish brew derived from nightshade. It can be a useful remedy in small doses, but deadly poison in higher doses. During the fifteenth century, it was used in an ointment by witches to produce the sensation of flying."

"But, did the count apply the ointment to his own foot?"

"Aye, there were traces of the ointment beneath his fingernails. He was suffering great pain and sent his butler with a note to his apothecary for the strongest pain-relieving medicine possible. The chemist compounded a belladonna ointment with directions to apply no more than a quarter teaspoon to his gouty foot. He foolishly used the whole batch at once."

"Ah, so he accidently killed himself."

"Aye. He made a fatal mistake."

21 August 1881

Recent events have left me with frightening, disorienting flashes of memory. Am I going insane?

I am not even certain of the date, since the Russians use the old Julian calendar that is some twelve days behind our European calculations of time. If it wasn't for Mr. Tatum, I would no longer be keeping this diary for fear the secret police will discover its contents and send us all to prison or worse.

Days after the belladonna episode and my futile attempt to save Old Igor, I went with Dr. Bell to his rounds and lectures. It was at one of these lectures that Vera invited me to attend a student meeting. She asked if I could explain the theories of Darwin to the workers in order to wean them from the Church. Even with my scientific education, I was uncertain, but Tatum made it clear that I should mingle with the students. There might also be an opportunity to be alone with Vera, and I had the wild thought that Penelope might be there.

I hailed a droshky, a two-wheeled cab. The grubby driver understood my poor attempt at Russian when I asked him to take me to the Imperial Library. He beat his tired nag and we went across the Nikolaevsky Bridge, then along the embankment to Nevsky Prospekt. I handed the driver five kopecks, but he wanted more. Money was in short supply, so I gave him another coin.

Vera was waiting by the cab stand in front of the library. I scarcely recognized her. She had cut her lovely, blonde hair until it was scarcely longer than a boy's. She wore a plain, white blouse with a simple, black skirt and clumsy workmen's boots.

"Were you followed?"

"Why would I be followed?"

"They are suspicious of students."

"I'm no longer a student. I am a doctor."

"Feh. That makes no difference."

I was taken aback by the severity of her appearance and behavior. She grabbed my hand, and we took off through winding narrow streets, past babushkas huddled under black shawls against the cool breeze blowing off the Gulf of Finland.

The buildings were old, decrepit, and filthy. There were signs of poverty — dirty children playing in the rubbish, disheveled drunks passed out on the streets, and young girls soliciting soldiers.

It was nearly eleven o'clock when we reached a dingy store on a small backstreet overlooking the Fontanka Canal. Vera murmured a password to a sentry and we went through the store, which was stacked, helter-skelter with dusty books, icons, and pieces of jewelry. In the back room, oil lamps illuminated long tables littered with pamphlets and books.

"This is a reading room for workers and peasants," she explained.

I recognized a few medical students and the leader, Golovinsky, whom I had met at Dostoevsky's flat. This was a far more radical group than the students who met in the café. The men had long hair and wore red shirts, baggy, black pants, and worker's boots. The women, like Vera, wore plain, white blouses, black skirts and rough boots. It was as if they were wearing a uniform. In the dim light, Vera appeared to no longer be a soft, sensuous woman but a hard-line revolutionary.

"Who are all these people? What do they call themselves?" I whispered to her.

" 'Narodnaya Volia' or, in English, 'The People's Will.' "

Ivanov attempted, over the din, to introduce me.

Golovinsky shouted him down. "Bah, have you not read your Marx? The peasants need their religious opium."

"Yes, but if we can teach them about the latest scientific discoveries in England, we can …"

"Nyet! All that is worthless. We can wait no longer. It is time to kill the noble class and do away with another tsar."

He spoke passionately and loudly and quickly had the students and workers in the palm of his hand. All eyes were on him. The room went silent. He shook his fist as he spoke. "Comrades. The secret police are treating the death of Count Ignatov as murder and are rounding up Jews, students, and writers. Everyone in this room is a suspect."

The room erupted into furious shouts. "Kill the tsar! Down with tyranny of the so-called nobility! Wipe them out!" Vera translated for me. Even though I didn't understand the Russian words, I felt the passion of his speech.

"Please, silence! Listen to me!" Golovinsky shouted.

The hubbub died out, but there was a muffled scream from outside and the distinctive pop of a pistol shot.

For a moment, there was absolute silence, and then, officers in sky blue uniforms stormed through the bookshop and burst through the door to the reading room. Golovinsky drew a pistol and fired three times.

Blood spurted from the chest of an officer, but more police rushed into the room. I stared straight into the face of a furious officer who slashed at my head with a huge cavalry saber.

Vera grabbed my shirt and dragged me to the floor just as the huge curved blade swished through the air above me and sank into the neck of a surprised, red-shirted worker standing behind me. The saber cleanly severed his head with its little goat's beard. The decapitated head flew through mid-air as the poor fellow's body remained upright for a moment. Blood spurted from his carotid arteries, spraying the room and splattering on my face. For an instant, I wondered if the brain in the severed head understood what had happened.

The saber-wielding policemen drew his sword back for another slash. The next killing blow would have severed my head. That is, until Golovinsky hurled an oil lamp that broke on the door casing. Flames enveloped the secret police officers while two students overturned a table blocking the room against another assault.

The fire spread from the officers to the walls and books, and the room filled with oily, black smoke. I was stunned, but Vera dragged me out the back door in the midst of escaping students.

We fled through darkened streets to a clump of bushes by the canal. There were flashes of gunfire, and red-coated Cossacks raced from the Admiralty down Voznesensky Prospekt towards the flaming building. We were lucky we escaped alive.

"Hold me," Vera said. "Please."

I enveloped her in a crushing embrace. She opened her mouth and we lashed one another with wet tongues. The intensity and aliveness of our momentary lust helped dissolve some of the fear and anxiety. She pulled away and we crept along dim paths, avoiding the streets lit with gas lamps. We headed north until we came to the massive columns of St. Isaac's Cathedral and huddled in the black darkness while the tumult in the streets continued.

"We aren't safe here. Shall we go to your room?" I asked.

She shook her head, wrenched free, and hurried away in the darkness. "Vera, wait. I didn't mean to …"

She didn't look back. I trembled and broke into a cold sweat. My heart thumped wildly. The streets were alive with armed soldiers and mounted police. I huddled in the shadows, too frightened to leave the comforting dark confines of the cathedral.

When, at last, the shouts and gunfire died away, I made for the Nikolaevsky Bridge and, keeping to darkened pathways, reached Professor Sechenov's home. In the grey light of a false dawn, I quietly went up the back stairs and, after a pause, knocked gently on Mr. Tatum's door. I had to confide in a trusted friend. Dr. Bell, for the past several days, was either lost in his own cocaine-induced dreams or was extraordinarily active.

I was still shivering when Mr. Tatum opened the door.

"It is rather early for a social call," he said.

I fell, rather than sat, on a stuffed leather chair, trembling with nervous exhaustion. I uttered a low groan mixed with a sigh. "It appears a bit of restorative is in order," Tatum said.

And aye, he was right. I felt much better after a tot of whiskey.

"So … What happened? What's wrong?" Tatum asked.

"I am in danger and must leave the country," I said.

"Tell me everything."

I related my adventure with the students and the police raid. "The policeman who tried to kill me had a long nose, thin lips, and sandy-colored hair swept back from a high forehead. He will remember me just as clearly. It is not safe for me to walk the streets of St. Petersburg."

"Mr. Doyle, please just listen. They will not harm you."

"No, I must go home immediately."

"Actually, Mr. Doyle, you must stay and help us. Great things are afoot since I delivered the message intended for Lord Asquith to the British ambassador."

"You delivered the message? What about Penelope? I thought she would go to the ambassador."

Tatum ignored my question. "The Government and our Queen are determined to protect the tsar at all costs. In the future, Russia must be a counterweight to the growing power of Germany. There are elements, within and without Russia, who want nothing less than the death of Alexander III. You could be instrumental in keeping him alive."

"That is a matter for the Secret Service and military," I replied. "Not for me."

"It is your duty as a citizen of our realm to continue meeting with the student groups and report everything you learn about the anarchists to me. We particularly must learn the whereabouts of Captain David Campbell, the officer who was tortured in Afghanistan."

"With my Uncle Declan?"

"Yes."

"I don't know the first place to look. Have you contacted Penelope? Where is she? She would certainly know more about Captain Campbell than I."

Mr. Tatum looked away.

"You must know her whereabouts."

"Well, let us just say that Miss Walshingham is a capable young lady and I trust that she needs no help."

"Was she kidnapped?"

Mr. Tatum stroked his chin, and the expression on his face hardened into a scowl. "She went away of her own free will. Now, mind you, Mr. Doyle, the ambassador insists that you keep a detailed record of your activities with the students and Dr. Bell requests your company on student rounds this morning."

"Yes, I keep a diary to record everything."

"Good."

I tried to argue with Tatum, but he would not listen. I gave up, made my way to my room, and slept fitfully for about an hour, haunted by visions of the bloody saber.

22 August 1881

At breakfast, Dr. Bell stared at his egg with a bloodshot eye.

"Good morning, sir," I said.

His hand shook as he cracked the egg, which splattered over the table. "Damn," he said. Dr. Bell was silent, morose, and hollow-eyed, certainly the results of his cocaine injections. He rose from the table and, with a curt, "Bring the instrument case," took up his hat and went to the waiting carriage. I barely had time to finish my slice of buttered black bread as I ran to catch up.

"We will meet Dr. Gerchakov at the municipal hospital for student rounds," he said, once we were in the carriage. I remembered him, the great bear of a man who had attended the clinics in Edinburgh. As we grew nearer to the hospital, Bell took a small pinch of white powder from a silver snuff box and applied it to his nostril.

Within a few minutes, his spirits lifted and, except for a slight tremor, he seemed to be his old self — or maybe a more frenetic, energetic version of himself.

The city hospital was a sprawling, dark, stone building with long wards filled with the dregs of St. Petersburg. Sick and dying patients were on cots lined against the wall with scarcely any space between. I was accustomed to the astringent smell of carbolic in the Edinburgh Infirmary, but this place smelled of human excrement, pus, and boiled cabbage. Professor Gerchakov met us with two dozen students, including Ivanov and several of the radical students. I searched for Vera but she was not among the students. I felt a pang of remorse. Had the police caught her?

Dr. Bell briskly asked for their names and assigned a patient to each student. This was a standard bedside teaching routine in Edinburgh. These students were not accustomed to our methods, but under Dr. Bell's guidance, they quickly learned to palpate for tumors, auscultate the heart and lungs, and examine the head and neck. When they finished their examinations, Bell, with sparkling eyes and his usual good humor, quizzed each student in turn.

For example, Bell felt the pulse and took in the gasping respirations and blue lips of an elderly man who sat straight up in bed. "Well, Mr. Khartsov, what do you make of this poor fellow?"
"It is a case of pneumonia."
"Excellent, I completely agree."

We went from one patient to another, with Bell questioning each student. He gently pointed out their errors of diagnosis with a smile and sometimes a joke. The Russian students took his criticism with more good nature than his Edinburgh students.

There was a child with a twisted leg as the result of a poorly set fractured femur, several old men with heart failure or pneumonia, and a young woman with bulging eyes and a goiter. Bell was in his element, but the cocaine seemed to have possession of him. He was more agitated than usual but appeared to be in good spirits.

Midway through the ward, we came to a drowsy, middle-aged man with long, unkempt, black hair swept back from his forehead, a short beard, and a long mustache. His head drooped down to his chest, and his purplish-red nose was covered with broken veins. One side of his face was slightly flattened. Both his hands rested on a dirty quilt that covered his legs.

An alert, quiet lad with wide, deeply-set, brown eyes — perhaps ten or twelve years of age and wearing a dirty smock belted at the waist — sat on an old army coat folded into a crude pallet at his bedside. As we approached the bed, he offered a glass of water to the patient's trembling lips; most of the water spilled on the quilt. All the while, the boy never spoke and there was a strange calmness about him.

"Von Diebitsch, what do you make of this fellow?"

Unlike most students who wore dark uniforms with high collars, Von Diebitsch was dressed in a double-breasted jacket, a vest, fawn-colored trousers, and a wide, purple ascot tie. To complete the picture of a foppish nobleman, he had pomaded hair. He smirked and attempted a military bearing. "You will address me as Baron von Diebitsch."

"Well, Baron von Diebitsch, can you give us a diagnosis for this fellow?"

"He is human rubbish — a bum, an alcoholic, and certainly not worth my time."

"Sir, that is a horrible attitude for a budding physician."

Dr. Bell turned to Ivanov. "Ask the little boy about the patient."

Ivanov questioned the boy in Russian. "A week ago, the man was unconscious, on the steps in front of the Mariinsky Theatre. He has barely recovered consciousness."

Dr. Bell, with his hand on his chin, shifted his eyes from the patient's face to his tattered shirt, then fixed on his hands. He examined first one hand, and then the other; Bell's fingers trembled, but his face lit up with one of his 'aha' moments.

"Now, Baron von Diebitsch, look at these hands. Do you still think he is a bum?"

Von Diebitsch adjusted his pince-nez and barely leaned forward. "I see nothing that would lead me to change my opinion."

Bell gave the man a withering glance, and then, his gaze swept over the students. "It is essential to observe every detail of every patient if you expect to make a proper diagnosis."

He lifted the patient's hands from the bed. "Look here. The nails are clean and well-trimmed. The hand is flexible, the skin is soft, and the abductor pollicis brevis that moves the thumb laterally is well-developed. Likewise, in the hypothenar eminence, the flexor digiti minimi and the opponens digiti minimi that control the fifth finger are all hypertrophied. Gentlemen, these are the hands of a musician. I would wager that this man was an accomplished pianist."

The students crowded forward, eager and completely captivated by the professor. He stood back, lit his long curved pipe, and waited a moment before speaking. "Dr. Doyle, if you please, conduct a neurologic examination."

The boy sat as still as a Buddha on the ragged army coat, while I, with reflex hammer, pin, and tuning fork, tested the patient who gave no response to my questions. His left arm and leg were weak, and the reflexes on that side were nearly absent. I then noticed the dilated pupil in his right eye.

"His left side is weak, and the right pupil is dilated as if he had a lesion in his brain," I said.

"Please, make a more specific diagnosis," Bell asked.

"A tumor or a blood clot," I replied.

Bell commenced a minute examination of the man's scalp. He brushed back the long hair and probed with his fingers. He drew himself erect and faced the students, but spoke directly to Von Diebitsch. "As Dr. Doyle mentioned, there is a slight hematoma over his right ear. Gentlemen, this patient has suffered a blow to his head, perhaps when he fell on the steps of the Mariinsky Theatre. He undoubtedly has a blood clot pressing on his brain."

I felt a glow of triumph at making a good diagnosis, but Baron von Diebitsch gave me a look of pure malevolence and bent close to my ear. "You and your damned professor will not publicly ridicule me. I know where you go at night and the filthy company you keep. Watch your step and your mouth, Doyle, or you might find yourself on the wrong end of an Okhrana sword."

My blood turned to ice. How did he know? Was there an informer among his fellow students? I again thought of the officer with the saber. He would surely recognize me again.

In the midst of these black ruminations, Dr. Bell demanded attention. "This man needs an immediate operation. Dr. Gerkachov, can you arrange the operating theater?"

"I am sorry, but I am due at my private clinic within an hour, and no other surgeon is available. So, an operation is quite impossible at this time."

"But this man requires immediate surgery to remove a blood clot on his brain."

"Yes, I agree. And you can demonstrate your technique," Gerkachov replied. "But as I've said, I can't assist."

"I, um, well, let's see …" For the first time, I noticed Dr. Bell was perspiring and had gone slightly pale. He made no reply. There was a coarse tremor in both his hands. I had never seen him hesitate at an opportunity to operate. Surgery was the love of his life. It was the damn cocaine. He must have realized that the drug has affected his surgical skills. This was the jolt he needed to overcome his dependence and quit using the rancid stuff.

"Of course, Dr. Bell and I will be happy to operate," I said, on impulse.

Bell shot me a sharp glance as Gerkachov embraced Dr. Bell with an enthusiastic bear hug. "Capital, capital. I shall send for my anaesthetist. I might be able to watch you open him up and then, regrettably, I must go."

The operating room was dingy and poorly-equipped with enamel pans, bottles of antiseptics, and a stack of greyish towels. Light poured in from an enormous skylight and there were a few gas lamps. Tiers of seats for students rose from the floor to near the ceiling. Eager students placed the nearly-unconscious patient on a white, painted, wooden table in the middle of the room while I soaked the instruments in a solution of carbolic.

The anaesthetist — a bustling, young, bespectacled man — arrived with his bottles of chloroform and a gauze-covered cone. Dr. Bell positioned the patient with his head turned to the left and indicated that I should shave the side of his head with a straight razor. That done, I scrubbed the area with carbolic.

Dr. Bell's forehead glistened with sweat, and his hand shook as he selected a scalpel from the instrument table. He hesitated, and at one point, I thought he might throw down the knife and leave the room.

Instead, with great fortitude, he applied the scalpel to the skin and made a curving incision above and forward of the ear. Not a word was spoken as he turned back the flap of skin, selected a drill, and bored holes in the skull. His head dropped until his chin nearly rested on his chest, and he took several long deep breaths.

When he was steadier, he picked up a chisel and connected the holes. The operation had lasted nearly an hour, since it was not possible to hurry for fear of drilling into the brain. The diagnosis was correct; a purple blood clot bulged against the dura mater, the tough membrane that surrounds the brain.

The students crowded closer to get a better look. Meanwhile, I held my breath for fear of what might come next. A cut in the wrong place could be fatal. With unerring skill, Bell made a perfect incision and swept the clot out with his finger.

It should have been a triumphal moment, but with a choking voice, Bell turned to me. "Doyle, I am not well. Please finish. Excuse me."

Dr. Bell walked away as took his place. I had sutured a bit of skin in the emergency ward, but I had never been responsible for closing a major incision, much less one close to the brain. If the dura mater was not closed, water tight, spinal fluid would leak and eventually become infected. I threaded the finest silk sutures on small needles and set to the job.

This man's life rested in my hands and I was horribly worried that my inexperience would lead to his death, but alas, I had no choice and carried on.

It's not like I didn't know what to do. I did. It was just that I had never done it before, and one false move, one tiny little slip, and I'd surely kill him. So, I tried not to falter.

First, I sutured the dura with closely-placed stitches, then replaced the bone, and finally, closed the skin. If the operation was a success, the patient should show definite signs of re-awakening when the chloroform was stopped.

To my horror, blood oozed from the wound; first, there was one drop at the site of a suture, then more, until there was a steady flow of blood. I feared that I had failed and doomed this man to an unnecessary death.

I pressed as hard as possible, hoping to staunch the flow, but each time I released the pressure, there was more blood. It seemed impossible that a major vessel was pumping blood. It appeared to be a general ooze from the entire incision. I had made no mistakes, had done everything properly. I just couldn't stop the bleeding. Was it me, or did this man suffer from a bleeding disease?

Dr. Bell, reclined on a chair outside the operating room. He was of no help. For the first time since the surgery began, I noticed the ragged little boy sitting in a corner of the operating room, hugging his knees and swaying from side to side.

I gave up my feeble attempts to control the oozing blood and we moved the patient to his bed. The ragged little boy came to him, whispered in his ear, and stroked his face. The bleeding continued, drop by terrible drop, until the bandages and then the bed sheets were soaked with blood.

The patient moved his hands, flexed his fingers, and opened his eyes. These were wonderful signs of recovery. It should have been a triumphal moment, except for the terrible, unrelenting bleeding.

I had an inspiration. "Send for Dr. Pavlov. Tell him we need his blood-clotting plasma!" I shouted. We continued the bedside vigil.

Over the next ten minutes, the pulse, which had been slow and strong, was now growing faster and weaker. I looked in vain for Dr. Bell, but he had left. I needed Pavlov and his plasma, but his laboratory was far away. All seemed lost.

The Baron spoke with an air of triumph. "Bah. He will be dead soon. Look what you've done. I've had enough of you and your arrogant Dr. Bell." He stormed off with most of the students.

He was right and now I was alone — well, except for Ivanov and the silent child. My patient only had a few more moments to live. I had surely killed him.

But then, the little boy, the strangely calm little boy with the deeply set eyes, reached out to the patient. The blood continued to trickle from the bandage, seemingly unabated, while the boy, now with his eyes tightly clenched, took the man's hands.

He stroked them gently and seemed to enter a trance state. There was an intensity which one rarely sees in children and, I will swear, there was an aura of light about his face. The boy muttered a prayer. At that very moment, the trickle of blood stopped. The pulse under my fingers grew stronger and definitely slower.

Somehow, the boy had staunched the flow of blood and saved the man by sheer psychic force. I am a man of science, but I will swear on a bible that something supernatural happened in that moment. The magical little boy used his psychic powers to clot my patient's blood.

I turned to Ivanov. "The boy is a miracle worker."

"Da."

"What is his name?"

"Grigori, Grigori Rasputin," Ivanov replied.

Suddenly, there was a commotion at the end of the ward. Pavlov rushed to the bedside with a syringe filled with a yellow fluid. “Plasma,” he said. He plunged the needle into a vein at the patient’s elbow and pushed the plunger. “There, now we shall see.” The patient’s color and heart rate improved. Pavlov believed that he had saved him, but I knew better. It was the boy. Definitely the boy. If not for the boy, he would’ve been dead before Pavlov even arrived…

“Thank you, laddie. Thank you… Can you tell me the patient’s name?” I asked.

The boy looked up in surprise and said a few words. Even in the Russian, I made out the name. “Modest Petrovich Mussorgsky.”

23 August 1881

I was tired and tense with worry today over Dr. Bell and my involvement with the radical students. So, it was a lovely surprise when an old university chum, Dick Ferguson, sent me an invite for dinner. Dicky wasn't in the medical program, but was an engineering student. We played on the same rugby team and had downed many a pint after an afternoon on the field.

It was an easy walk across the bridge over the Neva to his comfortable rooms on the English Embankment. He greeted me warmly and invited me into his library. My old friend wore a finely-tailored tweed suit, a silk tie, and his elegant shoes were polished to a high gloss. When I was seated in a padded chair, with my feet stretched out on an ottoman, Dick poured me a tot of fine single malt whiskey. The aroma of heather made me a bit homesick. Only a few weeks ago, I was excited to get out of Scotland, and now, my heart ached to return.

"Dick, you appear to be prospering in St. Petersburg, while I'm still wondering what to do with my life."

Dick laughed. "It was a pure stroke of good luck. I landed a job with a Glasgow firm that is building an electrical system. Soon, all the aristocrats will have Edison lights in their homes and the street trams will run on electricity."

I told Dick of our adventures on the ship and Dr. Bell's extraordinary powers. I then mentioned the meeting of the students.

"Oh, laddie, stay away from those bastards or you'll wind up rotting away your life in a cell. They are hoodlums and anarchists, intent on killing the tsar and all the nobles," he warned.

"Is it as bad as all that?" I asked.

"Ever since the radicals murdered Alexander II, his son, Alexander III is deathly afraid of assassination. The city is practically under martial law. He has established a new secret police force, the Okhrana. The government is sending students, anarchists, and Jews to prison every day. St. Petersburg has become an unfriendly and dangerous place. But enough of that, let's go to dinner and drink some good Russian vodka."

It was one of those eternal, lovely St. Petersburg nights, so we trotted along the embankment to Nevsky Prospekt and the Grand Hotel Europe. It was nine o'clock in the evening, but a warm sun lit up the street so it felt like a midday stroll. We walked through the grand lobby and into the entrance to the gilded dining room. A uniformed waiter bowed and led us to a table in this most sumptuous of surroundings.

Dicky spoke enough Russian to order beef in sour cream and then salmon and rice with hard boiled eggs, which was followed with a dish of herring layered with grated boiled potatoes, carrots, beets, and onions. I stuffed myself with the luscious dishes and savored every bite. It wasn't until we finished lemon pie and coffee and were sipping brandy that I asked about the tsar. "Maybe I'm naïve, but please tell me. Why do you think so many people hate the tsar?"

Dicky wiped his mouth and cleared his throat. "His father was a liberal who had, in fact, signed documents granting more freedom to the people just before they killed him. Unfortunately, since his death, his son has grown fearful and, as a result, repealed his father's proclamations and keeps the status quo through fear and violence. The new tsar is in virtual seclusion for fear of assassination. He is not a bad sort, from what I hear, but is an autocrat who thinks Russia must be ruled with an iron hand. Aye, the intelligentsia wants democracy, but they won't get it from this tsar."

We talked about politics late into the night when I bid Dicky farewell and made my way back to my room.

3 September 1881

Though I am writing the following entry after the events took place, and my memory may be a tad faulty, I will set down the events to the best of my ability.

I was still thinking about my conversation with Dicky, when, the next morning, just before a lecture, Vera dashed into the hall and, without so much as a "Good morning," took my arm. "Come immediately! We need your help."

Her hair and clothing were more disheveled than usual, and there were deep worry lines around her eyes.

She led me across the university square to a maze of streets that led to a poor residential area on the industrial side of Vasilyevsky Island. She knocked softly on a wooden door until an aged housekeeper let us in to a weed-choked courtyard. Vera crossed to another door, which led to a corridor and to still another door.

I followed her. Golovinsky came out of the shadows with an angry grimace. "Why isn't he blindfolded?" he asked.

"I trust him," Vera said.

He shook his head angrily. "Nyet! You are too soft!" He roughly grabbed my right hand and twisted it behind my back. "Why must I do everything myself?"

"Damn you, fool! Don't break my arm!" I shouted.

"Then don't fight me." He twisted even harder. There was a mad quality to his voice and his eyes radiated the fury of an enraged fanatic. I wilted and made no resistance when he tied a dark rag over my eyes. The door creaked open and he led us outdoors.

I struggled to keep up, but each time I faltered, he yanked my arm. Suddenly, my mind cleared and I remembered Dr. Bell's oft-given advice to use all your senses.

We had made a left turn out of the door and walked on squishy mud. I tried to count the seconds, but lost track after four minutes. We turned left again into another street or alley.

A door opened and there was raucous laughter; a tavern, I thought. I could still hear the tavern when we stopped and Vera tapped softly on a door. By turning my head a bit, I could peek under the mask and had a fleeting glimpse of a narrow alley and an unpainted, wooden building.

Golovinsky pushed me into a room that smelled of cooking and down another flight of stairs. I was nearly overcome by the powerful, acrid odor of burning chemicals. Golovinsky jerked the mask away from my eyes. I was in a laboratory.

The acrid chemical odor was from large flasks of liquids boiling over Bunsen burners. There were benches, retorts, and other chemical apparatus; all tended by two young men with singed eyebrows and an older woman.

Vera led me to an adjoining room where the remains of a loaf of bread, a cut of cold meat, and a bottle of brandy were on a table next to an oil lamp. I first heard their piteous moans, then, when my eyes accommodated to the light, I could see three poor souls huddled on cots with their faces and hands swathed in dirty rags.

"What happened?" I asked.

"There was an explosion," Vera said.

"Gunpowder?"

"No. It was a chemical explosion. Fulminate of mercury."

"Great God, it is a wonder anyone is alive!" I recalled that fulminate of mercury is made by adding mercury to nitric acid and used as a detonator for explosives. If there was more of the stuff, the entire building could go up in smoke.

"What do you want with me?"

"You are a doctor. Take care of these people."

There was no way to run, and this could be another challenge to my budding surgical skills. Golovinsky had settled into a chair, swigged from the bottle of brandy, and gestured with a revolver.

"English Doctor, if you wish to live, save our comrades."

My anger at the abduction was overcome with pity for these poor wretches.

"I will help," Vera said. She set about removing the bandage from the face of a young man with a horrible injury. His skin was seared to a crisp, and a there was a deep gash from his forehead to the corner of his mouth. Shards of glass were embedded in his neck, face, and forehead. Worst of all, a thick fluid dripped from his left eye where a shard of glass had penetrated the cornea.

"This man should be in a hospital. He needs expert care from an ophthalmic surgeon or he will lose both eyes. I can do nothing for him. Maybe Dr. Bell could ..."

"No, we have no choice. You must do it. Make a list of medicines and instruments," Vera said.

"We need everything — morphine, antiseptics, chloroform, bandages, sutures, surgical forceps, and, most of all, a bright light," I said.

Vera sent a pale, sallow youth to fetch the supplies. I rolled up my sleeves and went to work with soap and water to sponge away the worst of the dirt and soot from the burns and deep lacerations. The flesh was blown away from the thumb and index fingers of the man with the horribly injured face.

Both hands of another poor fellow were mangled with exposed bone where there should have been fingers and a thumb. I had been at work on the two men for perhaps twenty minutes, when I became aware of a soft whimpering moan from the furthest, dimmest corner of the room. "Bolli, oh, boll, bolli, oh."

"Bring the lamp," I said.

The moaning, young woman was lying on a pile of rags. Her eyes were closed, her face was deathly pale, and her hair was softly braided in the Polish style. Any man could fall desperately in love with her delicate nose and softly-curving lips. She seemed to offer a bit of peace and sanity in this awful setting. I thought she was untouched by the explosion until I saw the long, tapering shard of glass, like a dagger, protruding from her chest, just beneath the left breast.

I instinctively reached to pull it out but drew back. The glass quivered with each heartbeat. In absolute horror, I realized the point had to be embedded in the heart muscle; its removal would cause an immediate fatal hemorrhage.

"Great God! What is the point of this insanity? Are you totally mad? How can you allow such injuries to occur?"

"You are so British. So foolish. So naïve." Vera had steel in her voice. "A few lives don't matter. Hundreds have already died for the cause. We must destroy the tsar and the nobles to free all of Russia. If hundreds more die, it will be well worth it."

I was a trained doctor but with no surgical experience to help these poor wretches. When the supplies arrived, I set to work doing the best that I could. There was enough morphine, chloroform, and carbolic, but the instruments were old and crude. I gave a double dose of morphine to the poor girl and wished I could do more.

Vera gave chloroform to the men while I cleaned the wounds, removed broken glass, and sutured the deep lacerations with a plain sewing needle and cotton thread.

It took hours to remove the dead tissue and shattered bone from victim's hands and to preserve bits of fingers for a serviceable hand. Meanwhile, the poor girl with the lacerated heart gave one last sigh and died while I was at work on the men. At last, I sank into a chair, drained the last of the brandy and, overcome by fatigue and chloroform fumes, passed out.

When I awoke some hours later, Vera was gone, but my foggy mind registered a strange sight. A grey-haired man, with a jeweler's magnifying loop screwed into his right eye, worked at a treadle that turned a small, circular saw.

Incredibly, he held an egg cradled in his hand. There was a gently whirring sound as he held the egg against the saw, cut away the top, drained its contents into a bowl, and took up a second egg.

He raised his head and shouted at the door. "Comin sie hier, bitte!"

Suddenly, the two young men with seared eyelashes and Golovinsky, carrying a beaker of thick greenish liquid, stepped on tip-toe into the room.

"The nitro is ready," one of them said.

I shrank back away from the madness while Golovinsky, with great care, poured the liquid nitroglycerin into an open egg, which was nestled in a small, straw-filled basket. He deliberately placed the beaker on the table and then, with infinite care, replaced the sawed-off bit of eggshell and sealed it with melted candle wax.

"There, that will be a nice treat for the tsar," he said.

One of my patients, the fellow with mangled hands, raised himself. "We did our job. Now, how will you do yours?" he asked, through clenched teeth.

"It will not be difficult. The tsar pretends to be a man of the people. He prepares his own breakfast, coffee, black bread, and boiled egg. He is in for a deadly surprise."

"Yes, but how will you deliver it?"

"The English woman will do it."

"When?"

"Tomorrow morning."

Who was the 'English woman'? Had they recruited Penelope? My thoughts whirled, but it became clear; she had been devoted to my uncle and David Campbell. Both men had been captured, tortured, and left to die by the Russians in Afghanistan. She had every reason to hate the tsar, but would she turn against England and the Queen?

If she succeeded and it became known that an English woman was responsible for the death of the tsar, there would be an international catastrophe or a great world war. I had to stop her. I had to escape.

Golovinsky left the room with the egg, which was carefully packed in straw. In the distance, I heard his heavy tread on the stairway and, then, only an occasional murmur and the clink of glassware next door. Surely those people had orders to prevent me from leaving.

I knew I couldn't idly wait. I had to create an opportunity to escape.

My only weapon was a small pen knife, but most anarchists carried knives or a pistol. I went to the dead girl who I thought might have a weapon. She was already cold and stiff with early rigor mortis. I went through her clothing, pocket by pocket. At first, I found nothing. Then, I felt a hard lump — a holster strapped on the outside of her thigh held a small, nickel-plated revolver loaded with five brass cartridges.

I blew out the oil lamp and, with infinite care, opened the door into the laboratory. Golovinsky had spoken in German, and many of our medical textbooks were in German, so I had a decent proficiency in the language. With great bravado, I waved the pistol and shouted in German. "Don't move! Hold your hands up!"

"Nein!" growled a large, blonde fellow as he balled a fist. He backed down at the sight of the pistol for a moment, then, with a deep, low growl, hurled himself across the room. I stepped aside and accidentally bumped against a bench covered with flasks and burners.

"Watch out, you idiot! That's nitroglycerine!" the second man screamed.

The bench tilted, and a thick, green liquid in an open flask sloshed with a small wave against the glass. The big man gasped and froze. I gently took up the flask and, again, spoke in German. "If you move, I will blow us to kingdom come. Into the other room — both of you. Now."

They gave up and, with great care, went to the next room. There was only a flimsy lock on the door. I gently placed the flask of nitroglycerine on the floor against the door. "Open the door and the nitro explodes. Don't follow me," I said.

A few moments later, I was on the dark and empty street. I turned to the left but remembered that, on returning, the direction should be the opposite of the way we came. My impulse was to run, but I walked at a normal pace to avoid attracting attention. There were a few drunks in the tavern, but the streets were empty.

I recognized the muddy street and soon came to the Neva River. The English Church was on the other side. I ducked in the shadows as a squad of police cantered across the bridge headed in the direction of Professor Sechenov's house. Were they searching for me? Going home might be risky, so I turned away and kept to the river bank in the other direction.

Dicky Ferguson's rooms were only a short distance across the river. I slipped from shadow to shadow and finally reached his quarters. My old friend listened to my tale of woe. He pulled a long, unhappy face. "Go straight to the police, Doyle."

"No, no, they'll surely put me in prison, and if the English woman is Penelope, it's curtains for her. Think what a black eye that would be for England. I must stop her. Please, my friend, you must help. Send for Mr. Tatum, our valet, at once."

Ferguson saw my point as much to protect the Crown as me. "The tsar is at the Gatchina Palace, nearly forty miles away. There is no time."

"We must try," I said.

"My chaise is fast, but I don't know," he said.

"We have no choice." By the time Tatum arrived, I had cleaned most of the blood and soot from my clothing and, after a cup of tea, felt much better. It was, however, nearly midnight. There was little time, but Ferguson had called out his driver, and with two fresh horses, we were on our way in his light, two-wheeled chaise.

Mr. Tatum gave the driver a handful of coins. "There will be more if we reach the palace before dawn."

The driver took up the challenge and applied the whip with good will. The horses strained at their traces, and off we went at a gallop towards the palace.

There was light in the east when the parapets of Gatchina palace came into view. The horses were flagging, and we were within a mile or so from the moat that surrounded the parade ground when the right-hand horse threw a shoe.

I was all for going ahead, alone on the one horse, but Mr. Tatum sighed. "Sorry, it's already within a few minutes of six-thirty." He had scarcely finished speaking when a terrific explosion shook the earth. Smoke and debris rose in a great cloud.

"We had best get away as quickly as possible," he said.

We had no sooner turned back, with the one horse in the traces and the other limping behind, when a troop of red-coated Cossacks raced by, standing in their stirrups, lances at the ready. Within a few minutes, a dozen blue-uniformed police drew up and surrounded our open chaise.

They would have shot us on the spot had not Mr. Tatum showed his papers to an officer and explained that we were merely eccentric Englishmen out for an early morning sightseeing trip. All seemed well until they found the revolver in my coat pocket. I had forgotten the weapon. It was damn foolish of me. The officers manacled my hands and threw me onto a wagon with other prisoners.

Two hours later, I was in Fontanka 16, headquarters for the secret police, which was overflowing with suspects who pushed against the officers and screamed their innocence. At first, the genial interrogator accepted my excuse for having the revolver for self-protection against the anarchists. It was all just a big misunderstanding . . .

I was surely in the clear, especially when Tatum arrived with the British consul, an affable fellow with nicotine-stained hands. They persuaded the police to set me free and remove my manacles.

As we left the secret police's headquarters, there was a shout. "Don't let him go! That man is a student anarchist!" It was the sandy-haired, saber-swinging policeman. The game was up. They pulled me away from Tatum and shackled my hands. Soldiers with bayonets jabbed and pushed me into a black carriage with dazed students and workers.

As the carriage bounced down the street, crowds of people shouted and danced with joy.

"What are they saying?" I asked a fellow student.

"The tsar lives! God saved the tsar!" The student slumped against my shoulder and sobbed. "The stupid people of St. Petersburg are filled with joy that their beloved tsar still lives."

The carriage jostled over cobblestones until it arrived at the Yoannovsky gate of a gloomy and dark fortress. "Where are we?" I asked.

"The St. Peter and Paul Prison," the student said. "No one has ever escaped from this rotten place."

(Though my hand is shaking as I write, and I dread revisiting the horror of this last week, I know it is important to put it in writing. I shall, therefore, try my best to recount it and then forget as much about it as I can, if that is at all possible. I was not allowed pen or paper during my incarceration inside the St. Peter and Paul Prison, hence the gap in dates of this diary. My memory is still clouded by lack of sleep and I still feel the mental turmoil of being inside such a hell-hole, almost as if I were still there.)

When we arrived at the prison, soldiers with fixed bayonets herded the twenty or so of us out of the carriages, across an open courtyard, and down stone steps to a subterranean cell furnished with piles of moldy straw and a bucket overflowing with excrement. There was barely room to stand, let alone sit or lie down. The terrible odor added to our general misery and sense of hopelessness.

Once the soldiers left, the prisoners traded stories about their capture by the secret police. My fellow sufferers were mostly social activists whom the authorities had rounded up on the basis of reports by spies. It was a mixed group. There were students, Jews, and workers, as well as posh, upper-class men and women who had expressed sympathy for the dissidents or antipathy to the tsar.

There were many rumors milling about, but the only certainty was that the tsar had escaped an assassination. After less than an hour of confinement, the cell door clanged open. Two guards seized a victim at random, a boy of scarcely twenty years, for interrogation. The *thwack* of truncheons against flesh, the *crack* of a broken bone, and the howls and screams of the victim commenced immediately and went on for half an hour or more.

The same guards dragged him back, threw him into the cell, and selected another suspect. This went on for most of the afternoon. Two prisoners did not return. The rest were bleeding from their nose and mouth and suffered excruciating pain from dislocated fingers or broken bones. Each time the guards returned, every prisoner was frightened that they would be next. We suffered from fear of being picked, as well as the guilt of not being picked and remaining uninjured.

As a physician, there was little I could do but offer sympathy and soothing words. The police became more and more enraged and cruel when they learned nothing from us suspected regicides. I was at the side of one poor soul, attempting to straighten his broken arm, when a man knelt at my side. “It’s no use, Doctor, we are all doomed,” he said, in English.

“They cannot be so confounded inhumane. Why does the tsar allow the police to mistreat his subjects so?” I asked.

“It is the tragedy of Russia. In this terrible prison, Peter the Great strangled his own son, and Catherine buried her enemies alive. The best you can hope for is sudden death; the alternative is to slowly die by torture or to lose your mind in a lonely cell.”

He spit as he spoke and glared at me with piggish eyes. "A guard called my name. I steeled myself for torture and resolved to reveal nothing of my involvement with the student group or the bomb makers. Two officers led me to a small, plain room on the ground floor where a civilian, or at least an officer in plain clothes, offered a glass of tea. I lifted the glass with trembling hands, and as I drank, the officer began to speak. "The British ambassador spoke with Prince Vladimir and demanded your immediate release."

My heart leaped with joy and I put down my tea.

"Thank you. Thank you."

"Not so fast, Dr. Doyle..." Instead of removing my manacles, he folded his hands and smiled. "We would normally comply with the wishes of the Prince. However, since the case involves a plot against the tsar, it would be unwise to let you go without further investigation."

"And so how long might that take? A few more hours?"

"Maybe... But maybe days... Months... or even years."

"That is completely unjust!" I shouted. "I have done nothing to deserve a long prison term!"

"Dr. Doyle, you're in serious trouble. We have more than enough evidence to hang you, but since we, like you British, are a civilized people, we will not keep you in the usual pigsty, but will place you in a more — shall we say, pleasant — cell."

Two guards marched me, still in manacles, across an open courtyard to a sort of reception room where a fat, old man in the uniform of a general sat behind a desk. He examined the ambassador's note and roared with laughter. His French was terrible, but I understood enough. "Comfortable quarters? Ha!"

A foreigner, an Englishman, like the scum filling our cells." He leered at a non-commissioned officer. "Find a place for the Englishman where he will be comfortable until he hangs with the rest."

The bastard was still roaring with laughter when a detachment of soldiers took me through an iron gate further into the fortress to a damp room. I waited while a silent guard entered my name into a large book and ordered me to remove my clothing.

They commanded me to dress in their prison garb, an ankle-length flannel gown, wool stockings, and high, felt shoes. There was no sound as we tramped through a long, cold corridor through another locked and guarded gate to a small courtyard. I looked at the angel at the top of the cathedral and wondered if this would be my last breath of fresh air and my last sight of an open blue sky.

The Trubetskoy Bastion was a long, low building with individual cells that faced an open, gloomy corridor. The heavy door to the cell on the very end of the building had only a peephole and a small portal for the passage of food. The guards removed my chains and thrust me into a narrow cell. The heavy door clanged shut. My heart sank.

The room was dark; not a single ray of sunshine came through the small, barred window. When my eyes finally adjusted to the gloom, I made out a small, moldy threadbare carpet, a paper-thin cot, and bare damp walls.

Then, my heart stood still and my limbs grew weak. I had never believed in ghosts, but the apparition that I saw rising out from the shadows — from behind a small writing desk in the far corner of the cell — could not be real. It was a horrific, ethereal monster, a supernatural being. Or was my overactive mind hallucinating?

I blinked and looked again. The apparition was still there — small, white-haired, and hunched. A threadbare garment, a sort of caftan, hung about the creature's shoulders and dragged on the floor. The apparition's features were almost obscured by a flowing beard and long, tangled, curly, white hair. The rheumy eyes were vacant, dark, deep-set globes. The wide nose and thick lips might have reflected facial aspects of an African ancestor. It moved forward, with its arm and skeletal fingers outstretched. I heard the *swish, swish* of felt boots on the floor and nearly screamed. I realized the apparition was human, and in horror, I retreated until my back pressed against the heavy door.

"Natalya, ma cherie?"

I caught my breath. "No, my name is Doyle," I whispered, responding in French.

My first instinct was to strike the creature, but then my good sense took over and I stood stock still. This was a poor human being who must have been imprisoned for years and who certainly deserved pity. I held out my hand. "I am your new cellmate. What is your name?" I asked, in broken French.

"I have no name. I am officially dead — dead to the world, dead with a bullet in my spleen, dead to my dear wife, Natalya. Oh, Natalya, is that you?"

"Please, I am not your Natalya, but I am a trained physician."

"I have waited so long for them to send you." And with that, the old man tottered and fell into my arms. I carried him to the cot, where he lay back, folded his hands over his chest, and gave a great sigh.

"So many years. So many years… I have saved a candle for such an occasion as this. Light it, please."

I groped my way to the desk and found an old-fashioned flint and steel and a candle in a brass holder. After a few strikes, I caught a spark on a bit of charred cloth then blew until the glow was sufficient to light the candle.

I anxiously surveyed my new world; there was no possible escape. The bars in the window were set in a wall several feet thick. Next to the candle holder, on the desk, was a worn bible and a slate with a bit of chalk.

There were no loose bricks, only solid stone walls. I held the candle to a yellowed, cracked calendar on the wall and painstakingly deciphered the date — 10 February 1837. This was beyond comprehension. Why was this poor gent here? Had he truly been imprisoned here for more than forty years?

I listened for some human sound, but the silence was broken only by the old man's raspy breathing, the scurry of rats, and the drip of water. Finally, utterly exhausted, I threw myself onto the threadbare carpet and went soundly to sleep.

I awoke many hours later. Or was it all a dream?

The old man's voice rose and fell in a sort of rhyme that seemed familiar. The words were Russian, but sometimes, he lapsed into French. “Tatyana, Natalya …” he murmured. Once, with great clarity, he shouted the name *Eugene*.

In the morning, the old fellow’s eyes were glued shut with thick, yellow pus, and his eyelids were swollen. I led him to the window and, by the light of a single ray of sunshine, saw pustules at the base of his eyelashes. He was in pain and nearly blind.

I didn’t have my bag or any medicine. What could I do for him?

My only remedy was to apply a wet compress with a bit of cloth soaked in the weak tea that came with breakfast. I plucked out several infected eyelashes, and over the course of several days, the infection resolved. His eyes cleared, and his gratitude was touching.

During the days, he scratched on the slate and then erased what he had written. I hoped that he could teach me a few phrases in Russian, or explain his nightly recitations, but his mind was too far gone.

The days dragged one after the other with no communication, no outside human sound. The guard passed our two meals of coarse bread with thin soup and took away the slop jar but remained absolutely silent. I paced back and forth, back and forth.

Day by dismal day, I sank into the most dreadful despair, broken by dreams of my mam or of crushing Penelope in my arms, her lips warming mine and bringing my dying body back to life. I knew not how long I was there, but it seemed like an eternity. One especially dreary morning, the guard opened our door.

A nun of the Orthodox faith put a gold coin in his hand. Her shapeless, black garment and a thick veil covered her body from head to foot. She offered the heavy cross that hung on a gold chain to the guard. He knelt, and with great reverence, kissed the cross. “Thank you, little mother,” he murmured. The guard took his rifle and left his post.

She motioned for me and the old man to follow. Was it my imagination, or was there a whiff of orange blossoms? Most of her face was covered, but her eyes looked familiar, and the way she swung her hips as she walked was not like any nun I had ever seen. My heart began to race, and for the first time in days, I had a spark of hope that I might live.

The nun spoke to the old man in Russian. His features broke into a twisted smile. He nodded. "Ah, an escape. No, I am too old and frail to leave. This is where I shall stay, but I will help you get away. If, in return, you could take this, I shall die in peace." He withdrew from the depths of his old caftan a rolled bit of paper and pressed his greatest treasure into my hand.

"I will guard it with my life. Be well, my friend," I said.

The nun led us across the courtyard towards a side door of the cathedral. My cellmate, the old man, stumbled, and after a few steps, he clutched his chest and cried as if in pain. He collapsed and fell to the ground. The guard ran to his side, put down the rifle, and knelt by the old man.

I wanted to help but the nun pulled my arm. "It is part of the plan. He is acting. We must go."

We hurried and, in an instant, entered the cathedral and then the mausoleum between the tombs of Romanovs.

"Here, quickly, put these over your clothing." She handed me the cassock of an orthodox priest, a bishop's hat, and an enormous pectoral cross.

I pulled the black robe over my prison garb as fast as I could. "Walk, just ahead of me, slowly through the gate. There will be a waiting carriage. The driver will wear a blue coat," she whispered.

At the gate, a guard with rifle and bayonet barred our way. I wanted to run, but, after having seen the first guard kneel before the nun, had the presence of mind to offer the cross to be kissed. The young guard put down his weapon. "Thank you, Your Excellency," he murmured.

The slow march from the cathedral to the carriage seemed to take hours. At every step, I expected a bayonet thrust or a saber slash from one of the lounging soldiers. Suddenly, one of the guards ran towards me. All seemed lost. I was determined to smash his head with the heavy cross and run, but at the last moment he stopped, kneeled, and spoke with great urgency. "Please, Father, my son is sick. If you could give him a blessing?" he asked.

The soldier kneeled. I made the sign of the cross and recited a soft Latin blessing that I had learned as a child. When it was over, I helped him to his feet and he kissed my hand.

A few moments later, I assisted my companion into the carriage and slumped at her side. The driver did, indeed, have a spanking dark blue coat. We crossed the bridge over the Neva at a bare walk, and only then did the driver whip the horses to a gallop and the carriage lurch ahead. We were off.

The nun gave no inkling of her identity, and a scarf muffled the driver's features. I wanted to hug my savior, but she kept her distance and remained silent. When we were well away from the fortress, on a deserted street, she finally spoke. "Remove the cassock, and remember, not a word — not one word to a single soul."

She pulled off her headdress and long, chestnut curls tumbled out. "Penelope, what… How… Who are you?" I asked. She put her finger to her lips. "Don't ask. It is better that you remain ignorant. But it has been great fun," said she. I fell into her arms, happy beyond words to be with her again. She returned my gratitude with a long kiss, full on the lips, and then wiggled out of her black robe. She was, once again, transformed — now a demure young lady in afternoon dress. I was delirious with joy but no less mystified. She was a great actress, but how had she known I was in prison? Why had she come for me? Despite the fact that she had just saved me, the thought still plagued me — whose side was she on?

We took a roundabout route to Professor Sechenov's home, and once there, I went around the back way to the servant's entrance and slipped into my room unseen. I drew a bath and scrubbed away the prison dirt until Mr. Tatum knocked on the door.

I settled into an easy chair and told of my escape. He listened attentively, as if he was hearing this for the first time, but I wondered if he knew more about my adventure than he let on. Had he contacted Penelope through the British Secret Service?

Mr. Tatum rather solemnly recommended that I not leave my room. Thus, for days now, I have remained sequestered — eating, resting, recuperating and working with a Russian dictionary to decipher the tiny writing on the slip of paper from my mysterious cellmate. What follows is the most accurate translation I have been able to come up with.

d'Anthes' bullet ruptured my spleen, but unfortunately for the tsar, I did not die. My doctor, with the aid of brandy and opium, performed surgery and saved my life. The tsar was enraged and announced my death. He then ordered me to prison where I have languished for I know not how many years. Nicholas arranged the scandal, the duel, and claimed my death to have my beautiful Natalya as his own. Once the world knows the truth, I can die in peace.

Pushkin

10 September 1881

The past week has been one of further recuperation, reading, and study shrouded in a constant fear of being arrested. All the while, I have been remiss in making daily entries, so I shall remedy that situation with this update.

I have not left the confines of Sechenov's house. After my bloody horrific stay in the Peter and Paul Prison, I dream of returning home, sitting in my mother's kitchen and eating her blissfully good bangers and mash.

So what do I do all day?

Well, I spend my days in the library surrounded by books. At the end of each day, I do sprints and calisthenics within the walled garden to regain strength after my inactivity in prison.

What has made the past week tolerable is my daily Russian language lesson. I enticed a sweet, little kitchen maid named Marya to visit my room each night. She teaches me peasant Russian and cuddles in a most delightful manner. Her grammar is imperfect, but I am learning enough of the language to get by and she corrects my mistakes with a delicate kiss. I eagerly return each kiss and tend to make a few more mistakes than necessary. I have learned a great many terms of endearment and can carry on a very limited conversation in the Russian language.

In truth, I would be much better off taking Marya as my wife than Penelope, but I am mad about Penelope and my thoughts are of her even when I hold Marya. Would it be wrong to wed my own aunt? Could I even trust her? I know it would disturb many people, but there is something wonderfully compelling about the idea.

My rest was broken when, this morning, Mr. Tatum tapped on my door and announced that Dr. Bell requested my presence. I had scarcely seen him since my return, and as my own troubles faded, I was again worried for his health and deeply distressed about his proclivity for cocaine.

Fortunately, my concerns evaporated. He was erect, attired in a handsome dressing gown, and polishing off an omelet, a large beefsteak, and toast with marmalade. His cheeks were pink and he had gained weight. He leaned back, lit up his large, curved pipe and breathed out a wreath of fragrant smoke.

"Doyle, help yourself to coffee. There is another omelet and enough bacon for a whole battalion."

I thanked him and was soon stuffing my face with delicious vittles. "Sir, you seem to have recovered your usual robust health."

"Aye," Dr. Bell blew a large smoke ring. "I have determined the proper dose of cocaine to avoid unpleasant side effects. It is a capital nerve tonic. A seven percent solution of cocaine is beneficial."

It would be better if he had given up the drug but he seemed to be his old self. I said no more on the subject.

Bell delicately patted his lips with a damask napkin. "If you'd be so kind as to take a moment to refrain from eating so rapidly, I'd like to discuss some matters of great import with you," he said.

I put my fork down on my plate and sat back for a moment. "Aye, sir."

"I'd appreciate it if you could tell me what you've observed over the past few weeks."

"I've seen a great many exciting and awful things."

"No, not what you've seen. Anybody can see, but only a trained eye can observe. What you have you observed, laddie?"

Mr. Tatum bustled in with an overflowing tray of delicious sugary pastries with more eggs and bacon. Between mouthfuls, I related an abbreviated version of my involvement with the bomb makers and my arrest and incarceration. I ended with an announcement about how I am in great danger, and if the police discover my whereabouts, they will surely put me to death.

Bell helped himself to a lemon tart. "Well, Doyle, you are indeed fortunate. The Russian government cannot admit that escape is possible from the fortress. The third section is particularly adamant that you make no public mention of your mysterious cellmate. If this person was truly the famous poet, it will be a great embarrassment to the tsar. In that you are lucky. His government is eager to see that this all gets swept under the rug and has given a solemn assurance that, in return for your silence, your record will be destroyed and you will be granted complete amnesty," he said.

I was overwhelmed by this good news. After my prison ordeal, all I could think about was returning to Edinburgh. "Sir, does that mean that we are now at liberty to return home?"

Tatum squirmed. "Mr. Doyle, please …"

"I am sorry, but I almost died in that prison. I have done enough and should be allowed to go home," said I.

"Aye, I understand." Bell cleared his throat. "We cannot hold you against your will, but I cannot go, and as a favour to me, I was hoping that you may remain with us just a bit longer."

"Haven't you finished your course of lectures and demonstrations?"

"Aye, but the English Church has organized a clinic and a sanitarium for the care of children with tuberculosis. Professor Sechenov is anxious to test my theory that fresh air, good food, and cod liver oil is curative for these poor children. I have also developed a practice among the wealthy foreigners who live on the English Embankment. You can earn a bit more money by assisting me."

"That is a kind offer, sir, but after all I've been through, I've had enough adventure. It is time for me to return home."

"Laddie, we are involved in more than a bit of adventure here."

"Aye, and I have done my share for the Crown." I answered.

"Before you run back to Edinburgh, laddie, have you any notion of the importance of our mission?"

"The lives of many students hang in the balance."

He struck his clenched fist against his open hand. "Nay, hanging in the balance is more than the lives of a few students. We have fallen into a nasty situation that may affect the bloody balance of power in all of Europe."

"Sorry, but I don't see …"

"Doyle, has your head been so deep in medical books that you have no knowledge of world affairs?"

"Are those affairs so important?" I asked.

"The Queen and parliament are concerned because Germany is gaining power and may soon eclipse our empire. There is bad blood between the Kaiser and our Queen. The tsarist government is far from perfect, but Alexander is a friend of England. If an anarchist were to kill the tsar, there would be a power vacuum in Europe. The Germans would run rampant through Europe, and a Russo-German alliance could endanger millions of lives."

"Dr. Bell, surely the Crown has others who are better trained for this work."

"Nay, the British Secret Service has failed to infiltrate the student groups. You have earned credibility and trust with the students by the time you served in prison. Duty calls. Rise to the occasion. Your involvement could be the factor that keeps all of Europe from engaging in a massive war. Are you man enough for this assignment, Doyle?" Dr. Bell extended his hand.

I grasped his hand. "Yes, sir, I will do my best. There will be students at Pavlov's laboratory. I will talk with them."

Dr. Bell went off to the children's tuberculosis clinic, and despite an underlying sense of nervousness, I had a pleasant walk to the laboratory. Pavlov gave no indication that he was aware of my imprisonment and allowed me to perform several experiments under his expert guidance. Despite his insensitivity to human suffering, the man is a genius and far ahead of his time, especially in the field of blood transfusion and the nervous system. Together, with Ivanov, I succeeded in severing all the nerves to the heart in a dog. Much to our amazement, the heart continued a steady beat as if it had an intrinsic regulating mechanism.

I continued the work, and as we were preparing to operate, Dmitri, the animal keeper, brought a fine-looking female spaniel to the operating table. Most of the curs snapped their teeth or barked viciously, but this handsome animal licked my hand and allowed me to fondle her silky ears. She was mostly white, with brown spots and a handsome, brown muzzle. Her bushy tail thumped against the wooden table, and her large, dark eyes melted all my scientific instincts.

"Dmitri, put her back in the cage," I said.

For the first time, a fleeting smile passed over the poor man's face. It was as if something had awakened in his soul. Sometimes he has an air of refinement, quite unlike a peasant. For the next several days, I brought pieces of meat or bread soaked in gravy to my new friend. When I opened the cage, she put her head between her paws and licked my hand, then gently accepted my offering with all the elegance of a queen.

I couldn't think of a good Russian name, but her royal demeanor deserved a regal name that was equal to her dignity. I settled on the diminutive form of Alexandra — Sasha.

"Sasha, Sasha, come." she wagged her tail and delicately took a bit of meat.

I had not been involved with the transfusion experiments, but with nothing else to do that morning, I went to the blood laboratory. Two subjects were strapped on tables. At first, I did not recognize the poor wretch who was selected for transfusion. His beard was matted with old blood clots and his face was a mass of bruises and torn skin. Blood dribbled from each ear and his nose. The secret police had done their work. With a start, I recognized Golovinsky, who had chosen death by medical experiment rather than death by more torture at the hands of the Okhrana.

Ivanov and Dmitri held his hand and each bent close to his lips as if hearing a last confession. Over the hissing and rattling of the snakes in their cage, I could make out little of their conversation. The words made little sense, but I heard, "German" and "American." At my behest, Pavlov gave each subject enough morphine to dull their sensibilities during the gruesome experiment. I actually assisted Pavlov in isolating and canulating the donor's brachial artery and prepared the tubing for a direct blood transfusion.

Dmitri caught one of the giant rattlesnakes with a loop behind the creature's head and, with obvious reluctance, held the snake's body. He brought the terrible head, with its open jaws and exposed fangs, to Golovinsky's arm. The creature struck repeatedly, injecting its deadly venom. Golovinsky convulsed and his clotted wounds again dripped blood. The venom was, indeed, an anticoagulant.

Pavlov quickly placed a tube in a vein at his elbow and started the direct transfusion. Blood flowed from the donor into Golovinsky, but it was too late. With a last cry, his body stiffened and he died. "We could have kept him alive for another day. The damn fool," Pavlov swore.

I was about to leave for lunch, when a wild-eyed young man in a military uniform burst into the laboratory. "Dr. Doyle, there's been a terrible accident. You are wanted at the military hospital."

We climbed into the waiting droshky, and on an impulse, I shouted to Ivanov. "Come quickly, and bring Pavlov's serum."

We were away. The driver, sensing a tragedy and perhaps a large tip, whipped the horse to a frenzy. We dashed away to the other side of the city.

"What happened?" I asked.

"I'm in the Corps of Cadets. We double-loaded the noon gun, an old, bronze six-pounder. It exploded during the changing of the guard," the boy sobbed.

It was a scene from hell. Bodies were strewn about and the floor was slippery with blood. They were young boys with their limbs blown to smithereens and chunks of metal in their chests and bellies.

Dr. Bell was already at work on a head wound, and a half-dozen Russian surgeons were amputating limbs, suturing wounds, and ligating bleeding arteries. Dr. Bell pointed to a fellow on a makeshift table in the corner. "Doyle, make that lad comfortable. He is far gone. We can do nothing to save the poor fellow."

He was a slender boy of perhaps fifteen years with blonde, curly hair and a pale, bloodless face. His right arm was horribly mangled and his uniform was drenched with blood.

He was already lifeless. There was no need for morphine to relieve pain. By force of habit, I felt his wrist. Was there a flicker of a pulse? I put my ear to his chest and heard a distant thump. I resolved to do everything possible. "Orderly, please, over here. I need carbolic, ligatures, a scalpel, and a saw."

I snipped through the bit of skin that held his elbow to the upper arm and found an oozing brachial artery and vein. A single ligature controlled the bleeding. It was necessary to remove the lower humerus with a saw, and then, I stitched the skin over the stump. The entire affair had taken only a few moments, but the boy remained lifeless.

I was afraid that the shock of surgery had carried him off. I pressed my ear against his chest, but aye, there was still that distant thump. Almost as an answer to prayer, Ivanov appeared with a flask of Pavlov's serum.

We injected fifty, then one hundred, cubic centimeters of the fluid into his arm. I felt a weak pulse at his wrist. The boy was still alive. I straightened my aching back and noticed an older man, dressed in a frock coat and dark blue trousers, leaning on a cane, watching my every move.

He was obviously a gentleman and maintained his composure in the midst of chaos. "Will my son live?" he asked in refined French.

"He has a chance now," I said.

The man made a slight bow. "I am Prince Chernovsky. If my son, Konstantine, lives, I will owe you a great debt."

"I will do everything in my power to see that he lives."

"Thank you."

My patient rallied after a coffee enema. Prince Chernovsky insisted on removing the boy to his home. We placed him on the velvet seat in a splendid, gold and white, four-horse carriage. I stayed at the patient's side through the entire journey to his mansion and the boy's bedroom. A dozen liveried servants rushed about, securing pillows, fresh bandages, hot tea, and brandy.

The boy's mother burst into tears and had to be led from the room. At last, the child opened his eyes. It was as if he had returned from the dead. I felt a tremendous sense of accomplishment and slumped in a chair with overwhelming fatigue.

"Doctor, would you like tea or coffee?" a voice asked, a few moments later. The speaker was a rather plain, angular, young woman, dressed in a modest, floral-patterned dress from her neck to the floor. Her hair was tightly pulled back from her forehead into a bun. She was my age, or a little younger, and spoke perfect English.

"Coffee, please."

“I am Konstantine’s sister, Agafea, but mother calls me Kitty,” she said, with a smile. “And you are a doctor from England?”

“Edinburgh, Scotland actually, although my family is originally from Ireland. My name is Arthur Conan Doyle.”

The coffee arrived in a lovely silver service along with an assortment of cakes, biscuits, pâté, and a dollop of caviar. I was let down and had a case of nerves after the operation, and was rather overcome by the richness of the room, the silver tray, and her kindness.

“Our family is grateful to you for saving my brother.”

“Aye, but he is still in great danger.”

“I will be his nurse. You should go to your home and rest, but tomorrow morning, you must return to care for the antiseptic dressings.”

“Excuse me, but how do you know about antiseptic dressings?”

“Must all women be idiots?”

“Sorry. That’s not what I meant.”

“I trained as a nurse in London and plan to teach in the country. We must educate the peasants if we are ever to have true democracy here.”

For all her gentility, anger simmered just beneath her surface, an unspoken resentment of a sort. I said no more, finished the excellent coffee, and wolfed down enough biscuits and cakes to make a substantial supper. Agafea plumped the pillows and spooned broth into the boy’s mouth.

“His youth saved him,” I said.

She brushed aside a lock of mousy brown hair. “Don’t be so modest. Father said you saved his life when everyone else had left him to die,” she said.

I was preparing to leave when Prince Chernovsky stepped into the room.

“I want to engage you to care for my boy until he has recovered,” he said.

“Of course, I will visit him as often as necessary.”

“I will pay you well. What is your fee?”

I had no idea what the charge should be. He could easily pay one thousand pounds, but would he be insulted if I didn't charge for my services? "I am Dr. Bell's assistant and work at his direction. Perhaps you could make a donation to the new sanitarium for children with tuberculosis."

He paused, perplexed at my novel suggestion. "Yes, I will do that." I sensed his embarrassment. "Dr. Doyle, there is to be a ball for the Duke and Duchess of Edinburgh. Agafea has no escort. Would you be so kind as to take her to the party?"

My mind whirled. Agafea was plain-looking and no beauty. I didn't know how to dance nor even how to address the nobility, but I knew it was too good an opportunity to turn down.

"Yes, sir, I would be honored if Agafea is willing."

She blushed and smiled, but I sensed she was not taken with the idea. "Please call me Kitty," she said.

The prince provided his carriage for my ride home. It was late, and as usual, I went around to the servant's entrance. There was a rustling sound and then a low whimper at the door.

It was the dog, Sasha. I petted her silky ears and she licked my face. I took her into the kitchen. She daintily polished off the leftovers from the Sechenov evening meal and followed me up the back stairs. At the side of my bed she laid down, put her head on her paws. I am writing this in my diary under her wistful gaze.

18 September 1881

I haven't written in over a week since I've been waiting for Vera and Ivanov to tell me what really happened with their assassination attempt at the palace. In the meantime, Sasha has captivated Mr. Tatum and the kitchen servants with her doleful eyes and her tail-wagging gratitude for food. The poor dog was semi-starved but quickly filled out on leftover lamb chops and salmon filets.

I have been attending the chemistry lectures, hoping Vera and Ivanov will show up. The police and official St. Petersburg claimed a gas leak caused the palace explosion, but I knew that was not true. Vera and Ivanov finally appeared this morning. We decided to have an early dinner at the Idiot's Café, a low, smoky place overlooking the Moika River and a favourite student haunt.

I arrived early and watched boats plying the river while a couple of scruffy fellows drank tea and played chess. The sun was low, and the buildings around the square cast long shadows. Vera and Ivanov arrived together, dressed in casual student garb rather than the semi-uniform worn by the dissidents prior to the wave of arrests.

I had collected a few fees from some of Dr. Bell's English patients and generously ordered tea with salmon, sour cream, and pickled mushrooms. Vera and Ivanov were subdued and nervously glanced over their shoulders. The chess players picked up the pieces and left.

"What happened at the Gatchina palace?" I asked, rather bluntly, after a bit of small talk.

"Didn't you read the paper? It was a gas explosion," Ivanov answered.

"I don't believe that. I risked my life to help your comrades and spent a miserable time in prison and deserve to know the truth."

They looked at one another with hooded eyes. "The Okhrana raided the apartment and killed everyone on the spot," Vera said.

"What about your injured comrades?"

"Dead."

"And your other comrades?" I asked.

"The police executed the leaders, and most of the members are in prison."

"What caused the explosion?"

"Doyle, we appreciate you help but it is none of your business. For all we know you could turn informer to save your neck," Ivanov said.

"He deserves to know." Vera said.

"He deserves to know nothing."

"What difference does it make? The movement is finished anyway," Vera said.

"Ack, you're right." Ivanov ground his teeth and then his countenance wilted. "Buy me a vodka and I will tell you."

I waived at the waiter and ordered a vodka. He soon brought a bottle and glasses. I poured and Ivanov downed a glass. "Golovinsky delivered the eggs to an English woman."

"Do you know her name?" I asked.

"No. but she had connections with the royal family."

"Golovinsky bound and gagged the babushka who tended the tsar's hens and who usually delivered the eggs. Our friend waited in the woods and watched while the English woman, disguised to look like the babushka, delivered the eggs to the kitchen. She left them in a pan of water on the stove ready for the tsar. Timoshenko, the wood cutter, filled the stove with wood and started a fire. Five minutes later, the eggs exploded."

"Why wasn't the tsar killed?" I asked

"That is the tragedy. Every morning, like clockwork, he usually makes his own breakfast like a common working man. But on this morning, of all mornings, he had a headache and stayed in bed."

"How do you know?"

"Golovinsky told me everything just before the snake bit him," Ivanov said.

In my excitement over saving the boy, Konstantine, I had forgotten the whispered conversation just before Golovinsky died. "Yes, I remember that. What did he say about the Americans and Germans?"

Ivanov's eyes widened and he dropped his glass. Bits of glass and vodka splattered on the floor and, for a moment, we were busy cleaning the mess.

"Well?" I asked, "Will there be more attempts on the tsar's life?"

"There are always plots; we will never stop until he dies."

"Have you heard of an Englishman who has sworn vengeance on the tsar?"

Ivanov was clearly startled, as if I had touched a nerve, but he recovered in an instant. "No, that is foolish talk," he said. "And why are you so interested?"

"I don't want any more deaths."

Vera and Ivanov were too fearful to tell more, but I had learned enough to guess the truth. Was the English woman — Penelope? Was she that involved? Whose side was she on?

I bid them farewell and set off for a short stroll to the Chernovsky mansion. Prince Chernovsky was pale and tired from lack of sleep. Young Konstantine had no fever but was very weak. The skin about the stump was slightly inflamed and a drop of pus oozed from the incision.

"I will remove the infected stitch. Please soak a forceps and scissors in the carbolic solution."

Agafea put down her book and sterilized the instruments.

"You are reading *Origin of the Species* by Darwin," I said.

"Yes, I enjoy reading about science," she answered.

"Instead of the great psychological works of Russian literature?"

"Our authors are dark and often depressing. I suppose it is our chilly northern climate. But, then, I enjoy Poushkine's poetry, so …"

"Poushkine?"

"Yes, you English call him Pushkin," she said.

"Ah yes. The great poet of Russia. Tell me about him."

"Pushkin's great work was *Eugene Onegin*, a tragic love story, but he wrote many other poems. He died after a stupid duel with a Frenchman."

"You say he died?"

"Yes." She paused a moment. "Although, there have always been rumors that he survived and was sent to prison or Siberia. There was also talk about Tsar Nicholas' role in his death and how, afterward, he supported Pushkin's wife and children." I thought of my old cellmate and said nothing more on the subject.

When the instruments were well soaked, I removed the stitch in Konstantine's stump and drained a bit of yellow pus.

Agafea saw the pus. "Oh dear, does he have a deep infection?"

"It is nothing, Agafea. He will be fine."

"Call me Kitty. I hate the name Agafea. It sounds like a witch's name."

"Aye, Kitty." She forced a smile and took my hand. She was trying to appear brave, but I could tell she was worried.

"I have never been fond of dances and balls, but my father insists that I go, so I shall … But please, you don't have to escort me if you don't want."

"No. Of course I will go, but I am not especially fond of balls."

"Well, we can wallow in misery together."

She wore a nondescript dress, and her hair was tightly pulled back into a bun at the back of her head. I was not attracted to her and wondered if I had made a mistake in agreeing to what might be an utterly painful experience. "About this ball," I stammered. "Is there anybody else you'd prefer to go with?"

"You shouldn't miss the ball. The empress is giving the party in honor of the Duchess of Edinburgh, the tsar's sister."

"Still …"

"It is a masked ball. You will see true Russian excess. There is nothing like this in England and might be your only chance to witness our decadence first hand." She squeezed my arm and gave me a cold kiss on the cheek.

Despite Marya's best efforts to brush and iron my once-elegant, black dress suit, it was shabby in comparison with the Russian's colorful uniforms. Sasha perked up her ears at the tap on my door. There was a twinkle in Dr. Bell's eyes when he placed a bulky package on the table.

"Open it. We can't have you attending a royal ball with a princess looking like a common tramp."

The package contained a Scottish evening suit. "Oh my!" I exclaimed. The trousers were made of fine wool in the black and dark green Black Watch tartan pattern, and the light grey Barathea jacket with silver buttons had the Edinburgh Medical School crest. Its dark red, light red, and yellow colors stood for liver, blood, and pus. A white waistcoat completed the outfit.

"It is quite grand," I spluttered. "Thank you."

"Put it on," Dr. Bell said.

I pulled on the shirt and stepped into the trousers while Mr. Tatum fussed with the studs. He held out the waistcoat and then the jacket. It all fit perfectly.

"I almost forgot. It is a masked ball," I said. "What should I do?"

"Here, go as a Scottish highwayman." Dr. Bell unfolded a large tartan handkerchief.

A while later, I was sitting in a spindly chair in the Chernovsky's grand reception hall waiting for Kitty. After an hour, I paced about, pausing to look at a vase, painting, and gilded ornaments while the footman watched as if I were a potential thief. With nothing better to do, I visited Konstantine. He was pale and his breathing was shallow. His mother was crying. The wound was slightly red and swollen, but it was not that bad and required no further treatment. I reassured his tearful mother and returned to the foyer.

There was a rustle at the head of the marble staircase. It was Agafea, wearing a sparkly, small tiara in hair that fell to her shoulders in soft waves, and a cream-colored ball gown that revealed her shoulders and just a hint of bosom. When she reached the foot of the stairs, I had the presence of mind to bow and take her hand. "Miss Kitty, you look quite lovely tonight," I said.

"You are too kind, Arthur."

She smiled and her dark blue eyes twinkled with humor. Her mother trailed along behind, wringing her pudgy hands. "Please Kitty. I beg you not to go."

"Mother, stop it! Father wants me to go and I need to show my face."

"If Konstantine was feeling better, I'd go with you, but we should both stay here with him."

"I am going to the ball, Mother."

"Oh dear, what will people say? All the respectable ladies in attendance will have a chaperone."

"Mother, please. I am of age. Besides it makes no difference what people say." We went off in the great family carriage. Nevsky Prospekt was jammed with carriages, armed guards, soldiers with fixed bayonets, and mounted officers. The guards who stopped us at the great columns of the palace were satisfied with Agafea's curt answers, but it was well after ten before we crossed the parade ground and reached the entrance of the Anichkov Palace.

We ascended the great staircase lined with white-wigged footmen dressed in splendid black satin and gold velvet costumes. The entire expanse of galleries, ballrooms, and the great hall were lit with hundreds of candles. I felt like a true pauper in the midst of this Russian splendor.

A mazurka was in progress when we entered the great hall. Wild dancers stamped to the right and then the left, whirled in a circle, and then formed a grand chain. There were officers of the Royal Guard in white and green uniforms, Hussars, aides to the royal family, diplomats and government officials, all with gold braid and glittering medals. Even the waiters and servants wore bright red and blue uniforms that outshone my Scottish attire. A seventy-piece orchestra filled the air with waltzes, the polonaise, and folk dance tunes.

I indicated a particularly resplendent captain in a gaudy green and gold uniform. "Who is that?" I whispered.

"A fool in the Seminofsky Regiment." Kitty replied. She adjusted her silvery mask and led me to a quiet corner. "You are quiet. Are you enjoying this ostentatious display?" she asked.

"I cannot but help contrast this opulence with the charity hospital. The money spent on champagne alone would feed the poor of St. Petersburg for a week." I said.

"I agree. I am a liberal and a terrible disappointment for father."

A waiter offered tiny, delicious pies and crystal glasses with vodka. Despite our liberal instincts and good intentions, we couldn't refuse. We wandered among the throng, sipping and nibbling while observing Russian high society.

"Come. We must pay our respects to the duke and duchess," she said.

We drifted with the revelers through the red and gold rooms to the concert hall where the English duke with his Russian duchess held forth. The duke scowled, as if he wished he was on the deck of a ship in the Royal Navy, but brightened when he noticed my Scottish outfit. "The University of Edinburgh. Ah yes, a fine school," he said. I glowed with pride.

I mumbled a reply and then, out of the corner of my eye, caught sight of a masked woman with orange blossoms in her long, chestnut hair dancing with none other than the be-medaled German Count. Could it be Penelope?

I took Kitty by the waist and madly whirled her through the dancers, bumping into couples and drawing hard looks in my attempt to reach the couple. I saw her once more, on the arm of Count Carl von Wittenberg before she disappeared in the crowd. "Who is that woman?" I asked Kitty.

"I believe she is Miss Walshingham, a lady-in-waiting to the Duchess of Edinburgh."

The mystery deepened. If it was indeed Penelope in the entourage of the Duchess and living under the same roof as the tsar, he was in great danger. It explained the 'English woman' who delivered eggs to the kitchen.

"I am tired, please. Let us leave." Kitty said.

We took a carriage back to the Chernovsky mansion. Instead of a darkened, sleeping mansion, every light was on. Servants ran to and fro with packets of pills, bottles with colored liquids, and a bowl of steaming soup.

"What is wrong?" Kitty demanded.

"The young prince has taken a turn for the worse," the old footman said.

We ran to his bedchambers. Prince Chernovsky' face was as dark as thunder. He was about to strike me with his fist but held back when Konstantine cried out. His poor wife sobbed uncontrollably and wrung a handkerchief. A maid applied cold clothes to the boy's hands and face while he nestled on silken pillows in a canopied, four-poster bed. At first glance, he appeared to be more frightened than ill.

An elderly, bearded doctor, introduced as the surgeon to Prince Chernovsky's regiment, sat at the bedside. "In cases of this nature, it is sometimes necessary to amputate the arm at a higher level," he said.

Great God! I thought. *Have I committed a terrible error? Was the bone infected?* The boy had fever but also a runny nose, and he sneezed. There were swollen lumps in his neck but no further discharge of pus from the amputation stump. The old surgeon was already sending for his surgical kit when I remembered a child in the infirmary with similar symptoms.

"Kitty, wait! Please hold a lamp to his face." She brought a gilded oil lamp to the bedside.

"Konstantine, open your mouth." I gave the order in French. The boy understood and opened wide. There were spots inside his cheeks. I gave a great sigh of relief. "Ah yes, these red spots are typical of measles."

"Dear God, another complication," the Prince said.

"The boy is suffering from a common case of the measles. There is no need for an amputation. Tomorrow, he will have a rash all over his body, and within a week, he will be fine."

The old doctor looked at the strawberry spots inside the boy's mouth and pulled his beard. "He is correct; Konstantine has measles. I am sorry, sir, for not checking his throat," he said.

The Prince pumped my hand, and his wife embraced me with a tearful hug.

"We are again in your debt."

As I prepared to leave, the Prince pressed an envelope into my hand.

"My dear Dr. Doyle, take this."

"That is not necessary."

“These are ballet tickets. Please use my box at the theater. There is plenty of room for your friends and, as a favour, take Agafea. The poor girl is worn out from looking after Konstantine. Please, take them. You have done so much for us.”

It was near dawn when I finally crawled into bed, which was already warmed by Marya, my dear scullery maid and comforting friend. She was drowsy, but delightful, and more than made up for Agafea’s cold peck on the cheek. Marya giggled when I gently squeezed her bottom and whispered a Russian phrase of love in her ear. Of course, I said a few words incorrectly so she would kiss me again and again …

19 September 1881

Prince Chernovsky's box at the Imperial Bolshoi Kamenny Theater was in the second tier to the right of the great stage. We had a glorious view of the boards and the gilded rows of box seats. Before the ballet began, we watched the milling crowds of people finding their way to the gold and blue chairs on the first floor. These preliminaries were as entertaining as the performance.

Kitty pointed to a box on the first tier, just below us and opposite. It was similar to ours, but roomier and more luxurious. "That is the Imperial Box, but the tsar doesn't like opera and rarely attends," she said.

The orchestra tuned up and then blasted away for the opening act while the gigantic blue and gold curtains swung back to reveal the cast. The performance was the ballet, *Tsar Kandavi* or *Le Roi Candaule*. It was terribly confusing, and I was never exactly sure about what was transpiring onstage. It seemed that Tsar Kandavi seized power, and then, King Gyges went to live with the shepherds; after that, I became hopelessly lost.

Very quickly, Mr. Tatum went to sleep, but Dr. Bell followed the performance with attention and apparent enthusiasm. Once I lost track of what was happening onstage, my eyes and mind inevitably wandered to a strikingly beautiful girl in the dim shadows of the Imperial Box. A large, bearded gentleman stood in the shadows with his hand on her bare shoulder. I nudged Kitty. "May I borrow your opera glasses? I think the tsar might be here tonight."

I focused the glasses and pretended to watch the stage but really fixed mostly on the girl's bare shoulders, rather striking bosom, and lovely features. As I admired the girl, the tall, portly man kissed her lips. I passed the glasses back to Kitty. "Is that the tsar?"

This was definitely turning out to be more interesting than the ballet. "I can't be certain, but he does not appear to be the tsar," she said, after several minutes of study.

"Then who is it?"

"I would wager that it's the Grand Duke Vladimir, the tsar's brother."

I tried paying attention to the ballet, but the amorous scene in the Imperial Box was much more interesting.

"It's my turn. The glasses, please." I said.

Dr. Bell scolded me with his eyes for the slight commotion.

"Sorry," I whispered and took the glasses from Kitty.

Things heated up during the "Pas de Venus". The nubile, young girl in the box climbed on the duke's lap and was deep in the old boy's beard.

"How scandalous. The grand duke is a notorious playboy and drunkard. The opera company regularly supplies him with girls, but I never dreamed that they would carry on so… so blatantly," whispered Kitty. Her eyes were glued to the Imperial Box.

Scandalous or not, I enjoyed the passionate scene, which was more interesting than the ballet. Suddenly, the girl slid off the duke's lap and collapsed. The duke adjusted his trousers and made a fast exit.

The girl lay motionless on the floor of the box, but the audience, intent on the performance, paid no attention. Of all those hundreds of people, I alone had witnessed the scene.

"Dr. Bell, a girl in the Imperial Box is sick or injured."

"The authorities need to be informed," said Kitty. She spoke rather imperiously to an usher who, in turn, found a military officer who led us, pell-mell, past guards to the Imperial Box. The girl was dead on the floor with a smear of dark blood and a neat, small hole in the back of her head. "This is a case for the police. As witnesses, you all must remain here until the police arrive," said the officer.

"What exactly happened?" Dr. Bell asked.

I told him everything. "I am certain it was the grand duke, but he does resemble the tsar," Kitty added.

Dr. Bell gazed at the stage, lit his pipe, and breathed out a cloud of smoke. "The dancers in this ballet are quite beautiful, are they not?" he remarked.

"Yes, lovely creatures. But sir, shouldn't we be searching for a killer?" I asked.

"Think before taking action," he said.

The police were not Okhrana thugs, but a polite, uniformed policeman and a pleasant, smooth-faced, blonde man of about forty who introduced himself as Inspector Marti Koivisto. As we shook hands, I thought the slim, pale inspector appeared more like a scholar than a police officer. He kept our little group in the wings of the Imperial Box, out of the view of the audience while he questioned the security guards. They shrugged and pointed to us. Kitty introduced herself as Agafea and explained who we were, with emphasis on Dr. Bell, the distinguished university lecturer.

"Dr. Joseph Bell of Edinburgh?" the inspector asked, in heavily accented English.

Dr. Bell bowed slightly. "Yes."

"I have read your articles on scientific crime detection and spent a week in London, observing Scotland Yard. You are far ahead of us in criminal investigation procedures. Tell me, what do you make of this young woman's demise?"

"You are most kind, but my associate, Dr. Doyle should first tell what he observed," Dr. Bell said. "He had a much better view of the incident."

"Inspector, could this be an assassination attempt on the tsar?" I asked.

"I am only concerned with this murder. It is best to make no mention of the royal family," Inspector Koivisto replied. My brief description of the man and woman and her sudden collapse lasted only as long as scene three in the third act. The audience was still oblivious to our little drama.

Inspector Koivisto listened carefully and made no comment. He motioned for us to enter the box. "Dr. Bell, your opinion, please?" he asked, after a minute inspection of the scene.

Dr. Bell motioned with his pipe. "Dr. Doyle, will you be so kind as to place the young woman in the position you noted immediately prior to her collapse?"

With the aid of the uniformed policeman, we turned the young lady over, noting a bruise on her right nipple, and then placed her in a sitting position, facing the back of the chair. "Hold her head in the exact position as you remember," Dr. Bell said, when her head flopped to one side.

"I don't see how this will …"

Dr. Bell interrupted the inspector rather impatiently. "Please, Inspector, if you will, indulge me."

I had the uniformed policeman hold her arms around the back of the rather high upholstered chair, as if she was embracing a lover, while I held her head as if she was in the act of kissing lips slightly above her level. The smudge of blood and the hole in her skull was centered at the top of her head. Dr. Bell sighted from the hole up and across the great theater.

"We must probe the wound, but unfortunately, I don't have my instruments."

"Sir, would a lead pencil suffice?" I asked.

"An admirable suggestion."

My almost-new lead pencil fit nicely into the small skull defect. Dr. Bell slowly advanced the pencil deep into the skull, withdrew it once, and then again. "I must follow the exact tract of the bullet if we are to find the killer," he said.

"A bullet? Come now, it would be impossible to fire a rifle without a single person hearing the shot," Inspector Koivisto said.

"I will explain in a moment. Ah, here, Inspector, push the pencil ever-so-slightly."

The inspector held the pencil delicately between his thumb and index finger, closed his eyes, and pushed the pencil, millimeter by millimeter, until the tip was approximately four centimeters inside the girl's head.

His eyes lit up. "Yes, the probe touched a hard object within the brain."

"It is a bullet lodged in her brain. An autopsy will provide proof of my observation." Dr. Bell said.

"Why are you so certain?"

"Elementary, my dear Inspector. Trust me, you will find a bullet of approximately .30 calibre lodged in the woman's brain. Now, Doyle, this is most important; hold the head in the exact position," Dr. Bell said. He dropped to his knees, as sighted along the pencil, and pointed to the top tier of boxes. "Based upon this angle, the assailant had to be there, in the last row, between the two entrance doors. Inspector, see for yourself."

"Yes, but..." Inspector Koivisto positioned himself and sighted along the pencil. "I still don't understand how it could have been a gunshot. There was no noise and no smell of gunpowder."

"If you followed all the latest scientific advancements, Inspector, you'd know that an inventor at the Krupp works in Germany has developed a powerful gun that operates on compressed air. It fires a conical lead bullet and makes almost no sound. I suggest we have a look at the upper tier directly opposite to discover the shooter."

Inspector Koivisto gave instructions to the uniformed officer to discreetly remove the body through the wings to the morgue for an autopsy, while we made our way through back corridors to the opposite galleries.

During the entire proceedings, which to a layperson must have seemed gruesome in the extreme, Agafea had maintained her composure and appeared to be intently interested. Even when I placed the pencil deep in the dead girl's head, she did not flinch.

"Would you prefer to go home, Miss Kitty?" I asked.

"Why?" she tossed her head. "Just because I am a woman? Besides, you may require an interpreter."

There were only a few scattered spectators in the upper gallery where the presumed assailant had fired the fatal shot. Dr. Bell moved back and forth until we had a clear view of the Imperial Box. "The assassin fired the fatal bullet from this vacant seat. He probably aimed at the girl's companion but, in the dim light, hit the girl instead."

Inspector Koivisto sniffed the air. "There is no odor of gun smoke."

"Believe me, Inspector, the assailant used a powerful air rifle." Dr. Bell said.

The light was so dim we could hardly make out the individual chairs. Dr. Bell, on hands and knees, inspected the aisle from one entrance door to the next. "Doyle, please light a match."

I struck a lucifer and held it, while he, as intent as bloodhound, minutely inspected the carpet and sniffed beneath each chair.

In the meantime, Inspector Koivisto discretely questioned the nearest spectators. No one had heard or seen anything unusual. I was beginning to doubt Dr. Bell's theory, when the match burned down and scorched my fingers.

I struck a new match and, in the flare, noted a sparkle as if from a metallic object beneath the chair. "There, sir. What is that?" I cried.

Dr. Bell took up a small circlet of paper with a bit of gold leaf that had sparkled in my match light. On the outside was the letter 'H'. "It's a discarded cigar band." Dr. Bell said. He held the band to his nose and inhaled deeply. "Latakia. Yes, I am positive the cigar was made with tobacco from Latakia. Those who appreciate tobacco consider Latakia to be the world's finest."

Koivisto shook his head. "I am sorry, Dr. Bell, but anyone could have left a cigar band."

"This is not just any cigar band, Inspector. This is from a Hirschsprung cigar, made in Denmark, and favoured by wealthy Germans. This brand is not available in Russia and far too expensive for most people," Dr. Bell replied.

"I am sorry, but there is so little evidence," Koivisto said.

"The evidence is there, Inspector, it is just up to one to extract its meaning. The owner of the Hirschsprung Cigar Company is a distinguished physician with strong ties to Germany. Discrete enquiries at the German Embassy will prove that I am correct."

"We shall see about that." Inspector Koivisto placed the cigar band in an envelope. "I will arrange the autopsy for ten tomorrow morning. Will you join me, Dr. Bell?"

"Doyle and I will be there, with pleasure."

We all departed and I walked Kitty home. In the Chernovsky drawing room, she rewarded me with a cold peck on my cheek. There were no cabs. During my long walk home, I turned over in my mind the recent assassination attempts. Had the killer expected the tsar, or were there plots to kill the entire royal family? Once again, my thoughts turned to Penelope — was she involved?

I was disappointed to find only Sasha in my room. Marya, the little tramp, must have found more pleasant company. I have passed the time by rubbing Sasha's belly and reading a medical text, but I can no longer keep my eyes open.

20 September 1881

The pathologist had already made the usual Y-shaped incision from neck to pubes and the girl's viscera were in a messy pile on the table. Inspector Koivisto seemed about to regurgitate his breakfast, even though the odor of rotting human flesh and excrement was no worse than usual. As a medical student, I had learned to cope with noxious odors in the dead house with copious amounts of cologne, cheap tobacco, and breathing through my mouth.

"Ockk, dere is nozzing in the chest or belly," The pathologist said to us, in his heavy accent.

He made an incision from one temple to another around the back of the head and yanked the scalp forward over her face. Then, with a saw, he removed the top of her skull. The bullet was embedded deep in the pulpy mess that was her mid-brain. She had died instantly. The lead was dented where it had first struck the skull, was hollow at the base, and measured three tenths of an inch in diameter — exactly .30 calibre.

Dr. Bell was, as usual, correct. It was hard to tell if Koivisto was angry or impressed. His lips were compressed in a grim line. "Inspector, find the owner of a .30 calibre air rifle who smokes Hirschsprung cigars and you have your killer," Dr. Bell said.

"Come, let us go. I will be sick if we stay here any longer," Inspector Koivisto said.

We went to lunch at a small café. We finished bowls of Solyanka, a spicy soup with pickled cucumbers. While we waited for a platter of pickled mushrooms, cured fish, and deviled eggs, Koivisto leaned back in his chair. "We have a spy in the German Embassy," he said.

"Is it ethical to spy on a foreign government?" I interrupted.

"Ethical or not, it is a must. There is so much tension between us and the Germans. You see, over the past year, Grand Duke Vladimir has instituted a government policy to force Germans in the provinces to speak only Russian. They are resisting, and Duke Vladimir is as unpopular as the tsar. My spy reports that a

Count von Wittenberg, the new naval attaché, is quite vocal about his disdain for Vladimir."

"And the count regularly smoked Hirschsprung cigars, yes?" Dr. Bell asked.

"Yes, and the count did not return to his quarters last night."

The inspector toyed with a bit of deviled egg. "You are very astute and deserve to know more. I have a source in the palace who keeps us informed so we can better protect the family. The tsar and the empress planned to attend last night's performance but, at the last minute, changed plans. The grand duke arranged a little tryst and attended in their place."

The inspector offered to pay the bill, but Dr. Bell waved him away. "It is our greatest pleasure to be of assistance and service to the Crown."

"What do you make of it?" I asked Dr. Bell, as we left.

Bell tossed a ruble to a street beggar before he answered. "I suspect the real target was the tsar. The cigar band could have been planted to lead us astray, but there are indications of German involvement. There are many German professors at the university. Are they inciting the students?"

I had to think about that. We were nearing the river before I replied. "The students don't need an outside influence to kill the tsar. The Germans, however, may supply money and advice to aid in the job."

22 September 1881

Yesterday and today have been, well, quite difficult, and I did not get a chance to write in this journal last night.

Yesterday, I was dreaming of going home to Auld Reekie when, at breakfast, Mr. Tatum, rather more forcefully than necessary, took me away to the British Embassy. I was tired and hungry and did not enjoy the ride, even though the carriage was drawn by four splendid, matching black horses.

At the embassy, an armed guard passed us on to an undersecretary and thence to the inner sanctum of Sir John Ecclestone, her Majesty's Ambassador to the Russian court. Sir John, for all his sixty years, was a handsome man and a flinty, hardened veteran of many a diplomatic war. He offered no refreshment and didn't waste time with small talk, but bore into me with his stern, grey eyes. "Mr. Doyle, Her Majesty, the Queen, is disturbed by the recent attempts on the life of Tsar Alexander III, and rightly so."

I stood rigidly at attention, wondered what was coming, and dared return his penetrating gaze.

"Mr. Tatum has made you privy to the Queen's request that we do everything possible to prevent his assassination. Is that not correct?

"Yes, sir," I replied.

"Then, why does the Russian Secret Service claim you were involved with an assassination plot?"

"I was actually attempting to STOP the plot."

"You are an embarrassment to the Crown, Mr. Doyle."

"Sir, I came here to assist Dr. Bell, but now, I would actually prefer to be home in Edinburgh!" I was about to make a more impudent reply but Mr. Tatum pinched my arm. "Mr. Tatum and I did our best to warn the tsar, but the police took me in custody and I spent several bloody miserable days in prison on false charges. I have done more than my fair share for the Crown, sir," I choked out.

The ambassador made the smallest hint of a smile as if he was laying a clever trap. "Yes, that is in your favour, and as a result, you are well positioned to be of further service to the Queen."

"I would be honored to help, sir, but I must decline."

"And why is that, Mr. Doyle?"

"I am sympathetic with the plight of the Russian people."

"Your sympathies are of no concern to me. You will do your duty or face the consequences."

"Consequences?"

"Your father could find himself incarcerated for his debts. His brother, your uncle, is a known supporter of the Irish cause. He may find himself under lock and key, and you may be tarred with the same brush. It could be difficult to practice your profession with such a stigma attached to your name."

I had never been threatened in such a way before. I gulped, thought for a moment, and then chose my words carefully. "I understand the global ramifications if the tsar and his government are brought down, but, with all due respect, who is to govern Russia is a matter for the Russian people and of little consequence to the British Empire."

"You are quite naïve, Mr. Doyle." Sir John beckoned us to a map of Europe and the Middle East on a large, well-polished rosewood table. "The Franco-Prussian War upset the balance of European power. Germany has the upper hand — not only in Europe, but in the Ottoman Empire. The Germans have financed and engineered railroads from Istanbul to Damascus and Baghdad that threaten our lines of communication from Egypt to India through the Suez Canal. The death of another tsar will lead to chaos in Russia. Germany will dominate Europe, the Middle East, and Russia all the way to the Urals."

"What is Germany's motive?"

"The age of coal and steam is over." He tapped his finger on the map and traced a line from Baghdad to the Black Sea. "The future is oil, Mr. Doyle, oil. If Russia falls into chaos, Germany will control the world's greatest oilfields. In a few years, the world will run on oil. A strong tsar is necessary to hold Russia together and to be Britain's ally against Germany."

"All that is well and good, sir, but what do you want of me?" I asked.

"Nothing more than what you've already done. Continue your involvement with the student anarchists and keep your eyes open for the British officer, David Campbell, who intends to kill the tsar.

The ambassador clipped the end of a cigar and sniffed its aroma. "You have had some involvement with Miss Walshingham, a clever woman who has made herself indispensable with the Duchess of Edinburgh," he said, rather offhand. The ambassador lit a lucifer and thoughtfully rotated his cigar in the flame until it glowed. "That clever lady is an enigma. Where do her sympathies lie?" *Aha*, I thought. *This must be the real reason for my summons to the Ambassador*. "I am sure she is a loyal British subject," I said. I hoped the ambassador did not detect the lack of certainty in my words.

Sir John waved us away with a curt dismissal. "My secretary will fill you in with the details."

Adrian, the secretary, spoke in a condescending, plumy, upper-class English voice. His large, red nose showed the effects of an affectionate relationship with the bottle. I hated him on the spot, especially when he compelled us to take an oath of allegiance to the Queen.

He then handed me a small document. "This will identify you as an agent of the British government. It may be of some use if the Okhrana stops you again." Next, Adrian's well-manicured hand pushed a small box across the desk containing a two-inch, .40 calibre derringer pistol and twenty brass cartridges. His voice turned cold. "Conceal this on your person. You are to kill, if necessary, to protect the tsar and his relationship with the crown. Miss Walshingham and her deceased husband's associates may be enemies of England. Kill them, as well, but only if necessary."

I abruptly left Mr. Tatum at the embassy, went straight home, found Sasha lazing in the kitchen, and set off at a near-trot with the dog running at my side. We left the large homes and bypassed the factories. The whole time, my mind was in a whirl; I could not possibly kill Penelope. Would that make me a traitor? I desperately yearned to return to Edinburgh, remove myself from all this deadly international intrigue, and get on with the practice of medicine.

The exercise cleared my head, and it was good to get away from the stench and noise of the city. After a few miles, we came upon summer houses with green gardens. Sasha's comic antics soothed my troubled soul. She gaily chased rabbits, and when her eyes fastened on a bird, she pointed with her nose and delicately raised her front paw.

After a long, invigorating walk, we came to the dockyards, rested on the embankment, and watched ships coming and going in the harbor. There were many Russian navy vessels and ships with every European flag in the anchorage. It is getting to be fall and a cold wind whipped a chop in the water. I shivered, found shelter in a cheap tavern, and made a hearty workman's lunch of beer, black bread, and soup.

Sasha, with a grateful wag of her tail, finished the scraps, while the jovial proprietor explained how business had picked up with the gathering of the Baltic fleet for the tsar's review. It seemed as if all of St. Petersburg was anxious to see the tsar come out of his self-enforced isolation to review the fleet.

I dawdled in the long, northern evening and didn't arrive home until late. Marya fluttered over Sasha. "They are waiting for you, Arthur. You must hurry to Dr. Bell's room," she whispered.

I sniffed the fragrant blue smoke from Dr. Bell's great, curved Meerschaum even before I arrived at his room. It meant he was deep in thought or troubled by a new case. Professor Sechenov paced the room in a state of high agitation, but Dr. Bell at his desk, sorted surgical instruments and peered at the labels of medicine bottles. "One cannot predict whether these cases require an operation or will be amenable to medicines," he said.

Sechenov wrung his hands. "We must hurry. Countess Tolstaya's message indicated great urgency and it is a long way to Tsarskoye Selo. The royal carriage is waiting and we must go."

I was tired from the long walk, but sensed another adventure.

“Ah, Doyle, lad. We must leave at once. Take the instrument case and let us be on our way. Professor Sechenov will explain everything,” said Bell, as he packed the last bottle.

The gold gilt carriage with red wheels drawn by four shiny, white horses was indeed a royal means of travel. The driver and his assistant, in green and gold uniforms, could have passed as generals in the army.

The assistant leaped down from his high perch and handed us in to the spacious interior with soft velvet seats. There was room to stretch out and sleep, but Professor Sechenov aroused my curiosity. “Professor Sechenov, you mentioned Countess Tolstaya. Is there any chance we will meet her husband, Count Tolstoy, the great writer?” I asked.

“Bah, I think not. The man has become a socialist reformer. Many think he is mad, especially when he speaks of anarchy. The fool is totally out of favour, but his wife, the countess, is not. She is a lady-in-waiting to the empress, Maria Feodorovna.”

“What is the medical problem?”

“The empress was enjoying the gardens at Tsarskoye Selo when she became ill with terrible abdominal pain. I fear it may be an inflammation of the appendix, the American disease. Her physician thinks it is a medical problem,” Professor Sechenov said.

“Who is the physician?” Dr. Bell asked.

“It is quite awkward. He is a German specialist and physician to Princess Yurievskaya.

“Who is this princess?” Dr. Bell asked.

Professor Sechenov pursed his lips. “It is a sorry episode in the lives of the royal family. When the wife of Alexander II became ill, he took a commoner, a woman named Dolgorukov as his mistress. After his wife died, he married the woman, but instead of making her his empress, he gave her the title, Princess Yurievskaya. She is jealous of the Empress Maria for taking her place in the royal household.”

“Where is the tsar?” Dr. Bell asked.

“Somewhere in the wilderness with his friends, hunting bears.” The lengthening Russian night was upon us, when, beneath a misty full moon, we rolled into the courtyard at the gates of

Catherine the Great's palace. Servants with lanterns led us through gilded corridors to the bedroom of Empress Maria Feodorovna.

In the light of a single candle, I could appreciate magnificent gilt chairs, carved tables, velvet wall hangings, brocade curtains, and, in the middle of the room, our patient was covered by rumpled quilts in a great four-poster, canopied bed. Except for the sound of raspy breathing and her occasional moan or a low scream, the room was deathly silent. A servant girl with trembling fingers first rubbed the empress's hands and then applied a compress of cold water to her face.

Professor Sechenov was clearly in awe of his surroundings. "C-countess Sophia Tolstaya, may I p-p-present Professor Joseph Bell," he stammered.

The countess Tolstaya, a middle-aged woman with a tired, lined face, was dressed in severe, black, mourning clothes in respect for the assassinated Alexander II. She wracked with sobs and held a tear-soaked handkerchief to her face. She said nothing, but nodded briefly to Dr. Bell.

The other person in the sick room was a handsomely-dressed gentleman wearing a monocle attached to a long, red ribbon who hovered at the bedside holding a large syringe. He clicked his heels and made a little bow. "Boris Meyer, Doctor of Medicine, University of Berlin and senior physician to Princess Yurievskaya. I am about to administer a stimulant." I remembered Vera saying that the Russian elite preferred German or French doctors to Russian physicians.

Dr. Bell approached the bed, pushing the German aside. "More light, please."

The servant girl rushed to ignite gas lamps, and in their bright glare, I could see the pale, sweaty face of the empress. She was beautiful, with large, round eyes that were dimmed with pain and fever.

The German, Dr. Meyer, lowered the syringe and he sadly shook his head. "The empress is in extremis. You have made a needless trip. If this injection doesn't restore her to health, she is doomed."

Dr. Bell ignored the man and took up her wrist. “It is too fast to count,” he said. The German was a thickset fellow with big shoulders, a pointed beard, and wooly eyebrows. He carefully placed the syringe on a table and stepped between Bell and the patient. “I say, there is no need for your examination. This is my case.”

Bell ignored the man and pulled away the quilts.

Meyer attempted to restrain him and there ensued a pushing match. “Listen, you damn English pest, leave her alone!”

Nothing angered Bell more than to be called English. He was Scottish to the bone. I barely saw his short punch, but Meyer staggered back. His face reddened. “Gott damn you!” he bellowed.

He came back at Dr. Bell, but with an old trick learned on the rugby field, I caught his foot with my ankle and tripped him up before he could reach Bell.

Meyer fell, sprawling on a bright blue carpet, blood spurting from his nose. The Countess Tolstaya and Professor Sechenov huddled in a corner, aghast at the display of professional temperament. “I will get the guard!” Meyer shouted.

“Good riddance to you, sir. Doyle, lock the door and we will go to work,” Dr. Bell said. I turned the lock. Bell first held a candle to her eyes. Then, with his ear to her chest, he listened to the heart and lungs and finally palpated her abdomen. “What is this?” He pointed to a purple swelling on her left arm. “Countess, please tell me exactly the sequence of events that led to her illness.”

In that moment, the empress clutched her abdomen with both hands and a long, drawn out scream came from her blue lips. Then, her head drew back and her limbs went rigid. Her back arched, and her legs and arms beat an angry, painful rhythm against the bed. At last, in the mere flicker of a candle, the convulsion ended, her eyes opened in terror, and her breathing just stopped. All her muscles were in spasm.

“Crivvens! Doyle, give her ether — NOW! We must break the spasm or she will die!”

I could not imagine giving ether, a drug known to depress respirations, to a patient who was not breathing. Bell pulled the bottle of ether from his medicine case.

"Sir, she isn't breathing. Ether will surely bring her end sooner," I said.

"Damn you! Just start the ether!"

With shaking hands, I poured a few drops of the pungent anaesthetic on a folded handkerchief held over her face. For a horribly bloody-long moment, all seemed lost.

But then, after what must have been thirty seconds, she made a choking noise deep in her throat and took in a short, strangled breath. I took away the ether.

"Michty me!" Bell shouted. "Keep giving the ether!"

She took another short breath and her spasms eased. Her neck relaxed and her arms went limp, but she continued to breathe.

I touched her forehead. "Sir, her skin is hot, as if she were on fire."

Bell ran the back of his hand over her face. "Sechenov, Madam Tolstaya, please, we need ice. Get ice and cold water."

The maid flew out of the room, followed by the countess. It seemed like forever, but in what must have really only been five minutes, they returned, accompanied by two sleepy young men, each carrying two buckets of ice. They left their cold burdens and, with terror in their eyes, departed in haste.

"Lock the door again," Bell said. He then stripped the quilts and bedding away from the empress.

"No, you mustn't expose the empress!" Countess Tolstaya shouted.

"Cover her with sheets soaked in ice water," Bell said.

Outside, Dr. Meyer demanded entrance and guards pounded on the door. The noise aroused the entire palace, but we refused to unlock the door.

Through the uproar, we heard shouting. "The empress is dead! They murdered the empress! Oh, God save us. Where is the tsar? Call the tsar!"

"Och!" Bell removed the Webley revolver from the instrument case and handed it to the professor. "Sechenov, shoot anyone who comes through that door. We must not be disturbed."

The whole mad ordeal continued until the grey light of a false dawn seeped through the windows. As tiny fingers of light poked into the room, the empress's fever came down and the spasms grew less frequent.

I gradually reduced the dose of ether as her breathing became deep and regular. Dr. Bell sat at the bedside and timed her pulse with his folding gold watch. "Her heartbeat is down to one hundred."

Dr. Bell put away his watch and, after examining the swollen purple bruise, turned to Countess Tolstaya. "Countess, now please tell us the exact sequence of events."

The countess, who had been violently sobbing wiped away her tears. "We were in the English garden, admiring the flowers and having tea, when Princess Yurievskaya sent her maid with a gift for the empress, which was wrapped in beautiful red silk…" She took a deep breath and continued. "The note said the princess wished to make amends and be friends with the empress." Countess Tolstaya was again wracked with violent sobs.

"Please, go on," Dr. Bell said.

She collected herself and continued to speak. "We returned to this room to open the present. There, on the table… The crumpled silk wrapper lay next to five beautifully-carved matryoshka dolls, each smaller than the next so they nestled inside one another. The dolls represented traditional peasant girls, except for the smallest, a baby."

"Interesting," Dr. Bell said.

"Princess Yurievskaya had them specially carved. The empress removed the dolls, one by one. She was almost childlike with her delight, but after removing the last doll, she cried out with pain and clutched her wrist. I thought she had a minor sprain, but almost immediately, she complained of pain in her stomach and went to bed."

"And then?" Bell asked.

"I sent for Professor Sechenov, and later, Princess Yurievskaya kindly sent her personal physician. He was about to administer an injection when you arrived. He left the syringe on the dresser."

"Ah, ha…" Professor Bell inspected each of the dolls and, with a certain amount of theatrical flair, removed the remains of a brown insect from inside the last and smallest doll. “There is our culprit.”

He held up the tiny, brown object. “The remains of a male of the species, *Latrodectus Theridiidae*, better known as the Black Widow Spider. The female devoured her mate and then bit the empress on the wrist.”

“Are you certain?” Professor Sechenov asked.

“Aye. See here.” He pointed to the empress’s wrist. “A small punctuate wound in the middle of the purple swelling. Severe abdominal pain and muscle spasms are typical symptoms. The question remains, how did the spider get into the dolls?”

The empress opened her eyes and gazed about the room. “The noise, please stop the terrible racket,” she whispered.

“ENOUGH!” The countess flew to the door. “The empress lives. Do not disturb her. She needs peace and quiet.”

The shouting subsided, but Dr. Meyer continued to demand entrance. The countess admonished him and he skulked away.

“It would be difficult for a spider to enter the smallest doll. Could it have been placed there on purpose?” Professor Sechenov asked.

“I believe so… And there is more.” Dr. Bell closely examined the syringe with its contents that Dr. Meyer intended to administer to the empress. “I suggest you analyze the contents of this syringe for strychnine.”

“Strychnine?” Professor Sechenov asked.

“Strychnine causes the exact same symptoms as the bite of the Black Widow Spider. The venom causes muscle spasm, a high fever, and death by asphyxia. Meyer may have intended to poison the empress, and if there was suspicion, he would have produced the spider and claimed the death was accidental. Perhaps it is just as well that the spider bit her before he had a chance to give the poison.”

The door flew open. A captain of the guards entered with a drawn saber and Meyer at his side. “Arrest these men!” Dr. Meyer shouted.

In an instant, Dr. Bell snatched up the syringe and placed the needle against Dr. Meyer's arm. The German doctor's face contorted. "No, please… Not that, please!"

"Confess, or I will inject the contents. It is strychnine, is it not?"

Meyer blubbered, broke down, and under Dr. Bell's prodding with the needle, admitted he had planned the empress's death. The guards took him away. The unknowing servants continued to clamor for our deaths, but thanks to Madame Tolstaya, we hurried away unmolested.

This evening, I was enjoying a bit of Dr. Bell's single malt whiskey while Professor Sechenov soundly beat Dr. Bell at chess. "Dr. Bell, congratulations, you were entirely correct about the empress and the strychnine. I must say, I am impressed," Sechenov said, as if to make amends.

The Professor bowed, and just the tiniest hint of a smile crossed his lips.

Mr. Tatum looked up from a two week old *London Times*. "Where have you gentlemen been?"

"Oh, out and about," I answered, cheekily.

"Well, when you were out and about, I gleaned some interesting information through a friend. I have been told that The Russian Secret Service brought in a German physician for the attempted murder of the empress."

"Really?" I smiled at Dr. Bell who did not return the smile.

"Yes, and during the interrogation, a very agitated Princess Yurievskaya arrived and accused the poor man of attempting to murder both her and the empress. She insisted on immediate punishment by burning his tongue with a red hot poker. The doctor died almost instantly."

Dr. Bell leaned back, extended his long legs, folded his hands over his chest and muttered to himself. "Was he acting alone, or was he part of a more sinister plot to destroy the royal family?"

"My concern exactly," Mr. Tatum said.

Dr. Bell puffed his pipe for a moment. "There may be three factions interested in killing the tsar — the student anarchists, perhaps the Germans, and we still haven't found the English officer, Campbell."

"The Okhrana has effectively destroyed the student groups. What is Penelope up to? Is she working with the German or is she still loyal to the Queen?" I asked, both out of curiosity and hoping I might get some inside information which I could use to ultimately win her affections.

"Mr. Doyle, that little problem may be in your hands," Mr. Tatum said.

Dr. Bell blew a perfect smoke ring. "In the meantime, Doyle, don't neglect your medical education. You have a woeful lack of knowledge concerning common poisons."

Bell had not lost his knack for making me feel inferior, but with twinkly eyes, he tossed a well-thumbed volume of Lucifer's *Common Poisons* onto my lap. "Study this with care if you have any interest in forensic medicine."

23 September 1881

During the night, a cold, white mist settled over St. Petersburg. This morning, when I went out, eerie spires and steeples loomed above the fog only to vanish seconds later. On the streets, heads and shoulders of ghostly people appeared above the mist, then mysteriously dissolved. Except for the muffled ringing of a church bell, the streets were silent.

It was disorienting and I had a queer sensation of foreboding. Perhaps it was the growing cold; I had brought clothes for the summer, thinking we were only going to stay for a few weeks. If I knew that we would be here this long, I would have brought my heavy tweeds. As it was, I pulled the collar of my jacket tighter and found my way through silent streets to Pavlov's laboratory.

The secret police had rounded up all their suspects, and during the past few days, there were too few victims to continue the blood coagulation experiments. Further work would depend on another purge or pogrom.

Pavlov remained convinced that a substance in the plasma portion of blood influenced clotting and that he would eventually cure the royal bleeding disease. He concentrated more than ever on conditioned reflexes and brain function.

Dmitri has taken a special interest in the snakes and, to Pavlov's great joy, taught them to search for food at his whistle. This has supported Pavlov's hypothesis that even the primitive brain can respond to secondary stimuli.

Unfortunately, poor Dmitri has become absent-minded. On several occasions, he forgot to clean the animal cages and, more than once, left the cage doors open.

When I arrived, Dmitri sat at his crude table, rocking back and forth, holding his head in his hands. I was sure he said, "Pain, the terrible pain ..." in English, but then I was probably mistaken. At my questioning, he knocked his head with a fist and merely shrugged his shoulders, like any poor peasant.

I assisted Pavlov in an intricate operation to stimulate the vagus nerve within the skull, but we had hardly opened the animal's head when he died. That ended the operation.

On the way out, I pointed to my head and, with signs, asked Dmitri if he felt better. Dmitri's face was an ashen mask, without expression. He rocked back and forth and didn't respond. I assumed he simply wanted to be left alone.

Ferguson had invited me to lunch at the Hotel Europa, and since the fog had lifted, I decided on a leisurely walk along the Embankment. Immediately outside the laboratory, a poorly dressed, but pretty, girl stepped in my way and timidly held out a scrap of paper. I tried to brush her off, thinking she was a beggar or a prostitute. The girl shivered, either from cold or from fright. "Please a message for you, sir," she said. I barely grasped her meaning, but took the paper. It was a hurried, penciled scrawl on a cheap bit of foolscap paper. "Tonight, Pen —"

"Who gave this to you, and where?" I asked.

The girl barely whispered. "La Maison de Beaux Rêves."

Before I could question her further, she ran down the street and turned into an alley. I followed, but she was fleet-footed and I lost sight of her. After another minute, not knowing in which direction to run, I stopped, out of breath, and examined the slip of paper. It must be a message from Penelope but what and where was La Maison de Beaux Rêves?

Ferguson was at the bar, but a waiter whisked us to a table near the window. Dick was eager to tell me about his latest sport, a thirty-foot sailing yacht. I didn't have such interesting news and waited to talk until we had finished the main course and were spooning up a chocolate pudding and sipping a nice Madeira.

"Dick, what is La Maison de Beaux Rêves?"

"Oh, Doyle, that is no place for a nice Edinburgh lad. The House of Beautiful Dreams was once a fine hotel but is now a notorious gentleman's club. The worst dregs of the Russian officer corps and dissolute noblemen engage in the vilest sort of vice there. When they are finished with a girl, her body often ends up in the river."

"Is it open to non-members?"

"Absolutely not! The members pay a big initiation fee for the privilege of keeping rooms for their women and to have a private place to gamble and drink. They allow guests, but the place is heavily guarded and there is a password. I am shocked that you would even consider going there, my friend." Dick said.

Dick paid the bill and clapped me on the back. "If you want a woman, there are plenty of actresses and dancers in St. Petersburg. You don't have to go to the Beaux Rêves. Come with me. You will have more fun sailing. There is to be a regatta when the tsar reviews the fleet."

"I am just curious. Where is this den?"

Dick lit up a cigar and puffed, thoughtfully, before speaking. "Don't even think of going there; more than one visitor has lost his life in a drunken brawl or a duel. These Russians are unpredictable."

"I wouldn't but it's, just, well, I have an old friend who …"

"Ahhh yes, an old friend… Well, if your *old friend* really must know, it is the yellow building in Suavaroskaya Place next to the Embankment."

I was totally confused. Penelope had brushed me off and disappeared. Why should I care about her? But was she in the clutches of evil and in desperate need of my help?

By the time I arrived at my quarters and took Sasha for a walk, I was resolved to ignore the message and mind my own business. I mentioned the incident to Mr. Tatum who snatched the slip of paper from my hand and held it to the light, searching for a hidden message.

There was nothing more. He became serious. "This could be a genuine plea. If so, she had only seconds to write, meaning she is in danger. On the other hand, it could be an attempt to lure you into a trap."

"Either way, Mr. Tatum, I don't see how anything dealing with Penelope is really any of my business," I said, though it really wasn't the truth.

"If this involves a threat to the tsar, it is our business, yours as much as mine. Penelope is either onto something or else she is part of another plot. I must investigate; don't do anything until I return." Mr. Tatum clapped on his hat, immediately dashed away, and hailed a droshky.

Sasha put her head on her paws and whined while I paced the floor. I simply wanted to return home, start a medical practice, and do a bit of writing.

I wrestled with my thoughts. *Penelope doesn't care about me, so why should I care about her?* But then, I couldn't forget those brief, but passionate, kisses. Perhaps I might have a chance with the girl. I brooded over the single word 'tonight' that indicated urgency and suggested danger. But whose side is she on? She did save me when I was in prison . . . *If she is in trouble*, I thought, *I should save her . . .*

The idea of visiting a gentleman's club aroused my interest. I had heard of the 'hells' of London, where young rakes gambled and indulged in every vice. In Edinburgh, the most sinful evenings were student club haggis dinners, an academic lecture, and a debate about some obscure issue. At the end of the evening, a half-dozen of us or so would get tipsy with a bottle of port.

A very grim-faced Mr. Tatum returned shortly after seven o'clock, just as Dr. Bell and I sat down to a light supper. He removed his coat and accepted a cup of tea with a boiled egg.

"Mr. Doyle, Penelope has been secluded in the palace with the entourage of the Duchess of Edinburgh. Our agents have observed her leaving at night to visit various suspicious groups and the German Embassy. We don't know if she contacted her husband's colleague and is working to kill the tsar or if she's still on our side."

"I am interested in Penelope, but is she really our affair?"

"Aye." Dr. Bell lit up his pipe. "There is a great deal at stake. We must see this affair to the bitter end."

Mr. Tatum pulled his ear and made a sad face. "Penelope is very resourceful, but she may be over her head with a Count Lopukhof, an especially handsome man from an Ulan regiment. The army is heavily influenced by the German military and many officers are bitter about the tsar's reforms. They may well be plotting another assassination. This Count is a ruthless killer, known for beating soldiers without mercy. His colonel seconded him to the

Palace Guard, ostensibly as punishment, but perhaps to place him close to the tsar. Penelope and the count have disappeared. He may have taken her against her will, or she may be working with him. The count frequents the Maison de Beaux Rêves."

"If this is so important, why not send a trained agent who could do a better job?" I asked.

"This is a delicate situation; it would not do for a British agent to kill this Lopukhof. If you goad the man into making the first move, then succeed in killing him, it will appear to be a simple crime of passion."

I put my head in my hands. Mr. Tatum's argument made sense, but I wasn't a killer. On the other hand, I was intrigued by the prospect of seeing the Maison de Beaux Rêves. Furthermore, I couldn't let Dr. Bell down.

"What do you suggest?" I asked.

"You will gain entrance to the club, dressed as a debonair young dandy in your evening suit. The Maison de Beaux Rêves is heavily guarded by off-duty secret police officers, but you will not be going in blind. One of my informers told me the password, 'Sevastopol.' "

"How does he know it is correct?"

"He learned it from a drunken friend and assured me it is valid. Even better, he also knows the location of the valve that shuts off the gas to the entire building."

"What good is that?" I asked.

"If you get into serious trouble, fire a single pistol shot. At the signal, he will shut the gas valve and the lights will go out. In the darkness, you will have a better chance to escape. Early in the evening, women will mainly be on the first floor on the lookout for customers, and most of the regular members will be upstairs in the gambling den with their own mistresses. That is where I expect you will find Penelope, but remember, this Lopukhof is an expert swordsman and has killed men in duels," Mr. Tatum said.

I carefully fastened the studs, polished my shoes to a high shine, and smoothed the wrinkles from my dinner jacket.

"You will attract less attention if you are disheveled and drunk. Rinse your mouth with brandy and put a few drops on your collar, but drink no alcohol after you arrive. Keep your wits about you," Mr. Tatum said.

"He should look a bit older. A light powdering of flour in the hair will do the trick. You had best take the Webley," Dr. Bell said.

Unfortunately, I could not conceal the big pistol and would have to rely on the little derringer. Even then, it made a bulge in my coat. We decided on the waistcoat pocket where it would appear to be a pocket watch.

"Now, laddie, one more thing. You must stagger a bit to appear as if you are drunk." Dr. Bell said. "Please, give it a go for us."

I wobbled across the room in my best imitation of a drunken gait. Dr. Bell watched closely. "No, no, no. That won't do. Think what a drunk really looks like. Practice a wide-based gait, like a patient with tertiary syphilis." That was the clue I needed, since I had studied many patients with syphilis of brain.

"Now, pronounce Se-VAST-o-pol like a Russian," Mr. Tatum said.

Dr. Bell gave me a brotherly clap on the shoulder and took one hundred rubles from his wallet. "Doyle, stealth and deception tend to be superior to brute force, but there are also times when this may be helpful." He then handed me his cane. "Be careful."

The driver had apparently taken many a customer to the Beaux Rêves, for he made a knowing leer when he held out his hand for a tip. Once on the street, I wobbled on a wide gait, feeling my way over the cobblestones with the cane. The red door was flanked by two grim, uniformed guards who barred the entrance with crossed sabers. I mumbled the magic word, "Se-VAST-o-pol." With no change of expression, the guards opened the door to a warm, darkened room filled with semi-naked men and women.

The light was low, the windows were hung with crimson velvet drapes, and the furniture was covered with red damask. There were several large, stone fireplaces with roaring fires. Gas lights, shaded with red glass, cast a scarlet glow over the room, and huge mirrors reflected wildly gyrating women and men. A hairy man with a naked girl on either arm splashed in a giant pool. With a roar of delight, he turned his face to a stream of foaming yellow liquid that spurted from the mouth of a woman's statue in the middle of the fountain. Marble cherubs gaily pissed streams of foam over the cavorting women.

The hairy man caught a mouthful and sprayed his companions who laughed with apparent glee. To my utter amazement, the fountain was filled with champagne. Beyond the pool, a dusky Nubian, wearing only giant gold earrings, swayed to an African rhythm sawed out by a trio of women with strange, stringed instruments.

I leaned on my cane and stared, dumbfounded, at exotic blondes, brunettes, tall girls, short girls, and several with oriental features who twisted their hips to the music. Others reclined on lush, upholstered divans. A woman exuding a musky scent appeared out of the reddish gloom and took my arm. "What is your preference?" she whispered.

I slurred my words. "A glass of champagne."

She breathed into my ear. "We have three enchanting ladies experienced in the arts of love, from Paris — or would you care for a fresh, young virgin?"

I mumbled in French and accepted a glass of the bubbly, but remembered Mr. Tatum's words of caution. I spilled the drink which added to my appearance of a bumbling drunk.

Meanwhile, I lurched on my cane, seemingly in search of a companion for the night. I could hardly tear my eyes away from the myriad varieties of voluptuous women, with breasts bared to the fondling of men. I had never dreamed that such a place existed. I tried to remove all lustful thoughts from my head and remember my mission; it was not easy…

Even though it was early, many of the officers were in the last stages of intoxication and reeled about, from one woman to another. The main sport appeared to be ripping off their clothing and dragging women into the pool. I sank onto a plush divan with a doll-like oriental girl who spoke neither Russian nor French. Without a word, she sat on my lap and immediately began to loosen my trousers, but I brushed her off and looked over her shoulder.

At first, in the reddish glow, all the women looked alike, but I gradually distinguished the blondes from the brunettes, the slender from the plump, and the exotic from the plain. None of them resembled Penelope, even if she was disguised. From Mr. Tatum's description, I recognized the curving staircase that led to the second floor gambling den.

I gave the oriental, doll-like girl a friendly squeeze and wobbled up the grand marble steps to yet another double door, flanked by two guards. Once again, my mumbled "Se-VAST-o-pol" did the trick.

Despite clouds of tobacco smoke, the vast room glittered beneath brilliant gas lamps in great chandeliers. I was arrested by the sight of a mural, *CRIMEA*, depicting the Russian flag waving over valorous Russian cannons blasting away at English soldiers. One wall was filled with paintings of nude women and another showed a mounted Cossack driving a lance into a great, bleeding stag.

Men in full dress uniforms or evening clothes, and women in the latest Paris fashions, surrounded green baize tables with roulette wheels or games of baccarat. The scene was beyond my wildest imagination. Scantily-clad women went about carrying trays with glasses of champagne or stronger drink. Aside from the loser's sighs, or the occasional happy shout of a winner, the room was relatively quiet.

I nearly lost my balance on the step that led down to the room, but my misstep surely gave credence to my assumed drunkenness. I hobbled to the nearest table where officers and painted women were assembling about a roulette wheel and numbered squares. I bumped into a short, troll-like fellow with a penciled mustache standing next to the wheel.

"Will the gentleman place a bet?" he asked.

I was at a loss, but wordlessly took Dr. Bell's one hundred ruble note from my wallet. The fellow whisked it out of my hand and, with a disdainful grimace, gave me one blue chip.

The others piled chips on numbered squares, seemingly at random. Since my mother's birthday fell on the seventh day of July, the seventh month, I placed my single chip on the red seven.

The croupier, the same fellow who snatched my one hundred rubles, spun the wheel and sent a small, white ball on a tilted track in the opposite direction. The wheel spun and spun, then slowed. After an eternity of waiting, the ball dropped into a red pocket, number seven.

The croupier raked in stacks of red, white, and blue chips from the other players, then, disdainfully, pushed a pile of blue chips to me. I counted twenty-seven, worth the incredible sum of two thousand seven hundred rubles, more money than I had seen in months. "The money, please," I mumbled in my drunken voice, despite my urge to continue.

"No, no, it is not done. You must not stop," the other players muttered.

"It is customary for the winner to continue play," the croupier said, his face an angry mask.

I rapped the table with my cane. "Je veux mon argent," I said, with great emphasis on each word. The croupier and players were silent.

I pushed the stack of chips toward the croupier who, with a show of anger, tossed ruble notes fluttering down the table. I counted each one, stuffed them in my pocket and, with a nod, hobbled on.

I went a few steps, leaned heavily on the cane, and caught midst the acrid tobacco smoke a faint familiar scent. I sniffed again, but there was nothing. I went in the direction of a buffet table at the end of the room.

There it was, again, unmistakably, a whiff of orange blossoms — but there was no sign of Penelope. I hoped to sharpen my wits and accepted a cup of coffee from a sweet young waitress. All the while, people were muttering in French, "That drunk young man took his winnings" and "That damn cad's no gentleman."

I tensed when a heavily-muscled man with black, mutton-chop, side whiskers rose from a baccarat table, threw down his cards, and bared his teeth at me with an angry scowl.

I gave my best imitation of a silly, drunken smirk, went on sipping my coffee, and paid him no attention. A moment later, his scowl changed to a wicked smile, as if he had found a new toy. It was then I noticed his arm locked around a woman's neck. Was it a fond embrace or was she a prisoner?

Her face was heavily rouged, and her mouth was a red slash, like any common harlot. I squinted over my cup at that brute of a man. His dark blue, double-breasted jacket and skin-tight, blue breeches with a red stripe tucked into black, knee-high boots, gave every indication that he was a cavalry man. A gold, hilted dress sword hanging from his belt added to my sense of alarm.

"Who is that man?" I whispered to the nearest waitress.

"Count Lopukhof," she replied.

It was then that I saw wilted orange blossoms in the woman's tight ringlets. Penelope? My heart skipped a beat. Was there warning in her eyes or was she daring me to action?

The count's wicked smile in an instant turned to a mean grimace. "Your name, sir?" he asked.

"Conan Doyle."

"A damn Englishman?"

"Scotch-Irish, actually."

He roared with laughter. "Oh, dearie, where is your quaint little plaid skirt?"

I threw my coffee dregs in his face. Lopukhof tensed, and in a flash, he released Penelope, drew his sword, and slashed the air only inches from my face. There were scattered cheers and a shout of "Down with the English!"

I released the sword blade from Dr. Bell's cane and made a clumsy attempt to parry his thrusts. It was no use. He flicked the razor-sharp steel back and forth, from one side to another, slicing through one arm of my dinner jacket, then the other.

With a look of wicked joy, he made a long slash down one trouser leg but did not draw a drop of blood. He showed off his expert swordsmanship and total mastery over me, his hapless victim. The crowd stamped their feet and roared their approval at this new sport.

I side-stepped, dodged backward, and stabbed at his chest with the cane-sword, but there was no escape from that slashing blade. He lunged forward with a wicked grin while swinging the cruel steel blade hither and thither.

Then, apparently tired of sport, he smashed the flat of his sword just above my ear. I saw stars and fell on one knee. Another blow struck the other side of my head and I went, almost insensible, flat on my back.

The roaring in my ears subsided, while the bloodthirsty crowd noisily urged him to finish the job. Through blurred eyes, I watched the sword deliberately approach until the tip broke the skin of my throat.

Before he could give the final, killing thrust, a slender officer — in a resplendent white and gold uniform with a visored, black cap drawn down over his eyes — stepped over my prone body.

He thrust a slender rapier into the count's bulging crotch and then slashed with the tip of the blade until there was a gaping, bloody hole. The count bawled with pain, and blood streamed down his leg.

He roared and turned on his new assailant with bare hands. My savior adroitly side-stepped and drew the tip of his rapier across the count's face, leaving a scratch on his nose.

I came to my senses, fumbled in a side coat pocket for the pistol, and found the derringer in my waistcoat. The count was going back for another bare-handed attack when I drew the pistol to aid the gentleman who had saved my life.

My poorly-aimed bullet nicked the count's left ear, but he was unfazed. The onlookers howled for blood. It looked like my savior was going to be slaughtered by the count and then, surely, I would be next.

And then, just as the count was about to execute a killing blow, the gas lights dimmed and sizzled out.

I was lost in a strange room filled with hostile enemies and black as a tropical night. It was then that I heard a familiar voice behind me whispering in my ear. "Come with me."

Was I dreaming, or was it the voice of — Agafea? I was stunned.

How did she come to be in this place?

I was confused but didn't argue as hands dragged me on wobbly legs through the darkened room. We bumped against bodies, rammed tables, and reached a stairwell, where, I realized, there were two sets of hands pulling me along. We didn't stop until we reached a room on the third floor.

The small, slender soldier who was my savior lit a candle, and without the hat, I realized that he, or should I say she, was indeed — Agafea!

I couldn't believe it. What was she doing here, and why was she dressed like an officer? I practically burst into tears because I was grateful for her assistance.

And then I recognized, beneath her heavy rouge and paint, the pert, upturned nose of the second woman. My dear Penelope suddenly threw her arms around me and planted a smeary kiss on my lips. She pulled away and, with her hands on her hips, glowered at me. "What took you so long?" she asked.

"No, the question should be, why are you here and why is Agafea dressed like an officer?" I asked.

Agafea smiled. "The ladies here find my uniform very attractive."

I stared, speechless, and then averted my gaze.

Agafea shook her head. "I thought you would have guessed by now. I prefer girls to boys. In this place, I can satisfy my desires and the women keep my secret. I am much kinder than the men."

I turned scarlet. "It is unnatural," I mumbled.

"Ah, yes, I should've expected as much from you, Scottish Calvinist. From the day I was born, my father desperately wanted a son to take his place in the regiment. As a child, I learned to become that boy he never had. It was not hard since I never played with dolls or liked dresses but loved to dress as a boy. Father let me take fencing lessons instead of sewing and taught me to shoot. So, now, I have certain propensities and I don't intend to change," Agafea said.

There was no time to learn more because, as we spoke, the shouts and disorder downstairs increased to a tumultuous, angry roar. Before Penelope wiped the paint from her face, feet pounded up the stairs and fists rapped on doors.

"Open up! Who is in there?"

“The two of you, in the bed, cover up. Quick!” Agafea whispered, as she removed her uniform, flung it over the back of a chair, and literally dove into the bed. The door was still ajar.

“Shouldn’t we lock the door?” I asked.

“They will be less suspicious of an open door,” Agafea said.

Three men, holding candles and pistols, shoved their way into the room.

“Can’t you see we have a customer?” Agafea said, in French, with a low, seductive voice.

The officers saw the uniform flung aside on the floor and me in bed with two women. Penelope planted her painted face on mine and Agafea made violent motions beneath the blankets. To all appearances, we were in the midst of an orgy of love-making. It worked; the men backed out of the room with a curt apology, but left the door open. If it wasn’t such a tense encounter, it would probably have been the most exciting moment of my life. I had never enjoyed the focused attentions of two women at the same time and it was heavenly to be in their arms and have their warm bodies so close, even though I knew Agafea would have preferred to be alone with Penelope.

We continued our charade until the men were gone and it was safe to leave. Despite fearing for our lives, I savored being enveloped in the warmth of Penelope’s arms until, with a bit of wriggling, Agafea crawled next to Penelope and shared a squeeze and giggles. I was left alone on the cold side of the bed. My head ached from the count’s blow, but I got out of bed, shut and locked the door, and surveyed the room. There was an oversized bed, a mirror on the ceiling, a table, chairs, and a closet filled with an assortment of clothing. My suit was in shreds, but I still had the sword cane and one bullet left in the derringer.

Penelope rolled away from Agafea. “How do we get out of here?” she asked.

“We wait until they are asleep from alcohol or opium. There is a secret passage to the street and I have bribed the guards,” Agafea said.

When the commotion died down, Agafea dressed in her uniform, put her hair up in a tight bun, and pulled the cap's visor down over her eyes. The transformation was remarkable.

"Now, we need a shawl for Penelope and a long woman's cape for Dr. Doyle." Agafea laughed. "They will think I am an officer leaving with two women. And here, you will need this candle."

I put the candle, matches, and the derringer in a pocket and hid the cane beneath the long, dark cape. We clasped hands. Agafea led the way along a pitch-black corridor to a hidden door, down one flight of creaky stairs, then another, to a locked door. She produced a key and opened the door onto a dark alley. I took Penelope's hand and commenced to run, but tripped and went flying, head over heels. My cape fell away.

"Halt!" A match flickered; a bullseye lantern flared and lit up the alley. My slashed trousers and dinner jacket were the giveaway. Two uniformed men with bayoneted muskets blocked our escape route.

Penelope opened her shawl, revealing a nearly-bare bosom, and cooed seductively. "Boys, you must be lonesome out here all by yourself while the officers party. Come, let's have a good time."

While the two young soldiers admired Penelope, I rolled over, found the derringer and, with a lucky shot, put out the bullseye light.

We were off and running, with bullets zinging over our heads. The guards raised the cry while we ducked in and out of alleys. Within minutes, there was the clatter of hooves, and random gunshots popped in our direction.

We had not gotten far enough away; all seemed lost. We would be shot or captured in the next few moments. "Follow me. NOW!" Agafea said softly, but with urgency.

And then, with what seemed insane recklessness, she led us across the open Palace Square just as a troop of horses came down Nevsky Prospekt and cantered beneath the Triumphal Arch.

We put on another burst of speed and zigzagged across the open square. We were surely lost, but Agafea ran into shadows between two large buildings and led the way to a small, hidden, side door. She twisted a key in a well-oiled lock, opened the heavy door, and dragged us down uneven stone steps into what could have been in a tomb.

Water dripped in the distance. I felt my way along a cold, damp, stone wall while carefully placing my feet on stone steps leading down into a dark, cavernous room. There were loud rustlings, and something small brushed against my leg. Penelope uttered a strangled scream. “Rats!”

“It is nothing. Be quiet and light the candle,” Agafea said.

I fumbled for the matches and struck a light. In the still air, the candle burned with a tall flame revealing a room with stone walls and immense pillars that went on endlessly in the gloom. Everywhere I looked, cats lounged on stacks of wooden crates. A large orange tom flicked his tail and regarded us with suspicious, orange eyes until he leaped down and rubbed against Agafea’s leg.

She stooped and petted the cat. “Strays from all over the city find shelter in the cellars beneath the Hermitage and volunteers give them food. Every week, I bring all the scraps from our kitchen and look after the sick animals,” she said.

“Why are they tolerated here?” I asked.

“They control the rats and mice that would destroy the paintings. There is no time to lose. Follow me.” She led us up flight of stairs to a splendid room with an arched ceiling and giant columns. The walls were hung with paintings. Even I could recognize the work of old masters.

“This is part of Catherine the Great’s collection.” Agafea said. She hurried us through galleries, into another hall filled with Egyptian mummies and statues of ancient kings and queens, and then through the Greek and Roman gallery. I was getting a private tour of the Hermitage, so magnificent it was almost easy to forget that we were in danger. However, Agafea hurried us along until we came out a back way onto the bank of the Neva River.

She extinguished the candle and, in the dark, led us down a bank to the water’s edge where mist drifted in from the sea.

Agafea felt in the dark. “We are in luck, the skiff is still here.”

“What are we to do?” Penelope asked.

"Take the skiff and drift with the current on this side until you reach the English Church. Then, and only then, go to the other side. You will be safe if you do exactly as I say. I will leave you now. Good luck."

I helped Penelope into the little boat, cast off, and, as Agafea said, the current carried us, hidden in the mist, until the homes along the English Embankment and then the church loomed above.

I rowed hard to cross the current until our skiff touched the muddy bank of Vasilevsky Island. We stood on the muddy shore for a time, listening to the burbling of little eddies on the Neva.

I could hear her soft breathing, but Penelope was an indistinct shadow in the dark, wispy fog. She shivered and pulled the shawl tighter. A fish jumped. A sea bird squawked and rose on urgent flapping wings. If only I had wings, I would fly away with Penelope. Dawn was not far away.

I pulled the skiff to higher ground. "Penelope, why were you with that man, in that place?"

"The count is a real man, not a damn silly boy."

"Then why did you send a message for help?"

"It is part of the game, a great game that you and that doctor are in — one that is way over your heads."

She beat on my chest with her fists and burst into tears. I was confused. Why did she cry? I hated seeing her distress. Was I in love with this strange girl? I dried her tears with my torn sleeve.

"But, Penelope, we are under orders from the Queen."

"Oh, who cares about that wretched woman? What has she done but persecute your people and make war?"

"Are you a traitor?" I asked.

"A traitor? What is a traitor? Words, words, you will never understand. It is time for a new Europe and we must embrace new words and thoughts!"

She clutched my lapels and spoke with a new urgency. "You must choose sides." She melted into my arms and I feverishly sought her lips. I wasn't sure what she meant, but at that moment, I would have done anything she asked. "Penelope, dear …"

I leaned in to kiss her and she pulled away. In an instant, without another word, she was gone. I was stunned. Every time, just as we were getting closer, she would run away. Where did she go? Half an hour later, I crept into Dr. Sechenov's garden, removed my muddy shoes, and slipped up the back stairs to my room. Mr. Tatum, in a tattered dressing gown, sat in my leather covered chair with his feet on a leather ottoman. The room was lit by the stump of a single candle.

Sasha sleepily rose and licked my hand. I sat on the bed, took off my slashed suit, and carefully stuffed the ruble notes I had won inside a book. Mr. Tatum regarded me through lowered lids, as if he was half asleep, but his voice was crisp. "Tell me every detail of your encounter with Count Lopukhov."

I couldn't lie, but I didn't provide every detail of my singular adventure. I mentioned a 'young officer' who came to my rescue, without giving away Agafea's secret, and said only that I had spoken with Penelope for a few minutes. He looked at me with those hooded eyes for a long time.

I suspected he knew I was not telling everything. Perhaps, the person who shut off the gas had already reported to him.

"Mr. Doyle, I thank you, and the Crown thanks you. Sir, you have put yourself in great danger for service to the Queen." He rose and clapped me on the back. "If it was up to me, I would give you a medal for bravery."

24 September 1881

This morning, when I put one foot on the floor, the room whirled and, all of a sudden, I went down. I was still dizzy with a pounding headache when Marya arrived with the morning tea.

She immediately fetched Dr. Bell, who listened to my story. "Arthur, my boy, you should get a medal for your work. Unfortunately, you have a bit of a concussion. Cold compresses and a day's rest will set you right," he said, after a bit of poking and prodding.

Marya arranged pillows so I could have tea in bed. The dear girl ran to the kitchen and returned with towels soaked in cold water which she applied to my poor head. Within an hour, when Dr. Bell returned, I felt much better.

"Arthur, the American ambassador sent an urgent message requesting my assistance. Since you are in good hands, I will be away most of the day," he said.

"Is it a medical problem?" I asked.

"An American citizen is dead."

"Is it anyone we know?"

"The Texan who brought the snakes to Pavlov."

"Cowboy Bill?"

"I believe that is what he was called. Aye," Dr. Bell replied.

"I am coming with you," I said.

"No, you must rest."

While we were on the ship, Cowboy Bill was the picture of good health. I could not believe he was dead. "I insist on going with you," I said.

"Hmm, well, maybe some fresh air will be good for you. If you insist on going, fetch the instrument case and follow me," he said.

I was up and dressed when the ambassador, a middle-aged fellow named John Foster, arrived in a troika, a light carriage drawn by three horses. Poor Sasha was outside and, to my embarrassment, leaped into the carriage and settled herself at my feet. Mr. Foster was a typical Yankee with a top hat, bow tie, a black frock coat, and the most amazing long, flowing, white side whiskers.

"My, oh my! That's a good looking dog. Reminds me of my Rover."

"What kind of dog was Rover?" I asked.

"He was a good bird dog, probably with some Pointer and Beagle. When I was a boy, we hunted together on our farm back in Indiana," the ambassador said.

I was relieved that he did not object to Sasha and was mystified that an ambassador could have such a humble beginning on a farm out in the wilderness. His low background made mine look almost aristocratic. "Sir, if you grew up in the country on a farm, how did you end up being an ambassador?"

"Well, that's the beauty of America, boy. Anybody can become anything they want if they are willing to work hard enough for it. Yes, I grew up on a farm, but I didn't stay there. You see, I walked for many miles to hear Abraham Lincoln talk at one of his great debates with Stephen Douglass and that changed my life. Lincoln inspired me to go east to study and get a college degree. Then, I got into politics and became Secretary of the Navy under Grant," he said. "Anybody who is willing to work as hard as me might be able to do the same."

"Aye. May I ask … There was a navy man on our ship, an engineer, named Gritz, claimed he built electric boats," I said.

Mr. Foster squinted and looked away. "Never heard of the fellow," he snapped.

He was abrupt and said no more; I settled back and scratched Sasha's ears. The driver whipped up the three matched, grey horses to a fast pace. I knew little about horses, but Dr. Bell became excited. "What breed are these horses?"

"Orlov Trotters, came out of an Arabian stallion years ago. There is nothing like them; when hitched to a troika, the center animal trots while the two on the side canter," the ambassador said.

We were flying along. "How can I help with this business?" Dr. Bell asked, once we left the city streets.

"I love horse racing and, you see, this fellow, Cowboy Bill, had a remarkable way with horses. He was clever, too. Learned the language well enough to get a job training race horses for a Colonel Shirapov." the ambassador said.

"How did he die?" Dr. Bell asked.

"They say he took his own life. But I knew Cowboy Bill and I just don't believe he was the type of man to commit suicide."

"Yes, I can look into it for you."

"I have to tell you, I don't trust these damn Russian officers. They don't do a damned thing but drink and gamble. I want someone who speaks English to look into this matter and you are well known for your ingenious detective work. I am grateful that you have agreed to accompany me today."

The rains had settled the dust, so the drive through the country was pleasant. The leaves were turning yellow, and the birch trees were already dropping leaves. Within an hour, we reached a regimental summer camp with a race track, stables, and officer's quarters. We paused to watch grooms exercise horses, and then, the ambassador directed our driver to Captain Shirapov's stables.

A half-dozen somber grooms and trainers idled under a tree with wide, spread limbs in front of the stable. Inspector Koivisto of the St. Petersburg police met us at the stable door with a wide smile and an extended hand. He shook hands with the professor. "Welcome, Dr. Bell. It's good to see you, but why are you here? The cowboy's death is a clear case of suicide."

"I would be interested in your findings, especially, since we have come a long way," Dr. Bell said.

"The man clearly killed himself with his own pistol."

The ambassador puffed out his cheeks and spoke in a loud voice and in poor French. "The dead man was a citizen of the United States. And as a representative of the U.S.A., I demand a full investigation. If you don't cooperate, I will go the tsar himself."

"Well…" Inspector Koivisto scowled and jutted out his chin in a fit of anger, but his demeanor quickly changed. "Fine! Out of respect for Dr. Bell, I will allow him to view the scene. But I am certain he will merely confirm my conclusions."

Sasha scampered at our heels as we entered the long, low shed with stalls where a half-dozen horses fed on hay and oats. A small double door led to the trainer's room. The stables were clean, with the pleasant smell of hay and horse. The room where Cowboy Bill had lived was comfortable though spartan. Cowboy Bill, dressed in a blue shirt and tan trousers, leaned back on a chair with his legs folded beneath. He looked almost jaunty with a red scarf at his neck, but his dim, sightless eyes were glazed.

"This is exactly how we found him," Inspector Koivisto said. "I opened his shirt to inspect the wound, but touched nothing else. He does need to be buried or shipped back to the United States at once."

Dr. Bell, chin in hand, surveyed the room. There was one window, a small, black, iron stove, and a neat, made-up bunk. The body faced a table with a nearly empty bottle of brandy and one glass. It appeared as if Cowboy Bill had been drinking alone. A pair of high, cowhide boots stood next to the door. The floor was spotless. Nothing was disturbed and there was no blood. In a way, the death scene was serene; too serene.

"May I see the wound, please?" Dr. Bell asked.

Inspector Koivisto casually pointed. "Here is a hole in his shirt over the entrance wound on the right side of his chest. There is no exit."

Dr. Bell went to his knees next to the body and gazed, intently, at the small bullet hole just beneath the breast on the right side. He gently palpated the surrounding skin and, after a moment, deliberately moved his index finger medially towards the breast bone. "Hmm, strange. There is very little blood."

"Yes, I commented on that in my report and concluded that he was dead before he had a chance to bleed."

"Where was the weapon?" Dr. Bell asked.

"In his right hand with his finger on the trigger." Koivisto replied.

"May I see the weapon?"

The inspector removed the revolver from a leather bag and passed it to Dr. Bell. It was an old-fashioned pocket pistol that had seen hard use but was clean and well-oiled. The wooden handle was scratched, and the brown finish on the barrel was worn down to bare metal. The barrel was marked, 'Patented 1855, Samuel Colt.'

Dr. Bell removed the cylinder and examined the chambers. "Inspector Koivisto, will you permit me to fire a shot?"

"Sir, I don't see the point. I must be leaving here soon; this isn't my only case, you know." the inspector said.

"Please, in the interest of truth, allow me just one shot. It will require but a few seconds."

"Very well."

"Dr. Doyle, kindly place a wad of paper just to the right of that hole in the wall."

I had not noticed the rat hole, perhaps two inches or less in diameter in the far wall, right at floor level. I tore a page from my notebook, wadded the paper into a small ball, and placed it as directed.

Dr. Bell took careful aim and pulled the trigger. There was a soft *bang* and a puff of smoke. The wad of paper 'jumped,' with a bullet hole left in dead center. Behind the paper, a small lead ball was about half-embedded in the wood.

"There! Your evidence! This was not a suicide."

The inspector balked. "What? I don't see how you can say that after firing one shot."

"It is basic ballistics. The ball is only .31 calibre. The powder charge was sufficient to kill a rat, but it would hardly scratch a man. Cowboy Bill could not have killed himself with this pea-shooter of a pistol."

Not a word was spoken while Dr. Bell spent a great deal of time filling and tamping his curved pipe with Cavendish. When it suited him, he lit up and puffed a cloud of fragrant, blue smoke.

The inspector coughed. "This is preposterous. Of course he died by his own hand. There could have been a heavier load in the chamber. There is certainly no other cause of death."

"Hmmm." Dr. Bell put down his pipe and minutely scrutinized the body. "Dr. Doyle, maybe you can shed some light on this case. If you will, tell us what you observe and your conclusions."

Why did he always have to treat me like a school boy, especially when I was not feeling up to par? I walked about the room glancing here and there.

I idly noted a plate, fork, and spoon, with another glass on a shelf. A dish towel hung from a nail next to the sink. To stall for time, I took another look at the body. Damn, why hadn't I noticed it before? There was bleeding in his eyes. "Sir, there are sub-conjunctival hemorrhages in both eyes."

The tiniest hint of a smile appeared and disappeared on Dr. Bell's lips. "Ah yes. How could I have missed it? So sloppy of me. Thank you, Dr. Doyle." He then looked around the room. "Gentlemen, Cowboy Bill was dead before he received his gunshot wound. This is murder and should be treated as such," Dr. Bell said.

"Bah. Preposterous! How can you say that without demonstrating any other cause of death?" Koivisto responded.

"Dr. Doyle, kindly remove that red scarf from his neck."

The red scarf, what the Americans call a bandanna, was tightly knotted in back and folded in a triangle in the front of his neck. The knot was so tight that I had to pry it apart with a surgical probe. There was a slight bruise over Cowboy Bill's windpipe but nothing else.

Dr. Bell pointed at the bruise with his pipe. "Hemorrhages in the eyes indicate compression of the jugular veins causing severe intracranial pressure."

"They could've been caused by sand or dirt that got in his eyes while he was working with the horses."

"No, Inspector. An assassin garroted Cowboy Bill with his own scarf."

"I am sorry to say this, Dr. Bell, but that's impossible. That bruise is nothing. I say he died by his own hand."

"I most respectfully disagree, sir. He died by the slow compression of his jugular veins and the carotid arteries with his own scarf. It had to be a slow, painful death by strangulation. The knot was pulled tight when a stick or other instrument twisted the scarf about his neck." Dr. Bell said.

"But how can you prove it was murder?" asked Mr. Foster.

"Mr. Foster, since the deceased is an American, I need your permission to prove my point with one simple skin incision."

"Well, I don't know. This is highly irregular," the ambassador said. "We don't know if he has family and if they would approve of such a thing."

"Even if I can prove that he was murdered?" Dr. Bell asked.

Mr. Foster dithered, pursed his lips, and pulled at his side whiskers. “Is it absolutely necessary?”

“Yes, with one small incision I will prove that a bullet did not cause his death.”

“Very well, Doctor.”

“Doyle, a probe and a scalpel, please.”

I placed the instruments on the table while Dr. Bell rolled up his sleeves and removed Cowboy Bill’s shirt. No one spoke while Dr. Bell deliberately inserted the steel probe into the wound. The probe slid along the top of the fifth rib for a distance of four inches and obviously did not penetrate the chest cavity.

With a quick slash, he laid open the skin and demonstrated the round, lead ball buried in muscle tissue. There was no bleeding and it had not struck a vital organ.

Dr. Bell plucked out the harmless ball. “This bit of lead did not cause his death. The assailant first killed Cowboy Bill then fired the shot to make it look like suicide,” he said.

The ambassador turned white, covered his mouth, and ran from the room. “Inspector, you must search for an exceptionally powerful man. The murderer was probably a soldier trained in the killing arts,” Dr. Bell said.

“Da.” Inspector Koivisto wrote in his notebook. “I stand corrected, Dr. Bell. It does appear to be murder, but still …” he said, rather sullenly.

“If you need more proof, Inspector, here it is.” Dr. Bell rinsed the instruments and his hands at the sink and picked up the dish towel. He inhaled deeply and glanced up at the empty glass on the shelf. “If you look closely, you will note that both the towel and the empty glass have traces of brandy. Another person drank with the victim and then rinsed the glass in hopes of misleading us to think that Cowboy Bill drank alone.”

Damn, I had missed another clue. In the hope of redeeming myself, I again examined the corpse. I saw nothing new, though idly wondered why the left hand was open but the right was tightly clenched. The fingers were rigid even more than one would expect with rigor mortis.

I did not want to touch that cold, dead hand but forced down sour bile and pulled on his middle finger with all my strength. It broke with a sickening snap as I pried it open. At first glance, there was only a handful of horse feed inside his fist, but on closer inspection, I could see that a coarse brown powder was mixed in with the oats.

"What is this brown substance?" I asked.

"Ah, Doyle, you might amount to something, after all." Dr. Bell said, as he rolled the brown powder between his fingers. He smelled it, placed a small amount on his tongue, and poured the remainder into a glass jar. "It is quite bitter and appears to be some type of ground root that has been mixed with the oats."

Sasha came dashing into the room, her bushy tail sweeping back and forth. She immediately laid back her ears and, with her nose in the air, circled the corpse on stiff legs. She sniffed the dead body and, with surprising tenderness, licked the outstretched left hand.

At that moment, a carriage drawn by a fine pair of chestnut bays dashed into the little, grassy yard in front of the stable.

The driver, a white-haired but heavily-muscled man in the uniform of a Cossack sergeant, dropped the reigns and slowly stepped down. The fellow, with a hard, weathered face of an old campaigner, opened the carriage door and carefully assisted an army officer with a colonel's epaulettes and gold braid out of the carriage.

The colonel, nearly as old as his servant, stumbled, but the servant caught his arm and spoke gently to him. "Batya, take care. Please take care," he said.

"Batya means father, a term of endearment for a good commander. His driver was an old *denshchik*, or as the English say, a 'valet' or 'personal servant,' " Inspector Koivisto whispered.

The colonel tucked his chin into his chest and stood very erect, facing the crowd as if he were reviewing troops. He had the air of a man accustomed to command. Unlike many high ranking officers, he was clean shaven, except for a long salt and pepper mustache.

We came to attention and Koivisto saluted. "Good day, Colonel Shirapov," he said.

The colonel turned and gallantly assisted a strikingly handsome woman down from the carriage. She was an inch or two taller than the colonel and clung to his arm with a possessive air while holding a bright red parasol. She was at least twenty years his junior, dressed in the latest Parisian style and adorned with rings, bracelets, and a diamond necklace.

"Where is the American?" she asked. "I want to see Mercury."

"I am sorry. The American is dead." Inspector Koivisto said.

"Oh, that is too bad. He was so good with Mercury." She shook her head. "Still, I'd like to see my horse. Would someone please bring out Mercury? I am looking forward to seeing my husband ride him in the steeplechase tomorrow."

Colonel Shirapov said nothing, but he tensed and one eye twitched. We waited at the open stable door while a groom went to fetch the horse. The groom hesitated, was about to say something, but unlatched the gate. Mercury, a great, black stallion, laid back his ears, feebly kicked, and attempted to rear.

"I can't." The groom backed away. "The horse is too dangerous. Only the American could handle him. I will not," he said.

"That horse is sick," exclaimed Mr. Foster.

Colonel Shirapov walked a few steps. "He is just high strung… If you have finished your investigation, please leave my property," he said, in a low voice.

"He was perfectly gentle when Cowboy Bill worked with him," Mr. Foster said.

"I am a doctor. Please let me see him." Dr. Bell edged his way closer to the stall and peered intently at the stallion. "His nose is congested and there is sweat on his hindquarters. He does indeed appear to be ill and he should not be ridden."

"No!" The old Cossack growled. "Obey my colonel! That is an order. Prepare the horse."

And so they did. There was nothing else to do; we trudged away to the troika while Inspector Koivisto arranged for the body to be delivered to the American Embassy.

I whistled for Sasha. I called again and, in defiance of the colonel, returned to the stable. The poor dog was lying on a pile of hay, frothing at her mouth. Her eyes were closed and her head lay on her paws. She barely moved when I picked her up and carried her to the troika. What had happened to her? I felt bloody awful.

I petted her tangled fur and talked to her as if she were a baby. She didn't respond, and mucous bubbled from her nose. I was convinced she was dying, but she feebly raised her head when Dr. Bell looked into her eyes and applied his stethoscope to her chest.

He sighed and sat back with his legs outstretched, silent and deep in thought. What did he think happened to poor Sasha? What was wrong with her?

Dr. Bell said nothing and seemed unconcerned about my obvious distress. I hated him at that moment, but then I realized that maybe he had larger issues than the health of one poor dog on his mind. Had cocaine hardened him to all suffering?

It was my fault. I should not have brought poor Sasha on this trip. If I had left her at home, she would be fine now. What had she gotten into here that had made her so sick? I felt so horrible about saving her from the lab only then to lead her to her death here …

I stroked her silky ears and begged her forgiveness. She made a low *woof* and licked my hand. It was as if she sensed my distress and, even though she was ill, wanted to comfort me. I carried her to the troika and we set off for home.

The ambassador talked about horses most of the way home. "Mercury is a great horse, but hard to handle. Cowboy Bill claimed he could talk to horses like an Indian. Within three weeks, he had Mercury eating out of his hand, and damn, was that horse ever so quick. You've never seen such a fast horse, especially when Cowboy Bill took the reins. Now, that young woman expects Colonel Shirapov to ride him and win the steeplechase, but the colonel can't handle Mercury the way that Bill did. If you ask me, the whole thing is going to end badly."

We arrived home in the late afternoon. I carried Sasha to my room and gave her a bowl of water. She took a bit but gagged, spit, and went to sleep.

I prayed that she would feel better and stayed by her side for the next few hours, petting her as she slept. When she awoke at nine p.m. or so, much to my relief, she stood on shaky legs and walked about the room. I was overjoyed. Later this evening, she lapped up a bowl of soup, breathed normally, and thumped her tail just like her old self.

I went to tell Dr. Bell the good news and found him pacing the room with excited, glittering eyes. Blue, fragrant smoke hung over the room like a mist. "Ah, Doyle, that is wonderful news! Pour a dram for yourself and sit with me for a moment."

Ah, so he did care after all. I cupped the glass of whiskey in my hands and inhaled the peaty smell of prime Scottish single malt while Dr. Bell paced the length of the room and back. He stabbed the air with his pipe. "Well, there is still one piece of missing information, but by tomorrow afternoon, we will see the case solved," he said.

"But sir, all we know is the method of the murder. We have no motive, let alone a culprit."

"Au contraire, my lad. It is perfectly clear, and you and your canine friend helped us find the missing clue."

What was he talking about? How was he always one step ahead of me or, for that matter, everybody else? "I don't understand, sir."

"You will soon, laddie. You will soon. Now, go and get some rest. I have work to do. Goodnight."

Reluctantly, I went off to bed and was drifting off to sleep, when Sasha pounced on the bed and licked my face. I cuddled with her and soon we were both floating off into dreamland.

25 September 1881

I slept like a dead man until the grey light of early dawn. My head felt better, so I dressed and took Sasha for a short run before breakfast. Sasha frolicked and barked at a carriage that came to a halt on the side street by Professor Sechenov's garden.

The driver, as well as the passengers, wore peasant's garb — dark trousers tucked into high boots, long shirts belted at the waist, sheepskin vests, and wooly astrakhan hats. It took a moment to recognize Mr. Foster, the ambassador, who held the reins, and Mr. Tatum. Dr. Bell was heavily disguised with a sort of Muslim scarf about his face.

"Ho there, Doyle, my lad. We are perfectly famished from a hard night's work. Would you like to join us for breakfast?" Dr. Bell asked.

An hour later, we tucked into ham, omelets, a heap of dark bread, smoked salmon, succulent lamb chops, and gallons of sweet Turkish coffee.

I knew better than to enquire about their mysterious nighttime adventure until Dr. Bell lit his pipe, sighed, leaned back, and blew a perfect smoke ring. "Doyle, read this paragraph." He tossed a book in my lap. It was *Oriental Herbal Remedies*.

I read the paragraph, "*Rauwolfia Serpentina* or Indian Snakeroot: The dried root, an ancient remedy, is an effective tranquilizer in cases of insanity. An overdose may cause collapse and even death. When accidently ingested by horses or cattle, there is nasal congestion, sweating, lethargy, and, occasionally, death."

"How did you know about this drug?" I asked.

"Aye, 'tis a doctor's job to know about the properties of all of God's herbs."

"Your knowledge is encyclopedic, sir."

"Books help refresh it, Doyle ..."

"Do tell all, sir."

"Well, your friend, Cowboy Bill, had gained the trust of Mercury, but the horse would not tolerate another rider. The murderer is afraid to let the colonel ride in the race and attempted to poison Mercury with the powdered root of *Rauwolfia Serpentina*. I knew this for certain when Sasha had identical symptoms after licking a small amount of the residue from Cowboy Bill's hand."

"Aye, I figured something along those lines when she got sick, but still . . ."

"I would wager that Bill was killed when he confronted the murderer with the evidence."

"Do you have proof?"

"The proof is in this little bag of feed from Mercury's stall."

"But how did you get it?"

"We just paid a little visit to the stables last night. While Mr. Tatum entertained the grooms with vodka, Mr. Foster and I removed the feed from Mercury's stall."

"But, he is a vicious animal."

"Mr. Foster knows a trick or two from his days as a farmer. There isn't a horse in the world that can resist peppermint candy."

"We not only removed all the adulterated feed, but left new clean oats, hay, and two buckets of water. Mercury will be as good as new by this afternoon."

Mr. Tatum chuckled. "I bet one hundred rubles on Mercury. The grooms were happy to give me ten to one odds."

"We still don't know who murdered Cowboy Bill," I said.

"We will soon. Now, off to the races. Dress in your best day suit and a top hat."

Mr. Foster met us with his fine carriage and greeted us with twinkly eyes. "Ah fellows, it is a grand day. Inspector Koivisto is my guest."

The inspector drew himself into a corner of the carriage and barely nodded to Dr. Bell. "Frankly, I don't understand what a horse race has to do with murder," he said.

Dr. Bell chuckled. "You will see, Inspector. All in good time. All in good time."

The circular track wound through birch and spruce trees. Steep slopes, fences, piles of logs, and small streams were obstacles to test the jumping skill of each horse and rider. Grooms decked out in silk shirts, tight breeches, and high boots exercised horses, while a throng of spectators with telescopes and opera glasses crowded the open fields that surrounded the track.

The race was a highlight of Russian social events. Even the Tsar was drawn out of seclusion. He, with his splendid entourage, was seated in an enclosure near the starting line. His body guards and company of soldiers were scattered among the crowd of ladies in bright gowns and large flowery sun hats, men in uniforms, and civilian officials with medals, top hats, and walking sticks. The gay crowd moved to and from tables set with champagne and edibles. It was utterly decadent and, at the same time, grand and fantastic.

I took a glass of bubbly and a helping of caviar while listening to whispered rumors. Mercury, the favoured horse, was nowhere to be seen. "The grooms are afraid of him," one anxious fellow said.

The crowd cheered as the first horse, a fine-looking, chestnut mare ridden by a guard's captain and led by a groom, came to the starting line. More horses, riders, and grooms followed until only Mercury was missing.

The crowd became quiet. Then it cheered when Mercury, ridden by the colonel in jodhpurs and high glossy boots and led by the old Cossack sergeant, came onto the track. The horse was stiff-legged and his ears were twitching.

Colonel Shirapov sat rigidly in the saddle and held the reigns with both hands. The horse balked just short of the starting line. The colonel raised his whip, but the old man whispered in the horse's ear. Mercury settled and pranced to the very outside position. Mercury was nervous and dashed across the starting line. The colonel turned him back to the line, and after two attempts, the umpire shouted. "Away!"

Mercury balked and was last to start. Then, with a shake of his great head, he shot down the track. Colonel Shirapov's face was set in a rigid mask. I was struck with the thought that he was bloody terrified.

Mercury gracefully leaped over the first obstacle and gained two lengths on the nearest horse. He sailed over a pile of logs and went into the lead.

The crowd cheered when he went high in the air over a small stream to land on a steep precipice. The colonel bent forward, with both arms around the horse's neck. Mercury was now well in the lead, his forelegs reaching out with every stride and his strong hindquarters driving him onward.

The crowd screamed and surged toward the finish line.

Looking like a black demon, Mercury came into the homestretch a half-dozen lengths ahead of the nearest horse. He pounded toward the finish but hesitated, tossed his head, and triumphantly crossed the line.

The crowd's loud cheers quickly turned to stunned silence as the horse abruptly put out his forelegs and kicked up his hind legs.

The old colonel shot over the horse's head and landed on his back. Mercury, with a deadly gleam in his eyes, reared up and came down with both forefeet on the colonel's chest. The hooves crushed the colonel's ribs with a sickening crack. Geysers of blood shot in the air with each heartbeat then subsided into a red pool on the track.

The old Cossack was there in an instant, kneeling at the colonel's side. With all the tenderness usually seen in a mother with a sick child, the old man lifted the bloody corpse in his arms while tears rolled down his cheeks.

"Oh dear lord, what have I done? What have I done?" Dr. Bell sighed.

I will never forget the image of the weeping, devastated old man who stood in the sun before the silent crowd, refusing to give up the crumpled body to the doctors.

Dr. Bell pointed. "Inspector, there is your man."

I elbowed my way through the crowd with a grim-faced Inspector Koivisto. Just as we arrived at the track, a giant of a man came through the silent crowd. He spoke a word to the old *denshchik* but took the colonel's body in his own arms to the tsar's enclosure.

"My God, the colonel must have been a favourite of the tsar himself," Koivisto said.

The old man stood stock still, his arms outstretched and tears rolling down his face. Koivisto and I led him away to a quiet spot where, between heaving sobs, he talked. Later, Koivisto interpreted for me.

"I was a good *denshchik* and cared for him like my own son for nearly forty years. He was done with racing until he married that damn woman. She gave him that wicked horse and expected him to ride like a young captain. I tried to stop it, but the American found out. So I had to kill him." He held out his strong, gnarled, scarred hands. "I thought it was the only way to protect the colonel."

It was a slow, sad walk back to the carriage. During the journey home, Dr. Bell huddled in the corner of the carriage, his arms folded tightly over his chest. He didn't say a word, but stared into the distance.

Ambassador Foster was garrulous after imbibing more than his share of champagne, while Mr. Tatum, under the guise of polite conversation, drew him out. "Oh yes, we have Alaska. Next, we take Siberia and the Pacific Ocean is ours. The United States Navy, by God, we are building a navy that will show the world we can fight," the ambassador bragged.

"Do you have any special ships?" Mr. Tatum asked.

Mr. Foster belched and patted his stomach. "That is a secret, my man." He leaned forward and put his mouth to Mr. Tatum's ear. "But I can tell you, the future is not floating on the surface of the ocean, but beneath it."

30 September 1881

Dr. Bell has not left his room all week and has taken only small morsels of food since the race. He blames himself for the colonel's death and, aside from regular injections of cocaine, remains slumped in a chair staring into the distance.

I have taken on most of the work at the children's tuberculosis clinic. There is a little girl there with straw-colored hair — five years old at the most — who is at the point of death. Without a doubt, her entire left chest is filled with pus. An operation is indicated, but I dare not attempt such a capital procedure.

So, this morning I went to his room and begged him to help. "Please, Dr. Bell, you must operate."

"I cannot." He waved me away. "Doyle, you have seen these operations. It is nothing. You can do it. Just incise the skin, remove a bit of the seventh rib, and probe through the pleura until you encounter pus and drain it."

"But I can't …"

"Aye, you can, lad. And you must. There is no one else to do it."

So, I will try tomorrow.

I only pray that I do not do further harm to that poor, suffering little girl.

1 October 1881

Early this morning, with Ivanov administering a few drops of chloroform, I did the operation exactly as Dr. Bell directed. There was a great gush of green pus and, by noon, Katrinka — for that is her name — took some food for the first time in days.

I am elated, literally walking on air, at this small success. Not only that — but the arm stump of young Konstantine has also healed.

I bubbled over with excitement this afternoon when I reported the result to Dr. Bell. A smile flickered over his lips. "Good, good, Doyle. You have been a bit off-color, lately. This is exactly what you needed."

It is most amazing. His eyes were clear, and there wasn't the slightest tremor when he knotted a silk cravat that matched his fine, grey, tweed suit.

"It is a fine day. Let us walk to the clinic," he said.

He set a fast pace and, in high spirits, twirled his new walking stick with a bright silver knob. Once he stopped and eyed a small, round stone, took a stance, swung the cane like a golf club, and sent the stone flying down the road.

"Dr. Nikolay Pirogov will visit the clinic this afternoon. Do you know of his work?" he asked.

I had to dredge through a distant anatomy lesson and finally came up with an answer. "There is Pirogov's aponeurosis over the biceps muscle. An amputation through the heel of the foot is named for him, is it not?"

He sighted along the cane at a duck rising off the Neva. "Yes, good memory. Pirogov is known for surgical work during the Crimean war and is a first-class scientist. Sadly, he is no longer active in surgery."

At the clinic, we donned clean, white aprons and carefully washed our hands between each patient. I glowed with happiness as Dr. Bell examined my little patient and said I had done well.

Professor Pirogov arrived just as we commenced a most difficult operation on a ten-year-old boy with infected nodes in his neck. I studied the famous man, hoping for inspiration. He was not the imposing great surgeon I had expected, but was stooped, walked with a limp, and was nearly bald. He sat on a high stool with his chin resting on one hand while Dr. Bell gently dissected nerves and arteries in the neck away from tubercular lymph nodes. Sweat trickled down my brow when he inserted the last stitch and I stopped the chloroform anaesthetic.

"Well done, sir. Well done." Pirogov said.

Dr. Bell rinsed his hands. "Thank you," he muttered.

Pirogov pulled at his well-clipped beard. "I must put to you a most difficult situation. The tsar's son, Grand Duke George Alexandrovitch has tuberculosis of the glands, not unlike this lad. The tsar requested my opinion about surgery but I am no longer operating. Dr. Bell, would you be good enough to see the boy?"

His fatigue dropped away, and he straightened his stooped shoulders. "There are many capable Russian surgeons, aye?" Dr. Bell asked.

"They are all afraid of the consequences if the boy should die."

"Ah, now that is a challenge I'll accept. I shall be happy to see young George tomorrow morning."

And so, in the morning, we will journey to the tsar's Palace. I dread to think what will happen to Dr. Bell if the surgery fails and the boy dies. But Dr. Bell seems confident in his surgical skills, so I hope all goes well … Certainly, if anyone can save the boy, it is Dr. Bell.

2 October 1881

After breakfast, we were in the royal coach with the gilded Romanov crest, galloping off to the Gatchina palace some twenty miles south of St. Petersburg.

Once we arrived, a silent, rather cowed, young aide-de-camp led us to the tsar's study. The royal family's quarters were not what I had expected, but were simple and plainly furnished.

Alexander III, Emperor of Russia and King of Poland, is a mighty figure — tall, solid, with a long, reddish-brown beard and a high forehead. He was not covered with medals, as I had expected, but wore a simple military jacket with no decorations. The tsar sat on a plain chair in front of a desk covered with documents.

Professor Pirogov stepped forward, bowed, and introduced us. The tsar spoke in French and Dr. Bell replied in French. The tsar went to the point. "Dr. Bell, can you cure my son?"

"I can operate, but only God can cure your son," Dr. Bell replied.

The tsar's heavily-lidded eyes showed a flicker of respect. "True," he said, and beckoned to his aide-de-camp. "Fetch my son George."

The tsar went back to his papers while we waited. A rather plain-looking governess carried the sickly, pale boy in her arms. He was an attractive little fellow dressed in a blue sailor suit but was stick thin and rather lethargic for an eight-year-old.

"Remove his shirt please," Dr. Bell, rather unceremoniously asked.

The flustered governess looked to the tsar, who nodded. Dr. Bell said not a word, but examined the boy's neck, then listened to his chest, and prodded the abdomen.

"Dr. Pirogov, do you agree these lumps are infected tuberculous nodes?"

The old surgeon clasped his hands in thought. "I do agree and have advised an operation."

"It should be done. Make your arrangements," the tsar said, and held out his arms for the boy, who eagerly went into his embrace. The tsar fondly stroked little George's hair and murmured into his ear before handing him back to the governess and returning to his work.

I could've been mistaken, but there was a bit of moisture on the tsar's cheeks after the boy left. There and then, no matter what I had heard about him, I concluded that Tsar Alexander was not a bad man, and I resolved to do my best to protect him.

Dr. Bell, with Pirogov and an elderly footman, selected a bright, airy room immediately across a corridor from the tsar's private quarters for an operating theater. Dr. Bell wasted no time but scheduled the operation for the next day.

So, now we shall see Dr. Bell in action. I would never want to have to perform surgery under such pressure, but he seems to relish the challenge.

We shall see…

3 October 1881

Professor Sechenov, Pirogov, and three of Russian's foremost surgeons observed our meticulous antiseptic preparations. The poor governess had tears in her eyes when we placed the small, quivering grand duke on the solid oak table.

I whispered to the boy and dripped ether on gauze over his face. He bravely coughed just once, inhaled deeply, and went under the anaesthetic. Dr. Bell made an incision from the angle of his jaw downward, spilled a few drops of royal blood, and dissected the infected nodes from the nerves and vessels in the neck. We could hear the tsar's heavy tread in the corridor all through the operation, which lasted over one hour.

There was one particularly ticklish moment after Dr. Bell nicked the external jugular vein with his scalpel. He pressed the bleeding vessel with one finger and adroitly applied a stitch with one hand. There was a collective sigh of relief when he removed the last infected node.

The boy awoke from the anaesthetic but vomited and vomited until there was nothing left in his stomach. Dr. Bell and I maintained the vigil throughout the afternoon and evening. The tsar, with his face set in a rigid mask, held his son in his arms and paced the floor when the poor child whimpered with pain.

After midnight, the tsar retired to his quarters just across the hall, but he returned within half an hour.

"Bah, how can I sleep when my son is near death?"

"Your Majesty, you must rest, for tomorrow may be another trying day. Dr. Doyle will stay with him through the night. Here is a sleeping draught."

The tsar downed an extravagant dose of laudanum with one gulp and returned to his quarters. A little after midnight, the governess coaxed little George into taking a few sips of milk, and at last, he settled into a light sleep, breathed quietly, and had a strong pulse.

For all my determination to remain alert, I, too, dozed off…

4 October 1881

In the wee hours of the morning, I was awakened by a strange thumping sound. George was resting easily, and the governess was lightly snoring. Had I dreamed, or was there, again, the sound of a dull *thump* in the corridor?

Perhaps, the tsar was returning to see his son, but then the sound was gone. I went to the door and listened, but there was nothing…

Then, I heard something which sounded like a faint rattle. Was it the wind stirring a tree branch? An animal scratching in the garden? I listened for a long minute. There it was again, a faint rattle.

I took the single candle from its holder and gently opened the door into the corridor. There, immediately at the entrance to the tsar's bedroom, his personal guard was unconscious on the floor with a gash on his forehead. At first, I thought he must have fallen and cracked his skull, but he was a healthy young guardsman and there was no smell of liquor. Someone had attacked him.

Before I examined him, there it was again — a faint rattle from within the tsar's bedroom. The scene in Pavlov's laboratory, with snakes sinking their deadly fangs into the poor old caretaker, rose like a dread scene from hell in my mind.

I had no weapon, was in stocking feet, but sensed there was a rattlesnake in the tsar's bedroom.

The candle flame flickered from the slight draft as I opened the door into the tsar's small, plain chamber. Was it a hallucination? No.

Why was a uniformed British officer in the tsar's bedroom?

A single oil lamp in a far corner cast a flickering, yellow light over a garish scene. I guttered my candle with two fingers and moved further into the room. The figure in the uniform of a British officer set a large basket on the floor and, with the tip of his boot, lifted the top. The rattling increased, then there was hissing and, finally, the scrape of scales on the basket. I watched, as if in a hypnotic trance, while a reptilian head as large as my fist rose from the basket.

In the dim light, there was no mistaking the flat head and dull, venomous eyes of a gigantic Texas rattlesnake.

As if responding to a charmer's melody, the snake rose from the basket, its head swaying back and forth. The entire seven-foot reptile coiled, uncoiled and, in a nightmarish moment, was suddenly at full length on the wooden floor.

It was only then that I saw the massive bulk of the tsar resting, fully clothed, on the top of an oversized soldier's cot in the far corner of the room.

Unfortunately, I was too far away to stop the venomous creature and no match for a deadly rattler. The tsar was out cold from the laudanum, on his back, with one arm hanging almost to the floor.

With a sibilant hiss, the snake raised its head as if sampling the air, hunting for food. I should have cried out, aroused the palace, but there was no time and the tsar was still deep under the influence of the laudanum. The snake, as if sensing the helplessness of its prey, raised its head and flicked its tongue.

I huddled with my back to the wall, in the shadows, as the officer picked up the basket and slowly backed away.

I waited, then threw an arm around his neck with a stranglehold. He struggled. I administered a short chop to the back of his head. He wilted in my arms.

With his head thrown back, I stared at his face. My God, it was Dmitri, the caretaker from Pavlov's laboratory. Why was he dressed as a British officer?

Could this man be David Campbell, the British officer who had sworn vengeance on the tsar? Aye, my mind was in a whirl.

Ivanov had deliberately placed him in Pavlov's laboratory. I had not been mistaken when I heard him muttering in English. Penelope must be behind this diabolic plot. Who else could have helped him gain access to the tsar's quarters?

There was no time for idle thoughts. The great, horrid snake made the sibilant rattle, his warning of an impending strike. The creature was within a foot of the tsar's dangling arm. It seemed helpless, but I had to save the tsar.

Ah, the whistle, the whistle Dmitri used to call the snakes for food. At first, I couldn't produce a sound from my parched, pursed lips, but I finally managed a feeble, high-pitched tone. The snake did not respond. It was again coiled, its great head moving back and forth, on the scent for food. I whistled again and, slowly, the head turned. Was it my imagination, or were those dull eyes searching for new prey?

It was an utterly terrifying moment. I whistled again. The snake turned and, with one coil after another, silently moved in my direction. The snake's primitive brain had followed a dim Pavlovian instinct to find food in the direction of the whistle. I had saved the tsar. For now…

Unfortunately, it appeared as if I was now the chosen food source. I pushed the unconscious officer, Dmitri — or was it David — into the corridor. I retreated, completely terrified and without a notion of how to save myself from the snake that kept slithering faster and faster towards me.

For a moment, I thought of slamming the door, leaving the snake and the tsar alone. But then, I thought of the tsar holding his son just as any loving father and backed further into the hall.

I stumbled backward onto the felled guard. He groaned and rolled over. There, beneath his body was a rifle with a fixed bayonet.

The snake was now halfway out the door and into the corridor when I, with trembling hands and not a moment to lose, took up the guard's rifle and commenced a terrible dance with the poisonous beast. We parried, back and forth, now thrusting, now retreating. The whole time, I fixed my focus on those awful fangs.

The rifle was a short cavalry carbine, so even with the bayonet, my reach was not even as long as that terrible, thrusting body.

In short, I had only made the reptile angry.

The snake had ignored the two unconscious men; the eyes in that flat, deadly head were only for me. I whistled and retreated down the hall where the only light came from a single candle in a wall holder. Any further and I would be in total darkness. The guard groaned and, for just a moment, the snake turned aside.

I thrust the bayonet behind the creature's head but missed the vital spinal cord. He struck with lightning speed and barely missed my leg. With one more thrust, I drove the tip of the blade through the body and impaled the writhing snake to the wooden floor.

It was still alive, writhing and striking out but unable to slither forward or back. Yet, the open mouth and deadly fangs were as dangerous as ever.

The snake struggled, but the bayonet did not give. I had a moment's reprieve. I removed the light dress sword from the guard's scabbard and, in one fell swoop, I severed the snake's head from the body.

Now, what to do with the mess? A dead snake, an injured guard, and a sick English officer. The tsar, even after a heavy dose of laudanum, would rise at first light and the palace would come awake. I wrapped the snake's body in bedclothes soiled by our patient's vomiting.

Later, I convinced the governess the bundle was infectious and must be burned. A dash of medicinal brandy on the face of the unconscious guard provided an explanation for his dereliction of duty.

That left a very sick, dazed English officer who I had known as Dmitri but was almost certainly the missing officer, David Campbell. His trousers were not so different from a Russian officer. Perhaps, without his jacket and British insignia, he might pass as a palace guard. I dragged his limp body into a corner of the sick room and covered him with a quilt.

Little George opened one sleepy eye and said just one word. "L'eau."

I held his head while he sipped from a cup of water. The governess awoke immediately and took charge of the boy. It then occurred to me that the poor guard would be shot for neglecting his duties. Out of sympathy, I roused the poor man, put a bit of sticking plaster on his wound, propped him up, and replaced the carbine into his limp hand. If needed, I could claim the brandy was a wound disinfectant.

All in all, it was not a bad night's work.

Nothing was amiss, when, at the crack of dawn, the tsar tramped into the room on heavy feet and swept little George into his massive arms.

An hour later, Dr. Bell arrived, as fresh as ever, and after examining George, allowed the boy to go with his governess to his own room. We were alone with nothing to do but to pack our instruments and leave.

"Sir, we have a problem," I said.

"Oh come now. It is a fine morning and our patient is recovering nicely," he said.

"I believe I have discovered the English officer. He is there, under a quilt."

I carried the poor man to the oak table. He was light as a feather and clearly suffering from a chronic illness.

"He is very near death," Dr. Bell said.

I related what I knew of Dmitri's headaches, confusion, and loss of memory. Dr. Bell commenced his usual sleuth-like examination, noted the scars on both hands, more scars on his torso indicating old bullet wounds, and the emaciation. "Ah, Doyle, he is certainly the British officer. What do you make of this?" He had pulled down the lower lip to expose a blue-black line on the lower gum, just beneath the teeth.

I recalled an old patient, a lead miner, in the insane asylum. "Burton's line!" I cried. "Lead poisoning."

"Very good, Doyle. Excellent. Sadly, his brain is affected and he is near the last stages of the illness. If his kidney's fail, he is a dead man."

"But why?" I asked.

"The wounds, Doyle. Think about it. From the looks of these old bullet holes, he has one and possibly two lead balls within his body." Bell set about, with his long, sensitive fingers, to palpate every inch of the man's torso. His index finger came to rest high in the officer's armpit. "It is here, lodged in the subscapularis muscle. We must remove it."

"Shall we take him to a hospital?"

"There is no time to lose, and there is no better operating room in all of Russia than right here. Quick — carbolic and open the instrument case."

It made sense. The sooner the lead ball was removed, the better his chances. The royal family and the entire household was either with little George or at breakfast. We had the room to ourselves for at least an hour.

Bell kept his finger on the place where he had located the bullet while I splashed carbolic on his hands over the patient's chest. He needed only a probe, the sharp curved scalpel, and a rat-toothed forceps to remove the bullet, a .65 calibre musket ball.

Our patient uttered a sigh but scarcely moved during the brief operation. "Now, fetch that young aide-de-camp; demand a carriage and four fast horses."

We told the young man that our patient was a visiting physician who had swooned at the sight of the great tsar. He understood completely and helped us carry the English officer to the carriage.

"We could have used Mr. Tatum," I said. "Where is he?"

A look of exasperation — or was it worry — passed over the professor's face. "I am sorry to say that he never appeared this morning. It does not bode well for him."

Indeed, there was no Mr. Tatum at our quarters either. During the rest of the day, I forced tea, broth, and water into our patient with the intent of washing the lead from his system.

He roused a bit by late afternoon, but by then, and even late into the evening, Mr. Tatum was still missing.

5 October 1881

This morning, David Campbell came around when Sasha licked his face. An inscription on an antique gold watch in his trousers pocket proved he truly is the lost English officer. Bloodletting has gone out of fashion these days, but Dr. Bell decided to take a pint of his blood to reduce the amount of lead in his body.

It did seem to help. He can now walk a few steps and no longer holds his head in pain. Marya has taken over his nursing care, and when she takes breaks, we have resumed our delightful language lessons.

There is still no sign of Mr. Tatum. It would seem something awful has happened to him. I visited the embassy, spoke with the ambassador's secretary, and made enquiries at the Hotel Europa. No one has heard from him.

Just before dinner, the footman ushered Inspector Koivisto with two uniformed policemen into Dr. Bell's sitting room.

"I regret to be here under these circumstances," the inspector said.

"Is it about Mr. Tatum?" I asked.

"Yes, very likely. You must come and identify the body."

The police cab, drawn by two aged hacks, took us to the waterfront near the western end of Vasilyesky Island. We alighted and, led by the inspector, walked to the very end of a wooden wharf where two officers and several sailors in high boots and thick sweaters stood by a canvas-covered corpse.

"We don't have all day. Remove the canvas," Koivisto brusquely said.

Without ceremony, a young policeman pulled the rough canvas aside. The body was bloated from immersion in the sea, and part of the face had been gnawed away by fish. I instantly turned away and did my best not to vomit. Dr. Bell remained stolid and studied the corpse.

Most of the corpse was intact and it was indeed our valet, or rather, our friend, the British secret agent we knew as Mr. Tatum. I had become very fond of Tatum with his quiet good humor and common sense.

I refused to look at the dismal body and choked back a sob. This whole trip was just a bloody awful mess and I yearned to go back home and try to forget it all. I just prayed that Tatum's life, and the lives of the others who had died, were given for the sake of a lasting peace in Europe and not in vain!

Dr. Bell, in his usual professional manner, knelt and continued to inspect the remains. "Where was he found?" he asked.

"A fisherman discovered his body, tangled in old cables, immediately beneath this wharf."

"When?" Dr. Bell asked.

"Just before noon," Koivisto said.

Dr. Bell consulted a small, black notebook, turned several pages, and marked the place with his finger. "I last saw Mr. Tatum on the morning of October the first. He was at the embassy during the mid-afternoon and did not show up on the morning of the second as was his usual habit. He disappeared sometime during the early evening or night of the first."

He again consulted his notebook. "There was a full moon that night which would have produced an exceptionally high tide early on the morning of the second. During the late evening, up to perhaps two a.m., there would have been a strong incoming current."

One of the onlookers spoke up in Russian and said something that sounded like he agreed with Dr. Bell about the strong tide currents over the past several days.

"Tell me, please, what is the direction of the incoming current at the end of the wharf?" Dr. Bell asked.

The fisherman pointed. "Go to the end of that dock and see for yourself."

He was indeed correct; flotsam and bits of seaweed drifted our way from the end of a dock where two vessels were moored side by side, perhaps a half a mile away.

Dr. Bell snapped open his watch and intently observed the floating debris for a full five minutes until Inspector Koivisto impatiently broke the silence. "Come, come. It is getting late. We shall deliver the body to the morgue for an autopsy in the morning. We shall be happy to deliver you to your rooms."

"Nay." Dr. Bell waved him away. "We shall remain for a while. Come, Doyle, let us walk. This clean, fresh, sea air will clear our minds."

It was a classic example of Dr. Bell's perfectly innocuous statements that were loaded with foreboding and gravity. I was not surprised when we set off at a good pace along the sea wall towards the dock with the two moored ships.

The nearest vessel was a screw-propelled warship of the latest design with forward and aft turrets, each with powerful cannons. German colors flew from her stern.

The dock extended five hundred feet from the embankment, and the second ship was partly hidden from view. She appeared to be an older cargo vessel with both sails and steam. A peculiar, tattered ensign fluttered in the dying breeze from her aft mast.

I made out a black cross with a circle containing the figure of an eagle in the center and an anchor in the lower left hand corner. "Ah, it is the ensign of the German commercial fleet," Dr. Bell exclaimed.

Two blank-faced guards stamped back and forth from one side of the wharf to the other, blocking our way to the pair of ships.

"We are visiting friends," Dr. Bell said.

The guard halted and held his rifle squarely in front of his chest. "Verboten."

"Why?" I responded in German.

"Eintritt untersagt," the second guard replied, in a most unpleasant, surly manner.

"Seems like we are forbidden," I muttered to Bell. He nodded, and I realized that he spoke better German than me and I should let him do the talking. I was all for barging past the guards, but Dr. Bell thought otherwise. "They are up to no good. It is best we leave now," he muttered, in English.

We strolled, chatting in French, appearing to be aimless sightseers, but we were fully alert and surreptitiously observed the German ships. The sun was nearly at the horizon, casting long shadows, but we made out crewmen scurrying about the two ships and more rifle-toting guards. "There must be a way to get close to those vessels," Dr. Bell said.

"I shall nip around and see my friend with the sailing yawl," I said.

Later, that evening, I called on good old Dicky Ferguson. We shared a bottle and a bit of cheese. He said he would be more than happy to take us for a sail tomorrow. So, we have a plan and now need a good night's rest.

I cannot not know for sure, but I have a feeling that the fate of the tsar — and all of Europe, for that matter — rests with our little sea journey on the morrow.

6 October 1881

"We must not be recognized," Dr. Bell said. The professor had secured a natty yachting outfit; cap, blazer, ascot, and white, duck trousers. When we met at a rickety dock on the Neva, Dicky Ferguson provided me with a black, wool cap and fisherman's garb. This meant that I had to haul on sails, lift the boom, and bail the bilge like a common hired hand.

Within minutes, my once well-manicured physician's hands were covered with sticky tar. When we entered the bay, the yawl heeled over in a brisk breeze and skipped along over a light chop. We tacked out over clear water and, with quick changes of sails, tacked and dodged between the anchored ships.

"Now, turn back to the German ships!" Dr. Bell shouted.

Dicky brought the tiller around and the yawl spun on her keel, while I desperately hauled in the main sail and pushed it to the other side. The jib sail came over with considerable flapping, and we went off on a course for the moored Germans.

Dr. Bell, to all appearances, looked the part of a casual nautical observer, training his long, brass telescope first on one ship and then another.

"Did you know," Ferguson shouted, "The entire Russian fleet is in port for the tsar's review? There . . ." he pointed. "Carr and McPherson, our countrymen, built those three cruisers, the *Ozight*, *Rasboynik* and the *Opritchnik* here in St. Petersburg." They were older, three-masted ships with iron hulls and steam engines, mounting Hotchkiss guns on either side.

We were hull down, flying past a great, Russian, armored cruiser, close enough to make out an officer with three golden eagles on his epaulets. "That's the admiral!" Dicky shouted. "On Sunday, the tsar will review the whole fleet from his flagship, the *Nakhimov*." She was a grand four-stacker with a sleek iron hull. There were more ships, gunboats from France and Sweden, and a late model cruiser from Germany.

"Our fleet arrives tomorrow with Her Majesty's yacht, the *Victoria and Albert*, just in time for the festivities on Sunday." Dicky said.

We swept down on the German ships, tacked, and came about. Dr. Bell crouched low behind the coaming, with his telescope trained on the Germans. “Can you stop for a better look?” he asked.

Dicky immediately flung over the tiller. “Doyle, let go the main halyard!” he yelled.

Without knowing one rope from another, I let go of the main sheet. The boom went out and the sail shivered. “No, no, you fool! The main halyard.”

I finally got the idea, un-cleated the right rope, and the main sail came crashing down the mast into a tangled heap. Our boat wallowed on the waves while Dicky and I ran about like maniacs to set things right.

Meanwhile, Dr. Bell, hidden among folds of the heavy canvas sail, trained his telescope on the German cargo ship. “Doyle, focus on the space between the two ships.”

I took the brass instrument and managed a close look at a most peculiar structure. Low in the water, almost invisible, was a black object supporting a wooden platform that appeared to be a landing stage between the two ships. “There is a semi-submerged vessel beneath the wood platform,” I said. “It seems to be similar to what I saw in the hull of the ship that we came here on.”

“Did you note the black pipes extending up from the mystery ship?” Dr. Bell asked.

We set the sails again and rolled down wind back to our dock on the Neva. While we tied up, a grizzled old fellow shouted out to us. “Be you English?” he asked.

“Scottish!” Dicky shouted.

“Close enough. An Englishman rented my skiff and hasn’t returned. I need my skiff,” he said.

Dicky translated for us. “Ask him what the Englishman looked like,” Dr. Bell said.

The description was close enough. Tatum had rented the skiff. We could not help the man further, but assured him that, soon enough, he would be compensated.

As a thanks to Dicky, Dr. Bell offered dinner and drinks at the Hotel Europa. I had a quick change of clothing and enjoyed enough fine food and drink to be a bit tipsy on return to our quarters.

I left Dr. Bell at the door to his sitting room but turned when he spoke. “Come, Doyle, we have a guest,” he said.

Colonel Sir Cameron Beachy-Edwards, pale, slender, and as impressive as ever, sat bolt upright on a straight chair, with both hands folded over the knob of an elegant, ebony walking stick. “Where is Sergeant James O’Grady?” he asked, without so much as a greeting.

“Unfortunately, the sergeant is dead.” Dr. Bell said.

The colonel hunched forward and leaned heavily on his cane. For a moment, he lost his aplomb, but recovered his British stiff upper lip. “No! What was the cause of death?”

“Apparently, he drowned.” Bell said.

“I find that hard to believe. James O’Grady or, as you called him, Tatum, was a strong swimmer.” the colonel said.

“The Russian police have arranged an autopsy for tomorrow morning,” I said.

“This presents us with a most troublesome situation. The sergeant was looking after security for Her Majesty’s yacht, which arrives tomorrow. His dispatches suggested trouble from either the anarchists or the Germans. He was so concerned, I rushed from Paris by rail across all of Europe. We must be especially vigilant because Edward, Prince of Wales, is aboard the yacht. If there is an attack on the tsar while he reviews the fleet, the Prince would also be in danger.” Sir Cameron said.

“O’Grady’s body was in the harbor not far from two rather suspicious German ships. Perhaps he died during an investigation” Dr. Bell replied.

“Indeed. Why do you suspect the German ships?” the colonel asked.

“A cargo ship is moored next to a well-armed German naval vessel and something, perhaps another boat, is hidden between the two.”

“In one of his dispatches, O’Grady said the American ambassador let slip something about a submersible vessel. It is hardly possible that the Americans would have a submarine boat in these waters."

When Colonel Beachy-Edwards paused, Dr. Bell spoke. "And we thought you should know. The lost English officer, David Campbell, is here with us."

Colonel Beachy-Edwards brightened. "Indeed, I wish to speak with him."

"He is suffering from severe lead poisoning as a result of an old bullet wound. His illness explains his rather strange behavior since he left Afghanistan," Dr. Bell said.

"Poor Campbell was actually quite brave in the war," The colonel said.

We had placed David Campbell in Mr. Tatum's room. He was attired in Tatum's tattered dressing gown, and when we walked in, Marya was spooning gruel into his mouth. Beachy-Edwards took his hand, and for a moment, Campbell's eyes lit with recognition. "Ah, ah, colonel," he mumbled. He did indeed show signs of improvement, but then, as quickly as his lucidity had appeared, it slid away…

The colonel, yawning and claiming exhaustion from his arduous train journey, insisted on sleeping on a spare narrow cot in the sitting room.

7 October 1881

Over breakfast, the colonel complained about overcooked eggs and that we didn't have proper marmalade. By the time we were able to scrounge up enough marmalade to satisfy his rarified tastes, we were late for the autopsy.

The pathologist had already made the long, Y-shaped incision from chest to lower abdomen. The organs were disintegrating from bacterial action, but the stench didn't faze the colonel. He had seen death at first hand on many fields of battle. He looked at the gnawed face for several minutes, squinting, from one angle to another. "Indeed, it is O'Grady," he said.

"Ah, what have we here?' Dr. Bell exclaimed. Blood clots and free blood oozed from the open peritoneal cavity. "Doyle, five pounds says this blood is from a ruptured spleen. You may have the honor of proving my point or winning my money."

I accepted his challenge and, with some reluctance, removed my jacket, rolled up my sleeve, and thrust a hand up to my elbow into the rotting mess of intestine. The soft, spongy spleen, in the left upper quadrant of the abdomen, was ruptured into three pieces. Dr. Bell was correct, as usual.

"Mr. Tatum suffered a traumatic rupture of the spleen. The loss of blood explains his inability to swim, or else he was dead before he entered the water. He either fell from a height or an assailant gave him a terrific blow to the abdomen," Dr. Bell said.

"O'Grady was expert with knife, gun, or fists and was agile as a cat. I can't believe he fell or was defeated by a single opponent," the colonel said.

"I agree. This was most certainly murder," Dr. Bell said, and added, "Let us repair to more comfortable surroundings." So, we returned to our quarters.

While Marya served tea in the sitting room, the colonel withdrew a sheaf of papers from his leather dispatch case. He fixed me with his piercing grey eyes. "Mr. Doyle, you provided Sergeant O'Grady with detailed accounts of your activities on the *Servia*, but I am unclear with regard to your discovery of an unconscious American engineer and your encounters with Miss Walshingham," he said. He drained his cup of tea and scowled. “I demand a full explanation.”

“Sir, I fully expected Miss Walshingham, or rather, Mrs. Foley, would make a report to you and there was no need for me to …” I said.

“Young man, Miss Walshingham suffers from hysteria. Her father sent her to school in Zurich, where she fell in with radical Russian students. The Secret Service recruited her because she is a brilliant linguist, even knowing she had a tendency towards emotional and other psychological disturbances. She can assume any role or personality and, indeed, serves admirably as lady-in-waiting to the Duchess of Edinburgh. She had an affair with Captain Foley and planned to accompany him to Russia —”

“Excuse me, you said an affair. I was under the impression that they were married?”

“No. They never married.”

I was speechless. Penelope had lied and led me on? Why would she claim to be married to my uncle if it wasn’t true? Nothing about that women made sense.

“Speak up, Mr. Doyle. Explain your encounters with Miss Walshingham.”

I could not lie to the colonel or to Dr. Bell, but I chose my words carefully to protect Penelope. “In truth, it was a chance meeting, but we indulged in a romantic tryst in the hold of the ship. An intruder, brandishing a gun, interrupted our bit of romance. I thought he was the murderer and struck a blow that rendered him unconscious.”

“Could you identify the cargo?”

“No, there were three large wooden crates and, ah, yes, I remember, they were labeled ‘Brooklyn Naval Yard.’ ”

“Crates that were unloaded in Kiel?” the colonel asked.

“Yes, sir. I observed cranes remove them from the ship.”

The colonel studied his papers and sighed deeply. “I hope you were careful in your dealings with that woman. She is involved with the anarchist students, the German naval attaché, and rebellious Russian officers. She is the link connecting several plots on the tsar.”

"But, sir, she saved my life by extricating me from prison and, well, say what you will, but isn't it also possible that she is working to keep the tsar alive?" I asked.

The colonel heaved a great sigh. "I wish I could believe that."

Dr. Bell, with eyes closed and hands folded over his chest, had listened to our conversation. "None of this explains the death of Mr. Tatum, or rather, Sergeant O'Grady. I suspect the Germans were responsible."

"Sergeant O'Grady assumed, wrongly, as it turned out, that Count von Wittenberg murdered Lord Asquith. He searched of the count's cabin and found diagrams that correspond to the crates in the hold of the *Servia*. Here is his rough copy of the drawings. Our experts in the Royal Navy are convinced that the crates contained sections of a new type of submersible vessel. There are questions about how the crew can obtain breathable air in such a vessel. Dr. Bell, kindly look at this sketch and give us your expert opinion as a man of science."

I peeked over his shoulder as Dr. Bell examined the drawings. "Incredible," he said. "The Americans have solved the problem of travel beneath the sea." The vessel was pointed at either end and powered with an electric motor. If the batteries failed, the crew, with a system of pedals, chains, and gears, could turn the propeller. "But, sir, how can the crew obtain oxygen? I asked.

"These two pipes extending above the water have manual pumps to draw in fresh air and to discharge the used air. When totally submerged, they have canisters of sodium hydroxide to absorb carbon dioxide, and a cylinder of compressed oxygen. The most incredible feature is this system of mirrors within a tube, which allows the captain to see above the surface."

"But what is the use of such a vessel?" I asked.

"Think, boy!" Colonel Beachy-Edwards replied. "This ship will revolutionize naval warfare. Furthermore, the Americans have improved upon the Whitehead torpedo. It has an effective range of three hundred yards and, if used with this submersible vessel, they would instantly become unbeatable at sea. Unbeatable!"

Bell studied the drawings. "Ah, yes, the firing mechanism uses compressed air to start the torpedo on its way, and then, a small electric motor turns a propeller that propels the torpedo to an enemy ship. The Germans and Americans have created a most diabolical instrument of naval warfare."

"You are quite correct. The torpedo has a plunger, which strikes a detonator to explode on contact with another ship." the colonel said.

"Why are the Americans involved? Dr. Bell asked.

"Some Americans think a Russian anarchist killed their President, Garfield." I said.

"Either way, things don't look good for the tsar on Sunday." Dr. Bell jumped to his feet. "I tried to convince the tsar to let young George rest, with cod liver oil and sunshine to complete his cure, but he insists on taking his entire family on board the *Nakhimov* when he reviews the fleet on Sunday."

"Good God, man! A single torpedo could sink the ship and kill the entire royal family in one fell stroke!" the colonel exclaimed.

"The Germans killed Tatum when he discovered the submarine boat between the two German ships. We must report this to the Russian police at once," Dr. Bell said.

"No, the Queen insists that the matter be handled quietly. She does not want to precipitate a full-blown European war," the colonel said.

"Well then, how can we prevent this atrocity?" Bell asked.

"I might have a plan," I said. "It is a bit risky, but …"

"I'm sorry, son, but I have to say your reliability is questionable, at best," the colonel said.

"I can vouch for Mr. Doyle, but if O'Grady, a well-trained practitioner of espionage, met his death in this crusade, I fear that there is little a common citizen like Mr. Doyle or I can do," Bell said.

"My lack of credibility with you might just be my strength. You see, the student anarchist groups trust me. I can talk to them tonight and learn if they are involved in the plot." I said.

The colonel was not eager to follow my plan, but he had little alternative. That evening, I went in search of Vera or Ivanov. My friends weren't at the Beranger or the Idiot's Café. The whole time, I kept thinking, *was Penelope involved*?

I could not forget her lips, her body, her passionate embraces … I knew that Vera and Ivanov must have means to contact her. She must not be hunted down and shot as a traitor to the Queen. If I could just get to Vera or Ivanov…

After a few hours, I dejectedly approached Dr. Sechenov's home, when a dark figure emerged from behind a tree. "Doyle, we must speak." It was Vera. I had spent all night looking for her, and only when I had given up did she find me.

She held me close, and I put my arm around her. We walked as lovers do, and like lovers, we whispered in the night, but they were not whispers of love. Rather, Vera asked if I was still sympathetic with their cause.

I hesitated for a second. Where would this lead? "Yes, I would like to help. Have you heard from the English woman?"

"We will meet her tomorrow, Saturday night."

"Where?"

"Alexander's Column at midnight. Bring warm clothing."

From my wanderings about the city, I knew the impressive column with the cross and an angel atop a great red granite base. It was in the open Palace Square, safe from surprises. So, I felt certain it wasn't a trap…

Or was it?

9 October 1881

I did not sleep well yesterday. Too much was riding on my shoulders. It was Saturday, and if I failed to do my job, and the Germans killed the tsar, the next day might explode into a huge European conflict. It was hard to believe; I could be the only person standing between the tsar's death and a disastrous war.

I did not feel confident, but I could do nothing less than carry on. The odds were against our small group, but then, Dr. Bell and I had saved the American president from a Confederate plot during our journey to America. The thought renewed my confidence.

Early in the morning, I dressed in a dark sweater and high boots and took Bell's telescope in a leather case. With Sasha, I loped along a path leading to the harbor. When the great fleet came into view, I dodged into a clump of trees and tied Sasha to a branch.

The Russian cruiser, *Nakhimov,* was on the far side of the harbor, perhaps five miles from the German ships. The Queen's royal yacht was anchored a quarter-mile off the cruiser's stern, and other ships were arrayed about the harbor.

According to the colonel's informants, tomorrow, the ships will pass in review, firing salutes to the tsar on the far side of the cruiser. Short of a long, cold swim, I could see no way to get near the German ships or the submarine boat. If there was a plan to kill the tsar and his family and set Europe ablaze with war, I had no idea how I might prevent it. I got Sasha and returned to my room.

Later, I had a substantial supper, alone, since Bell and the colonel were at the embassy. It was with some misgiving at my rather hasty decision to join the students that I ventured into the unknown for the midnight rendezvous. It wasn't until then that I wondered, with great anxiety, *Great God, what have I done?*

I was to meet with both Vera and, perhaps, Penelope. I hesitated, unsure whether to brave the love — or was it the wrath — of two women. But then, a deeper emotion, a sense of duty, won over. I went ahead, not knowing what to expect, but with the full knowledge that I had no choice but to continue walking down a potentially deadly path.

The streets under a fine, misty rain were deserted. I stood in the shadows, observing the Palace Square. A few minutes after midnight, two figures and then a third strolled past, turned back, and huddled on the side of Alexander's Column facing the Winter Palace. I eased forward and joined the group.

I did not recognize Penelope, who wore a dark, wool cap that obscured her face, a shapeless sweater, and trousers. "Why is he here?" she hissed.

"You requested four crewmen to help the count," Vera said.

"Damn, why didn't you bring a Russian student?"

"The reliable ones are all dead or in prison. Dr. Doyle has aided us in the past. I trust him," Vera said.

"It will be very dangerous. We might all die." Penelope said.

I listened to the exchange, totally flummoxed. Neither woman cared a good damn whether I lived or died. I called on my Irish backbone. "It is a good cause," I said.

Vera shook my hand. "We are all together. Wear this."

I put on a dark student's jacket and pulled a visored cap over my eyes.

"Excellent," Vera said.

We walked towards the Neva where we met a four-horse carriage coming along Dvortsovaya Street. "Get in, quickly," Penelope ordered. I hesitated but climbed into the closed carriage.

The two men wore naval uniforms. When my eyes adjusted to the gloom, I recognized the German, Count von Wittenberg, and Gritz, the American engineer. We clipped along, in silence, for over an hour, turning into one street, then another, apparently to avoid followers. It was a dangerous mission, but there was no other way to see the submersible vessel.

The driver doubled back to the square and paused for long minutes. "Good, we are not being followed," the count said in English, which I presumed was for the benefit of Gritz.

At the wharf, the guards came to attention, saluted the count, and waved us on. We alighted from the carriage, crossed a gangway to the cargo ship, and climbed down a ladder to a landing stage where the submersible was hidden. I immediately noted how three sections were bolted together and recognized the breathing tubes and the periscope.

We descended through an open hatch into the belly of the beast, which was dimly lit with two Edison electric bulbs. I quickly scanned the interior, which was truly an engineering marvel. The navigation station was near the center, just forward of a huge electric motor connected to a series of batteries. Further aft, there were gauges, levers, and electrical devices I could not recognize. There was no doubt, however, about the rack containing new Mauser repeating rifles next to the navigation station.

When we reached the bottom of the ladder, Penelope gave the count an enthusiastic embrace. "This time, we must not fail," she said.

The count pushed her away. "If we prepare properly, we cannot fail. First, we assign stations, and then, we practice for the final run."

"We shall test the motor, but must save electricity. Hans, Fritz, Adolph, show this young man how to pedal," Gritz said.

Ivanov joined the German sailors at a series of pedals that turned the propeller shaft. The count led Vera to the forward-breathing tube pump and, for a moment, left me near the navigation station.

I peeked through the periscope for a minute and noted the steering wheel and depth control levers. While the count and Gritz were busy demonstrating the various pumps and pedals to the students and Penelope, I studied the compass. Whether or not the American, Gritz, was as much of a drunk as he appeared when we had first met, it was clear he was an experienced engineer.

Evidently, the captain navigated with the compass while submerged below periscope depth. It was a larger version of the simple magnetic compass I had used during hikes in the highlands. The black end of the needle pointed north, while the white aimed south.

Gritz came aft, pulled a switch, and the electric motor started with a whine. The deck vibrated, and immediately, the compass needle reversed itself. After the test, when he switched off the engine, the compass returned to normal.

"You," the count ordered. "Man the aft breathing-tube pump."

My job was to sit on a sort of saddle and turn bicycle pedals that, through a chain, ran a pump which brought in draughts of fresh air. *This will be hard, monotonous work,* I thought. The count seemed satisfied with my efforts, then took Penelope by the hand and went forward to what I deduced to be the torpedo firing station.

"Penelope, dear, you may have the honor to press the trigger to fire the torpedo that will kill the tsar," the count said. Would Penelope go with their plan or was she playacting? It was hard to tell. I had no choice but to let things play out.

The hatch remained open, and after the practice session, the count ordered us to rest. Meanwhile, he had turned the steering wheel and worked the lever, which moved a rod near my station.

I dredged up a memory from my brief look at the diagram. When the rod moved forward, the fins turned downward, so the boat went deeper. Moving it backward made the boat return to the surface. Could I move the rod by hand to control the boat's depth? There had to be a better plan.

Hours went by. I hated this ship, but tried not to let anybody see my distress. It was impossible to stand erect in the horribly cramped space. The atmosphere was hot and dense with humidity, even with the open hatch. I had been in dangerous situations during our American trip, but being entombed in an iron coffin was far worse. To make matters worse, I was far away from home and family and, not for the first time, yearned to return to dry land and lovely Edinburgh.

Then, I thought about how even Dr. Bell was unaware of my whereabouts. Sweat rolled down my face, but I shivered with cold fear. No one would know if I died.

I had been such a fool to meet these lunatics at midnight. What was I thinking? It was the day of the Naval Review. I was in this crowded space, close to Vera and Penelope — once, or perhaps, still, the love of my life — but visions of being in the open air with Ferguson on his yacht beckoned. The rascal would be sipping champagne with a couple of ballet dancers while he watched the parade of ships.

Then, I kept reminding myself that my comfort was of no consequence today. My task was to save lives at all costs. These people hated the tsar, but I knew him to be a good and kind father to little George, and the lives of everybody back home might be at risk if I failed.

Then, with a start, I thought of Sasha. Would someone care for her, or would she be returned to Pavlov's dreadful laboratory?

I felt sluggish and developed a headache. The air smelled stale. Nine people used a great deal of oxygen. I pedaled and, immediately, there was a breath of fresh air. I sucked in several lungs full and my headache cleared. The others sagged or held their heads in their hands.

In a flash, I realized that I controlled the amount of fresh air in the boat. If I pumped slowly, there was enough air for me, since the vent emptied out close to my head, but not enough for the others. The chemical, sodium hydroxide, would take up carbon dioxide too slowly to clean the air breathed out by nine people. This might turn out to be a valuable bit of knowledge.

Hours went by until I judged the sun to be nearly overhead. "Start the pumps and close the hatch," the count suddenly ordered.

In the dim light cast by the Edison bulbs, I watched the German crewmen and Ivanov pump pedals that turned the propeller. The boat moved sluggishly, then gathered speed. The count was glued to the periscope with his hands on the steering wheel. He moved the lever forward and the deck inclined downward.

"Five feet, continue to descend. Ah, good, maintain ten feet. At this level only the tips of our tubes are visible," Gritz said.

I pumped for all I was worth to maintain fresh air in the boat.

"Course, thirty-two degrees to the *Nakhimov*," the count said. He turned the periscope one hundred and eighty degrees and watched intently for several minutes. "Ah, right on schedule, our cruiser is following us. After we fire the torpedo, she will provide cover for our escape."

Gritz went forward and tapped a gauge connected to a large steel cylinder. "Good — two thousand pounds pressure, enough to fire the torpedo."

The count and Gritz kept up a steady patter. “Clear of the wharf. Five miles to target,” the count said. “You fellows, more speed.”

The big German sailors and Ivanov pedaled furiously. Sweat dripped down their faces and they gasped for air.

“Let us start the engine,” the count said.

“Not yet. We must conserve electricity for our escape,” Gritz replied.

I gradually slowed my pedaling until there was only a soft draft of fresh air on my face, but hardly enough for the others. Vera’s head drooped, and the German sailors took in great gulps of air. All of them sagged and lost great quantities of sweat in the hot, closed space. Hans, one of the German crewmen, stumbled and nearly fell.

“Damn, the air is stale in here. You, British boy, pump harder!” the count shouted.

I pedaled furiously for a few minutes, but when the count went back to the periscope and attended to steering the boat, I slowed my pedaling and the intake of fresh air diminished to a trickle.

“Ah, my dear Gritz. Come, see a beautiful sight. There she is, less than a mile away,” the count said.

Gritz took the wheel and put his eye to the lens and system of mirrors. “Ah, yes. Very good. The tsar’s cruiser is anchored, broadside to us. The other ships are passing in review on the far side. At a range of six hundred yards, go deep and navigate by compass. No one will see us.”

Gritz shook hands with the count. “Our approach is perfect. When we close to three hundred yards, fire the torpedo.”

“Penelope, dear girl, see for yourself — the fruits of all our planning.”

Penelope was pale and stumbled when she went to the count’s side and peered through the periscope. “I feel ill,” she said.

“The air is rotten. You, boy, pump harder!” the count glared at me. “Pedal, pedal, pedal faster. We need oxygen.”

I went through the motions and pumped furiously, but when he turned his back, I slowed.

"Close the breathing tubes. It is time to descend to twenty feet," the count said.

Gritz studied his depth gauge, and the count pushed the lever controlling the fins. The deck inclined downward. The Germans and Ivanov pedaled furiously to maintain speed.

"We are below periscope depth!" The count shouted.

"Level the ship," Gritz said.

"Target, three hundred and fifty yards."

Gritz opened the oxygen cylinder. The gas hissed but the air was still dank.

A long two minutes elapsed. I waited, furiously thinking of a way out, but it seemed helpless. My mind was foggy, but when the count shouted "Fire!" I reacted by instinct and screamed. Penelope had both of her hands on the firing mechanism. Her eyes were glassy with fatigue and lack of oxygen. "NO, Penelope! Don't!" Penelope dropped her hand from the mechanism and turned those lovely eyes on me.

I left my post and lunged forward, down the middle of the crowded boat, brushing against the count. He swung a clenched fist that grazed my head. The violence of his attack knocked away my visored cap. I nearly went down but regained my feet and continued plowing ahead.

There was no escape. "You damn English! Curse you, Penelope, for bringing saboteurs on my boat!" he shouted, between ragged breaths.

In an instant, the count pulled a Mauser rifle from its rack and pressed the barrel against my chest. I kicked him in the groin. He fell backwards, but the deadly rifle was still aimed at my chest.

"Stop! Don't shoot! You will put a hole in the boat!" Gritz yelled.

The American lunged forward and pushed the rifle barrel upward. The count's features contorted into a dreadful mask of hatred and fear as he pulled the trigger.

A terrific *boom!* reverberated inside the iron hull. The powerful blast drove the bullet through the hull over my head. There was an immediate trickle of water, which increased to a stream the size of my finger.

"Hans, the plugs, get the plugs. SURFACE, SURFACE!" Gritz yelled.

Hans gazed at the thickening stream of water and drew his finger across his throat."Kaput," he said.

Gritz pointed at the hole. "HANS, THE PLUGS!"

Hans smiled. "Ah, Verstopten."

Hans fumbled in a tool box, found the wooden plugs, and, with dull German efficiency, hammered a wooden bung into the bullet hole. The leak stopped, but the deck inclined upward so rapidly, I rolled in a heap against the air pump. "Surface! Surface!" Gritz cried.

The count lunged forward and struck Penelope across the face, grabbed her hair, and pulled her head back.

"You damned traitor! You brought him and the others. Saboteurs!"

"No! No! NO! They are loyal to the cause," she said.

"There isn't enough air for all of us if we descend again," said the count. "When we surface, leave the damn traitors to freeze in the water. We can still fire the torpedo and be gone," Gritz growled.

The count peered through the periscope. "We have surfaced. Open the hatch."

Fritz leaped up the ladder, twirled the opening bolts, and in a moment, we had air and sunshine. Vera and Ivanov, dull from lack of oxygen, slumped in the arms of the German sailors who carried them up the ladder. Penelope was next, then me. I offered no resistance when the three muscular German sailors dragged me up to the deck, barely awash with the sea.

In a moment, I was sprawled on the deck and gasped for air. Gritz slammed the hatch, and the submarine started its slow slide beneath the waves. Instantly, the four of us were floating in the freezing sea. We couldn't last long. I prayed for rescue.

My first thought was to shout and wave at the Russian cruiser, only three hundred yards distant, but sailors at attention looked to the starboard side where ships passed in review. Their backs were turned, and the booms of saluting cannon drowned my feeble shouts.

The cold penetrated my flesh like deadly, icy daggers deadening my limbs. I could only think of death by freezing; the blood congealed, the heart slowed to a standstill, and the brain became a lifeless pound of flesh.

I was on my back, nearly covered with arctic water, when Vera's face floated into view. Her lips were blue and she seemed lifeless. I struck out and slammed my open hand into her face. "Wake up, damn you! MOVE! Don't give up!"

She opened her eyes. I rubbed her arms and legs with as much energy as I could muster until she moved both arms and feebly kicked with her legs.

Ivanov had the good sense to grab the periscope tube and was making feeble efforts to stay above water. The effort brought life back, and I vigorously beat the water with both hands while taking great gulps of fresh air. But the icy water was so frigid that I feared I couldn't last long.

It was like a blow to the solar plexus when I again realized the Russian cruiser with the tsar was within firing range of the submarine.

Penelope started off, thrashing the water with strong strokes as if she planned on swimming to the distant shore. Her efforts soon diminished, however, and she paddled back to where the three of us clung to the periscope tube.

Penelope sucked air. "Damn, you Doyle! We will drown or be killed by the blast. Do something!" Her voice dwindled to a pathetic whimper but she was right. The others could do nothing to save themselves, and I was the only strong swimmer.

"Everyone, keep moving! Kick and hold on to the periscope tube with one hand."

It was difficult because the boat was slowly picking up speed as it headed directly towards the Russian ship. The count intended to destroy the tsar and start a European war. He would escape and no one would know of the German and American involvement.

We clung to the periscope tube, with water over our waists, but the boat was diving deeper. The cold penetrated into my bones, and for a moment, all I could think of was a warm fire. Then, I thought of the count, down below, peering at his prey and ordering Hans or Fritz to fire the deadly torpedo.

I gulped icy seawater and, in a flash, thought of a solution. Without the periscope, the count would be blind.

"Ivanov, hold tight. I have an idea. Just try not to move."

I stepped up on his shoulders, which were just above water, and clung to the periscope tube. I hoisted myself up, like a monkey on a coconut tree. "Ivanov, help hoist me up."

Ivanov gave me a great upward push with as much energy as he could muster, and I grasped the very top of the periscope tube. Somehow, I found the strength to tear off my student's jacket and wrapped it around the lens.

I slid in a heap down the tube, but now, even standing on tip-toe, the water was nearly over my head. We could not survive the cold for more than another five minutes. Vera was already blue and scarcely breathing.

I desperately slapped her again until she roused. The boat was diving deeper, so the breathing tubes were just breaking the surface.

Penelope again struck out, paddling and treading water. I grabbed her and held everyone together, hoping to conserve any last remnants of body heat.

I gasped and spit out a mouthful of salty water. "Stay together. Hold onto one another. Keep moving. Our only chance is to stay close for warmth," I spluttered.

We were now floating and drifting away from the periscope tube. I forced everyone to kick and to hug one another. Ivanov felt the vibration first. "They've started the electric motor," he said.

I felt a commotion in the water. The submarine turned erratically, first one way, then another, as if lost. For a moment, the boat came to its original course towards the *Nakhimov,* then made a one hundred and eighty degree turn.

In my mind, I could see the compass. When Gritz started the electric motor, the electro-magnetic field caused the compass to swing a complete half circle, one hundred and eighty degrees from north to south.

The count must have been confused, but, trusting his compass, came to the new course, away from the Russian ship. We had all been concentrating on staying afloat, but by chance, I raised my head and looked over the waves.

To my great amazement, the grey hull of the German cruiser was no more than three hundred yards away, directly in the path of the submarine. I remembered the count saying that the cruiser would cover their escape. For a moment, we floated, holding one another under a sunlit sky on a calm, cold sea. There were many ships and smaller pleasure boats about, mostly in the distance toward the Russian cruiser and the tsar. I idly remembered Ferguson's invitation to watch the review from his sailboat. If only we could stay alive long enough to be rescued …

Suddenly, I felt a mild a concussion — like a gentle punch to the gut — when they fired the torpedo. Bubbles rising to the surface were on a course towards the German ship.

"That would be the compressed air," Ivanov said.

There were more bubbles, then a small wake, heading directly towards the midsection of the German cruiser. The count depended completely on the accuracy of his compass, not realizing it was completely reversed.

It was a rather pleasant thought that we had deceived him. If we died, at least our deaths would not be in vain.

I treaded water and, with one hand, held Vera and Ivanov afloat as we watched the bubbles rising from the torpedo streaking directly on target. It hit dead center just below the water line.

There was another *boom!* and flames and black smoke rose from the German ship. We were left rocking on a great wave, stunned by the concussion.

When the shock wave receded, I waved my arms wildly, hoping someone might see us. But, alas, all seemed lost.

We were destined to die from exposure at sea. It was just too cold and we'd been in the water too long…

As I gave up the last shreds of hope, I caught the welcome sight of a white yacht with twin masts flying in our direction. It rounded up with sails flapping in the mild breeze.

Was it possible? Aye…

Dicky tossed a rope with a life preserver.

"Old boy, what a show, eh? Best fireworks of the day!" Dicky shouted. "Grab the lifesaver!"

Ferguson, along with Dr. Bell and Colonel Beachy-Edwards, dragged us, one by one, aboard the little yawl. I had never before been so grateful to see my dear friends. I was still sprawled on deck, vomiting sea water, when one hundred yards away and, not far from the flaming German cruiser, the snout of the black submarine shot to the surface, like a breaching, wounded whale.

The periscope tube and the breathing tubes were torn away. It must have taken on water after the torpedo blast. By some miracle, Gritz, the engineer, had saved the boat.

In a moment, the hatch opened and Hans, the huge German sailor, pulled himself on deck. He lay, face down, perfectly motionless.

"If you please, Mr. Ferguson, let us pick up the survivors," said Colonel Sir Beachy-Edwards, hardly raising his voice.

Dicky put down the tiller, and I helped bring over the main sail. We went tearing down towards the submarine and drew alongside.

Hans was a mass of bruises, and there was a huge gash on his head. "Gott mit uns. Alle tot. Alle tot," he said, with a final gasp.

I recognized his words, "All dead. All dead." He then slipped away beneath the waves.

Then, before our eyes, a bloody hand came up out of the open hatch. With what had to be a tremendous effort, the count's blonde hair, then the rest of his head, appeared just at the level of the hatch opening. The submarine was slowly sliding beneath the waves.

Penelope sighed. "Oh, please, save him, please," she said in a weak voice.

I had no intention of diving back into those frigid, heart-stopping waters. I glanced at Dr. Bell for support. He shook his head and seemed to indicate to me not to risk my life. His face remained impassive; he was no longer a teacher-mentor.

Yet, it was my decision, and time was of the essence. *A life is a life*, I thought, and dove overboard. With a few thrashing strokes, I reached the submarine, sliding slowly beneath the waves. Another inch and water would pour down the hatch. I managed to kneel, grasp his hand, and drag Count von Wittenberg's dead weight to the deck. He lay on his back with those cruel, light blue, Prussian eyes that for the past thousand years had stared straight through common people.

The submarine commenced its last fatal dive. I slid into the water with my arm across the count's chest. It was then I realized his massive injury. The blast had stoved in his chest. Every broken rib on his right side grated with each of his torturous breaths.

"Take care. He has broken ribs!" I shouted.

Ferguson and Dr. Bell leaned down from the deck and, as gently as possible, heaved him to the yacht's deck. He was on his back, having his last glimpse of the sun and sky, when I pulled myself, hand over hand, into the cockpit.

Penelope cradled the count's head on her lap, stroked his forehead, and shed tears.

"Schatzi, mein liebling," he whispered.

She put her mouth next to his hear. "Carl, Ich liebe dich," she said.

So, they were lovers, a perfect match. It was still difficult to believe that lovely Penelope, woman of gentle English blood, was a traitor to the crown. I felt sick to my stomach, yet the worst was still to come.

With great effort, he pulled a packet wrapped in oiled silk from his jacket pocket. "Dear Penelope, the money is yours." He coughed and blood splattered on Penelope's face. With his last effort, the count withdrew a small, glass vial from an inner pocket and pressed it into her hand. "Take it. An honorable death is preferable to a life in prison."

I watched in horror as Penelope took from him the deadly vial of cyanide, the suicide poison chosen by spies. Count von Wittenberg drew in a long, lingering breath, turned his head to one side, and was dead.

Penelope's lips drew back in an ugly rictus — was it of fear, anger, or did she say "Good riddance?"

She tossed the vial over the side just as another ship passed the Russian cruiser and fired a noisy salute to the tsar. Amid the great firing of guns, Colonel Sir Beachy-Edwards removed the packet from Penelope's hand and, with great care, opened the water-proof package.

Inside was a stack of fifty pound Bank of England notes. "Ah, how unfortunate," the colonel said. "The Secret Service provides these notes to our operatives. Dr. Bell, may I see the note you recovered from the Chinese Cook who killed Asquith?"

Dr. Bell opened his wallet and passed the crisp new note to the colonel.

"Ah, yes. The serial number of this note indicates it was the first in the series that the service provided to Miss Walshingham."

Penelope shivered, but wrapped her arms around my neck and planted a hearty deep kiss on my lips. "Doyle, you are magnificent. You saved us from that fiend."

"Young lady, you are an accessory to murder and guilty of traitorous and duplicitous conduct. A prison sentence will be your just reward," the colonel said.

Penelope smiled. "Actually, you are mistaken," she said.

"No, Ma'am."

"Yes, colonel. I have a friend at court."

Dicky had brought the yawl on a new course, and within minutes, we passed under the bows of Her Majesty's yacht, the *Victoria and Albert*.

Penelope set up a shout and waved at a portly figure on deck. "Yoo-hoo, Bertie! Bertie!"

"Penelope, dear, is it really you in those dreadful clothes? You are just in time for Tiffin. Come, dear girl, I have an extra frock just your size," the Prince of Wales replied.

The colonel and, for that matter, the rest of us, were stunned. But Penelope just smiled as if all that had occurred over the past few hours was nothing but the events of another ordinary Sunday afternoon.

Dickie dropped the sails, and we glided up to the landing stage at the base of a ladder leading up to the port side of Her Majesty's yacht. The portly figure — with a spade beard and dressed in perfect nautical attire — descended the ladder, took Penelope in a great bear hug, and cooed at her. "You dear, sweet girl. It has been so long."

Before any of us could say or do anything, Penelope and 'Bertie' were gone. She did not even look over her shoulder as she departed. For once, I was not upset to see her leave.

A few minutes later, we went off with tight sails and passed near enough to the *Nakhimov* to see the tsar and his family happily waving to the passing ships.

Colonel Beachy-Edwards sadly shook his head. "Imagine, calling the Prince of Wales, the future King of England, 'Bertie.' The foolish sod does nothing but gamble and chase women. I pity the future of our homeland."

Dicky brought the yacht on a course for home and gave me the tiller while he opened a magnum of champagne and a hamper filled with glorious edibles. We all set about devouring the picnic, and I tried to shake off the cold and the memory of the past twenty-four hours. I tossed off a tumbler of bubbly but was overcome with a shaking chill and pain in every muscle.

"Such a pity. We may never know if Walshingham or the count paid for the murder of poor Asquith," said Colonel Beachy-Edwards, between bites of smoked salmon.

14 October 1881

I am now on the night train to Paris and have completed my report to Colonel Sir Cameron Beachy-Edwards. It's been days since the submarine boat episode, and things have settled down quite a bit. My thoughts have returned to the start of this adventure, when the Colonel identified Uncle Declan. I had regretted our failure to save his life, but would he have wanted to live without legs? Would he have wanted to be a half a man? He had endured suffering, but his search for truth and justice never ceased. His teaching during our visits to the museum was similar to Dr. Bell's. He told me to observe carefully before deciding on a course of action. It is essential to gather facts in order to know the truth. Uncle Declan courageously gave his life in honor of that noble pursuit. I am proud of that legacy in our family and hope it will help lessen mam's grief.

David Campbell is reading a novel by Dostoevsky while Sasha sits at his feet, twitching and whining, as if, in her dreams, she is chasing a rabbit.

After the near-catastrophe on Sunday, Dr. Bell had convinced the tsar to take his son south for fresh air and sunshine and ensure that the royal family was well out of danger.

And in the end, since Vera and Ivanov had committed no crime, I convinced the colonel and Dr. Bell to stay mum about their involvement with the plot. They were chastened and vowed to be good citizens of the tsar. Pavlov even agreed to employ both in his laboratory.

Ah, Dear Dr. Bell. At present, he is with Sir Cameron Beachy-Edwards in a separate compartment. The two of them have become quite companionable while they enjoy a tot of single malt and compare notes on criminal investigation.

Sadly, he still uses cocaine, but his use seems to be in moderation.

And Penelope? Dear, unfathomable Penelope returned to England on the royal yacht with Bertie. It is rumored that he has taken her as a mistress. I may never hear from her again. I will miss her, but perhaps that it is just as well. Who knows? Maybe one day, she will marry the prince and be the next Queen of England. Perhaps, instead, she will continue her dangerous double life. Or maybe — just, maybe — she might miss me and come back to cover me with her sweet kisses. Is that even what I want?

Oh well. At least with this adventure over, I am free to go back to my beloved Scotland and focus on my medical career. If I am lucky, and it is not Penelope who is destined to be Mrs. Doyle, perhaps I will fall into the arms of that pretty Scottish nurse back home. Even if those plans don't work out, Sasha will certainly be my faithful companion for many years to come. After all, dogs are said to be man's best friend…

Perhaps, someday, I will publish the stories in this journal so the world can learn about how I, in a small way, assisted Dr. Bell. It was really through his keen mind that we saved Europe from a great war!

In the meantime, last night I had a dream that gave me a glimmer of an idea for a story. I imagined a great detective in the very image of Dr. Bell who solves the most difficult crimes. Of course, he would require an assistant, perhaps a rather bumbling physician, such as myself . . .

Adventures in America, 1883

15 May 1883, Bush Villas, Southsea

I attended the butcher's epileptic fit until he was out of danger and left him with a packet of bromide powders. His wife paid with a pound of bacon and twenty pence. This afternoon, I opened the door at a knock only to see a one-horse gypsy caravan. I expected they were begging until I heard a piteous cry. It was a baby with pustules, a clear case of measles. I dabbed carbolic ointment on the sores and gave the poor mother a bottle of very dilute laudanum so the exhausted babe could sleep. They offered three pence, but I surmised that would leave them with nothing for food. I took their coppers and gave them the butcher's twenty pence.

A typical day . . . Earnings: a pound of bacon and three pence.

16 May 1883, Bush Villas, Southsea

I awoke to fierce banging on my door in the grey light of early dawn. I hurriedly put on a pair of trousers and ran downstairs. It was the constable, William Beade, whom I knew from the rugby club. He wore no hat, his clothing was disheveled, and there was a two-inch, bleeding gash on his forehead. "Come right in. You need stitches," said I.

"No, No, come immediately. Lady Stanhope has gone berserk again," said he. I snatched my medical bag and raced after the constable to the most fashionable part of Southsea. The Stanhope sisters were widows and definitely upper-class gentry. *My fortunes are taking a turn for the better*, I thought.

As we turned the corner, I heard screams interspersed with pitiable wails. "Have mercy! Oh, oh, the rats! The horrible rats! Get them off me!" Lady Stanhope, a woman of about sixty, was in the street, half-naked, with her back against a brick wall. Her eyes were wild, her hands trembled, and her disheveled, grey hair hung like coiled snakes over her bare shoulders. She flailed the air with a stout cane that was thick enough to disable a strong man.

"She hit me with the cane," said Constable Beade. A second constable darted close to the poor woman in an attempt to snatch the cane. She gave him a terrific smack on his right arm. He yelped with pain and retreated. It could have been bedlam, but this was one of our better neighborhoods, and the normally well-behaved Stanhope sisters were in the upper echelons of high society. My mind raced with the diagnostic possibilities. Could it be a brain tumor, an unusual stroke, or was she insane?

"Hold it, men. This calls for a change of tactics," said I. The poor woman trembled, cursed, and tried to remove the rest of her already-shredded night dress.

"Oh, get them off me! Oh, please!" she screamed. She beat the cobblestones with her cane and dragged her fingernails across her naked breasts, leaving trails of blood. The neighbors were out in force. Some offered suggestions and others demanded an end to the commotion. I then noticed on the doorsteps another woman, also in a nightdress.

"Are you the sister?" I asked. She dabbed her eyes with a soggy handkerchief.

"Yes, Lady Jane is my older sister," said she.

"When did this start?" I asked, aiming to retain my composure.

"Oh, the poor dear never went to bed, hasn't had a wink of sleep, but kept up all night long, walking and muttering to herself until she ran out to the street."

I was even more perplexed. The screaming stopped for a moment, then resumed, more intense than ever. "Help me God… The spiders!" Lady Stanhope had thrown down her cane and was tearing her hair with both hands, apparently in an attempt to remove what she imagined were spiders. Constable Beade quickly snatched up the cane, while the second constable managed to grab both of her arms. I hastily filled a syringe with a generous dose of morphine sulphate and jabbed the medicine into her arm. It should have been enough to subdue a strong man, but it had little or no effect; she managed to tear loose from the constables and fled down the street. Beade grabbed her with a flying tackle, and I administered a second dose of morphine. Lady Stanhope went limp, though continued to whimper piteously about spiders, rats, and a rabbit that she claimed was clawing her ankles.

We put her to bed and securely wrapped her in a sheet, but she continued to moan and, at times, cry out. Exhausted by the wild chase and chaos, I finally slumped into a chair before again addressing Lady Jane's sister.

"Has this happened before?" I asked.

"Oh yes. She has gone off like this twice in the past five years."

"How long do the spells last?"

"Three or four days or until Dr. Jones comes and prescribes for her." Jones was one of Southsea's most respected physicians who mainly looked after the upper-class gentry.

"What is the medicine?" I asked.

"That is the problem. She took two bottles on Friday, forgot to get more on Saturday, and the shops were closed yesterday. Perhaps I can find an empty bottle." She left and returned with a bottle on which a pink label, illustrated with a picture of a kindly lady, read: 'AUNT MARY'S FEMALE TONIC.' It was a six-ounce bottle, and at the bottom of the label, in fine print, it read: 'forty percent alcohol by volume.'

"Your sister is suffering from delirium tremens," said I. "This medicine is no different from whisky and she is in alcohol withdrawal."

"Well, I never heard of such a thing! This is medicine, not drink! How dare you suggest she is withdrawing from alcohol use? I shall call Dr. Jones. Young man, leave and never set foot in this house again!"

Later, I stitched Constable Beade's forehead where Mrs. Stanhope had hit him. "Thank ye, sir," said he. It is customary for physicians to treat the police and firemen for free. Thus, my day's efforts added nothing to my cash balance. Fortunately, I still had a half-pound of bacon.

I have been making more time for photography as of late. It is a fine way to view the world and often helps soothe any agitation, such as that I was feeling after my visit with the Stanhope sisters. So, I picked up my folding, bellows-body, half-plate camera, and a tripod, and went for a short stroll. After attempting to capture an image of the setting sun, and spending the time outdoors in great contemplation, I made two decisions about my life. The first is to qualify as a Doctor of Medicine, with the hope that the added degree will attract more patients. Secondly, I shall finally achieve the dream I have long held and write a novel of great deeds, derring-do with a bit of history. I shall begin in earnest by joining the Portsmouth Literary and Scientific Society and taking leave from the practice for just a few days. During that time, I plan to venture to Edinburgh where I can visit my family and further observe the source of inspiration for my novel's main character, my former professor at the Edinburgh Medical School, Dr. Joseph Bell.

20 May 1883, Edinburgh

When I arrived in Edinburgh, I left my bag with my mam and hurried so as not to miss Dr. Bell's afternoon clinic. I slipped into the third row in the great amphitheatre, hoping to evade notice, but nothing escaped the observant professor, who witnessed my entrance and gave me a sly wink. Though relieved to no longer have to spend every day in lectures and labs, it was grand to be back in the old place with the familiar, lingering odor of chloroform and carbolic from the morning's surgery. The floor was swept clean except for a small heap of blood-stained sawdust beneath the operating table.

Dr. Bell's clerk — a callow, second-year student — stood like a dummy, thumbing through his notebook after he brought in his patient. I felt a pang of sympathy, having been in his place only a couple of years ago. The patient was a solidly-built fellow with streaks of grey in his reddish-brown beard and a fine Scottish face. He was dressed like a countryman in a clean, flannel shirt and faded, black and green plaid trousers, which were tucked into cowhide boots. He lurched when he walked and favored his left foot.

"Well, now, Mr. Weeks. Have ye lost your tongue? Please tell us the patient's history and your diagnosis," said the professor. The other students, cruel boys in their youth, howled and stomped their feet at their fellow student's misery. I recalled being in that same situation and felt pity for the poor clerk. If history shows anything, however, in a year or two, they will settle down to learn decorum and the proper business of our profession.

The poor clerk found his voice at last. "Sir, the patient is sixty years old and has a limp. I suspect he has a sprain."

"Is that all, Weeks?" Dr. Bell asked.

"Aye, sir…"

The professor ran his hand through his head of pure white hair and stood to his full height. With twinkling eyes, he pointed me out with a long, slender finger. "One of our recent distinguished graduates has granted us the favor of his presence. Mr. Conan Doyle, if you please, give us your diagnosis."

I was nonplussed and afraid the professor would embarrass me as he had done so many times in the past. Then, I spotted a tattoo — a faded anchor surrounded by a white circle — on the back of the patient's right hand. "Sir, the man was in the navy and, during his world travels, contracted syphilis. His lurching gate is due to *tabes dorsalis*," said I.

"It's a mistake yer a makin'. As a lad, I was in the volunteer lifeboat service at Arbroath. I ne'er been in the navy or left Scotland. The anchor and life ring tattoo is a badge of service," said the patient. A wide smile spread over his weather-beaten face.

Dr. Bell circled the patient, sniffed like a bird dog on a scent, sat down, extended his long legs, and folded his hands over his chest. "Now, Mr. Cameron, your cows are giving an abundance of milk?"

"Right, sir."

"You have lost almost two stone of weight in the past weeks."

"Nearer to three stone, sir."

"And you must get up at night to pass water?"

"Aye, I'm a spending most of me night at the pot."

"Mr. Weeks, kindly take your patient into the side room and secure a sample of urine," said Dr. Bell.

In a few moments, the clerk returned with the patient and a flask of urine.

"Now, observe carefully . . ." Dr. Bell said, as he squinted at the yellow liquid. He shook the flask until the urine foamed, then inserted his finger, brought the finger to his mouth and tasted the urine. There was no expression on his face, but the students cried out with astonishment. I was amazed at his performance. It was unusual, even for a showman like Dr. Bell. "Now lads, pass the jar and each of you sample the urine exactly as I demonstrated," he said. The flask went from student to student. Each carefully inserted a finger and, grimacing with disgust, tasted a sample. I took the tiniest drop on the tip of my tongue. It had a sweetish taste. I knew the diagnosis, but kept my peace and watched the students squirm.

Dr. Bell pointed to a chubby student in the first row. "What did you taste?" asked he.

"Sir, it was sweetish, like honey," said the student.

"You are quite correct. The diagnosis is diabetes mellitus. As you all know from your Latin, *mel* is the word for honey. I am sad, however, that not one of you noticed how I sampled the urine even though I asked you to do exactly as I had demonstrated. Remember, I have told you many times to observe every detail. Gentlemen, if you had paid close attention, you would have observed that I inserted my index finger into the urine but tasted my third finger."

The students groaned but wrote furiously in their notebooks.

"Gentlemen, you are about to see wet gangrene. Mr. Cameron, will you be so kind as to remove your boot?" asked the professor. A foul odor rose in the cockpit when the patient removed his boot and sock. His foot was dusky blue in color, blistered, and dripped green pus.

"Mr. Cameron, I am indeed sorry, but there is no alternative to an amputation of your foot. My house officer will arrange a bed for you in the infirmary," the professor said in a soft, sad voice.

It was another of Dr. Bell's great triumphs of observation and diagnosis. The students were too shy to ask, so I raised my hand. "Yes, Mr. Doyle?" he asked.

"Sir, tell us how you knew his name, his trade, and made the diagnosis so quickly," asked I.

"Elementary observations! His trousers were of the Cameron plaid. The manure on his boot was from cattle, not sheep. The white splatters on his boots and trousers indicated he had been carrying overflowing milk pails. You may have noted that he limped but did not complain of pain. Painless gangrene is typical for diabetes. Any fool should have deduced his weight loss by observing that his belt was buckled three notches down from its usual place. Sadly, there is no cure for Mr. Cameron. An amputation will remove the gangrene and a restricted diet may help for a few months."

The professor waved his hand. "That is all," said he.

After the students left, I greeted Dr. Bell. He shook my hand with a strong grip. There was no sign of the cocaine use that had plagued our trip to Russia two years ago when he was introduced to the drug as an anaesthetic. “Sir, you are looking well,” said I.

“Lad, what brings you to Auld Reekie?”
asked Dr. Bell.

“I intend to qualify for a doctorate in medicine and need your advice,” said I.

“You must take an oral examination and write a thesis. Do you have a topic?”

“I am thinking of writing on *tabes dorsalis*. I am quite convinced that the poison of syphilis causes the disease.”

“Hmm, not everyone will agree with that notion. I suggest you ask Dr. John Brown for his opinion.”

John Brown, one of my other former professors, was the most beloved and wisest physician in all of Scotland. He was also a great writer, which only added to my admiration of him. I immediately called on his office to make an appointment for the next day. Unfortunately, the ancient lady who kept his office said Dr. Brown would be indisposed tomorrow and suggested that I visit his home at 29 Rutland Street the following day.

22 May 1883, Edinburgh

When I arrived at Dr. Brown's today, he greeted me with great cordiality. I presented my proposal for a thesis on *tabes dorsalis*. He was enthusiastic and agreed that the cause was probably syphilis. After we spoke for a wee while, he lay back on a pile of cushions with a great sigh. The color drained from his face. I suspected he had a weak heart but said nothing. He would know his own diagnosis only too well.

"Arthur, will you do a great favor for me?"

"By all means. I would be most happy to do anything for you."

"I am unable to visit a patient. She is Mrs. Samuel Clemens who is residing in the Veitch's family hotel. Would you be so kind as to take a jar of Arnica liniment to her?"

"Yes, indeed," said I.

"Please instruct her to apply the ointment to both knees and then cover them with hot wet towels," said Dr. Brown.

We bid our farewells. Upon my arrival at the home of Mrs. Clemens, a tall man of about fifty years of age, dressed in a white suit and smoking a long cigar, opened the door. He had remarkably unruly, curling, grey hair, a bushy, unkempt mustache, and was surrounded by clouds of tobacco smoke. He extended his hand.

"Mr. Sam Clemens," said he.

Sam Clemens. I knew that name... Could he be THE Samuel Clemens, the writer who had adopted the pen name of Mark Twain? Was this really the great American author here in Edinburgh? I trembled with excitement at that possibility. His books of adventures were among my favorites, especially after having traveled to the Midwest of America with Dr. Bell nearly five years ago and seen firsthand the land and people as he had so vividly described. I was amazed, but remembering the reason for my visit, I composed myself.

"Ah, ahem, sir, I am Arthur Conan Doyle, here to deliver medicine to Mrs. Clemens," said I.

"Aah, yes. Welcome, Mr. Doyle. I will take you to Mrs. Clemens," said he.

"Sir, by any chance are you Mark Twain, the author of Tom Sawyer?" I asked, just to be sure.

"Guilty as charged," said he.

"I have laughed over whitewashing the fence many times, and I have often dreamed of writing as well as you someday," said I.

"Young man, I would advise you to stick with medicine or find another more useful occupation than writing; drive a steamboat or learn to cheat at cards. Hell and damn, I wrote those stories, but liars and cheats have taken all my money. I've gone broke a half-dozen times."

"But sir, is the money as important as leaving a mark on the pages of history?" I asked.

Mr. Clemens simply paused, waved away a cloud of smoke, and led me through a large drawing room — part of an extensive suite of rooms — and into an adjoining bedroom. "My wife, Olivia," said he.

Mrs. Clemens was in a large bed, dressed in a nightgown and a shawl, even though it was not yet evening. I observed a half-dozen bottles of medicine on her bedside table, and the curtains were closed.

"Good evening, ma'am. I am Arthur Conan Doyle and have brought you some liniment to ease your pain."

"I was expecting Dr. Brown," said she.

"Dr. Brown is ill."

"Oh, the dear man. I hope it is nothing serious. Young man, are you a physician?"

"Yes, Dr. Brown was one of my professors."

"I suppose you will do. My knees hurt so much. Rheumatism, you know. Please, I am so weak, apply the ointment for me."

She swung her legs over the bed. Though her knees looked to be perfectly normal, I assumed my best bedside manner, sat on a chair, and carefully massaged a generous dab of the ointment into the little depressions beside her kneecaps. "Oh, that feels so good," she said when I applied towels, which had been soaked in hot water and wrung out. “I am so much better. You are a kind young man. Will you visit tomorrow?” she asked.

I bowed. “If Dr. Brown is unable to make a call, I will be happy to see you again.”

I was making my way out of the suite when Mr. Clemens plucked at my elbow. “Livy has been in such pain . . . We are grateful for your service. Say, I am lecturing at the Queen’s theatre tomorrow evening, and after my lecture, the Siamese twins, Sui Fong and Wei Fong, will sing and dance. Kindly accept these two tickets. Who knows? It may inspire you to seize upon an idea for your first novel.” He winked and showed me to the door.

“Thank you, sir. It would be an honor,” I said, before taking the tickets and making my exit.

24 May 1883, Edinburgh

Since I came here to focus on my novel, I have begun to carry my notebook with me as often as possible in order to capture and recall moments such as those I have experienced in the last few hours. It is near dawn. I am at the bedside of a most beautiful woman, writing the events of yesterday by the light of a single candle.

It began when I invited Miss Jean McGill, a student at the university, to accompany me to the performance. Jean is a little on the plump side, but I had been in love with her for almost two weeks a couple of years ago while I was finishing medical school and right before I left for Russia with Dr. Bell. She reluctantly agreed to join me only after I explained that Siamese twins were a medical curiosity. Jean desperately wanted to be a doctor, but the faculty of medicine would not allow her to dissect in the anatomy laboratory.

Thanks to Mr. Clemens, our seats were front row, center. The Queen's Theatre was packed to the top gallery with spectators anxious to hear the great American author's talk, see the famous Siamese twins and listen to them sing. Gas lights lit the stage as bright as day, but the far recesses were in shadows.

When the curtain went up, a young man came out and announced the arrival of 'Mr. Mark Twain' who sauntered in from the left wing, sat on a high stool, and winked at the audience. He puffed at his ever-present stogie, removed it from his mouth, and peered at the ash on the end. "I never can get rid of the damn ash," he said.

He squinted at the audience, shrugged his shoulders and, after another moment of silence, went off on a mile-a-minute monologue.

"This morning, when the sun was bright and shining, a Scotch banker loaned me his umbrella. It was mighty kind of him although there was no rain in sight. I supposed he was just mighty kind and generous. Well, by and by, clouds came in and water poured out of the heavens. I would have been drenched had it not been for the kindness of the banker, but in the midst of the downpour, he not only demanded I return the umbrella but insisted I pay a dollar interest for its use." The crowd clapped tepidly, mostly out of politeness. There wasn't much enthusiasm for jokes at the expense of Scotsmen, not even if the butt of the joke was a banker.

Mr. Twain puffed his cigar, took a long look at the lengthening ash, and launched into a story about a frog named Dan'l Webster that "could jump further than any other frog in the entire state of Californy." The owner of the frog took bets on how far the frog could jump, but someone loaded Dan'l Webster with birdshot and he couldn't jump even one inch. When the laughing and feet stomping stopped, Mr. Twain told another whopper, this time about a duel between two newspaper editors in Nevada who lit out at each other with Colt six-shooters. They were bad shots, and no one was seriously hurt. He left the stage with a flourish. The cigar was down to about one and one-half inches, but the ash had never fallen off. I suspect he had a pin down the middle of his stogie.

Miss McGill never cracked a smile. She didn't care for Yankee humor, and when I was romantically inclined, she pushed away my hand. She perked up when a small, black-haired Italian man, Signor Bellini, introduced the Siamese twins, Wei and Sui. According to the program, the twins were trained in the Italian school of bel canto singing. Signor Bellini claimed the twins were favorites of the Chinese emperor and had performed before the heads of state of every country from China to Scotland. They swept onto the stage, dressed in a large, white, gossamer gown that floated in the air and enveloped both of them as if they had the wings of butterflies. Wei and Sui were beautiful, with an exotic Eurasian cast to their features. Their eyes were as dark as bits of obsidian, and their long, coal-black hair appeared to have been varnished. There was, however, a distinct English cast to their features. They bowed in unison. Then, Sui Fong — on the right — played a long, stringed instrument that made a noise like a wailing screech owl, and both twins sang trills and long runs of high notes with turns and leaps of sound. Jean was spellbound and clapped with great emotion at the end of each song. I was relieved to see how much she enjoyed that portion of the evening's entertainment.

After the last encore, the stage lights dimmed while the crowd cheered and clapped. On stage, a tallish man, dressed in a formal evening suit and wearing a top hat with the brim pulled down over his face, emerged from the shadows. He carried a cloth-covered tray with two flutes of what appeared to be champagne, and it looked as if he were a part of the final act. For a fleeting moment, I was certain that Wei Fong smiled in recognition of the man. She took a glass and downed the champagne in a single gulp. Sui Fong took the second glass, hesitated, and took a delicate sip. The fellow dashed from the stage and disappeared into the shadows, but as soon as the crowd hurrahed at this presumed encore, Wei dropped her empty glass, grasped her throat, and collapsed onto the stage, dragging down her sister. Sui's barely-touched glass fell and shattered, splashing the stage with champagne. The crowd was stunned into silence, which was followed by a great, collective gasp. At first, individuals, then entire rows of people, dashed to the exits as if someone had shouted "Fire!" The Italian agent, Bellini, came out of the wings and, with an anguished cry, wiped Wei's face with a frilly handkerchief. She had evidently suffered some form of an attack and needed medical attention. I leaped onto the stage and knelt by the stricken woman. In a moment, her face took on a blue tinge and she went perfectly limp. I felt for her pulse at the wrist. Nothing! Then, I dug my fingers into her neck. The beat of the carotid artery was too rapid to count, became fluttery, hesitated, and then resumed its frantic, erratic pace. Sui rolled and twisted on the stage as if attempting to separate herself from Wei. "Is she going to die?" she asked.

"I, I don't know," said I.

"If my sister dies, I shall die with her. Oh, it was so bitter …"

I crouched by the sisters, helpless as newborn babes, with my finger on Wei's fluttery pulse. "Arthur, you are a doctor! Do something!" Jean McGill shouted in my ear.

"We shall both die. Oh, it was so bitter …" Sui whimpered.

Bitter, bitter, what would be bitter? I thought. *Some sort of a poison, but what?* It came to me in a flash; Wei had the symptoms of an overdose of Gelsemium; she was weak in her extremities, her respiratory muscles were paralyzed, and she had rapid, irregular heartbeats.

"Send immediately for Dr. Bell!" I shouted. I then pressed down on Wei's chest to drive out the old air and pulled her arms over her head to force fresh air into her lungs. It was a technique called 'artificial respiration,' and I had seen it used on patients who had been overdosed with chloroform. I pressed her chest and raised her arms again and again with a ferocious sense that I must save her life. Color did return to her cheeks for a few minutes, but I was unable to force enough oxygen into her body. Sui moaned and she, too, appeared to be on the verge of collapse. Had she taken a fatal dose of the poison? I should have pumped out her stomach, but had no tube. At that moment, Mark Twain rushed onto the stage, still chewing his cigar. I snatched it out of his mouth and jammed the saliva soaked wad of tobacco into Sui's mouth. She gagged, choked, coughed, and vomited up the contents of her stomach. This had taken just a moment, but by the time I turned my attention back to Wei and resumed pressing on her chest, she had already faded away. Her heart stopped. I knelt by her side, overcome by a sense of utter helplessness, when Sui gave a great sigh. To my utter horror, she had become pale. Her eyes rolled up, and the color had drained from her cheeks. Drained . . . Drained? God, I was such a fool. Wei was dead, but the twins were connected so that Sui's heart pumped blood into Wei's circulation. That was what Sui meant when she said they would both die. I tore away the gossamer dress and found a band of tissue as big around as my arm connecting the twins at their waist.

"Great Scott! She is bleeding into her dead sister. Ye damn fool — a tourniquet, use your belt man!" I heard Dr. Bell shout. He had arrived with Willum, his man, who carried an instrument case. I removed my belt, wrapped it around the band of tissue and cinched it down as tight as possible. Sui was still alive, but just barely. Dr. Bell kneeled on the stage and stroked Sui's hair. "I will not let you die," said he. A bit of color returned to Sui's cheeks, but she breathed rapidly and I could barely feel her pulse. "There isn't a moment to lose. We must remove her to a place suitable for surgery," said Dr. Bell.

"But, sir, in the history of surgery, no one — absolutely no one — has separated Siamese twins," said I.

"We are duty-bound to save her life if we can and must make the attempt," Dr. Bell replied.

Mark Twain listened to our conversation, lit another cigar, and looked down at the poor twins. "I have a spare room in my hotel across the street," said he.

Willing hands carried the live girl, attached to her dead sister, through the theatre, out the lobby, and across the street to the hotel. It was a grim procession made even gloomier by drizzly rain and the curtain of yellow fog that enveloped Edinburgh. It occurred to me halfway across the street that the killer could be lurking about. "Jean, I can call a cab to take you home," said I.

"You can't get rid of me that easily. I shall stay and help," she snapped.

Dr. Bell decided on the dining room in the Twain apartment, where there were bright, gas lights. We placed the twins on a wide, mahogany table and rapidly soaked the instruments in a basin of water and carbolic acid. We rolled up our sleeves and rinsed our hands. Despite the urgency, Dr. Bell strictly adhered to the antiseptic technique. A bit of color had returned to Sui's cheeks. It was a good sign, but she opened her eyes like a startled fawn and looked in horror at the array of steel knives, forceps, needles and thread on the table.

"Miss McGill, give the chloroform," said Dr. Bell.

"I have never given an anaesthetic," Jean said.

"Pour the chloroform, a few drops at a time, on a folded cloth held over her face until she goes to sleep. If her breathing slows, stop pouring. If she moves, give more," said Dr. Bell.

Sui struggled at the first whiff of chloroform, but soon settled into a light sleep. Jean gained confidence and was able to adjust the dose of chloroform so our patient remained unconscious. Dr. Bell, with sleeves rolled to his elbows and his sharpest scalpel in hand, surveyed the band of flesh that connected the abdomens of the live and dead twins.

"Arthur, move the tourniquet closer to Sui, if you please," said Dr. Bell. I adjusted the belt. The incision was perfectly bloodless, since no blood circulated on Wei's side and my tourniquet cut off the blood flow from Sui. He pressed the knife deeper into the tissue until a layer that looked like the lining of the abdominal cavity came into view. There was indeed a cavity, and within the space, there was a solid, brownish-colored organ. "Aha, they shared a common liver," said Dr. Bell.

"It is hopeless," said I.

"Perhaps, but we shall see." He cut into the liver and exposed a nest of blood vessels which he sutured with a silk thread.

"Now, release the tourniquet." I loosened the belt. A gush of blood literally exploded from the cut surface of the liver.

"I can barely feel her pulse," said Jean.

"Tighten the tourniquet and stop giving chloroform," said Dr. Bell. He sutured more blood vessels, but each time I released the tourniquet, there was a gush of blood.

"Damn me. An old fashioned hot iron would sear these vessels," said Dr. Bell.

"Sir, I will heat an amputation knife in the flame of a gas light," said I.

It seemed to take hours, though it was only a few minutes until the blade glowed red hot in the gas flame. Dr. Bell held the wooden handle and pressed the blade against the surface of the liver. There was smoke and a *sizzle* as the blade burned the tissue. I released the tourniquet again. This time, there was only a slow ooze of blood from the cut surface. With two more slashes, Dr. Bell divided the liver with the red-hot knife. There was only a little bleeding, which he controlled with sutures. He incised through the remaining skin until he had separated the dead from the living. Bell sutured the skin so that only a neat row of stitches showed where Sui had once been connected to her twin.

"The pulse is stronger," Jean said.

Angry voices came from the next room, and in a moment, Detective McPherson and a constable from the Edinburgh Police burst into the room. McPherson was a big-shouldered bully who had played rugby on the town teams against us students. He took in the blood-soaked table, the instruments, and the dead girl at a glance. "A murder was reported, but this is more than murder. What foul deeds are you up to?"

"We saved a life. Yes, there was a murder — a foul murder — but in the theatre, not here," said Dr. Bell.

"Yes, murder by poison, namely an overdose of Gelsemium," said I.

"The doctors are correct. I witnessed the death of the twin, Wei. The other would have died as well, without these medical gentlemen," said Mr. Twain.

McPherson's face grew red with frustration and anger. Having the chance to arrest a professor and an old school boy would enhance his reputation. "This is no regular hospital. How do I know she did not die under your knife from a dastardly experiment?"

Sui fluttered her eyes and came awake with a low moan. Miss McGill stroked her face and spoke softly. "I saw the whole thing." I could have kissed her as she told the story from beginning to end, effectively ending the detective's tirade.

"An autopsy on Wei will prove everything," said Dr. Bell.

Willum carried Sui to the spare room while the constables wrapped Wei's corpse in a blanket and carried her away to the morgue. Dr. Bell packed up his instruments and ordered me to stand vigil over Sui. I commenced my bedside duties and, in my focus on keeping watch, I forgot about Miss McGill, who must have found her own way home.

I had no nursing skills, could not even make up a bed, but kept my fingers on her pulse, offered sips of water when she stirred, and said soothing words. Fortunately, the girl slept most of the time that I was on bedside watch. Promptly at six a.m., a Nightingale nurse, dressed in a pure white uniform with an apron that reached her ankles, bustled into the room. "A gude mornin' to ye, Meester Doyle. Dr. Bell directed me to care for the poor lass. Miss Angeline McTavish at your service," said she. Miss McTavish was a plain lady, approaching middle age, and wonderfully efficient. She fluffed the pillows, changed the sheet, wiped Sui's face with a wet cloth, and swabbed her lips with glycerin. The girl came awake with a startled cry and wild, frightened eyes.

"Oh, where is my sister? Where is Wei?" She flung herself about the bed until I worried about the stitches. "I am all alone!" sobbed Sui.

I took her hand, gave it a reassuring squeeze, and floundered as I grasped for the right words. "There was an accident. You are fine, but Wei is dead." This was not the first time I had told a poor, grieving soul about their relative's death, but this was different. After all, a part of Sui had died, as well, since they had been together every minute of their lives.

My words were totally inadequate, but Miss McTavish came to my rescue. "There, there, dear. Time for some wee rest. Ye'll be needin' all o' yer strength to get back upon your toes, y'know. I will be here wi' ye today so yer nae alone. Mr. Doyle, dinna' forget you are to meet the good doctor in the morgue promptly at eight this very mornin'. He will surely be upset if you are late. Rest assured, I will stay here with Miss Fong and take good care o' the lass," said she.

After thanking Miss McTavish for her assistance, I brushed out the wrinkles in my suit and took a cup of tea in the hotel lobby before rushing away to the infirmary. I was a few minutes late. The old morgue in the basement of the Royal Infirmary was cold, dark, and as depressing as ever. To my surprise, three of Edinburgh's leading surgeons had gathered to witness the dissection and see Dr. Bell's handiwork. With clouds of their tobacco smoke, Spence, Arbuthnot, and Archer masked the odors of rotting flesh, intestinal gas, and the general putrefaction that permeated the very walls. McPherson and two constables hovered in the background well away from the body. The surgeons intently examined the liver in the band of flesh that had connected the twins.

"Confoundedly impossible. Bell, old boy, how did you stop the hemorrhage?" asked Spence. Before Dr. Bell could answer, Professor Lewis made the long, Y-shaped incision typical of an autopsy, which commenced at Wei's upper chest and extended down her abdomen. One by one, Professor Lewis examined and removed each organ until the heart, lungs, liver, spleen, and intestinal tract lay on a steel dish. Detective McPherson groaned with disappointment as Professor Lewis pronounced each organ normal. “I understand there is a suspicion of death by poison,” said Professor Lewis.

“Aye,” said I.

The professor had left the intestinal tract from esophagus to intestine with its contents intact. With great care, he opened the stomach and drained a half-pint of yellow fluid into a flask. “Now we cum ta tha meat o’ the case. What killed this bonnie lass? There are no signs that the operation was to blame. Meester Conan Doyle ha’ you tha answer?” he asked.

I repeated my story about the strange man who had appeared from the shadows and given the twins the fatal draught. “Wei died with all the symptoms of an overdose of Gelsemium,” said I.

“What makes you an authority of Gelsemium?” asked McPherson.

“I published a paper on the toxic effects of the drug in the *British Medical and Surgical Journal*,” said I.

“It was a well done paper,” said Dr. Bell.

Professor Lewis sniffed at the yellow liquid from Wei’s stomach as if it were a fine wine. “Ah, I will wager the young man is correct. I shall analyze the contents later today. Now, laddie, tell these gentlemen about Gelsemium,” said the professor.

“It is an extract of the roots of Yellow Jasmine, a flowering plant found in the southern part of the United States of America. It is used in appropriate doses to treat nerve pain and muscle spasm,” said I.

“Arthur, you made an astute diagnosis. Well done, lad. I am proud of you,” said Dr. Bell.

“Thank you, sir.”

“Will you kindly join me for dinner at my home this evening? Would eight o’clock be convenient?” asked he.

“Yes, of course, but I don’t have an evening suit with me.”

“Quite alright, my boy. We shall be informal.”

I immediately returned to Sui’s bedside. To my amazement, she was sitting with her back against fluffy pillows, taking strong, beef broth. When she finished, Miss McTavish gave her a spoonful of tincture of iron. Sui spluttered, and although she appeared wan, her face was wreathed in a smile that melted my heart. In a moment, she took my hand in hers. “Mr. Twain told me everything. You saved my life,” said Sui.

“Ah noo, but I am leaving you in good hands,” said the nurse. She threw on her cloak and swished out the door, leaving me alone with Sui.

“I must thank you. May I give you a kiss for saving me?” Sui put her arms around my neck, lowered her eye lashes, kissed my cheek, and let her soft lips linger as they brushed across my skin.

It would be unethical to kiss a patient, but oh how I wished to turn my face and feel the smoothness of her lips on mine. As she leaned towards me, Sui’s nightdress dropped ever so slightly, revealing perfect shoulders and a hint of bosom. I caught my breath, wishing the situation were different and I could act on my desire and meet her open lips. It was difficult not to get caught up in the blissfulness of the moment, especially when she made a slight groan, but I managed to retain my professional composure and quickly pulled back.

“Dear Sui, I am forgetting myself. Did I hurt your incision?”

“Now that you have saved me and we are better acquainted, you may call me Julie. My real name is Julie Pembroke. My sister’s name was Mildred. Sui and Wei were only our stage names.” She spoke in perfect, rapid English, as if she urgently needed to tell her story. My head swam. I was confused. Who was this delightful woman? Was she Chinese or English?

“I don’t understand. Why did you perform under different names?”

“When Papa died — was killed, actually — in the Afghanistan war, Uncle Peachy became our guardian and arranged for our education in languages and music. We already spoke Chinese and English, but he said we must make our own way in life, and being Siamese twins, that meant performing on the stage or joining a freak show. Uncle Peachy had other ideas as well. We actually did a bit of work for Uncle.”

“What kind of work?” I asked.

Julie blushed and turned away. “Oh, at first it was just for fun. We, especially Mildred, attracted men, and a certain sort wanted both of us. They talked, and sometimes, we learned secrets for Uncle Peachy."

I wanted to reach out to her and offer the comfort of my firm embrace. Instead, I held back, especially since, at that moment, Julie's face twisted with fierce intensity as if she were remembering something painful. "Did you see him? Could you recognize the man who killed my sister?" she asked, after a long silence.

"It was very dark. I had only a glimpse, and his face was hidden. I thought for a moment that Wei, er, Mildred recognized him," said I.

"It must have been one of them, one of her visitors. Uncle Peachy warned us to be careful. I thought he had a scent, something with spice," said Julie.

At that moment, another Nightingale nurse bustled into the room carrying a covered tray. I bid both ladies good evening and went home to Mam for a bit of rest before dinner with Dr. Bell.

I arrived at Dr. Bell's promptly at eight o'clock. Willum met me at the door, took my umbrella, and led me into the study. I immediately recognized Colonel Sir Cameron Beachy-Edwards who I had met when my Uncle Declan was murdered years ago. He also came to Russia when Dr. Bell and I traveled there in 1881 and helped us save the Crown from a potential war. Now, he sat opposite Dr. Bell by a grate with glowing coals. A bottle of Old Glenmore sat on the table between them. With the help of his walking stick, Colonel Beachy-Edwards rose to his feet with some difficulty and extended his hand. "Arthur, dear boy, how can I express my deepest gratitude? Your quick thinking saved Julie Pembroke," said he.

As usual, in the presence of the regal Colonel, I came to attention and, as if still a poor, young student, felt shabby in my threadbare tweeds. Though he was impeccably dressed in striped trousers, a black, frock coat, and the ever-present Victoria Cross ribbon over his breast, his clothing was looser than I remembered from our Russian adventure. He had lost weight and appeared ill.

"I am sorry that I could not have done more," said I.

A tear glistened in his eye. "You did your best. I am responsible for the twins, but sadly, I now realize I put them in too great a danger. You see, the twins are my wards."

"You are 'Uncle Peachy'?" I asked. The colonel blushed to the roots of his hair.

"Yes, the twins called me Uncle Peachy from the day I became their guardian. Their father was an officer in my regiment. He married a Portuguese-Chinese woman. It was a dreadful scandal, but she was beautiful and kind and ultimately won the hearts of every officer." The colonel paused and, before continuing, wiped a tear that trickled down his cheek.

"She was quite small and died in childbirth. Captain Pembroke, fearful of ridicule, kept the twins in seclusion but provided them with a superior education. I was their godfather. When he died of wounds in Afghanistan, I became their guardian and, later, brought them to England. There was very little money in the captain's estate, so they had to make their way in the world. I arranged for music lessons, and they became fluent in Mandarin, Russian, and French, as well as English. Men with strange appetites were drawn to them, but the twins were skilled in fending them off. As they got older, however, they insisted I give them assignments in service of the Crown. It was their way of repaying what they thought of as a debt. Because of their unique circumstances, they offered to gain secret information that some men spilled in moments of passion. They insisted on performing these covert activities against my will. They were headstrong, and I have had no experience controlling young ladies. Mildred was especially skilled and could easily have become a courtesan except for her highly developed sense of right and wrong. One of those men could have been the murderer, especially if he was afraid he had 'spilled some beans' as they say."

"Sir, they were inseparable. I don't understand how Wei, er, Mildred, could have had a private tête-à-tête without the knowledge of Julie. I should also think that a man would be embarrassed," said I.

When Sir Cameron Beachy-Edwards assumed his role as a professor, I felt inadequate — and even stupid — because he seemed to think that I should be aware of the most obscure information. "Arthur, surely you must know that a Siamese twin has the ability to go into a trance-like state and be completely oblivious to the activities of her sibling. In fact, Mr. Samuel Clemens, under his nom de plume, Mark Twain, remarked on this in his essay of Chang and Eng, each of whom were married and had children. I can assure you, Julie had no knowledge of the men whom Mildred entertained," said the colonel.

"Arthur, would you like a drop of a fine single malt?" asked Dr. Bell, as if to offer me a reprieve from my confusion.

"Indeed, sir," said I.

Willum brought up a chair, and I joined the group around the table. The smooth whisky easily slid down my throat, and I sunk into the comfort of a deep cushion and the warmth of companionship. My days in practice at Southsea had been lonely.

Dr. Bell took a sip of Old Glenmore, put down his glass, and folded his hands across his chest. "Arthur, we have traveled over oceans to America and Russia together and you have proven yourself to be a fine companion, doctor, and even life-saving sleuth. Are you up for another adventure? Dr. Reginald Fitz at Harvard has invited me to Boston for a series of lectures and demonstrations. It seems as if the Americans still don't believe in Lister's work with antisepsis. Professor Fitz has not yet convinced the Americans to operate for appendicitis. We will then go on to San Francisco where I am to lecture on surgery in children with tuberculosis at the American Society of Surgery."

I considered the prospect of traveling to America again and exploring even farther west than we'd gone back in 1878. We certainly had our share of discoveries and daring adventures, and the remembrance of surviving many mishaps together — on land, at sea, and even aloft — made me smile.

Returning from my nostalgic daydream, I realized it would be difficult to leave my patients for more than just a few days and could even diminish my practice further. "I would like to go but cannot leave my practice in Southsea," said I.

The colonel tapped his cane. "I insist you accompany Dr. Bell," said he.

"I am afraid that would be impossible right now, sir. My patients depend on my services."

"You swore allegiance to the Queen and are still under oath to serve the Crown," said the colonel.

"Yes, sir, but my practice is my only livelihood and I must help support my mam and family," said I.

"You see no more than two or three patients a day, is that right?" asked the colonel.

I hung my head in shame. How could he know that I was a failure, that the practice did not yet even support the rent? If I left the patients I did have, even if only for a short while, they would quickly find another doctor and I would lose everything.

The colonel's voice grew cold. "If you don't agree, the Crown will revoke your medical license. There is no need to worry about your practice. I have a friend, an army surgeon who has recently retired, who is now taking a refresher course at St. Bartholomew's Hospital. His name is John Watson, and he would be happy to take over your practice for two months."

I had known a John Watson at university, but I did not know this man. I got so angry at the colonel for cornering me this way, I could have punched him in the face. Why would he put me in this position? Had I not done enough for the Crown when Dr. Bell and I last traveled to Russia and helped prevent an international conflict? The colonel, as head of the Secret Service, held the power of the British Empire in his hands. The damn empire had done nothing for us Scots and Irish, but I knew better than to argue, so I just held my tongue and glowered with suppressed rage.

"Doyle, my boy, the game is afoot yet again. I assure you this will be an opportunity for you to advance professionally, and you will be well paid, to be sure," said Dr. Bell.

Something in me softened at hearing Dr. Bell's words. I did enjoy the adventures with him and seeing the world. "What duties must I perform, if I go?" asked I.

The good doctor rose and rummaged through the smoking paraphernalia that littered the mantle. From the heap of pouches, straight-stemmed churchwarden pipes, and lovely old meerschaums, he selected an enormous calabash that he deliberately filled with

Cavendish. When he had tamped down the tobacco and lit the pipe with a coal from the grate, he exhaled a cloud of smoke. "Ah, the gourd stem ensures a cool smoke. Now, Arthur, you will assist me during surgery and arrange patients for demonstration. As with our other trips, there may also be some risk involved, so we need to be vigilant. The colonel will explain your ancillary duties," said Bell.

Ancillary duties? It was clear they had already discussed the matter and decided that I would accompany them. Despite no longer being his clerk, I found it difficult to say no to Dr. Bell. Assisting him on this journey would mean I would learn more medicine that would be valuable in my practice. And the additional compensation would certainly help pay rent, and then some. However, I was wary about what else might be required and what they meant by 'ancillary duties' . . .

The colonel again rose stiffly and went to a large globe of the world. "Here is the North Pacific, rimmed by the United States, Russia, China, Japan, the Philippines, and …" He paused to tap the globe for emphasis. "The damn Yankees control the Sandwich Islands and have what was formerly Russian-America. They have recently acquired a coaling station in Korea, are making inroads into Japan, and are contemplating a canal through Central America. The Americans have never forgiven us for supplying the Confederate States during their Civil War and are still demanding reparations for the battle cruiser, *Shenandoah*, which we outfitted for the South. The Americans are determined to have total control over the Pacific Ocean. Our only port on the North Pacific is British Columbia."

"This is all very interesting, but doesn't involve me. I did enough for the Crown in Russia and nearly died in the process — with no thanks, I might add," said I.

The colonel ignored me and went on, as if I was a mere insect. "The Russians claim that the land they sold to the Americans also included the entire west coast down to the Oregon Territory. Now, the Americans want that as well. The Queen appreciated your work, but, as you well know, the affair with the Tsar is so sensitive the international repercussions would be disastrous for England.

Your work must never be made public. You are still under oath to the Crown."

"Sir, I think I have had enough of our fanciful and risky trips and desire only to get on with my practice of medicine and finally writing my novel," said I.

The colonel took a generous measure of the single malt and forced a wan smile. "Would you not value the opportunity to solidify your finances, learn about the latest medical trends, and show your loyalty to the Crown while also working to track down the man who murdered Mildred? Poor Julie might recognize the man and be in danger. Duty demands that I send her to America, since the killer might well be in a plot against England."

What an enticing prospect. Momentarily drunk with the fantasy of finding Mildred's killer and having Julie show her gratitude with her soft lips on mine, I almost agreed on the spot, until I reminded myself that I cannot afford to become seriously involved with a woman until my practice is flourishing, to say nothing of the fact that she is still my patient.

"Lady Penelope Walshingham will accompany Miss Pembroke to America as her traveling companion," continued the colonel. Was that a smile or smirk on his face as he made this announcement?

I gasped at the thought of seeing Penelope again; blood rushed to my face. I had been madly in love — was it love — with the ever-mysterious, tantalizing Penelope during our Russian adventure, despite believing her to be a double — or was it a triple — agent. She worked for the Crown, but may have also been a German spy, the mistress of the Prince of Wales, and who knows what else . . .

"Sir, Miss Walshingham is a treacherous double agent and should have been executed for treason. How can you trust her?" asked I. Though it was a real question, the prospect of seeing her again was, admittedly, intriguing. I had not thought of Penelope and our many stolen kisses — and the way she would inevitably leave — in quite some time.

"Penelope expected to marry the prince and be the next queen, but he would not divorce his wife. Penelope threatened to expose the prince for the gambling, womanizing playboy that he is. The Crown was happy to buy her off by dropping charges and re-instating her in the Secret Service."

"Gentlemen, it is time for dinner. Let us continue this discussion later," said Dr. Bell.

The food was good, plain Scottish fare; barley soup, mutton, boiled potatoes, and haggis. I had second helpings of everything. After the rice pudding, we filed back to the study where Willum had laid out a bottle of Madeira and a round of cheese.

"Look at it this way, Arthur. Julie is in great danger. You could be of service to her," said the colonel. "And to Miss Walshingham, as well…" he added.

He had touched my weak spot and he knew it. I love nothing more than old tales of chivalry and derring-do, especially when they involve me and a beautiful woman, or women. Dr. Bell knows me well. He had been wise to take a break in the conversation after the talk of going with Julie to America and the first mention of Penelope. He must have figured that pondering the idea of another international quest while being sated by indulging in a delicious meal was the best way to gain my acquiescence. It worked. "I have given it some thought and agree to accompany Dr. Bell," I said.

"You are a wise and brave lad. You will accompany Dr. Bell to America and render what assistance you can to Miss Pembroke. I will arrange for Dr. Watson to cover your practice while you are abroad. We will let your patients know you are temporarily away in pursuit of new techniques so they can be assured they will get the best, and most current, care on your return."

With the decision made, and more briskness than he had exhibited so far in the evening, Colonel Beachy-Edwards opened a large carton and brought out a black walking stick with a peculiar handle. "This may be useful." He twisted the handle to reveal a revolving cylinder. "The outer layer of ebony covers a .32 calibre rifled barrel. It is capable of firing three shots. You simply twist the cylinder and press the concealed trigger. When the muzzle is pressed against a vital spot, one shot will kill instantly, and it is accurate up to a distance of some thirty feet."

He next produced a lovely, leather gentleman's traveling case, which contained a razor, soap, spare buttons, needle and thread, a small nail file, and a silver liquor flask. "By pressing this button, you can open a secret compartment, which contains spare bullets for the cane and a small stiletto. You have everything necessary for self-defense, and this." The colonel rather gingerly picked out the silver liquor flask. "Be extremely careful. This flask contains black powder. Twisting the lid ignites a spark and a ten-second fuse that, in turn, sets off an explosion with sufficient smoke and noise to confuse your enemies."

"Will we be in constant danger?" asked I.

"You must be willing to take risks because the empire may be at stake. I would go with you, but duty calls in London. You and Dr. Bell have the particular skill of making keen observations, which, in your previous travels, has proven to be advantageous. Once again, you will need to be aware and use your wits to stay out of trouble," said the colonel.

"Arthur, I am indeed pleased with your decision. I am sure we can learn something new from the Americans. Professor Fitz has much to teach us about this new disease, appendicitis," said Dr. Bell.

"Gentlemen, I must take my leave." The colonel rose, rather stiffly. Willum immediately appeared with his hat and cloak.

Dr. Bell was as excited as a schoolboy when he pushed aside the bottle and unrolled a map of North America on the table. "We leave from Liverpool on the *Oregon*, a new Cunard Liner, on the thirtieth of May and will arrive in Boston seven days later. She is the fastest ship afloat. We shall spend nearly a week in Boston and then onto Chicago. You will recall our good friend from our last trip to America, the railroad baron, Angus Duncan. He has arranged first-class accommodations all the way to San Francisco."

Perhaps it was the meal and wine, but I had already warmed to the idea of another adventure and traveling again with Dr. Bell. My practice had been dull and unsuccessful thus far, to say the least, and as with our previous experiences in America and Russia, I would commit to keeping a diary of each experience in order to have an official record and amass more material for my novel. "We shall see the Rocky Mountains and perhaps a herd of buffalo," I said. "I have read that the Indians are still ferocious and there are bandits in the west."

"The American Army has the Indians under control. Besides, I have my sword cane and a Webley .455. Thanks to the colonel, you are also well armed. We have more than enough firepower to subdue aboriginals and ruffians," said Dr. Bell.

It was nearly time to leave. "Now Arthur, we will be in a first-class salon on the ship and you must look the part of a respectable physician. Since at least one of the suits you had made for our journey to Russia was destroyed by that swordsman, I suggest you acquire some new clothing, as you have done with our last two trips."

25 May 1883

I had only enough time to be measured for a lightweight summer outfit and a new evening suit at the local haberdashery today before racing back to Southsea to meet Dr. Watson and gather personal belongings for the journey. Dr. Watson appeared to be a perfectly competent physician. I am happy to leave my practice in his able hands. Unfortunately, there was no time for us to become better acquainted, but I trust the colonel's judgement. Truth be told, I am grateful I will get some time away from a practice which reminds me I have not yet achieved success, and if Bell is right, I will return better able to serve my patients and build my practice.

27 May 1883, Edinburgh

This morning, I went directly from the train station to the bedside of Miss Pembroke. Mr. Twain greeted me with a wave of his cigar. I have never met such a friendly man. Oh, that all Americans were so delightful. Julie had made an amazing recovery. She was up, and I couldn't help but notice that she was dressed in an adorable gown that showed her trim body to the best advantage while concealing the site where she had been connected to her sister.

"I am here to inspect your incision," said I.

"There is no need. Dr. Bell changed the dressings this morning." I had hoped for at least a friendly smile, but she was distant. I attributed her demeanor to a post-operative, depressed mental state. I thought surely, despite her great loss, when she learned that I was to be her guardian on the journey, she would be delighted and even melt in my arms, knowing I would take care of her. Instead, she simply brushed aside a stray lock of hair and sipped from a cup of tea.

"Uncle Peachy said you will be traveling on the *Oregon*," said she.

"Aye. Perhaps we will meet on the ship," I said.

Julie simply tossed her head and made no response. I should have been more sensitive to her great loss. After all, her twin was really a part of her.

30 May 1883

Last night, I collected my new outfits from the haberdashers, packed everything in my portmanteau, kissed Mam goodbye, and arrived at the station a little after midnight in time to board the train with Dr. Bell. The trip to Liverpool was uneventful. We hired a cab drawn by a pair of fast, chestnut mares for the mad dash from the rail station to the docks. I was excited by the prospect of our upcoming travels and had come around to feeling completely at ease with taking leave from my humdrum medical practice. The bustling Port of Liverpool was crammed with towers, cranes, and machines of all sizes and description for the handling of cargo. The yellow waters of the Mersey were busier than ever with steamships carrying immigrants to the new world. Tug boats chugged back and forth while stevedores, all hooting and shouting, unloaded cargo amidst a tangle of horses and wagons. Our cab drew up next to the *Oregon* amidst carriages and broughams, which had carried the hundreds of impatient passengers now attempting to board the ship at the same time.

The *Oregon*, moored to the Prince's Dock at the foot of Bath Street, was over five hundred feet in length and powered by enormous steam engines. She also carried four masts to catch a following wind. *Soon*, I thought, *even these auxiliary sails will be obsolete*. The Union Jack and the Cunard pennant fluttered at her stern.

We boarded at the first-class gangway with the rich and famous, all excited to be aboard for the fastest crossing of the Atlantic ever made. Back aft, the poor, the lonely, and the unwanted struggled up the gangway for the sole purpose of escaping old Europe for a better life in the New World. Sailors wearing smart uniforms lined her deck, while Captain Cottier welcomed us first-class passengers. There was great excitement because the *Oregon* had made the crossing from Boston in seven days. The captain promised the return voyage would take only six and one-half days. The Royal Marine Band, with trumpets flashing in the sun, played a rousing version of "Rule Britannia." Stevedores took Dr. Bell's bags and trunk, and my lone portmanteau, but the professor insisted that I carry his precious instrument case. I was at his side, feeling hot and a bit shabby in my old, tweed, traveling jacket, when Julie and Penelope swept up in a four-horse carriage. They had an immense load of trunks, cases, and hat boxes. Julie curtsied to Dr. Bell and gave me a fleeting, but winsome smile. Penelope gave me a cold look of complete disdain and walked away without a greeting. Did she still blame me for the death of her German lover, Count von Wittenberg, when we were in Russia? She hadn't been upset when he died and had even run off with the Prince of Wales that same afternoon! Perhaps she was disappointed that I had not stayed in touch with her when she was having her dalliance with the prince. As always, though, she was the one who had left — not I. Why would she be angry with me?

As we settled on board, I followed our familiar travel ritual — first suggested by Dr. Bell years ago — and chewed ginger root to ward off the mal de mer that I suffered during our first passage to America. When tugs pushed the *Oregon* away from her dock, the band struck up "Heart of Oak" and then the rather mournful "Navy Hymn." I spent a splendid afternoon watching the flats and low hills of Liverpool Harbor, but when the ship turned south at Anglesey Island, I reluctantly went to our stateroom.

A handsome, black steward in a resplendent white uniform had put our clothing away in the spacious closet. He and Dr. Bell chatted as if they were old friends. "Arthur, meet Samuel Wallace. He has news of Rufus," said he. I was all ears. Rufus had been our steward during our first passage to America and became our friend and all-purpose assistant who helped identify the culprits in a scheme to assassinate the U.S. president. Though I have been told I am still not to mention it in public, the details of the journey remain secure in a diary I kept of the entire trip. Rufus, a black man, had been uneducated, but proved himself on that trip to be smart and skilled. He dreamed of becoming a doctor and help people around the world. With Dr. Bell's influence, Rush Medical College in Chicago had accepted Rufus into medical school.

Samuel grinned and showed a row of impeccable white teeth. "Ah knowed Rufus as 'Bub' when we worked together for a time on the *Servia*. He was ma best fren' and he tol' me about how you fixed those Rebs. He be Dr. Rufus Freeman now an' done hung out his shingle in Memphis. I's right proud of him." Though not surprised, I was delighted to hear that Rufus was accomplishing his dream.

Samuel efficiently put away our clothing, stacked books on the shelves, and arranged toilet articles in the bathroom. When he was about to take his leave, Dr. Bell put a gold coin in his hand. Samuel flinched and held his wrist. "Ah got this swellin' that hurts when ah uses ma hands," he said.

There was an egg-sized lump on the back of his right wrist. "That is a ganglion, also known as a synovial cyst. I can cure it in a jiffy," said Dr. Bell.

"What you goin' to do?" asked Samuel.

"Sit here and place your hand and wrist flat on the desk. This will be quick."

Samuel clearly trusted Dr. Bell from all Rufus had said, and he plunked his hand down on the desk. "Now, close your eyes," said Dr. Bell. The good doctor ran his fingers over the swelling, made a minor adjustment in the placement of Samuel's hand and selected from the shelf a thick volume, *Lewis's Textbook of Surgery.* He hefted the book in both hands, then brought it down with great force and hit Samuel's wrist with a sharp *thwack!*

Samuel caught his breath, snatched his hand away, and looked at it in awe, as if it belonged to another person. "Glory, it be gone!" said he.

Dr. Bell applied a dab of menthol salve and wrapped a bandage around the wrist.

"There, all fixed; it will hurt for a day or so and then you will feel no pain," said Dr. Bell.

"I be always grateful to you doctors. Anything you need, just call on me," said Samuel.

When I went topside to catch a breath of fresh air, the ship was well down the Irish Sea, known to my ancestors by its true name, Muir *ÉIREANN*. The wind was whistling in the rigging, and a nimble fellow — with a smart sailor's queue bound with a black ribbon that hung down the back of his neck — ran up the shrouds.

He stood on one foot just beneath the very peak of the mainmast and sang out.

"Heave away, boys. Heave away."

A half dozen sailors sprang to the halyard and bent their backs to the work.

"Heave and haul, boys. Heave away."

"Our Davy says heave and haul away!" the sailors shouted. They stamped their feet and chanted louder. "Heave, heave!"

The sailor, Davy, high in the rigging, gave a merry shout. "Heave, you sailors, heave away!"

I thought of my pleasant months on board the *Hope*, while whaling in the high Arctic, and wanted to leap to the rigging to chant with these good sailors and experience, once again, the camaraderie of a crew sailing together. Instead, I scribbled their cries in my notebook so as not to forget the experience.

Heave and haul away, you say.
Our Davy says heave and haul away!
Down we haul. Down with the Queen's knickers!

The chant continued as the great sail rose and caught the wind. The sailors laughed while doing their work. Davy, way up in the rigging, seemed to be a favorite among the sailors and a natural leader. I envied him his freedom.

A glaring, short, squat, red-faced fellow with the stripe of a petty officer swaggered up a ladder to the deck. "Damn you, Davy! Damn your lazy hide. Enough of that tomfoolery. Get down and help haul on that halyard!" the man shouted.

"Right-O," replied the sailor. He grabbed a line and, fast as a bullet, slid down the rope, facing the mast and away from the cluster of men. A gust of wind caught him and the rope just before he reached the deck. His feet struck the petty officer's shoulder, knocking him to the deck. With a dancer's grace, Davy landed on his feet and, before joining the other sailors in their work, offered his hand to the fallen officer, who smacked it away. The petty officer rose from the deck, glowering with rage.

"Damn! You struck me! Smashed my shoulder on purpose. It's the brig for you, you stupid sod!"

The men slowly and deliberately cleated the halyard and turned on the officer. "It war' an accident and you ain't hurt," growled a huge sailor. Davy, their leader, clenched his fists.

"Oh, it is mutiny you want? Right, then!" screamed the officer. I watched with utter amazement as the man drew a revolver, took deliberate aim, and fired a single shot. Davy grabbed his upper leg, but bright red blood spurted over the deck and down his leg. He collapsed on the deck.

"You swine! All of you, back to work!" shouted the petty officer.

The other sailors shrank away and went back to toiling with the halyards. I bounded forth, removed the blue bandana from the fallen sailor's neck, made a compress, and jabbed it into the wound. I put all my weight on the wound until the bleeding slowed to a trickle. The bullet must have severed his femoral artery in the groin. He had lost at least a pint of blood, though Davy neither screamed nor groaned but forced a smile as he looked up at me. "Thankee," he said.

I had not noticed before, but at my side, there appeared a smallish fellow with a full beard cut square across. "He is a brave man and you saved his life," said he.

"He will live if we can stop the hemorrhage," I said.

"Sad. So sad. Petty officers can be so cruel to hardworking, honest sailors," said he.

It seemed to be an eternity before the captain and the first officer appeared to restore order. "Quiet! You and you, take this man to sick bay. The rest of you — to your quarters," commanded the first officer.

The sick bay, with an examining room and five beds, was bright and clean. A woman with tightly-coiled blond hair and wearing a long, grey dress buttoned to the neck, was behind a desk. "Send for the ship's surgeon. This man has been shot. The femoral artery is bleeding," said I.

The woman sat straighter and glared. "I am Dr. Maude Topenham, the ship's surgeon," she said.

I was taken aback and momentarily released pressure from the wound. A geyser of blood erupted from the wound and splashed on the wall and floor. I leaned in to the job again until the bleeding stopped and composed myself. "I apologize, ma'am. I thought you were a nurse," said I.

"I have a medical degree from the Woman's Medical College of Pennsylvania," said she. The woman doctor — I can't say she was a lady — rose from her chair. She was tall and not unattractive, but neither was she appealing. Her skirt swished as she went to the wounded sailor and felt his pulse at the wrist. "Pshaw, there is no need for surgery. Echinacea powder and a tight bandage is all he needs. A one-in-a-thousand dilution of Cinchona will prevent a fever," said she.

Sailors were lurking at the door, wondering about their fellow crew member. "Call for the captain and Dr. Joseph Bell. Run for it!" I shouted. Captain Cottier arrived a moment before Dr. Bell and took in the situation at a glance. My arms were bloody to the elbows and there was a scarlet splatter on the wall. The captain had most likely been in the service during the days when officers treated sick sailors and performed rough surgery.

"This is no case for homeopathy. Dr. Joseph Bell is one of the world's foremost surgeons. We shall let him decide." said the captain.

The good professor, with Samuel trailing behind carrying the instrument case, hurried into the room. He scarcely glanced at the woman doctor and took charge. She had a hand across her bosom. A look of malignant hatred crossed her features, and she then broke into a stiff smile. "I shall happily offer my services," she said.

Dr. Topenham bustled about, getting in the way, until an orderly — a wizened little fellow with bright, intelligent eyes — arranged clean towels and basins for the carbolic antiseptic solution. "Henry Burns, at your service. I can administer the chloroform if you wish," said he.

"How very kind," said Dr. Bell. We soaked the instruments in a carbolic solution, cleaned the skin, and set to work. The fumes of chloroform rose from the folded towel over the patient's face.

Bell slashed through the sailor's clothing with a curved bistoury. "Samuel, press here with all your weight." Dr. Bell indicated the right lower quadrant of the patient's abdomen. I understood immediately. Pressure on the iliac artery would stop the hemorrhage while we searched for the femoral artery. It is an important surgical principle to have proximal control of a bleeding vessel. The scene could have been a surgical demonstration at the medical school. Dr. Bell rolled up his sleeves while I removed my blood-stained coat. We soaked our hands in the carbolic, and Dr. Bell selected his sharpest scalpel and incised the skin above and below the bullet wound just under the crease that separates the upper thigh from the abdomen. I recited to myself to ensure I was accurately considering the anatomical details. *The femoral artery emerges from beneath the inguinal ligament about halfway between the pubis and the iliac spine and enters Hunter's canal over the sartorius muscle just medial to the femoral nerve.* There it was, the femoral artery, with a ragged hole. Without pausing, Dr. Bell passed stout ligatures around the artery above and below the wound. He mopped up a blood clot and wiped the area with a solution of carbolic.

"Samuel, please release the pressure," said he. There was no more bleeding. I heaved a sigh of relief, but we were not finished. Dr. Bell removed bits of clothing and plunged a forceps into the tract of the bullet. "Ah, there it is, embedded in the femur." He worked the forceps up and down and then extracted the smashed bullet. "I fear the femur is cracked. Doyle, if you please, stitch the wound and apply a Thomas splint to immobilize the leg," said he.

After he packed his instruments, and with a slight bow to Dr. Topenham, Dr. Bell took his leave.

Davy came out of the anaesthetic without a whimper, thanks to the skill of Henry Burns. Burns again demonstrated his ability by applying the Thomas splint, a clumsy contraption of a padded ring and steel rods to the injured leg.

"You have had medical training," said I.

"A year at Guy's, but the book learning was above me. I could nae pass the examinations" said Burns.

Dr. Topenham had taken her small bag and left sick bay. "She goes to make her rounds of the women this time o' day," said Burns.

"Why does the ship have a woman doctor?" I asked.

" 'Tis a sad tale. The last doctor was a good man, a kindly man, but he mixed laudanum with drink until he went daft. They carried him off the ship in a straightjacket to a hospital in Boston. The lady doctor was the only one available at the last minute. The captain signed her on for the last voyage and so, here we are," said Burns.

"Can she perform surgery?" I asked.

"She claims to be a natural healer. I admit, she is good with women troubles but not much else."

I pondered this state of affairs and was happy to leave a capable man like Burns in charge of our patient. "Give him a light diet and no more than a teaspoon of laudanum for pain," I said.

I left and took a turn around the promenade deck, glancing into the ladies' drawing room as I passed, hoping to see Julie. The room was beautifully appointed and furnished in the most costly manner. I spied Penelope at a damask-covered table; an empty glass was by her elbow. She held a Sobranie Black Russian cigarette between her second and third fingers. Smoke curled upwards towards the ceiling when she exhaled through her nose. She was as I remembered her — a modern, sophisticated woman. My mam would say she was 'a bad un' and should nae be trusted,' but I couldn't stifle a feeling of yearning to spend time with her.

"May I join you?" I asked. She looked over and gave me a sour glance, though that turned, in a moment, to a lovely smile. She put the cigarette to her lips and took in a lungful of smoke as she eyed me from head to toe. There were fine wrinkles around her eyes, something I had never noticed before. She exhaled a cloud of acrid smoke.

"If you wish," said she.

"Would you care for a drink?"

"Yes."

I ordered two of the new 'cocktails,' brandy with a dash of Angostura bitters and lemon.

I tapped my fingers on the table. We remained silent until the drinks arrive.

"Are you working for Her Majesty again?" I asked.

She tossed her head, and I caught a whiff of orange blossoms, her favorite scent. "I had no choice. My father drank up his inheritance and no longer has any influence. Prince Bertie turned out to be a fat playboy and I lost interest." She snuffed out the cigarette and downed her drink. "I may settle in America and marry a rich man."

She gave me one of her most radiant smiles. My heart skipped a beat or two when she then leaned forward and caressed my hand. She was still beautiful.

"Order another drink," said she.

"Only if you allow me to escort you to dinner."

"Yes, but aren't you really interested in Miss Pembroke?" she teased.

"Oh, dear Penelope, Julie is a patient," said I.

It was nearly time for the first gala dinner at sea when I left Penelope to change into proper attire. Oh, the luxury of a first-class stateroom. Just think — we had our very own bath. I had a hot soak and then dressed for dinner. I cursed the links and studs but managed the starched shirt and winged collar before struggling into my waistcoat, which fit perfectly. Dr. Bell was resplendent in his usual black, velvet, Barathea jacket, a tartan waistcoat, and his dress blue kilt. He was indeed a noble Scotsman. "The captain invited me to dine at his table this evening. I must do justice to our great city," said he.

Edison electric lights flooding the Grand Salon set the gold and white ceiling decorations and the satinwood, paneled walls to glowing. The first-class passengers were already mingling, tapping their feet in tune with the string orchestra, and swigging down cocktails. Dr. Bell immediately went off to find the captain's table, while I wandered in the crowd until I caught a whiff of orange blossoms and spied Penelope. At that moment, I forgave all of her sins and the way she had repeatedly lured me in and then rejected me. She was absolutely bewitching in a frothy green, satin gown that revealed delicious, creamy shoulders and enough bosom to set my heart beating faster. I was about to proudly take her arm and escort her to a table when a handsome chap, in red trousers and a dark blue jacket, bowed low and kissed her hand. I had pangs of jealousy until Julie Pembroke came out of the crowd, diverting my attention, and offered me her hand. I bent and caressed her dainty fingers with my lips. She rewarded me with a beatific smile. In light of Penelope's dismissal, I was especially grateful for her kindness and attention and could have instantly fallen in love, except that the companion to the cad who had swept away my dear Penelope came over and bowed to Julie.

"Shall we make up a foursome?" asked he. The fellow had an American accent, a carefully trimmed mustache, and rather long, sandy-colored hair. He was as elegant as any British toff. He swept her away, leaving me feeling like the lower-class working man I am. I guess it just confirms I need to follow through on getting my doctorate. I slunk away and took a seat at the dinner table next to a heavy-set gentleman with curly, dark red hair flecked with grey, and an enormous mustache. There was what appeared to be a scar, like an old rope burn, on the back of his neck.

"I am Arthur Conan Doyle," said I. The man rose and made a sweeping bow.

"Colonel Ned Buntline, at your service," said he.

"Do you have business in the States?" I asked.

"Business? Great Jehoshaphat, no. Business is for those poor fools with no imagination. I write stories and entertain the public. Why, sir, I have just arranged a show starring Buffalo Bill Cody to take place in London. Damn it all, it is time for the Europeans to learn about the real Wild West of America," said Mr. Buntline.

We took our seats, and after partaking of a glass of very fine wine, I resumed our conversation. "I have heard of this Buffalo Bill. Wasn't he an Indian scout on the Great Plains?" I asked.

He glared at me for a long moment. "Hell's Bells! Haven't you read my story, *Buffalo Bill, King of the Border Men*?"

"No sir, but I have a great interest in writing, though there is little money in such an endeavor," said I.

"No money? Damn it all, you can make a fortune, boy. Why, I can dash off a story in one afternoon that will sell for thousands of dollars."

I nearly fell over. Most writers had complained of poverty and advised me not to try my hand at writing. "You must have a secret," said I.

"Hell no. Every great story has romance, a dastardly deed, and revenge. Start with a cowboy — let's call him Slim — who is in love with the boss's daughter. He is poor, but honest, and has no chance with the girl until a gang of desperados murders her father and kidnaps her. The leader of the gang is one of the best gunfighters in the west, but Slim leaps on his horse and gives chase all by himself. He kills all the gang with his trusty six-shooter and, even when shot and bleeding, he knocks out the gunfighter with his bare fists. He rescues the girl and collects a ten thousand dollar reward. He gets the girl and the ranch. It is a sure-fire formula."

I plied Mr. Buntline with questions while I indulged in the meal's multiple courses. It was after the oysters, when I was spooning clear consommé, that the frosty dowager across the table gave me a cutting look and spoke to me sotto voce, though it could be heard around the table. "Young man, you are using the spoon intended for cream soup." How was I to know the difference? My face became hot, and as the meal continued, I watched how everyone else at the table ate and focused on my food in order to avoid her further judgement. I had grilled lobster, beef steak, roast pheasant, lamb with mint sauce, creamed peas, a sorbet, buttered new potatoes, fresh asparagus, pâté de foie gras, and, at last, peaches in jelly with a chocolate éclair. I surreptitiously undid the top button of my trousers, which had grown tight after indulging in the delicious food, and woefully looked across the salon.

Julie was in animated conversation with the American gentleman. The fellow in red trousers alongside Penelope must have told a joke, because Julie giggled and then laughed out loud. The only jokes I knew were mostly anatomical and wouldn't do in mixed company. Just before we rose from the dinner table, Mr. Buntline clapped his hand on my shoulder. "Remember … the bad man always wears a black hat and carries a gun on each hip."

After an hour or so in the smoking room with a fine cigar and more than one brandy, I went, unsteadily, out on deck and leaned against the railing for a breath of salt air. After a few moments, Dr. Bell appeared out of the gloom. "It is a fine night," he said.

"Yes, indeed, the stars are brilliant," said I.

"I am worried about that boy's leg. Let us visit sick bay," said Dr. Bell.

Henry Burns' head was down on folded arms on the desk; he snored softly and smelled of beer. I nudged his arm. He came awake with a start and rubbed his sleepy eyes. "How is our patient?" I asked.

"Right as rain, sir, right as rain. I shall switch on the Edison lights so's you can see for yourself."

Davy was dead white. His lifeless body was still warm and showed no sign of rigor mortis. Dr. Bell quickly examined the body. "He has not been dead for more than an hour. There is no sign of bleeding or gangrene," said he.

There was nothing amiss that I could see. "Perhaps he had a delayed reaction to the anaesthetic," said I.

Dr. Bell continued his examination. "What is this?" he exclaimed.

"I see nothing untoward," said I.

"Come, lad, the pupils of the eye become widely dilated just before death and remain fixed in position."

I looked more closely at the open eyes. "Yes, yes, now, I see. His pupils are about halfway between pinpoint and normal," said I.

"Does that suggest anything to you?" asked Dr. Bell.

"An opiate, such as morphine, produces pinpoint pupils," said I.

"Mr. Burns, did the patient move at all after we left?" asked Dr. Bell.

"Oh, no, sir. The splint kept him immobile, just as you asked," said Burns.

"Did you pull his undersheet tight?" asked Dr. Bell.

"Yes, sir, tight as a drum, it was, hospital-like," said Burns.

Dr. Bell's questioning of the little man made no sense. I was puzzled, and Burns quivered under Dr. Bell's unrelenting gaze. "Were you with him all evening?" asked Bell.

"I slipped out for a bite of supper and some refreshment wi' the port watch," Mr. Burns said.

"Has Dr. Topenham been here?"

"Oh no, sir. The doctor takes her meals in her quarters and retires early unless she has to visit a sick passenger."

"I gather she treats the passengers in their rooms and sees the crew here in sick bay?"

"That is correct, sir."

"Now, Arthur, a bit of sleuthing. Is there anything unusual about the bed?" asked Dr. Bell. I looked closely and remembered that Burns said he had made the bottom sheet 'drum tight' like a proper hospital bed, yet there were wrinkles on the bottom sheet.

"If the patient was completely immobile, how did he wrinkle the bottom sheet next to him?" I asked.

"Very perceptive," Dr. Bell said. He traced the wrinkled sheet with his index finger. Was it my imagination, or had he outlined a vague impression of a human form?

"Mr. Burns, see to the body. I shall request a captain's investigation of the death," said Dr. Bell.

Despite a fogged brain, I sat up until the wee hours of the morning, setting down every detail of this day. I am counting on the idea that my compulsion to write and record everything, especially the expertise of Dr. Bell, will provide fodder for my novel.

31 May 1883, at sea

The inquest was a farce. Dr. Topenham testified that the patient died as a result of our unnecessary surgical meddling and anaesthetic shock. The captain ignored my eye-witness account of the shooting, as well as that of the small, bearded gentleman who was on deck at the time. "My officer enforced discipline and prevented a mutiny," said the captain. I left the hearing with my bearded friend, and together, we strolled aft on the promenade deck. We leaned on the railing and watched the small white-capped waves driven by a gentle northeast breeze.

"My name is Arthur Conan Doyle," said I. He languidly shook my hand and offered an absentminded smile.

"Herman Melville," he said.

"The author of *Typee* and *Moby Dick*?"

"The very same," said he.

"Sir, I have read your books. They are remarkable adventures! I have looked for more, but it seems you have written nothing during the past few years. Is that so?" asked I.

"So, young man, have you really read my stories?"

"Yes sir, every word."

His kindly face was sad. "The critics said I was mad, totally mad. In Boston, the clergy burned my books."

"I would give up medicine if I could write half as well as you."

"No, don't give writing a moment's thought. Medicine is an honorable profession. Writing only leads to poverty. I can write about sailing men and sailing ships, but the age of sail is almost over. Now the poor fellows are in a dark, steel cage shoveling coal instead of up there in the rigging enjoying a fresh breeze and sunshine," said he.

"Yes, I understand. I have traveled on multiple ships and even served as ship's surgeon on an arctic whaler. The conditions were often terrible, but the men had a fair life. They were cruel to the animals, however."

"The life of a sailor can be brutal. On one of my ships, the second mate falsely accused a topsail man, named Billy, of thievery. The captain ordered a hundred lashes. Of course, the poor fellow died. Yesterday's episode reminded me of poor Billy.

"Why not write a story about him?" I asked.

"Perhaps, someday."

We pushed through the crowd to the bar. Mr. Melville ordered brandy and water while I, still feeling the effects of last night, had a lemon squash. In the far corner of the room, Penelope and Julie played whist with their escorts of the night before. Penelope was partnered with the American this time, and the bounder was fondling her knee. I could not help but stare, with more than a twinge of jealousy. But for which girl did I feel more? Julie was ravishing and appeared to be under the spell of the damned fellow who had swept her away from me last night.

A fellow nudged my elbow. "A couple of lovely dishes, eh?" He had a pleasant twinkle. "Giles Stevens of the London Times," he said.

"Pleased to make your acquaintance. I am Arthur Doyle and this is Mr. Herman Melville, the great author," said I. Mr. Stevens toyed with his drink and stared across the room with a hungry look.

"Look at them — a damn Russian and an American with the two best looking women on the ship," said he.

After my escapades in St. Petersburg, I was interested in anything Russian. "I didn't realize that the other man was Russian. Who is he?" I asked.

"Count Nikolai Borovsky, a distant cousin to the new tsar. He was a director of the Russian-American Company before they sold out to the Americans," said Stevens.

"So, this Borovsky must be wealthy," said I.

"In the early days, the Russians made a fortune in furs, but they fell on hard times. Borovsky was more interested in minerals, and he may have swindled the company before Russia sold Alaska to the Americans," said Stevens.

"Who is the American?" I asked. "Not certain, but he claims to be a California mining engineer and I believe I heard someone address him as Mr. Dawson."

Our little group broke up, and I whiled away a half hour or so attempting to learn the game of whist, but it was no use. After a time, I wandered into the library to search for the book by Henry James, *Principles of Whist Stated and Explained.* Dr. Bell was there surrounded by books and stacks of newspapers. "Laddie, I am troubled by that boy's death. It reminded me of a brief note in the London papers about a series of mysterious deaths in Boston." He pushed a month's worth of the *Boston Herald* across the table. "Look for reports of unusual deaths, especially in young men."

This is one of the Doctor's methods for solving mysteries. He is convinced that criminals repeat their crimes and the solution is always to find a common thread. I didn't expect to find anything, but set to work looking through the stack of papers. There were long stories about the completion of the Brooklyn Bridge and the end of the spoils system in politics. I read about the man named Buffalo Bill — who Colonel Buntline had mentioned was organizing a Wild West of America show — and about a telephone line connecting New York with Chicago.

I grew tired and was struggling to focus when a story in the paper from the twentieth of April caught my eye. It was about a young man who died in a nursing home after a trivial injury. It happened in Quincy, a city not far from Boston. An attendant had found the young man dead in bed, and an unidentified doctor pronounced the death as due to a fractured tibia and a shock to his nervous system. I had seen a number of fractures of the tibia, but had never known of that causing a death. I read the story to Dr. Bell.

"It may mean nothing, but I don't believe in coincidences. Arthur, here is your chance to use your wits. Why should a young, healthy man such as the one in the Quincy nursing home or Davy die after a trivial injury?" Dr. Bell asked.

"Perhaps, a sudden stoppage of the heart or a stroke," said I.

"Oh, stuff and nonsense! Think, man. Use your training. Observe, deduce, and connect. Remember the pupils of his eyes." I thought hard. There had been no signs of distress, no contortion of Davy's limbs to suggest a fit. His face was peaceful in death.

"Some sort of poison," said I.

"Close … Have you heard the expression, 'in the arms of Morpheus'?"

"Yes, an overdose of morphine would cause a peaceful death and explain the near pinpoint pupils of his eyes. But who could have administered the fatal dose?" I asked.

"I first suspected Mr. Burns, but in the annals of crime, women are just as likely to be serial killers as men. Deranged killers, such as Jack the Ripper, combine a longing with hatred for the opposite sex."

"But why? I asked.

"Disturbed sexuality," replied Bell.

"Only two people would have had access to a supply of morphine — Mr. Burns and Dr. Topenham. If the death in Quincy is related, it could not have been Burns because he was on the ship at the time," said I.

"There, you have it. Dr. Topenham came on the ship in Boston after the Quincy murder. We must set a trap to catch her and be sure she is the killer. I shall leave that to you," said Bell. I felt pleased that Dr. Bell was giving me responsibility in solving the case.

I was preparing for dinner with Penelope when Samuel entered with fresh towels. "Mr. Arthur, you dasn't go to dinner with dat bristly face. You jes set still, right here, and I will give you the best shave of your life," said the steward. I relaxed under the steaming towel until he brushed on foaming lather and, with all the deftness of a surgeon, gently passed a wicked straight razor over my face. "Now, this here lotion is goin' to make you feel like a million dollars," said Samuel. He slapped on a fragrant lotion and rubbed until my skin fairly glowed.

"That feels wonderful. What is it?" I asked.

"Dat's bay rum. Folks down in the islands soaks mashed up fresh bay leaves in Jamaica rum and add a little lemon and orange," he said.

I whistled on my way to their stateroom. If fortune smiled on me, even if Penelope continued to rebuff my romantic attentions, I might end up whirling Julie around the dance floor after dinner. As I arrived, daydreaming of dancing in Julie's arms, she opened the door to my knock and, to my shock, immediately clutched her throat, rolled back her eyes, and went absolutely rigid. She appeared to be in a deep hypnotic trance. "Penelope, bring Dr. Bell! This instant, please!" I shouted. I led Julie to a chair. She sat down, but appeared to have no awareness of her surroundings.

Dr. Bell arrived and, in his usual manner, first listened to my story and intently observed the girl. His concentration was uncanny. I explained the abrupt onset of her trance when she had opened the door. As I spoke, Julie remained quiet and rigid. Her eyes were half open but clearly sightless. She made no response to questions nor appeared to hear any sounds we made, such as clapping our hands.

"Arthur, please leave the room for at least five minutes," said Dr. Bell. I was totally mystified, but did as he ordered. I lingered on the deck for five minutes by my watch and re-entered the room. Julie was awake and seemed perfectly normal until the second I appeared. Her eyes rolled upwards, she went rigid, and was totally unresponsive.

"She knows you. The only change is that powerful scent. Charcot, the French neurologist has described a sort of self-hypnosis induced by smell," Dr. Bell said.

"Sir, is it possible to reach her mind when she is in the trance?" I asked.

"Let us make the attempt," said Dr. Bell. He knelt by Julie, stroked her hand, and spoke softly as one would with a frightened child.

"Julie, dear, we are friends of Uncle Peachy. You are perfectly safe with us." There was a flicker of movement in her eyes.

"Julie, listen closely. Uncle Peachy wants to know about the man who visited Mildred. Did he smell nice?" Her hand jerked convulsively and she giggled with girlish amusement.

"You remember him. Was he amusing?" Dr. Bell asked. She giggled, then burst out laughing.

"He smells nice, but looks like a boiled egg. Oh, Milly, put it back," said Julie.

Dr. Bell stroked her arm and spoke in a soft, reassuring voice. "Julie, was he the same man who killed Mildred?" The poor girl went rigid. She clenched her eyes and, after a moment, shook violently.

"Must not bother Milly. Must not tell. Oh, Milly," said she.

"A small mirror, please," said Dr. Bell. Penelope produced a mirror from her purse. Dr. Bell adjusted the electric lamp and repeatedly reflected bright flashes of light from the mirror into Julie's eyes.

There was no response until she batted at her face. "Bright, too bright," said she. Suddenly she burst into tears. "Oh, where is my sister? Has the awful man left?"

"You are safe. You smelled a scent, but it was only Arthur, not the man who was with Mildred," Dr. Bell said. She stretched and seemed disoriented, like someone coming out of a deep sleep.

"Why did the man look like a boiled egg?" Dr. Bell asked.

Her face again went blank. "I don't know," said Julie.

The evening was ruined. There would be no dinner and dancing. No hugging and kissing. Julie went from the quiet blankness to hysterical sobbing to pacing the floor. Penelope agreed to watch over her for the night.

It is now much later and I am about to collapse into bed, leaving Dr. Bell puffing his favorite meerschaum pipe and frowning in deep concentration.

1 June 1883, at sea on the *Oregon*

Giles Stevens, the London Times reporter, is in his early thirty's, not a young man, and he limps on a trick knee. We were enjoying a rasher of bacon, poached eggs, kippered herring, and an assortment of pastries. The tea was first rate. "Giles, would you like a bit of excitement and to help solve a crime?" I asked.

He wiped egg from his chin. "Only if it involves good-looking women," said he.

"You will be bait to catch a killer and, yes, a woman is involved, but I would wager she is not your type," said I.

"I smell a story. Do I get an exclusive if we catch the killer?"

"Of course. You can leave us out of it. Dr. Bell loathes the press," said I.

Mr. Stevens didn't even need to put on an act as his knee did bother him. He hobbled into sick bay and made sure to groan at the approach of Dr. Topenham. She made a cursory examination, prescribed a harmless homeopathic remedy, and ordered Mr. Burns to bandage the knee. "Stay in bed. I will visit you this evening to make quite certain you are comfortable," said Dr. Topenham. Giles put on another realistic display when he put his arm over my shoulder for support and limped to the lounge for a much-needed brandy.

"Giles, if this Dr. Topenham is indeed the killer, you may be in danger. She must be incredibly clever to get away with murder. Are you certain you want to go through with this?" I asked.

"I have been in danger before. Never fear," said Giles.

"I admire your bravery, but still, I will have Samuel, the steward, look after you. Take care," said I.

A few hours later, I met Mr. Melville for a stroll on deck. We paused to admire the ship's arrow-straight wake and her trail of black smoke. "Fast and more reliable, but not as romantic as a sailing ship," said I.

Melville shaded his eyes and peered over the sea, which sparkled in the bright sunshine, as if he were on the lookout for a whale. I expected him to shout, "Thar she blows!" Instead, to my surprise, he cried out something far different. “Man overboard!” he shouted, and pointed to a small body entangled in a rope ladder that dangled over the side. Within seconds, a sailor threw out a life ring, a whistle blew, and the ship’s engines shuddered and shut down. Officers and a crowd of spectators swarmed to the rail. The bosun’s mates lowered a boat. The sailors cut away the tangle of ropes and, within minutes, hoisted the boat with its dreadful cargo.

Death is a failure for every doctor, perhaps more so to a newly minted physician like me. Even though I have seen cadavers in medical school, and witnessed several deaths when we were last in America and in Russia, I couldn’t help but choke back bile when I pressed my fingers to her ice cold neck. I had not expected a pulse and there was none. Even the faintest flutter of her carotid artery would have meant life, but Julie was dead. She wore only a light nightdress, which was half off her shoulders. I covered her with my jacket. Even in death, Julie was beautiful. I couldn’t stomach the thought of my patient and potential love being dead and barely made it to the rail before heaving bile into the ocean.

“Davy was meant to haul up the ladder after the pilot left,” said the bosun. “With his death, and in the chaos, it was never done.”

“But then, had the ladder been lifted, she would have disappeared without a trace,” said Mr. Melville.

The first officer supervised transfer of the body to sick bay. Bad news spreads quickly. Dr. Bell arrived immediately and watched Dr. Topenham perform a cursory examination.

“The woman was addled by drink and fell overboard. It was a simple accident,” she said.

“You must perform an autopsy,” said Dr. Bell.

“No need to disturb the passengers,” said the first officer. “The captain would never approve such a thing. She obviously drowned.”

Dr. Bell flicked open his penknife and, with one motion, made an incision down the center of Julie’s neck. The first officer lunged forward, but I smashed my fist into his face. He staggered back, blood pouring out of his nose. “Damn you!” He lurched forward, but I blocked him with a kick to his knee that dropped him to the floor.

"Arthur, stop the fisticuffs and assist me. Mr. Burns, two small retractors, if you please," said Dr. Bell.

Burns opened a glass-fronted case and secured two small retractors, instruments with a sharp hook on the end to hold open wounds. Bell made a precise incision that opened the trachea. I inserted the hooks into the wind pipe and pulled it open. It was empty. Dr. Bell pushed gauze down the wind pipe. It was perfectly dry.

"There is no water in her windpipe. Miss Pembroke was dead before she entered the water," said Dr. Bell.

"Is it a case of murder?" I asked.

"We shall see about that," said Dr. Bell.

Dr. Topenham, with her hand over her mouth, rushed out of sick bay.

"Arrest that woman!" I said.

"Not so fast, laddie. Let her be for now. She was most likely taken with a sudden nausea."

I had expected Dr. Bell to demand a full autopsy, but he merely proceeded to a methodical examination of the body. There were no bruises, wounds, or other signs of violence. Dr. Bell filled his meerschaum pipe with Cavendish, lit up, and blew a cloud of smoke. After a full five minutes of silent contemplation, he withdrew a small magnifying glass from its case and minutely examined dear Julie's face. "There! Arthur, look carefully. There is a shallow indentation on her cheek to the right of her mouth and minute indentations on the left side. The killer placed a hand over her mouth and, with his thumb and forefinger, choked off her nose," said Dr. Bell.

"Someone with a strong hand suffocated her and then threw the body overboard," I said, feeling the bile again rising in my throat.

"Exactly; but for the rope ladder, she would have disappeared, leaving no evidence that she was murdered."

"Would the handprint show in a photograph?" I asked.

"If we arrange the light correctly," Dr. Bell replied.

I hastened to get my equipment. Mr. Burns helped arrange the lights and I took several photographs. Later, I developed several excellent photos that demonstrated an unmistakable outline of a hand — the hand that choked the life out of dear, sweet Julie. I was determined to bring the killer to justice with my own bare hands. I had dreamed of holding her in my arms and kissing those soft lips that were now cold and dead. She hadn't hurt anyone. Why would someone murder dear Julie? While mourning the fact that I would never be able to be with her, I suddenly remembered Penelope. Was she in danger as well? I couldn't bear to experience another loss, so I ran up a ladder and forward to their stateroom on the promenade deck. Thankfully, Penelope opened the door, though she was still in night clothing. Her eyes drooped with fatigue, and her hair was disheveled.

"Julie is dead," said I.

Her expression hardly changed, but her hand shook as she lit a Sobranie cigarette. She flicked out the lucifer and sat with a bare leg crossed over her knee. "Julie was hysterical until quite late, then she slept for an hour or so. I watched over her until nearly dawn. She felt better and went out for air. I finally fell asleep," said Penelope.

Could I believe her? Penelope had been a double agent. I wanted to trust her, to believe she would not lie again — especially to me — but I couldn't be sure. Was she loyal to the Crown or was she working with an enemy to England? Did she care about Julie, or was this just pretense?

Later, in our stateroom, I put the question to Dr. Bell. "Did one killer commit both murders?"

"No, the methods are completely different. The sailor died with an overdose of morphine. Whoever killed Julie had an entirely different motive," said Dr. Bell.

"Could the same person have killed both twins?" I asked.

"Yes, the methods were different, but the killer must have had a motive to be rid of the twins" said Dr. Bell.

"What about Penelope? Could she have committed both crimes to put us off the scent?" I asked.

"No, Penelope is devious, but not a cold-blooded killer. In fact, we must combine forces with her to find a man who looks like a boiled egg," said Dr. Bell.

"Come, now, it must be a silly joke," said I.

"It came from her subconscious. Julie told the truth. The killer is bald. He must have an excellent toupee. We must look for a gentleman who brushes his hair the exact same way every day," said Dr. Bell.

I rang for Samuel. He arrived promptly. "Samuel, be a good fellow and invite Lady Walshingham to our quarters for tea," said I. Penelope arrived and took the tea but waved away the scones and jam.

Dr. Bell went right to the point. "Do you have any thoughts on who could have murdered Julie?" he asked.

"Colonel Beachy-Edwards is investigating a plot against England that involves the Pacific coast of Canada. Mildred obtained information for him during a tryst. The killer naturally would have thought that Julie had overheard him speak in a moment of passion," said Penelope.

"Do you suspect anyone?" asked Dr. Bell.

"There are dozens of Americans on this ship. Could be any one of them," she said.

"What about that Dawson fellow?" I asked. She waved off my question with an enigmatic smile and abruptly went her way.

2 June 1883, at sea

I had completely forgotten Giles until we met at breakfast. He walked with an exaggerated limp but appeared to be cheerful. "Giles, what happened?" I asked.

He slathered a bit of toast with marmalade. "The nice lady doctor arrived just before midnight, enquired about my health, and left a small dose of laudanum. She was very solicitous. You medical blokes could take lessons from her in bedside manners," said he.

"Look sharp," said I.

The ship's officers soothed the passengers' fears by claiming that Julie had fallen overboard accidently. She was quickly forgotten because everyone was more focused on placing bets on the exact day and hour of our arrival in Boston. Dr. Bell spent the day working on his textbook of surgery while I strolled the deck and occasionally looked in on the game room where Penelope avidly played whist with Borovsky the Russian, Dawson the American, and a bejeweled dowager. I studied the game and was still confused by the strict rules of bidding, tricks, and trumps. Dawson appeared to have an eye disorder since he blinked, winked, and raised his eyebrows from time to time. Periodically, Penelope swept a pile of banknotes off the table.

3 June 1883, at sea

For most people traveling by ship, one day is much like every other. The ship leaves a straight wake, passengers lounge on deck, and we all eat and drink too much. The English talk of troubles in Afghanistan, and the Americans chatter about horse races, politics, and the economic depression. No one has mentioned the murders. The ship's officers have no leads, and at Dr. Bell's instruction, I have kept our plan a secret. If we do not catch the culprits soon, we will arrive in Boston and the killers will be free.

4 June 1883, at sea

Giles was remarkably cheerful. "You have it all wrong about the lady doctor," said he.

"She may still kill you. Is Samuel keeping watch?" I asked.

"Oh yes. He fixed a comfortable spot in a far corner of my stateroom."

I grumped about because the captain predicted we would dock in Boston a day earlier than expected — by noon tomorrow. This would be our last day and night at sea and we had not apprehended either killer. Dr. Bell seemed completely unconcerned. Dinner was again a sumptuous feast, and I overindulged on wine — at least that is my only explanation for my behavior later in the evening.

I can hardly write because my hand is swollen, and though I may have a broken carpal bone in my wrist, it is probably a mere sprain. Sometime after dinner, while many first-class passengers had crowded into the lounge for drinks, the dynamo failed and the Edison lights went out. Most passengers stumbled off to their staterooms. Penelope, the Russian, Borovsky, Dawson, and the same old dame, whose husband was apparently in the House of Lords, continued playing whist by gaslight. Penelope was partnered with Dawson, the American. I could not stop thinking about finding the murderer and was all for getting a full night's sleep so we could start fresh again tomorrow. Dr. Bell sat his chair at our small table with his legs stretched out and his hands folded on his chest. A casual passerby would think that he was half asleep. He had not touched the tot of single malt whisky but raised a hooded eyebrow every time Dawson and Penelope won a trick.

"Arthur, what have you observed about the foursome?" he asked.

"Nothing in particular," said I.

"Have I taught you nothing? Look closely. Dawson and Penelope are cheating."

"Do you mean the winks and raised eyebrows are some kind of a signal?" I asked.

"Of course," said Dr. Bell.

My mind whirled. Yes, Dawson! A man who cheats at cards is capable of any nefarious act, even murder. Before Dr. Bell could stop me, I sprinted across the room and caught the odor of bay rum. "Aha, it is you! Damn you!" I shouted. I snatched at Dawson's hair with all my might. He yelled. I yanked out a few hairs, but his coiffure was perfectly intact. Penelope pulled in a pile of banknotes and overturned the table on the Russian's lap. The count fell backwards but came to his feet with a growl. His locks of hair had become unhinged.

"No, YOU are the boiled egg!" I shouted at Borovsky.

He responded by lunging at my midsection. I went down, gasping for breath, but came up and smashed a haymaker into his face with my right fist. The Russian snatched a derringer from his pocket. "You dare to lay a hand on a nobleman!"

Penelope lifted her skirt with practiced ease, withdrew a small revolver from a holster on her ankle, and fired twice. The first bullet grazed the Russian's shoulder but the second struck dead center in his chest. The count groaned, clutched his chest, and theatrically collapsed on the floor. I ducked out of the way. Dawson rubbed his head, and the dowager remained perfectly calm, as if fisticuffs and gunplay were a regular occurrence. A blood stain rapidly spread over the Russian count's shirtfront, but he was very much alive. Dr. Bell calmly lifted the count's wig. His head did resemble a boiled egg. He inspected the wound and found that the low-powered .22 bullet had not penetrated the count's sternum. It was hardly more than a flesh wound.

Two ship's officers and the master-at-arms quickly took charge. "Take this man to sick bay and don't let him out of your sight. He may be a vicious killer," said Dr. Bell. He pulled me away from the excited group of passengers and officers. "Arthur, we must search his room. Be quick," said Dr. Bell.

Off we went through darkened passageways until we halted at room 201. The professor jimmied the lock with a twisty surgical instrument suited for removing deep foreign bodies from wounds. "Strike a light," said he. By the light of a candle, we opened drawers, riffled through clothing, and searched a trunk. There was nothing unusual until Dr. Bell found a locked, red, leather case beneath the bed. He probed the lock until the lid sprung open to reveal small compartments filled with dozens of small stones wrapped in bits of paper. Each piece of paper had numbers written on it. We took one small, pale, white stone and a second, orange-colored bit of crystal wrapped in a paper with the numbers 62:48 132:12.

In sick bay, Mr. Burns had already removed the small bullet from the count's chest. The captain and first officer questioned the count and looked upon me with suspicion.

"You are under arrest for attacking a fellow passenger," said the captain.

"Sir, this man murdered Miss Pembroke," said I.

"Bah, where is the proof?"

At this point, Count Borovsky put on a great show of bravado and innocence. "The fracas was all a mistake, a question of cards. I forgive the impetuous young man," said the Russian count.

Dr. Bell huddled with the captain. "We have evidence. Arthur, fetch the photographs, if you please," said Dr. Bell.

The dim outline of the hand in my photograph matched the count's. This might have been the first time in the history of crime detection that a photo incriminated a murderer, but it was not enough to convince the captain. He ordered the count to be confined to his room until officials in Boston could investigate.

I suddenly remembered Giles and had a terrible sense of foreboding. I confronted the first officer. "Come with me, quickly," said I.

We dashed down a flight of steps to the second-class section and, at the end of the corridor, found the door to Giles' room ajar. I will never forget the scene. Samuel, the steward, violently shook Giles who lay in a coma. "Wake up, wake up!" he screamed.

"What happened?" I shouted.

"I musta dozed off and thought it was a dream. De lady doctor was all sweet talk when she gave Mr. Giles a glass to drink. He took little sips, den a long pull, and sank back on the bed. She waited a minute or two, den lay down next to him, kissed his mouth and run her hand along his body. He groaned once or twice, like he was havin' a good time. I figured it warn't non o' my bizness. I lay quiet until I couldn' hep but sneeze. De lady doctor rised up and run right out of the room. Dat's when I figured somethin' was wrong."

Poor Giles was scarcely breathing. "Samuel, soapy water, quick! A pitcher of water with soap!" I cried.

Giles made automatic, feeble attempts to swallow when I poured the liquid into his mouth. Some went down his windpipe and he coughed. I pinched his skin and slapped his face until the soapy water worked. He vomited a gush of soapy water and emptied his stomach. At last, the poor fellow opened his eyes.

"Samuel, damn your hide . . . Coffee, a jug of hot, black coffee, now!" said I.

By the time daylight streamed through the porthole, Giles had finished the pot of coffee and walked with assistance. "Oh, what wonderful dreams; there were the sweetest lassies and wonderful kisses," said Giles. He sagged back on the bed. I shook him awake.

"What happened?" I asked.

"She was kind and so sweet. She gave me a drink of the most delightful medicine. I had to have more and more," said Giles.

"You barely survived a lethal dose of morphine. Thank goodness you are alive! Now, you have a first-hand account and can tell the world how you helped identify — and survived — a serial killer," said I.

5 June 1883, Boston Harbor

The pilot boat met us as we drew near the Boston Light on Little Brewster Island. After the pilot boarded, the captain sent an urgent message on the returning boat, requesting police and an official from the British Consulate to meet the ship. The weather was glorious. Passengers crowded the deck to see the islands in Boston Harbor. The English hissed and booed when we steamed past the very spot where the rebels staged the Boston Tea Party. Horns tooted when tugs pushed the *Oregon* alongside Long Wharf in Boston Harbor. A dozen armed police held back a crowd of relatives and onlookers while excited passengers crowded against the railings. Everyone was thrilled to have been part of the record-breaking Atlantic crossing. The moment deck hands lowered the gangplank, I noticed Penelope, hand in hand with Jack Dawson, dash away and get lost in the crowd. I caught sight of them again, just as they entered a cab. Dawson carried the red, leather case that belonged to Count Borovsky. Penelope looked up at me, waved, and blew a kiss.

"This is not the last we will see of those two," said Dr. Bell. I felt a terrible pang. Why could it not have been Julie and me dashing away, hand in hand, to romance?

A ponderous, fattish, middle-aged man with woolly sideburns made his way up the gangplank. Despite a walking stick, he staggered as if he'd had a drink or two. A thin man with a bowler hat followed him. The second officer insisted that we accompany the two men to the captain's quarters. The captain offered tea, and we made introductions all around. The thin fellow was police detective William Kennedy. The other man introduced himself. "Baron Sir Edmund Runcie, Her Majesty's Consulate," said he.

The damn fellow was probably the worthless third son of a baron who found a place in the diplomatic corps, but he expected us to bow and scrape. Dr. Bell looked him over with his usual keen eyes. "Sir Edmund, you are not long from your posting in Hong Kong?"

"By jove, that is correct. Quite correct. We have never met. How did you know?"

"The rash on your face and your unsteady gait indicates an overdose of quinine. Hong Kong, of all the Crown Colonies is the worst for malaria. The carved dragon head on your walking stick is of Chinese origin," said Dr. Bell.

"By Jove, you are correct. Um, now, captain, you sent a message. Murders, eh? Do you have the scoundrels in custody?"

"We have no real proof that either death was a case of murder. There is only circumstantial medical evidence," said the captain.

"I proved the young woman was dead before she entered the water. A handprint on her face matches the hand of Count Borovsky, and there is an eyewitness for an attempted murder," said Dr. Bell.

Runcie twirled his mustache. "A count, you say? Must not create an international incident with a false accusation," said he.

"You should also know that Dr. Topenham, the ship's doctor, may be a serial killer. Her case is one for the American police," I said.

"Where is this Dr. Topenham?" asked Detective Kennedy.

Captain Cottier turned to his first officer. "Well, is she in custody?" he asked.

"I am afraid, sir, that the ship's surgeon has disappeared. We have searched everywhere," the officer said.

"Damn! I will not stand for incompetence in my officers," Captain Cottier said.

"She is extremely clever," said I.

"Baron Runcie, Dr. Reginald Fitz at the Massachusetts General Hospital is a world renowned pathologist. I insist that he perform an autopsy on the Julie Pembroke to prove she was murdered," said Dr. Bell.

"Oh, very well. Where is this Count Borovsky?" asked the baron.

Two tough masters-at-arms brought in the manacled count. His nose was swollen and he favored his right shoulder. When introduced to the Baron he bowed low.

"The Runcie line, a most noble family," said the count.

The damn fool baron fairly beamed with pleasure. "I say, we must not manacle a nobleman. Will you be my guest, sir, until we resolve this unfortunate affair?"

Despite Dr. Bell's objections, the thing was settled. The baron took Count Borovsky off to the consulate as if he were a visiting dignitary.

I loitered on deck. The first-class passengers continued disembarking in grand style to awaiting carriages, while the poor people in steerage shuffled by with their load of belongings wrapped in blankets or carried in small trunks. The women were dressed in long skirts, colorful blouses, shapeless cloaks, and bonnets. They all looked alike. It seemed hopeless. Dr. Topenham must have mingled with the steerage passengers and managed to disguise herself. I was growing anxious thinking she would go scot free and kill again, when I caught something amiss. I spotted a tallish, but stooped, woman who wore a ragged black shawl and a grey skirt that dragged on the deck. The hands of the lower-class women were red, rough, gnarled by hard work. Yet her hands, which clutched her shawl, were lily-white, and her fingers were clean and well tapered.

"Stop that woman!" I shouted, while pointing towards her. She heard my yell, pushed aside the other passengers, dashed down the gangplank, and disappeared in the crowd. I shouted for the police and set off after her but bumped into people at almost every step. It was no use. I caught a glimpse of her more than a block away. She crossed a main street, looked back to see if anyone was following her, and, in doing so, stumbled on the iron rail of a streetcar track and fell beneath the hooves of four dashing horses pulling a streetcar. It was indeed, Dr. Topenham. Her crushed head leaked brains onto the street. It was a dreadful death, but it had saved her from hanging, and she would never again be able to murder another innocent person.

Professor Fitz agreed to perform the autopsy. Samuel helped load our baggage into a two-horse cab and off we went. The driver, a loquacious Irish-American, drove slowly from one cobblestone street to another. He took great delight in pointing out the church where a fellow named Paul Revere hung lanterns and a hill where a band of farmers killed over a thousand British redcoats. We at last arrived at the Massachusetts General Hospital facing the James River. Despite its pretentious dome and portico, it was not nearly as impressive as the Royal Edinburgh Infirmary. It was, however, famous in the medical world as being the place where ether was first used as an anaesthetic. Reginald Fitz was a jolly, balding fellow with a great bushy mustache. I instantly liked him. His laboratory, in a tiny room on the first floor, was filled with specimens and books. The news of an interesting case traveled fast, and soon, the room was crowded with students and physicians.

Professor Fitz pulled his mustache. "Won't do. Won't do. Much too crowded. We shall use the Bigelow auditorium."

We marched to a glum, ill-lit auditorium that had creaky wooden floors and the overwhelming stench of dead bodies. Students and observers lined the tier of benches that overlooked Julie's body reposing on a plain, wooden table. Even in death, Julie was still exquisite. I wiped away a tear and struggled to keep calm. Dr. Bell and I squeezed in between students on the lower bench nearest the body. At that moment, a diminutive, frail man wearing a large bow tie and a grey, frock coat entered the auditorium. The students stomped their feet. "Hurray for Dr. Holmes!" they cheered.

The little fellow spoke with a wheezy voice. "Now, Reginald, be gracious to our guests. After all, they are from Edinburgh," he said.

The new arrival was none other than Oliver Wendell Holmes, the 'Autocrat of the Breakfast Table' and America's greatest poet. There was a brief, polite exchange concerning who should perform the autopsy, Dr. Bell or Dr. Fitz. The corpse, after all, was English. Graciously, Dr. Bell said that Dr. Fitz should have the honor of opening the body.

"Arthur, explain what happened to Julie," said Dr. Bell.

The students became very quiet when I described the events; the historic operation of separating the twins, Julie's apparent suffocation, and her ultimate and untimely death. I also exhibited the photograph of the hand print on her face.

From his first, careful midline incision in the abdomen, Dr. Fitz worked with Germanic precision to dissect the organs.

“Gentlemen, observe the liver that was shared by the twins,” said he.

The students became more attentive, and Dr. Holmes stood on tiptoe to peer into the abdomen. “A miracle of surgery,” he said.

Dr. Fitz dissected, organ by organ, and demonstrated that the lung floated in a basin of water. “This young lady did not die by drowning. She was definitely dead before entering the ocean,” he said.

When we followed the students out of the auditorium, Dr. Holmes, with a twinkle in his eyes, grasped Dr. Bell. “By all means, stay at the Parker House and join our literary group on Saturday afternoon. The food is the best in Boston. Try the clam chowder and don’t miss the Boston cream pie,” he said.

“Arthur, we have the proof. Now we must convince that oaf, Baron Runcie, that the Russian count, Borovsky, is a killer,” said Dr. Bell.

6 June 1883, Boston

The five-storied Parker House hotel at the foot of Beacon Hill has high, arched windows, marble steps, thick carpets, and comfortable beds. A pleasant surprise in this uncouth country. Worn out by the yesterday's activities, I slept like a dead man and awoke today to leaden skies and driving rain splattering against the windows. Dr. Bell, still in his dressing gown, barely responded to my rather glum "Good morning." An empty syringe and a needle rested on the small table. My spirits, none too bright after witnessing Julie's autopsy, sank even lower. When we were in Russia, the good doctor had become addicted while self-experimenting with cocaine as a local anaesthetic. After several weeks of ill health, during which he could barely perform surgery, he learned to adjust the dosage. Since then, I have known him to use the drug only when bored, in order to produce a state of euphoria. In a moment, he bounded to his feet, full of vigor, lit up his favorite pipe, and blew a cloud of fragrant smoke. "Arthur, Runcie has not contacted London. The confounded man is besotted with Borovsky's title. Typical. The British upper class will believe a nobleman instead of a commoner. He may very well allow Borovsky to go free without more evidence," said the doctor.

"Sir, what about the stones we took from his case?" I asked.

"Yes, they may be significant, but we are likely to require the assistance of a geologist if we are to learn more."

I gave the orange-colored stone to Dr. Bell, who examined it with a magnifying glass by the window. "Hmm, yellow flecks embedded in stone. Merely fool's gold, iron pyrites, or the real thing?" He paced the floor, turning the stone over and over in his hand while puffing his pipe. "Arthur, after you get something to eat, dash out to the nearest chemist and purchase one ounce of nitric acid and three of hydrochloric acid. And, yes, a small quantity of liquid mercury and a small glass flask," said he.

I paused long enough to have a capital breakfast of eggs, bacon, and a dish recommended by the waiter, Boston baked beans. After a second pot of tea, I had strength sufficient to face the rainy day. The chemist's shop was on a delightful cobbled street with posters advertising potions for every conceivable ache and pain. There was medicine for the liver and kidneys. Most, such as 'Lydia Pinkham's Vegetable Compound,' were for female ailments. They all contained a considerable amount of alcohol or opium.

The chemist raised an eyebrow at my request, but measured the acid into bottles. "Be careful. Either will eat through solid iron," said he. He also had liquid mercury for barometers. I also purchased a small glass flask and a sack of licorice candy.

When I returned to Parker House, Dr. Bell chipped a yellow speck from the crystal and placed it in a porcelain dish filled with nitric acid. The intact speck gleamed like a gem at the bottom of the liquid. It was unaffected by the acid. Next, he added the hydrochloric acid. When the two liquids mixed, we watched as the yellow speck dissolved. "Ah, the mixture is *aquia regia*, also known as the 'acid test.' Now, one more test." He chipped off another yellow speck and placed it in the liquid mercury. The speck promptly disappeared. "This rock contains gold. Where is it from? Why did Borovsky have it?" asked Dr. Bell.

"Yes, and why did the American, Jack Dawson, carry away the sample case with Penelope? What else might be in there?" I asked.

"The best minds in Boston will be at the literary club this afternoon. Surely someone will know of a geologist," said I.

Boston is called the Athens of America for good reason. The Saturday Afternoon Literary Club met in a fine room on the second floor of the hotel. There were many notables. James Russell Lowell and John Greenleaf Whittier each read a bit of poetry. The highlight was Oliver Wendell Holmes. He stood before a cheery fire, as tall as his slight frame allowed, and read from one of his most famous poems, "The Chambered Nautilus."

Build thee more stately mansions, O my soul,
As the swift seasons roll!
Leave thy low-vaulted past!
Let each new temple, nobler than the last,
Shut thee from heaven with a dome more vast,
Till thou at length art free

Leaving thine outgrown shell by life's unresting sea!

There were huzzahs and applause when he finished. Dr. Holmes immediately made for Dr. Bell. "I knew nothing of the germ theory or of antisepsis, but I recommended cleanliness for childbirth many years ago. The profession laughed when I suggested that fevers of childbirth were carried on the hands of physicians," said Dr. Holmes.

"Pasteur and Lister have proved that you were absolutely correct. Can you recommend someone on the Harvard faculty who is a geologist?" asked Dr. Bell.

"Indeed. Alexander Agassiz is just the fellow. He is a geologist, as well as a miner and a zoologist. You can find him in the Peabody Museum," said Holmes.

Later, we tucked into green turtle soup, oysters on the half shell, venison chops, and delicious Parker House rolls.

8 June 1883

Yesterday, Bell immersed himself in the newspapers and his books. With nothing else to do, I chose to stroll about Boston. Bostonians are a sober bunch, and the streets were crowded with black-clad people on their way to church.

Today, physicians and surgeons occupied the lower benches in the Bigelow auditorium for the first of Dr. Bell's demonstrations and lectures. The medical students in the upper tiers were more gentlemanly than the ruffians we had encountered at the Rush Medical School in Chicago five years ago. Dr. Bell lectured on Lister's antiseptic techniques in great detail using innumerable case histories of compound fractures of bones and joints infected with tuberculosis. In America, the surgeons still amputate limbs for these diseases, but Dr. Bell showed how patients could be healed while saving the limb. Professor Bowditch, wearing a black, frock coat and a purple, satin vest, theatrically gazed about the room. "I have looked everywhere and have never seen a germ," said he. The students roared with raucous laughter. "Now, Mr. Shattuck will present a patient to our distinguished guest," said Bowditch. I felt sorry for poor Shattuck, a student.

The patient was about forty years old, pale, and a bit yellow, with hollow cheeks and a rather stumbling gait. His face contorted into a painful grimace each time he placed his right foot on the floor. He had a particularly severe spasm of pain when Mr. Shattuck assisted him onto the padded table. "Reverend Ebenezer Hale has had fevers, been sick to his stomach and, during the past month, has had severe pains in his right leg," Mr. Shattuck read aloud from a notebook.

Professor Bowditch stood, twirled his watch chain, cleared his throat, and spoke. "My diagnosis is malaria. However, there has been little response to Cinchona," he said.

I tingled with anticipation. Dr. Bell observed the patient and the poor student through half-lidded eyes. "Mr. Shattuck, our students in Edinburgh examine patients. I presume you performed the usual observations, palpation, and auscultation. What did you find in the Reverend Hale?"

"Ah, sir, we students are not allowed to examine patients," said the quivering Shattuck. Dr. Bell fixed his gaze on the patient. His restless eyes roved back and forth from face to hands and settled for a moment on Mr. Hale's coat. He counted the pulse for a full minute and then pulled down Mr. Hale's lower eyelid. He stood away from the table. "Mr. Hale, how long were you stationed in West Africa?"

"I was in Mali four years before I became too ill to preach the Gospel," said Mr. Hale.

Professor Bowditch came to his feet. "How the deuce did you know he had been in Africa?" he asked.

"A religious tract with a portrait of an African is protruding from his coat pocket. He does suffer from malaria." Dr. Bell dramatically paused, while Bowditch turned bright red. "He also has a second disease that is most commonly found in West Africa. Mr. Shattuck, please roll up Mr. Hale's right pant leg. Gentlemen, you are about to see a blister. A blister typical for Dracunculiasis." The students and physicians gasped in astonishment when Mr. Shattuck revealed a blister nearly a half-inch in diameter on the lateral side of Mr. Hale's leg. "Bah! Means nothing. It is a mere skin irritation," said Dr. Bowditch.

"Arthur, prepare a small bistoury and a toothed forceps," said Dr. Bell. I found the instruments in his case, prepared the carbolic acid, and soaked the instruments. "Now, if you please, administer a light anaesthetic to our patient." Mr. Shattuck volunteered.

When the Reverend was peacefully asleep, Dr. Bell removed his coat, rolled up his sleeves, and dipped his hands in carbolic. I swabbed the leg with the antiseptic. It was a perfect demonstration of Dr. Bell's method of preventing infections in wounds. He took up the bistoury, opened the blister, and made an incision that extended three inches up the leg. "Gentlemen, you are about to see a Guinea worm, also known as the fiery serpent because of the intense pain." He grasped a white, worm-like object that was about an eighth of one inch in diameter and gently pulled it from the wound. He paused after he had delivered perhaps six inches. "The female Guinea worm can be up to three feet long. One must remove them slowly and avoid breaking the worm. If a portion is left in the patient, the worm will die and cause a fatal infection."

It took well over an hour of patient traction to deliver the entire worm. The audience remained in their seats, speechless, as if mesmerized by the performance. The Brahmin feathers were severely ruffled by Dr. Bell's acute diagnosis.

After lunch, we took a brisk walk to the consulate. An undersecretary ushered us to Baron Runcie's office. The fellow was still in a soiled dressing gown and smacking his blubbery lips over a tumbler of gin and tonic. "Only thing for one's health," said he.

"Have you had instructions from Colonel Beach-Edwards concerning Count Borovsky?" asked Dr. Bell.

"Damn it all. Can't bother the home office with trifles. Enough trouble with these Americans. Now, the count — a fine fellow, a real sportsman. He has shot polar bears and tigers. Couldn't ask for a better man," said Runcie.

"Please, the man murdered an English woman. You must consult the Secret Service," said Bell.

Runcie waved a chubby hand. "Stuff and nonsense. Besides, an American — damn me, his name, his name is Stanford, a rich railroad man — wired the American Secretary of State to intervene and insists we set the man free," said Runcie.

"You must not do that without permission from the home office," said Bell.

"Yes, must not let the Americans interfere," said Runcie.

We left it at that and took our leave. I felt let down and disappointed about Her Majesty's servants, but then, I was only a lowly doctor.

9 June 1883

Immediately after a hearty breakfast, we set off to see specimens of appendicitis at the laboratory of Professor Fitz. It is an amazing collection of appendices pickled in alcohol. Everyone came from an autopsy of patients who had died with abdominal pain. "I cannot convince our surgeons to operate," said Fitz.

We examined appendices with perforation. Others were gangrenous. "Clearly, an operation to remove these might be curative. It only requires the antiseptic technique," said Dr. Bell.

Dr. Bell waved me away. "Arthur, I intend to study these specimens the rest of the day. You are on your own." He was scheduled to attend a medical faculty dinner at the Harvard Club that evening. It was time for me to do a bit of sleuthing, bring Borovsky to justice, and get to the bottom of why he had murdered Julie.

I set off to find Professor Agassiz at the Peabody Museum of Archaeology and Ethnology at Harvard University in hopes of learning the origin of the rocks we had taken from Borovsky's room. I entered the two-story, red brick building and was immediately confronted with fearsome skeletons of long extinct animals, a huge turtle shell, and a Dodo. I wandered about and at last found a droopy, ancient curator who informed me that Professor Agassiz was away in Peru seeking a copper mine. "Is another geologist available?" I asked. The old fellow rustled the pages of a day book while I shifted from one foot to another.

"Ah, you are in luck. His assistant, Mr. Manfredi, is out for the day, but will return this evening. I shall put you down for an appointment. Would nine o'clock be convenient?" he asked.

"It will do," said I.

Next, I stopped in at the consulate. Baron Runcie was unavailable. The officious clerks didn't say if he was out for a long lunch or an early tea. By great good fortune, I happened on the communications officer, a nice young man named Codlington. "Have you by any chance sent a cable concerning this Borovsky fellow to Sir Cameron Beachy-Edwards in the home office?" I asked.

"No, no, nothing like that at all. The baron treats Borovsky like visiting royalty," said Codlington. I invited Codlington out for a spot of supper and a drink. He turned out to be a jolly fellow and knew all about the new telephone system and the miraculous trans-Atlantic cable.

"Would you mind sending a personal message to Sir Beachy-Edwards?" I asked. "Glad to," said he.

I rapidly wrote a few lines on a sheet of note paper. *Dear Uncle Peachy, J.P. dead. B. suspects Nikolai Borovsky. Arthur*

We strolled back to his office in the consulate. "Some of us have rounded up a few girls for a party. Are you free later tonight?" Codlington asked.

"No, I have an appointment with a geologist at the museum," said I. Was it my imagination? There had been a slight rustle at the door and a soft tread in the hall outside of the office. I dismissed my unease and took my leave of Codlington.

I had developed a limp and a swollen right ankle, due to an old rugby injury, so I first went to our room to fetch my walking stick before proceeding to the museum. The geological section was rather isolated in the southwest corner. After losing my way in darkened corridors and rooms filled with skeletons, I found Mr. Manfredi at a large desk facing a wall, in a large room lined with cases containing rocks, various types of earth, sand, and specimens of minerals. "I am Arthur Conan Doyle. Thank you for seeing me," said I.

"I have not yet had supper and am about to leave for the day, so you will need to be quick," said Manfredi.

I produced the two rocks we'd taken from Borovsky's room. "Please, before you go, can you tell me anything about these specimens?" I asked.

He pulled an oil lamp closer and withdrew a large magnifying glass from a drawer. He scrutinized the specimen that I handed to him. "Quartzite, with a rich vein of gold," said he. He turned the second specimen over in his hands. "Ah, this is much more interesting. See these orange crystals?"

"Yes, are they of any importance?" I asked.

"It is wulfenite, also known as lead molybdate, a rich source for molybdena," said he.

"What is molybdena and the origin of the specimen?" I asked.

His eyes and hand went to a bookcase over the desk. He seemed to be pointing at a small, brown, cloth-covered book when, at the same instant, a shot rang out. The left side of Manfredi's skull exploded. Bits of shattered skull, blood, and brain splashed on my coat. I turned just in time to see a dark figure in a cloud of acrid gun smoke. He was less than twenty feet away and taking aim again. The second shot came less than a second later. The bullet tore at my sleeve, but I suffered no injury. I recalled Colonel Beachy-Edward's explaining how to use the cane, so I dropped to one knee, raised my walking stick, and pressed the trigger. There was a surprised yelp, and the assailant dashed away down a darkened corridor. I could do nothing for Manfredi and gave pursuit. It was useless. The killer got away through an open window. I returned to the room where the remains of Manfredi's lifeless body still lay. I glanced up at the bookshelf and retrieved the small volume he had pointed out. The title was, *Exploration of the Yukon Territories and Alaska, 1878-80*, by Nelson Miles, General, U.S.A.

I was still hunched next to the dead Manfredi, and had only turned the first page, when there was a cry of alarm. A guard arrived and flooded the room with light from a bulls-eye lantern. I had the presence of mind to shove the volume into an inside coat pocket just before a beefy, red-faced policeman rushed into the room. He crashed his nightstick down on the back of my head. It was at least half an hour before I came to my senses, lying in a sticky pool of blood on the floor. For a long while, I saw two faces, then they merged into one. It was Detective Kennedy who had met us at the dock on our arrival.

"You are in a bit of trouble, Mr. Conan Doyle," said he. I struggled to a sitting position and, still inarticulate, pointed towards the back of the room. "Sho — shots from there," said I.

Kennedy paced the length of the room then returned. "Explain yourself," said he.

I rose, unsteadily, to my feet and attempted to explain what happened. “There, in the wall …” I pointed to the two holes.

Kennedy went to work with a pocket knife and soon extracted two large bullets. The detective weighed one in each hand. “At least two hundred grains, .44 calibre,” he muttered. Without another word, he inspected my .32 calibre cane.

“You fired this weapon,” said he.

“Yes, I may have winged the assailant. He escaped down the corridor and out the window,” said I.

Kennedy was still not satisfied with my explanation. My mind did not clear sufficiently to give a detailed account of my actions until we arrived at police headquarters. I was still bleary-eyed when word came to the police headquarters of a murder at the British Consulate.

“Come, Mr. Conan Doyle. You may be of assistance,” said Kennedy. He beckoned me to join him in a two-horse cab. The consulate was in an uproar. The baron, still in his dressing gown, could hardly speak. My newest friend, Codlington, was dead. His head was down. One arm was stretched out over his desk. His dead hand clutched my scribbled message. The handle of a dagger protruded from his back. This was too much. I was surrounded by death. Was I responsible for this latest murder? I felt like weeping, but struggled for control.

“Mr. Kennedy, I suggest you call in Dr. Bell,” said I, before turning and getting sick on the floor.

Dr. Bell arrived within the hour. He was clean-shaven, dressed in a houndstooth jacket, grey trousers, and freshly shined shoes. His cravat was tied perfectly. Without a word, he surveyed the communications room and stooped to inspect a crust of dirt on the floor. He rose, tore a page from his notebook, scooped the bit of dirt onto the page, and folded it carefully. He then moved to the body and gently touched a spot of blood on poor Codlington’s jacket. “The blood clot is almost dry. The wound was inflicted within the past three hours,” said he. “Please, bring a lamp.” He then stooped, minutely inspected the handle of the dagger, and circled around to the desk, where another pool of dried blood had seeped out of the victim’s mouth. “A long blade. First, the lung.

Then, it penetrated either the aorta or the left ventricle. Death was instantaneous. He may have recognized his assailant," said he. Bell stood quite still for several minutes, surveying the room with his quick, grey eyes. He nodded to Detective Kennedy. "Remove the dagger," said he. The blood-stained dagger came out of the body easily. The blade was at least eight inches long and was sharp on both sides. "This is a type of dagger used by Cossacks," said Bell.

"Then it is of Russian origin. Where is Borovsky?" I shouted.

There was a dead silence until Baron Runcie coughed and cleared his throat. "He did not come for morning tea," said the Baron.

A search of the consulate revealed no trace of the Russian.

"Could he have been at the museum? Dr. Bell should investigate the crime scene at the museum," said I. Kennedy readily agreed and off we went, back to the Peabody Museum on the Harvard campus.

Dr. Bell lingered to admire the many specimens, especially the Dodo skeleton, until, with a sigh, he entered the geology section. There were still fragments of Manfredi's skull, a splash of blood, and bits of soft brain tissue on the desk. The mind sometimes turns to seemingly irrelevant items in emergency situations, and I wondered for a moment why the brain is called 'grey matter,' since fresh brain tissue is pink and covered with bluish veins.

"I fired a shot at the assailant. He was there," said I, after regaining my focus. I pointed to the end of the room, just at the entrance to a corridor. Bell wandered about, apparently looking at specimens of minerals and plain rock, before he went to the back of the room. He stood, chin in hand, and surveyed the wall and then the floor. He stooped, rose, walked a dozen steps, went down on his knees, and scooped up a bit of dirt onto a sheet of paper.

At the desk, he beckoned to the mystified detective Kennedy and displayed the two sheets of paper with a few crusts of grey-black soil. "These are identical specimens of loamy, alluvial soil," said he. The caking suggests they were embedded on the cleat of a boot. One man committed both murders," said he.

"Hah! Your companion, Mr. Conan-Doyle, admitted to being at the consulate and was here at the time of Manfredi's murder," said detective Kennedy. He was right! Would I spend months in a Boston jail attempting to clear my name? I had been falsely accused of crimes during our last trip to America, when I saved the president from assassination. The police, instead, accused me of attempting assassination. *Why did I ever think it would be worthwhile to venture again to this godforsaken country?* I thought.

"Please remove your shoes, lad," said Dr. Bell. I removed my rough brogans. The soles were worn and smooth. There was no trace of earth. "Now, come along," said Bell. He beckoned to Detective Kennedy. The good doctor easily climbed out the window used by the escaping murderer. There on the moist ground were deep prints of a cleated boot. The footprints went off to the northeast in ever-lengthening strides. "The man you seek is wearing heavy boots. Now that he has killed an American citizen, I hope that the Boston police will finally take an interest in Count Nikolai Borovsky," said Bell.

We returned to the Parker House, where, despite a throbbing head and still-sore leg, I have written down these notes and am now exhausted and ready for sleep.

10 June 1883

Today, I awoke, yawned, and rubbed the sleep out of my eyes. I was sore all over, but no worse than after a game of rugby. Dr. Bell, fully dressed and bright of eye, thrust a mug of hot, bitter coffee into my hands. "You need this. We must hurry. Our train departs before noon," said he. I drank the bitter brew and finished off the buttered toast and a slice of cold ham that remained from Dr. Bell's breakfast.

Bell thrust a cable-gram in my hands. "I threatened to report that damn Runcie as an incompetent fool unless he sent a cable to Beachy-Edwards. I have spent the past hour deciphering his response. This is the result," said he. *Regret death of Julie. Nikolai Borovsky, Russian, brilliant scientist, known assassin, assumes many disguises, very dangerous. Has contacts with Americans and Russians on west coast. Peachy*

The bullet had torn away a portion of the sleeve, ruining my tweed jacket. I was about to dispose of it when I remembered the moment just before Manfredi died. I thrust my hand into the inner pocket and found the small book by an American general. The two rock specimens and a balled up bit of paper fell out as well. I packed the lot into my bag.

We hurried away to the Boston, Albany and Chicago rail station, found our car, and had just enough time to settle into our compartment when the whistle blew and off we went. Our car became incredibly hot and stuffy as the train wound up and down hills, past fields and the picturesque villages of New England. In the evening, just before going to bed, I rediscovered the small, brown book by the American general. I became wide awake when, on the title page, I saw the name Nikolai Borovsky listed as both a member of the expedition and its geological consultant. The book described a survey of the mountains and rivers of Alaska and the Yukon Territory of Canada. There did not seem to be an agreement as to the location of the border between the two. There was a hint, even a statement, that Russian-Alaska had included a good deal more territory than appeared on maps. The book suggested that the United States had purchased all of the Yukon and British Columbia.

The only passing reference to geology was a short note about the latitude and longitude of a hill named 'King Solomon's Dome.' I sighed at this new mystery and went off to sleep.

11 June 1883, Chicago

Upon our arrival in Chicago, Angus Duncan, Dr. Bell's old university chum, met us in his splendid carriage driven by a jolly Scotsman dressed in a black top hat and all the finery of a London footman. Angus, a railway magnate, had generously hosted our previous trip to the states. When we arrived at his home, I left Mr. Duncan and Dr. Bell in the lavish drawing room, refreshing themselves with tots of single malt whisky. I immediately went to the kitchen and embraced Mrs. O'Flynn, the cook, who had become a friend during our last trip to America. I gazed into her wrinkled, motherly face, thought of my mam, and had a momentary pang of regret that I was not home looking after my family. She bustled about the kitchen and, in no time, fixed an enormous roast beef sandwich with mustard and a tankard of cold beer. I munched on the pleasant repast and listened to her prattling. "Well, lad, now ye are a regular doctor ye can prescribe for me knees," said she. She shyly hoisted her apron and black, wool skirt. Her knees were knobby with bony lumps from scrubbing floors on her hands and knees.

I remembered Dr. Brown's prescription for Mrs. Samuel Clemens. "I will get Arnica ointment from the chemist. It is the latest thing for rheumatism," said I.

An hour or so later, I unpacked my bag and again found the two rocks I had taken from Borovsky. While admiring the orange crystal, I replayed in my mind the assailant's booming shot and Manfredi's head exploding and leaving shards of skull and brain scattered over the desk and floor. He had just said something important about the orange crystal. In a flash, I remembered; molybdena. Manfredi had pointed to the brown book. I searched its pages, but found no reference to molybdena. I went back to the bits of rock, one with gold and the other supposedly containing the strange element. *Exploration of the Yukon Territories and Alaska* described mountain peaks, rivers, and other landmarks. There were occasional numbers indicating latitude and longitude, but none matched the numbers on my slip of paper.

Mr. Duncan, with his usual magnanimity, put on a splendid dinner to celebrate our arrival. The guests were mostly business men, but there were professors from Rush Medical College who remembered Dr. Bell's extraordinary diagnostic skills and were eager to hear the latest medical advances from Edinburgh. Our fellow Scotsman, Alan Pinkerton, the detective, arrived late. His gait was unsteady, his face was pale, and his bushy beard was completely grey. I thought he was ill, but his eyes were as keen as ever. After drinks in the drawing room, we tucked into breast of passenger pigeon, roasted new potatoes, asparagus, and a delicious Lake Michigan trout in a tomato sauce. I couldn't wait to talk with Pinkerton and went up to him immediately after dinner.

"Have you caught the James gang?" I asked. Pinkerton scowled.

"Young fella named Bobby Ford shot him in the back a year ago. He earned a handsome reward," said he. I thought Mr. Pinkerton would mention the bit of work I had done for him, but the mission was still a national secret. "There is a worse gang out west. Damn outlaw name of Butch Cassidy is robbing banks and trains. My men can't lay a finger on him," said Pinkerton.

The talk of outlaws brought the recent murders to mind. Pinkerton began walking away, but on impulse I clutched his arm. "Sir, have you heard of a Russian, Nikolai Borovsky?" I asked.

"Never heard of him." Mr. Pinkerton turned away and joined the group smoking cigars and drinking brandy. I followed him through clouds of smoke and listened to discussions of the decline in railroad building, mine closings, and the ongoing depression. Thousands of men are still out of work.

"Leland Stanford's got the right idea. He is building a mercenary army with all those out of work Irish." I could not identify the speaker but pushed through the crowd.

"And who is Leland Stanford?" I asked, recalling that was the man who had wired Baron Runcie to release Count Borovsky.

"Well, if that don't beat anything. Young fella, everyone knows Leland Stanford, one of the richest men in the world. Owns railroads, mines, companies, and most of California," said a fattish man who poked a cigar in my face.

"The man is a robber baron," said Dr. Gunn, a Rush surgeon.

"If he is so rich, why is he interested in a Russian assassin, Nikolai Borovsky?" I asked.

Alan Pinkerton came across the room to my side in an instant. "If you value your health, don't ask questions about Stanford," said he in a low voice, directly in my ear.

I knew enough to heed Pinkerton's advice and drifted away to a group of Rush doctors who surrounded Professor Bell. "Is there an analytic chemist at Rush?" I asked.

"Well, no, but there is a new fellow, name of Lange, at the Chicago Medical School," said Dr. Gunn.

"Oliver Marcy at Northwestern in Evanston is a good all-around scientist," said Angus Duncan.

12 June 1883

I rose late, had leftovers for breakfast, and was determined to learn more about the orange crystal. I walked to South State Street, boarded a cable car, and paid my ten cents. Immediately, the driver pushed a handle that grabbed the cable and off we went at ten or even twelve miles an hour.

The Chicago Medical School appeared to be deserted, since there were no summer classes. The front door of the school was locked, but at the rear of the building, I found an open door leading to the basement. The room was ice cold. By the light of a single oil lamp I saw a half-dozen naked cadavers on tables. I shrank away from a pale fellow who stared up at the ceiling with open eyes. He looked pretty fresh. It was a storage room for bodies awaiting anatomical dissection. Out of the gloom came a beetle-browed man with a barrel chest and arms that seemed to hang down to his knees. "I am looking for Professor Lange," said I.

He said nothing but beckoned me to follow. We went up two flights of stairs, through a lecture hall, and into a laboratory which housed tables covered with retort flasks and bottles of various chemicals. Without a word, my guide motioned me into a tiny, cluttered office just off the laboratory. An elaborate diploma on the wall written in German proclaimed Johan Frederick Lange as a Doctor of Science from the University of Tübingen. A middle-aged fellow with stern, Teutonic features and short, bristly, grey hair was twirling a flask over a gas flame. There were chemical stains on his shirt.

"Professor Lange?" I asked.

"Yes," said he.

"I am Arthur Conan Doyle, of the University of Edinburgh. I have a question for you."

"Only one? Most people have dozens." He spoke with a strong German accent, but I was encouraged by his pleasant response. I placed the piece of orange crystal on his desk.

"Can you identify this specimen?" I asked.

His eyes widened and he half rose from his chair. "Where did you find this?" he asked. His hand clenched my bit of rock. His entire demeanor changed in an instant. He could barely control his voice. "It is nothing, nothing at all, an insignificant piece of quartz . . . I mean, it looks like it is nothing, may not be significant, but if you want to know for sure, why don't you leave it with me for analysis? Yes, that is it. Leave it here as I will need to analyze it just to be sure of what it is, and of course, I will let you know my findings, though I am sure it is nothing," said he, almost as if I wasn't even there and he was talking to himself.

"No, thank you. I haven't the time. Give it to me," said I, suspecting there was more to his interest in the specimen than he was stating.

He crouched like a cat, and with a cunning look, he moved to drop the crystal into a drawer. I grasped his arm with all my strength, but he still held the specimen in a death grip. "If it is of so little importance, then why don't you give it back?" I asked.

"It may have some value. I will trade a much more beautiful specimen if you are a collector," said he.

"I am not interested," I replied, sure by this time that he was hiding some information about the crystal.

Lange turned to the beetle-browed fellow who was still at the door and nodded. The man's long arms, moving like a professional fighter's, grabbed my neck with a vicious choke hold. I couldn't breathe and would have collapsed if he had not let up the pressure. "Now, Dr. Doyle, I am serious. You must leave this specimen and inform me of its origin. You are trespassing in my laboratory. For all I know you are a common thief. My friend, Gunter, has room for you with the other thieves and derelicts in our basement cooling room."

He was right. No one would recognize another corpse awaiting anatomical dissection. I tensed the muscles in my neck and raised my shoulders a fraction of an inch. It was enough to loosen his grip. I managed to take in enough air to clear my mind and kicked back with the heel of my shoe against Gunter's knee. He grunted and loosened his grip just a fraction. I landed another kick on his knee. He let out a *whoof* of pain and wilted just enough for me to reach down and grasp my ankle stiletto. I turned the blade outward and brought the point along his leg to the groin and then to his mid abdomen. It cut through his clothing but could not have penetrated his skin more than a fraction of an inch. His surprise and pain gave me the advantage. In a moment, I had the knife at Dr. Lange's throat. "Give the crystal to me. I will leave and say nothing about this encounter," said I. He released the orange crystal.

"Now the key to this room." His eyes bulged. I dug the point of the stiletto deeper into his skin until he reached into his pocket and produced a brass key. I closed and locked the door as fast as I was able and made a run for it.

I kept up a fast pace on Prairie Avenue, past fashionable mansions, until I was certain there were no followers. My heart raced, but instead of panicking, I grew even more determined to get to the bottom of this mystery. Mr. Duncan had mentioned a Professor Marcy, so I went into the business center and asked directions to the Northwestern University. The policeman directed me to the Chicago, Milwaukee, and Northwestern station. "Get off in Evanston, walk east to the lake. Can't miss it," said he.

University Hall was a gothic building with a grand tower set in a grove of trees overlooking the wide expanse of Lake Michigan. It was a lovely setting for a university, but not as imposing as the University of Edinburgh. A young assistant led me up flights of stairs to the Natural History Museum on the top floor of the building. There were skeletons of a whale and an elephant at one end of the room. Display cases along the wall held specimens of animals, minerals, and fossils from all over the world. Professor Oliver Marcy was at a long table surrounded by fossils. He was about sixty years old and dressed in a black frock coat. Pince-nez glasses were perched on the bridge of his nose. If nothing else, he looked like a real professor, a description I hoped was accurate given my experience with the sinister Professor Lange.

He was tracing the outline of a fossil fish on drawing paper and did not look up.

"Sir, I am Arthur Conan Doyle of the University of Edinburgh. Can you spare a moment?" I asked. He removed the glasses and squinted my way.

"Edinburgh? Do you know of John Hutton?" he asked.

"He was before my time, sir, but I know of his work with fossils. He proved the world is millions of years old," said I.

"Ah, splendid. Quite right. How may I help you?"

"Can you identify this specimen?" I asked, not wanting to waste a moment. I placed the orange crystal on the table.

The professor adjusted his spectacles and weighed the rock in one hand. "It is lead oxidate molybdenum and very rare. So far as I know the only source is a small mine in Sweden," said he, as he patiently and methodically viewed the specimen, rolling it in his hand and looking at it from all angles.

"Is it important?" I asked.

"Young man, molybdenum is almost priceless. When mixed with iron, it produces a steel alloy of incredible strength that resists high temperatures. The world's industries, especially the munitions makers, would pay millions of dollars for a reliable source of molybdenum."

"But, sir, are there not other, more readily available, alloys?" I asked.

Professor Marcy took a long look out the window at the tranquil blue surface of Lake Michigan. "With sufficient molybdenum, any munitions maker, such as the Krupps in Germany, could manufacture a cannon so strong and so light that it could be transported by a team of horses and fire a half-ton missile across the English Channel. It would also be possible to build light, powerful, steam engines that would increase the speed and safety of railroad engines," said he.

I suddenly felt overwhelmed by fatigue, slumped in a chair, and sighed. "Do you mind telling where you obtained the specimen?" he asked.

I glanced about the room. The wooden floor creaked when I moved in my chair. Dust motes danced in sun beams shining through west facing windows. The door to the corridor was closed; we were alone. I moved closer to the professor, deciding that he seemed trustworthy and knowing I would need to find out more if I was to help bring Borovsky to justice.

"I am not certain, but I believe this sample came from an expedition to Alaska." I unfolded the crumpled paper with the numbers, 62:48 132:12 and placed it on the table. Without a word, he leaped to his feet, went to a shelf, and returned to spread what turned out to be a large map of North America on the table. He used a pair of dividers and a protractor to measure from the lines of latitude and longitude on the map. After a moment, he drew an X.

"This point is not in Alaska but in the Yukon, a part of Northern Canada. It is surrounded by high, cold mountains, rivers, and impenetrable forests. For most of the year, the land is covered with ice and snow. It is one of the most inaccessible places on earth," said he.

"If it is so rare and can only be found in such a remote area, making it nearly unobtainable, then why is this specimen so important?" I asked.

The professor had a faraway look in his eyes, removed his spectacles, and tapped them gently on the table before he spoke. "The fact that molybdenum is rare and nearly inaccessible means that whoever gets his hands on it will attain great wealth and power. Some men — greedy, ruthless men — will do anything, go anywhere on earth, to find what they believe will enable them to acquire such dominance," said he.

I pondered this new information. "But sir, would it not take the power of a government with a great army of men to mine and transport the mineral?"

"No lad, a ruthless man could build a transport system with imported labor, just as a few men managed to build our railroads," the professor answered.

When I rose to leave, he offered a word of caution. "Forget you ever found this. Stick with medicine, young man," said he.

After I left the professor's, my head was swirling with more questions than answers. I momentarily yearned for home, then decided it would be wise to go back to Angus Duncan's, eat a good meal, contemplate all I had discovered, and share the information with Dr. Bell. Sure enough, a huge slab of rare beefsteak and a glass of port, delivered with a warm smile by Mrs. O'Flynn, restored my sense of well-being. After dinner, over cigars and brandy, I relayed the story of my day to Dr. Bell and Angus Duncan.

"I know of Professor Lange. Since he is not a physician, the Chicago Medical School pays him very little. He acted out of greed. The police would pay little attention to your story. Forget that episode," said Angus Duncan.

"Let me see the book about the Yukon and Alaska," said Dr. Bell. I handed him the book and he immediately began perusing its pages. "Arthur, how often have I told you to pay attention to details? Look here, on the title page. Did you see this? You did not mention it. Nikolai Borovsky was not only a member of the expedition, but also a consultant to the Alaska Mill and Mining Company. That must be American." said Dr. Bell. Despite my now being a doctor, I felt the same sense of inadequacy that I had often experienced while I was Bell's clerk so many years ago. The information was in fine print, but why had I not noticed it before?

"Sir, in the day's chaos, I merely skimmed through the book," said I, hoping that would serve as a reasonable excuse for missing such an important detail.

"Oh, yes, lad. To be sure," he responded, almost absentmindedly, while keeping his eyes focused on the book. "Aha, look … page forty-five, at the far eastern edge of the map here, written in small numbers, 62:48 132:12, marking a small peak, 'Catherine's Dome.'

"Ah, that is the same latitude and longitude on the specimen" I said. Mr. Duncan put down his glass and examined the page over Dr. Bell's shoulder.

"Catherine became empress of Russia in 1773. The location of the dome on this map that is named for her suggests the Russians explored Western Canada. When Russia sold Alaska to the United States in 1867, the eastern border was in dispute. The United States could claim a good bit of Western Canada," said Duncan.

"In that case, the United States would have the molybdenum," said I. Angus Duncan, the wily Scot, paused to re-light his cigar.

"It is more likely that Russia would claim the area beyond the boundary and even attempt to buy back all of Alaska in order to have sole access to the untapped resources like molybdena. America is in a depression, so the country needs money. The new president, 'Elegant Arthur,' must support his grand lifestyle," said Duncan.

"But wouldn't the United States back England's claim to the area?" asked Dr. Bell.

"The Americans still hate the British because of the *Alabama* affair," said Duncan.

"What is that?" I asked.

"The British built the *Alabama* for the Confederates. She was a heavily armed cruiser that sunk sixty-five Union merchant ships. The United States is still demanding reparations."

"What does Nikolai Borovsky have to do with this?" I asked.

"He is very likely out of favor with the Russian government and is attempting to sell information to the Americans. The Russians are building a trans-continental railroad that will reach the Pacific Ocean within a year. The Russians and Americans could control the entire North Pacific Ocean and, with very little force, take over Western Canada. The British are stretched thin all over the world, from India to Egypt, and the Trans-Canada Railroad is bogged down. It would be easy for the Americans to take over British Columbia," said Mr. Duncan. Dr. Bell stretched his long legs and clasped his hands over his chest.

"Borovsky is up to no good. Perhaps he hopes to gain by playing off the great powers against each other. What else is in his specimen case, and where is it now? The American and Penelope snatched the case. It is quite likely Borovsky is seeking it." said Dr. Bell.

"If that is so, Penelope may be in danger," said I.

13 June 1883

As soon as Angus Duncan let us off at the Union Station so we could get on our way to San Francisco, he hailed a uniformed Negro porter. “George, take this luggage to these gentlemen’s sleeping car, number four,” he said.

Our quarters were a veritable hotel on wheels. The interior was of shiny, varnished, walnut panels, and we had two berths that were, during the day, comfortable seats. George, the porter, bustled about, putting away our luggage on convenient racks, dusting the seats to remove every speck of dust. Dr. Bell gave him a five dollar bill.

“George, how did Mr. Duncan know your name? Are you a friend of his?” asked Dr. Bell. The porter flashed a mouthful of white teeth.

“No suh. My name is Willy, but all us porters are called ‘George’ after Mr. George Pullman who makes these here fine sleeping cars.”

Within an hour, we had left Chicago and were speeding across western Illinois past small farms, fields of knee-high corn, cows, and pigs. It seemed like every farmer out tending his fields waved at the train. I always waved back. Along towards dusk, we crossed a fine, new bridge over the Mississippi River at Davenport and were in Iowa. After our sumptuous dinner, I listened for a while to the rhythmic *clickety-clack* of the wheels, which lulled me into a renewing sleep. I woke to the mournful sound of the train’s whistle, which hooted each time we passed one of the many small towns along the way.

14 June 1883

We crossed the Missouri river at Council Bluffs, where the west really starts, but we made a dogleg to Omaha where the trains stopped long enough for us to get out and stretch our legs. There was a fine new station and a bustling town, but there was no time to explore.

I had planned to study for the doctorate examination during our trip, but I was glued to the window, just watching the plains roll by. After we passed the Mississippi bluffs, the land was flat and the sky so big you could see for miles and miles. At first, there were fields of green wheat with windmills, farm houses, and men and boys hard at work. After a while, there was just grass so high that a man on horseback could scarcely see over the top. We stopped at little towns, like Elkhorn, that weren't much more than a half-dozen saloons alongside a dusty street, a bank, a store, and, at the end of the street, maybe a courthouse. I kept on the lookout for buffalo and wild Indians, but there weren't any, not a one. After a while, the landscape changed again. Amazing! There were no trees, except a few stragglers along a creek bed, the grass grew shorter, and the land was mostly sand and dust.

Late in the day, we stopped for a whole twenty minutes at a little town, Grand Island, where a sorry band of Indians with sway-backed horses met the train. The young ones put on a little show and the passengers threw nickels and dimes to them. Dr. Bell gave them two silver dollars. There were a couple of old fellows with handsome, brown, creased faces and feathers in their hair. Because of their dress and the way they stood apart, I supposed they were chiefs. They kept off to the side and seemed to scowl at us whites. I was sorely disappointed. Where were the stalwart Redskins I had dreamed about as a boy? For a while, I had planned to write a novel about a great battle with bows and arrows pitted against rifles, but the Indians would win and capture a fair maiden. A hero, like Sir Walter Scott's Ivanhoe, would go to her rescue.

We followed the wide, muddy Platte River, and off to the north, there were rolling sand hills and a lot of dust that turned the sky grey. One time, a couple of cowboys raced alongside the train on their horses. They waved and fired pistols, but they couldn't keep up with the iron horse. The big thrill of the day was seeing a herd of antelope, leastwise that is what Willy, our porter, called them. They are fine animals — long-legged, with curling horns and a patch of white on their chest. I never saw an animal run so fast. I watched all that landscape slide by until the moon went down.

15 June 1883

It was a long way across the state of Nebraska before, in the far distance, we could see snaggle-toothed, snow-covered mountains. Folks said they were fifty miles away, but they sure looked close. The Wyoming territory had the same grass but was more barren and dry; even the people looked sort of dried out. We came to Cheyenne about the middle of the day. The two trains ahead of us were stopped on the tracks. Willy brought the bad news. A landslide had destroyed the west end of the Dale Creek Bridge and our train would be stopped for at least two weeks. Dr. Bell hardly ever lost his composure, but he was sorely disgruntled.

"I am scheduled to give lectures and a demonstration in San Francisco ten days from now," said he.

"Mebbe you can take the Denver and Rio Grande through the mountains to Salt Lake City. It's a run-down little train that sometimes don't run on account of the owners are broke, but it's as good a chance as any fo' getting' there," said Willy. That sounded promising, but the train for Denver wouldn't leave until late in the afternoon. Our train wasn't even up to the depot, so Willy dumped our luggage out on a dusty road beside the tracks.

"You can get something to eat and rest at the Cheyenne Club" said he, pointing the way.

Every horse and wagon in town was busy hauling passengers and their baggage to rooming houses or hotels. Dr. Bell carried the instrument case, and I picked up my bag and tossed his trunk on my shoulder. It was hard going until an old fellow came by in one of those contraptions called a buckboard. It was nothing but a wooden box on four wheels hitched to a pair of horses.

"Hey, you boys need a lift?"

"Yes sir," said I. We climbed aboard.

"You kin call me Bearskin Charlie," said the driver, a runty man with tobacco-stained whiskers down to his belt. He had a double-barreled shotgun across his lap. The wagon didn't have springs or cushions and the horses mainly switched their tails against the flies, but it beat walking. We plodded for a mile or so over a street thick with horse manure and dust. Once, we had to stop for nearly a half-hour while cowboys drove a herd of cows down the middle of the street. Every man in town carried a big Colt revolver in a holster and a Winchester by his saddle. The driver, Bearskin Charlie, spit a stream of tobacco juice and hit a fly.

"You fellows will like the club. Got the purtiest girls in the territory and any kind of gamblin' you want. Food ain't bad neither," he said.

Dr Bell gave him a silver dollar. "Wait for us and there will be another," said he.

The Cheyenne Club was about the grandest building west of Chicago. The main room on the first floor had plush carpets, gas lights, and comfortable easy chairs. Two gilt staircases led to the private rooms upstairs. I guess that's where the 'purty girls' stayed. Dinner was listed for seventy-five cents. I ordered antelope steak, mashed potatoes, beans, and cherry pie with coffee. The antelope was stringy and tough as an old cow. The coffee was bitter and still had egg shells and grounds. We were about finished with the meal when a waiter came and poured a tumbler full of clear liquid for the man at the next table. The fellow took one swallow, commenced to cough, then his legs kicked out and his eyes rolled back. I went to his aid immediately, thinking he was having a fit. I clapped him on the back and his eyes opened.

"Are you alright?" I asked.

"Jest finer than a damn fiddle. That there moonshine will make a prairie dog spit at a mountain lion," said he.

After dinner, Dr. Bell retired to the reading room with his pipe and a pile of newspapers while I went upstairs to look around. There was a lot of giggling and carrying on behind closed doors, but no girls were in sight. A fellow with a big pistol on his belt looked me over outside a closed door.

"I wouldn' go in there if I was you," said he.

"Why not?" I asked.

"A poker game's been goin' on all day. Dangerous Dan McGrew is playing a woman. Don't that jes' beat all?" he answered. I went in anyway, carrying my walking stick like a fine English gentleman. The room was maybe sixty or seventy feet long and about as wide, with a long bar down one wall and a little stage.

The windows were covered with black curtains, and the room was lit with gas lights. In spite of a big crowd of tough-looking men and a few painted ladies, it was quiet as a graveyard. Over in one corner, a woman in a long, red dress was sitting alongside of an upright piano. The crowd was around a table in the middle of the room. I squeezed close enough to see a man in a black frock coat with a black hat shuffling cards. His face was like a piece of granite, and he had the meanest blue eyes I ever saw. I figured he was Dangerous Dan. The woman's back was to me, but when I pushed my way around, I saw she was Penelope, known in polite society as Lady Walshingham. I caught my breath. Her hair was done up in a bun, like a school teacher, but instead of her fancy gowns, she wore a satiny, purple shirt with long sleeves tucked into a pair of men's pants. There was a big pile of gold eagle coins, silver dollars, and greenbacks in the middle of the table. I wanted to call out to her, but out of curiosity, and with good sense, I stayed quiet and watched the play. Dangerous Dan shuffled and dealt the cards. Penelope threw down a card and picked another, then showed her hand. Penelope had three aces. She reached for the pile in the middle of the table, but Dangerous Dan pulled a two-shot derringer.

"You pulled that last ace out of your sleeve," he said. The crowd howled.

"I knowed it! I knowed for sure, that woman cheats!" one young cowboy yelled. I didn't even remember if it was loaded but I poked my walking stick against Dangerous Dan's head.

"Put down that pistol or I'll blow your head off," said I. My hand trembled worse than if I held a scalpel to a sick patient. The room went quiet. Dangerous Dan held that little pistol on Penelope and never batted an eye. Did he know I was bluffing? All of a sudden, the lady in red brought her hands down on the keys and beat out a lively tune on the piano. The whole place calmed down. She looked back over her shoulder and smiled at Dangerous Dan. The scowl never left his face and his jaw clenched until I thought he would crack a tooth; after a whole minute, he nodded his head just a little and lowered the gun. I shoved the pile of money to McGrew, grabbed Penelope, and we charged out of that place like two scared rabbits.

I called to Dr. Bell when we passed the reading room and picked up our luggage.

"Do you have a bag?" I asked Penelope.

"Not a thing. Just what's on me. I'm cleaned out," she said.

I had to give Bearskin Charlie a whack to wake him up. We put Penelope on the bottom of the wagon and covered her with feed sacks.

"Head for the Denver station," said Dr. Bell.

It was a dinky little train, on account of the rails were only three feet apart and it didn't go near fast enough to suit me. I expected Dan McGrew and a band of armed men would hold up the train any minute. As soon as we settled down, Penelope spit like a cat.

"He ran away on the last train to San Francisco and left me with nothing," she said.

"Who left?" I asked.

"Why that damn Jack Dawson, that's who," said Penelope.

"What happened to the red leather case?"

"Took the case and all the money. I had to sell my clothes and jewelry to get a stake. Now it is all gone. Damn that Dan McGrew."

****

Editor's note: Arthur Conan Doyle met and indeed sought out prominent literary figures during his lifetime. This episode with Dangerous Dan McGrew may be the only time he encountered a fellow who would become a literary character rather than an author. Dangerous Dan McGrew met his death in the Malamute Saloon in the Yukon Territory during the Alaskan Gold Rush. The Lady in Red (known as 'Lou') was there, but that time, she could not protect her lover from a 'man in a buckskin shirt that was caked with dirt.' In the poem, "The Shooting of Dan McGrew," (from *Songs of a Sourdough*, Barse &Co. New York, N.Y. Newark N.J. 1916) Robert W. Service, the English Poet, described the murder scene.

"But I want to state, and my words are straight, and I'll bet my poke they're true,
That one of you is a hound of hell . . . and that one is Dan McGrew."

Then I ducked my head, and the lights went out, and two guns blazed in the dark;
And a woman screamed, and the lights went up, and two men lay stiff and stark.

Pitched on his head, and pumped full of lead, was Dangerous Dan McGrew,
While the man from the creeks lay clutched to the breast of the lady that's known as Lou.

16 June 1883

We arrived in Denver covered with soot, sweat, and grime. Straw and oats were stuck in Penelope's hair, and her face was streaked with dirt. Despite our meager appearance and the need to lose no time, we were happy to be in Denver, the only city with real amenities between San Francisco and Chicago. On the advice of a depot lounger, we hailed a one-horse cab and set out down the street for the Windsor Hotel. It did our hearts good to see the Union Jack flying from one turret and the flag of Windsor Castle on another. An English syndicate owned the hotel; we expected a royal welcome. The cab driver hauled our baggage to the front entrance beneath an elegant, iron porte-cochère that was flanked by two electric lampposts. Instead of a royal welcome, however, a porter in a swell gold-braided uniform and a top hat looked at our disheveled appearance and refused us entrance. He was totally without grace until Penelope turned on her upper-class English charm.

"My dear man, please announce my arrival to your manager. I am Lady Penelope Walshingham," said she in her best plummy English voice. The manager rushed out and swept Penelope right up to the lobby. We were only halfway up the front staircase when a body tumbled past our startled eyes and crashed onto the first landing. I immediately ran to the man and put my finger to his carotid artery, but he was already dead with a broken neck. Two porters removed the body with speed and nonchalance as if a dead body tumbling down a staircase was an everyday occurrence. Dr. Bell demanded an explanation.

"It is those miners. They go up to the cattlemen's room and bet all the gold they found after a year's work. When they lose, the damn fools go crazy with rotgut hooch and jump from the fifth floor to end it all," the porter explained.

Penelope bowled over the manager who, after a lot of bowing and scraping, ensconced her in a suite with a gold-plated bath tub. We took a room that cost two dollars and fifty cents. It was pure luxury, but nothing compared with the Roman bath area that was connected to the hotel through a tunnel. I hustled to the baths and sunk down in hot artesian water that bubbled up from way underground.

17 June 1883

Dr. Bell insisted we leave at the crack of dawn. The Denver, South Park and Pacific train was nothing more than a dinky steam engine, one wooden passenger car, a baggage car, two box cars, and one car for cattle. We flung Dr. Bell's trunk and my portmanteau into the baggage car and climbed aboard. Penelope sat next to Dr. Bell, since he was the best dressed and most respectable looking man on the train. I took the only seat left, next to a grizzled miner who smelled of old sweat and booze. "This shore beats packin' in grub on mules," he said. The old boy punched me in the chest and slapped his leg. "This here train goes ta durned near every town in the state of Colorado. We might even make it to Leadville, if'n we don't run off the tracks," he said.

I settled down to watch the valley of the South Platte River roll by while we chugged along a bubbly little stream. "That there is Buffalo Creek. Found a nugget there once," said my companion. Dr. Bell unfolded a week-old newspaper, *The San Francisco Morning Call.*

"Well, it says here, that Leland Stanford is donating six Gatling guns to the Bear State Militia," said he. I came out of my sleepy reverie with a jolt.

"We heard that name before," said I.

"That damn Jack Dawson said he was going to make a fortune with Stanford," said Penelope. I wondered why a millionaire was interested in the most lethal weapon known to man but let it go when I remembered that Alan Pinkerton had warned me not to mention the man's name.

We stopped at a little town named Como to fill the boiler with water and, in Garo, all the passengers went into a dirty saloon for lunch. All they had was beef stew, but the hunks of meat could just as well have been rhinoceros it was so tough. We kept going up and up and still higher as we got into the mountains. I thought we had great mountains in Scotland, but these were the highest, most rugged, and beautiful mountains in all the world. My seatmate got off at a little cluster of shacks, called Climax, and we pulled into Leadville in the late afternoon.

Leadville is a thriving little city with no less than five churches and six banks. We made for the Clarendon Hotel. Next door there was a fine brick building, the Grand Tabor Opera House. Emblazoned across the front of the building was a notice for an address on 'Art Decoration by Oscar Wilde.' I had heard the name and recalled having read one of his poems. Dr. Bell was all for meeting him since Wilde's father was a notable eye and ear surgeon.

The program started at seven o'clock in the evening; the place was packed with unruly minors and cowboys who hooted when Wilde appeared on the stage. After a coughing fit that seemed to last minutes, a tall, skinny fellow with a silver badge hollered at the men to behave themselves or he would shoot the first one who let out a squeal. The man next to me nudged my elbow. "That there is Doc Holliday. He used ta' be a darn good dentist — coulda' pulled a tooth from a wild buffalo if he had to. Then he done fell ill with the tuberculosis, came out west here, and became more of a gunslingin' gamblin' man. Folks claim he's the fastest gun in the west. Word has it he and the Earp brothers won a gunfight in Arizona. Place called the O.K. Corral. Thirty shots in thirty seconds. Fancy that! One of the bloodiest street fights in our country's history and that man you see 'afore you walked away with just a wound. The men on the other side weren't so lucky, I can tell you that. That man got more lives in him than a damn cat," he said.

Wilde had long, black hair and was pale of face. He wore a black coat, knee pants and silk stockings. He got everyone's attention from the moment he spoke the first words. "A man can be happy with a woman as long as he does not love her," he said. There were also loud guffaws when he said that we are all in the gutter. When he shared his philosophy of aestheticism, though, most of the crowd seemed to fall asleep.

Penelope, ever on the lookout for a savior, figured he was rich and was excited about meeting him. At the end of the lecture, Dr. Bell went up to the stage and invited Mr. Wilde to the bar in the hotel for a drink. Penelope gave him the eye and twitched her hips, but Wilde didn't pay her any attention. I wasn't sure if I felt bad for the poor woman or glad that she was being treated the way she had oft-times behaved towards me. We were talking about writing, poetry, and the like when he looked up at a sign above the bar, ***'Don't shoot the piano player. He is doing the best he can.'*** "That is the best art criticism you will ever see," Wilde said.

Though Dr. Bell went off to bed, I found Wilde easy to talk with, and pretty soon, we found a common interest in sport, especially boxing. The patrons of the Clarendon Hotel bar were a quiet bunch, but near midnight, three miners came through the swinging doors. They were all muscle and gristle and looking for trouble. Folks backed up against the walls, leaving a clear space in front of the bar.

"There's them dam furiners." The speaker swayed in his boots and pointed at us with his fist.

"That one, there, the pretty boy with hair like a girl. Fellows, let's give him a haircut," said the brutish miner. Oscar Wilde leaned with his back to the bar, propped on his elbows. I stepped aside while Penelope ducked away.

"Let's give 'em a good thrashing," said the second man. The miner who came at Wilde had an ear that looked as if it had been beaten by a hammer and a broken nose, likely from many a battle. I had a sinking feeling that we might not survive a fight. Wilde stood his ground until the big fighter came at him with flailing arms, then stepped aside and landed a solid punch on the fellow's nose. The miner backed up a couple of steps, with blood pouring down his face. He let out a tremendous roar, put down his head, and held his enormous clenched fists with arms together out in front of his body. He started out at a run, but I managed to get my foot between his ankles. He tripped forward, and Wilde landed an upper cut on his chin. I couldn't keep track of all that happened next, but there was a general melee. The three miners were throwing wild punches while Wilde and I held them off, mainly by keeping out of their way and occasionally landing a well-aimed blow. Thankfully, three deputies with tin badges came through the swinging doors. One fired a deafening pistol shot and ended the brawl. The law officers took the three bloodied miners off to spend a night in jail. When it was all over, Penelope counted a wad of greenbacks on the bar.

"I bet on you boys, had five to one odds," said she.

18 June 1883

The train for Salida, our next scheduled stop, was waiting for a shipment of silver ore. We couldn't leave until almost noon. It started out as a fine afternoon. We traveled down a valley next to the Arkansas River with mountain peaks up to fourteen thousand feet on either side. When we pulled in to Buena Vista, a collection of shacks and saloons along one street, the train stopped and the engineer banked the boiler fire. "When do we get on to Salida?" I asked.

"Next train to Salida leaves on Monday," said the conductor.

"But we bought tickets for Salida leaving today," said I.

"You kin sure enough use yer tickets next Monday when we got a load of cargo," he replied. We were in a fine fix. Dr. Bell was anxious to get on to San Francisco.

We were in the middle of the dusty street, with our baggage, hoping for a stagecoach or some means of conveyance, when two young fellows came busting out of a place called The Palace Manor. The boys stumbled and landed in the dirt as if they had been kicked in the backside. It was peculiar because both had on big hats, but their pants were down around their knees, as if they had left in a big hurry. A belligerent, cross–eyed woman followed the pair out the door and threw two belts with holstered pistols and two sets of leather chaps into the street.

"You good-fer-nothing, cheap, scoundrels! Next time you pay, ya' hear?!" said she.

"Old cock-eyed Liz sure gets mean," one boy said. He looked up at Penelope and a big smile crossed his face. "Why you are the purtiest woman I ever did see," said he.

Penelope blushed and pushed a lock of hair back from her eyes. "Why, thank you! That is the nicest thing a man ever said to me." The first fellow had a boyish grin on his handsome face. He had a square jaw and even, white teeth. Both boys had fuzz on their upper lip as if they were trying to grow a mustache. They couldn't have been more than sixteen or seventeen years old. The boys got up out of the dirt, pulled up their pants, and buckled up their belts with leather holsters that held ancient revolvers.

The first young fellow tipped his hat to Penelope, "I'm Butch. This here is Sundance. Happy to be of service," said he. "We are looking for a means of transportation to Salida," said Penelope. "Shucks, if you don't mind ridin' horseback, we kin get you there, easy as pie," said Butch.

"How much?" asked Dr. Bell.

"Let's say ten dollars apiece, and we will go along and guide," said Butch.

The boys took off down the street, turned a corner and, within half an hour, returned riding nice-looking horses and leading four more. "We figured you needed an extra horse to carry that there trunk and bag," said Butch. Dr. Bell gave them forty dollars, and the two of them lashed our baggage on top of a sway-backed mare. Sundance held his hands together for Penelope to mount her horse, but instead, she leaped into the saddle as if she had been born to ride. The boys were clearly impressed. Dr. Bell did a credible job of stepping into the stirrup and swung his leg over the saddle. My horse was a big roan gelding named Tom that sidestepped and shook his head when I put a foot in the stirrup. "Scratch his ear and talk to him," said Butch. I gingerly got close enough and rubbed his forehead. Tom looked at me with huge eyes and twitched his tail. I had only been on a horse twice before, during our last trip to America, and I had lost the knack of climbing aboard. Sundance had to give me an extra push before I got a leg over that big, leather saddle.

We set off on a road that was no more than a couple of dirt tracks. After we left the flat valley, the trail turned steep and rocky. Butch and Sundance seemed to be in a hurry and kept us going at a fast trot. When the horse bounced up and down, the saddle slapped my backside until I was sore and bruised. We followed a tumbling stream that was dimpled with trout coming to the surface to eat insects. I saw a little herd of deer and a huge elk higher up the mountain to our left. Butch and Sundance kept looking back over their shoulders, as if watching for followers, and kept up a fast pace. We had gone about ten miles, or maybe a little more, when I thought I heard something behind us, peered back, and saw a growing cloud of dust. Within a few minutes, black dots came out of the dust cloud, and pretty soon, it became clear a bunch of men on horses were following us and they were moving at a good clip.

"Oh, Oh. Time we skedaddled out of here!" Butch yelled. The two boys splashed across a creek and galloped into a patch of pine trees. Within a minute, they were out of sight. Dr. Bell, Penelope, and I looked at each other, astounded. In less than two minutes, three men with drawn pistols had us surrounded. Three others fired their guns and went off after Butch and Sundance. Their leader had a scar that went from his forehead, across an empty eye socket, and on down his cheek. He wore leather chaps, big spurs, and a battered felt hat. All three were covered with red dust, and their horses were winded.

"Damn horse thieves! We oughta string you up right now!" he yelled. His two companions uncoiled ropes from their saddles and shook out a big loop. I was too scared to talk, but Penelope blushed crimson, wiggled in her saddle, and looked at the men with puppy dog eyes.

"Gentlemen, I think there has been a misunderstanding. We did not steal anything from anybody. When our train meant for Salida was postponed, we rented these horses for ten dollars apiece from those two boys who rode off into the woods," said she. The leader took off his hat, scratched his bald head, and took a long look at the three of us. Dr. Bell was wearing his deerstalker hat to keep the sun out of his eyes and a light brown suit with a cravat and waistcoat. We were dressed for train travel and had clearly never expected to go on horseback.

"Are you damn Yankees?"

"I am English and they are Scots," said Penelope. The fellow with the scarred face relaxed a bit.

"Get down off my horses," said the man. We all slid off the horses and stood there, uncertain what to do next.

"Paw, kin we shoot em?" asked one of the riders.

"Don't go wastin' a bullet, now. It's them two boys what stole our horses. They's the ones to shoot." The youngest of the group untied our baggage and flung Dr. Bell's trunk down in the dirt. They rode off, leading the horses across the creek and into the woods, leaving us in the middle of a dirt road that was hardly more than a path.

The sun had already disappeared behind the mountains and a chill wind came down the valley. Penelope's teeth were chattering and I shivered with cold. We picked up our belongings. Dr. Bell led the way to a clump of trees by the stream where we were out of the wind. He gave Penelope his heavy cloak, and I put on another jacket. It was still cold. I had the presence of mind to collect dry wood to start a fire. We huddled together, not saying anything. Penelope went to sleep leaning against my shoulder. An animal made a mournful howl back in the woods and Penelope snuggled closer. I had dreamed about such a moment when she would lean on me for comfort, and it should have been romantic, but I could not stop shivering.

19 June 1883

I must have dozed off, because when I opened my eyes, it was daylight. The fire was dead, and we hadn't had a single morsel to eat since leaving Leadville. My stomach growled. Dr. Bell lit up his pipe and got the fire going. We were about ready to set off walking along the stream when from around a corner came a barefoot boy leading a plodding, grey horse. He wore only a leather vest and a breechclout. He also had a leather case slung over his shoulder, which held a bow and arrows. A skinny, old man sat on the horse with his feet dangling down. There was no saddle or stirrups, only a wool blanket, but he sat on the horse straight as a ramrod. The old man wore leather breeches and a patched, cotton shirt. There was a leather circlet with a feather around his long hair. He also had a necklace of polished, curved teeth around his neck. The boy gave us a surprised glance, but the old man remained stiff and upright. He looked straight ahead. I limped up to the trail and held up a hand. The old fellow paid no attention, but the boy stopped and stared at me. I pointed down the trail.

"Is that the way to Salida?" I asked. The boy pulled the rope and started the horse. "Yes," said he.

"Are you an Indian?" I asked.

"I am Ta Pu Chet of the Tabaguache. The white people say we are Mountain Utes," said the boy.

"Who is he?" I asked.

"Taiwai, my grandfather, a great medicine man."

"Where are you going?" I asked. The boy pursed his lips and did not answer for a long time. "Are you going to Leadville?" The boy pointed to the highest snow covered peak.

"I am taking grandfather to the sacred mountain. The bear will tell him how to find the hole in the sky so he can see the sun and the moon and the stars. Then Grandfather will go off on his own to die," said the boy.

Dr. Bell had been watching the old man thoughtfully while smoking his great calabash pipe. Its smoke drifted over the trail. "The old man has cataracts and is blind," said Dr. Bell. I moved closer. Sure enough, the old man's eyes were milky white and completely opaque. Without saying a word, Dr. Bell slowly reached up and gently touched the old man's hand. The man still sat straight, but opened his fingers, whereupon Dr. Bell lightly placed his great calabash pipe into the medicine man's palm. "Please accept this pipe and tobacco," he said. The old man sat still for a moment, then moved his lips, as if in prayer, while raising the pipe to his left side, front, right side and up towards the sky. He brought the pipe to his mouth, clenched the stem between his teeth, and took in a lung full of smoke, which he slowly blew out in a great, round cloud.

"I am also a medicine man. Have your grandfather come down from the horse," said Dr. Bell. The boy spoke softly to the old man and then helped him down off the horse. He could hardly stand. We helped him to sit on a rock where Dr. Bell peered into his eyes before reaching for his instrument case. He examined the old man's eyes with a hand lens.

"The cataracts are mature. I can easily remove them and he will see," said Dr. Bell. The boy and the old man chattered back and forth in their language.

"He says the white man's tobacco is very good. If the medicine for eyes is as strong, he will take the medicine," said the boy.

"Sir, you can't operate here," said I.

"Arthur, surgeons have operated on cataracts in the open air ever since the Hindu's invented the operation. Now, fetch some water from the stream and make up the carbolic," said he. I watched, fascinated, as Dr. Bell cleaned his hands and put a sharp, curved scalpel with a wooden handle, a slender forceps, and a dainty pair of iris scissors on a clean metal tray. The old man happily puffed on the calabash, stopping only while Dr. Bell put belladonna drops in his eyes and then two percent cocaine.

"Tell him he must stay still while I do this," said Dr. Bell. The boy said a few words to the old man. I held the leather circlet about his head, but the boy motioned me away.

"Do not touch his head. He will remain still," said the boy. Dr. Bell sat on a rock beside his patient and, with one hand, held his lids apart. With his other hand, he made a small incision in the sclera and then inserted the small scissors into the globe of the eye.

When he was satisfied, he plucked out the white lens with his forceps. Instantly, he closed the lids.

“Arthur, apply a tight bandage.” He shifted position to the left eye and repeated the operation. I had bandaged each eye as tightly as possible.

“He must lie absolutely still until tomorrow,” Dr. Bell said. The old Indian was light as a feather when we carried him to the clump of trees by the stream and put him down on the saddle blanket.

“Sir, do you plan to stay here another day? Shouldn’t we be on our way?” I asked.

“Tut, tut, my boy. We must not abandon our patient, even if we are late,” said Dr. Bell.

There wasn’t much to do but keep the fire going and drink water directly from the stream. After saying a few words to his grandfather, the boy set off up the mountain with his bow and arrows. He returned in late afternoon with the skinned carcass of a small deer slung over his shoulder. I never tasted anything as delicious as that venison roasted over an open fire. The boy carefully cooked slices of deer heart over the fire and fed them to the old man. That night, we slept well under the stars.

20 June 1883

We woke with the sun, and Dr. Bell removed the medicine man's bandages. The old man blinked his eyes, looked into the face of the boy, and then turned his eyes to the high snow-covered peak. Dr. Bell selected a small convex lens from his case.

"Tell him to look through the glass," said Dr. Bell. The old man's dark face creased with a huge smile. He spoke rapidly to the boy.

"He says you have made great medicine. He can see an eagle flying." It was necessary to bind the old man's eyes again, but he was clearly pleased.

We finished the last of the roast venison and helped the old man up on the horse. Then, we tied the trunk and my bag on behind and set off together down the trail to Salida. At first, it was steep and rocky, but after a few miles, we came upon a broad, flat valley. After a while, we passed fields of barley and oats where men plowed. Just at the outskirts of town, the boy stopped.

"We turn here," said he.

"He must keep the bandages on his eyes for two weeks," said Dr. Bell.

The old man untied the leather thong around his neck and gave Dr. Bell a polished tooth. "Grandfather is grateful for your medicine and wants you to have this. He says it is a tooth from a great bear. It will give you good luck," said the boy.

We said our goodbyes and got a ride from a farmer in an empty hay wagon, who took us to the Monte Cristo Hotel, a fine new establishment on First Street in Salida. It was the middle of the afternoon, but we descended on the dining room like a flock of hungry wolves. The only food left was a sandwich they called the Monte Cristo, which had layers of turkey, swiss cheese, and ham, all smothered with currant jelly and fried in butter. I never tasted anything so good. The bad news is that the next train west doesn't leave until noon on the twenty-second.

22-23 June 1883

There was no hurrying the Denver and Rio Grande Western Railroad. We crept along the sides of mountains on a track that was only three feet wide, stopped for water and coal at dinky little towns, and stayed overnight in Gunnison, a dusty mining town. Today, we went through the scariest part of the trip yet, the gorge in Black Canyon. We were surrounded by sheer rock walls — which were thousands of feet high and seemed to stretch to the sky — and a fierce river roaring below the narrow, rickety track. Luckily, we got to Cimarron without falling off the track and just in time to catch a train to Salt Lake City. More and more, it appears that we will be late for Dr. Bell's San Francisco lecture at four o'clock on the afternoon of the twenty-fifth of June.

24 June 1883

We had a piece of good luck today because a brand new line of the Denver and Rio Grande and Western Railroad went straight through to Ogden, Utah. We made good time over the flat, desert land and, with only one short stop, went straight through to Salt Lake City. We pulled into the depot at about noon and ran to the Central Pacific ticket office.

There was a near riot as shoving men and women attempted to buy tickets, but they were turned away. My attention was drawn to a fellow wearing a black sack coat, buttoned to the neck, and stovepipe pants. He stood quietly, and I would not have picked him out of the crowd until he turned his head and I saw a glint of steel in the brim of his derby hat. I became instantly suspicious, as an English thug could slice an opponent to ribbons with only his derby for a weapon. I clutched Dr. Bell.

"Hold back. That fellow looks like trouble," said I.

Dr. Bell leaned to Penelope, "Do you recognize that man?"

"No," said Penelope.

He was not a large man, but I began to imagine scenarios in which he attacked us, even though I knew I could handle him if I could dodge the slicing edge of his hat. I didn't think that Manfredi's killer would have been able to follow me, but I had still been anxious since his murder. The heavy barrel of my walking stick gun would give me an advantage if I could club him before he closed in. I had worked myself into such a frenzy that I broke into a cold sweat as we approached the ticket window.

A fat woman with a half-dozen kids knocked me out of the way with her umbrella. "We been waitin' for a train near t'all day. Don't push yourself ahead of the line." I fell back, almost into the arms of the man in the derby hat. Expecting trouble, I half-cocked my arm back to get in the first blow when he coolly held out a picture of Dr. Bell.

"Claudius Pew, at your service. I am a Pinkerton railroad detective. We've been looking for you all up and down the line," said he.

"Are you arresting us?" I asked.

“No sir. I got orders to escort you on a special train all the way to San Francisco,” said he. I breathed a sigh of relief.

“Why?” Dr. Bell asked.

“They never told me, but I heard they want you for a special consultation on a sick chink. If he dies, they say Chinatown will riot and burn the city,” said he. With a sense of relief at having averted potential danger — and the opportunity to be escorted to the west without further trouble — we climbed into a grand sleeper coach, the only car connected to an engine that already had steam. I have never seen a train go so fast. We swayed around curves and barely slowed for hills. There was no dining car, but the conductor had a small stove to heat coffee and tea, and he had laid in enough cold chicken, roast beef, bread, and butter to last the trip.

25 June 1883

We came out of the hills to Oakland and reached the Union Pacific Dock by mid-morning. The Pinkerton man whisked us onto a ferry, and we crossed the bay to the San Francisco side.

"There is no time to lose. I have telegraphed ahead for a carriage and the proper officials," said Claudius Pew. The huge bay was enveloped in a cold fog, but in clear areas we could see Chinese fishing boats, mail steamers from across the Pacific, a frigate flying the Russian flag, and a variety of smaller craft. The clocks on top of the ferry terminal chimed noon when we exited the building to a crowd of horse-drawn cabs, produce wagons, and streetcars. The delegation of city officials waiting for us was not a welcoming committee from the American Society of Surgery as I had thought. Instead, the uniformed chief of police and the city mayor stood to one side, glowering with anger and impatiently shifting from one foot to another. The fellow who offered his hand was dressed in a cutaway morning coat with a very large, diamond stickpin in his collar.

"Professor Bell, I presume. Welcome to our city. I am R. Beverly Cole, dean of the medical school and the city health officer. We have an unfortunate situation with an injured Chinaman named Chin Ten Sing. His physician refused our recommendation to perform trephination when he learned of your visit, and he insisted on waiting for you. The fellow believes in that damn Listerism," said Dr. Cole. Dr. Bell bristled, his features hardened.

"I was invited here to lecture on the antiseptic method and did not expect to have the method criticized," said Dr. Bell. I drew my jacket tighter against the cold fog, and out of the corner of my eye saw a slender, young man with oriental features standing well away from the group.

"See for yourself. The patient's physician is also a chink." said Dr. Cole.

"Gentlemen, this is not a time to quibble over medical matters. If the man dies, the chinks will riot and burn the city. Sir, we will appreciate anything you can do to help," said the mayor.

"In that case, I will speak with the man. Will you kindly take Lady Penelope Walshingham and our baggage to the Palace Hotel?" asked Dr. Bell. Penelope flashed her usual come hither smile. Dr. Cole raised his hand, bowed, and whisked her into his elegant carriage. I had the presence of mind to take up Dr. Bell's instrument case before we went to the waiting Chinaman. He bowed until the topknot of his cap almost touched the ground. Despite the cold, he wore a dark blue, silk blouse and pajama-like trousers. His hair hung halfway down his back in a single braid.

"Esteemed Dr. Bell, I am Lam Qua, physician to Chin Ten Sing. Please, kindly accompany me," said he. Dr. Bell immediately plied him with questions.

"Who is this Chin Ten Sing?" asked Dr. Bell.

"He is my uncle and also the leader of the number one tong. One week ago, a gang of whites beat him senseless. He has not awakened since. If he dies, all Chinese will rise against the whites," said Lam Qua.

"How did you learn of Listerism?" asked Dr. Bell.

"I attended the mission school in Canton and assisted the doctor who was from the Yale University. He and my uncle, Chin Ten Sing, arranged for me to attend the Yale medical school. I learned of the antiseptic technique from the British medical journals. The doctors here do not believe in Lister," said Lam Qua.

We climbed into a curious conveyance, a cable car, similar to the one I had ridden before in Chicago, and went up Market Street to what I presumed was the border of Chinatown. A line of angry Chinese beat drums, clashed cymbals, and brandished hatchets at policemen, who were armed with clubs and revolvers and stood across the street. A hundred or so rough-clad white men, armed with rifles and shotguns, threatened both the police and the Chinese.

"They are the militia," muttered Lam Qua.

Under the protection of Lam Qua, we scurried through an alley to a street festooned with yellow banners over shops of all kinds and description. It was a different, exotic world, unlike any I had seen. The roofs were of green tile, and the buildings were red and gold with carvings of dragons, lions, and murals of soft mountains wreathed with fog. We passed doors opening into small rooms where men lay on a dirty floor smoking small pipes. The air was filled with a sweetish smoke, which Lam Qua said was opium. The men all wore the same type of blouse and pajama-trousers, and some carried wicker baskets at each end of a bamboo pole held across their shoulders. Lam Qua knocked three times on a heavy, oaken door that was studded with iron bolts, until an elderly man with a wispy beard opened a small window next to the door. After a few words, the door opened. We passed through a large room filled with men playing with black and white buttons.

"A game of fan tan," Lam Qua informed us. We went through another heavy door also guarded by a look-out window into a room lavishly furnished with heavy, dark furniture, paintings, and a golden statue of a goddess. The place was heavy with incense, and at the end of the room, there was an enormous bed covered with a red, silk quilt. Two young women with smooth, black hair and cheeks tinged with red powder stepped aside as we approached the bed. At first, I could not be certain if the man was alive. He lay perfectly still; his hands, with skin like pale parchment, were folded over his chest on top of the silk quilt. His eyes were closed, and the yellowish skin of his face was nearly translucent. His eyes and cheeks were sunken. Most amazing of all, his scalp was clean-shaven except for a ragged patch of hair on the top of his head. There was a small bruise over his right ear. He has had nothing to eat or drink in three days," said Lam Qua.

Dr. Bell sat at the bedside and, with infinite care, lifted the patient's right wrist and placed his index finger on the pulse. "Tell me what happened," he said.

"A gang of ruffians beat my uncle and cut off his queue. He has never regained consciousness. The American doctors recommended trephination," said Lam Qua.

"Why did they cut his hair?" asked Dr. Bell.

"Since the building of railroads has finished, there is no longer any need for Chinese. There is now a law against more Chinese coming to this country and the Americans want us to leave. We wear a queue, a long braid, as a sign of respect for our emperor, but the Americans have ordered us to cut our queues," said Lam

Qua. At that moment, I distinctly thought I heard the old man sigh. Dr. Bell lifted the silk quilt and tapped the patient's knee tendon. There was a slight reflex response on both sides. He then stroked the soles of his feet. The great toe bent downward.

"A candle, please," said Dr. Bell. Lam Qua produced a lighted candle. Dr. Bell held open each eyelid and placed the candle directly in front of his face. Each pupil responded, equally.

He then sat silently, chin in hand, for almost ten minutes, before turning to me. "Arthur, what is your diagnosis?" he asked. I thought of all the usual causes for coma, drugs, head injury and diabetes but could not come up with an answer.

"The loss of his queue must have been a great shock. Please, my instrument case," said Dr. Bell. He removed the bear's tooth from a small compartment, placed it in the palm of Chin Ten Sing, and closed the old man's hand around the tooth.

"This is the tooth from a great and powerful bear. It is very strong medicine," said Dr. Bell. At that moment, I could have sworn our patient eyes fluttered and he took in a deeper breath.

"Lam Qua, explain to the women that they must prepare a soup with the necks and feet of two chickens, rice, and shredded ginseng root. They are to add this tooth to the soup." said Dr. Bell.

Lam Qua smiled and his eyes twinkled with delight. "Ah, your prescription will replace the power of the lost queue," said he.

I was dumbfounded. Why was the professor, the epitome of scientific medicine, stooping to black magic? Professor Bell had held his finger on Chin Teng Sing's pulse during the entire time.

"My fee will be one hundred American dollars in gold eagles," said he. This was most unusual. I had never heard Dr. Bell discuss his fee with a patient, but I knew better than to question him. Without a word, Lam Qua went to a brass, bound chest and removed five gold coins. He dropped them, one by one, in Dr. Bell's hand. *Clink, clink, clink, clink, clink*. At each *clink*, the old man's lips twitched.

"I shall return in two days," said Dr. Bell.

Lam Qua escorted us to the edge of Chinatown, where we hailed a hackney cab. "You are very perceptive," he said.

"Your treatment was most unusual," said I, once we were in the cab.

"My dear Arthur, it is elementary. The length of a Chinaman's queue is dear to his heart. Cutting the queue removes his sense of importance. When I mentioned the queue and the bear's tooth, his pulse rate increased, and it fairly leaped when I mentioned my fee. The old boy was wide awake and understood English. The cure will give him 'face' and he can brag that his treatment cost one hundred dollars. I shall see him again in two days," said Dr. Bell.

The streets were lined with aimless, ragged men, sitting on the sidewalk or leaning against a storefront looking out with vacant eyes. "Is it a holiday? Why aren't these men at work?" I asked.

"Ain't no work. The goldmines went bust, the railroads are built, and the damn slant-eyes work all day for nothin' but a bowl of rice," replied the driver.

We jogged along past shuttered shops and more ragged men. "The millionaires on Nob Hill gotta do something fast," said the driver.

The Palace Hotel, a vast, drab, nine-story building of iron and brick loomed on Market Street. We drove in through the splendid, skylighted garden court. The lobby was swarming with doctors from all over the country, as well as stranded, eastbound travelers waiting for the railroad to open. Penelope, still in the traveling clothes she had worn since Denver, was in a towering rage. Not only was there no room for her, but the clerk refused to believe she was an English 'Lady.' Since the surgical association had reserved adjoining suites for each of us, Penelope took my room and I moved in with Dr. Bell. We ascended to the ninth floor in a swell hydraulic elevator. Our rooms were equipped with every luxury, even an electric call button in case we needed a bootblack or refreshments. Dr. Bell hurried away to give his first lecture. I decided to accompany Penelope to a ladies haberdashery. The dear girl tried on evening dresses, day suits, frilly hats, sun bonnets and, behind closed doors, various undergarments. I was entranced by her transformation from a dusty, travel-stained woman to a real English lady. She preened and sighed and basked in my admiration, but I knew her too well to revive a romance. Still, she was bewitching and paid for the new outfit with the lucre she had won by betting on me and Mr. Wilde in Leadville.

26 June 1883, San Francisco

The morning clinic at the San Francisco City Hospital was an unexpected surprise. Here, at the very end of civilization, doctors were doing work which equaled that in Boston or Chicago. Dr. Bell fielded questions and demonstrated the antiseptic method on a jaw excision and a displaced fracture of the wrist in a twelve-year-old boy. The medical students and faculty from the medical division of the University of California were quite up to date except for a few holdouts who did not believe in the germ theory of disease. The third patient was a fifty-year-old man who worked as a coal stoker on a ferry boat. A medical student ushered him into the amphitheatre and tried to seat him on a chair, but with an enraged howl, the patient flung his arms and bared his teeth at the poor student. His face, pitted with old scars and marked with coal dust, was drawn back in a hideous rictus that exposed yellow teeth. He emitted animal-like moans and howls that expressed fear as much as rage. A woman with frazzled, grey hair and a lined face, who I presumed was his wife, trailed along. She calmed him sufficiently that he took the chair for a moment before he jumped up and fitfully changed position. He again bared his teeth and seemed as if he would bite the student. After a few minutes of frantic activity, the poor fellow, tamed by sheer exhaustion, returned to his chair. The patient's face, indeed his entire chest, was contorted with his effort to breathe. He would sit for a moment, but the paroxysms or spells would recur despite the best efforts of two medical students to restrain him. His mouth was dry, and he talked at great length but made no sense. I could only think of a strange form of epilepsy, criminal psychosis, or a brain tumor.

Dr. Levi Cooper, the senior surgeon who seemed to be very quick with the knife, advised an exploratory trephination searching for a tumor or blood clot. "Dr. Bell, do you agree with the need for surgery?" Dr. Cooper asked.

Dr. Bell observed the poor man with great intensity. "Nay. These movements are not convulsions. They are not lateralized to one side," said he. As if a light had flashed, his eyes twinkled. "Fetch a glass of water," said he. When the student returned, Dr.

Bell held the tumbler in front of the patient's face. The poor man attempted a sip of water, but as soon as the liquid touched his lips, he made a most agonizing cry, clenched his lips, and attempted to strike Dr. Bell.

Dr. Bell sprang to one side, then took the wife's hand in his. "When did the dog bite your husband?" he asked.

"Never. We have no dog," said she. Dr. Bell, with a perplexed look on his face, again approached the patient and examined his hands and arms at length.

"What do you make of these marks on his right hand?" Dr. Bell asked.

"Sir, they are just scratches, certainly not important," said the student.

"When did the cat bite you?" asked Dr. Bell. The poor man clenched his teeth, and only after great difficulty did he respond.

"Tried to pet him, but he bit. Mebbe six weeks ago," said he.

"If you please, take your patient to his room," said Dr. Bell. Two students led the patient and his wife away from the amphitheatre. "There we have it. The diagnosis is hydrophobia, also known as rabies. The ancients termed it 'the furious disease' and knew that venomous poison in the saliva of infected animals carried the disease. Dr. Louis Pasteur in Paris has proved a germ causes the illness and is working on a preventative vaccine. There is no hope for a cure. The best a mortal can do is make his life tolerable with morphine until death releases him from misery," said Dr. Bell.

The students applauded, and the attending physicians stood in line to shake Dr. Bell's hand. He went off to a luncheon while I spent the rest of the day attending lectures and demonstrations.

29 June 1883, San Francisco

There is a gap since my last entry because so much has transpired, but I have not yet managed to remember it all. I took notes and made a sketch of the room during our visit to the Bohemian Club. Penelope has described some of the events and Dr. Bell filled in the remaining blanks in order to ensure that this entry is accurate.

I believe it was noon on the twenty-seventh when Lam Qua ushered us into the inner sanctum where Chin Ten Sing sat, cross-legged, on a cushion before a low table. His merry eyes twinkled with delight when Dr. Bell made a slight bow. "Please be seated," said Chin Ten Sing. We sat on cushions and, with difficulty, crossed our legs beneath the low, polished table.

Our host clapped his hands. "Cha," said he. Instantly, a lovely girl with glistening, black hair and a body-clinging, silver-colored dress appeared with a tray. She knelt by the old man's side, deftly placed small cups on saucers before each of us, and put down a tea pot beside Chin Ten Sing. With his left hand, he poured tea for Dr. Bell, who sat on his left, and Lam Qua. Then, he pushed the pot to Lam Qua, who poured for me and his uncle. This most delectable girl left and reappeared, then put plates on the table filled with tiny morsels of food. I was nonplussed because there was no knife, fork, or spoon. The girl returned and placed small trays containing slender sticks by each of us. While holding the sticks in one hand, Chin Ten Sing dexterously picked up a tiny steamed bun, tossed the morsel upwards, caught it in mid-air, and brought it to his mouth. Lam Qua imitated this amazing feat with an even tinier bit of fried shrimp. Dr. Bell — noted for his dexterity with knife and forceps — attempted, without success, to pick up a tiny dumpling. Another delightful young lady, whose slit skirt showed a lovely leg, knelt between Dr. Bell and me. With great hilarity, she placed the sticks in our hands; one resting at the base of the thumb and held stationary by the fourth finger, the second held like a pencil between thumb and index finger, resting on the tip of the third finger.

“Her name is Lotus Blossom,” said Lam Qua. After a few minute’s practice, I was able to pick up a small, steamed bun that contained delicious, barbecued pork. We ate shrimp dumplings, bits of pork, deep fried beef, and morsels of vegetables between slurps of delicious tea.

“Ah, you learn quickly. Catch this,” said Chin Ten Sing, as he tossed a bit of fried prawn in the air. I snatched with my sticks and missed, but Lam Qua, in a flash, managed to catch the morsel before it touched the table. Lotus Blossom clapped her hands, and we all laughed. Her peal of laughter was a merry tinkle. She then swept away the dishes and returned with tiny cups, which she filled with a clear liquor poured from a porcelain bottle.

“You are English?” asked Chin Ten Sing.

“No, Scottish,” said Dr. Bell.

“But you have the same queen,” said Chin Ten Sing.

“Yes, that is true,” said Dr. Bell.

The old man raised his cup. “We drink to the English queen,” said he. I nearly choked. The liquid burned all the way down but left a warm feeling in the pit of my stomach. Lotus Blossom re-filled our cups.

“To the emperor of China,” said Dr. Bell. I have never tasted such strong liquor, though, this time, the burning sensation was not as severe.

“It is rice brandy,” said Lam Qua.

“Does the English queen value her distant possessions and her people?” asked Chin Ten Sing.

“But of course,” said Dr. Bell.

“The Queen is very rich. She could pay well for information about a threat to her lands,” said the old Chinaman. Dr. Bell carefully folded his hands on the polished surface of the table. His lids were half closed. Except for distant street noise, the room remained quiet.

“It would depend on the source and the reliability of the information,” said Dr. Bell.

“My nephew, Johnnie Chan, is number one boy in the house of Mr. Leland Stanford. Mr. Stanford thinks he is a stupid, illiterate Chinaman, but Johnnie studied in Paris and knows English, as well as French. He has learned of a threat to the Queen's lands in Canada," said Chin Ten Sing.

"We are only doctors, but have great interest in the affairs of the Queen. We would appreciate any knowledge about threats to Her Majesty. Thank you for the lunch. I must give a lecture within the hour," said Dr. Bell. We made our bows, and again, Lam Qua escorted us to the edge of Chinatown. As if by magic, a skinny, bright-eyed boy of ten or twelve years appeared at my side.

"This is Pow Chan, my messenger," said Lam Qua. The small boy bowed and held out his hand with my wallet.

"I believe this belongs to you," he said.

"You picked my pocket!" I shouted. I wasn't sure whether to be impressed or horrified.

Lam Qua smiled. "Pow Chan is very talented and can be very helpful," said he. We walked for a while along Market Street, marveling at the sparkly day, the hills, and the vast bay.

Dr. Bell lit his old brier-root pipe and seemed deep in thought as we walked. "Chin Ten Sing is an old rascal who may or may not have useful information. This Stanford fellow offered Borovsky protection while we were in Boston. He is rich and powerful and may be working with Borovsky. Given what we know, and the fact that, at one time, the Russians claimed Northern California, we can assume the Russian is here in San Francisco. Miss Walshingham spent time with Borovsky; perhaps she has more information. We must take her in our confidence," he said.

Dr. Bell went off to give a lecture, which I skipped since I had heard it many times. Penelope strutted into our suite as if she owned the hotel. She sniffed. "You have been with a Chinese floozy," said she.

"A lovely Chinese girl served lunch for us and two Chinese gentlemen. You could take lessons in courtesy and female behavior," said I, hoping that she might be even a wee bit jealous.

"You damn men are all alike," said she, before turning away.

"Now, Penelope, be a dear girl. Let's kiss and make up," said I.

"Bah, why should I make up with a penniless doctor, even if you are handsome in a rugged sort of way?" It was her usual two-handed way of making me feel like a fool.

"Enough! Our Chinese friends think this Stanford fellow is plotting against the crown. Have you any leads on Jack Dawson or the Russian?" I asked.

Penelope smiled. It was one of her radiant, heart-throb-inspiring, appealing looks that I had succumbed to so often in the past. "What do you want?" I asked. Penelope moved closer and touched my cheek with her lips. I turned just enough so our lips met and, rather clumsily, clutched her to my bosom. I had forgotten how delicious it was when we were together. Though our passionate embraces only lasted for brief moments before she would flee, I was grateful for each one. Unfortunately, this kiss lasted all of fifteen seconds until the vixen suddenly pulled away.

"Jack Dawson often mentioned the Bohemian Club. We might find him there or at least learn of his whereabouts," said Penelope.

"Why then, let us visit the place," said I, with an exasperated sigh, knowing that was it for today's romantic interlude.

"It is a private, men-only club, mostly for newspaper men or literary types," said Penelope.

"Dress up in trousers, a shirt, a jacket, and a cap. You can pass for a man if you try," said I.

The club was dingy, smoky, and filled with men wearing soft shirts, corduroy jackets, and with pencils stuck behind an ear. Most were at the bar. A few slurped oyster stew at wooden tables covered with checkered cloths. A huge fireplace dominated the room. From the mantelpiece, a wood carving of a one-eyed owl looked out over the crowd. We had no sooner gained entrance when a rough-looking fellow laid his hand on my collar.

"You a member?" asked he. I was about to explain we were seeking guest privileges, when a voice began to bellow.

Comrades, leave me here a little, while as yet 'tis early morn:
Leave me here, and when you want me, sound upon the bugle-horn .
. .

The speaker stopped for lusty drink from a tall glass. I responded with the next lines, which I knew by heart from having read them many times.

'Tis the place, and all around it, as of old, the curlews call,
Dreary gleams about the moorland flying over Locksley Hall.

We went on to the very end, reciting, in turn, all eighty-five or so stanzas of Tennyson's grand poem of lost love. At the end, my throat was dry. There were huzzahs and shouts of "More! More!" The rough fellow who had been set to throw us out thrust a whisky toddy in my hand and led us to a table. My fellow poet made his way to us through the throng and, with no invitation, flung himself into a chair. He wore a checked coat, a soft cap, and, for a fellow who had been tossing down whisky like it was water, was remarkably steady. I felt an immediate kinship with the man. He had the build of a rugby player, a ruddy face, a longish nose, and hooded eyes. He looked down his nose as if he were above it all.

"By God, you know Tennyson! I am Ian Blake, lately of Liverpool," said he.

"Arthur Conan Doyle of Edinburgh and my nephew, ah, David Doyle," said I, gesturing towards the newly-masculine Penelope.

"What brings you to our Paris of the Pacific?"

"A medical meeting. My professor is lecturing and demonstrating," said I. He rubbed his jaw and cast what seemed to be a suspicious eye on Penelope.

"Are you one of the saw-bones who treated old Sing?" he asked.

"Yes," I answered.

"There are people here who want to see him dead. You might be in big trouble for interfering," said Blake.

"Why? He seems like a nice old man," said I.

Blake burst out laughing and took another pull at his whisky. "The old devil owns half of Chinatown and is standing in the way of the Nob's grand plans," he said.

"How so?" I asked.

"The workingmen hate the Chinese, and both the chinks and the working men are about to take down the Nobs."

"Who are the Nobs?"

"Oh, you are really a greenhorn. The millionaires who live on Nob Hill; Stanford, Crocker, Hopkins. The bastards made a fortune on railroads and mines. Now it is all bust, but they still have their millions and damn the rest," said Blake. "Stanford tells the Chinese he wants to hire them to build another railroad, and he tells the working man he will 'send the slant-eyes back' to China."

Penelope had said nothing but sat with hands in her lap, eyes downcast. Blake suddenly grabbed her arm and pulled her hand into his lap. He leered at me, showing fine white teeth. "Such a delicate hand. Your nephew is more like a niece. Now, do you want to tell me what in Sam Hell you two are doing here?" he asked.

"If you must know . . ." I began, knowing it would be a lot worse if I didn't tell him the truth, "She is Lady Penelope Walshingham, traveling from England. A dastardly fellow named Jack Dawson robbed her of every cent, leaving her destitute. I am helping her find the wretch."

Blake winked and released his hold on Penelope. "If I know Dawson, he took more than her money."

"Do you know the man?" I asked.

"Half of California is looking for Jack. He staked every creek for miles around, then salted the area with fool's gold and a little dust. He let the suckers find a bit of gold, then sold the claims to gullible fools for thousands of dollars. He made a lot of money but lost most of it on cards and women. It is rumored that he is selling an Alaskan scheme to Stanford."

"Where can we find him?" I asked.

"He may be hiding out with the Nobs, hatching a grand plan. I'll keep my eyes and ears open. Watch your back and be careful. My dear Penelope, I apologize if I grabbed your arm a bit too tightly. One can never be too sure who they are dealing with in these times, don't you think? Please, allow me to help with your grief over losing Dawson. My card," said he. He lifted Penelope's hand, looked around — as if to be sure no one was watching —

enclosed a note in her palm, then gently closed her fingers around it before looking in her eyes and letting go. Though she watched his every motion, Penelope stayed silent the whole time. I must admit I felt a pang of jealousy about his attentions, but I was also glad she was still there with me.

His card read:

IAN BLAKE
San Francisco Chronicle

Blake left our table to join another group. He was remarkably steady, and the thought passed my mind that he mostly drank watered-down booze in order to keep a sharp mind. "Let's go," said I.

The night was cool, and dense fog obscured the buildings. No cabs were about, so we continued on foot, bumping into hitching posts and the occasional tree. We found our way to a recognizable landmark, the cast iron Lotta's Fountain. We set off on Market Street, arm in arm, not out of affection — at least on Penelope's part — but for protection. We had not gone far when a silent band of club-wielding men materialized out of the gloom. *Damn!* I thought. *My walking stick is back at the hotel.*

Before I could make a defense, one of the ruffians stifled Penelope's scream with a rough hand over her face. "Owee, he bit me!" howled her assailant. This was followed by a stifled moan when Penelope stabbed her elbow into his mid-section. I lashed out with a clenched fist. My wild haymaker struck a darkened face with enough force to break his jaw, but the fellow merely shook his head like a huge dog. I ducked when he swung a club at my noggin, but stumbled backwards against Penelope. The dear girl twirled and struck my assailant with the side of her hand. Much to my surprise, the fellow went down.

There was no respite. My fisticuffs and Penelope's martial arts skills were insufficient for conquering an entire gang. A powerful arm encircled my neck and twisted my entire head until I felt a *snap*, which was followed by a lightning bolt of pain in my legs. I went down, totally helpless, and my feet went numb, though

I could still see. I was sufficiently conscious to wonder if this meant a broken neck and permanent paralysis. I expected another blow, but out of the misty gloom came a crowd of screaming dervishes led by a tall, shrouded, slender woman. She fired a pistol, and in the spurt of flame, I also saw the boy, who I recognized as Pow Chan, hurl a small hatchet. The picture is still there, engraved on my brain. The hatchet flew, end over end, until it split the skull of a burly, dark-faced villain. There were more hatchet-wielding, rock-throwing boys who came out of the foggy mist. Was it my imagination, or did the female figure look like Lotus Blossom? My immediate assailant went down with a bullet through his spleen. Another hatchet whistled through the air and split the head of a wild-faced ruffian. Another of our assailants snarled and struggled to his feet. A diminutive, pajama-clad figure sliced off two fingers of the wretch's right hand with a small hatchet.

"You bastids learn not to mess with triads." The voice was Pow Chan's.

My next conscious moment was an awareness of being gently lifted onto a litter and swiftly carried through dark, silent streets. Next came the sweetish odor of opium and the clacking sound of fan tan players. A door closed. There was absolute silence for a moment until a gentle hand caressed my forehead.

"You are safe," murmured a distant, musical voice. I drifted into a sort of stupor, but all the time was aware of tingling and numbness in both feet. With the greatest of will, I attempted to move my right leg, but I was unable to discern motion. Would I ever walk again? I have never felt more alone and desolate.

It could have been several hours or minutes until I recognized Lam Qua's calm words. "Do not move your head, but swallow these pills and drink," said he. The rice brandy burned all the way down, but I was soon drowsy and totally relaxed. I then had a vivid dream of walking through a bright meadow to dark woods. Even in my dream, I interpreted the dark woods as death but had no fear. At what seemed the very depth of the dream, I felt incredibly soft hands holding my shoulders while another set of hands slowly manipulated my head from side to side with increasing traction. The motion lulled me into another state of utter relaxation until the hands forced my head and neck backwards and to the right, at which time I felt my vertebrae snap. There was a great burst of light, and an incredible pain shot up the back of my head. I thought I screamed, but I can't be sure . . .

Next, I felt cold as ice and drifted off into the cold dark woods. I came out of the deep stupor with a sensation of warm flesh, a soft breast nestled against my chest. Nothing could have been more comforting. "Do not move," said Lotus Blossom. The pain was gone, but there was a tickling sensation on the sole of my right foot and a soft giggle when I jerked it way. *Glory be!* I wasn't paralyzed! I hungered for the continued warmth of her body, wanting to touch every part of this being who seemed to have magically brought me back to life. It was as if by feeling her aliveness, I was reconnecting with my own. I began to run my fingers through her hair, over her eyes, cheeks, and full lips, sliding over two lovely, soft nipples, a flat abdomen and a delicately indented navel.

"No monkey playing. You are poor, sick man. I am only warming you cold body so you live again," said Lotus Blossom. I sighed and attempted to sit up. "You be still until Lam Qua says you can move."

I must have slept again, and when I next awoke, my head and neck were immobilized in a padded scarf wrapped around my neck. I tentatively moved each arm and leg until I was quite satisfied there was no paralysis.

"You have good joss. Pow Chan was on the lookout for you. Lotus Blossom and the boys arrived in time. You will have no permanent injury," said Lam Qua. I was on a couch in a small, wood-paneled room lit with candles that smelled of incense. I felt a sense of great ease, which must have come from the opium, until bits and snatches of memory returned, bringing anxiety with them.

"Penelope, what happened to Penelope?" I asked as the memory of the attack came more into focus.

"The English lady is quite safe in the hotel," said Lam Qua. I focused on Lotus Blossom, grateful she had brought me back to life. How much more was there than I first thought to this beautiful, slender girl who taught me to use chopsticks and then saved my life? Could she also be the leader of a deadly gang?

Somehow, Lam Qua must have understood my silent curiosity. “Lotus Blossom is the most fragrant flower of all of Chin Ten Sing’s ‘nieces.’ She is also known as the Tooth of the Dragon or simply, the Dragon Lady, one who has become both a great healer and warrior woman,” said Lam Qua.

Though it is hazy, I have a dim recollection of being given another pill, a brown one, and a glass of the fiery rice brandy, then being strapped onto a litter and carried again through the streets and an alley, through a dim back door, and up several flights of stairs. When I awoke, I was in my own bed in the hotel suite. Dr. Bell was at my bedside.

“What is the date?” I asked.

“June the twenty-ninth,” replied Dr. Bell. “My boy, you have had quite a night.”

He wore his ancient, red dressing gown, was surrounded by newspapers, medical journals, and his notebook, and was intensively studying a map of San Francisco. Clouds of fragrant smoke rose from his favorite calabash. “I suspect you are hungry,” said he.

“Ravenous.” I found I could rise from bed, though still felt shaky, weak, and sore in every joint and muscle. I haltingly made my way to the table, which was laden with boiled eggs, ham, smoked salmon, a dish of oat porridge, and a gallon-sized pot of coffee. Though I was still foggy-headed and ate slowly, I managed to finish every crumb.

“Where is Penelope?” I asked, after feeling my energy slowly starting to return.

Dr. Bell tamped more tobacco into his pipe, struck a lucifer, and puffed until the tobacco was a glowing, red coal. “Read this,” said he. The message, written on plain, lined foolscap, was in Dr. Bell’s own handwriting. He had obviously translated the message from a code. *Remain in S.F. until situation resolved. Employ Lady Walshingham as you see fit. Agent will make contact. Edwards.*

“I explained to Miss Walshingham that, since she had no funds, she was no longer welcome to accompany us at this juncture.

I then encouraged her to answer an advertisement requesting a tutor for Leland Stanford, Jr. The boy will accompany his parents on a grand tour of the continent next year and his parents expect Lady Walshingham will erase the boy's uncouth figures of American speech, convert him into a young English gentleman, and teach him fluency in French and Russian. She now has comfortable quarters in the Stanford mansion on Nob Hill," said Dr. Bell. I noticed the twinkle in his eye and the slight upcurl of his lips as he conveyed this news.

"Well, that is news. Has she heard anything of Jack Dawson or Borovsky?" I asked.

"It is too soon. Come, do you feel well enough to accompany me on a consultation? I suggest you take the various armaments provided by the colonel, as a precaution," Dr. Bell said. I was still somewhat befuddled but instantly became interested. Dr. Bell's consultations always led to new adventures.

"Yes, of course, I feel well enough. What is the case?" I asked.

"A military problem," he answered, with a mysterious little smile.

We set off in a hired cab. The day was marvelously clear, and as we came down the hill, we were treated to a remarkable view of the bay, islands, and along the foreshore, the hulks of innumerable ships. The cab driver explained that these were windjammers that had rounded Cape Horn from the east coast of the United States to California during the gold rush. The crews jumped ship to search for gold, leaving the abandoned ships. "There appear to be workers on some of the ships," said I. The driver squinted at the partly refurbished ships.

"Those 'uns be bought by the Occidental and Oriental Steamship line. Old Leland's got no more use for the Chinese and figures on sending them home, but them ships'll go down afore they reach the Farallones," said the cabby.

We went through Cowtown, a dismal neighborhood, turned onto Presidio Drive, and arrived at a military base. We trotted through a delightfully wooded meadow overlooking the bay, where curving streets were lined with barracks for enlisted men, bungalows for the lieutenants, and mansions for high-ranking officers. Artillery pieces aimed at the bay dotted the landscape.

"Here be Fort Point," said the cabby. We alighted before the stone and brick building, which was guarded by a single, slouching sentry whose boots and rifle were dirty. He barely acknowledged our request for the medical officer, Captain Hennessey, but dragging his rifle, he led us to a small infirmary.

"The American military lacks British discipline," said Dr. Bell.

"Aye, they have no one to fight, now that they have subdued the Indians," said I.

Captain Hennessey sat hunched over a littered desk in a small office. Cabinets contained medical equipment, including a scalpel still smeared with pus. Bookshelves lined the walls. The medical officer was bleary-eyed and had dirt beneath his fingernails. With seemingly great effort, he roused himself from a padded chair.

"Gentlemen, thank you for arriving so promptly," said he.

"Always delighted to see an interesting diagnostic problem," said Dr. Bell. "Orderly, fetch Duncan and Hancock," shouted Captain Hennessey.

Duncan, a sergeant, and Hancock, a corporal, were battle-scarred veterans well into their forties. "These white spots have me puzzled," said Hennessey. Duncan thrust out his hands. Although his face was tanned a deep mahogany brown, the skin of his hands showed blotchy patches of de-pigmentation that were pronounced on the ulnar side. Dr. Bell inspected each of his hands, first with his naked eye, then with a small hand lens. Without a word, he removed a pin from behind the collar of his jacket and pricked the skin of each hand.

"Ouch!" said Duncan, when the pin pricked his index finger. He made no response to the pin in the white areas. I instantly knew the diagnosis, but made no comment. Dr. Bell remained expressionless but nodded at Corporal Hancock who thrust both hands forward. Dr. Bell again carefully scrutinized a small, white patch and then felt the ulnar nerve at the patient's elbow.

"How long has the nerve been swollen?" Dr. Bell asked.

“ ‘Bout six months, more or less,” said the corporal.

“When were you men out of the country?” Dr. Bell asked.

“Back in ’78 to ’80, I was a guard at the legation in Shanghai,” said Hancock.

“I had duty in the Sandwich Islands from ’79 to 81,” said Duncan.

“Thank you, gentlemen, that will be all,” said Dr. Bell.

“Dismissed!” barked the orderly.

“The diagnosis is leprosy,” said Dr. Bell.

Hennessey recoiled. “No, that’s not possible. They are white men. The chinks get it from opium and filth,” said he.

“Hanson, a Swedish scientist, has definitely demonstrated leprosy to be caused by a germ that is passed from one person to another. You can prove the diagnosis by scraping the skin and applying the proper bacterial stains,” said Dr. Bell.

“You say it is contagious?” Hennessy asked.

“Yes. I advise you to examine every man on the base,” replied Bell.

“Does this mean quarantine?” Hennessey asked.

“Indeed, it does,” replied Bell.

Hennessy put his head in his hands. “The colonel won’t like this, but it won’t make a hell of a lot of difference. Half the garrison has syphilis and the rest are down with scurvy. The government doesn’t give a damn about the army anymore,” he said.

The ride and the day’s exertions left me with a recurrence of pain and slight weakness in my left foot. I am tired and still recovering, so I was glad it turned out there was no need for armaments. We have returned to our rooms and, though it is early in the day, I am ready to collapse into bed.

30 June 1883

I slept for the remainder of the day and night and awoke this morning with some aches and pains, but felt much better than yesterday. Dr. Bell had left, probably for another consultation, by the time I awoke. There was an envelope with my name — written in precise, perfect penmanship — on the breakfast tray. A note read: *If you please, Pow Chan will meet you at noon and guide you to Ah Toy's House of Pleasure for lunch. Lam Qua*

I adjusted the ankle sheath for my stiletto, dressed with care, placed the brandy flask in an inside pocket, and took up the walking stick. I felt a bit ridiculous with these armaments, but set off prepared for any eventuality and with a tingle of anticipation. What was the meaning of the invitation? Would the lovely Lotus Blossom attend the luncheon?

Near the hotel entrance, a small boy, whose features were obscured by dirt and a large straw hat, was polishing the boots of a well-dressed gentleman. When finished, the man withdrew a large wallet from an inside coat pocket and flipped a coin to the boy, replaced the wallet, and selected a cigar. The boy immediately struck a lucifer and held the flame to the cigar. While the man rotated the cigar to achieve a perfect glow, the boy, with his other hand, deftly removed the wallet. In the twinkling of an eye, the boy, whom I finally recognized as Pow Chan, squatted on the cobblestones before me.

"Polish your boots, sir," said he. The large gentleman, now unknowingly bereft of his wallet, was already in a cab, trotting down the street.

"You little rascal," said I. He looked hurt and beckoned me to follow. He set off at a fast pace to Grant Street, passed the Kow Chow temple, and stopped at a large, red door.

"Fifty-six Ross Alley," said Pow Chan. He rapped three times, paused, and gave two more taps. An elderly man opened a small window, and after they exchanged a few words in Chinese, he admitted us to an ante-room and then a second room, which smelled of incense and was decorated with dragons and paintings of temples.

A strikingly tall, beautiful woman wearing a clinging skirt, slit to her thigh, hobbled on bound feet across the room. "Welcome to the house of Madam Ah Toy," said she. Lam Qua and Lotus Blossom rose from the low table where they had been seated prior to our arrival.

"Welcome. Meet Johnny Chan," said Lam Qua. Chan was tall, had black hair combed straight back from a high forehead, and was dressed in fashionable western clothing. He gave me an imperious, hostile glance and made no greeting. It was hard to believe he was the house boy for Leland Stanford.

"Please, be seated," said Lam Qua. When we were settled on cushions around the low table, Madam Ah Toy clapped her hands. Servants appeared with tiny cups and pots of bitter tea. After the tea, they brought trays filled with small, delectable bits of meat, fish, shrimp, and tiny dumplings. I wolfed down pork spiced with garlic.

"My girls' lonesome. No soldiers come last night," sighed Madam Ah Toy. Johnny Chan gave me a look of pure hatred.

"Then it is true. The American soldiers cannot leave the Presidio. Very bad for business in Chinatown. Uncle Sing and tongs very unhappy," said Johnny Chan.

"You English doctors do this?" asked Madam Ah Toy.

"This could be very bad. With no American Army, the California Militia will be the only military in the state," said Lam Qua.

"This is not good for Chinese. The English doctors must rescind the order and let the soldiers go free." said Chan.

"Leprosy is contagious. It is necessary to protect the community," said I.

"Ha, you only protect the whites on Nob Hill," said Chan. We continued eating in silence, and when we had consumed the last bits of dim sum and the servants had cleared away the dishes, Johnny Chan rose to his feet and commenced speaking in rapid-fire Chinese.

Lam Qua raised a hand. "Johnny, please speak English for our guest," said he.

Chan's face turned into an angry scowl. "The English are no friend of our emperor and have no business here. He will do nothing for us," said he.

"The Americans are our enemies. We have a common cause with the English," said Lam Qua.

Johnny Chan's angry retort was blocked by shouting and the sound of gunfire from the street. The screams and cries became more distinct. "It is the California Militia," said Lam Qua. The crackling rifle shots were now continuous and getting closer and louder.

"They have come for my girls!" screamed Madam Ah Toy. The heavy oak and bolted doors were no match for heavy axes. The outer door opened with a crash, and when the inner door to our room trembled with powerful blows, we scrambled to the narrow stairway that led to the kitchen. Madam Ah Toy tripped on her bound feet, fell, and blocked the exit. For a moment, I crushed Lotus Blossom in my arms, then thrust her behind Johnny Chan. As if in a dream, I remembered Colonel Beachy-Edwards words, "flash" and "bang." I hastily withdrew the brandy flask, and just as a half dozen crazed militia men crashed through the door, I gave the lid a twist, counted to three, and threw the flask as hard as possible. It landed in the midst of — and surprised — the intruders, who stopped their forward rush. The flask went off with a *bang* and a *whoosh*. The room filled with a yellow, acrid smoke that drove the militia back into the ante-room. We escaped up the stairway to the kitchen, then down another flight of stairs into a subterranean room that connected with an adjacent building.

"Follow me," said Lam Qua. We found our way through a series of rooms hidden beneath the buildings until we exited on Grant Street at the edge of the Chinese district.

"You go to office of Mr. Ian Blake at the Chronicle. Tell him what happened," said Lam Qua. I remembered Blake from our recent Tennyson recitation and his flirtation with Penelope, and I left to go find him. The gunfire had subsided, and the streets were clear as I made my way to the newspaper office. Blake's office was a cluttered cubbyhole redolent with old tobacco smoke.

"We meet again," said he.

"A gang of white men from the militia stormed the Chinese district," said I.

"I heard the gunfire. It happens every month or so," said Blake.

"Damn! Why do they do that? They are murdering innocent people," said I. Blake twirled a pencil between his fingers and gave me a long, speculative look. He slammed the door shut, but we could easily hear conversations in the next office through the flimsy walls.

Blake drew his chair near to mine. "*Nos socii. Pater noster est Beachy*," said he. It took a moment to remember my grade school Latin. He had said, "We are partners. Our father is Beachy."

"Let's put our cards on the table. I keep an eye on the British interests. The Nobs need only the slightest excuse to take over the entire Pacific coast from Alaska to California," said Blake.

"Would a huge discovery of gold and other minerals in the Yukon be a sufficient excuse?" I asked.

"Yes, a big strike would be the perfect excuse," said Blake. He shuffled through a stack of paper. "Ah, here it is. Stanford and his associates have proposed building a railroad through British Columbia and the Yukon to Alaska. The British rejected the proposal, and most Americans don't think Alaska has anything of value. Stanford must have inside information about the gold and minerals," said Blake.

"I have another question. Why is Johnny Chan angry with us?" I asked.

"It is a sad story. Chan came with his father to work on the railroads. He carried spikes when he was ten years old. His father became ill, couldn't work, and a foreman beat him to death. Old Chin Ten Sing took care of Johnny. Chan is brilliant but hates all whites," said Blake.

"Get him! Stop the little bastard!" The shouts in the outer office were accompanied by a clatter of overturned chairs and broken glass. The door to Blake's office burst open. Pow Chan tumbled into the room.

"Lotus Blossom hurt … Come quick!" he shouted.

I followed Pow Chan through the streets as fast as I was able, to a tiny storefront on a dirty alley just off Grant Street. Johnny Chan cradled Lotus Blossom in his arms while an old lady held a compress on her neck. "They shot her," said Chan. She was unconscious, her skin was blue, and she wasn't breathing. I looked more closely to see how badly she was injured. The bullet appeared to have entered near the midline in front of her neck and exited at the left side.

"Where is Dr. Lam Qua?" I asked.

"The damn militia hurt many people. He is in the streets rescuing the wounded," said Chan. When I removed the compress, there was a torrent of blood. She should have been pale from blood loss, not cyanotic. Pressure on the wound stopped the external bleeding. I pictured the anatomy and suddenly realized the bullet must have opened her trachea and she was bleeding into her airway.

"Quick, hold her upside down!" said I. Johnny Chan gave me a questioning look, but obeyed and suspended the girl so her head and upper body hung down. I flung both arms around her chest and gave a great hug, released my pressure and gave a second squeeze as hard as possible. A great torrent of clots and blood erupted from her mouth. Lotus Blossom made a convulsive gasp, took in air, and coughed out more gouts of blood. I squeezed again. She coughed, more blood drained from her mouth, and she took in a long, gurgling gulp of air.

"Put her on the counter," said I. Chan swept aside boxes of tea, dried fish, and vegetables in order to create a space for Lotus Blossom.

"Tell Pow Chan to find Dr. Bell," said I. I held the compress for half an hour until a half-dozen ragged, little boys dragged Dr. Bell into the room. The boys chattered all at once, and Pow Chan proudly carried the instrument case.

"I am compressing the jugular vein. She had blood in her trachea," said I. Dr. Bell took in the situation and, with his usual aplomb, removed his coat, rolled up his sleeves, and placed an assortment of gleaming forceps, knives, scissors, and ligatures on a towel. He rinsed his hands and soaked a gauze compress with carbolic.

Lotus Blossom moaned and attempted to raise an arm. "A few drops of chloroform will not be amiss. I will hold pressure, while you give the anaesthetic," said Dr. Bell. At the first whiff of chloroform, she stopped breathing and her eyes rolled back. I placed my lips on hers and forced air into her lungs. She revived. Dr. Bell kept up pressure on the vein with one hand and, with the other, made an incision connecting the entrance and exit wounds. I have never seen such a deft bit of workmanship. The tissues were suffused with blood, but with unerring skill, he encircled the torn vein with ligatures and stopped the bleeding. He cleaned the area with carbolic swabs and sutured a bit of muscle against the perforated trachea.

"She will live," said Dr. Bell.

"I will take her to the home of Chin Ten Sing," said Chan. He looked into my eyes. I saw a softening.

"You are indeed a good friend," said he.

We followed Pow Chan to the Kow Chow Temple, where Lam Qua patched the wounds of blood-splattered victims. We spent the rest of the day working with the wounded.

1 July 1883, San Francisco

Our leisurely breakfast was interrupted by a knock on the door. The bellboy, dressed in an impeccable scarlet uniform, bowed. "A message for Dr. Bell," said he. Dr. Bell put down his cup and read the penciled note. *An interesting autopsy. Medical school auditorium, ten o'clock a.m. R. Beverly Cole, MD*

We arrived just as the deaner, assisted by a student, rolled a pale, naked body into the auditorium and placed it on a table directly in front of the tiers of students. Ian Blake was with the students in the front row, his pencil and notebook at the ready. Greasy, grey intestines spilled out of a great slash down the front of the body. The eye sockets were empty. Birds had evidently pecked out the eyeballs. I gasped, covered my mouth, and averted my eyes from the body. I recognized the long, sandy hair that I had once attempted to pull from Jack Dawson's skull. Dr. Cole bustled into the room wearing a blood-stained apron over his fashionable frock coat.

"The ferry boat men found him floating in the bay yesterday afternoon." He nodded to Dr. Bell. "You have never seen the likes of this in Scotland, I'll wager. Would you care to examine the body?" asked Dr. Cole. He strutted about like a pompous jay, obviously intent on showing up Dr. Bell before the students.

Dr. Bell approached the body and, chin in hand, observed every detail. He said nothing.

"Well, what do you make of it?" asked Cole. I had averted my eyes from the awful scene, but when Cole spoke, I looked more closely. The left hand had been amputated at the wrist and it was held with a spike, which had been driven through the hand and into his chest. Dr. Bell stooped and examined the hand.

"This is most peculiar; the thumb is extended up towards the chin, the three middle fingers are curled inwards, and the fifth finger is aimed downward," said Dr. Bell.

"Well, doctor, do tell us . . . What is the meaning of the hand?" asked Dr. Cole.

Dr. Bell shook his head. "I have never seen the likes of it," said he.

"Gentlemen, the upraised thumb represents the head of a dragon and the fifth finger the tail. This is the work of the Chinese triads. I will prove it. The man's gallbladder will be absent." Cole delved into the abdomen. "See, see here, the gallbladder was torn out. The fiends drink the gall of their enemies for strength," said he.

"Are you quite certain the man was dead before he was thrown into the water?" asked Dr. Bell.

"Yes, of course," said Cole.

Dr. Bell smiled at the students. "At times, the truth is not found at first appearances. Note the bulging spaces between the ribs on the left side, while the right, intercostal spaces are normal," said Dr. Bell. He then placed his middle finger on the chest wall and thumped it with his other index finger. The sound was a dull *thud.*

"Gentlemen, if indeed the man was dead when he entered the water, the lungs should be full of air. What explains the dullness to percussion and the bulging intercostal spaces?" asked Dr. Bell. The students shuffled their feet, but no one had an answer.

"What is this damn nonsense?" asked Cole.

"If you please, turn the body over to expose the back," said Dr. Bell. I took the shoulders and stared into the distorted face of Jack Dawson. I could barely stifle a cry. I had disliked the man, but hadn't wished for his death.

"Please, Dr. Doyle, assist me," said Bell. I swallowed bile and, with the aid of a student, rolled the body onto the abdomen. There was a small stab wound in the upper left chest.

"Bah, that little wound could have been a fish bite," said Dr. Cole.

"A knife, please," said Dr. Bell. He made a deep incision down to the ribs and spent a few minutes removing a segment of rib. The students fidgeted and Dr. Cole hopped about.

"Damn it. Doctor, the cause of death is plain as the nose on your face. The triad killed him," said Dr. Cole.

Dr. Bell paid him no attention and cut deeper until he encountered blood clots in the chest cavity. "Forceps, please." Dr. Bell withdrew a sharpened, white bone from the mass of clotted blood. The students gasped, and I was immediately awestruck by another of Bell's triumphs.

"It is a spear point from a harpoon. I saw many of them when I sailed on the *Hope* in the Arctic!" I cried.

Dr. Bell held the bloody spear point for all to see. "Here is the cause of death. This spear point penetrated the pulmonary artery. Indeed, this point is a weapon used by the Arctic Eskimo. Here is the toggle that releases the shaft of the harpoon," he said.

He bowed to the students. "Young men, in your practices, you will often be led astray by first appearances. Observe closely. Search out every detail before you make a diagnosis. In this case, the murderer attempted to fasten blame on the Chinese." The students clapped and stomped their feet, while Dr. Cole hurriedly left the auditorium.

"May I treat you gentlemen to lunch?" asked Ian Blake.

"Our pleasure," said Dr. Bell.

Pow Chan and his collection of scabby, little boys were playing dice beneath a tree when we came out of the medical school. Pow Chan waved them away and trotted after us while we walked to Powell Street and boarded the Powell-Hyde cable car for a ride down the hill to a busy collection of wharfs, piers, and boat landings. A cluster of small fishing boats were docked at a long wharf, and others were anchored in the bay. Gulls, cormorants, and terns flew and squawked as we made our way along the waterfront to a ramshackle building with a sign, 'Restaurante Italiano.'

"Achilles Paladine is the fish king," said Blake. Paladine, a weather-beaten man with a huge, drooping mustache, embraced Blake at the door.

"Welcome, my fren'. You want the usual place?" he asked.

"Yes," said Blake. We went up a narrow stairway to a room containing a single table that overlooked the Golden Gate. We were scarcely settled at a round table covered with a checked cloth when a young man arrived bearing a jug, long loaves of crisp bread, and small dishes of olive oil. Blake poured red wine from the jug and tore off chunks of bread that he dunked in the olive oil.

"Help yourselves," said he.

Next came a platter of shellfish and a bowl of melted butter. "Dungeness Crab," said Blake. He broke open a long claw and extracted white meat. One of the most satisfying aspects of our travels in America is feasting on the diverse foods. For the next thirty minutes, we gorged on the succulent crab, prawns, fish, and bowls of creamy noodles spiced with herbs and tomato sauce.

It was late afternoon before waiters swept away the remnants of our feast and left a pot of coffee. “Perhaps, I should establish my bonafides,” said Blake. He placed on the table one third of a bronze penny. I stared at a part of the face of young Queen Victoria and the word, ‘VICTOR.’ The rest was missing. Dr. Bell placed another third of the coin next to that of Blake’s. It matched perfectly. I was confused by this display.

“Where is the other third?” I asked.

“Lady Walshingham,” said Dr. Bell.

My confusion turned to ire. There were many instances, during our travels to America and Russia, in which I had given my time, and nearly my life, for the Crown. Yet, my loyalty seemed to go unappreciated. “Well, why don’t I have a part of the coin? Have my efforts on behalf of the Crown these last five years meant nothing? Penelope is someone known to be untrustworthy; a double, if not triple, agent. Why would she be the one to have that honor?” I asked.

“You are indeed a valued member of our group, but Colonel Beachy-Edwards could not know for certain if you would accompany me on this trip. He has implicit faith in Lady Walshingham and entrusted her with the final third prior to your invitation to join us,” said Bell.

Though not fully satisfied with his answer, I was slightly mollified.

“Do you know who killed Jack Dawson?” Blake asked.

Dr. Bell fussed with his pipe and tobacco until he blew a perfect ring of smoke. “The weapon is of Eskimo origin,” said he.

“There are no Eskimos in the entire state of California,” said Blake.

“The harpoon point is the type of artifact that an explorer would collect. Now that I think of it, Count Borovsky was a member of the Russian-Alaska Company,” said I.

Dr. Bell arched his eyebrows. “Count Borovsky is very clever. Had it not been for Arthur’s quick work, we never would have suspected that man's foul play in the murder of the twins. Yes, this could most certainly be the work of Borovsky," said he.

"Dawson stole Borovsky's case of specimens, so the count had a motive," said I.

Blake gestured at a black-hulled ship with three masts and a funnel. An ensign with the Saltire of St. Andrews and a Maltese cross flew at the stern. "That Russian warship has been here for two weeks. Most Russians have left the bay area, but there is a large colony at Fort Ross, up the coast. At one time, they claimed all of Northern California. The Russians are indeed up to no good," said Blake.

"Why would the killer want us to blame Dawson's murder on the Chinese?" I asked.

"It would be an easy diversionary tactic. Unfortunately, because the Chinese are different, or seem exotic, and Americans think they are taking jobs, they are believed to be sinister and are easy scapegoats for everything bad," said Blake.

We had been silent for some time, savoring the last of our strong Italian coffee and watching the last rays of sunlight reflected from a mass of clouds over the Golden Gate. Out of the dusk came three identical ships with four masts, square sails, high sterns, and forward cabins. The ships were festooned with red pennants bearing Chinese characters, and a great bronze cannon was mounted midship on the lead vessel.

"What strange ships," I said.

"They are ocean-going, Chinese junks that make the round trip from Shanghai twice a year. They always come in just before dark, when the customs inspectors have gone home." said Blake.

"Why?" I asked.

"The Chinese Exclusion Act is legislation that bars more Chinese from entering the country, so the men have no women. Chin Ten Sing buys women in China and smuggles them into San Francisco. Their families get money that is needed for their survival and they have the opportunity for a new life in America. The youngest and prettiest wind up in Madam Ah Toy's brothel and the rest he sells to men. It is the only way for the men to have Chinese wives. He also smuggles opium," said Blake.

"Can't the Americans put a stop to it?" I asked.

"Tonight, every woman and every bit of opium will be loaded into small fishing boats and will be gone. When the custom officials inspect tomorrow, they will find only bolts of silk, dried fish, and Chinese trinkets. You should not be surprised. Old Sing bought the lovely Lotus Blossom in Shanghai. She is now his number one concubine," said Blake. I almost choked on my coffee. I could not imagine dear Lotus Blossom in the arms of that old man. I am not sure I would have advocated saving him if I had known he was keeping her as if she was a slave. The more I thought about it, the more irate I became.

"The man is a slaver, a damn criminal!" I shouted.

Blake fiddled with a black, twisted cigar for a moment. "No. It is seen as a service to the Chinese since it is the only way for the men to have women and start a family. The women are better off here than in China, where they would starve. Lotus Blossom is fortunate and has great status here. Some people say she is a Lung Tao, or Dragon Head, in the Precious Tiger Society. In China, she would have suffered a worse fate," said Blake.

"What is the Precious Tiger Society?" I asked.

"The society is an ancient Chinese triad, a network of arch-criminals. Here, they run the opium dens and the cheaper brothels. They rarely become involved in affairs outside of Chinatown, but that may change," said Blake.

I have had the bad habit of falling in love with nearly every beautiful woman I encounter. As with many of those before, I knew the idea of possibly starting a romance with Lotus Blossom was a mere fantasy, but I still felt an emptiness at hearing this news. Even though she appeared to be well-respected, it didn't seem like this turn of events gave her a fair chance at a decent life of her own choosing. I could take her away from all of this, but would she be happy in Edinburgh? What was I feeling for her, anyway? Was it love, or was it just the wine talking?

2 July 1883, San Francisco

Despite the events of the last few days and the sense of deflation I felt yesterday upon learning about Lotus Blossom, today somehow started as a delightful morning. I figured it would be good to get some fresh air, so I took my camera and decided on a solitary stroll to photograph the astounding sights in this grand city. In the hotel lobby, a dumpy, middle-aged lady poked me with an umbrella. I did not recognize Penelope until I heard her voice.

"Meet me at the ferry landing," she said. I went out into bright sunshine, and after a half a block, I glanced back. Penelope wore a long, grey dress. A black shawl covered her head and shoulders. She appeared heavy around the middle, had a curious hump on her back, and waddled as if her feet hurt. I waited at the ferry ticket office until she caught up, and separately, we made our way to seats on the upper deck. Her hair was darker with streaks of grey, her cheeks were puffy, and her glorious bosom was flattened. We said nothing until the ferry was well out into the bay. Engine noise, the cry of gulls, and the wind swept away the sound of our voices.

"Dr. Bell did the disguise and it is a good thing. I saw Borovsky," said Penelope.

"Where?" I asked.

"In Stanford's library. He claims to be a direct envoy from the tsar," she said.

"Then he really could have been the one who killed Dawson," said I.

"Dawson was of no importance, a cheap con man. Borovsky got to Stanford first."

"Start at the beginning," said I.

"I took the job to teach Stanford's son French and Russian. He is a smart boy, an only child, and learns fast. We got along well, and within a couple of days, I had the run of the house. One evening, when the family was away, I slipped into Stanford's private office. The house boy, a big Chinaman, grabbed me around the neck and held a knife to my face."

"Johnny Chan?" I asked.

"Yes. First, he asked if I knew you. When I reassured him, he asked me to set up a meeting with you for today," said Penelope.

We followed wagons and carriages off the ferry to the Alameda landing. Penelope pointed south, along the shore of the bay. "About a half-mile past the marine railway, look for a boat flying a flag with a green turtle," said she. Penelope gave me a cool kiss and left the way we had come. I walked along a muddy, rutted road past an industrial shipyard and fishing boats tied to crumbling wooden docks until I saw the flag with a green turtle at the masthead of a small fishing boat. It was about forty feet long, flat-bottomed with a high stern, and tied to a crumbling, wooden dock. A dark-skinned Chinaman, wearing a straw hat with a conical crown and pajama pants cut off at his knees, squatted at the bow. He motioned for me to board, held out his hand, and I clambered onto the deck. The Chinaman grinned and pointed to the midsection that was partially enclosed by a curved bamboo overhead. I did not recognize Johnny Chan until he spoke.

"Sit here." Chan also wore dirty pajamas and a large straw hat that hid his features. The man at the bow shoved off, while another at the stern sculled the boat offshore with a long oar. When crewmen raised a huge, rectangular sail, the wind sent us skimming across the bay.

"Wear this," said Chan. I put on one of the straw hats and a dirty cloak that covered my western clothing. We were heading southwest towards the southern part of San Francisco. "There is Potrero Point and, over there, Hunters Point," said Chan, as he pointed out both locations. I made out a mass of smokestacks, dark, low buildings, and a locomotive. When we drew closer, I could see a huge dry dock occupied by a two-funnel steamship. Chan uncased a long brass telescope. "Take a good look," said he. At first, I focused on a low, sandy beach and swampland that rose to low hills. There, men were pushing carts, and steam-powered trucks scuttled about on tracks. It was a busy industrial complex. "That is the Union Iron Works, manufacturers of locomotives, mining equipment, and rolled steel. Further along is the shipyard," said Chan.

"It is huge," said I.

"It is the largest industrial complex of any Pacific nation. Look to the open space further north," said Chan. I focused on a row of tents, groups of men drilling on an open field, an array of field artillery, and Gatling guns.

"It looks like an army," said I.

"It is the California Militia. The officers are ex-Confederates."

We were skimming along a few hundred yards offshore. Chan gave an order, the boat rounded up, and the crew put nets overboard. To any onlooker, we were no different from a hundred other fishing boats on the bay. We were closer now. I again focused the telescope on the drill field. The smartly-uniformed men carrying Winchester repeaters at port arms leaped into view. They were crisp, disciplined, and drawn up in formation. At the crack of noon, a puff of smoke rose from a field gun, and in a moment, we heard the *boom!* Several carriages dashed onto the field and a half-dozen men alighted. An officer in a grey uniform saluted the civilians. They marched across the field and inspected the troops. I twisted the lens but could not make out the faces of the men.

"Who are they?" I asked.

"Leland Stanford, Charles Crocker, Mark Hopkins, and a Russian envoy," said Chan. I twisted the tubing and brought the flag waving from a tall pole into focus. It was not the stars and stripes of the United States, but a peculiar flag with a walking bear above a red stripe. In the top left-hand corner were three stars.

"What a strange flag," said I. Chan took the telescope.

"It is the bear flag, the original State of California flag, but it has three stars instead of one," said Chan.

"Three stars? But there is only one state." I said.

"They plan to annex more land," said Chan.

"Who is the Russian envoy? I asked.

"A big handsome fellow, arrived here a couple of weeks ago and immediately went to the Russian warship," said Chan.

"Could it be a Count Borovsky?" I asked.

"Yes, that is his name. He brought papers and maps to Stanford."

"Did you say Union Iron Works?" I asked.

"Yes, the company smelts iron and manufactures mining and railroad equipment," said Chan.

"The Russian, Borovsky, knows the location of molybdenum for making a super-strong, steel alloy that could enhance the railroad industry and result in great wealth and power for its owners and overseers," said I, recalling the words of Professor Marcy.

"Aah, this Borovsky will trade the secret of the molybdenum to Stanford," said Chan.

"What does Borovsky get?" I asked.

"He wants Alaska for Russia," said Chan.

"Impossible. The Americans will never return Alaska," said I.

"The Russians may retake it by force," said Chan. I again inspected the iron works with the telescope and made out what appeared to be a partially-collapsed balloon almost hidden behind a high fence.

"Can we get any closer?" I asked.

The men pulled in their nets and sculled the boat until we were no more than a hundred yards offshore. Guards ran down to the beach with rifles at port arms and waved us away. Our Chinese sailors calmly re-set their nets and ignored the armed men. The guards faltered, apparently unwilling to shoot, eventually turned their backs, and marched towards the fence. At the same time, the civilian dignitaries, with a group of officers, approached the fenced-in area.

"Stay low, keep out of sight," hissed Johnny. I stretched out on my belly and watched as the balloon took shape. It was, apparently, a demonstration for the visitors. I focused the telescope and noted heavy ropes dangling from the balloon. As the tethered balloon rose in the air, I noted something dangling from the ropes. Cautiously, I raised my camera between two burlap sacks filled with fish and snapped a series of photos. "That's enough." Johnny Chan began to speak in rapid Chinese, and soon we were off, sailing back to the Alameda shore.

From the upper deck of the returning ferry leaving Alameda, I carefully scrutinized the Russian steam frigate. She was the

Chesma, and carried an impressive array of breech-loading guns mounted on modern turrets. Sailors in white shirts with horizontal blue strips polished brass and worked on the big guns. *Were they on a wartime footing?* I wondered.

Back at the hotel, I had a lemon squash and looked through the newspapers. Ian Blake had written an article when the *Chesma* arrived in San Francisco on a 'courtesy call.' She was a part of the Siberian Military Flotilla out of Vladivostock.

3 July 1883

I spent this morning in a darkened closet developing the gelatin plates. They were still drying when, at noon, I went out for a bite to eat. Ian Blake nursed a glass of whisky at the hotel bar. I took the next seat.

"What is a 'courtesy call'?" I asked.

"The Russian ship?"

"Yes, a Russian warship and a vicious killer named Borovsky who claims to be an envoy from the tsar. It can't be a coincidence," said I. Blake shrugged his shoulders as if my question was of no importance. *Ding*; a low chime rang from Blake's vest pocket. He withdrew a gold repeater and snapped open the case.

"What a beautiful watch. May I see it?" I asked. Without thinking or waiting for his answer, I lifted the watch from his hand. "Oh, I am sorry, but what is this?" The inscription read, *From the 1st King George's Own Gurkha Rifles to Major Ian Blake, Marchess of Brecon.*

I stared at the glowing, gold inscription for almost a minute. "You are not an impecunious poet," said I. Blake sighed deeply, tossed down the rest of his whisky, and took the watch out of my hand.

"Why did you leave the army to be a newspaper scribbler?" I asked.

"I had a fling with the colonel's lady," said he. He toyed with the watch and called for another drink. "I was at loose ends, heard about the Secret Service, and offered my services. Colonel Beachy-Edwards assigned me to this godforsaken post," said Blake.

"With a title, you should get along well with Lady Walshingham," said I, wishing I could take it back as soon as I said it, since it sounded a bit petty. Did I really want that to happen?

"Penelope and I are old friends," said he.

"Damn! Am I always the last to learn these things? I should be home practicing medicine. Instead, I came on this goose chase, have been shot at, had my neck twisted and snapped, and nearly lost my life. Please explain this to me. What in the world is going on?" I asked, barely taking time to breathe between sentences. Who and what could I trust?

I felt disoriented at hearing his admission about Penelope, so I was glad to have the opportunity to get away when, instead of answering my question, he invited me to meet in Dr. Bell's room tonight. "Shall we say, ten o'clock?" asked Blake. "I promise to reveal more then."

Penelope arrived at Dr. Bell's room within minutes of Blake. Dr. Bell had laid out a cold repast with several bottles of a local wine. She immediately went into the bathroom, slammed the door, and didn't emerge until nearly half an hour later. The padding was gone, and in place of the solemn grey dress, she wore a long, red Chinese dress, slit halfway up her leg and embellished with a formidable dragon. She posed, Turkish cigarette in hand. "A gift from Johnny Chan," she said. My heart leaped. She was as lovely as ever and I wondered, in that moment, what I could do to win her heart. It was Ian Blake, however, who, without hesitation, gallantly rose and greeted her with a kiss.

"My darling, you are absolutely ravishing," said he. Penelope practically wilted in his arms. It is amazing what a title will do for a man.

Dr. Bell blew a cloud of smoke. "It is time for business. Mr. Blake, tell us of your observations." Blake removed a sheaf of papers from his coat pocket.

"In a nutshell, the British Empire is overextended. Mr. Gladstone has wars in Egypt and the Sudan. We are bogged down in Afghanistan and India; the Royal Navy is busy protecting the Suez Canal," said Blake.

"By my observations, the American Army is almost non-existent since the end of the Indian wars," said Bell.

"That is correct. Here in California, the militia is better armed than the United States Army, and the officers are experienced ex-Confederates. It is the only military force on the Pacific coast," said Blake.

Dr. Bell bit down on the stem of his pipe. "British Columbia refuses to join the Canadian Confederation until it is joined by rail with the east, but the Trans-Canada Railroad is bogged down in politics and opposition from the Indians in Alberta. Could the California Militia take British Columbia by force?" Dr. Bell asked.

"Yes, of course. Western Canada is a wilderness with no vestige of the British Army, but if the militia attacked, it would appear to be an invasion by the United States, and neither the Yankees nor the British want an international war," said Blake.

Penelope rose from her chair and stalked across the room. "Will you men listen to me?" she asked.

"My dear, if you have anything to add, please speak up," said Dr. Bell.

"Yesterday, three men abducted young Leland Stanford and said I was no longer needed. Johnny Chan says the militia and the Russians now have control over Stanford. Stanford is not a bad man, but with the militia holding his son, he will do what they command." said Penelope. The room went silent. Blake poured a glass of single malt for himself and another for Penelope.

"These are dangerous men. Something evil is afoot," said Dr. Bell.

"Is it my turn yet?" I asked.

"If you have more information, spit it out," said Blake.

I recounted my trip with Johnny Chan that Penelope had arranged and described the military display. "Now, here is a mystery. What could be the purpose of a great balloon?" I placed three photographs on table from the Union Iron Works. Blake and Bell rushed to inspect them.

"Strange, there is no gas burner. It is a hot air balloon. Aha, this tube must lead to a tank of compressed hydrogen," said Bell.

"Look at the heavy ropes," said I.

Dr. Bell withdrew his hand lens from his vest pocket and spent several minutes going over every inch of the photo. "The balloon appears to be lifting a section of railroad track," said he.

"The iron rails are pre-spiked to the wooden cross ties," said Blake.

"But to what purpose?" I asked.

"Hydrogen balloons have incredible power. A balloon this size can easily lift a section of railway track and move it over difficult terrain."

Blake clapped a hand to his head. "Of course! Stanford plans to build a railroad through British Columbia to the mines in the Yukon!" said he.

Dr. Bell sat, stretched out his long legs, and folded his hands over his chest in the very pose I had seen so often when he solved difficult diagnostic problems in the clinic.

"Mr. Stanford and his associates have extensive industrial works. A railroad through British Columbia to the Yukon would give them a monopoly on molybdenum. They would be the world's foremost manufacturer of locomotives, ships, and munitions. They would be incredibly powerful," said Dr. Bell.

"Bah! The British government would never allow a foreign company to build a railroad on their territory. It would mean war with the United States," said I.

"War is a distant problem. At this moment, I am more concerned about young Leland Stanford. He is a good boy, an only child, and the apple of his father's eye. The old man is ill. Borovsky must be the brains behind this scheme," said Penelope.

"Penelope is correct, but we must have more information before we can act," said Dr. Bell.

"Borovsky appears to be scheming on behalf of Russia, but he may be taking advantage of Stanford to gain power and enrich himself," said Blake. We polished off the last bottle and came to no conclusion about next steps.

"It is late, we must have our wits about us tomorrow if we are to stop a major international conflict. We have no time to lose," said Dr. Bell.

I could not sleep, so have resumed writing my diary. My thoughts are in a whirl. How grave is this situation? Really, what difference does it make? How can a frozen land, so far to the north, affect the world? Even if things are truly so dire, what can I do?

The picture of the twins, their gossamer butterfly-like costume, just flashed into my mind — and then death before my very eyes. Though I attempt to rub away the vision, as if in a waking nightmare I can see Manfredi's brains splashing on the floor, the Cossack dagger in poor Codlington, and the harpoon tip that killed Dawson. Now, I see clearly — I must pursue Borovsky to the end.

4 July 1883, San Francisco

At the break of day, gunfire, a band playing "Dixie," and raucous shouts disturbed my slumber. When the sound of firecrackers, drums, and trumpets overwhelmed my senses, I looked out on a wild scene. Marching men carried banners and fired pistols into the air, and small boys lit firecrackers under tin cans. It appeared to be the usual national exuberance when our ex-colonies celebrated their independence from Britain. Dr. Bell was already up and at breakfast, ignoring the sounds of bedlam from the streets. I scarcely had dressed and consumed a cup of coffee when Ian Blake burst into our suite of rooms. He paused, breathless, and waved the San Francisco Chronicle in the air. "Read this!" Great black headlines covered the front page.

CONFEDERATE STATES OF THE PACIFIC!
A NEW COUNTRY

CALIFORNIA HAS JOINED WITH THE OREGON TERRITORIES AND SOON BRITISH COLUMBIA WILL BE A PART OF OUR GREAT NEW COUNTRY.
LELAND STANFORD, FIRST PRESIDENT OF OUR GREAT REPUBLIC, ANNOUNCES PLANS FOR ELECTIONS

Dr. Bell tore the paper from my hands and read the next page out loud. It was a statement by Major General Buford T. Forrest, commander of the California Militia and late of the Confederate Army. "The California Militia is now the Army of the Confederate States of the Pacific. All able-bodied men, including members of the United States Army, are invited to join our glorious cause. The pay is fifty dollars per month, three meals a day, uniform and rifle, comfortable barracks." The next page was even more ominous.

RUSSIA FIRST TO RECOGNIZE THE CONFEDERATE STATES OF THE PACIFIC

Bell put down the paper. "They are losing no time. Nothing can stop them from invading British Columbia. There will be war, but neither the United States nor Britain has the will or the power to stop them," said he.

"They have taken the United States Mint and have plans to issue their own money. I have learned from multiple sources that the militia is forcing Chinese men into transport ships. They will be slaves for the new country and forced to work on the railroad in British Columbia," said Blake.

"There isn't a moment to lose. First, we need to free the boy, young Leland Stanford. Then, his father will be free to act sensibly," said Bell.

"I shall contact Johnny Chan," said Blake.

While waiting for Blake's return and further word, I went out for some fresh air to clear my head and immediately encountered soldiers herding long lines of Chinese men towards the waterfront. Armed guards prevented me from walking up Nob Hill, and messengers, smartly attired in grey uniforms, dashed about on horseback. Everything pointed towards mobilization and a war to overtake Western Canada.

While we continued to wait for word from Blake, our afternoon tea was a dismal affair. Dr. Bell appeared to be completely without spirit. "The best we can do is contact Colonel Beachy-Edwards and request naval support," said he.

"There isn't a British ship within a thousand miles, and how could the colonel contact a ship at sea?" asked Penelope.

"She is right. Perhaps the British could organize resistance at Vancouver," said I.

"There is only a small garrison. The Russian warship will subdue resistance with a massive bombardment," said Bell.

Ian Blake, more than a bit disheveled and completely out of breath, came through the door with a rush. "Johnny Chan has a plan to rescue young Leland and do some damage to their army. Chin Ten Sing had the foresight to smuggle three hundred Snider-Martini rifles into Chinatown. The Chinese stole the rifles from the British Army," said he.

"What use would old-fashioned, single-shot rifles be against repeating Winchesters?" I asked. Blake bared his teeth and grinned.

"Those old British Sniders will kill a man up to fifteen hundred yards and are deadly accurate to four hundred yards. The Winchesters fire a .44 calibre bullet that is only useful at a short range."

7 July 1883

The events from the early morning of the fifth of July until now are blurred through the lens of danger, pain, and near death. We survived an ordeal rarely experienced by human beings mostly through the ingenuity and courage of Dr. Bell. The following is a narrative of the events of the last days to the best of my memory.

Johnny Chan and Chin Ten Sing organized the diversions that allowed me, Dr. Bell, and Penelope to rescue young Leland Stanford. I thought the mission was too dangerous for Penelope, but she insisted on joining us. "The boy will trust me and no one else," she said.

Just after midnight, early on the fifth of July, girls from the house of Madame Ah Toy descended on the main gate to the military compound. The undisciplined guards opened the gates, and in the ensuing melee, more soldiers arrived from all over the compound, in varying stages of undress, thinking they were about to enjoy the pleasures of oriental lust. Instead, a dozen hatchet-wielding members of Chin Ten Sing's triad slashed at the soldiers' arms, legs, and exposed private parts. At the same time, Pow Chan and some twenty boys made their way through the fence, set fire to the officer's barracks, and set off many strings of firecrackers.

Under a light fog, Johnny Chan, with the three of us in tow, stealthily approached Hunters Point in a small sampan. The largest and most heavily armed of Chin Ten Sing's junks followed us down the bay. We lay crouched on bundles of rags and watched the frenzied activities in the industrial area. Under the glare of Edison electric lights, men fastened ropes tethering the giant hydrogen balloons to sections of railroad. The balloons rose, lifting the sections of rail to a height of twenty feet or more, while men leading horses attached to lines walked the rails to a ship. Once the balloon was in position over the ship, workers released hydrogen, allowing the balloon to lower the rails into the holds. It was an impressive display of industrial might and ingenuity. Our sampan, drifting with the current, silently approached the beach. When the shouts of soldiers and the sounds of Pow Chan's firecrackers reached our ears, a barrage of gunfire roared from the junk and extinguished the electric lights that had illuminated the shipyard. This was followed by an immense blast from the sampan's giant brass cannon. The shell exploded directly over the ship that was loading railroad tracks. One of the hydrogen balloons erupted in a great wall of flame. The Chinese fisherman sculled us close to the beach. Unfortunately, I lost my cane/pistol when I assisted Penelope over the side of the boat. Johnny Chan led us through the compound, past a giant locomotive and factories, and to the fence surrounding the military compound, which was guarded at intervals by armed sentries.

"Wait here." Chan wriggled away. There was the sound of a brief struggle. Chan returned with a large shears and severed the lowest of the fence wires. "The stockade holding prisoners and young Leland Stanford is straight ahead, but surrounded by another fence," he whispered. We crawled, faces in the dirt, to the stockade fence. Chan silently garroted another guard, and after waiting for a cloud to cover the moon, he clipped the wire of the second fence just enough for us to wriggle through. Chan led our party. I was second, followed by Penelope, and Dr. Bell was in the rear. We came to the back wall of a small, brick building, which was functioning as a makeshift jail. I followed Chan as he crept towards two men who guarded the front entrance. Bell and Penelope kept well back in the shadows.

"Damn," Penelope uttered softly, when we were some twenty feet away.

"Who's there?!" The guard's lit bullseye lantern caught us in the glare. Dr. Bell's Webley revolver roared. The light went out and the guard screamed. Johnny Chan leaped forward and garroted one guard while I caught the second with a rugby tackle that knocked him senseless.

"The boy is in the second cell," said Chan. "We must move quickly." Aided by the light of a lucifer, Dr. Bell shot the padlock off the door and Penelope swept the boy into her arms. Chan released half a dozen Chinese prisoners who ran towards the main gate, setting off new alarms. I took the boy from Penelope. The others ran towards the beach and the waiting boat. Young Stanford was light as a feather. He clung to my shoulders and was as good as any soldier. We would have escaped unscathed but for the Edison electric searchlight that swept across the beach. Though we ducked low to avoid being seen, we were caught in its glare. A platoon of soldiers, running with their rifles at the ready, charged at us across the field.

"There they are! Don't let them escape!" a leader shouted. The great Chinese junk with riflemen and cannon, was enveloped in a fog bank and could not come to our aid. When the searchlight swept away for an instant, we made a run for the beach. Penelope stumbled. I reached back to pull her onward while still holding the boy, but just at the water's edge, we were again caught in the light. There was a fusillade of rifle fire. Fortunately, the bullets whistled over our heads. I stumbled at the water's edge, but Johnny Chan took the Stanford boy and — at first running, and then swimming — finally made it safely to the waiting sampan. The soldiers were on us in a second. One whacked Dr. Bell with the butt of his rifle, another grabbed Penelope by the hair, and a third struck me with the back of his saber. It was all over. When I regained my senses, the soldiers had hobbled our legs together with lengths of rope.

We were disheveled and water-soaked to the knees, but after daubing grime from her face and adjusting her riding habit, Penelope was perfectly presentable. The Inverness cape had protected Dr. Bell's coat, vest, and cravat from dirt, and with his aristocratic features, he was as presentable as any English squire. I was a complete mess, with a ragged hole in my filthy, tweed jacket. An especially well-muscled fellow had my left arm in a hammer lock.

"Unhand my valet! Look here, young man, we are subjects of Her Majesty, Queen Victoria, and guests of President Stanford. Kindly call off these ruffians and provide us with a conveyance to our hotel." said Dr. Bell. The young, fuzzy-chinned lieutenant was momentarily overwhelmed by this statement and more than a little flustered by Penelope, who rewarded him with a most coquettish smile.

"My apologies for the misunderstanding, sir. Men, release these prisoners," he commanded.

As the soldiers untied the rope, a group of officers appeared on the scene. One wore the blue sash, red, striped trousers and the blue jacket of a Russian officer. He wore a large shako, and his right hand was tucked into his jacket. I almost laughed; it was Borovsky posing as Bonaparte.

"NO, they are state enemies! Do NOT release them!" shouted Borovsky. The guards obeyed the Napoleon imposter. We were as helpless as caged mice. With Borovsky in the lead, the platoon of soldiers, now rather more roughly than necessary, led us back to the jail and forced us into the cell recently vacated by young Leland Stanford.

Borovsky, seated on a straight-backed chair and smoking a long cigar, gestured towards Dr. Bell and me. "You have been a great nuisance, but, dear Penelope, I should have thought you would see that I am the only man who can truly take care of you; your fortune lies with me. It is very sad. So sad. You made a mistake by shooting me, then taking my things and running away with that idiot American, Dawson. Now, I shall have to devise an appropriate death for all of you." A strange light came into his eyes and his face twisted into a parody of a smile. He licked his lips, closed his eyes, and started to mutter underneath his breath. "Yes, such a delicious revenge I will not want to miss."

The man was completely mad. He gestured with his cigar to Dr. Bell. "My method of administering poison to the twins was unique, was it not? The twins could have been my concubines, my dearest companions in the new world order. But, alas, under the influence of drink, I spoke too much. They had to die before Beachy-Edwards discovered my plan to get back Alaska and overtake the Yukon Territory. He made every effort to stop me."

He paused to puff at his cigar before continuing. "I detested using the knife and pistol to kill those fools in Boston. It was altogether too messy and without art. You must admit that without your damn interference these local idiots would have thought Jack Dawson died by drowning or was killed by angry Chinamen."

"We are British citizens and protected by the Crown. The Secret Service will hound you to the ends of the earth if you hurt a hair of our heads, and you are very well aware of that fact," said Dr. Bell.

"That is so. I could arrange to have you executed by a firing squad or by hanging, but the press, even in this new nation, would report your death to the world and there would be embarrassing questions," said Borovsky.

Penelope bit her lip, and though I would have sworn I saw fear in her eyes — and, perhaps, even tears — she was resolute in her response to his diabolical tirade. "These ruffians captured us. I shot you, but it was only a flesh wound when I could have killed you. You know I followed Dawson simply to protect the case he stole from you. How dare you ruin my cover or even question that I would betray you?! You are the one who is not loyal. If you were true to me as you suggest, you would obtain the handsome reward the Queen would surely offer you for our safe return and give me my well-deserved half. Me betray you? Ha! You have betrayed me!" said Penelope.

"Is this a tantrum? Words, words, words. A paltry reward is nothing compared to the riches of the gold and mineral wealth of the Yukon. I shall use this new nation to restore Alaska to Russia." Borovsky made another twisted smile. "I may rule Alaska myself and make the greatest fortune ever seen," he said.

The sky was lighter towards the east. It promised to be a clear day, perhaps our last. Borovsky swaggered away. The guard brought us bitter coffee, bread, and cold eggs. Within an hour, the mad Russian returned.

"The Americans agree. We will not put you to death, but give you the freedom of the sky," said he. "If you happen to have an accident while on the ride, oh well, then. . . No one can blame anyone but you for what will appear to be your own incompetence at flying. Who has the power now? Ha! Da svidahnia, my British friends!"

The guards led us to a clearing where a large balloon was tethered to posts driven into the ground. Ropes suspended from the giant balloon led to a large wicker basket with a wooden floor, covered with a thick carpet. The guards hoisted us into the basket.

The rascals kept Penelope in their clutches far longer than necessary. She offered them nothing but a steely gaze.

"This is an observation balloon so the surveyors can see far ahead and plot our route through the wilderness," said Borovsky.

Dr. Bell carefully inspected the well-constructed basket. It was more comfortable than usual, presumably because the surveyors would be aloft for long periods of time. Ropes held the basket to the balloon, and a curious tube led from the balloon to the basket. The balloon itself was made of impermeable, waxed silk.

"How do we release gas in order to descend?" Bell asked.

"Very simple. Merely open this valve at the end of the tube. The wind will waft you over the mountains to the east. There you can descend and will no longer be of concern to us," Borovsky said.

Indeed, when the tethering ropes were released, we quickly ascended with a gentle, onshore breeze that swept us over the bay. Within half an hour we were over Alameda and flying towards the distant mountains. We were far higher than my one experience in a hot air balloon during our last American visit. People and houses below were mere dots. Though that last trip had at least started off pleasantly, with amazing views, this one felt much more ominous from the outset.

"I can't catch my breath," said Penelope. Dr. Bell was taking in one great lungful of air after another, and I found myself sighing more than usual.

"The atmosphere is growing rarified. I can scarcely breathe. Arthur, please open the valve," said Dr. Bell. I twisted the valve, a simple stop cock, but there was no egress of gas.

"What is wrong? We must descend immediately," said Bell. I looked upwards, following the black tubing with my gaze. There, at its junction with the balloon was a second valve — closed. The fiend, Borovsky, had sent us aloft with no means to release gas. The incredible lifting power of hydrogen would take us high into the atmosphere, where we would die for lack of oxygen.

"We must release the gas," said Dr. Bell. I thought of my stiletto, still strapped inside my stocking against my leg. The blade was four inches in length, attached to a wooden handle.

"I could throw the knife and perforate the bag," said I.

"No, if the blade does not strike and penetrate the balloon, we will be lost," said he.

There was only one alternative. I placed the knife in a coat pocket, grasped two of the ropes that connected us to the balloon and wrapped my legs around them, hoisting myself to the edge of the basket. I hung on to the ropes with both hands for dear life. The effort of climbing nearly took all my strength. My head began to pound for lack of oxygen. I was forced to rest after every painful attempt to climb towards the balloon, which rose rapidly, forced by skyward gusts of wind rising from the foothills. I almost lost my grasp when the basket whirled in the changing winds, but I summoned a burst of energy and made it to within an arm's length of the balloon. I made sure to wrap my legs tightly about the ropes and, with what seemed like my last ounce of strength, clung with one hand while I groped in my pocket for the knife. I grasped the handle, lifted my arm, and succeeded in stabbing a small hole in the waxed silk. There was a slight hiss of escaping gas. I slashed at it again to increase the size of the hole, but my arm was seized with a terrible cramp. The knife slipped from my useless hand and spun out of sight towards the distant earth. I may have lost consciousness for a moment, but revived enough to descend to the basket. Penelope was on the floor, lying on her side, gasping for air. Dr. Bell sucked in great quantities of the thin air, but his lips were blue. I remained upright, but sagged against the side of the basket. The world went black and fuzzy.

It must have been mid-afternoon when I awoke. We were again over the bay. Nob Hill and the city sparkled in bright sunshine a mile or two off to the northwest. The shifting wind had first carried us south, and now, a brisk east wind pushed us over the peninsula. We had lost altitude. Dr. Bell, with his head lolling on his shoulder, was still blue about the lips. Penelope stirred and made small mewling sounds. It occurred to me that Dr. Bell was in his middle years and did not have the resiliency of youth. As I thought of his possible death, a great black cloud — part despair and part grief — descended on my mind. It was one of the worst moments of my life. The wind shifted and came from the south with increasing force, carrying us to the north end of the bay over the Golden Gate.

We dropped, perhaps another few hundred feet. Dr. Bell stirred and showed signs of life. I grasped his shoulder and shook his inert body until he opened his unfocused, dull eyes. I continued rubbing his arms and speaking to him until his cheeks lost their bluish hue and the old twinkle returned to his eyes. I breathed a great sigh of relief, despite my own slowly-ebbing oxygen level.

Penelope sat upright, rubbed her glassy eyes, and smoothed her hair. When his breathing returned to normal, Dr. Bell raised himself and peered over the side. The wind switched to the east and blew with increasing strength. "Arthur, the wind will blow us out over the sea. Borovsky fully expected us to die from asphyxiation and be blown out over the Pacific so we would be lost forever."

My elation at the possibility of descent over land evaporated. The thought of being blown over the trackless ocean filled me with despair. Our rate of descent was very slow, possibly because hydrogen, being lighter than air, escaped out the bottom of the balloon very slowly. We were at an elevation of a thousand or more feet and drifting out to sea. We watched the sun creep closer to the horizon as the fishing boats and land disappeared from sight. When the sun was a red-purple line just above the horizon, the rising wind pushed us ever more rapidly over the endless Pacific Ocean. We were low enough to make out individual white-capped waves but seemed doomed to die somewhere on that vast, trackless ocean.

At that moment, I spied jagged rocks, resembling the teeth of a saw, rising from the ocean. "Look, islands!" I shouted.

"The Farallones," said Bell.

"It is no use. Our present course will take us beyond the islands," said I. We gazed longingly at the sheer rocky peaks and one small beach, but we were being whirled along by the wind at an altitude of at least one hundred and fifty feet. The Farallones were home to a huge colony of sea birds; gulls, terns, and gannets swooped around our balloon then dove into the sea. *If only we had the freedom of birds we could descend near the island,* I thought.

"Well now, when all seems lost, there is one consolation," said Dr. Bell. He removed a silver flask from an inner pocket. "The water of life. Double-distilled, single malt whisky from the Isle of Skye," said he.

I was struck with a wild idea, and there was nothing to lose. "Dr. Bell, whisky is inflammable and may be our salvation." I took the fine silver flask from his hand.

"Penelope, a bit of cloth from your blouse," said I. The dear girl immediately tore a strip of cloth which I soaked in the whisky, formed into a wick, and placed in the mouth of the flask. "I propose to light the wick and hurl it at the balloon, igniting the hydrogen," said I.

"Oh God, no! Are you crazy? The explosion will kill us!" cried Penelope.

"There is a slim chance that the force of the explosion and flames will rise. If we crouch beneath my cloak, we may, with luck, survive the burst and sudden descent," said Dr. Bell. The fuse ignited with a small, blue flame at the strike of a second match. Penelope and Dr. Bell crouched beneath his Inverness cloak on the floor of the basket. I gauged the distance and, with all my strength, hurled the flask with its small flame towards the rent in the balloon. Thankfully, my aim was perfect. At first, a small puff of yellow flame flickered, and for a moment, I thought the wind had extinguished our only hope. The yellow flame climbed from the rent up the side of the balloon. I shut my eyes, but the giant ball of fire seared red through my eyelids. A shock wave and a blast of heat struck my face. Our basket swayed wildly and commenced to fall. I could not help but open my eyes to look aloft. Three ropes were still attached to a remnant of smoldering silk that acted as a giant umbrella, slowing our descent, but the landing nearly knocked me senseless. I fell on Penelope who was curled in a fetal ball. Her forehead was bruised. Dr. Bell was crumpled in a heap, but had sustained no serious injury.

All that kept us afloat was the wooden floor of the basket. We bobbed on the waves like a cork. Our elation at the safe landing soon turned to despair when strong currents carried us beyond the islands. When the sun disappeared beneath the horizon, it appeared we were headed to a watery death on the open Pacific. Worse, the basket was starting to sink into the icy cold water. The water was above our ankles, and then the numbing cold rose to our knees. Penelope became violently ill from the basket's motion and would have sunk into the water had I not used remnants of rope to lash her upright in the basket. The dreadful night wore on; patches of fog gave way to moonlight and then incredible darkness. Dr. Bell kept up our spirits by singing snatches of hymns. Once, I recognized a fragment of Robert Burns, "A Man's a Man for a' that." His indomitable strength began to fade. I was forced to lash him to the basket, as well, to prevent him from sinking into the water that was now above our knees. The numbing cold was our greatest danger. Penelope's face felt like ice. Dr. Bell no longer responded to slaps on his face, and my strength was waning. Fragments of memories — dinner with Mam, lectures at the university, a winning game — flashed through my mind. Then, nothing … My mind went blank.

I thought it was a star, perhaps a shooting star coming to earth, but it was a strange flame, out of place. What was a flame doing in the midst of the Pacific? Where was I? What was happening? I scarcely felt the incredible strength of the arm that pulled me up, out of the basket over the side of a small boat, and then the bliss of stretching out on dry sacking. I was vaguely aware of Penelope and Dr. Bell beside me on the bottom of the boat. Sometime during that dreadful night, I was awake long enough to see an oil lantern at the very bow of the boat. The flame attracted fish, and a black bird with a noose around his long skinny neck dove into the water. In a moment, the bird surfaced with a fish clamped in its beak. An incredibly huge Chinaman took the fish and tossed it into a wooden box. It was a strange sight.

Sometime later, warm rays of sunshine warmed my numb limbs. I was desperately thirsty. My voice was a hoarse croak. "Water, do you have water?" I asked. The giant Chinaman paid no heed. I grasped his hand and pointed to my mouth. "We must have water." The fisherman opened his mouth. He had no tongue. He then pointed to his ears and shook his head. I finally understood. He was deaf and dumb. Again, I made motions of drinking. He grinned and produced a bottle of cold tea. I have never had such a wonderful drink.

Over the next hour, first Dr. Bell, then Penelope, stirred and came awake. I gave them sips of tea and rubbed their extremities with dry sack cloth. When the sun was a quarter ways up, the fisherman tossed another fish into a box, raised his sail, and turned the bow of our small boat east. The onshore wind sped us along until we ran into a fog bank. The wind dropped, and for several hours, we tossed on lonely waves. The wind picked up, and by mid-afternoon, land rose out of the mists. At dusk, we skimmed through the Golden Gate and, at last, came alongside the largest of the junks that belonged to Chin Ten Sing.

I climbed the ladder and, to my pleasant surprise, Johnny Chan extended a helping hand. Dr. Bell reached the deck with difficulty, and the giant Chinese fisherman carried Penelope with great gentleness.

"You met Big Chan," said Johnny.

"He saved our lives," said I.

"The poor fellow; our enemies cut out his tongue and drove chopsticks into both ears. He is Chin Ten Sing's most faithful nephew." I winced at hearing of this horror. How could people be so inhumane?

Johnny led us to the main cabin, a great, wood-lined room hung with crimson drapes and lit with oil lanterns. We told our story while consuming huge portions of fried prawns, pork in a sweet and sour sauce, and crisp duck, all washed down with copious amounts of tea and rice brandy. Near the end of the meal, Ian Blake arrived, accompanied by Chin Ten Sing and Lotus Blossom.

"Bring us up to date. First, what happened to young Leland Stanford?" I asked, after sharing about our wretched experience.

"The boy is perfectly safe at the house of Madame Ah Toy. His father knows his whereabouts and that he is safe. Unfortunately, Mr. Stanford is still in the clutches of the military and Borovsky," said Blake.

"They plan to remove him to the Russian ship and take him along on the invasion of British Columbia," said Johnny Chan.

"We must stop them," said Dr. Bell.

"How? We have no money to buy off their men, no effective military force, and the Chinese laborers are at their mercy," said Blake.

"There would have been plenty of money if Chin Ten Sing could have sold the fireworks to the eastern cities for the July celebration," said Lotus Blossom.

"Why couldn't he sell fireworks?" I asked.

"A landslide blocked the railroad," Lotus Blossom replied.

Chin Ten Sing sucked in his breath. "My Chinese rockets would have lit the skies over Chicago and New York," said he.

"Their plans are no longer a secret. Borovsky is the master mind. Stanford is the reluctant figurehead of the new country. The Confederate officers have made the militia into a well-armed military force. With the aid of Russian naval guns, they plan to overwhelm Vancouver, invade British Columbia, and start work on the railroad immediately. The Chinese slave laborers will clear the way, and with the aid of hydrogen balloons, construction will move forward at an incredible speed. The Chinese will then be forced to work the mines. Borovsky will have unlimited quantities of gold and molybdenum to feed an industrial empire and will be the most powerful man in the world," said Blake.

Dr. Bell, resting on a plush divan, stretched out his long legs and folded his hands across his chest. He gazed at old Chin Ten Sing through half-lidded eyes.

"Fireworks, you say. What else do you have besides rockets?" he asked.

"Oh, very huge rockets make great *bang* in sky and firecrackers that roar like cannon and the great dragons," said Sing.

"No commander, especially a Russian, wants to lose his ship. Most Russian sailors are brave, but illiterate, superstitious peasants." said Bell.

"Do you have an idea?" asked Blake.

"Aye, here are my plans," said Dr. Bell.

I had not realized the effects of the day's events and did not rise from the cushions of the floor by the dinner table. I struggled to stay awake to hear Bell's plans, but was overcome by exhaustion and drifted off in a deep sleep. I was unsure how much time had passed when I finally awoke, had a cup of tea, requested paper and pencil, and set about recording the last day's events.

8-9 July 1883

Overnight, the great cabin had become a veritable war room. Ian Blake, Johnny Chan, Dr. Bell, and old Chin Ten Sing were seated at the table, in deep conversation, studying a map of the Bay Area. I went on deck for a breath of fresh air. Our junk was anchored next to another, while the third blocked access to the area. Chinese laborers were busily constructing a bamboo framework on a crude, wooden raft. Chin Ten Sing came on deck and, in rapid-fire Chinese, instructed the men where to place a series of firecrackers and sparklers on the bamboo.

"The great dragon," he said.

I was mystified. "What do you mean?" I asked.

"You will see when the great dragon flashes and roars in a most fearful manner," said he. More small sampans and fishing boats came to the sides of our junk. Men feverishly loaded cartons and boxes onto their small boats. The old man directed the frantic activity with an authority that belied his frailty. By mid-afternoon, the boats left and were dispersed about the bay.

I returned to the cabin and listened to the plans. "We should kill as many of the bastards as possible," said Johnny Chan.

"Our aim is to frighten, not harm. We must persuade the Russian commander to give up and convince Stanford and his officers to stand down." said Dr. Bell.

"They have stowed their Gatling guns and light artillery on the ship, and their army is a rabble of miners and laborers. They will break and run," said Ian Blake.

"Arthur, do you feel you have sufficiently recovered to take on a special mission? We need a strong swimmer. Are you game?" Dr. Bell asked.

"I will consider doing anything to get revenge on Borovsky," said I, hoping that I had recuperated sufficiently and my will would help me find the way.

Dr. Bell explained the dangerous, desperate mission.

"I will do it, only if I can take Big Chan," said I.

"My cousin will be proud to accompany you," said Johnny Chan.

The first rocket burst over Hunters Point at midnight. More followed until the intensity and glare appeared to be a fierce artillery barrage. Ian Blake, along with hand-picked Chinese sharpshooters on a boat just off the beach, opened fire with ancient Martini rifles. Bullets punctured the two great balloons that were moored in the shipyard. A single, well-aimed rocket ignited the hydrogen, sending great balls of flame into the night sky. Johnny Chan, with his hatchet-wielding tong members, broke through the outer fence at the same time that Lotus Blossom led her ragged gang with clashing cymbals and strings of giant firecrackers. The hundreds of shouting Chinese swarmed over the encampment, sending soldiers, still dressed in their underwear, fleeing every which way.

The waters of the bay were pitch black. I shivered in the bow of a small sampan while Big Chan sculled our boat to within a hundred yards of the Russian frigate. We quietly dropped anchor and slipped into the water. I clung to a plank and paddled with one arm while Big Chan, with powerful strokes, propelled us towards the ship. At the first crack of a rocket over the Russian ship, I raised my hand. We remained motionless, and — we hoped — out of sight, as more and more rockets exploded over, on, and near the Russians. Sailors manned the big guns but had no target and did not fire. We were close enough to dimly make out a barge propelled by a single man, which came alongside the ship until the bamboo framework practically hung over the deck. A spluttering fuse ignited hundreds of multi-colored firecrackers and sparklers that outlined a green, writhing dragon with a wicked red tongue. Immediately, the red sparklers replaced the green, outlining an even more fearsome dragon that swung a great tail at the very edge of the ship. The noise grew deafening, and in the light of the rockets, Russian sailors began jumping over the sides of the ship.

I motioned again, and Big Chan resumed paddling. I grasped the ten-inch anchor line with one hand and started to saw away at the fibers with a long, razor-sharp knife. When Big Chan understood, he took the knife and, with one giant slash, severed the big ship's anchor line. The ship drifted with the incoming tide until bells sounded an alarm. By then, the ship went aground on a sand bar. We swam back to our small boat in time to see Pow Chan and dozens of boys swarm over the side of the Orient and Pacific steamer that held Chinese laborers in locked cages below deck. They quickly subdued the guards and hacked open the cages. Chinese laborers fled the ship and joined the mob to overcome the soldiers.

It was all over by morning. Dr. Bell and I, in the comfort of the great cabin, sipped tea and listened to the latest incoming reports. For the lack of clean, dry clothing, Chin Ten Sing had supplied us with silk pajamas and long robes, which were surprisingly comfortable. The Army of the Confederate States of the Pacific was a disorganized rabble. General Forrest and his California Militia officers fled inland. According to rumor, they went to the Yosemite land grant where it is said that thousands of men could live and hide for years and never be discovered. Penelope, in a stunning, long, slit skirt supplied by Lotus Blossom, collected young Leland Stanford from the comforts of Madam Ah Toy's House of Pleasure and returned him to Mr. Stanford, who immediately renounced the new country and pledged renewed allegiance to the United States.

There was a small sensation when, wearing our Chinese clothing and carried in sedan chairs, Dr. Bell and I arrived at our hotel. Long, hot baths, bacon, eggs, and coffee restored my spirits and re-energized my still-aching body. Dr. Bell looked longingly at his syringe, but settled for his best meerschaum pipe filled with Cavendish. He blew a long, contemplative cloud of smoke towards the ceiling.

"One question remains. Where is Borovsky? We must bring him to justice," said Dr. Bell.

I accompanied Ian Blake and Johnny Chan to the shipyard and to every lodging house in the city in search of the evil Russian. Pow Chan and his boys combed the streets, but there was no sign of him. We were famished and tired by the search, so we all ended the day together with dinner at the Restaurante Italiano on the waterfront. Other than the missing Russian, the news was fairly good. The inscrutable Lam Qua reported that the casualties among the Chinese amounted to only a few split heads and no deaths.

While fishing boats came to the dock, I toyed with noodles and shrimp in tomato sauce and a glass of red wine.

Two steam tugs, with cables attached to the bow, managed to pull the Russian ship off the sandbar and tow it towards the Golden Gate. The ship came opposite the restaurant, and before our eyes, a figure wearing a blue coat and carrying a revolver backed away from the forward gun turret. His head was bald as a cue ball. A half-dozen cutlass-wielding sailors slowly advanced, under the command of an officer.

"There, there on the ship! It's Borovsky!" I shouted.

"I have a rifle in the cab. One shot would bring him down," said Blake.

"Under our law, he is innocent until a jury pronounces him guilty. An American court would dither over who has jurisdiction, and it would take months to bring him up before a British Court." said Dr. Bell. Lam Qua made an enigmatic smile and nodded agreement.

"You will remember my successful treatment of the tsar's son in Russia two years ago?" asked Dr. Bell.

"That I do, but what does that have to do with Borovsky?" I asked.

Dr. Bell blew a great cloud of smoke. "A word to the tsar about Borovsky's perfidy will bring the man to a Russian dungeon and then execution in cold blood," he said.

"Ah, you are a very clever man," said Johnny Chan.

We heard a faint shout; the Russian sailors made a dash towards Borovsky, who fired a single shot. The sailors backed off until, again, the officer goaded them forward.

"The Russians must have found him out," said Bell, as he gestured towards the ruckus.

Quick as a cat, Borovsky leaped on to a hawser that connected to a port side tugboat and went, hand over hand, to the tug's deck. A great bank of fog rolled over the bay, and in an instant, we lost sight of the tug and its evil passenger.

10 July 1883

We were at dinner this evening when a tired Johnny Chan joined us. “We searched the city again. He has vanished into thin air,” he said.

“Where is Penelope?” I asked.

“I have not seen her since, well, since yesterday,” said Ian, suddenly sounding worried.

Though I know more than most how Penelope mysteriously comes and goes at her leisure, this is different. Something is not right . . .

15 July 1883

I have been in a funk, sick with worry over Penelope, these past few days. We have searched everywhere, but have not been able to find a single clue to her disappearance. Shortly after dinner tonight, a bellboy brought a folded sheet of cheap foolscap. My name was on the outside leaf.

Doyle, you can have her for a bank note of one million U. S. dollars. Come alone to the fall of fire.

Dr. Bell sniffed the paper and examined the bit of the gum that had sealed the folded page. “The message is crudely written with what appears to be a charcoal, it smells of wood smoke, and the gum is from an incense cedar, a tree that exists only in the upper alpine strata,” he said.

“Where is the fall of fire?” I asked.

“He is camping rough in the mountains,” replied Bell.

Ian Blake rested his head in his hands. “The bastard has taken her to the mountains. We don’t even know if she is alive,” he said. He lifted his face. I saw tears in his eyes and realized in that moment that Ian Blake was in love with Penelope. I may have felt passion or lust for the damsel, but Blake’s love was genuine.

“I will get Borovsky if it is the last thing on earth I do,” he said.

“Perhaps he is attempting to join the militia and go to Mexico,” I said.

“We need transportation and money. Leland Stanford owes it to us,” Ian said. Without wasting a moment, off we went to the home of Leland Stanford.

His study was lit by a single bulb in a lamp on his desk. Mr. Stanford was in the shadows, slumped in a chair at his desk. “Your Russian friend abducted Lady Penelope Walshingham,” said Ian.

“He misled me; the man is unscrupulous. I will do everything in my power to make amends,” Stanford said.

“He demands a banknote for one million dollars and we must have transportation. His is ahead of us by several days,” Ian said.

"Ah, well, I owe you at least that much for the recovery of my son," Sanford sighed. He withdrew a checkbook from the desk drawer and, with a heavy hand, signed his name for a million dollars. "Now, about transportation. Where is the rascal?" he asked.

"Chinese grapevine says he is in the Yosemite wilderness," Johnny Chan said.

"If that is in a mountainous area, the locations fit with my observations of his note," said Dr. Bell.

Leland Stanford unrolled a map of Northern California on his desk. "Here is the Yosemite Valley. A riverboat could take you to the upper end of the bay near San Jose, and then, my chief engineer will conduct you the rest of the way in his latest invention," he said.

"How long will it take?" Ian asked.

"You can be at the head of the bay by dawn, and should reach the valley by mid morning," Stanford said.

"Impossible . . . Yosemite is more than two hundred miles away, there are few roads, and the area becomes mountainous," replied Ian. Stanford smiled for the first time.

"You will leave this very night and will travel by air," said he.

We assembled warm clothing for the high altitudes, a basic medical kit, a revolver for Bell and I, and a Martini rifle for Ian Blake. Dr. Bell did not forget a repast of cold salmon, a generous roast of beef with mustard, and a loaf of crisp, sourdough bread.

It is just before midnight. We have boarded the boat and are underway on a southerly course down San Francisco Bay. Since the boat is for daytime passengers, we will have to sleep on the deck.

16 July 1883

"Far as we go, boys. Rise and shine!" the captain shouted. The water was shallow, and we were anchored well off the marshy shore.

I rubbed the sleep out of my eyes and became aware of slow, steady cursing that arose from the foredeck. The cook offered hot coffee with a boiled egg and a slice of bread. With these meager rations in hand, I went forward, only to become entangled in a skein of ropes and electric wires. I didn't get his name, but the engineer — a slender fellow with blond hair — swore oaths, alternately in German and English. "Da damn valve be stuck," he said. Two men worked feverishly with wrenches and hammers to free the valve that should allow hydrogen to flow from a series of tanks into a giant balloon that lay useless and collapsed on deck.

"Is that our transportation to the mountains?" I asked.

The engineer smoothed his hair, "Ya, ya, she will take you anywhere," he said.

"I have had enough of ballooning. The wind is just as likely to take us out to sea as to the Yosemite Valley," said I.

"This balloon can fly against the wind or in any direction you choose," he said. Then, I spied what appeared to be an engine with a propeller attached by braces to the basket. "The latest electric motor, from Germany, powered by lead acid batteries," said the engineer.

Ian Blake paced the deck, muttering to himself. At last, just before noon, he seized a wrench from Adolph, for that was the engineer's name. With a great heave, he moved the valve's lever a quarter turn. A bit of gas hissed into the balloon. With another mighty heave, he opened the valve completely. Slowly, the balloon filled and rose from the deck. When, at last, it was high enough to lift the passenger's basket, I understood how the balloon could fly against the wind. The electric motor, with a six foot, wooden propeller, was attached by a pivot to braces that extended from the basket. A tiller-like handle extended from the motor so it could be turned in any direction. It was nearly four o'clock in the afternoon when we entered the basket; Dr. Bell first, followed by Ian Blake, and then me, struggling with our provisions and the medical kit.

"It is very simple. This switch starts the motor, using current from battery number one. When the battery runs out of electricity, we switch to battery number two and then, with this hand cranked generator, re-charge the first battery. Above all, do not disconnect a wire. A single spark could ignite the hydrogen," explained the engineer.

With those simple instructions, Adolph sat on a bench and, with tiller in hand, ordered the boat's crew to cast off the tethering lines. We ascended to about one hundred feet. Dr. Bell, with a map spread on the floor and compass in hand, ordered the course. "A point north of due east will bring us to the Merced River where it arises from the mountains," he said.

Adolph started the motor and turned the tiller until the propeller faced in the direction ordered by Dr. Bell, the basket rotated, and we moved to the east. The engineer adjusted our height to about five hundred feet, where we found a favorable wind. With the combined force of wind and propeller, we fairly flew over the marshes and swamps that surrounded the San Francisco Bay. Soon, we were over cultivated fields and a series of rivers.

Dr. Bell ordered course adjustments from time to time. "There, there, below us is the junction of the Merced River with the San Joaquin!" he shouted. Yes, he was correct; according to the map, the Merced from almost due east joined the San Joaquin at an almost exact right angle. We were on course; the jagged saw-toothed Sierra Nevada mountains were dead ahead, but the sun was a red glow in the west. Soon, we were in darkness, but we were able to follow the glimmering river with little trouble.

"I do not like to fly in the mountains in the dark. We must stop for the night," said Adolph.

"No, every minute counts," said Ian.

"Adolph is right and there is little we can do at night," said Dr. Bell. Despite his words, we flew on with only the sound of the motor and the whirling propeller for company.

"Ach, I refuse to go further," said Adolph.

"There, just ahead — a glimmer of light!" I shouted. Adolph released hydrogen until we hovered less than a hundred feet above the river. The glimmer of light was a small campfire.

"We go down here," Adolph said. He gently let us down, and when we hovered a mere five feet above a bare, grassy area, I hopped out and secured the tethering lines to boulders along the river.

We warily approached the campfire and soon spied a solitary figure sitting with his back to a huge, smooth boulder. A blackened pot stood on coals alongside the fire.

"Be ye a seekin' a spot o' tae?"

"Aye, we are, and ye hale from East Lothian," said Dr. Bell. The fire flared up, and in its light, I made out a fellow with a flowing, white beard who wore a slouch hat and a leather vest over a flannel shirt. Adolph busied himself with securing the balloon while the three of us found places around the fire.

"Ye still have the accent of Scotland," said Dr. Bell.

"Aye, but I left Dunbar while I was a wee lad. I am called John Muir," said our new friend.

"I am Dr. Joseph Bell of Edinburgh. This fellow is Arthur Conan Doyle. The other lad is Ian Blake. Would ye care for a drop o spirit in your tea?"

We had already consumed our provisions, but Mr. Muir broke off a chunk of bread for each of us. "What brings ye to the valley of the Yosemite?" he asked. I explained our urgent mission.

"What is the fall of fire?" I asked.

Mr. Muir pulled his beard and sipped tea before answering. "That would be the Horsetail Falls that flow from El Capitan. On certain evenings, just at sunset, the falling water and the spray glows as if on fire," he said.

"Will you guide us to the falls?" I asked.

"Aye, for a fellow Scots, I will do that."

17 July 1883

We slept under the stars, rose early, and after tea and a chunk of Muir's rough brown bread, we started out together hiking towards the falls. Muir, in his kindly way, suggested we take only the necessities. "We travel light and fast," he said. Dr. Bell insisted that I carry the medical kit. We crunched over a gravel trail and jumped from one polished boulder to another alongside the Merced River. We were surrounded by tall lodgepole pines, and I spied flakes of obsidian that could have been arrow points. There were patches of summer snow in shady areas, and it grew colder as the day wore on to late afternoon. Muir insisted we stay close because grizzly bears are famous — or should I say infamous — in these parts. He pointed out plants and animal tracks as if he were a professor in nature's university.

Near evening, we came upon an open, grassy meadow with blue lupines, surrounded with towering granite ramparts. "There be the falls," said Muir. We flung ourselves down on tufts of grass in a grove of pine trees alongside the river. Every muscle ached, and I was bone tired from our hike but felt awed and enlivened by the sight of the falls, the river water cascading as if forever falling down, down, down from the glacial granite rocks above. It was, indeed, a gorgeous, majestic thing to witness.

We had been resting just a moment in the gathering evening light when a faint shout reached my ears. "Doyle, come alone, unarmed."

"There, there, he is on the second ledge. I can get him." Blake rested the barrel of the Martini rifle on a rock, but before he could adjust the sights, we were surrounded by a troop of mounted men. They dismounted, relieved us of our pistols, and smashed Blake's rifle against a boulder.

Their leader, General Forrest, tapped my shoulder with a cavalry saber. "Go alone to the falls," he said.

I set out across the meadow, and just as I felt the mist of the falls caressing my cheeks, the setting sun flashed on the falling water until it appeared to be a river of golden fire. The swirling mists turned bright orange. I was struck with great awe and paused for a moment before continuing on a narrow foot path next to a slick, granite wall on one side and sheer drop on the other. Suddenly, a faint, high-pitched shout came from higher up the path. Above the roaring water, I made out two figures.

"Arthur, go back! He will kill you!" a voice yelled out. A horrible strangled scream followed. It was Penelope.

"I will kill her if you don't come with the money!" Borovsky shouted. I paused for a moment, clung to a slight indentation in the rock and realized I was up against not only Borovsky but the powerful force of the torrential flow of water, which was swollen by melting snow plunging down from a great height. The spray rolled up like the smoke from a cathedral on fire. The shaft into which the river hurls itself is a huge chasm lined by wet, glistening stones and narrowing into a ravenous pit of incalculable depth, a pit which seems to go down all the way to the center of the earth. The long sweep of clear water roaring forever down and down and down, and the thick, flickering curtain of spray hissing forever up and up and up, are enough to drive a man mad. I was soaked to the skin and unutterably weary. I was tempted to descend and leave Penelope. *She has the wit to get out of Borovsky's clutches*, I thought. Yet, her voice carried a pitiful note of pain. Could she be sick or injured?

I looked up through the dying light and mists. A hundred feet higher up the trail, Borovsky, his bald head shining in the golden light, had his hand around her neck. After one look at her pleading face, I found new strength and bounded up the curving path that wound upwards to a ledge at the side of the falls. Just beneath the ledge, I fell over a root and nearly slipped away over the precipice. I clung to the wet rock at the edge of the trail but slipped, inch by inch, to the edge and was about to fall into the torrent, which surely would have carried me hundreds of feet to my death. A strong hand grasped mine.

"I won't let you go until I have the money," said Borovsky. He dragged me back to a wide spot on the trail and grasped my neck with a choke hold. I was helpless as he slowly tightened his grip.

"The money," he said. I tensed and attempted to crush his arm with my chin, but damn it all, he was strong.

"The wallet is in my breast pocket. Let go," I said. He released his grip while I fumbled for the wallet that was tied by a stout cord to my coat. I went completely loose and stopped all resistance. It was not what he expected, and in the instant when he relaxed, I tore the cord loose from my coat and, with a lightening flick of my wrists, got the cord around his neck, stepped behind, and bent him backwards. He kicked back and struck my knee. I buckled and lost my advantage. We wrestled back and forth on the narrow slippery ledge in a death struggle. We were both weakening, but with great effort, I sent him flying against the sheer cliff. The bastard pulled a long knife from a belt sheath, crouched, and, with the knife pointed at my belly, advanced step by step. I kept moving away from him until I balanced along the very edge of the wet trail above hundreds of feet of torrent and jagged rocks. If I stepped back one more inch, I would surely cascade to my demise.

Borovsky took another cautious step towards me and pressed the tip of the knife against my neck, close to the carotid artery. I dared not move.

"You bastard," he said. "I could have easily gotten Alaska and been rich but for you and that Bell."

He pressed the knife deeper into my neck. I felt a trickle of warm blood when a rock gave way. I lashed out at Borovsky with one hand and clawed at the slick rock as I went over the side. I slid a dozen feet before, in a desperate move, I grasped a bare root. My feet touched a small ledge. Borovsky fell back and his knife clattered over the edge.

I managed to crawl from one precarious hand hold to the next until I was behind the cascade of water where my narrow ledge widened to a half-dozen feet. He was on me again and crashed a great fist into my chest. I fell just at the edge and yanked at his ankles until he tumbled backwards, striking his head against the granite wall.

We rose at the same time, facing each other, laboring for breath, and soaked with water. I feinted to one side, then crouched and delivered a head butt to his solar plexus. He let out a great *wuff* of air and went down but, with his super strength, managed to grasp my right leg. I kicked, but he held fast and slid, inch by inch, over the slick rock. His kicking feet went first, then his legs, until he dangled while still holding on to me. In a second or two, I would surely have gone off the trail with him and been pulverized by the deadly rocks below. I wrapped my right hand around the stump of a gnarly tree embedded in the side of the trail and struggled and struggled, but I could not release myself from his death grip. Borovsky was too strong. Within seconds, we would both plunge to our deaths.

Then, I thought of Dr. Bell. My mind cleared. What would he do? Something unexpected. I squirmed around until our eyes met and reached my free hand down, as if to give him aid. For a split second, he reached out to me towards my helping hand, but our hands never met. The sunlight faded, and the glowing, falling water became dark and ominous. For a moment, we were bound together in a death struggle, but a gush of water struck his face. He coughed, gasped, and sneezed — as if by an ancient reflex — before releasing his grip on my leg and plummeting to what I was sure was his death. His scream of agony resounded and echoed over the Yosemite Valley floor and left me shaking.

Penelope's pitiable moans led me to where she lay in a pool of water in a crevice. Her ankles were tied, and a white splinter of her broken humerus bone protruded from her left arm just above her elbow. She was nearly unconscious and could not stand. A distant "Hello!" answered my shouts. Despite seeming like hours, it was only minutes before John Muir, with his crooked staff in hand, came bounding up the trail, followed by Ian Blake. Blake cuddled Penelope in his arms as if she were a babe. We followed Muir down the treacherous trail.

By the light of a roaring fire, Dr. Bell washed Penelope's wound with carbolic. I pulled on her arm until the bones were together under the skin. He applied a clean dressing and bound her arm to her chest. There was nothing more we could do.

18 July 1883

After warming myself by the fire last night, I fell asleep from sheer exhaustion. Ian Blake never left Penelope's side.

At dawn this morning, Muir went back down our trail to fetch Adolph in the balloon. I returned to the falls and explored every pool in search of Borovsky's body. Though I did not see him, he was surely dead. The torrent would carry his body downstream to the sea.

Hours later, the balloon floated down to a soft landing in the open meadow. Muir, as good an honest a man as ever came out of Scotland, wished us goodbye and refused Dr. Bell's offer of compensation for his good work. Despite variable winds and a shower of rain, Adolph, with his marvelous motor and whirling propeller, returned us to San Francisco before dark.

21 July 1883

Even when we had returned safely to our rooms in San Francisco, Ian refused to leave Penelope's side. She awoke sometime during that night. For a moment, I detected the old flash in her eye, but part of her spirit had vanished on that terrible ledge beneath Horsetail Falls. She gazed at Ian with a look that I had never seen. It was no surprise when she said she had decided to stay and seek her fortune in San Francisco.

I had planned to return the check to Mr. Stanford, but in my soaked wallet, the ink had run on sodden paper. The check was completely worthless.

In the afternoon of the next day, Dr. Bell and I crossed the bay for the last time. Pow Chan carried our bags. Lam Qua and Johnny Chan bid us farewell when we boarded the eastbound train.

During these last couple days of travel, we have dozed and enjoyed the food, but nothing of note occurred until a train with a brigade of U.S. Army soldiers heading west sidetracked our train in Nebraska. The eastern newspapers carried no news of the recent events in San Francisco, but the Chicago Tribune mentioned Leland Stanford's request for troops to quell rioting Chinese.

15 August 1883, our last day at sea

Though I am delighted to be on my way back home to Edinburgh and then Southsea, I have sunk into a strange lethargy, hence the lack of journal entries in some time. I am torn between following Mr. Mark Twain's advice about exploring, dreaming, and discovering, and my desire to return to Southsea, family, and friends. I will pursue my doctorate and writing my novel.

Dr. Bell, too, has seemed strangely dispirited and has applied himself to revising his textbook of surgery. He has not once used cocaine but, instead, continues to find solace in tobacco. This evening, immediately after dinner, we were idly watching for our imminent landfall. Dr. Bell put an arm on my shoulder.

"Laddie, I have had enough adventuring. You must decide whether to pursue medicine or a career in writing. Either way, you will be a great success."

"Thank you sir," said I.

Would this be our last parting? I wiped away a tear which I hid from my mentor and friend.

***

Editor's note:

Six months later, Leland Stanford and his family embarked on a grand tour of Europe. His only son, Leland Jr., contracted typhoid fever and died in Italy. Stanford endowed Stanford University in memory of his son.

There were no further entries in the diary. The last half-dozen pages were blank, but while we were leafing through the journal, three pages fell out from between the last page and the back cover; a one-page letter written in a lady's penmanship and what was clearly a draft of a two-page letter, which contained numerous scribbles and crossed out words. For the sake of clarity and ease of reading, we have eliminated all the errata and both are published below in a legible form.

The one-page letter:

8 April 1885

Dear Arthur,

It is such a long time since we parted. You may be surprised to know you are never far from my thoughts. I imagine you are successful in your medical practice and that your career in literature will be equally admirable. I am well. Ian discovered a cache of small arms left behind by the fleeing army/militia. He sold a number of repeating Winchester rifles and Colt revolvers to Chin Ten Sing and purchased a parcel of land in the Napa Valley. Our vineyard is not as grand as an English country estate, but we are content. Visit if you come to California again.

Kisses,
Penelope, [Lady Ian Blake]

The two-page draft letter:

Bush Villa
Southsea
1885

Dear Dr. Bell,

I hope you are quite well and in good spirits. Penelope sent word that she and Ian are happy together and enjoying life in California. Quite a change, I imagine, from international double agent to vintner, though she seems to have adjusted nicely.

Though that is news, it is not, however, the reason for my writing to you today. Rather, my intent is two-fold. First, I must thank you for all you taught me from the time you took me on as your clerk.

Indeed, you have been a most formidable figure in helping me become a doctor, and my practice is allowing me a comfortable existence. As well, you know of my life-long desire to create a more complete literary work of my own than the short story published anonymously years ago. Although it has been a long process, I am delighted to share that wish is finally and truly moving towards fruition. I first conceived of an idea when we ventured to Russia years ago. It is your skills of observation, deduction, and diagnosis which made me realize you would be the best model for this story about a consulting detective based in London who solves many great mysteries. Although I have yet to fully flesh out the tale, I am committed to publishing it within the next two years and have even been consulted regarding its ultimate publication by Beeton's Christmas Annual.

The second reason for this missive is to share news of my impending nuptials. You know, more than most, that I have always been an imaginative sort, especially as regards adventure and romance. Though it took me until now to realize it, there's surely a difference between believing a thing and knowing it. My dear, sweet, Louisa, who is soon to be Mrs. Arthur Conan Doyle, is better than any fantasy and will become my wife in August of this year.

Yours very truly,
Arthur Conan Doyle

Dr Joseph Bell,
The Model For Sherlock Holmes
and
The Medical Life of
Sir Arthur Conan Doyle

Sir Arthur Conan Doyle was born on May 22, 1859 at 11 Picardy Place, Edinburgh, Scotland. The original building was torn down long ago but a statue of Sherlock Holmes wearing his deer stalker cap stands at the site.

[Figure 1. Statue of Sherlock Holmes].

Conan Doyle's father was an alcoholic and his poverty-stricken family was forced to live in in the rat infested old town of Edinburgh. The family moved from one rented apartment to another in poor neighborhoods. His saintly mother took in lodgers to support the family. Fortunately, his well-off uncles provided the young Conan Doyle with a classic Jesuit education. His teachers encouraged him to write and in addition to the usual subjects, he learned Latin, Greek and German. Conan Doyle entered the University of Edinburgh Medical School at the age of 17 in 1876.

Edinburgh was and still is one of the world's great medical schools. Unlike schools in the United States that required only two years of lectures for graduation, the Edinburgh School provided four years of study in the sciences, humanities and clinical medicine. During the 19th century many American physicians, including Benjamin Rush, a signer of the Declaration of Independence studied in Edinburgh. The founders of the first medical school in the United States were Edinburgh students.

The faculty included James Simpson who discovered the anesthetic properties of chloroform and Joseph Lister, the founder of antiseptic surgery and the world's foremost surgeon during much of the 19th century.

Prominent students at the University included Charles Darwin who was repulsed by an operation in the days prior to anesthesia. Robert Lewis Stevenson, a law student preceded Conan Doyle at the University by one year. J. M. Barrie was a contemporary and the poet, William Ernest Henley was a patient of Lister's at the time Conan Doyle was a student. Barrie and Doyle became fast friends and Doyle corresponded with Stevenson.

[Figure 2. The medical school]

Conan Doyle described his medical education in one of his earliest short stories, “The Firm of Girdlestone”, as a long grind and a business arrangement between the students and professors. He studied botany, chemistry, physiology, anatomy, surgery, medicine and midwifery. Human anatomy is the cornerstone of a medical education but bodies were in short supply. Until the middle of the 19th century, grave robbers supplied bodies for dissection. The infamous pair, William Burke and William Hare, not satisfied with waiting for their victims to die, committed 16 murders and sold the corpses to Dr. Robert Knox an anatomy professor. Perhaps, Conan Doyle studied the skeleton of William Burke that resides in the anatomical museum of the Royal College of Surgeons, Edinburgh.

[Figure 3. Skeleton of William Burke, museum of Royal College of Surgeons, Edinburgh]

As a child, he may even have sung the skipping tune;

Up the close and down the stairs
But and ben wi Burke and Hare
Burkes the Butcher and Hare's the thief
Knox the boy that buys the beef

Dr. Joseph Bell, a fourth-generation Edinburgh surgeon was one of the most influential and charismatic professors. Dr. Bell was a keen diagnostician who could at a glance determine a patient's occupation, nationality and medical diagnosis. Although Conan Doyle claimed he was a mediocre student, Dr. Bell selected him, when he was a second-year student to be his clinical clerk. Dr. Bell later said, "Arthur was one of my best students. He was always interested in anything connected with diagnosis." The clerk took notes on each patient, arrived at a tentative diagnosis and presented the case to Dr. Bell in the great amphitheatre of the Royal Infirmary.

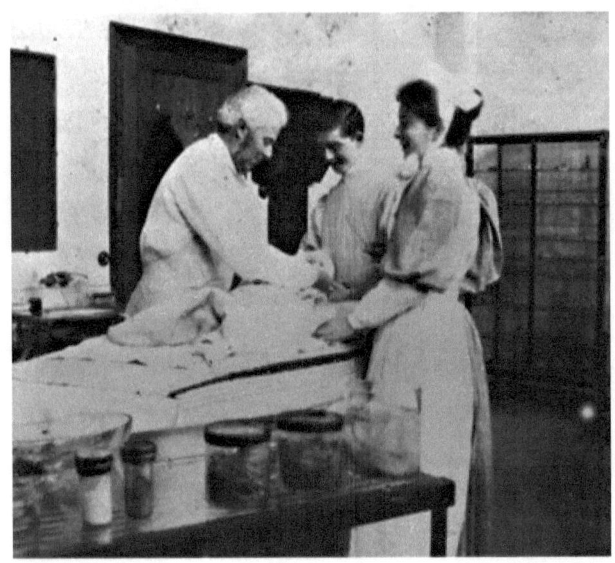

[Figure 4. Dr. Joseph Bell performing surgery]

Conan Doyle described the waiting patients, the clerk and the amphitheater in his short story, "His First Operation".

They passed under an archway and down a long stone-flagged corridor with drab colored doors on either side, each marked with a number. Some of them were ajar, and the novice glanced into them with tingling nerves. He was reassured to catch a glimpse of cheery fires, lines of white-counter-paned beds and a profusion of colorful texts upon the wall. The corridor opened upon a small hall, with a fringe of poorly clad people seated all around upon benches. A young man, with a pair of scissors stuck like a flower in his buttonhole and a note-book in his hand, was passing from one to the other, whispering and writing.

"Anything good?" asked the third year's man.

"You should have been here yesterday," said the outpatient clerk, glancing up. "We had a regular field day. A popliteal aneurism, a Colles' fracture, a spina bifida, a tropical abscess, and an elephantiasis. How's that for a single haul?"

"I'm sorry I missed it. But they'll come again, I suppose. What's up with the old gentleman?"

A broken workman was sitting in the shadow, rocking himself slowly to and fro, and groaning. A woman beside him was trying to console him, patting his shoulder with a hand which was spotted over with curious little white blisters.

"It's a fine carbuncle," said the clerk, with the air of a connoisseur who describes his orchids to one who can appreciate them. "It's on his back and the passage is draughty, so we must not look at it, must we daddy? Pemphigus," he added carelessly, pointing to the woman's disfigured hands. Would you care to snip and take out a metacarpal?"

"No thank you. We are due at Archer's. Come on!" and they rejoined the throng which was hurrying to the theatre of the famous surgeon.

The tiers of horseshoe benches rising from the floor to the ceiling were already packed, and the novice as he entered saw vague curving lines of faces in front of him and heard the deep buzz of a hundred voices, and sounds of laughter from somewhere above him. His companion spied an opening on the second bench and they both squeezed into it.

At the time, Joseph Bell was 39 years old, sparse, lean and tall, with unkempt hair and an angular nose. He had long sensitive fingers and his gray eyes 'twinkled with shrewdness'. This is almost exactly the same description that Dr. Watson made of Sherlock Holmes in their first meeting at 221B Baker Street in "A Study in Scarlet"

Bell, a dedicated doctor, had contracted diphtheria after he had performed a tracheotomy on a child. The disease left him with a limp and a minor speech defect. Despite this infirmity, he became a skilled surgeon and was in charge of the surgical wards in the Royal Infirmary. He was one of the first to take up Lister's antiseptic surgery, gave a course in clinical surgery, wrote textbooks and instituted the Nightingale system of nursing on his wards. In those days, surgeons operated rapidly to decrease the patient's shock. When a patient arrived with his legs crushed under a loaded wagon, Bell amputated both legs in 24 and half minutes. The man survived. When he left the Royal Infirmary, Dr. Bell became the first surgeon at the Royal Edinburgh Children's Hospital. There he developed operations for tuberculosis of the joints and lymph nodes in children, performed skin grafts for burns and repaired cleft lips. Among his many honors, Bell was president of the Royal College of Surgeons and was surgeon to Queen Victoria during her visits to Scotland. Bell took care of the rich and poor alike. A colleague, said, at the time of his death, "Every child in Edinburgh is indebted to this great man, rich, poor, churched and unchurched."

[figure 5. Dr. Joseph Bell, in his Royal College of Surgeons robe. Painting in the museum of the R.C.S.Edinburgh]

Dr. Bell's great skill in making a diagnosis after a mere glace at a patient impressed Arthur Conan Doyle. The physical description of Sherlock Holmes led Robert Lewis Stevenson to write; "can this be my old friend Joe Bell?"

In 1892, after publication of "A Study in Scarlett", Arthur Conan Doyle in a hand-written note, now in the archives of the Royal College of Surgeons, credited Dr. Bell with being his inspiration for Sherlock Holmes.

Arthur Conan Doyle worked to pay his tuition and to help support his family. One of his first jobs was ships surgeon on the arctic whaling ship, the Hope of Peterhead. He apparently had few medical duties, although he probably treated cuts, bruises and broken bones that resulted from falls or fights. He spent most of his time reading, hunting seals, harpooning whales and boxing with his mates. The ship's captain named him, 'The Great Northern Diver' as a result of his falls into the sea.

[figure 6. The whaler Hope]

The ship's doctor – Conan Doyle (third from left) on board the *Hope*, 1880.

[figure 7, Conan Doyle with his shipmates]

"I went out on the whaler a struggling youth, I came back a powerful, full grown man."

By working as a physician's assistant, he earned money and gained experience in minor surgery, filling prescriptions and delivering babies. He commenced writing short stories while he was assisting Dr. Hoare in Birmingham, but his first essay was on the serious side effects of the drug Gelseminine, a plant extract of the Yellow Jasmine. The drug which contains potent alkaloids was used to treat pain such as sciatica and migraine as well as muscle spasm and epilepsy. Conan Doyle discovered, by self experimentation, that with increased doses, the drug had serious side effects. He published his paper in the British Medical and Surgical Journal,

[1879. 2, 483]. It would be extraordinary, even today for a medical student to publish a paper in a prestigious medical journal. The drug is still available as an over the counter homeopathic preparation.

In 1881, he graduated with a Bachelor in Medicine and a Master in Surgery. By any measure, Conan Doyle had an outstanding medical education. Although he claimed to be a mediocre student Doyle had several 'firsts' for his studies. He acquired the finer points of diagnosis from Dr. Bell and as a physician assistant he learned the practical aspects of medical practice. Another student paid him a great compliment: "he had a kind and considerate manner towards poor people."

Figure 8. Conan Doyle's sketch of his elation at achieving his medical school diploma in 1881.

[Figure 8, self-caricature, 'license to kill']

Dr. Arthur Conan Doyle M.B. C.M., graduate of the University of Edinburgh.

[Figure 9. Graduation Portrait]

With no other prospects, he went as ship's surgeon on the steamship, Mayumba to the West Coast of Africa; he treated sea sickness and tropical fevers. On his return, still with no prospects, he took a position with a former classmate, George Turnavine Budd. Conan Doyle recognized Budd as unethical and soon left. Conan Doyle regarded medicine as a profession devoted to philanthropic altruism, rather than a way to make money.

In his autobiography and in the "*Stark Munro Letters*" He described the excision of a cancer from the nose of an old soldier who had for many years held a clay pipe between his chin and nose. He wrote, "*Of course, there could be no question as to diagnosis. It was an epitheliomatous cancer, caused by the irritation of tobacco smoke."*

In this statement, Conan Doyle demonstrated his diagnostic skill and was years ahead of his time by attributing the cancer to tobacco smoke.

It was about the same time, or perhaps during his practice in Southsea he removed a dermoid cyst from the eyebrow of a young man. Dermoid cysts are related to teratomas, a rare form of tumor that contains many different tissue elements. Conan Doyle not only recognized the pathology as a dermoid cyst but identified its contents, 'a rudimentary jaw and teeth'. He went on to say, "*I think that every cell in the body has the power, latent as it may be by which it may produce the whole individual.*" This extra-ordinary observation indicates a deep knowledge of human pathology and development. It wasn't until the 21st century that we understood the potential of stem cells to reproduce various tissues in the body.

In the summer of 1882, Dr. Arthur Conan Doyle hung up his brass plate, engraved

"***Dr. Arthur Conan Doyle, Physician and Surgeon***"

at 1 Bush Gardens in Southsea, a suburb of Portsmouth. He also hung out a red lamp, which instead of the usual meaning, indicated a physician's residence. For the next eight years, until January 1890, Conan Doyle practiced general medicine and commenced his career as a writer.

[Figure 10. The young doctor at 1 Bush Gardens]

His first patient was ‘a little anemic old maid, a chronic hypochondriac”. His practice grew slowly, prodded on with a bit of self promotion, such as the time he treated a man who had been thrown by a horse and sustained bruises. Conan Doyle immediately reported the incident to the local newspaper. He did the same after treating a man for a stab wound of the chest. He vaccinated babies, treated children with measles, an old man with consumption, [tuberculosis] another old fellow with cirrhosis, heart trouble, kidney disease and an enlarged spleen as well as patients with minor injuries. There was a grocer with epilepsy and a lady with dyspepsia who shortly after Conan Doyle made his visit died with a bleeding gastric ulcer. He had no way to make the diagnosis of an ulcer prior to her death, since there were no X-rays. Apparently, he did a good bit of obstetrics because in 1889, he delivered his own daughter, at home. He truly had a general practice and won a reputation as being a hard working, compassionate, skillful physician. He dispensed his own ointments, tinctures, pills and powders. As his practice grew he made a comfortable living. His interest in preventive medicine led him to advocate vaccinating soldiers and sailors against smallpox and the testing of 'harlots' for venereal disease.

In 1885, Dr. Conan Doyle submitted a medical thesis and took an oral examination to qualify as a doctor of medicine. This was unusual because most practicing physicians were satisfied with a bachelor's degree. His thesis, entitled, '*An Essay upon the Vasomotor Changes in Tabes Dorsalis and on the Influence which is exerted by the sympathetic nervous system on that disease'* is an 88 page, handwritten document.

He opens with "*It is with diffidence that a young medical man must approach the subject upon which so many master minds have pondered with views contrary to the authorities in a provincial town without pathology and histology.*" Conan Doyle compensated for his lack of access to a laboratory by extensively reviewing the English, German and French literature.

An Essay
Upon the vasomotor changes in tabes dorsalis
and on the influence which is exerted by
the sympathetic nervous system in that
disease, being a thesis presented in the
hope of obtaining the degree of the Doctorship
of Medicine of the University of Edinburgh.

by.

A. Conan. Doyle. MB. CM.

[Figure 11, hand written first page - Conan-Doyle's medical thesis.]

Tabes dorsalis is neurosyphilis but when he wrote his thesis, the medical profession was divided on whether syphilis caused the disease. The sailors who explored the new world brought syphilis to Europe during the 16th century. It spread rapidly. Since he practiced near Portsmouth, a naval base, Conan Doyle would have encountered cases of syphilis. He attributed the disease to the 'poison' of syphilis even though the causative bacteria, Treponema Pallidum was not identified until 1905. He reviewed the anatomy of the nervous system, the lightening pains, unstable gait, problems with vision, skin and bone changes, the dementia and the psychiatric aspects of the Tabes dorsalis. He even quoted the

German poet, Heine who suffered with neurosyphilis. Most of his thesis is still true today, but he wrongly attributed the disease to an interrupted blood flow to the spinal cord. He compared the symptoms of the disease to ergot poisoning that constricts blood vessels and even suggested a vasodilator for treatment. He tried nitroglycerine on one patient and was ahead of his time, when he insisted upon what we now term, 'informed consent'. He wrote, "*Empiric experiments of this sort should only be tried with the knowledge and consent of the patient.*"

Conan Doyle's doctoral thesis is for the most part scientifically correct, shows flashes of literary brilliance and demonstrates his interest in medicine.

In November 1890, Conan Doyle made a special trip to Berlin to investigate Robert Koch's claim of discovering a cure for tuberculosis. Koch was the world's pre-eminent bacteriologist who in 1884 had identified the bacteria responsible for cholera and tuberculosis. Conan Doyle decided that Koch's vaccine had little effect on tuberculosis. He then wrote about his findings in a letter to the Daily Telegraph. Very few young physicians would have the courage to contradict one of the world's most prominent scientists but he was correct.

During the later years of his practice he learned to do refractions and prescribe glasses at the Portsmouth Eye Hospital. In December 1890, Conan Doyle left his practice in Southsea to attend lectures on diseases of the eye in Vienna. He had difficulty understanding the lectures and left Vienna after a few months to establish an eye practice in London. He had no patients and after a bout with influenza, he gave up his practice to write full time.

His medical career was not quite over; Conan Doyle was honor bound to take part in the Boer war. As a voluntary physician, he helped organize a front-line military hospital. When he arrived, the hospital was filled with soldiers suffering with typhoid fever and cholera due to contaminated drinking water. The field hospital, built for fifty beds held three hundred and fifty sick soldiers. In his words the situation was "*death in its vilest, filthiest form*". An associate wrote of Dr. Conan Doyle; *It was difficult to associate him, [Conan Doyle] with the author of Sherlock Holmes: He was a doctor pure and simple, an enthusiastic doctor too. I never saw a man throw himself into duty as thoroughly heart-and-soul. – He threw open the door of one of the wards and what I saw baffles description. The only thing I can liken it to is a slaughter house.*

It fascinated me to watch the cheery doctor carrying the sunshine with him, wherever he went, worshipped by all." After the war, a soldier who had been under his care wrote; "*As one who was under your care at Bloemfontein in Langman's hospital, I and others owe my life to your kindness and care."*

In his book, "*The Great Boer War*", written two months after his return to England, he related his concern for the need of sanitation and better organization in the military medical department.

In 1910, he addressed the medical students at St. Mary's Hospital in London on "The Romance of Medicine". His talk, published in the St. Mary's Hospital gazette relates his experience as a practitioner and tells how diseases in world leaders, such as Napoleon changed the course of history. He warned the students against materialism and emphasized the humanness of medicine. He said, "*There is another fact which life will teach you,---the value of kindliness and humanity as well as knowledge—A strong and kindly personality is as valuable as learning in a medical man.*"

Conan Doyle introduced disease, drugs and doctors into his Sherlock Holmes stories. Two of his novels have a medical theme and he wrote nineteen short stories about doctors and disease. These stories include descriptions of difficult childbirths, an elderly doctor who had not kept up with scientific advances but had the healing touch and a poignant tale about a young man who committed suicide when he discovered he had congenital syphilis.

There are critics who claim Dr. Arthur Conan Doyle became a writer because he was a failure in medicine. It is true, he did not succeed as an eye specialist, but he was a skilled, highly regarded physician who took a special interest in syphilis and tuberculosis, two diseases that were common during the 19th century. More of Conan Doyle's literary output has a medical theme than other physician authors such as Somerset Maugham, Anton Chekov and Oliver Wendell Holmes, who was one of Conan Doyle's literary heroes.

In his later years, possibly as a result of notoriety for being the model for Sherlock Holmes, Dr. Joseph Bell consulted on forensic matters with Scotland Yard. Like Holmes, Dr.Bell used his powers of observation and character analysis to solve crimes. During the elections of 1904, Dr. Bell supported Arthur Conan Doyle's stand for parliament. Dr. Bell continued to visit hospital patients and make house calls until his final illness in 1911.

BIBLIOGRAPHY

The Real Sherlock Holmes and the medical life of Sir Arthur Conan Doyle

1. Footman, Ray, Young, Bruce; Edinburgh University, An Illustrated Memoir, 1983, University of Edinburgh, Information and Public Relations Services, Old College, South Bridge, Edinburgh, EH89YL
2. Conan Doyle, Sir Arthur, Memories and Adventures, An Autobiography, Wordsworth Editions Limited, Ware, Herfordshire, England, 2997
3. Liebow, M. Dr. Joe Bell, Model for Sherlock Holmes; Bowling Green University Popular Press, Bowling Green, Ohio, 1982
4. Guthrie, Douglas; The Royal Edinburgh Hospital for Sick Children, 1860-1960, E. and S. Linvingstone, LTD, Edinburgh and London
5. Booth, Martin, The Doctor and the Detective, A Biography of Sir Arthur Conan Doyle, Thomas Dunne Books, St. Martins Minotaur, New York, 2000
6. Rodin, A.E., Key, J.D. Conan Doyle's Tales of Medical Humanism and Values: Round the Red Lamp, Kreigler Publishing Company, Malabar Florida, 1992
7. Rodin, A.E., Key, J.D.; Medical Casebook of Doctor Arthur Conan Doyle from Practitioner to Sherlock Holmes, Robert E. Kreigler Publishing Company, Malabar, Florida, 1984
8. Stavert, G. A Study in Southsea; The Unrevealed Life of Doctor Arthur Conan Doyle; Milestone Publications, 1987
9. Conan Doyle, A. An Essay on the Vasomotor Changes in Tabes Dorsalis, [Doctoral thesis] Edinburgh Research Archives, http://hdl.handle.net/1842/418
10. Conan Doyle, A. letter on the toxic effects of gelsemium in The British Medical Journal, 1879, 2 483
11. Miller, R. A Biography, The Adventures of Arthur Conan Doyle; Thomas Dunne Books, St. Martin's Press, New York, 2008

12. Rodin, A.E. Key, J.D. Arthur Conan Doyle's Thesis on Tabes Dorsalis, Journal of the American Medical Association, 247.5 [1982] pp 646-650
13. Letter to Editor: The Consumption Cure: *The Daily Telegraph*, [London] November 20, 1890, pg. 3

Dr. John Raffensperger is a surgeon and medical historian who received his B.A., B.S., and M.D. degrees from the University of Illinois and was a medical officer in the U.S. Navy Reserve. He has served as staff surgeon, acting director of thoracic surgery, and chief of pediatric surgery at Cook County Hospital in Chicago, chief of pediatric surgery and surgeon-in-chief at Children's Memorial Hospital in Chicago, and visiting surgeon in Haiti and St. Lucia. "Dr. Raff" was a clinical instructor/associate professor of surgery at University of Illinois College of Medicine and an associate professor/professor of surgery at Northwestern University's Feinberg School of Medicine, where he remains a professor of surgery emeritus. He has been a visiting professor in Alabama, Connecticut, Texas, Bolivia, Canada, Cuba, Ecuador, Germany, Japan, Mexico, Poland, and South Korea, as well as a case report editor for the *Journal of Pediatric Surgery* and founder and editor of *The Child's Doctor*, a journal of Chicago's Children's Memorial Hospital. Approximately 300 of his articles have been published in the medical and surgical literature, and he has written book chapters on topics ranging from pediatric surgery to ethics and medical history, as well as non-medical essays on sailing, the environment, and art. Raffensperger has authored several books, including *Principals of Nursing Care for the Pediatric Surgical Patient* (Little, Brown & Co.), *The Acute Abdomen in Infancy and Childhood (*Lippincott), *Swenson's Pediatric Surgery (*Appleton, Century, Crofts), *The Old Lady on Harrison Street, the History of the Cook County Hospital, 1833-1995 (*Peter Lang Publishers), *Ward 41, Tales of a County Intern (*Discovery Association Press), *Two Scottish Tales of Medical Compassion (*Cosimo Classics), *Children's Surgery, A Worldwide History (*McFarland and Company, Inc.), and three self-published works.

Richard Krevolin is a teacher, writer, and director. A graduate of Yale College, he earned master's degrees in screenwriting at UCLA's School of Cinema-Television and in playwriting and fiction from USC. "Prof. K" has been an adjunct professor of dramatic writing at USC School of Cinema/TV, UCLA, Pepperdine, Emerson, Ithaca College, University of Redlands, and The

University of Georgia. During the last decade, he has taught the art of communication and storytelling to international executives, creatives, lawyers, and brand managers. The author of several books, including *Screenwriting From The Soul* (St. Martin's Press), *Pilot Your Life* (Prentice-Hall), *How To Adapt Anything Into A Screenplay* (Wiley & Sons), and *Screenwriting in the Land of Oz* (Adams Media/Writer's Digest Books), he has also written several young adult novels and over twenty stage plays. Krevolin has several scripts in development in Hollywood, including *SAFER,* with Tom DeSanto Productions, which will be produced in 2017. He was a documentary writer for *Fiddler on the Roof: 30 Years of Tradition*. He wrote, produced, directed, and starred in the documentary, *Making Light in Terezin*, which aired on PBS. Krevolin also wrote, directed, and co-produced the feature comedy film, *Attachments,* which stars Katharine Ross.

Kickstarter

A huge thanks to our Kickstarter backers who helped make this special hardcover edition happen. In particular to Nuno Robles and Mary Cardoza.

Also from MX Publishing

Also from MX Publishing

Our bestselling short story collections 'Lost Stories of Sherlock Holmes', 'The Outstanding Mysteries of Sherlock Holmes', 'Untold Adventures of Sherlock Holmes' (and the sequel 'Studies in Legacy') and 'Sherlock Holmes in Pursuit'.

Also from MX Publishing

"Phil Growick's, *'The Secret Journal of Dr Watson'*, is an adventure which takes place in the latter part of Holmes and Watson's lives. They are entrusted by HM Government (although not officially) and the King no less to undertake a rescue mission to save the Romanovs, Russia's Royal family, from a grisly end at the hand of the Bolsheviks. There is a wealth of detail in the story but not so much as would detract us from the enjoyment of the story. Espionage, counter-espionage, the ace of spies himself, double-agents, double-crossers . . . all these flit across the pages in a realistic and exciting way. All the characters are extremely well-drawn and Mr Growick, most importantly, does not falter with a very good ear for Holmesian dialogue indeed. Highly recommended. A five-star effort."

The Baker Street Society

The characters return in the sequel, *The Revenge of Sherlock Holmes.*

Also from MX Publishing

The Missing Authors Series

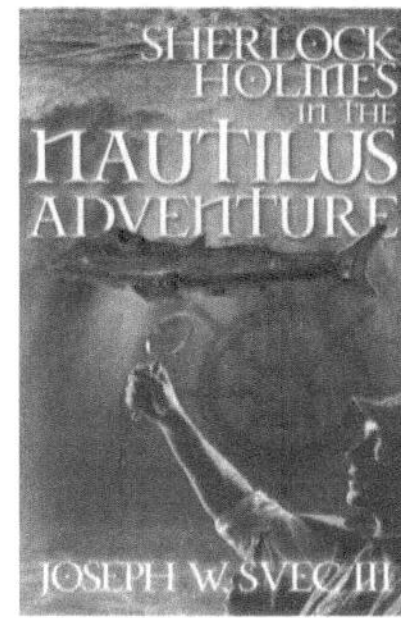

Sherlock Holmes and The Adventure of The Grinning Cat
Sherlock Holmes and The Nautilus Adventure
Sherlock Holmes and The Round Table Adventure

"Joseph Svec, III is brilliant in entwining two endearing and enduring classics of literature, blending the factual with the fantastical; the playful with the pensive; and the mischievous with the mysterious. We shall, all of us young and old, benefit with a cup of tea, a tranquil afternoon, and a copy of Sherlock Holmes, The Adventure of the Grinning Cat."
Amador County Holmes Hounds Sherlockian Society

www.mxpublishing.com

Also from MX Publishing

When the papal apartments are burgled in 1901, Sherlock Holmes is summoned to Rome by Pope Leo XIII. After learning from the pope that several priceless cameos that could prove compromising to the church, and perhaps determine the future of the newly unified Italy, have been stolen, Holmes is asked to recover them. In a parallel story, Michelangelo, the toast of Rome in 1501 after the unveiling of his Pieta, is tasked by Pope Alexander VI, the last of the Borgia pontiffs, with creating the cameos that will bedevil Holmes and the papacy four centuries later. For fans of Conan Doyle's immortal detective, the game is always afoot. However, the great detective has never encountered an adversary quite like the one with whom he crosses swords in "The Vatican Cameos."

"An extravagantly imagined and beautifully written Holmes story"
(Lee Child, NY Times Bestselling author, Jack Reacher series)

www.mxpublishing.com

www.ingramcontent.com/pod-product-compliance
Lightning Source LLC
Chambersburg PA
CBHW030827310726
48980CB00006B/673/J
* 9 7 8 1 7 8 7 0 5 1 6 6 9 *